THE 200mph STEAMROLLER!

BOOK TWO: THE ITALIAN JOB

MAY, 1962 - MAY, 1963

THE 200mph STEAMROLLER!

BOOK TWO: THE ITALIAN JOB
MAY, 1962 - MAY, 1963

BY
BS LEVY

THE SIXTH NOVEL IN *THE LAST OPEN ROAD* SERIES

THE SECOND NOVEL IN *THE 200MPH STEAMROLLER* SERIES

ART DIRECTION BY REBECCA STARR
COVER GRAPHIC BY ART EASTMAN

EDITING, PROOFING, FACT-CHECKING, HISTORICAL RESEARCH & OCCASIONAL "BS" REMOVAL BY
BILL SIEGFRIEDT
JOLINDA CAPPELLO
DON J. TRANTOW
SAM SMITH

MORE THAN YOU'LL EVER KNOW FROM THE TWO PATIENT,
WONDERFUL & HARD-WORKING WOMEN IN MY LIFE:

MY LOVING AND LOVELY WIFE OF 41 YEARS, CAROL

MY RIGHT ARM & OCCASIONAL KICK FROM BEHIND
BUSINESS PARTNER & FRIEND, KAREN MILLER

THINK FAST INK
OAK PARK, ILLINOIS
WWW.LASTOPENROAD.COM

2015

PUBLISHED BY
THINK FAST INK
1010 LAKE STREET
OAK PARK, ILLINOIS, 60301
THINKFAST@MINDSPRING.COM

WRITTEN AND PRINTED IN THE UNITED STATES OF AMERICA

PREVIEW EDITION
JULY, 2015
FIRST EDITION
OCTOBER, 2015

OTHER TITLES BY BS LEVY
THE LAST OPEN ROAD 1994
MONTEZUMA'S FERRARI 1999
A POTSIDE COMPANION 2001
THE FABULOUS TRASHWAGON 2002
TOLY'S GHOST 2006
THE 200MPH STEAMROLLER, BOOK I: RED REIGN 2010

LIBRARY OF CONGRESS CATALOGING IN PUBLICATION DATA:
LEVY, BURT S., 1945-
THE 200MPH STEAMROLLER!
BOOK II: THE ITALIAN JOB
1. AUTOMOBILE RACING   2. THE 1960S
LIBRARY OF CONGRESS CONTROL NUMBER
2015946029

ISBN: 978-0-9642107-8-3

IN LOVING MEMORY OF TWO WONDERFUL & INSPIRING PEOPLE:
MY BROTHER MAURICE
AND MY FRIEND, HERO AND COLLEAGUE
DENISE McCLUGGAGE

Chapter 1: Last Night

It was hard to make sense of everything that had happened. You never seem able to wrap your brain around what's going on while you're in the middle of it—*doing* it, you know?—and it's only later, looking back, that you find any apparent sequence or structure or even imagine yourself some sort of story line. But that's the way life is, isn't it? Things that seem random, chaotic and totally out of your control at the time appear to have some kind of meaningful plan or even—dare I say it?—cosmic destiny when you look back at them in retrospect. And the further back you're looking, the more clear and apparent that plan or destiny seems to be. And I guess that's what I was trying to explain to Audrey after a few drinks at the little pub around the corner from her father's row house the night after I got back from the Targa Florio in May of 1962.

"That's such rubbish, Hank," she pretty much scoffed. But she was smiling while she scoffed and she had that special, just-between-you-and-me glint in her eye while she was doing it. That was the thing about Audrey. She could make me feel grand even when she was telling me I was full of shit. You don't find that sort of thing just anywhere.

What I was trying to explain to her—and to myself, if you want the truth of it—was why, exactly, it might actually turn out to be a *good* thing that I got fired off the magazine when that asshole Quentin Deering caught me coming out of that brass-and-nickel, art deco twelfth-to thirteenth-floor elevator in Fairway Tower, and how my beckoning, insecure, thoroughly uncertain but undeniably more lucrative future as an amorphous motorsports spy/stooge/shill for Fairway Motors' still-top-secret "Absolute Performance" program could very likely upgrade my entire existence.

Only I wasn't doing a very good job of convincing either one of us.

Plus I wasn't making a terrific amount of sense, since I'd just got back from the Targa that very afternoon and desperately needed some sleep. Not to mention a shower. And a shave. And probably a bit more perspective. On that long, mostly silent ride back across France with Hal, I'd come to the uneasy conclusion (or been cornered like a rat by it is probably more accurate) that I was going to have to take that deal with Fairway Motors on whatever terms they wanted. And it wasn't sitting especially well with me. Then again, I was at a pretty low ebb seeing as how I was already in a desolate, hung-over funk when Hal and I boarded the ferry back to Naples after the Targa wrapped up, and things hadn't improved much since then. Although I did indeed stop in at Maranello on our way back—just as Bob Wright had asked me to—and explained to the gatekeeper as best I could in loud, slow English with a few Italian words and phrases thrown in that I was a star American motorsports journalist eager to get an interview with *Commendatore* Ferrari for a freelance story assignment for an important American business magazine that just everybody who was anybody in the world of finance and industry either read or subscribed to. Or both. I must admit I didn't look especially businesslike—I'd remembered to shave, but I was still pretty raggedy and it was hard to ignore the well-used Fiat Multipla chuffing away behind me on the Abetone Road—but the guard faintly remembered me from Ferrari's annual press conferences, and eventually he rang through on the guardhouse phone to find somebody from the office who spoke better English than I did Italian. Which was barely enough to order espresso and dessert, if you want the truth of it. That ultimately led to a few minutes with Ferrari's personal assistant's personal assistant, who had nice legs and hair, spoke English with an accent that made your earlobes swoon and didn't sound particularly convincing (or even that interested) when she finally told me she'd see what she could do. But at least I had something to report back to Bob Wright and Danny Beagle when I flew back to Detroit and donned my Fairway-blue blazer a few days later for another round of meetings.

"But you liked writing for the magazine," Audrey argued like the other half of my own brain, "and you don't seem nearly as keen on this opportunity."

"It's not like it's my choice to make," I grumbled into my gin-and-tonic. "The only other American outlet that covers any of the European races at all is *Competition Press,* and they're just a low-circulation, bi-weekly tabloid that can barely pay enough to get you from one race to another. Let alone eat. Besides, Henry N. Manney's been covering the European scene for them for years, and I really like his stuff."

"I've heard of him."

"Yeah, he's been doing it for years." I let out a long, slow sigh and took another swig off my drink. "I've just got to face facts, Audrey: there's no way I can make a living doing what I've been doing anymore. That's the way things have shaken out and I'm just going to have to figure something else out."

The corners of Audrey's mouth bent down into a frown. "So does that mean you'll be moving to Detroit?"

"God, I hope not. I've gotta fly there day after tomorrow, but I'm hoping they'll still keep me anchored over here…" I swirled the ice around in my glass, "…at least most of the time, anyway…."

"I like it when you're here, too," she said with a look that sent a heat wave shuddering through me. I took her hand under the table.

"Oh, I'm sure I'll still be over here a lot," I went on like I almost believed it. But the bare fact is I'd circled the drain a long, long time before finally coming to the unavoidable conclusion that I would have to take the Fairway deal lock, stock and barrel—including a hopefully temporary home-base relocation to Detroit—simply because I didn't have the imagination, gumption, self-belief or bank-balance reserves to try anything else. Hell, I couldn't even *think* of anything else. You may not know this, but a lot of your so-called "professional motorsports journos" have other jobs or some old family money or made a few bucks doing something else beforehand, so they don't need to rely on the so-called income from their magazine writing as their sole source of food, clothing and shelter.

And all of that was making me very blue indeed.

Audrey made it even worse when she said simply: "I'm going to miss you, Hank."

Jeez, that went right through me.

But there was no point in commingling our misery—it was just going to make things worse—so I gave her a big, fake smile that neither one of us believed and told her: "Oh, I'll be around. You can bank on that. A lot of my work is going to be over here and across The Channel in Europe. Starting off with that trip to Italy I told you about."

She eyed me suspiciously. "You think that's really going to happen?"

"I'm pretty sure it will," I nodded. "And I really will need you there. Really I will."

She looked even more suspicious.

"No," I protested before she could even say anything. "I'm going to really *need* a sharp interpreter if I get that meeting with Ferrari. If I have to do the interview through his people, it'll all be filtered down to nothing. Besides," I shot her a hopeful wink, "he likes pretty girls."

She gave me one of those embarrassed, exasperated looks that pretty women keep on tap for whenever you dare to call them pretty. But there was a little blush behind it, too, and that made me feel pretty good. Only then a waver of uncertainty passed through her eyes. I knew what she was thinking right away.

"Your father's not going to like that, is he?" I asked preemptively.

Audrey didn't say anything. She didn't have to.

"It'll only be for a few days."

I followed her eyes down to the table. You could feel the confusion swirling around in them.

"Just a few days," I repeated softly.

"It just seems so…" she searched for the right word "…*premeditated.*"

"If you mean 'planned,' well, I guess it is."

"That's not what I mean."

"I know."

"It's just Walter."

"I know that, too."

"He can be so…"

"*…Difficult?*"

"Yes. Difficult. Judgmental. Hurt. And it'll be in his eyes every time he looks at me or talks to me for a long, long time. Maybe forever."

"He's just being selfish."

"I know that."

"And it's not like…I mean, we've already…." I started to remind her.

"I know we've 'already,'" she pretty much snapped at me. And then you could tell she felt bad about it. "But this is different, Hank," she went on gently. "This is going away for several days together…"

"But it's business," I protested. "Really it is."

She gave me that look again.

"Really," I repeated again, sounding unbelievably lame.

"Don't get me wrong," Audrey said without looking up, "I really enjoy our time together, Hank, and I truly do appreciate the opportunity." Her eyes came up from the table and found mine. "And I really, really do want to go."

"So is that a 'yes'?"

"I suppose it is."

"Look, I can get us separate rooms if you like…"

"Don't bother…" she snorted. And then the corners of her mouth crinkled up in the wickedest little smile. "After all, it would be an unconscionable waste of money."

It was too late and I was too damn filthy and exhausted to even think about asking Audrey back to my flat that night, but she came over the next night—the night before my flight back to Detroit—and I was reminded all over again what a lousy sort of place it was to take a girl. Any girl. And particularly one you really cared about.

"This place is really bloody awful," she observed as we came through the door.

And that after I'd done my best to straighten the place up. Only I'd forgotten to turn the overhead light off before I left, and no question its harsh glare failed to flatter our surroundings.

"Next time we'll get a hotel room," I promised.

"I believe that's the way most proper gentlemen arrange it."

I let my eyes wander around the room, taking in the sink and my writing table next to the window and my piece-of-crap fake Chippendale dresser. "This really is a shit-hole," I said like it was just occurring to me for the very first time. I switched off the overhead light and put on the low-wattage one on the bed stand. The relative darkness made things slightly better.

"Have you got a candle?"

I rummaged around and found a couple votive candles in the drawer by the sink—the old Irish lady had left them there for emergencies, you know?—and so I got them out and found some stick matches and lit them. Audrey turned out the light on the bed stand. "Darkness becomes this place," she half-laughed. "And the more of it the better."

"Yeah," I sighed, "but I'm going to miss the hell out of it anyway."

"You're used to it, that's all."

"It's lonely as hell sometimes—particularly before I met up with you—but it still kinda feels like home to me…"

"Trust me on this, Hank: it's bloody awful." She was trying to cheer me up.

But I was already thinking about it too much. "I *like* living here!" I whispered to nobody in particular. My eyes went around the room in the half-light from the candles. "I mean, not *here*," I nodded to the dark, crappy flat around us, "but here in England. Where you are…"

"You'll be over here all the time to keep up on things," she echoed back to me, trying to sound encouraging. But she wasn't buying it, either. It was a shitty deal and we both knew it and felt it and couldn't do much of anything about it.

"It's just not the same…" I took one more visual inventory of the dark, cramped, dreary little flat I might never be coming back to and repeated: "I *like* living here…."

"You must be the only one," Audrey laughed, and I leaned over and kissed her hair. But it was like kissing a mannequin. It all felt wrong and odd and awkward. Like we were trapped in a scene in some stupid play that neither one of us particularly cared for.

"It doesn't feel right, does it?" I said out loud.

"No, not really."

"Don't you wish you could turn that stuff on and off whenever you felt like it?"

"It would make things easier, wouldn't it?"

"But then you'd just keep it on all the time, and it would lose its magic."

"You sound like a writer now."

"I am a writer."

"So you've said."

We were just going around and around, you know, because nothing was melting effortlessly together the way I'd hoped and imagined it would on our presumptive Last Night Together. Or Last Night Together for what could be a long, long time, anyway.

"You want to go to bed?"

"If you want to. I mean, it's what we're bloody well here for, isn't it?"

It felt all wrong. Like a soft organ chord with wrong notes in it. And I said so.

"It's because you're going away," she said simply.

And of course she was right. You worry about what's going to happen to things when you're not around to feed them and feed off of them. Plus I'd observed so many times that how things work out tends to pivot more around geography, opportunity and availability than emotions, hormones and compatibility. Like with Cal Carrington and Gina La Scala, for example. And now I was getting my own dose of it. And so was Audrey. I could tell. But what can you do? It's only in the movies where a character can give up everything just to be around the other person. Besides, if you do that, what on earth do you have left? What can you bring to the relationship except puppy-dog eyes and a lot of clinging? And I guess that's why we spent most of that night just lying there next to each other but feeling thousands of miles apart, staring up at the candle-lit cracks in the ceiling plaster like we were looking over the edge of a cliff.

Neither one of us slept much.

Then, what seemed like a long time but not nearly long enough later, some clumsy baker downstairs with his eyes still half-closed dropped a stack of muffin pans. You could hear their empty clanging off the wooden floor. That meant it had to be about 4:30. Maybe 4:45. Time to get up and drive Audrey home before her blasted father got up. Although we both knew Walter was surely wide awake and watching the luminous, ghost-green dial of his little bedside alarm clock, waiting to mark the exact hour and minute when her key finally jiggled its way into the lock. He didn't like me very much. In fact, he didn't like me at all.

He wanted her all to himself, the selfish bastard.

Oh, sure, I could turn it around in my head and see it all logically when I was having tea at the pastry shop down the street after I dropped her off. Walter was a proud, tough, bitter old bird who'd done a lot in life but couldn't get around too well anymore and had already had a couple mild strokes. No question he had to be scared shitless because he knew he was slipping inexorably into that last, clumsy, terrifying and humiliating downslope of life that we all eventually face if we live long enough. And I felt sorry for him for that. Really I did. At least when I wasn't around him, anyway. But he had his talons into Audrey, and he wasn't about to let her go, and I knew he'd do whatever he could—whatever he could think of—to fuck things up between us.

But it was nothing compared to what I would ultimately do to fuck things up myself...

Chapter 2: Texas Snake Oil

I returned to Detroit the next day to find that my unlikely blues- and country western-addict pal Ben Abernathy had put in a few words for me with Bob Wright and some of the other bigwigs on the executive corridor—as he'd promised— and helped convince them that I could be a truly valuable asset in their emerging "Absolute Performance" program. Even without my spy-cover position as European correspondent for an established and respected motoring magazine.

"You could still tell people you're working freelance, couldn't you?" Danny Beagle asked as we waited for Karen Sabelle to summon us into Bob Wright's office.

"I could, but racetrack press-relations people can get pretty sticky about that. You wouldn't believe how many people with no real business there try to get themselves press credentials."

Danny didn't look particularly surprised. "But you still know people there on the inside, don't you?"

"Of course I do." In fact, I'd done my best to stay on a friendly, first-name basis with the press-relations officers at all the major racetracks.

"Good, because I think Bob may want us to take a little trip to Le Mans this year."

"Oh?"

"Yeah, he might. He may want to get a firsthand look at what it's all about. Full VIP access, of course. But he'll want to keep it on the Q.T., too…."

My head started spinning. Le Mans was just over a month away, and there probably wasn't a decent hotel room available halfway back to Paris. And forget about four- or five-star. "You have any idea how many people he has in mind?"

"Don't have a clue. Just the three of us, probably. And maybe some of the staff…."

The spinning got faster. But before I could say anything, Karen Sabelle stood up, nodded like she was giving orders to a blessed firing squad and ushered us into Bob Wright's office. He looked up from the well-organized stack of papers on his desk and favored me with his usual, eagle-scout smile. "Good to see you again," he said with believable friendliness and enthusiasm. "Glad you could make it."

Like I had a choice.

"It's great to have you on the team."

I told him it was great to be there, and we shook hands like rail cars coupling. And after that it was all business. He had some numbered notes ready on the legal pad next to his elbow, and he went through them like he had a plane to catch.

"I think the first thing we need you to do for us is fly out to California to see what Carroll Shelby is up to. You already know him, don't you?"

"Sure I do. Pretty well, in fact."

Bob Wright glanced up from his legal pad. "What do you think of him?"

I gave off a noncommittal shrug.

"Don't beat around the bush, Hank. When I ask a direct question, I want you to give me a straight answer."

"Well," I started in, "he was one hell of a race driver. One of the best American drivers ever. He and Salvadori won Le Mans for Aston Martin…"

"I know all that. I wouldn't be doing this job if I didn't."

"I'm not sure what you're getting at?"

"I want to know what he's like. If he can come through for us like he says he can or if he's talking out of his behind."

I had to think that one over. No question Carroll was a great guy and a friend and I respected the hell out of him. But he was also something of an unknown quantity as an automotive entrepreneur, and he'd had a pretty checkered—you could even say dismal—record as a businessman. Hell, he'd started up and either faded out, fallen short or flat-out failed at a bunch of businesses already—a dump truck company, a chicken ranch, a sports car dealership, a struggling racing-tire distributorship, a driving school—and so I really didn't have a comfortable answer. But I did know he was a rugged, friendly, handsome sort of guy with a slow Texas drawl, an infectious smile, an unbelievable twinkle in his eye and a near-irresistible line of bullshit. He could turn on that down-home, "aw shucks" charm and sweet-talk you into damn near anything. Or that's how I sized him up, anyway. But I didn't want to say anything negative because I thought his new sports car idea was fantastic and I wanted to see it succeed. So I just kind of sat there and waited for Bob to start in again. It didn't take very long.

"Now don't get me wrong, Hank," Bob continued, "I like Carroll. Like him a lot. He's got drive and hustle and spunk and vision. But I've always believed it's safer to remain a little skeptical about people when you don't know all the facts. And sometimes even when you do. I worry sometimes that he's just another slick-talking, now-you-see-it/now-you-don't Texas snake-oil salesman like that Billie Sol Estes character who's all over the headlines right now. You've read about him, haven't you?"

"Sure I have." I mean, it was a hard subject to avoid in May of 1962. I wasn't really used to reading the American dailies again, and no question most of it was stuff I didn't much care about. Or, more accurately, stuff I couldn't do much about, even if I did care. I'd usually start with the fine-print agate type in the back pages of the sports section to see if there was any little scrap of racing news, most often followed by the funnies—I liked Walt Kelly's *Pogo* strip a lot— and then maybe the arts and movie section and only then on to the front page. But you couldn't avoid Billie Sol Estes. It was pretty shocking stuff, even if you considered yourself thoroughly jaded regarding shady business deals at the public expense, bribery and corruption that spread all the way up to Capitol Hill and maybe even a covered-up murder or two thrown in for good measure.

Like I said, it was pretty juicy stuff.

Now Billie Sol Estes was a poor, west-Texas farm kid with an unusual and perhaps even unholy knack for talking folks into things and putting convoluted business deals together, and his story read like something out of Horatio Alger. Only not quite so wholesome. It all started with the lamb he got as a birthday gift when he was 13. He sold its wool for five bucks, bought another lamb with the proceeds and, two years later at the age of 15, he'd run his herd up to a hundred sheep. That was pretty damn impressive for a backwoods Texas farm kid who started with next to nothing. But little Billie Sol was just getting started. He sold those hundred head of sheep for three grand, borrowed another $3,500 from a bank and made a real killing buying fixed-price, government-surplus grain and selling it at a whopping profit. But, like I said, Billie Sol was just getting started. He'd come from nothing and his goal was to be the biggest and richest damn wheeler-dealer in the entire state of Texas. Richer even than the Murchisons! So he set up another business selling irrigation pumps that ran on cheap natural gas to hardscrabble Texas crop farmers, and also wound up supplying them with anhydrous ammonia fertilizer. Only he'd learned from that early, government-surplus grain deal that legitimate business success couldn't hold a candle to what you could make scamming onto the largess of the Agriculture Department's half-assed and highly corruptible efforts to "stabilize prices" and "control commodities markets." Prosecutors claimed he made 21 million dollars a year off the federal government for "growing" and "storing" surplus cotton crops that never actually existed. Not to mention buying up, mortgaging and leasing back government-regulated cotton allotment transfers in an incredibly elaborate—you could even say "byzantine"—scheme that sneaked through a tiny loophole in the regulations and whose success depended on his dirt-level farmer-partners defaulting on their first lease payments (by prior arrangement, of course) in return for an under-the-table cash payoff.

Billie Sol was involved in a lot of other, mostly government-subsidized agricultural businesses and scams, and the one that brought things to a head was an ever-expanding Ponzi scheme of storage facilities to hold surplus grain (which the Agriculture Department happily paid him to store) in order to keep it off the market so it wouldn't erode price levels. That led to a partnership-of-necessity with the anhydrous ammonia fertilizer company he owed a *lot* of money to (as Billie Sol succinctly put it: *"you get into anybody far enough and you've got yourself a partner!"*) and that's what ultimately landed him in a cauldron of hot water and all over the front pages. Seems he'd been generating a little extra cash flow by getting some of his farmer friends to take out bogus mortgages on anhydrous ammonia storage tanks that didn't actually exist. Then they'd lend the mortgage money back to Billie Sol in return for a cash payment. Oh, the tanks had numbered identification plates so the banks could keep proper track of them, of course, but the plates hung from little metal hooks so you could take them off and put other number plates on and swap them around to your heart's content. And even the bank people, who might have gotten a whiff that something was rotten, were either paid off or afraid to say anything because then there'd be a scandal and they might lose their jobs. Not to mention take a massive loss.

So Billie Sol was flying high. He had a huge home with trucked-in palm trees planted in his front yard, a barbecue pit big enough to hold ten fat, sizzling steers and he owned most of the town in Pecos, Texas. But it all started to unravel when Billie Sol decided to run for the local school board. He offered the local, semi-weekly newspaper, *The Pecos Independent and Enterprise,* a luscious, lucrative advertising buy so long as it was accompanied by an under-the-table understanding that the paper would support his candidacy. Only the paper's editor, one Oscar Griffin Jr., responded with a strongly worded editorial to the effect that while the paper's advertising space was most certainly and aggressively for sale, their support of school board candidates (or any other type of candidates) most certainly was not. Billie Sol wasn't particularly happy about that, so he started up his own newspaper, the *Pecos Daily News,* and damn near drove Oscar Griffin Jr.'s newspaper into bankruptcy. So Oscar Griffin Jr.'s paper retaliated with a series of investigative reports detailing some of the shady mortgage dealings and Agriculture Department scams of an unnamed but wealthy and well-connected Texas wheeler-dealer that everybody and his brother knew had to be Billie Sol Estes.

That's when the shit hit the fan.

Followed by an investigation. And then, a week later, by a visit from several unsmiling gentlemen from the FBI up in Washington carrying an arrest warrant…

Now this was all pretty damn inconvenient—not to mention embarrassing—for the gentlemen over at the Agriculture Department. And the Kennedy administration as a whole, in fact, since Billie Sol Estes was a big-time Democratic campaign contributor and had long-standing ties to fellow high-profile Texan and current vice president Lyndon Baines Johnson. In fact, he'd been known to brag to whomever might be listening at the time that the President of the United States would "take my calls." Not to mention that Billie Sol, out of the goodness of his big old Texas heart, had occasionally bought custom-tailored suits, sports jackets and fine silk ties at Texas's famous and highly upscale Neiman-Marcus stores for a few high-ranking Agriculture Department officials. Like James T. Ralph and his assistant, William E. Morris, who both looked exceedingly sharp in the Neiman-Marcus outfits that somehow got charged to Billie Sol Estes' credit card. Morris was called in for departmental questioning about his Neiman-Marcus shopping spree with Billie Sol, but he must've forgotten to set his alarm clock that day because he never showed up. Far more circumspect and careful of his reputation was deputy administrator of the Commodity Stabilization Service Emery Jacobs, who waltzed into Neiman-Marcus one day with Billie Sol leading the way, tried on some nice things like a $245 suit, a $195 sport coat and enough pants, ties, shoes, socks and accessories to run the register up to just shy of fifteen hundred bucks. At which point he disappeared into the dressing room with Billie Sol and returned moments later with enough cash to square the bill. Under questioning, Jacobs vehemently denied any wrongdoing and maintained that he'd bought the $1433 worth of clothes with his own money. But that caused a few tongue-clucks and eye-rolls when it came out that he only made 6500 bucks a year....

Folks tend to shrug their shoulders, wink, nod or snort out a dry, disgusted sort of laugh when they hear about government corruption. I mean, what can you do? People are out for themselves and greed is a natural, born-in human frailty and why the hell would you want a job like that unless there was a little gravy available on the side? Been going on since forever, you know? Only the Billie Sol Estes deal had some pretty dark spots in it, too. Like those two convenient and mysterious "suicides" that cropped up down in Texas once the criminal investigation got rolling. I didn't really know all the details, but I did catch a piece in *The New York Times* that detailed what befell a sorry little lifer senior clerk from the Robertson County, Texas, office of the Agricultural Adjustment Administration named Henry Marshall. Seems he was tasked with investigating some of the details of Billie Sol Estes's business dealings—particularly the stuff about those complicated and most likely shady cotton-allotment land transfers—and what followed was genuinely amazing.

As soon as he started asking too many questions, old Henry (who was known to be a solid, trustworthy and diligent type) got offered a tasty job transfer to a much better position in another department. But it smelled an awful lot like a bribe to Henry Marshall, so he turned it down. And then kept nosing around and asking questions and firing his findings off to a bunch of pencil-pushing bureaucrats in Washington. At which point (on June 3rd, 1961, to be exact) he unexpectedly turned up dead. On his own farm. Stretched out next to his own pickup truck with a high concentration of carbon monoxide in his bloodstream and five fresh bullet holes in his abdomen that, at least according to the police report, had apparently been fired from his own, bolt-action .22 rifle. Think about that for a moment. Especially the "bolt-action" part. Not to mention the five holes.

As you can imagine, it raised quite a few questions—not to mention eyebrows—when the local county sheriff (and, later, the local grand jury) declared Henry Marshall's death a suicide.

But the Billie Sol Estes story was rich in hard-to-swallow suicides. Like what happened to suddenly deceased Texas accountant George Krutilek, who'd done books and tax returns for some of the farmer-partners who'd helped Billie Sol by taking out phony mortgages on a few of his equally phony anhydrous ammonia tanks. They found poor old George dead as a mackerel just a few days after the scandal hit the newspapers. And this time, it did indeed look like a suicide, what with George all alone in his car with the windows rolled up and a rubber hose leading from the car's exhaust to the interior. The odd part was, the coroner's office couldn't find even a trace of carbon monoxide in George Krutilek's lungs....

In any case, Billie Sol Estes was all over the newspapers and the TV and radio news shows, and so it wasn't the best time on earth to be an aw-shucks hustler/promoter from the Lone Star state because everybody had their antennae up regarding charming, smooth-talking Texans who wore nice suits from Neiman-Marcus and fancy Italian-leather shoes. And Carroll Shelby did indeed like nice suit jackets and fancy Italian-leather shoes.

"Anyhow," Bob went on, "we want you to go out there and take a look at things for us. Call it a reconnaissance mission. You came from California, didn't you?"

I nodded.

"That's why we think you're the right sort of guy to check things out for us. See who he's got working for him. See what they're up to. See if they're organized. See if the car's any damn good. We may even ask you to write some copy about it afterwards."

That was the first thing he'd said that actually sounded good to me. "I could do that for you," I told him. "That's something I actually know how to do."

"Good!" He raised a cautioning finger. "But you won't be doing it for me. You'll be funneling all your copy through Dick Flick's people. That's his department."

Suddenly, it didn't sound so attractive.

"But whatever you do, make sure you keep the company out of it."

"Keep the company out of it?"

"When it comes to Shelby, we need to keep everything at arm's length. In fact, when it comes to anything to do with races or racing, we need to keep things at arm's length. I had one hell of a meeting with Randall Perrune about that."

"Oh?"

He looked at me like I didn't have a brain cell in my head. "It's the liability issue. Do you have any idea how many lawyers are out there?"

I told him I had no idea.

"Well, there's more than you could ever imagine. And most of them would bare their teeth, lick their lips and start salivating like Pavlov's dogs if you dangled a shot at a lawsuit—*any* kind of lawsuit!—against a company as big and rich as Fairway Motors."

I could understand that.

"That's why Randall's people absolutely insist that we have a shallow set of pockets inserted somewhere in between. Something—how did he put it?—that will keep the company at least one legally defensible layer of deniability away from anything and everything in our 'Absolute Performance' field programs." He looked me right in the eye. "Do I make myself clear?"

I told him I understood.

"Good!" And then he favored me with a sly, insider smile. "You know what?" he started in. "I believe I'm going to let you in on a little secret." And then he waited, letting the words dangle like fish bait until I inched forward to hear the rest. "Do you have any idea what's going to happen next month?"

"Le Mans?"

He gave me an exasperated look. "Yes, Le Mans for sure. And by the way, did Danny tell you we may want to be heading over there?"

"*We?*"

He nodded like it was nothing. "A few of us from The Tower. Maybe a few staff people. Depends on time available, of course."

"Oh, of course."

"If we do, you and Karen are going to set up the arrangements. She'll give you all the necessary details once we get things clarified…"

I started to explain how difficult—how damn near impossible—it might be to try to set something like that up at this late date. But Bob just waved me off. He had more important things to think about. Then he summoned up one of his patented Dramatic Pauses—like the ones he used in that meeting about the new Ferret program—just to make sure I was giving him my full and undivided attention. He cleared his throat, then dropped down to a whisper: "On the 11th of June, H. R. Fairway is going to send a personal letter to the top men at GM and Chrysler and everybody else that matters. And do you know what that letter is going to say?"

I told him I had no idea.

"It's going to say that Fairway Motors is formally and officially opting out of the 1957 Automobile Manufacturers Association 'Safety Resolution' racing ban. And, although it won't say so in so many words, the obvious implication will be that we're jumping into motorsports and performance advertising with both feet."

"But everybody's already doing that, aren't they? I mean, look at Pontiac's program. It's pretty damn hard to miss. And Chrysler, too."

"Of course everybody's got one," he said like it made perfect sense. "But we're coming out in the daylight about it. We're sticking our collective corporate jaw out and putting performance and racing front-and-center on our entire marketing program. It's going to be our new identity. We intend to be *the* performance-car company—*worldwide!*—and we want everybody on every blessed main street in America to know about it!"

There was no stopping Bob Wright once he got rolling.

"…And that's where you're going to come in, Hank. You'll be our guide, consultant and confidant when it comes to winning big over in Europe. Especially at Le Mans. That's the one you think we really need to win, isn't it?"

I assured him that it was.

"And if things work out like I expect them to, you'll be the one writing the stories and turning out the press-release copy when we finally make it happen! People in that world know you and respect you, and that's going to give us a lot of credibility from day one. We're counting on that." He stuck out his hand again. "As I said when you first came into the office, it's great to have you on the team!" Bob Wright couldn't help throwing in a pep talk at the end. Just to let whoever might be there in front of him know that they *mattered*. And that he wanted and moreover *expected* the very best out of them, too.

And that was it.

Our meeting was over.

I saw Ben Abernathy out of the corner of my eye as I followed Danny Beagle towards the elevator landing. As usual, Ben was slumped over his desk like a dejected grizzly bear with one Marlboro dangling between his teeth and another dozen or so crumpled-up in his ash tray. He waved me into his office and summoned up half of a weary grin. "So how'd it go?"

"Well, I'm not entirely sure what my job is, but I'm pretty damn sure I'm in over my head…"

He gave me the other half of the grin. "Welcome to Fairway Motors."

"It's a little overwhelming."

He looked down at the confusion of papers, letters, memos and reports on his desk.

"Don't worry," he assured me, "it gets worse."

As I turned to leave, he called after me: "If you're still around on Friday, we could maybe go have a few beers and listen to some music."

"That'd be nice."

"No it wouldn't. But it'd beat hell out of going home and watching TV with the wife." He looked up at me sheepishly. "I love her to death, but she likes Lawrence Welk. Can you believe it?"

The company had me bivouacked over at the Fairview Inn again, and I didn't mind it much except for its singular lack of either charm or character. After all, I was used to living out of far cheaper hotels and crappy rented rooms, and this was a hell of a lot nicer than my usual accommodations. But it was empty and lonely and the only thing to do at night was watch a bunch of lousy TV shows or go down to the bar and get drunk. Oh, now and then I sat down at my little Olivetti and fooled around with the novel I was probably never going to finish, but it was hard to keep my concentration together. I missed my old life in London something awful. Missed scrambling together the race report that should've already been off in the post two days before or getting my clean socks, camera gear and travel plans gathered up for the next event. I missed having a couple pints with the guys from the Cooper Garage at the pub they usually went to after work and catching up on all the latest rumors and hot racing gossip. And I missed the living shit out of Audrey. Missed what it was like those few times she'd stayed over when we had sex or made love or whatever the hell you wanted to call it. But the point is it felt absolutely wonderful—except for that last night, anyway—and I was pretty sure it even felt wonderful on her end. Then, afterwards, we'd drift off to sleep like we were wrapped up in the same blessed dream. Or at least until the baking sheets and muffin tins started banging around downstairs and woke us up. I also missed just sitting around with her over her tea and my coffee at the little pastry shop down the street from her father's place or her glass of wine and my gin-and-tonic at the pub nearby and not really saying much of anything. In some ways, that was the best part of all, you know: just sitting there and not feeling like you had to be saying something or making some kind of bullshit small talk.

Oh, I called her, of course. Almost every day, in fact. But it always felt so damn distant and stilted and formal and stupid, and I could just about feel her father sitting there in his reading-and-telly chair, not saying a thing but with his jaw clenched tight and his eyes damn near vibrating. The only time it ever felt the same was when we weren't saying anything. When we were just *there* on the phone with each other, you know? But then the silence would get all awkward and edgy again and so I'd ask her what was going on over at Eric Broadley's Lola shop and how the Bowmaker Formula One car and that new GT project were coming along and how about Tommy Edwards and Clive Stanley's privateer Aston and their preparations for Le Mans and it would all turn into stupid racing chitchat that didn't mean anything. Then we'd hang up, and everything would seem even emptier and lonelier than before.

Like I said, I missed the living shit out of her.

Turns out my first official assignment as a full-time (if still somewhat hidden in the shadows) Fairway Motors employee was to fly out to California to check out Carroll Shelby's skunkworks in the old Reventlow Automotive garage at 1042 Princeton Drive in Venice, just a couple blocks from the Pacific Ocean. It's where the Reventlow Scarabs were built, and there was a lot of great American racing history associated with that building—not to mention a lot of designing, engineering and fabricating talent—and I'd visited there many times back in the late fifties and early sixties when I was still based in southern California. So I was eager to go back there and even more eager to see Carroll's new, Fairway V8-powered sports car project, and it was nice to see that a lot of the same keen eyes, weary faces and work-hardened hands were still clicking wrenches, pounding sheet metal and fizzing away with the arc welders in the old Scarab works on Princeton Drive.

By then of course Carroll's car was known as the Cobra and a truly dazzling, eye-gouge yellow example had been on the Fairway stand at the New York Auto

Show. It attracted an awful lot of attention (not in the least because Shelby had maybe the top custom car painter in all of Los Angeles, Dean Jeffries, spray on a flawless, six-or-seven-coat deep paintjob of glows-from-within pearlescent yellow) and all the mid-life married dreamers, crew-cut hot-rodders, closet racers, un-matured adolescent punks and especially the wild-eyed yahoos of the motoring press simply couldn't wait to get their hands on one. To that end, Carroll had the original, New York Auto Show prototype shoved into a hastily constructed paint booth in the back of the shop where Dean Jeffries's magnificent, pearlescent yellow paintjob could be masked over and re-sprayed with a coat of not nearly so perfect or magnificent bright red. And then white a few days later. And blue a few days after that. See, the magazine guys were just about lined up in the street to "test drive" Shelby's new Cobra (translation: beat the living shit out of it), and it was his idea that if he kept repainting that same one in a different color for each magazine, he could create the impression—or maybe illusion would be the better word—that there were really a lot of his new Cobras running around. Not to mention that you really didn't want to expose too many potentially saleable new Cobras to the so-called motoring press (see "translation" above) because they could be counted on to bring them back with the valves bounced, gear synchros graunched, clutch linings fried and the rear tires damn near melted off the rims.

Like I said, Carroll had hired on a lot of the old R.A.I. talent pool—including guys like Phil Remington and Warren Olsen and Ken Miles came over the following year after the I.R.S. put a padlock on his own shop—and they were all really sharp car guys and exceptional thumb-and-eyeball fabricator/engineers. Plus they were all thrilled to be getting a regular paycheck again for doing the same kind of crazy racecar shit they'd be trying to do on their own (and on their own nickel!) in their free time anyway. And it was impossible not to be drawn in by Carroll Shelby. He was a tall, relaxed, handsome, smooth-talking Texan with curly hair, a huge, friendly smile, a just-between-you-and-me look in his eyes and a singular knack for putting people at ease. He had this laid-back, folksy enthusiasm and a great sense of humor, and there was always this feeling that no matter what sort of crazy, outlandish scheme he was attempting, he'd conjure up some way or another to get it done. Carroll's charm, optimism and confidence were infectious as stomach flu, and you'd catch it off of him whenever he got close to you.

"You wanna go for a li'l spin?" he drawled at me from underneath his trademark cowboy hat.

"Sure," I told him. "Why the heck not?"

So he handed me the keys and had his guys pull most of the masking paper and tape off the primered-up New York Auto Show car and folded his long, lanky body into the passenger side. "Y'all do know how to work a damn stick shift, right?" And then he added an insider wink and a big, wide grin before I could even answer.

Like I said, it was hard not to like Carroll Shelby.

The Cobra fired up with a deep, lean, ominous sort of rumble that reverberated off the walls and made the paint and thinner cans dance on their shelves. I could feel the hair-trigger presence of an angry Detroit V8 without much weight to hold it back coming alive in my hands. Oh, the clutch was a little stiff and you could tell from the loose, rattley feel of the shift gate that a few ham-fisted journalists and VIP joy riders had already been slamming their way through the gearbox. That's because the soon-to-be-red Auto Show car was also Shelby's magazine test car and development hack, not to mention about the only Cobra anywhere near fit to drive at that point in time. He bragged that the first chassis had been air-freighted into LAX back in February, and that it only took his California hot-rodder crew eight hours to drop that new Fairway V8 and tranny between the frame rails, get all the plumbing and linkages hooked up and take it for a test drive. And it was fast as stink, right out of the box. As you'd expect from a roughly 2000-lb. sports car with a honking Detroit V8 under the hood. But there were a lot of weaknesses to sort out and rough edges to smooth over, and the more Shelby and his guys worked on it, the more they came to realize that it was pretty raw and that it was going to be a long, slow process to try and get it right...

Even so, the damn thing was magic!

We trundled down the drive and out into the California sunshine, and I was pleased to find that the steering was reasonably light and quick (even if there was kind of a dead spot right in the middle) and you had to love how the car looked and the way it made you feel to be inside of it. Shelby's new Cobra was about the most predatory-looking sportscar anybody had ever seen, and it could back those looks up every time you put your right foot down on the loud pedal.

Hell, it was the fastest damn thing on the street!

"Go ahead," Shelby grinned. "Punch it!"

"Here?" I asked as I stared over the throbbing dash cowl at the patched, uneven pavement up ahead and the occasional parked cars down either side of Princeton Drive.

"Sure!" he grinned some more. "Why not?"

So I did.

And the damn thing almost got away from me!

The acceleration was like nothing I'd ever experienced before. And it wasn't just the speed. No, it was the raw, explosive, hang-on-to-your-fucking-hat way it crabbed a little sideways, gathered itself up and damn near *leaped* towards the next intersection. But of course you couldn't do much more than just punch it, grab a heart-pounding fistful of second—the wind whipping through your hair and the V8 exhaust thunder splattering off the buildings on either side—before you had to lean into the brakes to slow it down for the next cross street.

Even so, I couldn't get the stupid grin off my face.

"It's pretty dang fast, ain't it?" Shelby deadpanned over the noise. But you could tell he already knew the answer to that one.

"Boy, I'll say!"

"We used to go looking for Corvettes with it, but it got to where it broke your heart a little to see the look on their faces…"

I punched it again, just to make sure it was as amazing as I thought it was.

It was.

"How does it handle?" I yelled over at him. To be honest, it felt a little squirrelly with all that power under the hood.

"It handles like a damn jackrabbit with JATO assists," Carroll drawled. And that was a pretty damn accurate description.

No question he—and, by extension, Fairway Motors—had a tiger by the tail. And that's exactly what I told Danny Beagle when I called him from the pay phone at a corner gas station.

"So it's *good?"* Danny asked.

"Hey, the magazine guys are gonna go apeshit."

"And they're building cars?"

I wasn't exactly sure how to answer that one, so I simply said: "Yeah, they're working their asses off," and let it go at that.

I drove my rental car down to Orange County the next morning to drop in on the *Car and Track* offices before I headed back to Detroit. And that turned out to be a mistake. It didn't do me any good with the magazine, but it managed to make Warren, Isabelle and me all feel pretty damn uncomfortable. But I was just starting to learn how things work inside the big Watch Your Step/Cover Your Ass/Take Care of Your Own and Fuck Everybody Else world of corporate commerce. Money was power and power was control, and if you had somebody by the purse strings, you had them by the nut-sack as well. Oh, Isabelle flashed me a big, welcoming smile when I stuck my head through the door and rushed up immediately to give me a big, warm hug—that was pretty damn demonstrative for her—only then this look of hurt, shame and helplessness descended down over her face like a window shade, and it all went straight to hell from there. If there was anything to be gleaned from the experience, it was that you should probably call first in situations like that and give the folks on the other end a chance to beat it out the back door.

So it was a long, somber, four-cocktail flight back to Detroit late that afternoon—plus I lost the three hours you always lose flying west-to-east across America, so I didn't land until well after midnight—and I knew I had to be back up on the 13th floor executive corridor bright and early the next morning to give my Shelby report to Bob Wright. And I tried to do it as honestly as I could, balancing my breathless enthusiasm for Shelby's raw but explosive new hybrid and my ongoing, positive opinion of Carroll himself with lingering concerns about just about everything else. Could Shelby really deliver? I wasn't really sure, but I told Bob and Danny Beagle I thought he could. Was he trustworthy? "Well," I answered back like it was actually an answer, "why wouldn't he be?"

"And what about the car?"

"It's fucking incredible!"

"You mean it's *good?*"

I paused to find the right words. "Like I said, it's incredible." And then I tried to explain the difference between a stoplight-to-stoplight, back-alley hotrod that can blast your eyeballs clear out of your ears every time you punch it and something you plan on selling to Fred Average and John Q. Public with your company name on it. Even if it's only on the valve covers. Plus I knew Shelby's new snake was a long way from a racetrack hero on anything much more challenging than a straight-line quarter-mile. "Don't get me wrong," I told them, "this thing could really be something special. I mean *really* special. But right now you've got a tiger by the tail and the last thing you want is for it to turn around and bite you."

"So what would you suggest?"

I had to think that one over. I mean, I loved everything about the project: Carroll, the car itself, and especially all those great L.A. wrench-twisters, lathe-spinners and racecar builders who were doing what they knew and loved again and moreover getting regular paychecks in the bargain. "If Carroll can't tame it or if the damn thing turns on you, you'll have to cut it loose," I told them solemnly. "But I'd stake everything I own that Carroll's guys can get the job done!"

And that was probably true.

Then again, I didn't own much of anything.

Chapter 3: Weekend Blues

Friday night I did indeed go out with Ben Abernathy, and I got the impression he really enjoyed my company. But then, he couldn't really invite any of his starched-shirt colleagues from the executive corridor to places like The Steel Shed or The Black Mamba Lounge. They just wouldn't fit in. Or have enjoyed it. And they probably wouldn't have been especially welcome, either. But I liked the music and the atmosphere and all the blue-collar characters letting off a little steam after work. And especially how different and yet how much the same they were. Plus it was nice hanging around with a guy who could listen to twangy, cornball country out of one ear and rolling, gut-bucket blues out of the other and not have to try to understand or explain it. Ben and I talked a lot about music when we sat along the bar at both places—not that either one of us knew much about it or could so much as pluck a chord on a guitar or fart through a trombone—but it got us away from all the tight, urgent, close-to-the-vest stuff up in The Tower (which we weren't supposed to talk about below the 13th floor anyway) and there was no point trying to discuss the ins, outs and prospects for the upcoming Formula One or World Manufacturers' Championship seasons with somebody who didn't give a shit about it. And Ben surely didn't. Going the other way, all he had to talk about was his extended family—so-and-so's baby was getting its teeth and keeping them up all night, so-and-so's father was dying of cancer but they couldn't bring themselves around to putting him in a nursing home, so-and-so's husband turned into a complete and total asshole whenever he had too much to drink—and the regularly disappointing efforts of Detroit's professional sports teams. So, with not much in the way of common ground, we mostly talked about music. Like the new crop of country hits they'd added to the jukebox at The Steel Shed, including Patsy Cline's *"She's Got You"* and Porter Wagoner's *"Misery Loves Company"* and Billy Walker's breakthrough single *"Charlie's Shoes"*—which I liked very much—plus a brand-new 45 called *"Wolverton Mountain"* from a guy I'd never heard of before named Claude King. It had a pretty catchy tune and a nice little story to it.

"Y'know why truck drivers always listen to country music?" Ben asked over our third or fourth round of Stroh's.

"You told me last time we were here."

"I did?"

"Sure you did."

"Last time we were here?"

I nodded.

"But wasn't that the first time we were here?"

He had me there. Besides, it was kind of a favorite topic of his—at least when we were at The Steel Shed—so he went right on. "Why, truckers'd fall asleep if they listened to anything else," he continued with a flourish like it was some kind of major revelation. "See, every country song has a little story inside. So you listen to that story and then you maybe listen to the DJ and a few ad spots and then there's another country song with another little story inside, and that's usually enough to keep you interested and awake while you grind out the miles from one end of the country to the other." He took another swig off his beer. "It's all-American, too."

I had to agree with that.

"And there's something else…"

"Oh? What's that?"

"Country music is comfortable. It's predictable. It's reliable. It's the only music on earth where you can sing right along with it the first time you hear a song."

I had an impulse to argue with him—the way guys do when they're out drinking and need a little difference of opinion just to pass the time—but it didn't seem worth the effort. So we just sat there and drank another beer and listened to a bunch of country tunes that you could indeed sing along with the very first time you heard them. At least by the second chorus, anyway. And by then, Ben was making small talk with the union guys next to us about the day-to-day, nuts-and-bolts crap that went on every shift around the foundries, forges, metal presses, spray booths and final assembly line across the road from us. Like about the various bits and pieces that didn't always fit together the way they were supposed to as those shiny new Fairway Freeways and Freeway Frigates came rolling down the final assembly line. And if you ever listened in on talk like that, you'd probably think twice before you ever bought another new car off a dealer's showroom floor…

"Them clips what holds the dashboard cover on ain't no damn good," a guy in a CAT Diesel cap groused. "More'n half of 'em snap off soon as y'hit 'em with th' damn tap hammer."

"You're not supposed to hit 'em with a tap hammer," Ben countered. "Those are plastic. They're supposed to be a press fit." You had to be impressed with Ben's knowledge of what went on at the plant-floor level.

"See these here fingers?" The guy in the CAT Diesel hat held up a set of digits that looked like they'd been gone over with a wood rasp. "Iff'n y'don't use th' hammer, they don't go inta th' dang holes. An' then the damn cover hangs loose and y' catch holy hell from th' assholes down at th' end of the line in Final Inspection."

"Did you try a plastic hammer?"

"Hell, y'can't drive a nail inta a slab a'shit with one a'them damn things."

"Maybe if you tried going a little slower? Being a little more careful how you lined things up first?"

"And fall behind?" He let out a grimy snort of a laugh. "Not on your life. Not this ol' boy. Union fought like hell t'git us the rate we got on this operation." He shook his head. "An' b'lieve you me, I ain't gonna be the one t'hit that red button over a damn dashboard cover. Not me. No sir. No thank you. I don't wanna spend half a day gettin' raked over th' damn coals in Scully Mungo's office."

Ben bought him a beer. He bought me another one, too.

"Has it always been like this?" Ben asked.

"Aw, hell no. Useta be fine with them metal clips that came in from Ohio. I saw it on th' box label that they came from Ohio. Used 'em for years with no problem. Only now we got them new plastic ones from some shit-ass place in Chicago, and they ain't worth a shit."

"Did you say anything to the shift manager?"

"'Course I did. At th' beginnin', anyway. But he's got a hard-on for me an' wants me t'fuck up bad enough that he kin git me transferred t'some dirty shit job in the foundry. Or with all them fuckin' fumes in th' paint shop. Or fired even better."

"Really? How come?"

The guy in the CAT Diesel hat flashed a smile with a couple bad teeth in it. "Ah'm fuckin' his sister…."

Later on, Ben explained that one of the hardest things to control in a huge manufacturing operation was what went on in P&P.

"P&P? What the hell is that?"

"Purchasing and Procurement…" he answered as he ordered us another round. "It's where fortunes are made…."

"Oh?"

And then Ben detailed for me how purchasing guys making well on the near side of ten grand a year sometimes retire to beautiful waterfront homes in tropical climates. And that's because they spend their days in a shitty little Tower cubicle passing out procurement contracts for millions and millions and millions of dollars worth of wiring looms and wheel covers and windshield-washer-squirter nozzles and whitewall tires. And every single company that makes or sells that sort of thing is on the make to get in (or get back in) as a supplier. So it's a very competitive environment and, when that much is at stake, you'd have to look long and hard to find some vendor who wasn't above offering a few 'side inducements' or cutting a few corners in order to secure a contract. I mean, the cost spread between Company A's chrome tail-light bezel and Company B's offering of the same exact thing might be fractions of a penny. And yet it could be the difference between whether the wife of Company A's president gave him certain special favors (or ignored him enjoying those same sort of favors with ladies of a less matrimonial bent) because she got a nice trip to Europe and wore a fancy fur coat and drove around in a nice, new Freeway Frigate Claude

Monet Special Edition with the embroidered water lily upholstery. That was one of Amanda Cassandra Fairway's personal favorites, and probably the only one of her "great artists" series that sold worth a shit.

In any case, three-martini lunches at upscale restaurants, bottles of expensive booze on birthdays and at Christmastime, all-expense-paid trips "to see our plant" (often by way of freewheeling vacation spots like the Bahamas or Las Vegas), tickets to must-see musicals or sporting events, nights with top-class hookers in pricey downtown hotels *("I've gotta work late again tonight, Madge…")* and good old reliable cash-under-the-table were constant threats and temptations in P&P. You couldn't get away from it. Although Ben tended to have a surprisingly live-and-let-live attitude about it. "I don't much care for it personally," he allowed, "but I don't really mind a guy negotiating a little side deal for himself if he's making a good deal for the company in the process." He was pretty damn certain that if the product was shit (or if it was blatantly and brazenly overpriced), it came to light sooner or later and then the supplier and his wife and her fur coat and all of his hardworking employees and even his side girlfriends would be out on their ass.

But they'd come sniffing around again in a year or two, trying to get back in.

There was just too much sugar to ignore.

To Ben, the bigger problem—like the one with the plastic dash-cover clips—was the continual "race to the bottom" by in-house engineers and P&P suppliers to see who could figure out how to do things cheaper. Like this case, where something that was perfectly serviceable had been replaced by something that, at least according to the guy with bad teeth and the CAT Diesel cap who was fucking his shift manager's sister, wasn't worth a shit. And meanwhile, the guy who owned the company that made the metal clips was drinking doubles and laying people off and thinking about closing up shop and probably wasn't getting any at home or anywhere else, while the salesman for the company who made the plastic clips had likely just spent a weekend in Atlantic City with a well-endowed manicurist named Monique.

"Sorting these things out is always a mess," Ben sighed. "First, you gotta get the problem identified and get your documentation together, and then you bring in the poor fish from the plastic clip company—if he is indeed a poor fish—and then you go through all the shit about if it's the lot or the batch or the mold or the fucking material and then he takes back the ten skids of clips you have in the system and sends you more stuff that's usually no fucking good, either. And meanwhile you've contacted the guy from the metal-clip company—if he hasn't jumped out of a window or wound up in the drunk tank—and ask him to drop in again for a chat." Ben shook his head. "I worked in P&P for a while after I came up off the line, and I'm here to tell you, it's the shits. You're fucking with people's lives and livelihoods every single day of the week."

"But people treat you nice, don't they?"

"Sure they do. Everybody and his brother wants to be your fucking friend."

"So what's so bad about that?"

Ben looked at me for a minute, lit up another Marlboro and creased his mouth into a phony, slimy sort of smile. "Tell me, Hank, how many friends you got?"

I gave him a blank look. "I dunno. I suppose I've got lots of friends over in Europe. Particularly in England. People who hang out at the races, mostly...."

"How about here?"

"Here in Detroit?" I thought it over. "Probably just you. And maybe Danny Beagle."

"Don't count on it."

"Don't count on what?"

"That Danny's your friend. Or me, either. Just because somebody makes themselves easy to get along with doesn't necessarily make them your friend."

Using that definition, maybe I didn't have so many friends.

"The point is this," Ben went on, "P&P floats on a sea of fake friends, veiled motives and bullshit. That's the way it is and that's the way it's always been. Oh, companies send a new sheriff in every now and again to try and clean things up. Set him up in a corner office so he can keep an eye on things and have him sign off on every single deal. But they don't tend to last very long, because they're usually guys on the way up who want to make a name for themselves and move up to a bigger office and a bigger paycheck in a department on a higher floor. Or they stick around and get dragged into it like everybody else." He gave off a shrug. "And I don't really give a shit, so long as I don't have to be the one doing it anymore." He sighed and snubbed out his cigarette. "You want another one?"

"I probably don't need it."

"Me, either," he agreed. Then swiveled his head around and hollered: *"HEY, FRED! HOW ABOUT TWO MORE STROH'S OVER HERE?"*

Saturday was a miserable day because I woke up in the middle of the night to pee some beer out and couldn't get back to sleep. So I just laid there, feeling miserable and hung-over and lonely as hell. And it was even worse because I knew I was missing qualifying for the first grand prix I'd missed since I left California to become *Car and Track's* European correspondent what seemed like three-quarters of a lifetime ago. The cold, sad emptiness of it put a hole the size of a moon crater in my gut, and it didn't help that you couldn't get any race coverage at all in the papers or on television or radio in Detroit. As far as those people were concerned, the grand prix scene didn't even exist (even though the reigning World Champ was an American) and the only time Formula One generated any coverage at all was when somebody got killed. Plus a scant few column inches when the circus crossed the Atlantic for the US Grand Prix at Watkins Glen in October. My only reliable print connection was the *Competition Press* subscription I'd started up with the very first temporary check out of the checking account I decided I really needed to open at a local bank. And I must admit *Competition Press* did a pretty good job of keeping you up-to-date and informed on the European and North American road-racing scenes. Including a lot of genuine insider stuff thanks to a semi-fly-by-night editorial staff that included people like Henry N. Manney and Dic Van Der Feen and Denise Mc-Cluggage (whom I always rated at the top of the game as a writer, thinker and racer). But it was just a skinny, bi-weekly, newspaper-format tabloid with decidedly iffy production values, occasionally suspect proofreading and, even though they tried very hard to stay up-to-the-minute, their European coverage was generally three-to-four weeks old already by the time your copy arrived in the mail. Even so, I always read mine front-to-back as soon as it arrived—even the damn classified ads!—but it never took very long because there were never many pages and it was all newspaper-style reporting (you know: a big, punchy headline—preferably with a hokey alliteration or two—followed by a wham-bam-thank-you-ma'am "who-what-where-why-when" column or two and not much at all in the way of details or background information). And in not very long at all I'd be done with it—even the classifieds—and start going into motorsports withdrawal again. In fact, my last copy was laying there in a rumpled-up heap on the carpet next to my bed. I'd read it cover-to-cover twice already, and was thrilled to learn that Stirling Moss was doing much, much better and amazing the doctors and nurses with his recuperative powers. He was apparently in good humor, getting around a bit on crutches and rumor had it he might even be leaving the hospital soon! And that was excellent news indeed. Although whether he would ever be fit to race again was still very much an open question. Also on the front page was a lead story on the Presidents Cup SCCA National at Virginia International Raceway, which was held in alternately hot and steamy and outright downpour weather conditions, and where Roger Penske's "Telar Special" Cooper Monaco (young Roger was quite a master at hustling up sponsorship dollars and subsequently making those sponsors glad they got involved) took first overall after Walt Hansgen's Alf Momo-built/Cunningham-entered Cooper-Maserati had to pit with wet electrics. That let Al Holbert's Porsche RS-61 through to take second place, but it was really just a glorified amateur club race, if you want the truth of it.

Meanwhile, over in Europe, the new Formula One season was nearly at hand, and both Henry N. Manney and new Porsche team driver/American fan favorite Dan Gurney weighed in on how they thought Ferrari's dominant but little-changed 1961 machines would fare against the new crop of 8-cylinder cars from

Lotus, Cooper, BRM, Lola and Porsche. The air-cooled, flat-8 Porsche 804 F1 car was very much an unknown quantity—from the pictures, it looked quite a bit sleeker and more purposeful than the old 4-cylinder cars, but they looked more or less like galvanized-tin piglets—while Lotus and BRM had each taken a non-championship, pre-season race win (BRM at Goodwood and Lotus at Aintree) while elegant little French vineyard owner/town mayor/race driver Maurice Trintignant, age 44, had taken Rob Walker's privateer Lotus 24 to a win at Pau in France. Ahead of—ahem—highly rated youngster Ricardo Rodriguez in one of Mr. Ferrari's latest, 120-degree V6s. But of course that wasn't the whole story, since Jim Clark had passed them both and been pulling away in the works Lotus 24 until a transmission bracket broke and put him out. It made me feel all sick and empty inside knowing that it was all going on without me and that I was on the outside now looking in…

Damn.

In any case, there wasn't much I could do except loll around some more in bed and order myself a room service breakfast that didn't sit too well as soon as the kitchen opened up. So I leafed through my dog-eared copy of *Competition Press* for yet a third time and watched a bunch of crap TV all day. I saw John Rotz ride Greek Money to an exciting, hotly contested win over Manuel Ycaza on Ridan—the horses bumped *hard* as they headed towards the wire—in the 88th running of The Preakness Stakes at Pimlico. The whole damn thing was over in one minute, fifty-nine-point-two seconds. And then I suffered through the hometown Detroit Tigers taking an endless 2 hours and 51 minutes to beat the Indians 9-to-3 in Cleveland. It seemed a lot longer.

I finally gave up and called my shooter pal Hal Crockett at his hotel near Amsterdam—I'm pretty sure I woke him up—and it turned out I'd missed a pretty damn eventful Friday and Saturday at Zandvoort. It all started when Colin Chapman opened up the Lotus transporter and rolled out his new Lotus 25 for Jimmy Clark to drive. It stopped people dead in their tracks because it was, by an obvious margin, the slimmest, sleekest, slickest, trimmest and tidiest grand prix car anybody had ever seen. Chapman managed it by using a revolutionary monocoque chassis folded up and riveted together out of aluminum sheet—like an airplane fuselage!—instead of the usual, skeleton-like, steel-tube space-frames that everybody else was using (and which Chapman himself had introduced way back in 1952!). In essence, the new 25 had its driver (and Jimmy Clark was pretty much jockey-sized anyway) lying down damn near prone between a pair of elongated, sheet-alloy chambers that made up the frame structure and also served as the fuel tanks. It was pure, unadulterated genius, Chapman style, and it didn't take long for all the other teams to realize that they were flogging around in last year's car. Which set off a chorus of groans and muttering from the Ferrari, Porsche, Cooper and BRM types along with cries of "foul!" from privateers like Jack Brabham and the U.D.T.-Laystall boys, who'd not long before shelled out a *lot* of pounds for the latest, tube-frame "customer" Lotus 24s which they'd been assured—by Colin Chapman himself!—would be "identical in every respect to what the factory team will be running this season." Fellow 24 purchaser Rob Walker summed it up rather succinctly (if bitterly) by noting: "Sure, Colin's car is exactly the same as mine. Only he's left the bloody frame out!"

Despite being hurriedly finished and bedeviled by the usual new-car teething problems, Clark qualified the stiletto-like new Lotus on the outside of the front row on the 3-2-3 grid, with Graham Hill's BRM V8 in the middle next to him and none other than ex-bike champ John Surtees somewhat amazingly taking pole in the Bowmaker Lola/Climax. That was pretty damn incredible for an almost-new F1 driver (even one with Surtees' impressive two-wheel credentials), a privateer team and a brand-new car from a brand-new constructor in its first-ever grand prix! It was starting to occur to everybody—me included—that Lola was emerging as a marque to be reckoned with and that John Surtees was apparently on his way to becoming one of those elite, one-cut-above drivers like Nuvolari and Fangio and Stirling Moss (and maybe, just maybe, Dan Gurney). But even though Surtees had qualified on pole, he wasn't all that thrilled with the new Lola's handling. Said it was a bit too nervous and darty. Which made you wonder what he could do with a car he really felt good about…

The 2-car second row featured new team owner Jack Brabham in the best of the Lotus 24 customer cars sitting next to his old teammate Bruce McLaren in the latest Cooper. Hal said it looked like the Ferraris and Porsches were in dead trouble, with Dan Gurney the quickest of the lot in 8th in the new Porsche flat-8 and Phil Hill mired behind him in 9th in the best of the Ferraris. But that was still two places better than Mexican phenom Ricardo Rodriguez in the second Ferrari and three slots better than team manager Dragoni's favorite-son Italian Giancarlo Baghetti in the third car. Good for Phil, even if it must have felt like a pretty hollow victory.

It was absolutely killing me that I wouldn't be there for the race on Sunday…

I didn't really know what to do with myself after I hung up on Hal. I was sick of watching TV and sick of hanging around my room at the Fairview Inn and I didn't really feel like going down to the lounge to sit there and get hammered with some stranded dash-instrument salesman or a guy from Dearborn Heights who'd just checked in because his wife had thrown him out of the house or the loud, leftover drunks from a wedding party down the hall. I guess what I really wanted was talk to Audrey, but it was past midnight in London, and I was pretty sure she was staying with the Monsters of Mayfair that weekend, so that wouldn't do at all. So I thumbed through the movie section of *The Detroit Free Press* to see if anything good was around, but all I came up with was an entirely-too-wholesome-sounding remake of *State Fair* with Pat Boone and Bobby Darin or a cheapie Roger Corman version of Edgar Allen Poe's *The Premature Burial* with Ray Milland or the much-talked-about (at least among those with advanced degrees and leather elbow patches) New Wave French film called *Last Year at Marienbad*. It was appearing at a so-called "art house" theater near Wayne State University, and although my gut was tugging me towards the Edgar Allen Poe offering (although it certainly would have played better at a drive-in with Audrey cuddled up next to me) my more-evolved self felt some sort of cranial obligation to see *Last Year at Marienbad* and find out what all the high-toned fuss was about. Besides, I felt pretty certain it was what Audrey would have picked, and that somehow seemed important.

So I got myself dressed and even shaved for the occasion, drove over to the theater and did my best to sit through a leaden hour and 33 minutes of artistically composed scenes and portentous French dialogue that made no sense to me at all. Not even with subtitles. If the goal of the French *Nouvelle Vague* movement was to confuse, bore and befuddle an audience, *Last Year at Marienbad* succeeded admirably. Especially once you realized it was going absolutely nowhere and moving in that direction at an agonizingly slow pace. By far the best part was listening to all the Wayne State college-professor/grad-student types sharing respectful nods, knowing critical comments and keen, insider interpretations as they meandered out through the lobby. I had to stifle the urge to holler *"WHAT A CROCK OF SHIT!"* at the top of my lungs, but that would have been rude. When the emperor has no clothes, you really don't want to get into an argument with folks discussing how nicely his ascot goes with his waistcoat.

But I was proud of myself for sticking it out to the end (although I really didn't have much of anything else to do), and I was pretty sure Audrey would have been proud of me, too. Better yet, if it happened to be playing in London next time I was there and she wanted to go see it, I could very politely and correctly decline on the basis that I'd already seen it. So on that score I'd actually accomplished something worthwhile that evening.

It was 9:30pm on a Saturday night and I was all alone with less than no place to go—the prospect of heading back to my room or the cocktail lounge at The Fairview didn't sound particularly appealing—and I caught myself wondering about maybe taking in a little blues music at The Black Mamba Lounge. Only I had never been there except with Ben Abernathy, and I wondered how I'd be welcomed—or if I'd be welcomed at all?—walking into the Black Mamba Lounge all by my lonesome. I could visualize the massive, muscular, bald-headed owner/bouncer in his wraparound sunglasses and two-sizes-too-small Banlon golf shirt and just about feel all those suspicious eyes staring at me over their beers and cocktails. But what the hell else was I going to do?

So my Fairway Freeway courtesy car pretty much drove itself back towards the plant complex from whence it came and wheeled with only the slightest hesitation into the packed gravel parking lot of The Black Mamba Lounge. The theater-style sign with one inner light burned out advertised "DIRECT FROM PARIS: MEMPHIS SLIM," and no question he was a popular attraction. I finally found an empty slot uncomfortably far from the door, switched the key off and just sat there for a moment or two trying to decide if this was something I really wanted to do. I really wished I'd had a drink or two beforehand to take a little of the nervous edge off. But finally I shrugged, muttered *"Hey, what the hell?"* like there was somebody else with me and headed for the door.

But before I got ten steps from my car, I heard the slow crunch of tires over gravel and felt the cold gleam of headlamp beams on my back. A phantom car was creeping along behind me at little more than a walking pace. Maybe it was just more Black Mamba regulars or some Memphis Slim fans looking for a parking space? But the icy tingle up my spine seemed to sense it was something more. And that tingle went damn near electrified when somebody yelled *"HEY!"* in a kind of squeaky, adolescent stage whisper. I didn't really recognize the voice, but there was something oddly familiar about it. And that's when the strange-yet-familiar left-front fender of a shiny, Bamboo Cream Pontiac Grand Prix with 8-lug aluminum wheels and a low, lopey exhaust note slid under my right elbow. *"Hey! You! The writer guy!"*

I knew before I even looked that it was Amelia Camellia Fairway and her unkempt, underage rich-kid friends from the Grosse Pointe suburbs again. What the hell were they doing back at The Black Mamba Lounge? Hadn't the big black bouncer shown them the door last time? Sure enough, the driver was the one with the raggedy flop of blonde hair on top and the perpetual adolescent sneer. The sullen brunette with the long, straight hair and the concave posture was looking up at me with dull, vacant eyes out of the backseat window. I stood there as the pale yellow Pontiac crunched to a halt next to me and I heard the passenger door open on the opposite side. And sure enough there was Amelia

Camellia Fairway, looking young and beautiful and bored and snotty and confident and angry and dangerous as the meanest sonofabitch in Detroit. She walked around to me through the headlight glare, and you couldn't miss the way it made her eyes glisten and lit up her hair like a tangled blonde inferno. Or how her boy's lumberjack shirt was open about four buttons so you could see she wasn't wearing anything underneath.

"You're the writer guy, arent'cha?" she asked as she planted herself in front of me. But her eyes were looking more through me than at me.

"I'm Hank," I reminded her. "Hank Lyons. You and I met at…"

"I remember," she interrupted like I was annoying her. "In the garden maze with Otis. And then right here in the parking lot." And of course that's precisely what was running and re-running through my brain like a film loop on a lousy projector. Especially the way she'd leaned up to give me what I'd thought was going to be a little-girl "thank-you" or "good-night" kiss that turned out to have an open throat and a slithering adder of a tongue hidden inside. And then she'd said: *"We ought to get high and ball sometime. I've never fucked anybody who worked for my father before"* like she was talking about the weather. To be honest, it scared the living shit out of me. And it did the other thing it was supposed to do to me, too…

"I remember," I told her.

She looked at me like I was something in a shop window. And then she just laid it all out: "You got us some weed that night, remember?"

"Some what?"

"Some weed. Some boo. Some pot," she said like I was eight kinds of dumb. And then, out of absolutely nowhere, she gave me a smile. A coy, flirty one. She tilted her head and used her eyes and everything. "We thought it was pretty good stuff…" she said like it was something I should be proud of.

"Look," I started to explain, but she cut me off again.

"We'd like to score some more of that," she went on matter-of-factly, but still working that come-on smile.

"We've got cash, man," the kid with the flop of blonde hair chimed in from the Pontiac. "We're set to buy a whole brick if we can, man. I mean, you know, if it's the same stuff..."

"A brick?"

"A kilo, man. We got enough cash for a kilo if you got one."

I glared at him. "Look, I don't have anything. I never had anything. I'm just a car writer. That's not what I do."

"But y'got us some last time, man," he more or less whined.

I did my best to ignore him and concentrated on Amelia. "Look," I told her. "That was just a lucky shot. I got it from your friend Otis. He just happened to have some. I don't know where he got it and I don't know anybody else in there, see. So I couldn't help you even if I wanted to. And I don't want to."

"But you could ask around for us, couldn't you?" Now she had the eyes and the smile and the unbuttoned lumberjack shirt all working together.

"This isn't what I do," I repeated as I tried not to look into her shirt. "And I don't really think I should be running around trying to buy drugs for underage kids, either. People go to jail for that sort of thing..."

"Aw, c'mon, man," the blonde kid whined some more. "You can get inside for us. Otherwise, we just gotta wait out here in the fucking parking lot until they start coming out."

"One time one of them took the money and just drove off with it," the girl in the back seat added in a dull, betrayed monotone.

"Don't be such a chicken," Amelia teased. I could feel the challenge in it. No question something inside of me wanted to wipe that fucking smirk off her face. Show her I wasn't chicken at all. But thank goodness I knew better. And that's when she let the other shoe drop. She sidled in real close so I could feel her against me and put her mouth up next to my ear. "I really, really like you, Hank," she began in a breathy whisper. "I really, really, really want to be your friend. And I can be the kind of friend you really want to have, too..." She pulled her head back a little so I could watch her eyes go hard like ice forming.

"…But you don't want me not to be your friend, Hank. That could get really miserable for you…" She ran her hands around my back and pulled in even closer. "…Didn't we kiss out here last time?"

I yanked myself away from her. "I didn't do anything!" I protested. "It was you. You did everything!"

"Hey, your word against mine," she shrugged. And then the coy, flirty smile again. "And remember, Hank: I'm only seventeen…"

"I'm going to tell your parents!" I growled at her. "That's what I'm going to do."

"Before or after my shithead father fires you?"

"And you don't have to *do* anything, man," the blonde kid whimpered in. "Just get us a connection is all."

"Yeah," Amelia agreed. "Just ask around and find somebody for us."

"You can even send them out here. We'll do the rest. You don't have to even touch it," the blonde kid added. "We'd do it ourselves, but that big, black ape at the door won't let us in there anymore…"

"Yeah," Amelia nodded, "and we're pretty sure you had something to do with that, too. So you kind of owe us this…"

I was starting to feel surrounded.

Amelia looked up at me with eyes full of insolent challenge: "C'mon," she urged, "do it for me, Hank. Show me the kinda guy you really are…"

So, God help me and against my better judgment—in fact, against any kind of judgment you'd care to think about—I agreed to go inside for them and see what I could do. It was a stupid decision, and I knew it even before I made it. But I knew she could wreck things for me at Fairway Tower if she decided to put her mind to it. And she would, too. In that respect, she was just like her father. She liked having that kind of power over people.

Besides, I really wanted to wipe that damn smirk off her face.

The Black Mamba Lounge was really rolling and rumbling inside, and you could smell a little hint of pot in the air along with the cigarette smoke, spilled booze and jasmine cologne. There were colored lights over the packed dance floor, and Memphis Slim was right in the middle of a throbbing, driving rendition of his rollicking blues hit *"When I Were Young."* He had everybody in the place bopping and jiving and swaying and nodding along with the beat. Memphis Slim was a truly striking figure: a tall, distinguished-looking black guy in a razor-creased sharkskin suit who wore his hair cropped tight to his head with his trademark, bleached-blonde Mohawk stripe right down the center. He had a deep, soulful, resonant voice that could plead or cajole or get angry and hurt and disgusted on command, and he could wail out blues and play boogie-woogie piano like crazy with his head rolling and swiveling around like a mean bulldog on a short leash while his hands flew over the piano keys in a blur. He had everybody so damn wrapped up and into it that hardly anyone even noticed when I came through the door. I scanned along the bar and the back wall as my eyes became accustomed to the darkness, but I didn't recognize anybody. I remember I felt a little scared.

"Hey, two dollas!" a deep, thick voice grunted behind me.

"Huh?"

"Two dollas, man." It was the barrel-shaped owner/bouncer again. He was wearing his wraparound sunglasses and his usual orange-knit golf shirt about two sizes too small. His chest, arms and shoulders filled it like an over-inflated inner tube. *"Gotta charge cover fo' a act like this here one."*

I fumbled for my wallet and gave him two dollars.

"Yo' frien' Ben wit' you dis tahm?"

I shook my head.

He reached up with a finger the size of a thuringer sausage and pulled his dark sunglasses down just far enough that he could size me up over the top. *"So you heah all alone?"*

I nodded.

"Y'all stay in the light then," he advised, and slid his sunglasses back in place.

By then the song was over and now people were noticing me and staring, and I was starting to think I'd made a big mistake. But I seemed to be getting more in the way of curiosity and annoyance than outright anger, so I kind of eased my way over to the near end of the bar and waited patiently for the bartender to get around to me. Memphis Slim helped out by rolling into his signature hit, *"Everyday I Get the Blues,"* and attention quickly drifted away from me and back to the stage. I swear, you could feel that music pounding right through you. The guy at the bar next to me gave me a soft elbow nudge and rasped: *"So y'all like th' blues?"* He was a skinny, wizened little guy with caramel skin, sunken cheeks, sly eyes, a creamy-white sport coat and a natty Panama straw hat with a creamy-white silk band around it, and he had to damn near holler to be heard over the music.

"Yeah," I nodded. *"I like it a lot."*

He looked me up and down. *"Not too many white folks comes in t'hear it."*

"Hey," I told him. *"That's their loss."*

He considered that for a moment, gave me an approving nod and stuck out his hand. *"Ah'm Willie Shorter."*

I shook it. *"Hank Lyons."*

"You fum aroun' here?"

"California."

He looked impressed.

"By way of London."

He looked even more impressed. Then he nodded towards the bartender—who had been kind of ignoring me—and he immediately came over so I could order myself a beer. Willie obviously wielded a lot of weight for a skinny little guy who couldn't have gone much over 100 pounds dripping wet. I asked Willie if I could buy him one, too, but he just smiled with a couple of gold teeth in back and said: *"Neva touch it no mo.'"*

In the back of my mind, I was already trying to figure how I could maneuver the conversation around to asking if he had any idea where I could find a loose kilogram of pot for some underage rich white kids parked outside, but it wasn't the sort of thing you wanted to shout out loud. Not even in a place like The Black Mamba Lounge.

"You work at the plant?" I asked, just to make conversation.

"Useta. But no mo'. I got me a bad back."

"That's too bad."

"Lahk hell it is!" he more or less cackled. *"Got's me a full disability now! An' a better job doin' somethin' else!"*

The song came to an end and Memphis Slim announced that the band was taking a short break. A few more lights came on as the dance floor cleared, and that's when I noticed Otis Jenkins and Zenobia Smith emerging from the middle of the crowd.

"Excuse me," I told Willie, "I think I see somebody I know."

I made my way over towards Otis and Zenobia, and you couldn't miss the eyes following me along the crowded bar. I felt like I was covered in luminous white paint. Zenobia noticed me first as I came up to them, but there wasn't even a hint of recognition in her eyes. Although it took me a moment to get my eyes up to them because it was impossible not to stare at her incredible, statuesque, even frightening body. Zenobia Smith was big and muscular and curvaceous and voluptuous and there was a shiny glisten of sweat all over her from the dancing. And you could see plenty of it, because she had a *lot* of skin showing. But above her magnificent breasts, broad shoulders and graceful, sculptured neck was that proud, angry face with *"don't you fuck with me!"* written all over it. Otis turned around from the bar with a pair of cocktails in his hand and pretended to notice me for the first time. He glanced over at Zenobia, but she didn't so much as flutter an eyelash. Then he looked back at me without much enthusiasm and asked: "Hey, how y'doin, man?"

"Fine," I told him. "Good to see you again." I saw a little sizzle of alarm shoot through his eyes and reminded myself that Zenobia could never, *ever* know about our first meeting in Amanda Cassandra Fairway's Androuet du Cerceau-copy garden maze the night of Amelia Camellia Fairway's seventeenth birthday party. "Great band, eh?" I quickly added.

Zenobia scowled at me like there was no way I could ever possibly appreciate —let alone understand—Memphis Slim's music.

"You like the blues?" Otis asked. You could tell he was eager to move the conversation anywhere else.

"Sure I do. Always have. We don't get much of it where I've been staying over in Europe."

"Well, you're about t'be getting' more of it," Zenobia more or less snorted.

"Oh? How's that?"

She tilted her head in the direction of the stage. "He's goin' back t'France soon as this tour's over."

"He?"

She glared at me. "Memphis Slim. He's leavin' all you o-fay crackers t'live in Paris."

I couldn't ever remember anyone being so angry at me when I hadn't really done anything. Otis gave me an invisible nudge in the ribs. "That's just Zenobia's way," he explained after she left for the ladies' room. "An' not just with white people, either." Although she surely ramped it up a few notches if you were white. All the way up to the fucking redline, in fact. And especially if you'd ventured onto her own, home turf. Otis swirled the drink around in his glass. "So'dja just come here for music?"

"That was my original intent," I pretty much laughed. And then I told him about Amelia Camellia Fairway and the Bamboo Cream Pontiac Grand Prix full of rich-punk white kids from Grosse Pointe that was idling away impatiently out in the parking lot.

"*Shit!*" he spit out between his teeth. "Can't have her still hangin' around when Zenobia an' me gets ready t'leave…"

"I'm in kind of a spot, too. I really don't want to get mixed up in this. Not at all. But she can really fuck me around if she sets her mind to it."

"She's trouble," Otis nodded. "Wisht I'd never laid eyes on her, honest I do." Only then a wistful look passed through his eyes and he half-whispered: "She really is sumpthin' though, issn'she?"

"I wouldn't know."

He shook his head, and you could see there were visions and memories and day-dreams and nightmares of Amelia Camellia Fairway floating around behind his eyes. "She's a wild one, all right…" He shook his head again. "But she's *trouble*…"

I took a long swallow of beer. "But can you help me out?" I asked again. "Help us both out? I mean, is there anybody here who could, you know, who might…"

Otis ran a finger around the rim of his cocktail glass. "You really don' wanna be messin' wi' dat, man." He shook his head. "It's trouble jus' waitin' t'happen."

"I know it is. But I don't know what the fuck else to do. And you're stuck in the middle of it just like I am. You want her waiting out there when you and Zenobia leave?"

I watched him wince at the prospect. And then he drained the rest of his drink. "Look," he finally admitted, "I might have a guy for you. But I'm not sure he'll even talk to you, man. He gots t'be real careful, y'know…"

"I understand."

Without a word, Otis nodded for me to follow him to the far end of the bar. In fact, right up to the empty bar stool where Willie Shorter had been sitting. He was gone now, but in spite of the heavy crowd pressing in around it, no one had taken his seat. We waited there a few moments while the bright lights dimmed over the dance floor and Memphis Slim and his band retook the stage. They all looked extremely relaxed and in extraordinarily good humor. And not long after that, while they were still getting their instruments together, Willie Shorter reappeared from the back of the room and made his way through the crowd. His eyes went back and forth between Otis and me as he approached—pausing to nod and smile or cackle out a *"hey, man!"* or *"how you is?"* along the way—but I couldn't read anything in his expression. He sat down between us and I watched Otis lean over and start whispering in his ear. It took quite some time and, while he was doing it, Willie Shorter looked me up and down again. And then, after Otis was finished, he looked me right in the eyes.

"You isn't a cop, is you?"

It kind of startled me. "Hell, no," I almost laughed. "I'm a car writer. A racing correspondent…" he looked at me like he didn't know what that was. "I live in London, for chrissake. I'm just here doing some, umm, 'motorsports consulting' for Fairway Motors."

He thought that over for a moment, then leaned in close and rasped: "Them's rich white kids outside, isn't they?"

I nodded.

He nodded solemnly. "Well, ah cain't be transactin' no bidness wit' dem."

"They just want to, uhh, make a purchase, that's all."

He shook his head. "That cain't be, man. That just cain't be."

Otis leaned in and whispered something more in Willie's ear. But Willie shook his head. So Otis whispered some more. As he did, Willie looked me over again, side-to-side and top-to-bottom, considering. But then he said: "Don' wanna be doin' no bidness wit' him, neither." He looked up at me almost apologetically. "No offense meant, man."

"None taken," I told him. And then I leaned over and whispered to Otis that Amelia and her friends were looking for a whole brick and that there was cash money outside in the Pontiac—plenty of it, in fact—just waiting to be spent. Otis bent over and relayed the information to Willie Shorter, and you could see just a slight glimmer of commercial interest come up in his eyes. So he thought it over some more while Memphis Slim's band started to play again and the two of them excused themselves and headed towards the back of the room to see if they could work out the details.

And that, in a nutshell, is how I wound up going out to the Pontiac in the parking lot again and telling Amelia and her spoiled-rotten, punk-raggedy friends that there was a guy inside who might be able to help them out, but he had less than what they wanted on him and it was already broken down into lids and he had to make some other deals and deliveries that night and so the best he could do was three lids for a hundred bucks. I had a suspicion it was actually three lids for 90 bucks and that Otis was making himself a little ten-buck finder's fee on it.

"That's highway robbery!" the blonde kid wailed. But Amelia shut him up with a glance.

"Is it the same stuff from before?" she wanted to know.

"How the hell would I know?"

So they went into a huddle inside the Pontiac and then the blonde kid passed me a crumpled-up wad of twenties out the window. "Hey, thanks man," he kind of whinnied. And then added a warning: *"Don't fuck us up now, man,"* in a shrill, reedy voice.

So I went back inside and finished up my beer while Otis danced some more with Zenobia, and then he and I went into the dark, stinky men's room in back and into that one stall with a door still on it and I passed him the money and my car keys and then we went back to the bar and I waited through the rest of the set while Otis and Zenobia danced some more and then he and Willie kind of separately melted their way outside while I stood there next to Zenobia, trying not to let her catch me staring at her shape while she made a huge point of totally ignoring me. What seemed like an awfully long time later, Willie came back in and took his regular place at the end of the bar and a little after that Otis came in and palmed me the keys down under the bar where nobody could see it. *"It's under the front seat, man,"* he whispered as he passed Zenobia another cocktail. I turned to go, but his hand snaked out and grabbed my sleeve. "Hey, finish up yo' beer, man!" he grinned like he was just being friendly. But I knew what he really meant was *"Don't be so fucking obvious."*

So I finished off my beer and looked at the empty stage and dance floor some more and listened to the music on the jukebox until the next two songs were done and then I kind of wandered my way outside, looked around over both shoulders—there were people outside around both the front and rear doors smoking and drinking between sets, and you could smell the heavy hemp stink filtering through the air. I was starting to feel pretty glad that my car was way over in a corner of the lot, hidden in the dark and far away from the building. But when I opened the door and groped around under the front seat, I didn't find anything. I felt a stab of stupid, rube panic go through me. Jesus, it was my first-ever dope deal and I'd been ripped off! Only that didn't seem like something Otis Jenkins might do. But you never really know about people, do you? I groped around under the seat some more, but again I came up empty. And I was just starting to run through possible scenarios and what the hell I might do next when it suddenly occurred to me...

Why not try the other door?

So I went around to the passenger's side, checked over both shoulders again—like nothing I'd done so far looked suspicious, right?—and sure enough, there it was. Just like Otis said it would be. Three little plastic bags of pot all rolled up like soft little logs. And that's when I thought about maybe taking just a little out for myself. As a sort of commission, you know? And that seemed like a terrifically reasonable idea. So I ripped a page out of the owner's manual in the glove box and creased it into a half-assed envelope and unrolled each plastic baggie and took just a little pinch from each one. And then maybe just one little pinch more. Then I folded it up and shoved it under the floor mat, carefully re-rolled the baggies, looked both ways again, locked up my car and headed back over to the Pontiac. They'd turned the motor and lights off and were listening to the radio with their heads ducked down below the windowsills. It was Shelley Fabares singing *"Johnny Angel,"* and it struck me how odd it sounded compared to the rolling Memphis Slim music that was once again pumping out of The Black Mamba Lounge.

"You got it?" the blonde punk asked.

I nodded.

"Lemme see it."

I eased the three baggies out of my pocket and dropped them in over the windowsill. The little idiot held them up right in front of his eyes. "They look awful skinny, man," he whined. "And what the fuck took you so long?"

To tell the truth, I'd had about enough of his crap. "Look," I pretty much snarled, "I just did you a fucking favor. A favor I really didn't want to do. And now you're giving me nothing but shit about it."

I heard the Pontiac's door open and close on the other side. And then Amelia Camellia Fairway came around the Pontiac's nose and kept on coming until she was standing right next to me. And I mean *really* close. "He's just an asshole," she whispered apologetically. "He's always been an asshole. He can't fucking help it."

"Then why do you hang around with him?" I whispered right back.

"I haven't got anybody else to hang around with," she answered with a lot of sad, adolescent innuendo. I could feel my nerve endings going on red alert. Only then she gave off a bored, half-hearted shrug like it really didn't make any difference. And then she moved in even closer. Like until I could feel her torso and thighs pressing up against me and smell her alley-cat scent in my nostrils. I think she mostly did it because she knew it made me really, really nervous. "Why don't you stay and smoke a little weed with us?" she whispered up into my ear.

"Right here?"

She nodded her chin against my neck.

"Right now?"

"Sure. Why the fuck not?"

I started to pull away, but she put her arms around my waist and ran her fingers through my belt loops.

"C'mon," she urged. "We'll just do one. He's rolling it up right now."

"Standing right here?"

"We can go in the car if it makes you nervous." She had that insolent, mocking tone back in her voice again.

I saw the orange glow of a lighter tip and then came the heavy, burning-jute smell of the pot. The blonde kid passed it out the window, and I watched while she took a long, deep drag. "Here!" she gasped, and handed it over. So I took some in and tried to hold it, but I coughed it out. So she pulled me in close, put her mouth over mine and blew the smoke from her lungs into mine. "There!" she grinned. And then she put her fingers over my lips to hold it inside. When the joint came around again, she put it in her mouth turned back-to-front, pulled in close again and blew a visible stream of smoke into my mouth and nostrils. She was right up against me with her lips just inches away, and I was starting to feel all sorts of things that couldn't do anything but get me into serious, serious trouble.

"Look, I g-gotta go," I pretty much stammered. I was really starting to feel the pot swirling around inside me. Like everything was overinflated and floating just a little.

Then, out of absolutely nowhere, she ran her hand down the front of my pants and laughed like hell when I jumped away from her. "You carrying a banana in there?" she giggled loud enough that her friends in the car could hear. Not that they were paying much attention.

"Look," I told her, "I gotta go back inside."

"Why?"

"I gotta go pay for it," I lied. "They're probably wondering where I am."

"Fuck 'em," she snorted. "Tell 'em you were out here with us."

"Can't do it," I told her as I backed away.

"You can run, but you can't hide," she snickered. "We'll be getting together sometime, you and me. Just the two of us. You can count on it."

Jesus, I'd never met anyone in my life like Amelia Camellia Fairway. Not ever.

I felt a little unsteady as I headed back into The Black Mamba Lounge. And at first it seemed a little overwhelming. Even a little scary. Everybody seemed to be looking at me. Staring at me. Leering at me. Seemed to know I was really, really stoned. But then I got a beer and the band's last set had started and pretty soon I was into it with Memphis Slim's music rolling and surging and pulsing through me like colored streams of molten lava.

I listened to some pretty damn good music that night, no question about it...

And that, in a nutshell, is how yours truly wound up becoming an irregular and mostly unwilling pot connection for Amelia Camellia Fairway and her rich, spoiled, arrogant, insolent, punk-ass Grosse Pointe friends. We made a deal that I'd engineer the buys at the Black Mamba Lounge and serve as a sort of a middle man, and in return, she agreed that she and her friends would pick it up there in the parking lot. Or, better yet, from where I'd leave it taped up under the kiddy slide late at night in the grammar-school playground down the street from the Fairview Inn. And she promised in return to never try to contact me at work—God knows Scully Mungo's guys probably had all the phones tapped in The Tower and probably had private-detective types   shadowing her and snooping through her phone records as a favor for H.R. Junior—or, worse yet, ever, *ever* come looking for me at the Fairview Inn. Then again, I knew what her promises were worth, so it didn't make me feel entirely secure.

But what choice did I have?

I also have to admit that every time I made a buy for Amelia Camellia Fairway and her friends in the Bamboo Cream Pontiac, I'd invariably sneak a little pinch or two for myself. Not that I was turning into a drug addict or anything. But I had a lot of downtime to kill at The Fairview—particularly on weekday evenings—and so sometimes I'd go out back where I had my stash hidden carefully away in an anonymous plastic baggie carefully rubber-banded to the inside branches of a thick juniper bush behind the trash dumpster. I mean, I didn't dare keep it in my room where the maid or some house detective might find it, and I didn't want it in my car in case I got pulled over in a traffic stop or if they surprised me by taking my Fiesta Flyer away one day and giving me a new company car. Then the cleanup guys would find it (although, considering who the cleanup shop guys were, they'd probably know what it was and smoke it themselves), but maybe a supervisor would get his hands on it and turn it over to one of Scully Mungo's security guys. And that would be serious trouble indeed. Plus the stuff reeked something awful, and you could smell it for sure whenever and wherever you smoked. So I always did it outside late at night in the darkness underneath the kids' slide in the grammar-school playground I told you about a half-block away from the Fairview Inn. Only then one night I got particularly euphoric or something—I remember there was a full moon like a neon-florescent silver dollar and a warm breeze that smelled of ancient rust and fresh pizza crust and you could hear the rumble of occasional, middle-of-the-fucking-night trucks passing by on the freeway a half a mile away and wonder what each one was carrying and what kind of music each of those truck drivers was listening to on the radio and…

…But I guess the point here is that I wandered my way back to the Fairview Inn lost in a great, swirling sea of important thoughts and feelings—and particularly of Audrey and how she smelled like jade, even though jade didn't really smell like anything—and suddenly realized, as I found myself standing at the locked side-door entrance of the Fairview Inn and needed my hands to go searching through my pockets for my damn room key—it had to be in one of them—that I was still holding the remains of a partially smoked (but very nicely rolled) marijuana cigarette (if you were in the know, you called it a "joint") between my thumb and forefinger. My God! I'd been smoking the damn thing while I'd been walking back from the playground! In fact, I'd probably been smoking it right while I walked across the damn Fairview Inn parking lot! Or maybe I was just carrying it? I couldn't really remember. But there it was, right there between my thumb and forefinger! And my first instinct was to throw the damn thing away immediately. Get it off the end of my fingers like it was a damn stinging insect or something! Only then somebody might find it. In fact, somebody—probably one of Scully Mungo's guys—might be in one of those darkened, parked cars, watching me right now! I looked around over my shoulders, but everything was as edgy and quiet as you might expect at one in the morning. And, in another impatient and selfish and ornery little corner of my brain, I was thinking how this was some *really* good stuff and it would be a damn shame just to throw it away. So I looked around over both shoulders again—real sly, you know—and then, nonchalant as can be, I slipped that two-thirds of an excellent marijuana joint into my pocket. I mean, I needed that thumb and forefinger to go looking for my room key…

…Only then, when I finally got back to my room—jeez, there were a lot of stairs to climb to get up to the second floor—I started worrying again about what the heck would happen if somebody found the damn thing in my room?

I mean, there was a cleaning lady and Lord only knew who else in and out of there every day. So I promised myself right away that I would never, *ever* put a match to it here in the room. I mean, people would smell it out in the hall. And then I had to find someplace to hide it. Someplace where nobody would ever, ever look. And I of course came up with all sorts of excellent and exotic ideas like hiding it inside the U-shaped trap in the drain pipe for the sink in the bathroom. Only then I'd need some sort of waterproof capsule to put it in and I'd need a couple monkey wrenches that I didn't really have and, even if I had all that, how would I keep it from just being flushed away with the water and soap residue and stubble the next time I shaved? Besides, it sounded like an awful lot of work. And, if you've ever taken one of those U-shaped sink traps apart, it's usually really icky in there...

And then I came up with a fabulously perfect and sneaky idea. I went over to the closet by the door, looked over both shoulders again to make sure nobody was watching, took one of the Fairway Motors ball-point pens out of the inside pocket of my Fairway-blue blazer, carefully unscrewed it, took out the ink cartridge and the spring and put my leftover two-thirds of a most excellent marijuana joint inside. Ha! Brilliant! And then I wondered and worried over whether I should just leave that stealth-stash pen in the desk drawer by the TV set or—did I dare?—put it back in the inside pocket of my Fairway-blue blazer and carry it with me wherever I went so I could avoid leaving it behind in the room where somebody, somehow, might find it...

Not that the stuff was making me paranoid or anything.

Chapter 4: The Brickyard

A jangling alarm shook me awake around noon the next day, and it took me a little while to recognize where the hell I was and try to figure out how the hell I'd managed to get there (and moreover crawl into bed and fall asleep under the covers with my left shoe still on?). It took me several blinks to realize it wasn't time to get up or a fire drill or a Russian missile attack but just the damn telephone on the bed stand. I reached out for it with fingers thick and numb as uncooked pork sausages.

Geez, my mouth was dry.

"Wh-wh-whozit?"

Pause at the other end. Then Hal Crockett's familiar, gravelly voice through the crackle of long distance: "That you, Hank?"

I ran my tongue over my lips to moisten them up a little. "Must be," I told him. "Doesn't look like anybody else is here."

"You sound like you had a pretty rough night."

"Nah," I lied. "It's just a bad connection."

"That's what happens when amateurs try to drink," he scoffed at me from somewhere or other in Holland. "Well, it's probably not worth much the way you're feeling, but I thought you might want a little update on the grand prix you missed a few hours ago."

"Of course I do." I scrunched myself around and propped my head up against the headboard so I could hear a little better. It took some doing, if you want the truth of it. But I finally got everything settled back down. "So tell me: what happened?"

Hal laid it out for me so it was almost like I was there. Come the start, Jimmy Clark and Chapman's new Lotus 25 shot off from the outside of the front row and simply ran away and hid. Left everybody else for dead! It wasn't even a contest. So Jimmy and the new, monocoque 25 looked set for a dominant, runaway victory—in the car's very first race, mind you!—but then they had clutch trouble and ultimately dropped down to 9th at the checker. But it was still one hell of a performance, and no question the handwriting was on the wall. Surtees gave chase early on in the new Bowmaker Lola— which amounted to one heck of a performance in a brand-new car from a brand-new Formula One constructor—but then he had one hell of a moment when a front suspension link snapped and sent him scything off into the barriers at truly frightening speed. It was just dumb luck that he hit at a shallow angle and didn't get hurt. But his confidence in the new Lola had to be severely shaken.

All of which left Graham Hill's BRM solidly in the lead, and he persevered on to score a welcome win for the BRM outfit. It was only their second-ever grand prix victory (their first had been with Joakim Bonnier at the same race in 1958, with four long, disappointing seasons in between) and everyone in the paddock was thrilled for them. Phil Hill had meanwhile pushed, cajoled and carried his reliable (but by now pretty much obsolete) Ferrari up to second place, but Trevor Taylor's older-style, tube-framed Lotus 24 was reeling him in and overhauled him in the late going to grab at least second place for Colin Chapman's Team Lotus. Afterwards, Phil got a highly public tongue-lashing from team-manager Dragoni for letting Taylor's Lotus slip past. Phil argued that the Lotus was obviously the faster car, but Dragoni countered that Phil was World Champion, and a true World Champion would never allow such a thing to happen! Hal said it was a pretty ugly exchange to witness, and we were both getting the feeling that Phil's days with *Scuderia Ferrari* might be numbered.

Still, it sounded like a pretty damn interesting race. But then, they all were if you knew what the hell you were looking at, and I was heartsick that I wasn't there to see it in person and report on it for the magazine.

There was more Lotus magic on tap at the 1000Ks Manufacturers' Championship round at the famously difficult Nurburgring the following weekend. From what Hal told me, I missed another rather startling display by Jimmy Clark, this time at the wheel of Colin Chapman's svelte and petite new Lotus 23 sports/racer, which had one of Chapman's new, in-house twincam engines in the back for power. It was only a 1500 (1498cc, actually), but the car around it was so light, low, lithe and sweet that it made for a formidable combination on the twisty, daunting, uphill-downhill mountain circuit. Clark was really coming into his own as a star driver, and he qualified the 1500cc Lotus a fairly astounding 9th on the grid—right behind the factory Ferraris and Porsches—but that was nothing compared to what he did with it on race day!

It was a typically damp, dreary race-day morning at the Nurburgring, what with a heavy mist hanging over the Eifel Mountains and intermittent spatters of rain around the entire, 14-mile circuit. Those turned out to be ideal conditions for the nimble little

Lotus, and Jimmy took full advantage, knifing through the cars ahead like they were running around on their wheel rims and then disappearing into the distance. He had such a huge lead at the end of the first lap that everyone assumed there'd been some sort of terrible accident. Only then, long after Clark had passed, the silence was broken by Gurney's new, flat-8 Porsche coupe pursued by teammate Graham Hill in the factory Porsche spyder, Phil Hill in the best of the Ferrari Dinos and then young Kiwi Bruce McLaren doing an incredible job under iffy conditions in John Oiger's borderline ancient Aston Martin DBR1. But the race at the front looked like it was already settled, as Jimmy and the Lotus continued to extend their lead on the damp racetrack. The 23 had almost two full minutes in hand over Gurney's Porsche at the end of the first hour and, as the weather began to clear, the only car that could match the Lotus' pace was wild man Willy Mairesse in a special, prototype-entry Ferrari GTO with a 4.0-liter V12 stuffed under the hood.

But a header tube had cracked on the 23's exhaust and, unbeknownst to the driver, the fumes were being drawn forward into the cockpit. A foggy and disoriented Jimmy Clark—he probably had no idea that he was being gassed by his own car!—eventually misjudged a corner, went off and crashed into a ditch. Fortunately without serious damage to either himself or the car. But Chapman's potent new flyweight (not to mention his new twincam motor) had made an indelible impression while they were still running. Of such things are reputations built. Not to mention envies and jealousies…

Following the Lotus's retirement and the first round of pit stops, things started sorting themselves out in more typical fashion. The 2-liter Porsches of Gurney and Hill lost ground to the more powerful Ferraris as the pavement dried and they also encountered some minor problems, and that allowed the Hill/Gendebien 246SP Dino to scratch its way into the lead and hold it all the way to the checker for yet another Ferrari victory. The Gurney/Bonnier Porsche uncharacteristically seized its gearbox right near the end (not typical of Porsche at all!) and that allowed the Mairesse/Mike Parkes 4.0-liter "prototype" GTO to take an unmolested second place. And a privateer Ferrari Berlinetta copped the bigbore GT win as well (and the coveted World Manufacturers' Championship points that went along with it!) to complete the Ferrari sweep. Maybe the most unusual thing was the surprise 1-2 finish by a pair of German-entered Volvo P1800s in the 2.0-liter Grand Touring class (although they were way down in 21st and

22nd overall and mostly beat a couple of Morgans and an aging A.C. Bristol and were three full laps behind the 1300cc Grand Touring-winning Alfa Romeo SZ and two more laps—and remember, those are 14-mile laps!—behind the factory-entered Porsche Carrera-Abarth that won the 1600cc Grand Touring class). Still, a smooth-talking, angle-shooting, curveball-master ad guy like Dick Flick could make a lot of mileage out of something like that. And without making a single false or actionable statement, too!

Oh, and our young yachting friend Count Volpi suffered through a pretty miserable weekend. He'd entered no less than four cars: his three Ferraris plus one of the hulking, mouth-breathing 151 coupes that Maserati was building for Le Mans. Only the Maserati wasn't ready yet (no big surprise, if you knew anything about how Maserati did business) and all of his Ferraris except the Sebring-winning Testa Rossa were either sitting in Ferrari's customer race shop in Maranello waiting for attention or sitting in Scuderia Serenissima's own shop waiting for their engines, transmissions or rear ends to come back from "rebuilding and refreshing" at Ferrari's customer race shop in Maranello. Which is something that can happen should your name somehow drop off the "preferred customer" list at Ferrari (if you know what I mean). And the remaining Sebring car crashed out on the seventh lap while the track was still drying. So it was a pretty dismal weekend indeed for our friend Count Volpi and Scuderia Serenissima.

I had a meeting with Danny Beagle first thing Monday morning to go over my official report on Shelby's operation, and then he took me into Bob Wright's office for a few minutes to go over our plans for Le Mans. I of course agreed that it would be a good thing for Bob to see and experience the race in person, and I told him it shouldn't be much of a problem making the necessary arrangements. After all, I still had a lot of friends and connections over there, even if finding a place to stay would be a bit of an undertaking. I mean, Le Mans was only four weeks away, and every decent hotel room was surely already booked halfway back to Paris. But I allowed as how you could almost always find something if you know where to look and whom to slip a stack of francs to. And then of course I mentioned Audrey and how she might very well be able to help us. It had already occurred to me that it would be unbelievably nice if she and I wound up working and traveling around together (and all of it at the company's expense and moreover away from her obstinate and cantankerous father!) not to mention that it would surely send some fat Fairway checks her way. Although Audrey never talked to me about her personal finances, I was pretty damn sure she could use the money.

I also made sure to mention Eric Broadley's Lola Shop in Bromley and about the doodled sketch I'd seen on Eric's drawing board. The one of the mid-engined Le Mans coupe with a big, amorphous blob of an American V8 nestled in behind the cockpit. Bob looked mildly intrigued. "Do you think it's any good?" he asked me.

"Well, this guy Broadley's done some pretty amazing things with everything he's designed so far," I allowed. "His new Formula One car sat on pole for its very first grand prix two weekends ago at Zandvoort..." I was careful not to mention the part about the front suspension shearing off. "...And this new Le Mans car looks like it could be pretty slick."

I saw a little glimmer coming up in Bob's eyes.

"He was thinking of putting a Chevy in it..." I added obliquely.

And of course that's about all it took to get Eric Broadley a couple of the new, reasonably lightweight Fairway V8s crated up and air-freighted over to Bromley. For "testing and evaluation" purposes, of course...

I thought our meeting was about over when Bob casually dropped his little bombshell about Little Harry Dick Fairway getting wind of the Le Mans trip and deciding that he wanted to join in. Along with most of his guys from the executive corridor who might ultimately be involved in any Fairway Le Mans program (plus some of their key staff members, of course), and I could see right away that was going to turn into a major logistical problem wrapped up in a travel agent's worst nightmare. Particularly when it came to lodging.

"I don't think we'll be able to find enough rooms," I tried to explain. I mean, I couldn't exactly see Little Harry Dick Fairway (or Bob Wright or Dick Flick or Wanda Peters and surely not Daryl Starling) sharing a set of Fairway-blue army tents in the public camping area near the esses or brushing their teeth at the communal sinks every morning next to a bunch of hung-over Brits and garlicky Frenchmen. Plus credentials would surely be a problem, since the Fairway bunch would undoubtedly want full VIP access—including all the places the race teams and organizers really didn't want any more in-the-way, know-nothing rubberneckers. Not to mention that Bob wanted "to keep a low profile on this" since he didn't want anybody to know or guess what Fairway Motors was up to.

Or at least not yet, anyway.

I cautioned him that we might encounter some difficulties trying to make it all happen on such short notice. But he just waved me off. "You've got four weeks," he said like that was an answer in itself.

"It-it's not quite that simple," I pretty much sputtered.

"Sure it is," he said through a large, confident smile. "We'll just put you and Danny and Karen on it. And maybe that girl you were talking about over in London, too." I could see he was watching for my reaction to that last bit, but he didn't skip a beat. "I have faith in you. You'll get it done."

And that was the end of it.

On the one hand, you had to respect the decisiveness of Bob Wright's decision-making process and his unshakable, almost evangelical conviction that a powerful, task-oriented company like Fairway Motors could do whatever the hell it put its mind to. At the same time, it was slowly and somewhat uncomfortably coming into focus what my job description truly entailed and what I'd be expected to accomplish on the company's behalf. And that I'd sure as hell better find a way to pull it off, too.

"So tell me more about this girl in England," Danny asked almost as soon as we left Bob's office.

I decided it would be best to try to make it sound as objective, unbiased, dispassionate and professional as possible. "Well," I started in, "her name's Audrey Denbeigh, and she's based out of London and by profession she's a school teacher—a private tutor, actually, and *very* well educated—but her father's been involved in motorsports all his life and so she grew up around it, and she kind of found her way into a side job making travel arrangements for several of the top English racing teams…" I could see Danny looked impressed, "…She's knowledgeable, experienced, personable and efficient and she speaks all sorts of languages and…"

Danny looked at me kind of sideways. "She wouldn't be the same one you were blubbering about on our way home from Amelia Camellia Fairway's birthday party?"

"I was?"

"You wouldn't remember. You were pretty fucked up. In fact, you were more than pretty fucked up."

"I was?"

Danny nodded.

Well, there was no point trying to hide it. "Yeah," I admitted. "It's the same one. But she's really, *really* good at what she does. Honest she is. And she could really help us out."

"Hey," Danny grinned. "I don't give a shit. You want to add on a consultant or an outside subcontractor with a few side benefits, go for it. No skin off my nose."

"You mean it?"

"Of course I mean it. Fuck the shit out of her if you like. Only not on company time. And make sure you submit a proper budget request."

"A budget request?"

"Sure. You can get the forms from Clifton Toole's people. Make sure to fill them out in triplicate. You keep the blue copy. They'll get back to you in a month or so if you're lucky…"

By then I knew he was messing with me. But I needed to know what to do. The idea of getting Audrey involved in Fairway's Le Mans expedition—and maybe even more projects down the road?—was too damn delicious to ignore.

"So what do I do?'

"See Karen Sabelle," Danny advised. "If you can convince her it's worthwhile, she can make it happen." He shot me an insider wink. "Shit, she runs half the damn company out of her top desk drawer."

"I see."

"And one more thing."

"What's that?"

Danny's smile evaporated. "Be careful, okay?"

"Careful?"

He nodded. "You know what I mean." He leaned in a little closer and whispered: "You don't want to be letting the little head do the thinking…"

"But it's not like that!" I snapped back at him. In fact, I said it loud enough that it seemed to echo down the corridor. I brought my voice down to barely a whisper and repeated: "It's not like that at all."

"Sure it's not," he chuckled with a nasty little twist of innuendo. "Hey, I don't mean anything by it. Like I said, I don't give a shit. I'm just trying to look out for you, that's all." He pulled me over by the closed door of Hugo Becker's office. "There are a lot of guys who fool around inside any big company—look at Dick Flick, for chrissakes—and most of 'em get away with it. I mean, it's nobody's business, right? But it's different when you're running your zipper up and down on company time. Y'gotta be careful about that sort of thing…"

I told him I understood.

But all I could think about was getting together with Audrey again.

Naturally I called her as soon as I got off the executive corridor and told her all about it, and the reception at the other end of the line was a little cooler than I expected. But it turned out her father had been feeling a little off and wasn't eating properly (and of course he refused to go see a doctor about it), and she was worried that he might have had another minor stroke. So the prospect of leaving him on his own while she went gallivanting all over Europe with me made her extremely uneasy. And of course I thought he might have been doing it on purpose just to ratchet up her guilt and concern. But I stopped short of saying anything.

"It's a hell of an opportunity," I told her.

"It sounds like it," she agreed without measurable enthusiasm.

"It should pay pretty good, too."

There was a long, tightly wound silence at the other end. I got the feeling that Walter was probably in the room with her. And then, in little more than a whisper, she added: "Don't get me wrong, Hank. It was kind of you to think of me and it sounds absolutely fabulous. It's just…" for just an instant, it sounded like she was going to cry, "…it's just that I'm not really sure I can, that's all."

Half of me wanted to keep telling her about it—to keep selling—but the other half knew better. So I backed off. There are times when you need to do stuff like that, and it's a measure of your sensitivity when you recognize such things. Or that's what I told myself, anyway.

"I miss you," I told her.

"I miss you, too."

I heard a kind of grunt in the background, and I could visualize Walter making a face.

"Your father's making a face, isn't he?"

That got me the first genuine laugh I'd heard in quite awhile.

"It stinks being this far away from you."

"Yes, it does stink, doesn't it?" I could tell she was saying it just to dig the needle in a little at her father. Make him wonder what the hell we were talking about, you know?

"If I can get Bob Wright and Karen Sabelle to approve it, I'll probably be over there in the next week or so to start setting up arrangements."

"It'll be good to see you again."

"It'll be good to see you, too."

And then we kind of ran out of things to say and just stayed there in the quiet together. It was nice just knowing she was at the other end of the line.

"This is costing you a fortune," she finally mumbled to break the silence.

"I'm pretty sure I've got an expense account to cover this kind of thing."

"That's no reason to abuse it."

"You're a real stick-in-the-mud when it comes to money," I laughed. "I think Clifton Toole's really going to like you."

"Who?"

"Clifton Toole."

"Who on earth is he?"

"You'll find out soon enough."

And that seemed as good a time as any to say goodbye. And I didn't mind, because I had the feeling that we were going to see each other again in the very near future.

In fact, I was pretty damn sure of it.

In the meantime, I found myself stranded in a severe state of motorsports deprivation and withdrawal, and although I'd missed that first grand prix of the season in Holland and the 1000Ks World Manufacturers Championship event at the Nurburgring, being in Detroit put me not too far up the road from Indianapolis on Memorial Day (which fell on a Wednesday that year), and it was a nice surprise when Danny Beagle told me Bob Wright wanted me down there as his "personal guest." Which meant traveling with a lot of the top-brass types from Fairway Tower, since Bob was eager to get them acquainted with the motorsports scene and thinking and formulating notions about how Fairway Motors should become involved. After all, the Indy 500 was without question the most recognized and important motor sports event in North America, and mainstream Fairway customers like John Q. and Fred Average and their buddies from the bar and the burger stand and the bowling alley and the grandstands at your choice of professional baseball or football games were convinced it was the most important automobile race on the whole damn planet. So no question Fairway Motors required a presence there. A massive presence. And preferably in the Winner's Circle.

It was quite an excursion. Bob (or really Karen Sabelle, of course) had arranged for about a dozen of us to fly down at the break of dawn Wednesday morning on the company Gulfstream turboprop, which was quite a revelation to a generally impoverished motorsports scribe used to sharing cheap rental cars or driving to races in my own dilapidated Fiat. Ben Abernathy didn't go because he had some family barbeque thing going on (plus, like I said, he wasn't all that interested in automobile racing and didn't really enjoy company junkets where Little Harry Dick Fairway was involved) so I sat with Hugo Becker. And was surprised to learn how interested and knowledgeable he was about what was happening at Indy that particular year. Particularly about the interesting new, mid-engined Harvey Aluminum car from Mickey Thompson with a Buick aluminum V8 in back. He'd read all about it in *Popular Mechanics*.

You couldn't miss how H.R. Junior sat by himself in a special, extra-wide seat in the very last row, so he could keep an eye on everybody while nobody could keep an eye on him.

We had a nice catered breakfast on the plane with eggs and thick-sliced bacon and orange juice and hash browns and pecan rolls so blessed sweet and sticky you had to wash your hands afterwards. So I headed back to the john to take care of that and let a little of the coffee out. But it was occupied, and I noticed that H.R. Junior's special seat was also empty, and so I was just in the process of turning around in a hurry and heading back to my seat so I wouldn't have to meet up with him face-to-face when he came out of the can. Not that I was frightened or anything. Or maybe just a little. I mean, he was powerful and unpredictable and he seemed to truly enjoy making people squirm, and the general consensus on the executive corridor seemed to be that staying off of his radar screen and out of the line of fire was by far the best course of action. But he burst through the little doorway before I could complete my escape and he gave me a withering, red-faced *"who the hell are you and what the hell are you doing in my way?"* sneer as I did my best to stand aside. He kept staring at me as he barged past, and you couldn't miss that his face was flushed and he was breathing a little heavy. I also noticed that he was carrying a blue folder under his arm, and I was pretty damn sure it was the same one I'd observed him, umm, "reviewing" by himself in the billiard room the night of Amelia Camellia Fairway's 17th birthday party. I was dying to know what was inside of it, of course, but figured that sort of curiosity was best reserved for people whose paychecks didn't have the Fairway family name printed across the top.

There was a fancy chartered bus with damn near a mobile living room inside waiting at the Indianapolis airport—the kind famous Hollywood stars and rock-and-roll idols use!—to whisk us away to the Speedway. Or sit mired in bumper-to-bumper race-morning traffic on Crawfordsville Road, which was really more like it. I hadn't been to an Indy 500 in several years, and it amazed me all over again what an enormous and uniquely American sort of spectacle it is. It makes the gladiator battles and Christians being fed to the lions in the old Roman Colosseum look like sandlot ball. To begin with, Indy is a truly gargantuan facility, and although it sits empty for most of the year, it fills the grandstands for two full weekends of one-car-at-a-time, four-lap-average qualifying every May and then up to overflowing on race day. Mostly with earnest, hardworking Midwestern types: gas station owners and their favorite mechanics, new-car dealers and their sales crews and service managers, construction contractors and their best customers, liquor salesmen ditto, machine-shop owners and their lathe, milling machine and drill-press operators and street-corner print shop, paint and hardware store proprietors and their neighbors and families who have been coming down to the same exact seats at the 500 for years. Most of them aren't your typical, informed, frothing-at-the-mouth motorsports fans and don't really follow the sport or go to a lot of races, but none of them would even think of missing an Indy 500. After all, it's an institution.

And especially when something controversial is going on.

Like I said before, the big hubbub in 1962 was over the radical little mid-engined, Buick V8-powered projectiles from California hot-rodder, drag racer and world-land-speed-record-contender Mickey Thompson. Now Mickey was a sharp car builder, a brilliant self-promoter and a true master when it came to brash, wild-eyed speed ideas that would attract a lot of attention. And he was even better when it came to hunting up the backers and sponsorship dollars necessary to actually make those ideas happen. No question he had the attention of some pretty important people over at GM. But he was a lot more than just another motorsports hustler, angle-shooter and bullshit artist. Sure, he flitted from idea to idea and project to project without ever really fin-ishing a lot of them. But he'd also been there in the cockpit himself, and whatever else you could say about Mickey Thompson, he knew how to put his foot down and hang on—no matter what!—even when things got scary. He'd hustled together a Bonneville streamliner with four blown Pontiac V8s under the hood (they really liked him over at GM's Pontiac Division!), and he even got Goodyear to build some special tires that might take the strain of a 400+ mph World Land Speed Record attempt. And he damn near pulled it off, too. Thompson actually managed to become the fastest man on earth (at least on level ground, anyway) with a one-way run across the salt flats at a timed-and-verified 406.6 miles-per-hour in that four-Pontiac monster in September of 1960. But he never got the actual record because a driveshaft broke and he couldn't get it fixed in time to make the return run within an hour required to make it official. And that was kind of the way it went with a lot of Mickey's projects: ambitious ideas, in-credible creativity, beautiful machinery and unbelievable effort, but not so much in the way of finishing kick or ultimate results.

But he sure knew how to generate ink and interest.

In any case, the top brass at GM loved him. Especially Pontiac Division general manager "Bunkie" Knudson and chief engineer John Z. DeLorean, who both thought racing (and the performance image and publicity it generated) was really good for business. Mickey was one of GM's "back-door" racing guys all through the late fifties and early sixties, and GM was more than happy to set him up with a few things he needed (but quietly, of course) for his new Indycar project. Including a bunch of the new, 3.5-liter aluminum V8s that they were touting for their new, mid-sized Buick, Oldsmobile and Pontiac "compacts." Which fit right in with Thompson's main sponsor, a relatively small but promotionally minded metals company out of Los Angeles called Harvey Aluminum.

As you'd expect from someone out of the California hot rod, drag race and Bonneville streamliner scene, Thompson's new Harvey Aluminum Specials were absolutely gorgeous to look at in their iridescent metallic blue-and-white livery with subtle red pinstriping—it reminded you of the Reventlow Scarabs—and he had no trouble punching the little pushrod aluminum V8s out to the 4.2-liter maximum. But they were down on power compared to the old but purpose-built and well-developed Offies everybody else was running, and a lot of the scribes and Indy regulars thought the project was too ambitious by half. The Thompson cars featured a brand new, mid-engined chassis designed by Englishman John Crosthwaite (who had worked for Cooper Cars), and so it was no huge surprise that it looked an awful lot like the Jack Brabham Cooper that had run so well at The Brickyard in 1961. But it was a brand-new car from essentially a brand-new Indycar constructor, and that plus the hogged-out and hot-rodded version of Buick's brand-new aluminum V8 amounted to an awful lot to bite off and chew all at once. Especially for a new team that had never run an Indy 500 before. Everybody else was running traditional, front-engined, solid-axle Offy roadsters, and nobody's ever had much success bucking the tide of tradition at Indy. Or at least not right off the bat, anyway.

Plus the cars had been rushed and hustled together in barely four months, and so there were a lot of details that looked finished but hadn't been properly sorted out or tested. So there were problems, and Chuck Daigh's #35 never even made it through qualifying. But Dan Gurney did an amazing job with the #34 Thompson car, qualifying it 8th on the grid and putting it in the middle of the 3rd row! Which was particularly impressive when you took into account that Dan was likewise a rookie at Indianapolis and, as a road-racer, didn't really have any oval-track experience to speak of. Then again, Dan was a racer—one of the truly elite ones in just about everybody's opinion—and no question the Thompson car was smaller, lower, lighter and poked a tinier hole in the air than the traditional Indy roadsters. According to the pit-lane gossip, it was also a wee bit spooky to drive…

I have to admit I was even more impressed by the "guest" Dan brought along with him on the flight over from Europe: Colin Chapman! They'd left Germany right after the Nurburgring 1000Ks on May 27th and would have to be on another plane as soon as the 500 was over so they could make practice for the Monaco Grand Prix two days later! But you could see pretty clearly—even behind his usual dark sunglasses—that Chapman had more than a passing interest in the goings-on at Indianapolis. He gave the new Mickey Thompson car a long, thoughtful walk-around, and to me it was like watching a high-school shop teacher inspecting a clever but overly ambitious and not-quite-finished student project. But that was quite a bit better than the ill-disguised air of contempt he displayed for the traditional Indy roadsters.

I stepped over to say "hello" and made sure to introduce Colin to Bob Wright, Danny Beagle, H.R. Junior and Hugo Becker. Hugo already knew all about him, of course, and Bob picked up right away that Colin was an important sort of guy and worthy of both respect and interest. All of which was pretty much lost on Little Harry Dick Fairway, who was already five or six drinks into his Memorial Day celebration and, as was his custom when he got a few drinks under his belt, Little Harry Dick was feeling expansive, gregarious and even a little pugnacious.

"So whaddaya think?" H.R. Junior demanded as if the entire Indianapolis Motor Speedway was his own personal backyard and Chapman was just some poor relation who just came over from the old country.

"It certainly is big," Chapman allowed diplomatically. He obviously knew who the hell Little Harry Dick Fairway was and the massive size and scope of the company he headed. Chapman was also obviously aware of the prize-money payout at Indianapolis. Hell, it was the richest damn race in the world!

"How d'ya like the fuckin' cars?" H.R. Junior continued expansively.

"They're awfully big, too."

Little Harry Dick's eyes narrowed. "You like them little sit-down-to-pee racecars over in Europe any better?"

"They're built to an entirely different formula," Chapman started to explain, but I saw Bob wince and so I gave Colin one of those hidden eye-rolls to shut him up. At which point Bob had Danny Beagle lead H.R. Junior away in search of more beer. Several more, in fact. It'd keep him occupied. And, after that, it would keep him quiet.

After those two had snaked off into the crowd, Bob Wright turned to Colin Chapman with a "now-you-understand-the-situation" sort of grimace.

Colin answered with a polite, almost imperceptible nod.

"So what do you really think of it?" Bob asked respectfully.

Chapman gave him half a shrug. "All you've got to do is get an engine with half the power of these great lumps of junk, build a decent chassis to hold it and you've won the bloody race." He didn't say it like he was bragging, either. More like it was a simple, irrefutable statement of fact.

I got the feeling I hadn't seen the last of those two together...

It was a pretty interesting race at Indianapolis that year. T.J. Huston was there with the same car he'd used to win it the year before. But he was in the middle of the front row instead of on the pole because Parnelli Jones and his crew (aided, no doubt, by a truly hefty dose of nitromethane in the fuel mix) had managed to eke out the first 150mph qualifying run ever seen at Indianapolis. Which was pure gold as far as publicity was concerned—even stick-and-ball writers can wrap their imaginations around a nice, round, dangerous-sounding number like 150mph!—and so Parnelli's qualifying run made headlines all across the country and sparked a lot of interest. But his crew knew they couldn't run the big dose of "pop" during the race because the engine would blow up like a blessed fragmentation bomb, so T.J. and the rest knew they were in with a fighting chance. And that's all T.J. ever figured he needed. The way T.J. Houston saw it, he'd never met a driver he didn't think he could lick even-up in a straight fight. In fact, he was a lot like John Surtees that way, even if Surtees had it covered over with a veneer of English manners and T.J. always came across like a chip-on-his-shoulder gunfighter who'd just barged through the doors of a saloon in an old-time western. And although some thought that came across as banty-rooster cockiness or plain old braggadocio, seven or eight times out of ten, T.J. could back it up out on the racetrack. And that made it a lot more than just attitude. He'd won the 500 and the USAC oval-track championship the year before, and even people who didn't much like him had to respect the living shit out of him.

I know I did.

He noticed me in pit lane just as he was strapping on his helmet and getting ready to climb into his white #1. As usual, T.J. was working on a big wad of chewing gum and keeping up the pre-race patter with his crew while *"Back Home Again, in Indiana"* crackled over the loudspeakers. But he stopped chewing and stood absolutely stock still all the way through the National Anthem, the invocation and the thoroughly mor-bid playing of *Taps* that always preceded the Indy 500 every year. No question he'd noticed me, and he shot me a big, snide sort of grin as soon as the last notes of *Taps* echoed through the Speedway grandstands. *"Hey! Lyons!"* he shouted over at me. *"You got that ten bucks y'all owe me from Daytona?"*

Jesus! I'd forgotten all about it!

But T.J. obviously hadn't.

I reached for my wallet as I headed over towards him.

"Nah," he said as he swung his leg over the side of the roadster's cockpit. "You hung onto it this long. You can hang onto it for another couple hours."

"I've got it now," I told him.

"Yeah, but you prob'ly got it all in nickels an' pennies—I know how you writer guys are—an' I really don't need th' extry weight in the car…"

I could see all of his crew guys smirking at me, and I could feel my ears starting to burn a little.

But T.J. just grinned at me some more. "Why don'cha jus' bet it on me if you can find us a sucker. That way we'll both come out ahead."

And that's when *"GENTLEMEN, START YOUR ENGINES"* came booming over the loudspeakers. T.J.'s crew waved me aside, stuck the big, plug-in starter into the front of the car, squirted some highly volatile starting fluid into the injector horns and spun the motor. The Offy barked to life with a harsh, spluttering roar and an eye-tearing cloud of fumes.

"I'll see ya in the winner's circle or in the fence!" T.J. hollered over the noise as 32 big, four-banger Offies and Dan Gurney's lone, stock-block Buick V8 thundered to life while the crowd stood and cheered and stomped and clapped and yelled and hooted so damn loud you could hear them right over the engines. It made the air throb all around me and the whole blessed Speedway seemed to shake. Right up through the damn concrete.

There was no race on earth like the Indy 500. Not anywhere.

Luckily I never tried to find anyone to take T.J. Huston's bet, because he didn't exactly win the Indy 500 that day. In fact, he dropped out right after his first pit stop thanks to a wheel nut that hadn't been tightened properly. It quickly unscrewed itself and sent one of his front wheels flying just as T.J. was approaching the end of pit lane and getting ready to scream out onto the racetrack again. The left-front dropped instantly down to the pavement and of course then the damn thing wouldn't steer, and all T.J. could do was sit there looking foolish as his roadster slewed into the end of the pit wall. He was pretty damn angry about it, too, since he'd been swapping the lead back-and-forth with Parnelli Jones and Rodger Ward up to that point.

I wouldn't have wanted to be the crew guy responsible for changing that left-front tire, that's for sure.

Hugo Becker and I were both keeping an eye on (and moreover quietly rooting for) Dan Gurney in the new Mickey Thompson car, but although its mid-engined chassis seemed a bit nimbler than the old, traditional, front-engined, long-wheelbase Indy road-sters heading into the corners, it didn't look nearly as settled or stable through the middle or coming out. You could see it if you knew what you were looking at. And the Buick engine didn't have nearly as much punch as the Offies on the straightaways. But Dan had it running solidly up in the top 10 nonetheless. Or at least he did until the rear end started making odd noises and sending worrying vibrations right up through the seat of Dan's coveralls. He said later that it felt like it was losing power, too. In the end, he pulled in and retired with a busted rear end a few laps shy of half distance. That was a shame, really. But you could see the potential was there. Not to mention that Dan and the Harvey Aluminum team picked up no less than $5,161 for completing

92 laps and being classified 20th out of 33 on the official results, and that was about as much as it paid to win a blessed grand prix over in Europe. Something that was surely not lost on Dan's very special British guest, one Anthony Colin Bruce Chapman.

Rodger Ward took the victory at the Indianapolis 500 that year at the wheel of a beautifully prepared Watson/Offy roadster entered by the crack Leader Card team out of Milwaukee. They pocketed a genuinely astounding $125,015 for their trouble. And his Leader Card teammate Len Sutton finished second, which picked them up another $44,566. That was a thoroughly eye-bugging, jaw-dropping amount of cash compared to the starting money and race purses offered up on the grand prix and World Manufacturers' Championship circuits. But it was still just one race, and it would be hard for even a committed English or European team to muster up the time, personnel and resources necessary to take a serious run at Indy. Or at least not unless they had a big, fat check in hand from someone who could afford it and moreover saw the possibilities and publicity involved in standing the Indianapolis establishment on its ear.

Someone like Fairway Motors, for example...

Chapter 5: Missing Monaco, Making Mosport

If you looked at a morning paper the day after the Indy 500—depending on which paper you picked up, of course—you very likely saw a picture of Rodger Ward swigging a bottle of milk or grinning at you (or at the crowd and the cameras, anyway) from the cockpit of the number 2 Leader-Card Watson-Offy in the storied winners' circle of the Indianapolis Motor Speedway. Sure, it was down at the bottom corner of the page with a headline like *"RODGER WARD WINS 46th MEMORIAL DAY RACING CLASSIC AT INDIANAPOLIS"* and then a little note at the bottom referring you to pg. 3 of the Sports Section for the full story. Or at least as much of the full story as a stick-and-ball sports writer who probably didn't know what the hell he was looking at could cram into two short columns. But it was still about the only time you'd ever see a racecar presented on the front page of your average American newspaper (unless there was some kind of cataclysmic wreck, of course—preferably with a lot of smoke and fire—where both drivers and a few spectators got killed), sharing space with legitimate front-page news like how Mr. and Mrs. Nikita Khrushchev attended a Benny Goodman jazz concert in Moscow or how the Israelis were going to hang Nazi concentration-camp mastermind Adolph Eichmann at midnight. Eichmann had somehow escaped to Argentina at the end of the war, but the Israeli secret service—they call it The Mossad—had tracked him down relentlessly over the years since the war, found him, essentially kidnapped him, drugged him and flew him back to Israel to stand trial for war crimes. It was all kind of a dog-and-pony show—he stood trial from inside a sort-of cage made of bulletproof glass so nobody could shoot him before they could find him guilty and hang him—and he was unremorseful and grimly defiant of the proceedings throughout. I mean, everybody knew they were going to execute him in the end. And everybody knew he deserved it, too. But there was no real feeling of relief or release or of the scales of justice finally coming into balance afterwards.

It was just one more body on the pile…

But Indy made car racing front-page news here in the states—for one day out of the year, anyway—and that made it thoroughly irresistible as far as Bob Wright's Absolute Performance ambitions were concerned. Although he made it pretty clear on the plane ride back that Memorial Day at The Brickyard was not going to be front-

and-center on my personal agenda. Other people would apparently be handling that. And I've got to say I was a little disappointed, since Dan Gurney's performance in Mickey Thompson's promising but problematic mid-engined car and the presence of Colin Chapman as an, umm, "interested observer" made you think that a lot of exciting new things were in the offing at Indy. And Fairway Motors was surely going to be a part of it. But, somewhat sadly, I wasn't in the frame on that. No, my focus was to be on Europe—hell, that's what I supposedly knew about, wasn't it?—and I would be working on it with Danny Beagle as my handler and Karen Sabelle as my facilitator, and that's just the way it was going to be. Period. End of discussion.

To be honest, I'd never really worked with anyone like Karen Sabelle before, and it was something of a revelation how she organized and prioritized things and got them done. Oh, Isabelle Bertrand was pretty good at that sort of thing back in the old *Car and Track* offices in California, and I had an inkling that Audrey probably had that kind of ability as well. But Karen Sabelle was World Class. She was sharp, unblinking, task-oriented, even-keel, methodical, patient when necessary, impatient whenever else and utterly, totally relentless. And she could keep more plates spinning and balls in the air than anybody I'd ever seen. Even Bob Wright himself. She quickly grasped the magnitude of the lodging and logistical problems we were going to encounter relative to the company's rapidly approaching invasion of France (especially H.R. Junior's idiotic desire to bring many of his executive-corridor department heads and some of their key staff people), and Bob Wright went along with the idea because he agreed that it would be good for them to see, feel, touch, taste and experience the 24-hour Le Mans classic for themselves. Besides, there was no point having an argument with Little Harry Dick Fairway over something as insignificant as that. It would only piss him off, and he'd win in the end anyway. Bob Wright was savvy enough to pick his battles carefully with those over his head, and he hadn't risen through the ranks at Fairway Motors by being impulsive, frivolous or capricious.

But I knew it wasn't going to be simple—not even with somebody like Karen Sabelle on the case—because you couldn't find an empty hotel room or house to rent nearby or even a ratty old bed in a hay loft over some peasant's livestock barn the weekend of the 24 Hours of Le Mans. Not anywhere close to the circuit, anyway. And my press-liaison friend from the track just laughed when I told him I was looking for all-access, top-level VIP credentials for a dozen or so of my close personal friends.

It helped a lot getting Audrey involved (and she got a few nice, fat checks for it, too) and, as I'd hoped, she made a good impression on Karen Sabelle immediately over the phone and became more or less our de facto overseas liaison person, language interpreter and interference runner. And that made sense because the French always seem to respond so much better when you speak to them in their native tongue. And particularly if you pronounce everything correctly. But that's probably also true of the Italians. And the Germans. And the Russians. And the Spanish. And the Portuguese. And the Poles. And the English. And everybody else who has their own native tongue, come to that, right down to the folks who speak nothing but Papiamento in the Dutch Antilles. But it's probably truest of all about Americans right here in these United States who, in spite of their immigrant heritage, tend to view the use of strange, incomprehensible offshore languages as some sort of personal cultural affront.

The good news on my end was that I got to talk to Audrey quite a lot—even if it was only long distance and usually early in the morning from an all-too-public, fluorescent-lit desk that Karen Sabelle had arranged for me in Hubert C. Bean's clicking, clattering, drowning-in-data-printouts computer-room office on the 6th floor. It was hardly a private or romantic sort of place to talk to someone you care about, but we got to do it every day (and on the company's nickel) and although it was mostly business, the silences in between tended to feel close, meaningful and intimate. And that was very nice indeed. Although it just made me more impatient about getting back across the Atlantic to see her again in person. More than see her, in fact.

It just about killed my spirit that I missed out on the Monaco Grand Prix the weekend after Indy. Hal called to tell me that Clark had once again demonstrated the magic of the new, monocoque Lotus 25 and put it on pole, but then wild, anything-but-risk-averse Willy Mairesse (who had qualified a pretty amazing 4th in his outdated Ferrari and was obviously out to impress team manager Dragoni) made a charging start, including a somewhat optimistic—you could even say impossible—dive up the inside heading into the very first corner, trying for the lead. And a lot of Ferrari supporters would tell you it was the right thing to try since passing is damn near impossible at

Monaco. Not to mention that a well-driven slightly slower car can keep a well-driven somewhat better car bottled up almost indefinitely on the narrow, twisting, barrier-lined streets in Monaco. But Willy left it a bit too late, locked up his brakes, got the Ferrari all squirrely in front of everybody and damn near lost it (plus all of his momentum) and that—along with the inevitable hard braking and *force majeure* avoidance maneuvers immediately behind—caused a huge, accordion-style jam-up. And that's when Richie Ginther's BRM arrived on the scene at full chat from his 13th starting slot (he said afterwards that his throttle stuck open) and ran *smack!* into the back of Dan Gurney's flat-8 Porsche. Then Ginther got rear-ended, which sent a sheared-off BRM wheel flying over the barriers and, quite sadly, it hit one of the track marshals. You couldn't really blame wild Willy—or Richie Ginther, for that matter—but it all started with the Ferrari driver's spectacular but perhaps ill-considered dive-bomb move into Turn One. In any case, there wasn't much of anything you could do about it, and the race went on. Polesitter Clark had taken evasive action to get around the melee and dropped all the way to 7th, and then Mairesse spun it completely around not half a lap later and dropped to the back of the field. There was no question that Willy was talented, fast, terrifically brave and frighteningly determined, but it was scary looking into his eyes—there was something hollow and hunted and haunted in them—and no question his will and adrenaline level tended to get the better of him under pressure.

In any case, the shuffled order at the end of the first lap had McLaren's front-row Cooper just ahead of Graham Hill's front-row BRM and then a typically calm, opportunistic, skillful and fortunate Phil Hill, who had to be somewhat amazed to find his Ferrari in 3rd after starting way back in 9th! But Clark was already hard at work trying to bring the new Lotus back up through the field. After a good battle, Graham Hill's BRM eventually managed to pass and pull away from McLaren's Cooper, Brabham's customer Lotus 24 got past Phil Hill's obsolete Ferrari and Clark's Lotus 25 worked its way past both of them, caught and passed McLaren's Cooper for second six laps later and closed inexorably on the leader. It was another pretty damn devastating performance from Clark and the new Lotus, and he had it right up in the wheeltracks of Hill's BRM and threatening to take the lead when a clutch problem reared its head and put him out of the race after 55 laps. After that, it looked like clear sailing for Graham

Hill's BRM, but then, very late in the race, the engine started to smoke. Followed by more smoke and some very ugly noises, and the BRM retired with just seven laps to go. Damn shame after a really fine drive. All of which left a somewhat bemused Bruce McLaren to take a welcome and well-measured win for Cooper (they hadn't had a grand prix win since Portugal in August of 1960, and no doubt the Cooper boys would be celebrating at the pub we all used to frequent when they got back to London!) while Phil Hill soldiered on and survived the attrition to take a fine second place in the archaic but stone-axe reliable Ferrari, over a minute ahead of rookie teammate Bandini in 3rd. That would give Dragoni something to stew over for sure. After the two Ferraris came the walking wounded (Surtees a lap down in the Lola and Bonnier a further six laps back in the second Porsche), and those were the only cars that actually managed to finish the race. As for the unfortunate flag marshal who got hit by the flying BRM wheel at the first corner of the very first lap, the news filtered through the pits as the teams were loading up their gear that he'd succumbed to his injuries. And that was a terribly sad note at the end of another parade of mistakes, breakdowns, attrition and luck of both varieties at Monaco.

Even so, I was mad as hell that I missed it!

And that's what prompted me to sneak away the following weekend and take a long, lonely drive up past Toronto for the big Players 200 pro event at Mosport. No question it was the biggest and most important sports car race in Canada—and one of the top events in all of North America, come to that—and I was really attracted by the unusual, two-heat format (two 100-mile, balls-out sprint races with no planned pit stops) and the fact that a lot of the top European drivers would be there in some really good cars. But I did it on kind of a last-minute whim and couldn't find anybody to go with me (or nobody in Fairway Tower I really wanted to ask, if you want the truth of it) and so what if I had to pay a damn admission fee like every other drool rubbernecker and stand there on the fences like an ordinary civilian?

It was still good to be back at a racetrack again.

And Mosport was a pretty special kind of racetrack. Oh, it was only two-and-a-half miles around—short by European standards—but it swept uphill and downhill through beautiful pine forests and had lots of dramatic elevation changes, some really fast, daunting corners and several spooky blind crests and hidden-away apexes that made most drivers' hands tense up just a little on the old steering wheel. Like Cal told me when I finally caught up with him in the paddock: *"I figure if you can race here at Mosport, you can race damn near anywhere."* But he wasn't complaining. In fact, he loved the place, because it was one of those flowing-yet-intimidating racetracks where a top driver can really make a difference. And the local Canadian hotshoes were amazingly open and honest about what it took to go fast there. Particularly an entertaining and slightly cantankerous half-pint Scotsman named Johnny Greenwood from the next paddock spot over. He was running a somewhat antiquated old Lotus Eleven in the Under-2 Liter class, but it still took some of the overseas stars a session or more to match him through Mosport's more deceptive corner complexes. And he was eager to introduce himself and make friends with the ex-Ferrari grand prix driver next door. "I was born on Christmas Eve," he told Cal in a rich Scottish brogue, "and I emigrated here to Canada on me 21st birthday. I suppose you could say it was a birthday present to meself." He nodded towards his clapped-out old tow vehicle, and more particularly to the license plate frame, which read: *"God made Scots just a wee bit better."* He was a character, all right, no question about it. But he was also well-versed in the track's nuances and subtleties. "Ach, you can learn this place in a lap or two," he advised Cal through a conspiratorial grin, "but never master the damned thing in a bloody lifetime…"

That made Cal like it even more.

"You wouldn't believe Turn Two," he told me later. "You're coming up to this blind crest with nothing but empty sky behind it—you're already well-out in top gear—and then the road just goes over this crest, plummets downhill and sweeps around to the left at the bottom like…like…" he paused for a moment, searching for the right words. But you could see the special glint it was putting in his eyes. "…My first time through there at any kind of speed—I guess it was my second lap—I backed out of it and downshifted to third and a couple of the local guys—including that Scottish sonofabitch in the old Lotus—blasted around me flat-out on both sides!" He shook his head, but he was laughing, too. "Oh, I finally got the hang of it. But believe me: Turn Two at this place is as close to jumping out of a damn airplane as you could ever hope to get in a racing car…"

So Cal loved the place. But he was significantly less impressed with the

Cooper/Maserati combination he was supposed to drive. To start with, it was based on one of the older-style Mk. II, transverse-leaf Cooper Monaco chassis, and no question the newer-style Mk III Monacos with the coil-spring rear suspension and the pointy tailfins in back (like the red Telar Special example Roger Penske was driving) had superior handling. But Cal said he could live with that. And the linkage to the Jack Knight gearbox in back felt strange, vague and baulky. But he could live with that, too. The real problem was the just-arrived-from-England-a-few-days-ago and supposedly "freshly rebuilt" 2.9-liter Maserati 4-banger, which had a recurring one-cylinder miss and was pumping oil out everywhere. The guy who owned the car was an engaging and enthusiastic old motorsports nutcase from Nova Scotia named Phil Lamont, who had raced for years at the club level and had actually planned to run the car himself at Mosport. But he was also involved with Dunlop as their Canadian racing-tire distributor, and that's how he got the connection with Cal. One of the Dunlop guys in England tipped him off that Cal was freshly out of a job at Ferrari and might be available for the Players race for little more than a one-way plane ticket and a share of any prize and/or appearance money. The organizers were eager to have him, too (although, as both Cal and Phil-the-car-owner noted, not eager enough to open up their wallets very far). As Phil explained through a laconic smile: "You need to understand something about us Canadians: we tend to have short arms and deep pockets…"

Now Phil Lamont was as nice, friendly and knowledgeable a motorsports guy as you'd ever want to meet. Plus he was easygoing and straightforward in that relaxed, open, do-the-best-you-can Canadian way that reminded me of wholesome American TV sitcoms like *Ozzie and Harriet* and *Leave it to Beaver*. I thought being up in Canada was a little like going back to the fifties down in the States. Although part of that was probably just an allergic reaction to spending too much time around the mendacity, maneuvering, corporate bullshit and hidden agendas in Dick Flick's 6th-floor advertising department and all along the executive corridor of Fairway Tower.

Things just seemed so much simpler and more agreeable up north of the border.

Or maybe it was just being back at a racetrack again.

Phil had two young Canadian guys working with him and for him—Del Bruce and Gord Ballantine—and they were all trying their very best to make the car run properly. But you got the sense that they were ever-so-slightly out of their depth. Not to mention worn out, since they'd been up for four days straight getting the damn motor installed (it was supposedly out of a wrecked Tipo 61 Birdcage and had arrived late from the "specialist shop" in England that supposedly rebuilt it) and then they'd towed straight-through all the way across Eastern Canada to make the race. That's a *lot* of miles and hours sitting upright and three-abreast in a pickup-truck hauler. And now the damn thing was refusing to run right. Oh, they'd put fresh plugs in it and Cal would go out for a couple laps and drive his ass off and then the flat miss would come back and he'd do maybe one more to see if it would clear up—it wouldn't—and then he'd come in and they'd pull the plugs and number four would look like it'd been dragged through the La Brea tar pits. They didn't have another gasket so they couldn't really pull the cylinder head, and most signs pointed to a broken or improperly installed piston ring anyway. Which would also account for the way it was pumping oil out, since bad rings tend to let the escaping combustion gasses pressurize the crankcase and push oil out wherever there's an opening.

The good news was that Cal was up there in the top six based on the few good laps he'd been able to run in qualifying. The bad news was that the miss and the oiling prob-lems were still there and the motor was starting to lose a bit of power now as well. "If we run it, we're going to blow it up," he told Phil Lamont and his guys.

Phil said he didn't care. They'd worked their asses off and gone without sleep for damn near a week and towed damn near a third of the way across Canada to race in the Players 200 at Mosport, and by God that's what they were going to do.

"I dunno," Cal allowed gently. "I don't particularly like oiling up the track for the other guys. And especially when it's never going to last through even one hundred-mile heat…let alone two." I'd like to think Cal was just being a good guy, but I knew he was also thinking about his somewhat stranded motorsports career and how another lousy race or a blown-up racecar was the last thing he needed on his résumé.

Phil looked down at the asphalt. And when he answered, his voice was subdued and even a little apologetic: "I'd kind of like to get that starting money if I could…"

Cal thought it over. "I'll do it if you really need me to, but I'll be honest: I'd like it better if you could find yourself another driver."

Phil understood how Cal felt and said he'd try to fix it with the organizers so he could drive the car himself. But Cal could see he was flat exhausted and also knew he'd never driven the car and didn't have a single lap of practice. So in the end Cal agreed to do it—I mean, there wasn't really time to do anything else—but he told Phil and the guys he was going to drop back behind the pack during the pace lap and pull in, and that they should spend some time with the bodywork up pretending to fiddle with the engine—just so the announcers in the tower and everybody else could see that the car was the problem and not the driver. And then he'd go back out and motor carefully around until he either completed enough laps to qualify for the starting money or they black-flagged him for dropping oil. Or it blew up…

Now everyone knows it's a privilege to be there in the pits during a motor race but, to tell the truth, I knew—hell, the whole crew knew—that Cal's race was pretty much over before it even started. Besides, you couldn't see much from the pits at Mosport— just the exit out of the last corner, the short start/finish straight and where the cars funneled out of sight as they disappeared into the fast, blind sweeper of corner one— and so I decided to honor the ticket I'd actually paid for with my own money and spend my first-ever Player's 200 hanging on the fences with the rest of the ordinary civilians. And I have to say it was a hell of a good time. I started at Turn One, which would have been fast but fairly simple if you laid it out in the middle of a desert somewhere. But it was blind on entry and slightly banked in the middle (although it flattened out at the end) and that made it extremely hard to judge. Plus there was an unsettling little dip in the road right where you needed to turn in. Oh, and not much of anyplace to go if you misjudged it and fell off the road at the end of the corner. It was fascinating to watch the difference between the guys who didn't really feel comfortable there and the more experienced drivers who had a handle on it. And things got even more exciting when I hiked a little further on to the shady hillside overlooking Turn Two. Just like Cal said, it looked like a damn blacktop waterfall. With a fast, double-apex left-hand sweeper down at the bottom. It was really something watching the true aces take it in one smooth, graceful, heart-stopping swoop! And the Canadian fans all around me were as enthusiastic and knowledgeable about motor racing as you'd find anywhere on the planet. Only friendlier. And did they ever know how to enjoy themselves! Like

I said, I'd gone on kind of a whim and didn't really have anyplace lined up to stay on Saturday night, and by the time I got done sharing their icy-cold bottles of Molson and Labatts (not to mention snacks and appetizers and side salads and campfire-cooked steaks, sausages, grilled chicken and bacon sandwiches!) I really wasn't in any shape to go find a hotel. Or even my way back to the highway. So one of them lent me some blankets and rolled a few towels into a makeshift pillow so I could crawl into the back seat of my Fairway Flyer Fiesta Flair courtesy car and sleep it off. I have to admit that my trip back to Detroit on Sunday afternoon was pretty damn rocky as well…

As for the race, Dan Gurney was on pole in the same, super-fast Arciero Brothers Lotus 19 that he'd coasted over the line to win with at Daytona four months and what seemed like a hundred years before. But Roger Penske was there with the Telar Cooper (which may have still had the rare, slightly larger, 2.7-liter Coventry-Climax "Indianapolis spare" engine), and Jim Hall had the Chevy-powered Troutman-and-Barnes Chaparral I liked so much. And the British U.D.T.-Laystall team was there with a nicely-prepared, pea-soup green Lotus 19 for Masten Gregory and a properly red Ferrari 246 Dino for Innes Ireland that the factory had "lent" (you can bet money changed hands!) to the UDT-Laystall team. The Canadian fans around me had a couple local heroes to root for with "world's fastest bus driver" Francis Bradley in a Canadian-entered Lotus 19 and Dan Shaw in the unusual, mid-engined, two-speed-gearbox Chevy-powered Sadler Mk. 5 and a particularly nasty (but neat-looking!) front-engined Chevy special called the "Dailu" that unfortunately suffered a serious oil leak in qualifying and didn't make the grid.

Come the start Penske shot away first with Gregory and Hall right behind while Gurney had some sort of fumble and slipped back to about 7th. And it was pretty damn entertaining for the first several laps, as Penske, Gregory, Hall and Shaw in the Sadler kind of separated themselves from the rest. Then the Sadler dropped out with gearbox problems, but the other three put on a hell of a show. The Cooper and the Lotus were definitely faster overall, but Hall's Chaparral had such a huge horsepower advantage that he'd barrel right past them on the steeply uphill back straight and then they'd have to work at finding a way around him again. And meanwhile Gurney was reeling all three of them in. Gregory finally got past Hall and made it stick, and then Hall did the gentlemanly thing and let Penske and then Gurney by so they could chase after Gregory. And it wasn't long before Dan caught the pea-green Lotus, found a way past and then just pulled off into the distance. And that was pretty much it for heat one: Gurney and Gregory in Lotus 19s, Penske in the Cooper and Hall in the Chaparral. I was happy for Dan—he really deserved the win—but then the old Gurney luck struck again in heat 2, and he had to retire with a blown head gasket. So it was yet another "we-wuz-winnin'-till-we-lost" day for Daniel Sexton Gurney. He seemed to have way more than his fair share of those.

For his part, Cal pulled in as promised at the end of the pace lap, waited while Phil and his crew guys lifted the rear bodywork, pretended to look perplexed and then lowered it back down again and sent him back out on track. After which he soldiered around, watched his mirrors (although conveniently ignoring the occasional plumes of oil smoke) and kept out of everybody's way just long enough to collect the starting money for Phil Lamont and his team. And then he pulled in and parked it. Although I did notice Cal was wearing somebody else's ugly orange helmet and a blue bandana over his mouth like a dirt-track racer so nobody could recognize him. And then, just to top things off, Phil's "freshly rebuilt" (and expensive) Maserati engine—the one that had just been air-freighted in from England at great expense not even a week before—made one loud, heavy *"CLANK!"* and locked up solid while they were trying to idle the damn car up the wooden ramps to its trailer.

Ouch.

But that's the way it goes in racing sometimes, and even when the results are nothing more than bitter disappointments, broken bits and bills yet to arrive, it's still nice to meet new people and make new friends at a racetrack. Or that's the way I'd always write it for the magazine, anyway.

Back on track, Dan Gurney's retirement in heat 2 left Masten Gregory with a big lead over Penske's Cooper, while Hall's Chaparral had dropped out with a busted rear end. And that put the Canadian-entered Lotus 19 of local favorite Francis Bradley (who'd had a wee off avoiding the Sadler Mk. 5 in the first heat) all the way up to third overall. Which was worthy of much comment and celebration among the campers on the hill. But there was damn near a lap separating Gregory from Penske and more than a lap down to Bradley, so it was a pretty dull procession towards the end and 1 more or less stopped paying attention. Except to my new Canadian camper friends. And their food. And their beer. And the bottle of better-than-decent scotch they broke the seal on to celebrate the waving of the checkered flag and the strange, still-vibrating silence that always comes after it...

Chapter 6: Over the Atlantic

Fortunately Karen Sabelle was impressed—or at least apparently satisfied—with how capable and organized Audrey seemed to be (in fact, I worried that she might be making me look bad by comparison), although it was slow going and one dead end after another regarding our housing arrangements for the Fairway Motors expedition to Le Mans. But at least the transatlantic phone calls were keeping me up to date on all the latest gossip and happenings at the Lola shop in Bromley. Even though Surtees had somewhat remarkably put the new Lola F1 car on pole at Zandvoort, he wasn't especially happy with it and Eric Broadley and his crew were busy adding frame tubes and strengthening gussets to try and take a little of the wind-up and liveliness out of the chassis. That's a very fine sort of balance to achieve as any F1 driver, designer or set-up mechanic will tell you. Make everything too stiff and the car launches off dips and skitters around corners like a roller skate on bumpy linoleum. Get it too willowy and the car takes forever to roll into a set (if it ever actually does), goes all wobbly over road undulations and falls hopelessly behind itself in transitions. And, for any racecar, the thing you're really looking for is a chassis that gives its driver confidence as well as speed. Which is never easy, since whatever you do over here with the chassis stiffness or the track width or the wheelbase or the ride height or the center of gravity or spring stiffness or shock dampening or camber or caster or toe-in or whatever will often have unintended consequences somewhere else. But that's what makes it all so damn fascinating, isn't it? I mean, where else in human experience do hard science, wild creativity, the laws of physics, blind hunches, bitter experience and sheer black magic blend together with such blinding speed, predatory instinct, hair-trigger decision-making, razor's-edge thinking and grace under pressure?

Not that I'm preaching or anything.

Audrey also told me that Eric was grateful for the pair of freebie Fairway V8s that showed up at his shop for him to ponder over and measure up, and the Le Mans coupe project was now progressing into the advanced technical drawing stage. The chassis frame had evolved into a full, twin-hull aluminum monocoque (surely influenced by Colin Chapman's amazing new Formula One car) and now there were exact dimensions and details penciled in on the engine fitment. The chief problem left involved locating a transaxle that could handle the brute torque of a hot-rodded American V8. None of the available units really looked up to the job, and Broadley was leaning in the direction of the Italian Colotti unit (which ace wrench Alf Francis had initially commissioned to replace the recalcitrant Lotus "queerbox" in the Rob Walker Lotus 18 that Stirling Moss drove so successfully at the end of the 2.5-liter formula) simply because there was nothing else on the horizon. Speaking of Moss, everyone in England was relieved and thankful that he had finally emerged from his coma and was embarking on what would surely be a long and difficult rehabilitation. And although somber, that was good news indeed. Even if it remained very much in doubt if he could (or should, or would) ever race again.

Even with Audrey's help and contacts, we were butting up against nothing but stone walls trying to secure appropriate lodging for the Fairway expedition. Especially since Bob wanted "to keep a low profile" so everything had to be on the hush-hush. The truth is, we were struggling. Badly. Or at least we were until H.R. Junior (who I'd honestly thought was pretty much useless up to that point and nothing but an obstacle when it came to making progress on anything) got impatient with our lack of results and rang up the son of the American ambassador in Paris. Who, it turns out, just happened to be an old fraternity buddy of his at one of the many upper-bracket schools he'd either left under a cloud or been dismissed from during his colorful so-called college career. And this particular onetime fraternity buddy/son-of-the-American-ambassador in Paris also just happened to be a freshman U.S. congressman from Kennebunkport, Maine, and not so incidentally married to one of Amanda Cassandra Fairway's onetime sorority sisters. And after the usual *"Good to hear from you!/Been a long time!/Fuck the damn Democrats!/How's the wife and family?/Are y'gettin' any?"* pleasantries, H.R. Junior got down to the business at hand and told him in the plainest, bluntest English imaginable—at least if he wanted another big campaign contribution when he ran for re-election and also incidentally to prevent certain embarrassing personal-history details (and/or photographs) from potentially being leaked to the supermarket tabloids—that his party sure as hell better have first-class accommodations close to the race circuit and top-level, all-access credentials waiting for, oh, say, fifteen or twenty of Fairway's top people when they arrived at Le Mans...

Making arrangements proved ever so much easier after that!

I was really hoping I could finagle a quick trip to London to "oversee" our Le Mans preparations (and hopefully with a little side jaunt over to Spa for the Belgian Grand Prix the week before, even if I had to go through the turnstiles as a damn spectator), but Audrey was thoroughly on top of the situation once Little Harry Dick got his congressman son of the French Ambassador fraternity buddy involved, and all I could get out of Karen Sabelle was an *"I know what you're really up to"* scowl and a dose of the old stink eye. Apparently she'd picked up on how Audrey and I had become a bit of an item over the past several months, and although I don't think Karen was congenitally puritanical or provincial when it came to such things (I mean, she'd surely seen or heard about plenty of fooling around on the executive corridor), she was old school enough to expect you to at least sneak around about it.

Not to mention that Audrey was doing a fine job—Karen told me as much—and she surely didn't need me around to muck things up. I was discovering that Karen was a hard person to warm up to (and, as far as I saw it, pretty much impossible to please!) and no question she'd already formed her opinions about me. To be honest, I'd have to say they were pretty damn accurate. And I know that's true, because I happened to see my employee review sheet on the corner of her desk one day. In fact, she probably left it there on purpose so I could see what I needed to work on. According to her list of notes, I was well-intentioned, intelligent, insightful, sensitive to others, marginally clever, reasonably loyal, possibly dependable, often unfocused, fairly goal-oriented but terminally lazy, plus I lacked discipline (I could have told her that) and that I was occasionally lax when it came to business attire and personal grooming.

Like I said, she had me pretty much nailed.

Anyhow, that's how I managed to miss the Grand Prix at Spa for the first time in years and wound up instead up on a chartered Boeing 707 the following Wednesday, June 20th, heading for Orly Field in Paris with about two-thirds of the Fairway Tower executive-corridor staff and with my white dress shirt buttoned all the way up and my skinny, Fairway-blue-and-Fairway-gray regimental tie tied so tightly around my neck it felt like a damn hangman's noose. Thanks to the employee review I'd seen on the edge of Karen Sabelle's desk, my pants were freshly creased, my shoes were shined until you could see window reflections in them and my cleaned-and-pressed polyester sport coat was folded neatly away in the luggage bin over my head. Through the laws of random selection, I wound up following VP of accounting Clifton Toole onto the plane, and I decided to take the end seat in the same row because I'd never really spoken to him before, even though his signature (or a printed facsimile of it, anyway) was on all of my paychecks.

Clifton Toole was pretty much famous around Fairway Tower for the way he could squeeze nickels out of thin air when necessary and make any column of figures stand up and do the hokey-pokey. He was old school, granite-faced, hollow-cheeked and severe, with cold gray eyes, neatly trimmed gray hair, a matching gray business suit and the grim look of a death-house executioner who took great professional pride in his work. Everybody said Clifton Toole was a stiff, brilliant, humorless, arrogant, Boston-raised, Harvard-educated, mean-spirited, dismissive, demeaning, tightwad sonofabitch bastard. But I thought I'd give him the benefit of the doubt.

"Hi," I smiled as he started to unfold his crisp, fresh copy of that morning's *The Wall Street Journal,* "I'm Henry Lyons."

He didn't even look at me. Just stifled a yawn. And then added: "I know who you are," in a disinterested monotone.

"I guess I'm going to kind of be your tour guide at Le Mans."

His eyes never moved from the page. "I know why you were hired and I know how much you make," he said like he found me mildly irritating. "And, up until this moment, I'd have to classify you as a needless expense." He favored me with the tightest, thinnest, driest smile you have ever seen from a warm-blooded creature. "I'm hopeful that you will manage to revise my opinion, but in all honesty I have no great faith that you will." And with that, he turned his attention back to the *Wall Street Journal* column about Wall Street financial vultures circling over the remains of Billie Sol Estes's fast-crumbling Texas agricultural empire. And that was something worth remembering about financial people. There was always money to be made, even off of catastrophes, collapses, meltdowns and disasters. It was just a matter of being on the right side of a proposition and buying in at the right price.

With Clifton Toole so occupied, there wasn't much else to do but bury my head in my own copy of *The Detroit News* and do my best to look like I was keeping up with current events. The front section was just more of the usual, dire, dark, unsettling political/military crap, with president De Gaulle's somewhat shaky French government doing its best to maintain an appearance of dignity, pride and decorum while essentially being thrown out of Algeria on their asses at the hands of the local populace. Next column over, I was sad to read that a couple American Army officers had been killed in a well-planned, well-executed ambush on a military convoy in Vietnam. To be honest, I hadn't quite figured out what the hell the United States Army was doing halfway around the world in Vietnam. But I was hopeful that, since it was apparently clear to President Kennedy and the rest of our government types in Washington, I'd eventually understand the need for it. And yet I had this nagging feeling that there might be some kind of parallel between what the French were experiencing in Algeria and what the United States might be destined to discover in Southeast Asia.

There was a little, two-column-inch follow-up piece at the bottom of the third page about the three guys who'd managed to escape from Alcatraz on June 11—that had never been done before—and now, since the police hadn't been able to locate hide nor hair of them, opinion was pretty much divided as to whether they'd drowned, gotten away with it or been eaten by sharks. That sent a bit of a shiver up my spine—especially since we'd be flying over the Atlantic for several long, worrisome hours—but it reminded me what Buddy's friend and partner Big Ed Baumstein always said about flying over water: "Hey, don't worry about it. The crash'll probably kill you anyway…"

I flipped over to the Travel Section for a little light relief, and right on page 1 was a big puff piece—complete with joyful little kids and smiling family photos—about riding the monorail and going to the top of the Space Needle at the much-ballyhooed Seattle World's Fair. It was billed as the "Century 21 Exhibition," and the writer made it sound like an absolutely glorious, fabulous, incredible, unbelievable, once-in-a-lifetime/don't-you-dare-miss-it experience. But that's what travel writers are paid to do, isn't it? I mean, their *real* job is selling tickets and filling up the airliners and resorts and hotel chains that advertise in the section. Not that I want to sound cynical or anything about the publishing business.

So I turned to the sports section and read way too much—three full pages, in fact—about how the Washington Senators managed to squeak out a narrow, 5-to-4 victory over the game but apparently unlucky (or unfortunate, or hapless, or character-less) Detroit Tigers. At home, no less! As usual, baseball filled almost the entire sports section, with just a tiny, one-half-inch blurb at the bottom of page three about Brazil beating Czechoslovakia for the World Cup in soccer (which was most assuredly front-page news all across Europe and South and Central America!) plus not even a lousy punctuation mark about the grand prix at Spa or the big 24-hour race coming up that weekend at Le Mans.

Now I usually looked forward to Le Mans with a combination of grand anticipation and nagging dread. Oh, there was always color and drama and spectacle and controversy and joy and disaster and plenty to write about, but I also knew in advance that it would ultimately turn into a long, painful grind filled with more boredom than genuine excitement and far more sad stories and anguished disappointments than exhilaration or euphoria. But, like Indianapolis, it was a one-of-a-kind event that always engendered a unique sense of occasion, and that alone made it a must every year. Even if it knocked the bloody stuffing out of you.

Only this time it was different. This time I was on the *outside,* no matter what sort of all-access VIP credential I might wind up wearing. Instead of teetering alongside Hal Crockett on the folding ladder he always dragged along so he could shoot over the crowd at the start or worrying my way down pit lane in the damp and dark at three in the morning to check out the pit stops gone wrong and get the latest word on the dead and dying, I'd be acting as tour guide for a crowd of important, well-groomed know-nothings who had no fucking idea what they were looking at. On the one hand, it's always fun to bring new people to an event like Le Mans to show them around and explain it to them and try to infect them with your enthusiasm. But it makes you a bit uneasy when they're also your overlords from way up at the top of the Fairway Motors' corporate food chain and especially when a few of them, like H.R. Junior and Dick Flick and Clifton Toole and Randall Perrune, were genuine pricks through and through. The major plus, of course—aside from the race itself—was the prospect of seeing Audrey again.

And who knew if we'd be able to sneak away and actually spend some time together?

But there were compensations. Starting with the chartered flight and the four-star food and service and the regular pay checks I was getting and ending with the fact that I didn't have any other kind of job. Or any other reason to be on my way to Le Mans, for that matter. And no question it was interesting (not to mention instructive) to get a little closer look at the Fairway executive-corridor staff when their feet were up and their guard was down. After I finished my *Detroit News,* I looked over at Clifton Toole—his head was now buried in a copy of *Barron's*—and so I stood up, stretched expansively and wandered off down the aisle like I was trying to get my circulation going again. But it was mostly just to get away from Clifton Toole. As I passed by, I caught a fleeting earful of Dick Flick leaning over and whispering animatedly into H.R. Junior's ear about a trendy and upscale Paris strip club called *Le Crazy Horse* that they should maybe check out together. And also about a somewhat more special and exclusive sort of place they could visit afterwards called *Madame Billie's,* which was even more upscale and very hard to get into. I'd never been there, of course, but I'd heard stories about *Madame Billie's,* and that it was the most elegant, expensive, exclusive and notorious bordello in all of Paris (and, by extension, all of France and all of Europe). It was a place where the right sort of person from the right sort of background, bloodline or bank account might enjoy the company of as many luscious, gorgeous, flexible, compliant, leggy, bosomy, uninhibited and eager-to-please young Parisian girls as he desired, and all of it in opulently outfitted theme rooms patterned after baroque, byzantine, neoclassic, art nouveau or high-renaissance bedchambers, the hall of mirrors at Versailles, the Imperial Palace in Tokyo, a Soho slaughterhouse, a medieval torture chamber or, if it was more to your taste and liking, the much-whispered-about horse stable from Catherine the Great's storied residence in St. Petersburg.

Eventually I found my way towards the back of the plane and took the empty seat next to my unlikely blues-and-country-music-enthusiast friend, Ben Abernathy. He hadn't really wanted to come—like always, he had too damn much work to do and too damn many problems erupting on his desk or exploding out of his phone line every day—but Bob Wright insisted. And you could tell Ben was a bit agitated about all the magnificent disasters, catastrophes and calamities he was missing by being away. "How y'doin?" he asked.

"Okay, I guess. I was just sitting with Clifton Toole."

Ben rolled his eyes. "Oh, he's good at his job—don't get me wrong—but he's a complete and utter asshole. But maybe that's why he's so good at his job. You ever have any poor, starving families you need evicted or orphans you need turned out in the cold, just put him and old Randy Perrune from legal on it. They'll get the job done."

"I never heard anybody call him 'Randy' before."

"Nobody does. It's a hanging offense. I only said it 'cause I've had a couple cocktails and he can't hear me."

"You ready for another one?"

"How far are we from Paris?"

"A long way. We're barely out over the ocean yet."

"Then maybe we should get a couple."

"Maybe we should."

So we had a cocktail or two and talked about music. Pop music and country music and rhythm-and-blues and jazz, and about Patsy Cline and Johnny Cash and Elvis and Ray Charles and how Ben had heard from the bulky, barrel-chested owner/bouncer of The Black Mamba Lounge that Memphis Slim was relocating to Paris because he liked the way he was treated and received over there when he was on tour. And that he apparently had a regular gig lined up playing blues and boogie-woogie piano at some underground jazz club in an old stone basement on the west bank in Paris, and he wondered if we could maybe find the time to drop by as long as we were in the neighborhood? But I had to explain that Paris was a long ways away and that we'd be pretty tied up at Le Mans and I doubted we could make it. Although it did sound like a hell of a good time.

We were well out over the Atlantic now, and all you could see was endless blue salt water all the way to the curvature of the earth. It was very peaceful out there, and I watched a great, weary calm descend over Ben Abernathy after our third or fourth round of cocktails and he drifted off into a deep, blissful sleep. He deserved it. But he also snored something awful (and drooled a little bit, too), so I eased myself up without waking him and meandered back up the aisle. Bob Wright was going over some meeting plans with Karen Sabelle at a little face-to-face conference table up at the front of the plane and Randall Perrune was in the next row with several stacks of bound papers in the seat next to him, waiting patiently for his attention once he got done going over his current plant acquisition or lawsuit or defamation case or property closing like he was picking fine bones out of a suspect piece of fish. Daryl Starling was sitting all by himself in the exit row in a powder blue cable-knit sweater, staring out over the wing with manic, fearful eyes and flinching visibly every time the 707 tripped over an air pocket or took a ride on a rising thermal. He didn't like flying at all, and it didn't help one bit that he'd read about the Air France Boeing 707 exactly like the one we were in that had crashed on takeoff at the same exact airport we were heading for—Orly Field, near Paris—just a few weeks before. It was heading back to America and loaded to the brim with art-museum tourists from Atlanta and 20,000 gallons of jet fuel, and it didn't get much more than ten feet off the runway before something as yet unexplained happened and it fell back out of the sky, barreled off the end of the runway, crashed and burned. And you could see that whole scene playing out behind Daryl's eyes every single time a wingtip dipped, the drone of the engines changed pitch even half a step from B to B-*flat* or the slightest little air-pocket hiccup shuddered through the airframe. I'd read that story, too, and it was pretty damn grim. But the amazing thing—the truly miraculous thing—was that not everyone was killed. Oh, all the passengers were. And the pilot and co-pilot. But two stewardesses way in the back somehow survived. And that was once again evidence (at least as far as I was concerned) that when it's your time, it's your time, and there's no point or benefit in worrying about it.

Except that now I was, too.

So I got myself another drink from the stewardess and wandered further down the aisle.

Hugo Becker was going over a sheaf of technical figures and test reports on the new Ferret prototype that he and his guys were wringing out over at the proving grounds. And to be honest, he was a little miffed (particularly at Daryl Starling, even though it wasn't really his fault) about how almost all of the budget was being allocated to how the car was going to look and what sort of gee-whiz ad campaign Dick Flick's people were going to come up with when it was finally ready to launch. There was damn little left over for practical, nuts-and-bolts details like driveline hardware, rear-seat leg room, trunk space or chassis development. In fact, in order to hit Hubert C. Bean's projected, Mr.-and-Mrs.-Mainstream-America price point squarely on the numbers, the whole damn car was going to have to come out of the existing Fairway Motors parts bins. But Bob Wright wasn't worried. After all, Fairway Motors had a *lot* of parts bins. Besides, the new Ferret was going to look like (and be launched like!) nothing anybody had ever seen before. And that's all you really needed.

I was a little surprised that Dick Flick had left his sultry private secretary Wanda Peters back in Detroit—much to her displeasure, I'm sure—but I guess H.R. Junior saw this as a "boys' trip," and so Karen Sabelle was the only female on the plane. Except for the two stewardesses, of course. And by now Dick Flick was hard at work chatting up the prettier one. He had a real knack for that sort of thing, and it was truly impressive to see him on the prowl. Dick was handsome, smooth, graceful, elegant and patient as a lion stalking a damn antelope. I kind of propped myself up by the lavatory at the back end of the plane just so I could watch him work. In his own scummy, amoral way, he was something of a master.

And then something heavy bumped into my arm. In fact, it startled me. But not nearly so much as when I turned around and saw it was Little Harry Dick Fairway himself coming out of the lavatory. Once again, his face was a little flushed and there were even a few beads of sweat showing on his forehead. He looked me up and down. "Say," he grunted. "You know how to play gin rummy?"

"Well, I know how…"

He pointed forward and I followed him down the aisle. And noticed along the way that he was carrying what appeared to be the same blue folder I'd seen him with through the crack in the billiard-room door at Amelia Camellia's 17th birthday party and again coming out of the john on the company Gulfstream on Memorial Day. To be honest, I was more than a little curious as to what might be inside.

"Siddown!" H.R. Junior commanded as we got to his row. So I sat down where he wanted me to in the window seat and he plumped himself down in the aisle seat and slid that mystery blue folder into the seatback pocket in front of him. He was terribly deliberate and precise about it, and you could tell he'd had a few cocktails. Maybe more than a few. Then he looked at me with a mixture of slightly inebriated, good-old-boy

sportsmanship and utter contempt. "Dollar a point Hollywood okay with you?" he asked as he dropped the tray table down between us.

"Uh…that might be a little rich for my blood."

"Suit cher'self," he snorted. "We'll make it half a buck."

I swallowed hard.

"Didn't know we'd hired on any ribbon clerks," he stage-whispered as he started to deal. But he paused long enough to order himself another double scotch when the stewardess went by.

Of course, what I didn't know was that Little Harry Dick Fairway was an absolutely terrible gin rummy player—he'd wait far too long for gut shots, pick up cards he didn't need, telegraph his hand and sit on way too many face cards waiting for a fill—and it got to where I was feeling pretty good about the way I was creaming him. Hell, if I kept it up, I was going to move myself into a brand new tax bracket before we got halfway across the Atlantic! Only I could see it was making him kind of sullen and petulant, and I didn't much like the color coming up on his cheeks and over his eyebrows. And then suddenly, without any warning, he jumped to his feet, bellowed *"IG-OTTATAKAPISS!"* like it was all one word and lumbered off towards the can. After the lavatory door was safely closed, Danny Beagle's head popped up over the seatback and announced in an urgent whisper: *"You'd better start losing!"*

"What?"

"You'd better start losing if you know what's good for you!" he repeated. And then his head vanished behind the seatback just as quickly as it had appeared.

It took a few blinks for that to sink in, and by then Little Harry Dick Fairway was ambling his way back from the john.

"It's hard as hell to pee in one a'those damn things," he groaned as he lowered himself into his seat. "They're built for fucking horse jockeys."

"They sure are!" I quickly agreed.

"I had 'em make the damn thing bigger on our Gulfstream," he bragged. "Cost me plenty. But a man can take a sit-down in there without bumping his fucking elbows against the fucking walls."

"He sure can!" I agreed some more. "I noticed that!"

He looked at me suspiciously. "You been in there?"

"Oh, sure I have. On our trip down to Indianapolis a few weeks ago."

"*You* were there?"

"You probably don't remember," I answered like the absolute nobody I was. And then added: "You were *awfully* busy that day...."

"Yeah, I'm sure I was," he nodded. And then he favored me with a big, self-satisfied smile. "A man can sit down and take a decent shit for himself in my Gulfstream. Even read the fucking sports section if he wants to."

"Or open up the centerfold in a *Playboy.*"

His eyes narrowed.

"You should be really proud of that," I continued. "It's a magnificent achievement."

"You think so?"

"Oh, absolutely!"

"Magnificent?"

"No question about it."

That earned me the first genuine smile I had ever received from Little Harry Dick Fairway. And the smile continued as he picked up the deck of cards. "Now where were we?"

"You were losing," I said playfully.

The smile vanished like he'd pulled a plug. But I knew what to do. I'd taken Danny's warning to heart. And so I proceeded to play the worst, stupidest, clumsiest, most amateurish and losing-est game of gin rummy in recorded human history. Like until I owed Little Harry Dick Fairway the rough equivalent of my next two paychecks. And the more I lost, the happier he seemed to become. To celebrate, he'd order himself another scotch and a sweet, sticky snack to push into his face every time the stewardess went by.

"You're not very good at this game, are ya?" he gloated as he totaled up the score of our most recent round of three-across Hollywood. I actually had to come out and fight a little right at the end to keep him from blitzing me in the third game. Hell, I was already well past what I could afford to lose.

"You're one hell of a gin rummy player," I told him.

"Nah," he gloated some more, "I just get lucky sometimes. That's all."

"You're entirely too modest."

His pig-like cheeks turned ever-so-slightly pink, and he regarded me with fleeting, inebriated friendship beaming in his vacant little eyes. "Lissen," he said with what I took to be genuine affection, "I gotta go take a dump." And then, just so I'd know he was telling the truth and not trying to cop a sneak while he was ahead in our game, Little Harry Dick farted loud enough so you could hear it right over the roar of the engines. It damn near made the whole plane shudder, and the smell that followed was like week-old fish on a compost heap, with just the slightest nuances of toe jam, soft cheese and vomit.

But before he waddled off for the can, H.R. Junior reached out for the curious blue folder from the seatback in front of him. And of course that made me wonder all over again what could possibly be inside. I knew it had to be jerk-off pornography of some kind. But what sort of jerk-off pornography would a man who could afford virtually anything carry around with him? That was the question. And I decided that somehow, someway, I was going to find out. I mean, you can take a beat reporter off a magazine staff, but you can never take the nosy, insatiable, need-to-know-everybody-else's-business curiosity out of a beat reporter. It's in the blood.

Danny Beagle's face popped up over the seatback again. *"Don't worry about the money,"* he assured me in low, conspiratorial tones.

"What's to worry about?" I almost laughed. "I haven't got it anyway."

Danny shook his head. "No sweat. Bob Wright'll have Clifton Toole's people write you a bonus check."

"A bonus check?"

"Sure."

"For how much?"

"For whatever you lost, of course."

"But that makes no sense. Why the hell would H.R. Junior want Bob Wright to tell Clifton Toole to write me a bonus check just so I can pay him back again?"

"Because the money comes out of one pocket and goes into another. They're two different pockets," Danny explained like it made perfect sense.

"Two different pockets?"

"Sure."

But I still must have looked perplexed, so Danny fleshed it out for me.

"H.R. Junior can have Bob Wright have Clifton Toole's people write you a check on the company account and have you pay all the taxes and withholding on it, and then he can have you take it to the bank and cash it so you can hand him over what you owe him in cash…tax free!"

"But it makes no sense," I repeated. *"I'm* still paying tax on it…"

"It's tax-free to him."

I couldn't get the sense of it.

"Look," Danny continued like he was talking to an 8-year-old, "in some ways, Little Harry Dick *is* Fairway Motors, right?"

I nodded.

"But in other ways, he's not. Sure, he's the biggest stockholder and he's chairman of the board and he has the final say on things whenever he actually gives a shit, right?"

I nodded again.

"But he also gets paid—and I mean a *lot!*—for being Fairway Motors's chairman. And you can bet your ass that the government taxes the living shit out of it."

"I'm sure they do."

"So if he has Bob have Clifton bonus you out enough to cover what you've lost to him and pays it out to you at *your* tax rate, and then you give it back to him in cash and he folds it up and puts it into his pocket for spending money and doesn't bother to mention it to his accountant, then he got it tax free, right?"

"I suppose," I agreed uncertainly. "But it just seems so damn stupid. I mean, a couple hundred bucks is a lot of damn money to me—a *LOT* of damn money!—but it's not even pocket change to him. Hell, I bet he spends a lot more than that just getting the grubs out of his wife's garden."

"Of course he does," Danny agreed. "It's not even close. But the money's not the point."

"It's not?"

"Oh, hell no. The money's not the point at all."

I shook my head. "I still don't get it."

Danny looked at me like I was too stupid to pair socks. "It's all about getting away with it, don't you see? It's all about fucking over the government and getting away with it!"

"But the amount doesn't *mean* anything," I argued. "At least not to a guy like H.R. Junior."

"Like I said," Danny went on to explain, "it's not about the money at all. It's about the *satisfaction...*"

Chapter 7: Totally Scru'd

With the help of Little Harry Dick's onetime fraternity brother, soon-to-be-up-for-re-election U.S. congressman and son of the ambassador to France, Karen Sabelle and Audrey had absolutely outdone themselves as far as race-weekend accommodations were concerned at Le Mans. As I'd told Danny Beagle repeatedly, you couldn't find a decent room (and surely not a decent *block* of rooms) anywhere in the vicinity during the 24 Hour weekend. But there was nothing wrong with going out and *buying* yourself a nice, cozy little château with a front courtyard, a rose garden, a four-car garage, a live-in servant staff and a pair of pointy stone turrets flanking the front entrance. Especially if it was less than 30 kilometers from the race circuit! And that's precisely what Karen Sabelle, Clifton Toole from finance and Randall Perrune from legal had organized. They'd found the place and made the deal through the good offices of a very close personal friend of the American ambassador in Paris (a friend who, by the way, just happened to already live there, although nobody at Fairway Motors was supposed to know about that part…or at least not until later, anyway).

In any case, that's where the whole bleary, bloodshot, sleep-deprived, drunk-or-hung-over Fairway expeditionary force headed via chartered bus straight from the airport. Or all of us except Dick Flick and H.R. Junior, that is, who said they had an important business meeting with the French Fairway Motors VP in Paris and took off in a Fairway Freeway Frigate Van Gogh Special Edition courtesy car (the one with the sunflower-and-iris-motif upholstery and the left-front door handle cut off) as soon as we landed. Although she wasn't there herself (she was handling timing and translating difficulties for Clive Stanley's Aston team that weekend, and so was at the circuit already) Audrey had arranged for some nice French appetizer trays and a cooler of chilled French champagne on the bus, so our crew enjoyed a champagne-fueled, recurring-toast tour through the pleasant French countryside all the way to the château. It brought into focus once again how different France looks compared to the States, what with narrow lanes flanked by rows of tall, skinny trees trimmed like poodle legs, quaint farm houses and stone fences older than our own constitution and occasional, half-crumbled reminders of the terrible wars that have been fought to death, despair and dismemberment across these same meadows and pastures. When you think about it, America hasn't really had a war on its own home soil (at least if you discount the one-off, sneak-attack sucker punch at Pearl Harbor in December of 1941) since the Civil War, while two totally devastating world wars have torn their way across Europe and used France as one of their favorite, home-court playing fields. And yet that unique French charm and personality have somehow survived. Along with a lingering sense of sadness, anger, shame and bitterness towards all the unwanted foreigners who have fought there. And I don't just mean the Germans.

It was very warm outside, and so we were happy that the bus had a decent air-conditioning system. According to the bus driver, the weather report called for more of the same throughout the weekend. And I wondered, as I watched the French country-side wheel by, how my Fairway Tower executives were going to react to 24 straight hours of heat, sweat, dirt, dust, crowds and noise. Le Mans is usually either hot and dusty or pouring and soggy, and you mix that in with the huge crowds and the traffic jams and the campers and the drunks and the carnival side shows and the race pounding around relentlessly in the background and, well, I guess you'd have to call it an acquired taste.

I learned from Danny Beagle that the company had engineered a rather unusual deal to secure the château—they'd essentially bought the damn place!—with the understanding that the company would have the run of the place through the middle of June while the previous owner (the close personal friend of the American ambassador, remember) and his family took an all-expense-paid vacation in Monte Carlo. They were then allowed to return and "lease" their own château back at a very attractive price throughout the rest of the year, so long as they skedaddled again (on another all-expense-paid vacation, of course) come the following June. Now you may wonder why any proud, well-established, upper-crust French family would want to sell their gracious old heirloom of an ancestral estate to some brash, bucks-up, low-brow American company with no class standing, culture or breeding to speak of. But things got a little clearer when you grasped the staffing and maintenance costs (not to mention taxes!) involved in living in such a place. Or what a colossal, oh-how-the-mighty-have-fallen hassle it had become to take in race-weekend boarders every year during the 24 Hours just to make ends meet. Plus things were still pretty tough in France for members of the landed gentry who'd thrown their lot in with Vichy during the war years. Even if it seemed like a good idea at the time.

Although stately and impressive on the outside, I'd have to say Château Fairway was a little run down when it came to things like plumbing, drafts, roof drips, plaster cracks and paint work. But it was still a million times nicer than anyplace I'd ever stayed before at Le Mans. Then again, it doesn't take much to beat sleeping in an old Fiat Multipla with the seats folded flat and peeing behind a tree.

To be honest, our Fairway crew was pretty much gassed after the long flight over and the bus ride down from Orly Field (not to mention the time change and all the in-flight cocktails and celebratory, bus-ride champagne we'd consumed along the way), so we all settled in around this massive old stone fireplace for a strange, early-afternoon breakfast of sausage, mushroom and asparagus soufflé and fresh croissants plus a couple more shooters of cognac before everybody started trundling off to try and get some sleep.

Except for me, of course, because I flat couldn't wait to get to the racetrack!

Sure, I was as tired as everybody else and it was hot and sticky outside, but I desperately needed to get to the blessed racetrack and find out what was going on! Not to mention seeing Audrey again, of course. Although we'd been on the phone almost every day setting things up for the trip, I hadn't actually seen her—hadn't actually *touched* her!—for what seemed like a hundred years. Maybe two hundred. But there was something of a problem with transportation. Sure, the chartered bus was parked out in the drive behind the two turrets, but the bus driver had already been off with someone he knew from the household staff enjoying some particularly fine Calvados brandy that the family usually kept under lock and key. But the head butler had "liberated" it (hell, the family would surely think the Americans had taken it!) and shared a large portion of it with our driver. Like until he was slumped over in the doorway of the charter bus with his cap pulled down over his eyes and great, sonorous snoring noises rising from deep in his chest. Which left me without any wheels.

I tried the garage, of course (which had been a horse stable for blue-blooded generations all the way back to Napoleon and still smelled like it) but the two Mercedes and the Citröen were all locked up tight and I couldn't find the keys. But I did find an old black VéloSoleX moped with a broken headlight lens and a bent front wheel leaning against the back wall with dust and cobwebs all over it. At first, I figured there was no way it would run. But I found a rag, wiped it off a little and rolled it out into the daylight. I'd ridden a VéloSoleX once or twice before—they were one of the staple forms of underclass transport in France, but were considered only a very small step up from a bicycle most other places—so I unscrewed the gas cap and peered into the tank. It seemed pretty empty. So I rolled the VéloSoleX back into the garage, found a length of rubber hose that tasted like it'd been pulled from a mummified baboon's ass and siphoned a little fuel out of the Citröen. And of course got a nice mouthful of vintage French gasoline in the process! But then I remembered you had to mix some oil in with the gas or you'd burn up that little 49cc 2-stroke. So I rummaged around the shelves until I located a blackened little squirt-can of oil that looked old enough to perhaps have lubricated armor suits, cart wheels and catapults during the Hundred Years' War. Only I had no idea how much oil I should add. So I aimed it into the fuel tank and just started squeezing the lever and counting the number of squirts. I did eight, but that somehow didn't seem like enough. So I did eight more. And then another eight after that, just to be sure. And then I shook the whole thing around to get it all nice and mixed. Then I swung my leg over, made sure the engine was properly engaged on the front wheel, pushed the choke full on, pulled the compression-release lever on the handlebar and started pedaling. The bent front rim made it wobble a little (okay, maybe more than a little), but I was tremendously gratified when I released the compression lever and the little 49cc 2-stroke sputtered to life. Accompanied by a truly impressive, Hollywood-special-effect cloud of bluish-white smoke. Which continued even after I took the choke off, and I got the distinct impression that I might have gotten a bit overzealous regarding the old oil-to-gas ratio. In fact, I had to keep goosing the engine to keep the plug from fouling all the way to the racetrack. And it became very clear along the way why that old VéloSoleX had been leaned against the back wall of the garage and pretty much left to rot. The bent front wheel made riding it in equal parts entertaining, comical and terrifying (not to mention potentially lethal), and the brake lever didn't do much except make the whole thing shudder. Accompanied by dry, horrid squawking noises like baby geese caught in a bench vise.

But I didn't care! I was wobbling and squawking and put-put-putting my way towards the racetrack, and it looked like I'd make it there in plenty of time to bluff my way through registration and be in the pits next to Audrey for Thursday evening's final practice! Not to mention that I was finally alone and on my own again instead of serving as tour guide and rudder man for the entourage from Fairway Motors. And that was really nice. Oh, maybe I looked a little odd, riding through the bucolic French countryside at little more than a brisk walking pace on a sputtering old VéloSoleX with an epileptic front wheel, horrible brakes and an enormous cloud of bluish-white smoke trailing behind, but I didn't care. Hell, I almost looked like a native...

There was the usual mob at registration, but I was surprised to find that the Fairway credentials were in a *very* special envelope (on the chief registrar's desk, no less) and so I was through the tunnel and into the paddock almost an hour before final practice was scheduled to begin. My first impulse was to go looking for Audrey, but I also wanted to catch up on all the latest news, rumors and gossip in the press room. It was a hard choice, but in the end I headed over to the media compound to check up on things there first. After all, Thursday evening practice would go on for quite a while and we'd be at Le Mans through Sunday, so there'd be plenty of time to catch up with Audrey later.

"Missed you at Spa," Eric Gibbon said through a wide, phony smile as I came through the press-room door. "It was a cracking good race." He never could pass up a chance to put the old knife in. And then, if he could, give it a twist: "I say, isn't that a VIP pass you're wearing?"

"Yeah," I deadpanned. "I'm special this weekend."

"Oh?"

I knew Bob Wright wanted to keep a low profile on our little expeditionary force from Fairway Tower—not that you could keep something like that under wraps, and especially from somebody as nosy, relentless and well-connected as Eric—but I was damned if I was going to be the one to spill the beans. So I tried the old switcheroo: "I haven't heard or seen a thing about Spa back in the states," I told him through the straightest face imaginable. "Could you maybe fill me in?"

And that worked like a charm, because there was nothing Eric Gibbon liked better or enjoyed more than serving and spewing forth as a font of wisdom, insight and invaluable insider information. He reveled in it. And so, for the next fifteen minutes, I was subjected to a full-disclosure dissertation on the grand prix at Spa. Complete with back stories, sidebars, behind-the-scenes revelations and even a few footnotes:

"Porsche didn't show because of a transportation strike in Germany, but I'd guess they were also giving their 804 a wee rethink after seeing the new job from Lotus and BRM's P-five-seven."

"So Gurney wasn't there?" I always tried to keep tabs on Dan, as he was not only an American and one of the very best and fastest, but also a really nice guy.

"Oh, he was supposed to drive a privateer Lotus 24 with BRM power—which should be quite a decent combination—but the car was barely finished and not really sorted and your fine Mr. Gurney declined to drive it."

Eric had a way of lacing in all sorts of nasty inferences and innuendos about drivers who didn't hail from England or Scotland. But I let it pass and told him to go on.

"The Lotus 25s were still the class of the field in most people's estimation, but Clark lost an engine in practice and had trouble in qualifying, so he was mired back in 12th spot on the grid. That left pole to Graham Hill's BRM P-five-seven. He's been damn near equal-quick with Clark and the new Lotus so far this year—luckier, too—and informed opinion holds that the BRM V8 is a bit stronger in the low and middle rev range than the Climax V8. Kiwi Bruce McLaren's works Cooper was in the middle of row one after another solid performance with Lotus number two Trevor Taylor in third slot on the outside of the front row."

"Good for Taylor."

"Good, indeed. Best he's ever done. But being number two at Lotus is never a very comfortable position, is it? And especially if you have Jimmy Clark as your number one…"

"How did Phil Hill do?"

"Oh, he did his usual, workmanlike job," Eric allowed. "His fourth-on-the-grid qualifying result was considered by many to be a commendable performance. The best teammates Mairesse and Rodriguez could manage was a row behind in 6th and 7th.

And you know Mairesse had the bit well and truly between his teeth in front of his home crowd."

"Mairesse doesn't lack for balls or bravery, that's for sure."

Eric looked down his nose. "What he does lack is imagination regarding what might happen if you take things a step too far. And one day it will get the better of him. Mark my words."

"The Ferraris seem to be struggling."

"Last year their grand prix cars couldn't be stopped, and now they almost look like antiques." I could see Eric warming to the topic. "Oh, the *Commendatore* still has things his own way in sports cars and GT—and will again this weekend at Le Mans, mark my words—but his cars have fallen into a shallow hollow in Formula One. The art and science of it has passed him by." Eric raised a warning forefinger. "But he'll come back. He always does. They're not far off the pace as it is, and the last thing you ever want to do is count Ferrari out. They made a strong showing at Spa against the best of the new cars. Although a lot of that was down to Mairesse's determination and fearlessness on a course that greatly rewards such things."

I couldn't wait to hear what happened.

"Mairesse made a demon of a start from the third row (and so, much more quietly, did Jimmy Clark back on the fifth row) and the high-speed nature of the circuit—the front-runners were lapping at a rather stunning 130mph average—along with the relatively underpowered cars of the current formula turned it into quite a slipstreaming contest, with Taylor, McLaren, Mairesse and G. Hill passing and re-passing for the lead as the cars in the queue behind got an enormous tow from the ones up ahead and could easily slingshot past at the end of the high-speed sections. And meanwhile, Jimmy Clark's Lotus had settled into a very comfortable fifth place and was obviously just watching and waiting for the right opportunity. The one who made you suck your breath in was Mairesse, as he fought and forced his way into the lead ahead of G. Hill and then ahead of Taylor a few times, and seemed hell-bent on making a race of it. But then whomever he'd passed would return the favor when it was their turn to slipstream by."

"Sounds exciting."

"Oh, it was. And, just a little ways behind that lot, we had the works Ferraris of Phil Hill and Ricardo Rodriguez engaged in the most fratricidal battle, passing and re-passing each other repeatedly—even when it wasn't really necessary—instead of working together at reeling in the gents up ahead. It was quite a show, really, and it lasted until the very end."

"But what was happening at the front?"

"Oh, McLaren's engine went soft and G. Hill's P-five-seven picked up a miss—still not positive if it was injection or ignition, but it made things difficult for him, that's for sure. Especially on down-shifting. He'd try to blip it down into the next gear and it simply wouldn't go sometimes. Even so, he could almost hold pace with the others."

"He's always had a lot of mechanical sympathy."

"Of course he does. He was a shop mechanic long before he was a racing driver."

I knew that, of course, but I pretended to be impressed by the insight.

"So what happened then?"

"On lap nine, Clark finally made his bid, swept past Taylor to take the lead and, with Taylor still highly involved with Mairesse, Clark began pulling out a margin." Eric gave a knowing nod. "And that was pretty much the size of it."

"So Clark won?"

He nodded again. "Clark's first F1 win and the first for the new monocoque Lotus as well. And mark my words: it won't be the last for either one."

Of that I had no doubt.

"So who finished second, Taylor or Mairesse?"

"Neither one…" He let that sit a bit to build up the suspense before he continued. "…Oh, they were going at it hammer-and-tongs—stupid stuff, really, on a track like Spa—and it all ended in tears with seven laps yet to run."

"Oh?"

Eric nodded solemnly. But you couldn't miss the giddy little smirk between his beard and moustache. "They came together in somewhat cataclysmic fashion at something like 100mph. Touched wheels. Bounced off of each other. Big accident. Fire. Alarm bells. Ambulances…"

"My God! Were they hurt?"

"Amazingly enough, not badly. The Lotus mowed down a power pole. Its remains looked like a squashed bug. A write-off, I'm afraid. And the Ferrari catapulted into the weeds, turned turtle and caught fire. Big flames. Tons of smoke. But apparently both drivers got away with it."

"And they were okay?"

"Taylor had some bumps and bruises and Mairesse had a few burns, but nothing serious. Amazing, really. They got Taylor back to the pits and paraded him right out front so Jimmy could see that he was all right."

"Damn lucky."

"Damn lucky indeed."

"And that was the end of it?"

"For all intents. Hill's stuttering BRM was still circulating and held on to take second—not to mention a useful lead in the world championship points after his win at Zandvoort and near-miss at Monaco—and P. Hill pipped teammate Rodriguez by less than a tenth at the flag to take third place."

"That must not have set very well with Ricardo."

"Oh, I think he was all right with it. I mean, Phil *is* the reigning World Champion," Eric eked out a sly wink. "The one who may not take it quite so well is *Poppa* Rodriguez."

I allowed Eric a wink of my own, excused myself like I had something important to do and headed for the door. Just as I'd hoped, he'd gotten so wrapped up in telling me about Spa that he'd forgotten all about my stupid VIP pass...

Still, I hated missing the race at Spa. I hated not being there and experiencing it for myself. And then writing about it afterwards for the readers back home. Even if I had to reduce it down so it would fit on two pages...including photos and room for a few ads. Damn.

And now, not even a week later, the scene had shifted drastically and we had a lot of the same players (plus many, many more) on hand for a grueling, twice-around-the-clock endurance grind at Le Mans. A race where teamwork, strategy, discipline and durability were far more important than driving finesse or flat-out speed. And, as is often typical at Le Mans, a lot of the high drama had already played itself out before final practice even began. In fact, one of the most compelling stories of the entire weekend—God, I wished I was writing it!—took place before the first car ever ventured on track. Oh, there was no mystery about the final results: everyone knew the prohibitive favorite for the overall was Ferrari's strange-looking "Experimental Class" Testa Rossa with a 390hp, 4.0-liter Super America V12 stuffed under the hood and proven Le Mans aces Phil Hill and Olivier Gendebien to see it home. Sure, Phil was going through a rough patch with team manager Dragoni—even after his fine 3rd place at Spa—but he and Gendebien had already won Le Mans twice for Ferrari in 1958 and again in 1961 and Gendebien had notched up a third victory co-driving another Testa Rossa with journalist/racer Paul Frére in 1960. So the wise thing was to put those two in the car, and that's precisely what Dragoni did. But there were rumors in the press room that the driver assignments might have been handed down from above (if you know what I mean) and that Phil and his team manager were still very much at odds. And remember that Ferrari himself never went to the races anymore, so all the reports and information he received from the field were filtered through team manager Dragoni. Plus a few undercover spies in orange coveralls, of course, but that went without saying at Ferrari.

In any case, Ferrari was hardly the type to bet everything on a single horse (prancing or otherwise) at a race as long, complex and tickled by the fates as Le Mans, and old Enzo had typically cleaned out his race shop and entered everything he had—and encouraged all his concessionaires to do the same—for the French classic. After all, you never knew what conditions were going to be like and breaks, dumb luck and reliability were always huge factors at Le Mans. So the factory brought a pair of the newer, quicker and handier (if not exactly faster in a straight line) mid-engined Dinos—a 2.4-liter V6 for the Rodriguez brothers and a 2.6-liter V8 for Giancarlo Baghetti/Ludovico Scarfiotti—plus the same, 4.0-liter "Experimental Class" GTO that had finished 2nd overall at the Nurburgring for Mike Parkes and Lorenzo Bandini. Although both cars were powered by the same engine, the 4.0 coupe figured to be more aerodynamic down that long, 6-kilometer straightaway towards Mulsanne, while the 4-liter Testa Rossa sports model was about 350 lbs. lighter. And, like my great race-mechanic friend Buddy Palumbo always said: "Sure, horsepower helps you in a straight line, but light weight helps you *everywhere!*"

As for the Scuderia's competition, there were two more standard, 3.0-liter privateer Testa Rossas to reckon with—one from Carlo Sebastian's New York team and the "factory-refurbished" Sebring winner out of Count Volpi's out-of-favor Scuderia Serenissima stable in Venice—and the driver lineups were pretty interesting. Dan Gurney and Jo Bonnier had season-long contracts with Porsche, but Porsche decided not to bring their 2-liter Type 718 prototypes (which didn't really have a chance at anything much beyond a slam-dunk class win anyway) and concentrated their efforts on the pair of full-works Abarth Carreras they'd entered in the 1600cc GT class in pursuit of those all-important World Manufacturers' Championship points. So, possibly as reciprocation for looking after their cars at the Targa, Porsche released Gurney and Bonnier to co-drive Count Volpi's just-freshened Testa Rossa at Le Mans. And you had to think they amounted to a pretty formidable combination. Especially if the new, 4.0-liter Hill/Gendebien "Experimental Class" Testa Rossa faltered. And I was thrilled to see that Carlo Sebastian had the faith, loyalty and backbone to put Cal Carrington in his Testa Rossa entry (alongside fast young Canadian Peter Ryan again) even though he'd been shown the door off the factory team. That didn't go down especially well with Ferrari team-manager Dragoni (although he told my Italian scribe friend Vinci Pittacora that he "didn't even think about it"), but you had to believe Carlo Sebastian had cleared it with the Old Man back in Maranello beforehand. And I wouldn't be surprised if some Cash American changed hands under the table. I'd heard whispers that Cal had come into a little of his inheritance money, and although that sort of thing always took place out of the public eye, there was a price to be paid for a good ride at Le Mans. I liked Cal a lot (even if he could be callous, conceited, self-centered and downright squirrelly sometimes), and no question he was a bona fide front-line talent. But he was on the outside now as far as his professional racing career was concerned, and I just hoped he wouldn't turn into one of those guys who spends out his inheritance trying to get his ass back in a good seat again.

Believe me, it's been done.

But even with Ferrari as the prohibitive favorite for both the overall and the big-bore GT category, there are always challengers to consider at a race like Le Mans. Aston Martin brought a broad-shouldered, bullet-nosed and sinister-looking (but surprisingly lightweight according to Aston insiders) one-off coupe for the "Experimental Class" powered by a bored-out, 3996cc version of the well-proven Aston straight-6 with triple twin-choke Weber sidedrafts and rumored to produce 350hp. Emphasis on "rumored." It was a full factory entry, officially labeled as "Project 212," and Eric Gibbon told me the French importer had begged Aston to do it since they hadn't really been back with a serious effort since their famous overall win in 1959. And people do tend to forget such things. John Wyer was overseeing the team, and I know Geoff Britten would have loved to be in on the deal instead of flogging away with Clive Stanley's slim-chance Aston Zagato. Especially considering that the factory team had signed BRM F1 team-mates Graham Hill and Richie Ginther to handle the driving chores, and both of those guys had extensive, nuts-and-bolts mechanical backgrounds and exemplary sorting-out expertise. Not to mention the kind of sympathy for the machinery that only comes with an accumulation of grit and grease under the fingernails. But not even the most rabid Anglophiles in the press room (and there were always a lot of them at Le Mans, with Eric Gibbon right up at the head of the queue) thought the Aston looked like anything more than a dark-horse longshot. Neither did the three monstrous, mouth-breathing "Tipo 151" coupes from Maserati, which most of the scribes pegged as about the most brutal-looking racecars anyone had ever seen. Two were in the white-with-blue-racing-stripes livery of Briggs Cunningham's team plus a red one with a French tricolor racing stripe down the middle from Maserati France. The struggling manufacturer had backtracked from the complex, hard-to-build, myriad-tube space-frames of its "birdcage" models and reverted to the simple, hefty, oval-section frame rails of Maserati's past (albeit with a perhaps slightly too clever "flexible" De Dion rear end) and powered by 4.0-liter versions of Maserati's big, bellowing V8 from the old 450S. They ran like absolute stink down that long, 6-kilometer straightaway that accounted for damn near half of each lap at Le Mans—fastest of all during practice!— but they were anything but stable or secure at that speed. I couldn't help noticing the scribbling on Eric Gibbon's note pad sitting next to his stupid little deerstalker hat in the press room, and he had this to say about the 151 threat: *The new Maseratis flirted with a genuine 180+ as they flitted from crest to crest down the long, undulating straightaway toward Mulsanne, their drivers' eyes wide as tea saucers.*

The little bastard could sure turn a phrase when he felt like it.

Although most of the speculating and "friendly wagering" in the press room pivoted around how long the 151s would last, rather than how well they would finish.

Ferrari looked like a sure thing in the Category One GT class as well, with no less than six 3.0-liter GTOs entered by various privateer and concessionaire teams plus a handful of older Short Wheelbase Berlinettas to back them up. I was pleased to see my favorite stock car hero Freddie Fritter signed on again to co-drive with experienced American ace Bob Grossman in Carlo Sebastian's new GTO, and Count Volpi's team had one entered for Targa expert Nino Vacarrella and Giorgio Scarlatti. That particular GTO had obviously been paid for and delivered before the young count fell from grace in Maranello. The buzz in the press room had it that he'd wanted a second GTO to run at Le Mans, but Ferrari flat refused to sell him one. Not at any price. So the young count had some of his ex-Ferrari "business associates" from Scuderia Serenissima and A.T.S.—led by the GTO's original chief engineer, Giotto Bizzarrini—whip him up a little something special to take them on. A kind of California-style Italian hot rod, if you will. Oh, it had to run in the "Experimental Class" because of its engine specifications and because it was a one-off, but everybody knew its real goal was to beat Enzo's GTOs and extend a sort of symbolic middle finger in the general direction of Maranello. And no question the thing turned heads, dropped jaws and captured imaginations the moment it rolled off the trailer. Even if it had been rushed together in such a crazy, last-minute frenzy that the paint job was uneven and splotchy. Not to mention still damp…

Now this particular car started life barely a year earlier as full-tilt, 250 Short Wheelbase Berlinetta "Competizione" racing model (lightweight alloy body, plastic windows, hotted-up engine, etc.), serial number 2819, and it was delivered to well-known Belgian aristocrat and Ferrari endurance-racing ace Olivier Gendebien in September of 1961 to run in the Tour de France. It came painted dull metallic silver with a Belgian tricolor black-yellow-red racing stripe (Gendebien and Tour de France co-driver Lucien Bianchi were both Belgian) and they brought it home a respectable 2nd overall behind wild Willy Mairesse/Georges Berger in another SWB Berlinetta come the end of the grueling 8-day, 3200-mile event. Count Giovanni apparently bought the car afterwards to add to his Scuderia Serenissima stable, and it finished 3rd overall a month later at Montlhéry and I'd seen it again at Daytona in March—still silver and with Gendebien driving—and then at Sebring (where it blew up) before heading back to Italy. And straight into the Scuderia Serenissima workshop, where a somewhat massive make-over began.

No question Bizzarrini and his guys tore into 2819 like a gang of hot-rodders in some back-alley garage in Los Angeles. They pulled out the blown motor and replaced it with a full-tilt, latest-spec Testa Rossa engine with six big downdraft Webers, hot cams and dry-sump lubrication (which allowed for a much shallower oil pan and a lower hood line) and then they shoved that motor as deep and as far back in the chassis as it would go. To the point that they had to squeeze the driver and passenger footboxes left-and-right to get around the damn engine! Then they stripped out everything that would come loose to lighten it and topped it all off with a low and sleek but very strange-looking Drogo body that hugged tight as a hooker's stockings around the car's wheels and running gear but ended in an unusual, chopped-off "station wagon" rear end that they hoped would make for more top end down that long, 6-kilometer straight-away at Le Mans. The shape was based on the theories and papers of German de-signer/aerodynamicist Dr. Wunibald Kamm, who began postulating his ideas back in the 1930s and worked with another German aerodynamicist named Reinhard von Koenig-Fachsenfeld (I hope you're taking notes, as this might easily come up in cock-tail-hour conversations sometime) on the radical, slippery-fronted/blunt-butted BMW 328 "Kamm-Coupe" that the company built for the 1940 Mille Miglia race that not-too-surprisingly never took place because of Germany invading Poland and World War II. But the important part is that most racecar aerodynamic studies and wind-tunnel work had transferred over from the aviation world up to that point, and it was pretty much agreed that the most aerodynamic shape of all was a sort of stretched-out, elon-gated teardrop that tapered off smoothly and gradually towards a pointy back end. Only that wasn't particularly practical for a racecar that had to operate on a real-life racing circuit (except for maybe a Bonneville streamliner), and Dr. Kamm and von Koenig-Fachsenfeld came up with the bright idea of simply chopping that teardrop off somewhere behind the rear wheels in hopes that doing so might kid the wind into thinking that a long, smooth, gently tapering tail was still out there in the breeze somewhere. Sure, the wind would get all pissed off about being deceived like that and there'd be all sorts of nasty turbulence following in the car's wake, but Dr. Kamm and his buddy figured that would be okay, because it would all happen *behind* the damn car. And a lot of racing designers started paying more attention to their ideas as speeds continued to rise. And particularly at Le Mans, with that looooong, flat-out 6-kilometer straightaway that made up damn near half of the entire circuit. But no one had ever taken it to the extreme of Count Volpi's Ferrari hot rod. That odd, shooting-brake rear end quickly earned #2819 a new nickname, *"Camionette,"* which roughly translates into English as "Breadvan." It was so unusual that it actually looked beautiful—in a strange and grotesque sort of way—but then, I'd grown partial to Count Volpi and his team anyway, and it was kind of funny and exciting and ironic and delicious that some rich young ex-customer was trying to stick it to Old Man Ferrari with one of his own damn cars! Only Ferrari apparently got wind of the project and wouldn't let his customer race shop sell them one of their new, 5-speed GTO gearboxes to put into the Breadvan, so the car was stuck with #2819's old, customer race shop-rebuilt 4-speed. Which was surely going to be a handicap on that long, long straightaway at Le Mans.

No question the Breadvan was one of the most intriguing entries of all that year—along with those bottom-feeder 151 coupes from Maserati and the broad-shouldered, bullet-nosed Project 212 from Aston Martin—but it didn't look like much of a GTO-beater to my Italian racing scribe friend Vinci Pittacora. Even so, the *Camionette* quickly became a sentimental favorite with the crowd thanks to its unique shape and all the intrigue, drama and discord swirling around it.

Although they didn't figure to finish ahead of Ferrari's 3.0-liter GTOs at the end of the 24 Hours, the 4.0-liter Grand Touring class featured a pair of better-developed, factory-supported Jaguar XKEs—one from Briggs Cunningham's American group and one from Peter Sargent's English team—accompanied by a rivalry you could feel like a temperature drop when you wandered past their spots in the paddock. Running against them were Clive Stanley's DB4GT Zagato plus another privateer Aston, and you had to figure Clive's team was in with a decent chance if they just had a little luck and reliability and the drivers kept it on the island. But that seemed less than certain, since now there were three drivers listed with a young English comingman named Trent Terry added to the mix. I didn't know much about him except that he'd done quite well for himself in British club racing, but I was suspicious as to what his presence on the team would do to Ian Snell. Some drivers can see all the way to the end of a race—even a very long race—from the instant the green flag waves, while others can't seem to see much further than the entry to the next corner. Or the next lap time to flash out at them on their pit board. That's not what you really want at a long grind like Le Mans. And I was terribly disappointed to see my friend Tommy Edwards listed as the "reserve driver" for Clive Stanley's team. But not nearly so disappointed as Tommy must have been.

There was a lone privateer Corvette from Team Scirocco in the 5.0-liter Grand Touring class, and it really only had to make the finish to win its class since it was the sole entrant. Only most of the smart money in the press room figured it wouldn't make the distance. Porsche's factory-entered Abarth Carreras were just about a dead-cert in the 1600cc GT class and figured to beat all the 2.0-liter GT cars as well (and very likely crack the top 10 overall if they performed with their usual, numbing consistency). Beyond that we had the usual muddle of middle-production factory teams and glorified club-racers hoping to survive to the end and cop a decent finish. Perhaps even class honors? Big news in France was that image-hungry Simca had forged an alliance with famous tuner/car-builder Carlo Abarth in Italy to essentially become their subcontracted racing department and hopefully get the same type of notoriety and results he'd already provided for Fiat and Porsche. The result was a trio of handsome little pumpkinseed-shaped "Simca-Abarth" coupes with bespoke twincam engines that owed almost nothing to the parent company. They had sweet, raspy exhaust notes and went *very* fast for 1300cc GT cars. But who knew if they could last the distance? TVR was there from Blackpool with one of their stubby little MG-powered coupes, Lotus had a pair of Elites, there were several Zagato-bodied Alfas—also with sweet, raspy exhausts (I don't know what it is about the Italians, but you just don't get that kind of music anywhere else)—a grumbling Healey 3000 for Sir John Whitmore and quick, steady South African Bob Olthoff, the factory-blessed Morgan oxcart of Chris Lawrence/Peter Baron (remember, their entry had been refused the year before because the Morgan was "too antiquated") and a pair of well-prepared, works-entered Sunbeam Alpines with subtly duck-tailed rear deck lids. And then you had all the small-displacement sports/racers and prototype coupes—mostly French, of course—with their eyes fixed solidly on the prestigious (and lucrative!) Index of Performance and *"Rendement Energetique"* (Index of Thermal Efficiency) handicap awards. And right there is where you had about the biggest damn news story of all at the 1962 24 Hours of Le Mans. A story that was settled, over and done with before I even landed in Paris.

Now there was no doubt anywhere that Le Mans was the biggest damn sports car race in the world, and it was also arguably the single most popular and important two-day sporting event in Europe. And particularly in France. But the French hadn't had an outright winner at Le Mans since the father-and-son team of Louis Rosier and Jean-Louis Rosier scored a glorious, all-French victory in their properly pale-blue Talbot-Lago back in 1950. Although French writers and racing enthusiasts regularly neglected to mention that the "Lago" part of "Talbot-Lago" came from ex-pat Italian industrialist/entrepreneur Tony Lago, who was originally from Venice and only fled to France after he got into a bit of a pissing match with Benito Mussolini and his Fascists. In any case, it rankled French fans something awful watching the English and then the Germans and the Brits again and then the Italians marching into France (or perhaps that's an insensitive choice of words?) and running the table at Le Mans every year after. Especially since there were no big, fast French sports cars to even make a race of it.

But the Frenchmen at the F.I.A. in Paris and the *Automobile Club de l'Ouest* at Le Mans still controlled the rules—don't ask me why—and so they elevated the Index of Performance handicap so it was second only to an overall win in terms of glory, prize money and prestige. The formula was basically distance covered divided by engine size, but skewed in such a way that it favored the dinky, elaborately streamlined little prototypes with tiny little demitasse engines that almost always seemed to be painted French blue. It was a glorious thing *por la France* when one of their beloved little CD-Panhards or René Bonnet Djets won the Index prize, and the French officials at Le Mans were proudly, zealously and even fanatically xenophobic about it.

Which is why the shit hit the proverbial French fan when Colin Chapman showed up at scrutineering with the expected pair of Lotus Elite coupes (they were established

Le Mans entries and had won the 1300cc Grand Touring class three years on the trot)
along with two of his tremendously quick new Type 23 sports/racers fitted with *very*
tiny engines: a 997cc twincam for the 1150cc Experimental Class in the factory car
plus an even smaller, 745cc Coventry Climax FWMC motor for the 850cc Experimental
Class in the U.D.T.-Laystall entry. And it was still fresh in everyone's memory what
Jimmy Clark's 23 had done to the big Ferraris and the 2.0-liter Porsches at the Nurburgring just four weeks before! Or how Chapman had brought a few of his new Lotus
Elevens over in 1957—one of them powered by a 750cc Climax—and came away with
two class wins plus the Index of Performance cash, celebrity status and cachet. As Hal
Crockett put it through a typically cynical smile, it was hardly lost on the French organizers that Chapman's 23s were likely to grind their beloved little blue cars into paste
as far as class honors and the Index of Performance prize were concerned at Le Mans.
And no one needed to be reminded that there were a whole pile of francs involved
along with all the honor, glory and prestige. And it was even stickier because French
manufacturer Panhard was in the process of introducing their new "CD" coupe in
dealer showrooms, and therefore were hoping—in fact, more than hoping—that one
of their factory-supported Le Mans entries would take the Index of Performance prize
and all the headlines, hoopla and hysteria that went along with it.

Now the Le Mans scrutineers could be notoriously picky, unpredictable, pompous
and political (as I already said, they'd rejected Morgan's 1961 entry because the car was
"too outdated," but accepted a damn-near identical car for the '62 race), and they re-
acted to the Lotus threat as only Le Mans scrutineers possibly could, walking around
and around the low, lithe little Lotus 23s before going into a huddle with much whispering, shrugging, head-shaking and gesticulating and subsequently presenting Colin
Chapman with a laundry list of things that were "totally unacceptable" and that would
have to be fixed.

If not, the cars would be refused entry.

Now most of it was pure, annoying bullshit (the turning circle was too large, the
ground clearance was too low, the oil reservoir was too big), but the real sticking point
concerned the wheels and hubs. The rules at Le Mans required every car to carry a

spare wheel "in case of emergency," and as the little pipsqueak chief scrutineer (who Hal said made his day-to-day living delivering trailers) pointed out—*"Zut! Alors!"*—the front wheel hubs on the 23 had only four mounting studs while the rears had six! So the spare (which would never be used in any case!) could not possibly fit both ends of the car! At which point he crossed his scrawny arms across his tiny chest and jutted his chin triumphantly towards the sky like a little half-pint, working-class French edition of Benito Mussolini.

But Colin Chapman wasn't about to go slinking back to England with his tail between his legs. No, sir! He called England and had his lads at the factory whip up a dozen or so four-stud rear hubs and four-hole rear wheels and had the whole lot airfreighted over while he and his on-site crew took care of the other items on the 23's laundry list. And he had the two 23s back in line at scrutineering late the next morning with all the problems sorted and four-stud hubs and wheels on both ends of the cars. At which point the scrutineering officials went into another desperate, whispery huddle with much animated shrugging, pointing, poking, head-shaking and gesturing. And they ultimately arrived at the somewhat incredible decision that, since the rear wheels and hubs were originally designed to be held on with six studs, they could not possibly be safe with only four. And, as safety was *always* the prime concern of the scrutineering officials at Le Mans, the 23s would not be allowed to run.

So there.

As you can imagine, Colin Chapman was livid! Along with several non-French F.I.A. officials who had taken an interest in the case (including the well-connected Count Johnny Lurani from Italy, who believed in fair play and wielded a lot of power within the F.I.A. community). That faction argued that the 23 had run successfully with a 50% larger engine at the Nurburgring and would shortly be entered in another race with a 2.0-liter BRM V8 for power, and while the torque of those motors might make six rear studs a good idea, four would surely be enough to handle the output of the pipsqueak 745cc and 997cc engines Lotus had installed for Le Mans. At which point the officials went into yet another huddle and ultimately ruled—finally, ridiculously and incomprehensibly—that Colin Chapman's little Lotus 23s were "outside the spirit of the regulations" and would therefore not be allowed to race. Period.

It was easy to imagine the muttered and not-so-muttered curses, clenched fists, bared teeth and barrage of Anglo-Saxon invectives that surely followed, but none of it did any good. The Lotus 23s were out and that was it. Before they ever turned a wheel in anger. The whole thing stunk like bad cheese. Bad French cheese, in fact. But such are the politics, polemics and proclivities you occasionally run into at Le Mans. It's part of the show.

I finally caught up with Audrey on the pit counter just as Thursday evening's final practice was about to begin, and it was absolutely great to see her again. We hugged and she gave me a nice, friendly kiss, but then she kind of backed away. Or at least that's what it felt like on my end. But Geoff Britten and Clive Stanley were standing right there, and it certainly wouldn't seem too professional to start petting and slobbering all over each other. Plus I guess it's always odd seeing someone you've been intimate with and really care about again after you've been apart for awhile. It's like all the closeness and intimacy you've shared turns somehow suspect, and you maybe wonder a little if it really existed. Or, even if it did, if you really want to risk it again? Because there is risk in letting anybody get inside of you like that, and everybody who's ever tried it knows what I mean. I also knew that whenever Audrey might think or feel about me, she was also thinking and feeling things about Walter and how anything she did with me would have an unwelcome ripple effect with him. Like she was somehow cheating on her own father, you know? And maybe even on the memory of her mother, if you wanted to take that trolley ride all the way to the end of the line.

Turns out Audrey was ahead of me on all of that and seemed to understand that you can't force these things—you can't *make* them happen—and all you can do is be patient and have a little faith and make dumb small talk while you wait for things to click again. Fortunately, we had plenty of time on our hands, since final practice was just about to begin and even the very quickest laps at Le Mans hovered right around four minutes that year and fell off steeply as you went down through the field. Plus the cars sorted themselves out pretty well on that long, long straightaway towards Mulsanne, so they didn't tend to come by the pits all bunched one-on-top-of-the-other like they did at the shorter tracks. So we had plenty of time to chitchat about our trips over and the Fairway arrangements she'd worked out with Karen Sabelle and that old fraternity buddy/son-of-the-French-ambassador guy Little Harry Dick brought into the mix. "Things got ever so much easier after that," she said with a hint of relief in her voice. "Plus it's very nice doing business when cost is no object."

"I wouldn't know what that's like."

"Neither did I, actually. But I'm quite certain I could get used to it."

I let out a little laugh. "Boy, are you ever getting involved with the wrong person."

"Is that what we are? *Involved?*" She said "involved" like it was something you'd scrape off the bottom of your shoe.

"I dunno," I shrugged. And then I volleyed it right back over the net: "What would *you* call it?"

She shrugged right back at me and quickly changed the subject. "The Aston's been running pretty well through practice," she said airily, and then proceeded to bring me up to speed on Clive Stanley's Imperial Tea campaign. It seems everything was a bit tense on that end since Clive had somewhat impulsively promised a Le Mans drive to an up-and-coming young Brit named Trent Terry, and that meant Tommy Edwards would be demoted to "reserve" status for the race. Needless to say, that wasn't sitting especially well with Tommy. Or with Geoff Britten, come to that.

"I saw that on the entry sheets in the press room."

Audrey rolled her eyes. "Then Clive conjured up some thoroughly suspect 'family business' excuse to keep him in London until race day, which left James to explain the situation to Tommy." She shook her head in disgust. It seems that James and Audrey were both pretty upset about it (although not nearly so much as Tommy), but Clive owned the team and signed the checks, and that gave him the right to call the shots and pick his own drivers. And poor Trent Terry was caught right in the middle. He was a genuinely promising young driver and a decent sort as well and, like all eager, hungry young drivers, absolutely desperate for a crack at Le Mans and willing to take any opportunity. And meanwhile Ian Snell was whipping the car mercilessly all through practice just to prove his position as team leader. Much to Geoff Britten's displeasure. And then Audrey whispered that James had been offered a plum second-in-command position with Aston Martin's Project 212 effort, but Clive refused to let him out of his contract. They apparently got into a hell of a row over it, but in the end, James had to knuckle under because he'd signed a piece of paper and taken responsibility for the team. Oh, he could have said *"You won't let me run things properly, so piss off"* and walked out, but, as an ex-military man who truly believed in duty, accountability and chains of command, it wasn't really in his nature. Besides, you don't want to get into a bunch of legal wrangling with someone whose family has lawyers on staff. But you could see how angry James was. It's really bad when things get like that on a racing team, because the sense of common effort and common purpose go right out the window and everyone feels like they're walking around on eggs.

Of course I complimented Audrey over and over on what a superb job she'd done on the accommodations for the Fairway crew, and she laughed about how, once the château had been located and its aristocratic but slightly distressed owners had been contacted (again, thanks to that son of the American ambassador), Karen Sabelle just kept relaying Bob Wright's message to up the price and up the price some more until the family finally caved in. "It's like they push money around with earth movers over in America!"

"Not everywhere in America," I assured her.

"I'm sure nowhere you ever lived!" We had a pretty good laugh off of that. And, in that exact instant, I saw that special light come up in her eyes and all of a sudden it felt like we were close again—just like that!—and that naturally got me thinking about where we might go after practice and what sort of accommodations might be available for the rest of the night. I even got the feeling that she might be thinking the same thing. So I gave her a kind of shoulder nudge and she kind of nudged me back and then, without actually getting into the graphic details, we talked about it. Like whispering kids, you know? And that made it kind of fun. It would have been, as Audrey put it, "conspicuously bad form" to try taking her back to Château Fairway with me (I was sharing a room with Danny Beagle anyway), and there was no way two human beings could ride there on my wobbly, asthmatic old VéloSoleX in any case. Even if the headlamp hadn't been broken. And she was staying in a tiny little side-closet of a room in a nearby farmhouse-cum-tourist-lodge where the rest of Clive Stanley's team was bunked in. Except for Clive Stanley and Ian Snell, of course, who were booked into a four-star hotel much closer to Paris. "All I have for privacy is a bloody curtain across the doorway, and the loo is way down at the end of the hall."

That didn't sound very promising, either.

And then she gave me a kind of mischievous look. "You know," she said slowly and deliberately, "Fairway's got a brand-new American motor home parked on the other side behind the grandstands."

"They do?"

Audrey nodded. "Karen had it shipped over as soon as the lot of you decided you were coming to Le Mans. I had to help them get it through customs and arrange to have it transported in from the coast."

"You did?"

She nodded and rolled her eyes. "It was an unbelievable amount of red tape. Just unbelievable. And the thing is absolutely bloody *enormous!* They had trouble getting it off the boat."

"Hm. Sounds intriguing."

"I understand it's got a full bedroom in back and a shower..."

"You don't say."

"...and a stocked kitchen..."

"Oh really?"

"...and a liquor cabinet…"

"Do tell."

Her eyes twinkled.

"Hm," I pretended to ponder. "Is the bed very comfortable?"

"I'm not really sure. I haven't tried it." She gave me a nudge. "But I do know who has the bloody keys…"

"Oh? Who?"

She jangled a set of Dodge keys in front of my nose.

"Then perhaps we should inspect it?"

"Perhaps we should."

"Won't James miss you?"

"I think he'll be all right with it once I've given him the time sheets. Peter and Georgie have to thrash on the car tomorrow, but it's an off day for me."

"I probably need to get my ass back to the château sometime."

"And what time is 'sometime'?"

"Well," I shrugged, "there's no way I can do it tonight." I didn't have to fumble far for an excuse: "I mean, my headlight's broken…"

"I see. So it's a safety issue then."

"Very definitely."

And that, dear friends, is how I wound up putting a nasty gash in my forehead stumbling around inside a dark, unfamiliar Dodge motor home after discovering that the light switch next to the door doesn't do much good if the master power switch has been left on and the battery has drained down to nothing. Naturally we couldn't find a flashlight or an owner's manual so we could figure out how to start the damn generator but, as our eyes grew accustomed it, we realized there was almost enough half-light coming in through the curtains that we could bump and grope our way around—that's when I banged my forehead into the edge of a blessed cabinet—until we found the sink and the stack of paper cups next to it and the cabinet below with the unopened bottles of top-shelf scotch, gin, vodka, rum and brandy inside. Not to mention a package of cocktail napkins for the gash over my eyebrow. I could feel the blood with my fingers.

"We'd better open one of these," I advised as I pulled out one of the bottles.

"For medicinal purposes only, of course."

"Yes. Absolutely. For medicinal purposes only."

So Audrey opened the vodka, put a little on a cocktail napkin and pressed it against my forehead. And it felt pretty good except for the sting.

"You think it'll need stitches?"

"Nah. It's just a bang on the head. I get them all the time."

"So you're all right?"

"Yeah, I'm fine."

"Good." And with that she leaned up and gave me a little kiss. And that made me feel pretty damn good.

There was some mixer in the fridge, but it was all warm and the ice was all melted, so we settled on the bottle of scotch. I poured a couple fingers (or maybe a little more, it was pretty dark in there) into a pair of paper cups and we shared one or three in the kitchen area and then took a couple more back into the bedroom with us. I'd have to say it was all kind of awkward at first—you know, when everything feels clumsy and strange and apologetic and you wonder what the hell you're doing there—but afterwards we just kind of lay there together and listened to the muffled, middle-of-the-night work on the cars issuing from the paddock and the party sounds coming from the spectator campground off in the distance. We didn't say much of anything, but we didn't really feel like we had to. And that was nice. So was the way we were kind of folded-up into each other as we drifted off to sleep. I couldn't ever remember a sleep so velvety, comforting and secure.

The smell of sausage frying and the dull thud of a mallet banging tent stakes into the ground woke me while the sky was just starting to get light. I looked over and saw Audrey's eyes were still closed, but I could feel her coming awake behind them. So I leaned over and gave her what I hoped was a sweet, soft sort of kiss on the forehead and she kind of shifted around and snuggled in a little closer and I swear I have never felt any more contented or complete in my entire life. But I also knew the sun was coming up and that I'd better be getting my ass back on the job at Château Fairway. "I'd better be getting back before they miss me," I mumbled into her hair.

"Just five more minutes," she yawned into my shoulder.

It was more like fifteen.

Or maybe twenty.

Not that it's any of your business.

But I remember us lying there afterwards with my arm around her and her leg over mine, looking up at the ceiling like it was some sort of wide-screen movie screen and just kind of drifting. "This is pretty damn special, isn't it?" I said out of nowhere.

Audrey propped herself up on one elbow and looked at me like she didn't quite know what to make of things. And then I watched her mouth bend down into a perplexed sort of frown. "Don't be an ass and spoil it."

"I'm not trying to spoil anything. I'm just trying to be a little romantic."

I could feel her drawing back away from me. Inside, I mean. It was like watching a train pulling out of a station. "You don't have to do that, Hank," she said evenly. "You don't have to do that at all."

"But I was just…"

"You were fine," she assured me like she was in some kind of hurry. "Everything was fine. It was lovely."

"Why are you…"

She put her fingers over my lips. "You don't always have to put things into words, Henry. It doesn't help things. It's superfluous."

"I don't think I've ever been called 'superfluous' before."

That made her eyes twinkle just a bit. "I'm sure people have thought it, Henry. They've just been too polite to say anything."

"Until you."

"Yes, that's right," she agreed. "Until me."

"Yes. Until you…And for God's sake, don't call me Henry."

"Alright, Henry."

I pinched her under the covers. "You're just jerking me around for the fun of it, aren't you?"

She did it right back to me, but never missed a beat: "I don't mean to, Henry. But you're such a grand target. And it's such good sport."

And then we kind of stopped and we were face-to-face with our noses a half-inch apart and I felt like I really needed to say something meaningful and poetic and memorable. I mean, that's what you're supposed to do, isn't it? But the best I could muster up was: "Would you like a cup of tea or something?"

"The stove doesn't work, remember?"

"Oh."

"And you'd best be off, shouldn't you?"

"I hate to leave," I told her, and tried to move in for another kiss.

She turned her head and gave me an elbow-jab under the covers. "Oh, no," she shook her head. "Not again. No way. It's been lovely and all, but I'm a bit sore down there and it's time for you to shove off. Besides, I've got to get myself together and this motor home in order before you and your entourage arrive."

No question she was right. And the moment had passed anyway.

"It was nice though, wasn't it?"

"Yes, it was," she nodded, sounding close again. "It was lovely."

Fifteen minutes later I was wobbling and put-put-putting my way back towards Château Fairway with a nasty gouge in my forehead, a huge cloud of blue oil smoke trailing behind the VéloSoleX and a huge, self-satisfied smile plastered across my face. I felt pretty damn magical if you want the truth of it.

Chapter 8: 24 Long, Hot, Boring Hours

While the rest of the Fairway brigade mostly rested, ate, drank and did their best to get their internal clocks in order on Friday (except for H.R Junior and Dick Flick, who were still apparently occupied with important company business at *Madame Billie's* upper-bracket relaxation and ejaculation spa in Paris), Danny Beagle and I went back to the circuit in the smaller, non-limousine Mercedes coupe to pick up everyone else's credentials so they wouldn't have to stand in line and also to make sure that all of our hospitality arrangements were in order. Turns out the keys to all the garage cars were sitting in a little ceramic dish right on the blessed kitchen counter! Even so, I was kind of glad I hadn't found them, as the wobbly old VéloSoleX with the broken headlight and the trail of blue smoke had turned into about the most perfect transportation device imaginable the night before. I mean, it got me there—right through stopped traffic, in fact—and then prevented me from heading back to Château Fairway before daylight, and you'd have to call that a pretty good deal all the way around.

I don't think Danny had ever ridden in a Mercedes 220SE before, and you could tell he was impressed. And maybe just a little bit envious of the way the Germans built automobiles. From the understated wood veneer on the dash to the firm but comfortable seats to the quality of fit and finish to the car's balanced, well-dampened ride and poised, even arrogant over-the-road manners, the Benz oozed confidence, security, class and breeding.

"Makes you wonder how they ever lost the war," Danny mused.

"Hey," I told him, "too much land to govern and too many peasants to kill…especially in Russia." I gave him a worldly-wise shrug. "Conquering territory and hanging on to it afterwards have always been two irritatingly different propositions."

"You'd think people would learn."

"Nah, they never have." And then, just to pass the time (and maybe to impress him just a little) I quoted pretty much verbatim from a borderline-plagiarized high-school term paper I'd done that was mostly slightly reworded paragraph snippets from *The World Book Encyclopedia:* "Alexander the Great, Cyrus the Great, Augustus Caesar, Genghis Kahn, Hannibal, Attila the Hun, Tamerlane, Charlemagne, William the Conqueror, Napoleon, Hitler…they all wound up giving it all back."

Danny didn't look too impressed. He just kept looking out the window at the quaint French countryside rolling by. "Boy," he finally sighed, "I wish we could build cars like this."

"Part of it is the roads," I started to explain. "Europe is all old, narrow lanes that date back to horse-wagon-and-chariot days, but in America, we've got these wide, smooth, near-perfect, near-endless freeways and long distances between our cities and…"

"You don't need to give me a fucking dissertation on it. I know all that. I'm in the car business, remember?"

I'd obviously hit a nerve. Or maybe we were both just tired. "Sorry," I told him. "I'm just so used to trying to explain these things to people."

We rode a ways in silence. You get edgy with other people—even people you usually get along with—when you're in a strange place and haven't had enough sleep and your inner time clock is twisted around all upside-down and backwards. Danny leaned back in the seat and closed his eyes. And when he spoke, it was little more than a murmur. "I just wish we could build cars that *felt* like this, that's all. That *rode* and *drove* like this, you know?"

"No offense, but I don't think people would pay 220SE coupe money for a Fairway Freeway. Not even a fucking Freeway Frigate Fragonard special edition…" I saw a smile sneak across Danny's face, "…Besides, most Americans would think it rides too damn hard. And that the seats are too firm and the styling's too dull and the interior's too plain. It doesn't have enough hot'cha or sex appeal or pizzazz."

"You sound like Dick Flick."

I made a face like I smelled old cheese. "Besides," I added, "you'd have to pretty much turn the company over to the engineers instead of Clifton Toole's bean-counters and Dick Flick's marketing hot-shots and those new market-research types."

I saw Danny wince out of the corner of my eye. "That Hubert C. Bean is really a pill, isn't he?"

I nodded instinctively. And two seconds later I felt bad about it, because Hubert C. Bean was really just a nervous, timid, awkward little rabbit of a guy who never asked to be an expert on anything. But H.R. Junior had recruited him personally to be the company's five-hundred-thousand-candlepower High Beam into the future—you could see it scared the shit out of him—but you also got the impression that, at least in some nightmarishly masochistic way, he was enjoying all the attention. At least when Little Harry Dick wasn't intimidating the hell out of him or Dick Flick wasn't ratcheting off snide, demeaning, impossible-to-answer questions at him in front of the whole fucking executive-corridor staff. Dick did it because he knew H.R. Junior approved of fine, well-focused cruelty—especially in public—and he thought it might be worth a few Brownie Points. And poor old Hubert C. Bean couldn't do much more than just sit there and take it. I shook my head. "The poor guy can't help himself. He didn't ask to be put in that sort of position."

"No, that was H.R. Junior's magnificent idea." Danny looked down at his fingernails. "But he took the job and he took the money that came with it, didn't he? So he's got to take all the shit that comes along with it. Just like the rest of us."

"Hey, doesn't it say in the bible that the meek will inherit the earth?"

"Yeah, it does," Danny nodded.

"Only they left out the part about how badly they'd fuck it up once they got their hands on it." Danny snorted out a little half-chortle of a laugh. "The worst part is, he actually believes all that crap."

"You mean about customers being able to tell us what kind of cars they really want?"

"That's exactly what I mean. He thinks you can sift through a million kazillion grocery-store-parking-lot questionnaires and find out what people really want."

Danny looked out the window again. "You'd best keep that stuff to yourself, Hank. Survival up in The Tower depends on following the power flow wherever it goes and not making any waves. The last thing you want is to do is challenge popular ideas."

"By popular ideas, you mean whatever kind of shit decides to float, flutter or fly through Little Harry Dick Fairway's head, right?"

"That's about the size of it…" he shot me a mean-spirited smile, "…at least if you want to keep drawing a paycheck."

"Even when you think he's full of shit?"

"Even when you *know* he's full of shit."

He wasn't telling me anything I didn't already know. But it still didn't sit too well.

Danny looked over at me. "I'm just telling you for your own good, Hank. Don't be a fucking hero. You want to make a stand about something, talk to me. Or better yet, leave me the hell out of it and talk directly to Bob Wright. That's what he's there for. Let him decide which fights are worth picking with an asshole like H.R. Junior. That's what he's there for."

To be honest, that didn't sit very well, either. But I could understand it. If there was one single, overriding goal on the executive corridor of Fairway Tower, it was to survive. And to prosper, of course, and enjoy all the power and prestige and fancy little perks that came along with it. Anything beyond that was pure gravy.

We got Danny through registration without much fuss and were able to sign for all of the other Fairway credentials (which you weren't really supposed to be able to do), and I was surprised—you could even say shocked—at how pleasant and deferential they were about it. The head registrar himself whisked us right through. And apologized for taking up so much of our time while he was at it! It's not like I was new to the politics, privileges and pecking orders in the world of motorsports—and particularly here at Le Mans—but it felt totally foreign indeed to be on the *"after you, sir"* side of it.

Audrey had done a splendid job cleaning up after us in the motor home, which was a huge relief. Why, if you didn't check the seals and levels on the bottles of vodka and Johnnie Walker Black, you'd have never known we'd been there. She'd even coaxed Peter Bryant over from Clive Stanley's team to sort out the generator and get the batteries charged. Although Danny just about shit when he saw the Dodge emblems and lettering all over the place. But of course there wasn't much you could do about that, since virtually all the popular American motor homes came on Dodge truck chassis. Ben Abernathy told me all about it later on that afternoon.

It seems the entire U.S. motor-home craze started with a Michigan farmer-cum-inventor-cum-engineer-cum-builder-cum-entrepreneur named Ray Frank, who'd cut a deal with Chrysler way back in 1953 for Dodge truck chassis to put under his new line of self-propelled motor homes. When the Chrysler brass saw that he was buying quite a few chassis and that his business was gaining both traction and momentum, they offered him access to their nationwide dealer network in return for re-badging his "Frank

Motor Homes" as "Dodge Motor Homes." Anybody with eyeballs could see there was a future in it. After all, Americans loved to travel and liked the outdoors and a few million misguided boy scout/Daniel Boone/terminal masochist types even liked to camp out. But most Americans were pretty attached to soft living at home with their cushy bedroom mattresses and plump living-room couches and favorite overstuffed TV chairs. Not to mention refrigerators to keep the beer and cheese cold and stoves to cook up eggs and bacon and sausage sandwiches and hot showers for the dust and grime and—most sacred of all—genuine indoor plumbing. So motor homes quickly evolved as the only and ideal choice for family road-trip vacations to national parks and such. Or homecoming weekends at college or horse shows out in the boondocks or racing-team housing and hospitality at racetracks.

It was becoming a genuine phenomenon.

Even so, Danny thought we'd be better off covering up all the Dodge emblems and lettering with tape. Or, better yet, with Fairway Motors stickers, banners and posters.

"Didn't Bob want us to keep a low profile on this?" I asked as passers-by stopped and gawked at the first big, American-style motor home anyone over there had ever seen.

But of course the whole "low profile" thing was out the window anyway when (again thanks to that American-ambassador father of Little Harry Dick's former fraternity brother/congressman-from-Kennebunkport friend) a sleek, wasp-like Alouette II helicopter arrived in the farmer's field across from Château Fairway at about 10:30am Saturday morning to shuttle the most VI of our VIP guest entourage—meaning Little Harry Dick Fairway, Bob Wright, Karen Sabelle and H.R. Junior's current best-buddy Dick Flick—to the blessed racetrack. And meanwhile the rest of the group had to get up hours earlier so they could sit in the damn tour bus for two hours in inch-at-a-time race-day traffic to make their way into the track. And it was hot as hell that morning, even with the air conditioner going full blast.

Or that's what everybody said, anyway.

Having been to Le Mans a few times, I told them all before breakfast that I'd "run on ahead and make sure everything's ready" and pedaled/put-putted off into the distance on my semi-trusty old VéloSolex. Only this time I only added six squirts of oil to the fuel mix, so the smoke cloud trailing off behind was a bit less conspicuous. In fact, it was damn near translucent. Smoky, rickety and wobbly or not, the VéloSoleX was still—by far—the quickest and easiest way into the track on race morning. And it was a real treat to scoot along the grass verge at the side of the road or shoot right up the middle between the still-life lanes of traffic. Sure, you had to be wary of the occasional car door swinging open to let a little air in—it was only 7:30, but you could already feel the makings of an oppressively hot and dusty day—and be on continual lookout for the glowing butt ends of still-lit Gauloises and Gitanes cigarettes flicking out through the side windows of French-registered Renaults, Peugeots, Simcas, Dyna Panhards and assorted Citroën models ranging from faded old gangster-profile Traction Avants to folded-sardine-tin Deux Chevaux to the 2CV's supposedly more stylish but still odd-looking and angular Ami 6 sibling to the genuinely svelte, stylish and modern DS19s. Mixed in of course with Fiat 500s, 600 Multiplas, 1300 and 1500 sedans, Alfa Giulias and Giuliettas, Lancias and even occasional Ferraris and Maseratis from Italy, VW Bugs, camping Microbuses, a few Opels, Borgward Isabellas, BMWs and rattly Mercedes diesels from Germany and the inevitable, bleary-to-bloodshot Brits who'd made the trip down—straight through, more likely than not—in their Austins, Morris Minors, Hillmans, Humbers, overheating Jaguar 4-doors and 2-doors and hot, cramped and noisy little MG, Triumph, Healey and Sunbeam sports roadsters.

You tended to wonder why they were smiling.

Then again, they'd probably been drinking along the way.

Race Day is always an overload experience at Le Mans, and I'd have to say that the Fairway brass were truly impressed—you could even say stunned—by the sheer size, scale and scope of the spectacle. The grandstands across from the pits were packed full by noon, even though the race was still four hours away. Danny and I made sure we had a couple well-paid security guards holding our little cordoned-off area in the very top row to avoid any arguments or incidents later. Audrey and I had set up a nice outdoor lunch at the motor home with good old all-American hot dogs and hamburgers (not to mention gin-and-tonics or vodka gimlets and plenty of good old all-American Stroh's beer flown in specially for the occasion), and then I took those who wanted to on a little tour of the paddock. Little Harry Dick, Dick Flick and Clifton Toole chose to stay in the motor home with the liquor and the air conditioning (which, to be honest, was struggling mightily to keep up with the heat), but Bob Wright, Hugo Becker and Ben Abernathy were keen to see everything, and most of the rest went because, heat or no, they didn't want to be stuck in the fucking motor home with the unpredictable and regularly hair-trigger Little Harry Dick Fairway and an ample supply of booze.

There were hordes of people meandering all over everywhere in the pits and paddock (particularly don't-really-belong-there hangers-on who'd somehow managed to obtain, steal or forge official, team guest or VIP passes), and we found ourselves wading through a near-impenetrable crush of gawkers, rubberneckers, crew members desperately trying to get tires, tools, spares and equipment to their pit stalls, wildly-jabbering TV and radio announcers interviewing anybody they could find with a team shirt and a decent haircut, wandering gendarmes, soldiers and band members in uniform, program vendors, tire-, oil- and spark-plug company pitchmen and PR flacks and a genuine infestation of self-important French race officials who seemed convinced that the entire scene had been provided for the sole purpose of giving them something to lord over with unbridled authority.

It was bedlam.

And then some.

I walked the Fairway bunch past the cars getting ready to take their places along the straightaway for the Le Mans start, and Hugo Becker was absolutely fascinated by the Ferraris and Maseratis and that odd, mid-engined Tojeiro coupe from Ecurie Ecosse. Then he saw Count Volpi's strange, chopped-off Ferrari Breadvan and stopped dead in his tracks. I did my best to explain the palace intrigue as well as the aerodynamic thinking behind it, and I could tell my stock went up hugely with Hugo (along with everybody else) when Count Giovanni himself came over to say hello and allowed me to introduce him around like we were great old pals. He got the gist that they were higher-ups and, as always, he really knew how to handle things in a social situation and was absolutely delightful.

"*That* guy owns the team?" Ben Abernathy whispered incredulously as we moved off through the crowd.

"Yeah," I nodded. "He's some kind of latter-day count back home in Venice. His father was a big businessman, politician and financier between the wars."

"Oh?"

"The way I hear it, he set up all the utilities that brought electricity to northern Italy and the Balkans…"

Ben Abernathy and Bob Wright looked suitably impressed.

"…and later on, he served as Minister of Finance for the whole damn country. Or at least he did until Mussolini sacked him."

Ben looked back over his shoulder at Count Giovanni and the Breadvan. "You have any idea how old he is?"

"Just twenty-four. Came into his inheritance last year and just knew that he wanted to go racing. The family wouldn't let him drive himself, of course, but they couldn't stop him from buying top cars and setting up a team. They're pretty damn good at it, too. They won Sebring for Ferrari this year—first overall—after all the factory cars crapped out."

Ben let out a low whistle. I could tell he was enjoying the notion of a kid with all kinds of money and power and family connections not only setting up a formidable international racing team, but acting gracious and deferential instead of strutting around and letting loose on people like Little Harry Dick Fairway. I knew what Ben was thinking and gave him a nudge: "See what a little breeding will do for you."

We went back to the motor home for some air conditioning and another round of drinks, and then I took everybody out to the pit straight to watch the cars being pushed into position for the traditional Le Mans start. Several of the Fairway types were surprised to see Tony Settember's near-stock, white-with-blue privateer Corvette take its place at the very front of the line, ahead of all the Ferraris and the Maseratis and that handsome Project 212 coupe from Aston Martin. So I had to explain all over again how the cars were lined up by displacement rather than qualifying times. And also that where you start doesn't really make shit for difference by the end of a 24-hour motor race.

As 4pm approached, we made our way high up over the start-finish straightaway to an exclusive little roped-off VIP section at the very top of the grandstands, and the Fairway contingent cheered like mad along with everybody else when the big clock ticked straight-up 4 on a dusty, sun-baked, broiling-hot June afternoon. Some of the drivers were already a few steps towards their cars as the tricolor fell—like it really made a fucking difference who got away first—and the Fairway bunch cheered even louder when that big, rumbleguts Corvette caught traction and squealed away at the head of the field. Even if it was a damn Chevrolet.

But of course that wouldn't last. In a little over four minutes, the field came streaming out of Maison Blanche and onto the start/finish straightaway with Graham Hill in the mist-green Project 212 Aston heading up the queue and driving like it was the opening lap of a blessed grand prix. He and the rest of the faster cars had gotten around the Corvette pretty easily, but then Mike Parkes in the 4.0-liter "Experimental Class" Ferrari GTO had come storming up the inside of the Aston on the run down to the hairpin, trying to grab the somewhat useless honor of leading the first lap at Le Mans. To be honest, that's not how you really want to behave on the opening lap of a 24-hour contest. And maybe the brakes were still cold or maybe one of them grabbed or maybe there was dust or sand on the inside or perhaps it was just a simple over-supply of adrenaline, but the end result was that poor Mike managed to out-brake him-self rather than the other car. He probably should have just gone straight up the escape road, but he tried to be a hero and save it, had it get away from him, steered like mad as it swung one way and then snapped around the other and the GTO wound up on top of the infamous sandbank on the far side of the corner. Which meant Mike had to spend the better part of the next hour trying to dig *Commendatore* Ferrari's one-and-only 4.0-liter GTO out of the sand. With his bare hands, no less, since there wasn't even a kid's toy shovel with the tool kit.

Then there was another close call when Ian Snell arrived on the scene in Clive Stanley's Aston Zagato and very nearly did the same thing trying to get under Chris Lawrence's Morgan (which never should have been ahead of him in the first place, but Ian got delayed at the start when the cuff of his Dunlop racing suit snagged on the shift lever as he leaped inside and reached for the key). Clearly flustered, he proceeded to grab third instead of first and lurch-stalled it twice before sorting it all out and getting away in a tire-melting broadslide that almost collected one of the pretty little René Bonnet Djets that was just trying to stay out of everyone's way. I could imagine the pained expression on Geoff Britten's face in the pits. Not to mention the thin, told-you-so smile that surely must have sneaked its way across Tommy Edwards' lips right behind him.

In any case, Ian was damn lucky not to wind up in the sandbank next to Mike Parkes's Ferrari (or even possibly on top of it?), but the Aston kindly swapped ends instead and wound up facing backwards on the inside edge of the road. Which was quite fortuitous, actually. Only then Ian had to just sit there, waiting and blipping the throttle like mad with adrenaline damn near spurting out of his ears while the whole bloody rest of the field funneled past. Right down to the tiny little René Bonnet Djets, Fiat-Abarths and CD Panhards at the very tail end.

Served him right, the way I figured.

But back to the race: Graham Hill and the Project 212 Aston got their moment of glory by leading at the end of lap one (which of course sent all the inebriated Brits in the crowd—and that would be most of them—into near-orgasmic spasms of joy). But Gendebien was gaining on him rapidly in that 4.0-liter Testa Rossa with the gnarly scoops, basket-handle roll bar and that odd, bulbous windscreen, and the red car duly stormed past to take the lead on lap two and immediately began pulling out a margin. Although nobody really knew it at the time, the race for first overall was pretty much over then and there.

Only a few minutes later, the stubby little Peter Bolton/Ninian Sanderson TVR Grantura from Blackpool, England (which had the approximate shape and build of a four-pound bullfrog), suffered the ignominy of being first car to retire when it limped into the pits with a serious water leak at the end of the third lap. Turns out it was just a radiator hose that had worked its way loose because a hose clamp either hadn't been tightened properly or had been tightened so zealously that the threads stripped. It would have been an easy thing to fix, but the Le Mans rules were very specific as to how many laps a car had to complete before you could add fluids of any kind. So that was it: just over 15 minutes into a 24-hour motor race and they were out of it.

Done.

Finished.

Time to pack up.

I tried to get the Fairway bunch to appreciate what it must feel like when you and your crew have been working your damn asses off for months—and at an absolutely killing pace over the past several weeks—and now you're finally here at Le Mans and you've made it through the gauntlet run of scrutineering and night practice and now everyone is all geared up to battle it out for 24 long, grueling hours. And then the bottom falls out just fifteen minutes into the damn race! Imagine an unseen hand opening up a tap on your heels and letting all the juices drain out. I figured the whole crew would get stinking drunk as soon as they pushed the car to the dead-car park and packed all their pit equipment away. I mean, what else was there to do?

Meanwhile, the odd-looking Testa Rossa with the pugnacious, twin-nostril nose, butt-ugly windscreen and squared-off back end continued to stretch its lead on the rest of the field. Next up was still Graham Hill in the Aston 212 and then the three nasty-looking Maserati 151 coupes all in a bellowing-V8 line followed by the V6 Dino of the Rodriguez brothers, which was the only one of the faster cars taking the daunting curve under the Dunlop Bridge without lifting. Pretty impressive stuff. But the little Dino was no match for the bigger-engined cars on top end (although it would surely get better fuel mileage). Behind the Rodriguez brothers came Gurney hustling along nicely after a fairly miserable start in Count Volpi's Sebring-winner Testa Rossa, Baghetti in the V8-engined Dino and then, wonder of wonders and ahead of *all* of Ferrari's vaunted GTOs—*take THAT, Enzo!*—the crowd-favorite Ferrari Breadvan from our friends at Scuderia Serenissima! I was damn glad to see that, and I did my best to explain to my Fairway people just why it was so much fun and such a great story. But Little Harry Dick Fairway didn't look too convinced. "Where is this Wazzizname Ferrari guy anyway?" he wanted to know.

"Enzo Ferrari. His name is Enzo Ferrari."

"What kind of fucking name is 'Enzo'?" H.R. Junior scoffed. You could tell he was getting bored and impatient. And that was always trouble.

"It's an Italian name," I tried to explain. "Like Guido or Giovanni or Giuseppe."

"I got a guy named Giovanni styles my hair. Same guy Dick Flick uses. Pretty sure he's a fucking queer." My eyes involuntarily focused on his expensive, chestnut-colored toupee and then over to the perfect, Cary Grant-style hair with distinguished silver dashes at the temples on Dick Flick. But I didn't say anything. In fact, I hardly even breathed. Little Harry Dick Fairway was staring at me with that dissatisfied, accusing, cocked-pistol glare that usually meant you were about to catch hell. "So where the hell is this Enzo Ferrari guy? As long as we're here at the fucking race, I think I need to meet the little dago. And I'm pretty sure he'd want to meet me even more."

Bob Wright shot me a worried look, but I finger-waved him off. "I'm sure he would," I quickly agreed. "But Mr. Ferrari never comes to the races…"

"He *doesn't?*" H.R. Junior snorted. "Why the fuck not?"

I really didn't want to go into the details because it was a subject of voluminous discussion, conjecture, argument and speculation all across the European motorsports scene. And Little Harry Dick Fairway was the kind of guy who liked short, simple answers. Especially when he had a couple drinks in him. "Oh, he used to come to the races all the time," I told him. "Ferrari was a pretty decent driver himself back in the twenties and then he was racing team manager for Alfa Romeo before the war."

"Alfa Romeos?" he scoffed incredulously. "Those shitboxes?"

It wasn't really the right time to bring somebody like H.R. Junior up-to-date on Alfa's glory years back in the 1920s and 30s when its Vittorio Jano-designed P2 and P3 grand prix models were winning just about everything. Or to tell him about the multiple Mille Miglia and Targa Florio wins or the four straight victories at Le Mans from 1931—34, or how the resurrected prewar Alfa 158/159 models so dominated Formula One in the immediate postwar era—Alfa drivers won the first two grand prix World Championships in steamroller fashion in 1950 and '51—that the F.I.A. switched to the less expensive (and less impressive) *voiturette* Formula Two cars for the 1953 and '54 championship seasons in hopes of generating some competition and improving the show. It was likewise a poor moment to tell him how much I liked and enjoyed the current generation of Alfas—warts and all—and, like a lot of my fellow motoring scribes, greatly respected their engineering artistry, history and heritage.

But Little Harry Dick Fairway wasn't interested in any of that shit. All he wanted to know was why the fuck Enzo Ferrari didn't come to the damn races.

"Oh," I started in kind of ambiguously, "he probably had his fill of it over the years. I mean, it's quite a grind. So these days he prefers to stay put in Maranello where he can keep his eye on the factory and the business and the development of the cars and let his team managers and mechanics look after them here at the races."

"Knowing how to delegate responsibility is a very important thing," Bob Wright chimed right in. "It's the mark of a successful chief executive."

I watched H.R. Junior's eyes un-cock. That was a relief. And later on I told Ben Abernathy in private how Ferrari always told members of the motoring press—tears damn near streaming down from behind his famous sunglasses—that he simply couldn't bear to be there when one of his brave, gallant drivers got hurt. Or, worse yet, killed. But Vinci Pittacora once said after a few too many glasses of grappa that the *real* reason Enzo Ferrari didn't go to the races anymore was that he couldn't stand to see and hear those same brave, gallant drivers over-revving his beloved engines or grinding the gears in his beloved transmissions or generally beating the living shit out of his beloved namesake racing cars.

They were almost like his children.

Gendebien brought the leading Testa Rossa in for fuel right towards the end of the first hour, and that allowed the Aston 212 briefly into the lead again until it also stopped for fuel. Ditto for the Cunningham-entered Thompson/Kimberly Maserati, which briefly held point before it pitted, and that left the lead to the Rodriguez brothers' Dino for about 10 minutes before it, too, had to pit for fuel. The fact that it could go further between fuel stops than the more powerful cars and that none of the 4.0-liter cars could quite make a full hour meant that the on-the-hour standing sheets in the press room often showed the Dino in the lead. And Lord knows the French track announcers and the radio and TV people were trying like hell to sell the David-vs.-Goliath aspect of the supposed battle between the big, bad, 4.0-liter Testa Rossa of Hill and Gendebien and the nimble, scrappy, feisty little 2.6-liter Dino of the Rodriguez brothers. And, to be honest, the two Mexicans were driving the bloody wheels off that car. Except for the little tiddlers, they were the only ones taking the fast, daunting sweeper under the Dunlop Bridge in a flat-out drift. Lap after lap. It took your breath away. By contrast, Gendebien looked like he was just stroking along at a canter with plenty left in reserve.

I could tell most of the Fairway people were getting bored—and particularly H.R. Junior—but, to be honest, watching cars howl or sputter past for hour after hour isn't much of a show unless you know something about them and the people behind them or are simply afflicted with a serious case of the racing disease. Without those things, it's just hot and dull and noisy and dusty and not much in the way of entertainment. So it was almost a relief when H.R. Junior rolled his eyes for about the fourth or fifth time, belched loudly, scratched himself below the beltline front and back and announced that he'd *"had about enough of this shit"* and headed back towards the motor home for a little air conditioning and another couple rounds of gin-and-tonics. Most of the others went with him, but Danny Beagle, Ben Abernathy and Hugo Becker decided that they'd rather hang out with me and see a little more of the race rather than being stuck in a closed (if air-conditioned) motor home with a well-lubricated and potentially combative Little Harry Dick Fairway.

I could understand that.

So I did what a good tour guide should and took them through the tunnel to the pits and paddock. By that point, Gendebien was holding about a 45-second lead on the Thompson/Kimberly Maserati 151 (which was sounding absolutely marvelous and clocking damn near 180 on that flat-out, undulating straightaway towards Mulsanne!), followed at discrete intervals by the Rodriguez brothers' Dino, the Project 212 Aston, Walt Hansgen in the other Cunningham Maserati, Baghetti in the V8 Dino, Count Volpi's brilliantly hideous Ferrari Breadvan still going like mad, the French Maserati with Trintignant at the wheel and then four Ferrari GTOs keeping an eye on each other as they cautiously aimed for the Category 1 GT honors and the manufacturers points that came with it. I was extremely pleased that the Breadvan was still leading all the GT Ferraris (even if it was technically running in another class) and even happier that Freddie Fritter was running smoothly, sweetly and serenely in Carlo Sebastian's GTO, staying on pace, keeping his nose clean and taking care of the equipment like you have to at a race like Le Mans. No question Freddie was turning out to be one hell of a decent long-distance sports car driver.

Sadly, two-thirds of our yachting friend Count Giovanni's Scuderia Serenissima effort pretty much fizzled out in unison at the beginning of the third hour, as both the

Breadvan and the Sebring-winning Gurney/Bonnier Testa Rossa retired on the same lap (their 30th) with terminal transmission woes. It sounded a bit coincidental that they both dropped out at nearly the exact same distance and with the exact same sort of problem, but then both cars' transmissions had been "rebuilt for Le Mans" by Ferrari's in-house customer race shop. Hmm. Nasty rumors circulated a few weeks later that when the Count's own mechanics pulled the gearboxes apart back at their home garage, they discovered a few shiny steel balls mysteriously missing from the races of the input shaft bearings in both transmissions. Which would of course allow those shafts to oscillate ever so slightly. And then, as time and wear and mileage accumulated, ever so slightly more. Until their predictable and inevitable failure. Hmm, again. But, as I said, those were only nasty rumors, and it could have just been sour grapes. Or perhaps an attempt to stick the old needle in at *Commendatore* Ferrari and his customer race shop one more time.

Not that he would have much cared.

It was coming on evening by the time we reached Clive Stanley's pit so I could check in with Audrey. They'd been going okay since Ian's needless spin on lap one, but the engine was running a little hot—no surprise, really, with the ambient temp in the upper nineties—and Geoff Britten had instructed the drivers to cut back on the revs. To be honest, it was kind of early to be nursing the damn car—I mean, we were barely four hours into the race—and I said as much to Audrey. She answered with a sour look. "I suspect Ian might be stretching a bit on the far side to make his times look better."

That was idiotic, of course, but the most difficult competition a driver ever faces is always his own teammate. Even the best drivers are prone to looking over the team's lap charts to see how they're doing compared to the other guy in the car. It can't be helped. What can be helped is acting foolishly and beating on the car in order to make your times look better. I leaned over Audrey's shoulder and whispered: *"Do you want to take in the carnival later on if it all goes to shit?"*

She stared at me. "Are you kidding? In this bloody heat?"

"It'll be cooler then."

"Like hell it will. Besides, we'll have to pack up. And I'll be hot and dirty and who the hell wants to be surrounded by a bunch of drunken Brits and rude bloody Frenchmen anyway?" She looked up at me with a wink. "I'd much rather spend a few more hours in the motor home where it's nice and air conditioned."

"Can't do it."

"Why not?"

"It's full of assholes right now."

"I don't mind. Really I don't. Just so long as the air conditioning is running and there's ice in the fridge."

"We'll see what happens later. Wouldn't surprise me if most of them head back to the château tonight anyway."

"That's what I'd do if I had the chance."

"And miss the race?"

She gave me a worn-down shrug. "It's one thing when you're running right, but it's another thing entirely when you're just bloody limping along and trying to make the distance."

The only good news was that Clive Stanley was plenty pissed off about Ian Snell's Keystone Cops getaway and subsequent spin at the hairpin (plus James had whispered in his ear about the lap times and that Ian might be pushing too hard), and so Clive was maybe, just maybe, toying with the idea of ordering Ian to come down with a phantom case of food poisoning so he could put Tommy in the car. I was all for that, of course, and so was Audrey. Not to mention Geoff Britten, Peter Bryant and Georgie Smales. But you never really know what rich team-owners are going to do. And especially guys like Clive Stanley, who could worry back-and-forth about things for weeks without ever coming to a decent decision and then, smack-dab in the middle of a race, erupt with orders, instructions and edicts like a sputtering volcano. Peter Bryant referred to it as *"throwing a wobbler,"* and apparently Clive Stanley was quite well known for it.

I could tell Ben and Hugo were getting bored watching me chat up Audrey, so I gave her a good-bye peck on the cheek and ushered us further down pit lane. It was well on into evening now, lights were coming on and Phil Hill had taken over the leading Testa Rossa from Olivier Gendebien. We watched the pit signals as Phil uncorked a couple sub-4-minute laps, one right after the other (just to show everybody—his pursuers in particular—what the car could really do) and in the process lowered the outright track record to a fairly stunning 3:57.7. Meanwhile, its factory team stable-mate, the 4.0-liter "Experimental" GTO of Parkes and Bandini (which had been in and out of the pits several times already with overheating problems) finally retired. Seems the motor had ingested a lot of sand down the intakes while Parkes was trying to rock it off the sandbank following his first-lap miscue, and that ultimately did them in. A few minutes later, the Project 212 Aston came in with a generator problem and spent several laps in the pits having the armature rewound. Too bad. On the Italian side, tire wear was starting to become a major concern for both the Cunningham and Maserati France Tipo 151 V8s, as either lack of sufficient tread cooling or the odd camber and toe angles of the 151's unusual, articulated deDion rear suspension was chewing up rear tires at an alarming rate. Hugo Becker came up with the possible diagnosis that air packing up underneath the back end of the car at 175+ was causing it to lift, which made the rear suspension extend into droop so the rear tires were more or less running on their outside edges. I have no idea if he was right or not, but that was pretty clever thinking for an engineer who spent most of his time taking the effort (not to mention the road feel) out of power steering mechanisms and packing Freeway Frigate suspension systems with marshmallows.

Then Dick Thompson had a hell of a scary moment in the Cunningham Maserati. He'd just come storming out of the pits following a refueling stop and a brake-pad change, and the pedal went straight to the floor when he stepped on it for the first time heading into the esses. That happens pretty regularly after the caliper pistons have been pulled back for a pad change. But this time, a pad had hung up or some air worked its way into the system, and although he pumped like mad, in a flash he was in way too deep and crashed heavily. Fortunately without injuring himself. But the car was too badly mangled to continue. And that's the way it goes at Le Mans: you can be droning on for hours—almost fighting boredom in spite of the terrifically high speeds and the oppressive heat and dodging dawdling backmarkers and the scenery whizzing by in a terrifying blur—and then it's over in the blink of an eye. Just one unguarded instant or unlucky moment is all it takes...

Dapper little Maurice Tritingnant also had a dicey moment when the Maserati France 151 suddenly broke loose—maybe a suspension problem or an unseen patch of oil on the road?—and banged off one of the earthen bankings that line the circuit. Damage looked minimal, but the whack was hard enough to bend a rear wheel rim, and it also apparently rearranged the suspension enough to make the tire-wear problems on the French Maserati even worse. In fact, it was looking like the remaining Maserati coupes might run through their entire tire supply before the race was over if both cars kept running.

Meanwhile Graham Hill was hustling hard to make up time in the repaired Aston 212 coupe, and accidentally grabbed third instead of fifth on an up-shift and ran a bunch of valves into the piston crowns. Doing no good for either, as you can imagine. But of course no proud manufacturer wants to admit that their engines or drivelines may have failed under pressure (and they surely didn't want to lay blame at the feet of ascendant British racing hero and current Formula One points-leader Graham Hill!), so Aston's "official" reason for retirement was listed as "ignition." Or, as Peter Bryant slyly explained afterwards: *"Y'see, when the bloody piston crowns break apart because they've been beaten to death by the bloody valves, everything essentially stops rotating. Including the shaft for the bloody distributor drive. And when that happens, y'can't help but lose your bloody sparks, now can you?"*

Dick Flick would surely have appreciated that line of reasoning.

The loss of the Aston threat and the tire trouble on the Maseratis meant that the Hill/Gendebien Testa Rossa was stroking along easily in first with the Rodriguez brothers Dino almost a full lap behind (although they could still get a brief peek at the lead each time the Hill/Gendebien car pitted for fuel) followed by the V8 Dino a few laps back in 3rd, so we had three of Ferrari's original four factory entries running 1-2-3 with the privateer Belgian GTO of Noblet/Guichet in 4th and Carlo Sebastian's GTO with Freddie Fritter up hovering not far behind. Then it was even more privateer/concessionaire Ferrari GTOs filling out the top 10 and, to be honest, not much in the way of drama anywhere. Just more and more cars running into problems, visiting the pits and either lingering there for repairs, heading back out again as walking wounded or being pushed away to the dead-car park. No question the hot, dry weather was taking its toll. "Everybody says they hate it when it rains here," I told Hugo, Ben and Danny, "and you don't even want to think what it must be like heading into the kink at three in the morning in a driving rainstorm…"

I watched their eyes grow bigger in unison.

"…but the fact is it's a lot easier on the cars when it rains. They run cooler and there's less strain on the motors and drivelines because there's less traction and so the drivers have to take it easier."

"The suspensions and brakes must like it, too," Hugo added as he wrapped his brain around the concept. "You can't put nearly as much load into them when the road is slick." You could see he was getting the bug. And so were Ben and Danny, come to that. But not nearly so much as Hugo. He was getting his head into the scientific fascination, mechanical intuition and engineering creativity that are so much a part of motor racing.

Pretty soon Ben decided he needed to go back to the motor home for another pack of Marlboros—no question he needed a sit-down, as all the heat and dust and crowds and walking were starting to get to him—and by then Little Harry Dick Fairway had gin-and-toniced his way into a second wind and Bob Wright had finished up the paperwork he was going over with Karen Sabelle and Dick Flick and the rest were going a little stir crazy from just sitting around and seemed up for a little diversion. So I loaded them all into the chartered bus—there was no way H.R. Junior was about to walk—and had the driver inch us along through the swarming race-night throng towards the carnival up by the esses, about a mile from the pits. We probably could have gotten there quicker crawling on our hands and knees.

Even so, it was an interesting ride.

It was nighttime now with the howls and wails of the racecars as a constant, droning background, and everybody on the bus seemed mesmerized by the streaking sweep of headlamp and driving-light beams and the red trails off the taillights as the racecars swooshed past, then disappeared underneath the Dunlop Bridge. They reappeared just a heartbeat or two later on the far side, charging pell-mell towards the esses where the colored lights of the carnival flashed, blinked and twinkled against the nighttime sky. They looked like a misplaced slice of Christmas.

I figured H.R. Junior and the rest would enjoy wandering up and down the carnival midway because there were all sorts of attractions and distractions to keep them entertained. Including the inevitable wine-and-beer tents and garlic- and hot oil-scented food-vendor stands and sleazy girlie shows with straw-hat barkers out front jabbering away in French and your usual array of carnival sucker games with weighted pyramids of milk bottles that you couldn't knock down with a wrecking ball and wooden rings that never seemed to quite drop over the top of the goldfish bowls with the best prizes inside. Plus there was an absolutely amazing Motorcycle Wall of Death act where two small-framed riders in helmets with streamers on top and colorful leathers took turns blasting noisy, smoky 2-stroke dirt motorcycles around and around inside a huge, horizontal wooden drum like crazy, armor-clad hamsters inside an enormous, laid-on-its-side exercise wheel. First they went one at a time and then both together—in tandem and then side-by-side as they weaved up and down the clattering wooden walls—and it made a heck of a racket what with the knobby tires pounding against the wooden planks and the 2-stroke engines popping and crackling and even spitting out flames now and then. They came so close to the upper edge that you could almost reach out and touch them! And then, for a finale, they split apart and started criss-crossing in a genuinely frightening, near-miss after near-miss display of balls, nerve and timing that made the crowd gasp and cheer. Ultimately they skidded down to the bottom in perfect, *pas-de-deux* unison, came to a back-to-back halt and took their helmets off. Much to everyone's amazement, one was a pretty young girl with a blonde pony tail, and the other was a tough, wiry-looking older guy—maybe her father?—and they held out their helmets while the audience clapped and hooted and tossed a shower of francs and coins at them. Then the lights came up and the crowd filed out and the two riders went behind the drum's wooden framework to open up their leather jackets, sweat a bunch and smoke cigarettes while the spectator gallery filled up again for the next show. God knows how many hours they'd been at it already. But no question it was impressive, and a couple of the Fairway people went back in to see it again.

Meanwhile, the rest of us wandered on past the crêpe stands and cognac stands and the noisy, worn-out carousel with its chipped pastel horses creaking up and down on once-shiny steel poles and the usual carnival hucksters and fortune tellers and a wrestling tent where a couple tough-looking retired pros would take on all comers (and preferably large, drunken young men with buddies or girlfriends to impress) for money. At the very end of the midway were the popular Ferris wheel and *Soucoupe Volante* "flying saucer" rides that carried people high up over the midway and gave a truly spectacular view of the racetrack below. Especially at night. Ben and Danny and I stood in line so that H.R. Junior and Dick Flick and Bob Wright could grab a crêpe or a cognac and then step in to take our spots once we got near the front. I knew from experience that it was pretty damn special to go wheeling through that warm night air, high up over the carnival lights with the laughter, shrieks and tinny calliope music echoing up from the midway and mixing with the blipping, downshifting race-cars hurtling through the esses—right under your damn feet!—with their exhaust pipes crackling and brake discs glowing and headlamps blazing arcs one way and then the other through the darkness.

By that time, you recognized most of them by sound.

At least if you were paying attention, anyway.

We got back to the motor home well after midnight and H.R. Junior, Dick Flick, a worn out-looking Ben Abernathy and most of the rest just stayed on the bus so it could take them back to Château Fairway for a few more nightcaps and a good night's sleep. But Bob Wright, Hugo Becker and Danny Beagle stayed behind. They wanted to see it all. So I took them on one hell of a hike all the way down to the hairpin so they could see the signaling pits and what the cars look like when they're squirming around up-on-tiptoes as the drivers heel-and-toe brake and double-clutch downshift all the way from flat-out top speed to something like 35 or 40mph. Even in long-distance survival mode, it's pretty impressive stuff. I was pleased to see Freddie Fritter still going smoothly and beautifully in Carlo Sebastian's GTO, holding down 7th overall and a well-paced second in class behind the experienced Belgian GTO team of Noblet/Guichet. Well done! And I was absolutely thrilled to recognize Tommy Edwards's green helmet in Clive Stanley's Aston Zagato. But you could hear he was short-shifting it, and the lingering stink after the Aston passed by left no doubt that the motor was running hot and boiling out a little coolant—head gasket, most likely—and that they probably weren't long for the race. Too bad.

The well-driven Bob Olthoff/Sir John Whitmore Austin-Healey 3000 was running like a freight train but understeering horribly at the hairpin (as I explained to Hugo, that's precisely what made it feel secure through the fast corners that really mattered) while the Hobbs/Gardner Lotus Elite leaned a lot but was extremely smooth and supple. Both English cars were running well up the order at that point—the Healey a short distance ahead of the Lotus—and they were leading all the factory-entered Porsche Carreras! Which certainly must have made for a few cautious smirks in the Lotus and Healey pits and a lot of grim faces over in the Porsche camp. But the Porsches always ran to a disciplined schedule at Le Mans, and even though it seemed like the race had been running for an incredibly long time, I had to remind my Fairway Tower friends that we weren't even at the halfway mark! You could see that the enormity of the challenge was beginning to dawn on them.

After the hairpin, I took them partway up the straightaway towards the Hippodrome Café, so they could see the cars at top speed, listen to the engines straining at max revs and watch the drivers of the faster entries fidget in their seats a bit as they approached the infamous, white-knuckle kink before the braking zone for the Mulsanne hairpin. Bob Wright was pretty much awed by the way some of the faster cars blasted flat-out through that kink—the Rodriguez brothers' Dino in particular—and you could tell he appreciated the nerve, skill and commitment of the guys who didn't lift. Even in the smaller cars, it had to be intimidating as hell.

We made it back to the pits a little before dawn—all of us feeling pretty used-up— and by then Clive Stanley's steaming Aston had been pushed to the dead car park, the Corvette was in and out of the pits repeatedly, essentially on life-support, and two of the privateer GTOs had also retired. I looked for Audrey but she was nowhere to be seen and all the team's equipment had already disappeared from their pit stall. It was kind of sad to see that empty space with nothing left but some stains on the concrete, a three-quarter full trash can and a short stack of worn-out tires. There were spaces like that all up and down pit lane by that hour of the morning, and a tale of disappointment and disillusion went with every single one.

I noticed my friend Cal Carrington leaning against a tool cabinet over in Carlo Sebastian's pit, and although they were still running, he was looking pretty glum. He and Peter Ryan had started out with what looked—at least on paper—like one of the strongest entries in the field. And in spite of his youth, relative inexperience and eager, wide-eyed, sometimes even boyish exuberance, Peter Ryan was potentially an excellent draw as a co-driver. He was bullet fast, smooth and steady, and he claimed to understand, even though he'd just turned 22, that there are really only two rules in endurance racing:

a) Take care of the car, and

b) Take care of the car

But you can throw all that handicapping crap out the window once the tricolor falls at Le Mans, and Cal had an unfortunate, not-his-fault-at-all coming-together with a backmarker during the very first hour. Cal swore the guy had signaled him to pass (but maybe he was just waving at a photographer friend or giving the finger to a corner marshal?) and, even with his brakes locked up solid and rubbersmoke pouring off the tires, the guy chopped right across the Ferrari's nose and gave it a hefty clout in the left front. The team lost half an hour straightening out the sheet metal and yanking the front end back into reasonable alignment, and the car never really handled right after that. Plus they'd had some niggling electrical problems during the night with the lights suddenly going dark—it took another couple stops and another half-hour lost to put that right— and three flat tires. And two of them happened on the far side of the track so the drivers had to limp the rest of the way in at little more than a walking pace. So they were really out of it as far as any kind of a top finish was involved. Only there were hardly any cars left running in the 3.0-liter sports class now that the Scuderia Serenissima Testa Rossa had retired. Just the two Dinos, really, and a lot of us doubted that either one would make it all the way to the finish. So, even though Cal and Peter Ryan were well down the order—behind even the Healey 3000 and the Hobbs/Gardner Elite and two of the Porsche Carreras and the quickest of the Alfa Giulietta SZs—there was still an outside chance at a high class finish and perhaps even a win if they could just keep soldiering on and accumulate enough laps to be classified as a finisher. That's how it goes sometimes at Le Mans. And now it was Cal's turn to get back in and grind out another stint. Only Peter was late coming around. First by a few seconds, then ten seconds, then twenty, then a minute, then two minutes, then…well, everybody kept staring into the darkness down towards Maison Blanche and wondering what the hell had happened.

We knew it had to be something bad.

Sure enough, Peter Ryan had arrived at the Mulsanne hairpin immediately after one of the Fiat Abarth twincams put a rod through its block and dumped a whole sump-load of oil all over the pavement. The driver was thoughtful enough to pull to the inside so as not to leave oil on the racing line, but then he had to turn in towards the apex because there was another car passing on his left and so when Peter got there, everything seemed fine until he got to the middle of the corner. At which point it must have felt like somebody had ripped the rug right out from under his feet. The marshal should have been showing a warning flag, of course, but he was more or less dozing and only woke up when Phil Hill (who had damn near lost it there himself on the previous lap!) brought the leading Ferrari to a complete stop and yelled and beeped the Testa Rossa's stupid little horn until the marshal woke up, brushed himself off with as much dignity as he could muster and hung out an oil flag. But it was much too late for poor Peter Ryan, who was doing an exhausted Mike Parkes replay, trying his best to dig the banged-up Testa Rossa out of the sand bank. He worked away at it for the better part of an hour before he finally gave up and headed disgustedly back to the pits on foot.

They were out of it.

The two remaining E-Type Jags were still running well—on the same lap with the British team a minute or so ahead of the Cunningham entry—and they'd both been progressing slowly but steadily up the order as the field thinned out and other cars ran into problems. Like the Maserati France Tipo 151, which finally retired with terminal rear-suspension derangement just as the sun was coming up. Then the sick-sounding Corvette couldn't be coaxed into going any further and it, too, was pushed to the dead-car park after 150 mostly slow and painful laps. Not unexpected, but sad nonetheless for the only American car in the entire field.

Even if it was a fucking Chevrolet.

And then we had major drama. Right in front of us, in fact. The second-place Rodriguez Dino came in a little after sunup for what should have been just another routine pit stop. But when they tried to re-start it after the tire change and refueling were done, the engine fired right up but the starter motor refused to disengage. It made a horrible racket—like scrap metal being fed through a meat slicer—and so they switched it off immediately and tried again. Same thing. They killed it again and popped the rear deck lid to look underneath. Then they jacked it up so one of the mechanics could go under and bang on the starter with a hammer. But it didn't do any good. So then the mechanics tried putting it in gear and rocking the car front-to-back to try to get the damn starter-motor gear to disengage from the blessed flywheel. But when they spun it over, the problem—and that horrible, gnashing, grating noise—was still there. So they shrugged and jabbered back-and-forth in Italian and finally sent the car back out with instructions to Rodriguez to try getting on and off the throttle really hard—repeatedly—to hopefully spit the stuck starter gear out of the flywheel.

But it didn't work.

The Dino never made it back around.

And that was a real shame after a truly valiant effort by both Rodriguez brothers.

By 8am, the race had turned into nothing more than a dull procession with most cars just struggling around to make the finish. Freddie Fritter's GTO had been leading the GT category and running an amazing 3rd overall behind the Hill/Gendebien Testa Rossa and the remaining V8 Dino of Baghetti and Scarfiotti, but then the Dino's gearbox got stuck in 2nd gear and the car suffered an agonizingly long pit stop to fiddle with the shift linkage. If it had been stuck in 4th or 5th, they could possibly have nursed it along, but there was no way they could run to the finish in 2nd gear. The mechanics finally got the linkage freed up, but the stop dropped them well down the order with no chance of making it back up the leader-board unless a lot of other cars hit trouble.

The last of the Maserati 151s (the McLaren/Hansgen Cunningham car) melted a piston and had to retire, and the Healey 3000 that had been doing such an incredible job—it was up in the top ten overall by that point!—also lost a cylinder. But the Healey guys weren't about to give up. They levered over the rocker arms for that cylinder, pulled the pushrods, yanked the sparkplug wire and sent it back out running on 5 with everyone's fingers crossed. But it came to no good, as another cylinder blew and this time there was too much internal damage to continue. So they were out of it after 212 laps and a genuinely gallant effort.

The Fritter/Grossman GTO had to make another long stop when the starter refused to engage after what should have been a routine pit stop—just the opposite of the Rodriguez Dino's problem—and meanwhile the remaining Scarfiotti/Baghetti V8 Dino started jumping out of gear around lunchtime and finally broke its transaxle for good with just a few hours to go. They were the final retirement, and I caught myself wondering if it was worse to have everything go to shit after all those long, hard, broiling-hot hours or just fifteen minutes into the race like the sad little TVR team from Blackpool. I came to the conclusion that it was shitty either way, and you couldn't miss that the odds were stacked against you at a race like Le Mans. Out of 55 starters, only 18 made it all the way to the finish that year. Think about that.

So when the end finally, mercifully came at straight-up 4pm, it was Hill and Gendebien scoring their third shared win in *Commendatore* Ferrari's overdog, 4.0-liter "Experimental Class" Testa Rossa, while a pair of privateer GTOs from Belgium (Noblet/Guichet and Dernier/Blaton) took the next two spots and wrapped up those coveted World Manufacturers' Championship GT points for Ferrari as well. The Cunningham "American" XKE and the Peter Sergeant "British" XKE provided most of the excitement right there at the end, as they staggered towards the finish with the Cunningham car smoking badly but nonetheless reeling in the Sargent/Lumsden Jaguar, which was also stuck in gear. In the end, they came home a more-than-respectable 4th and 5th overall with the Cunningham entry in front (and on the same lap, no less, which had to rankle the hell out of the English team!), and the Jags snagged 1st and 2nd in the 4.0-liter GT class in the bargain. Even if they did finish 16 full laps behind the 3.0-liter GT-winning Ferrari. Carlo Sebastian's GTO had surely had its problems but managed to keep running, and I was tremendously pleased to see my favorite new stock-car hero Freddie Fritter finish 3rd in class and 6th overall on his very first trip to Le Mans. Good for him! The lone remaining Porsche Abarth-Carrera finished a well-judged and wisely paced 7th overall and easily copped the 1600cc GT laurels and the Category II World Manufacturers' Championship points that went along with it (which, after all, is what they came for). And one of Colin Chapman's slick little Lotus Elites with comingmen David Hobbs and Frank Gardner sharing the wheel came in a rather amazing 8th overall, won its class (the fourth year in a row for an

Elite!) and also copped the obscure but oh-so-important—at least to the French or-ganizers, anyway—*"Rendement Energetique"* Index of Thermal Efficiency prize, which I explained after a few celebratory glasses of champagne had something to do with en-gine size, distance covered, fuel consumed and the drivers' combined hat sizes. In any case, it usually went to one of the little pale-blue French tiddlers, so Chapman came away with some small measure of revenge for what the French officials had done to his lovely new Type 23s at scrutineering.

Even so, Colin swore he was never coming back.

Chapter 9: Insights You Don't Really Want

Audrey and I kept missing each other towards the end of that long, hot weekend at Le Mans. I had my Fairway people to squire around, of course, and Clive Stanley's pit area was just a sad, empty space along pit lane by the time I got there following my long, early-ayem trek down to the hairpin and back with Bob Wright, Hugo Becker and Danny Beagle. So when they headed to the motor home for some much-needed coffee and rest, I stayed behind and wandered into the paddock to see if I could find Clive Stanley's transporter. Which I did. But it was dark and everything was locked up tight and nobody was around, and the only thing I had for company was the sound of surviving racecars droning, limping and sputtering through the last of the night. 55 cars had started the race, and by the sound of it, less than half of them were still running. And that's with just under half the damn race yet to run.

I was well past exhausted by then and headed back to the motor home myself, only to find that Audrey had been there looking for me, waited around for more than an hour but finally caught a ride with Tommy Edwards and Peter Bryant back to the farm house-cum-guest house where Clive's team was billeted. Missing her like that made me feel pretty damn miserable—and miserable always seems worse when you're so fucking tired and worn down you can't hardly focus—and I remember having this ridiculous brainstorm about how great it would be if everybody carried around these little private telephones so you could contact them whenever the hell you wanted to. But of course that was nothing but science fiction, right? I mean, what the hell would you do with the wires?

But by then I had other things on my mind. Like getting the local and somewhat worn-out Sunday-morning caterer Audrey had arranged for us (I think they'd done three separate trackside hospitality parties the night before!) hustling on setting up our *Omelettes Française* and *Crêpe Suzettes* brunch buffet before our tour bus arrived from Château Fairway. I wanted to make sure they were all really impressed by how nicely everything had been organized for them. And especially considering how it was all done in a mad, last-minute scramble with very little notice. The caterer didn't even want to take the job, but Audrey'd been told they were the best in the business and so, in the great American tradition, she just kept offering them more money and more money until they finally caved in. But it was important that the people from The Tower should see and appreciate the results, since I desperately wanted to work with Audrey again—as soon as possible and as often as possible and as closely as possible—as Fairway Motors' "Absolute Performance" program motored on into the future. Surely the notion of spending more time with her—particularly at lovely 3- and 4-star European hotels with airy, sunlit rooms, thick plaster walls for privacy, room service breakfasts on genuine china and 1000 thread-count Egyptian cotton sheets—had my imagination working overtime. Particularly since it would all be on the company's nickel! Or maybe that was just a wee bit far-fetched. But no matter how it worked out, I figured a lot of it would hinge on how they liked the way she'd handled things at Le Mans.

Still, I felt rotten about missing her—even though we were both worn down to nubs by that point and there was no place for us to go in any case—and I kept wondering and even agonizing about what my next Fairway mission might be, where the assignment might take me and how long it would be until I could see her again. I thought about that a lot. In fact, I couldn't *stop* thinking about it. And that's what was still rolling through my head as our chartered 707 lifted off for our long, droning plane flight back across the Atlantic. We were headed back to Detroit and Fairway Tower, and it was dawning on me all over again that it wasn't where I wanted to be. Not at all. Oh, sure, it was nice staying in a room that didn't smell like old socks and crumb cakes and where the banging of baking pans didn't wake me up before dawn every morning. Not to mention that my bed at the Fairview Inn was re-made fresh for me every day with clean, pressed sheets and there would likewise be fresh, fluffy towels over the chrome rails in the bathroom. Terry cloth, no less. But it was a sterile, lonely, anonymous sort of place, and the only life there at all was down in the lounge at the end of the day when some of the Fairway Tower executive brass would stop by for a few wind-me-down cocktails on their way home from work. That's where a lot of the planning and rumors and grousing and shop talk really took place, and that could be kind of fun. Especially the rumors and the grousing. But it was pale meat compared to the racing gossip I vacuumed up at the pubs around London where the Cooper guys or the Lotus guys or the BRM guys or the Lola guys stopped in for a pint after work. Jesus, I missed that. There's nothing more intriguing or entertaining or quicker to pivot on a dime than the art and science of motorsports, and the sense of being a genuine insider is pretty damn intoxicating. Not to mention addictive.

I missed the shit out of it.

Something pretty strange happened during that long, wearing plane ride back to Detroit. I was sitting in a row all by myself and just kind of brooding and feeling sorry for myself and every time I glanced down at my wristwatch, it didn't even look like the blessed second hand had moved. Out of sheer boredom, I wandered off down the aisle to take myself a sit in the john. And I tried to make sense of things as I sat there in that claustrophobic little closet of an airplane toilet and stared at myself in the mirror. No question the guy looking back at me wasn't used to the kind of thoughts and feelings he was having about Audrey. But I knew he was going to have to get used to it if he wanted things to progress any further. He'd also have to deal with her nasty, flinty, mean-spirited, ill-tempered, mad-at-the-world father and his entire fucked-up situation as well. And that was an unpleasant prospect indeed. But he was part of the package. And that's essentially what was meandering through my head when somebody knocked on the door. Or maybe pounded is more like it.

So I flushed the toilet like I'd actually been doing something worthwhile in there and re-entered the cabin. And who should be waiting there with an impossibly impatient look on his face and his infamous blue folder tucked under his arm but Little Harry Dick Fairway. His eyes were terribly bloodshot and he looked more than a little unsteady. "You shit a dead mule in there or what?" he snickered as he shouldered his way past, waving his hand in front of his nose like the stench was unbearable. Real Cub Scout stuff, you know?

The narrow little door closed behind him. And I caught myself wondering just what he was going to do in there and how he was going to position himself and…and just as quickly I was trying to get the whole, unfortunate image out of my head. That's the thing about imagination. You can't control the damn thing. It can elevate you with lyrical, magical visions or haunt you with horrid, grotesque images you simply can't get rid of. Like the terrible crash Buddy and I witnessed at Le Mans in '55. That whole thing was still waiting there on the inside of my eyelids, ready to burst out of the shadows like a silent, slow-motion explosion whenever things seemed too pleasant, settled and peaceful.

I wandered back to my seat and actually almost dropped off to sleep for awhile. But I was mostly just dozing and, as I dozed, I caught myself wondering what the hell might be inside Little Harry Dick Fairway's ominous blue folder. I couldn't help being fascinated by what manner of exotic jerk-off pictures or prose or drawings or whatever might be inside. I mean, what sort of pornography would you opt for if you were a rich, spoiled, mean-spirited S.O.B. who could afford any and every damn thing your twisted little heart desired? To be honest, curiosity was gnawing at me like a rat on an old cheese rind, and I made up my mind that somehow, some way I was going to find out what was in there...

That was for absolute certain.

Then I thought some more about Audrey and then I think I may have actually slept for a few minutes and then I got up and wandered the aisle some more and then I sat down again and went through my usual, too-much-time-to-kill rosary of worries and I guess that's about when Little Harry Dick Fairway ambled unsteadily up to my row. And no question he was well and truly soused. Oh, I'd seen him after he'd been drinking before—several times, in fact—but never like this. He had that lost, disheveled look drunks get when the liquor's really taken over. Then again, I'd seen him carrying a full bottle of Napoleon brandy onto the plane with him (liberated from the liquor cabinet at Château Fairway, no doubt), and my guess is he'd worked his way through most of it on his own. He looked down at me through a pair of bleary, barely focused eyes and asked—very softly, almost apologetically—if I'd like to play a few more hands of gin. It was the first time I'd ever heard him sound even remotely cordial (or even civil, come to that) and he'd obviously fallen into that deep, maudlin chasm all men seem capable of finding when they've been oversupplied with alcohol and undersupplied with sleep.

"Sure," I answered evenly, "I can play a few hands."

"Good," he exhaled as he more or less toppled his way into the aisle seat. "Thass really good."

I flopped down the center tray between us and watched as he attempted to remove a deck of cards from its packet with fingers thick and numb as frankfurters. It was actually kind of comical, but I didn't dare crack a smile. "I can deal if you'd like me to," I told him.

He eyeballed me suspiciously for a second—like I was questioning his manhood or something—but then he gave me a grunt of approval and pushed the cards in my direction.

"You're the writer guy, aren't you?" he said like he was simply reminding himself.

"Yeah."

He thought that over. "I beat the living piss out of you on the way over, didn't I?"

"That you did."

He looked at me with betrayed, Bassett-hound eyes, and when he spoke, his voice was thick with disappointment. "You know, I don't think you were playing your best game…"

The nerve ends at the base of my neck went on red alert. I didn't know what to say.

"…and I really *want* you to play your best game with me, see. It's important. That's what Bob Wright always says…" he mimicked Bob Wright: *"At Fairway Motors, we want your very best effort every single second of every single minute of every single hour of every single day."*

I told him I was sorry. And allowed that I was maybe a little afraid of beating him. I left out the part about Danny Beagle's head popping up over the seatback when H.R. Junior was in the john and telling me that's exactly what I needed to do.

Little Harry Dick thought it over, looking very serious indeed. And then he gave me one of those drunken, exaggerated, just-between-you-and-me nods of approval. "Oh, that's OK," he allowed like we were old chums. "People do that to me all the time…" He made it sound like one of the saddest things he could imagine. "I don't know why they do it, but they do." He gave me the Bassett-hound eyes again. "I just want to be treated like everybody else, that's all."

"Sure you do."

He nodded again. And then added, very slowly and deliberately: "But it's not easy."

"I'm sure it's not."

"You bet your ass it's not."

This was a side of Little Harry Dick Fairway I'd never seen. Hell, that probably *nobody* had ever seen! And I didn't really know what to make of it. But I did know that I'd better be careful about what I said, since I'd seen how he could change in half-a-heartbeat and strike out like a cornered rattlesnake whenever the mood hit him.

"…Sometimes I think people are actually *afraid* of me…" he went on like it was the oddest thing imaginable.

"No…*really?*" was about all I could manage in the way of a response.

"I mean, I used to get along with *everybody* back in college…"

"I understand you used to get along with everybody back in a LOT of colleges" I wanted to say, but fortunately another feeble "No…*really?*" was all that came out.

H.R. Junior nodded solemnly. "It's no easy thing running a company like Fairway Motors…"

"I'm sure it's not."

"People are always sneaking around and saying things behind my back…"

"I'm sure they are."

His eyes suddenly narrowed. *"Who are they???"* he pretty much demanded.

"Who are *who?*"

"The people saying things behind my back."

He was starting to look angry, and I was starting to get scared. I knew I had to come up with some kind of answer. "Well…" I allowed like I was giving it serious thought, "…the union guys, of course…"

He mulled that over and seemed to be satisfied. Only then his eyes narrowed even more. "Yeah, but I say *FUCK 'EM!* The rat-bastards wouldn't even have jobs if it wasn't for me an' my fuckin' family!"

"You're absolutely right," I quickly agreed. "You'd think they'd understand that."

"Fuckin' ay they should…the bastards!"

"It's not your fault you have the whole damn company to run."

"Damn straight it's not!"

"You give your best effort every day."

"Every single second of every single minute of every single hour of every single day!" he repeated, his head bobbing up and down. And then a strange calm came over him and he looked deeply into my eyes. Almost like he was noticing me for the very first time. And then, out of absolutely nowhere: "You know my daughter?"

Ice water shot through my veins.

"Uh…," I fumbled. "…S-sure I do…sort of…a little…I mean, you had me over for her birthday party and…"

"She stinks," he said definitively. "I swear, she's the worst kid ever…A real little snatch, you know? A real bitch. A real smartass…." He looked like he was having trouble focusing. "You ever try to talk to her?"

"No," I lied. "Not really."

"She's running around with those fucked-up so-called friends of hers…" he leaned in close and whispered: *"Bunch of fucking punks. They go down to that nigger bar by the plant to try and buy drugs…"*

That ice water in my veins froze solid. But I tried to keep looking calm, reasonable and supportive. Or at least I hoped I did. "How…I mean…how do you know that?"

H.R. Junior leaned his head back so he could look down his nose at me with the one eye that still seemed to be working. "Do I look fucking stupid?"

"Oh, no…I mean, hell no…I mean, not at all…I mean, if there's one thing you never looked, it was stupid."

His head bobbed faintly up and down in agreement. You could see he was running out of gas. That second eye was looking about ready to close like the first one. And it couldn't happen quickly enough as far as I was concerned. "Damn straight," he mumbled into his shirt collar. "My daddy built this fucking company by keeping an eye on things. I got people who make a damn good living doing just that…"

"Like Scully Mungo?" I asked so softly and sweetly it sounded like a lullaby.

"Oh…" H.R. Junior assured me as his head lolled forward into the fleshy little hollow between his shoulder and his breast bone, "…Scully's just the tip of the fucking iceberg…" his eyes sagged closed like theater curtains coming down "…just the tip…"

A moment later he was snoring.

And I just sat there, wondering what the hell had just happened? Thanks to long hours awake and that 2/3rds of a bottle of French brandy, I'd caught a glimpse of a human, vulnerable and possibly even sympathetic side of Little Harry Dick Fairway. I'd also come to realize that Amelia Camellia Fairway was, by a significant margin, the single most dangerous person I'd ever been in contact with in my entire fucking life. She was poison, no question about it.

Only then I couldn't stop thinking about her. Even though I tried. Lord only knows why she'd shown any interest in me—a way to get pot mixed up with a little spoiled-rotten teenage boredom and the sheer, kinky novelty of doing something unexpected and outrageous—and in my head I could see her looking at me like some young, predatory jungle cat eyeballing a slow, fat wildebeest and savoring the fear in its eyes. Jeez, she was trouble. And the thing I hoped and prayed for above all else was that Little Harry Dick Fairway would never get wind of any of it. I mean, I wouldn't just get fired—I'd most likely go to jail! And that's if I was lucky! I also hoped H.R. Junior wouldn't remember any of our conversation when the plane touched down in Detroit damn near four hours later. I had to pee something awful by then, but I'd been afraid of making my way across him to the aisle for fear of waking him up. Lord only knew what sort of face and demeanor he'd be wearing if that happened…

But luck was with me and he snored all the way to the gate.

Thank goodness.

I sat next to Danny Beagle for our bus ride back to The Tower, and along the way I asked him what was likely to be coming up next up on my corporate agenda.

"Well, first thing when we get back, you'll have to write your report."

"My report?"

"Sure. You always have to write a report."

"What kind of report?"

"Oh, just a routine post mortem. What we did. How we did it. What our budget and expenses were. How we'd do it differently if we had it to do over again…that sort of thing."

I let out a low whistle.

"There are accounting forms that'll have to go with it for Clifton Toole's people…"

Oh, great.

"…and then we'll have a de-briefing and you'll find out what you did wrong."

"But what if I didn't do anything wrong?"

Danny gave me a strange, sadistic little smile. "If you didn't do anything wrong, then you're perfect. And we all know nobody's perfect. So just start out by assuming you did something terribly wrong…"

I was beginning to wrap my brain around it.

"…and if, by some miracle, you didn't do anything wrong—and remember, H.R. Junior is going to be weighing in on this—then for sure they'll find something wrong with the way you wrote it up in your report."

"But I'm a writer. It's what I do."

"This is different. Especially the accounting stuff." Danny clapped a friendly hand on my shoulder. "Trust me on this, Hank: somebody is going to ream you a new asshole over this."

"But everybody said I did a good job. Even Bob Wright said I did a good job."

"Sure you did. No question about it. But no way are the assholes going to let you get away with it. Especially on your first-ever company project…."

"So I'm in for it?"

"Nah, you won't hardly feel it. They'll get somebody—probably Dick Flick or Clifton Toole or maybe Randy Perrune—to chew you out for something or other you did or didn't do and that'll be the end of it. The important thing is that you take it like a man and don't argue or make excuses and promise to do better next time."

"And then what happens?"

"Nothing at all. Then it'll be over."

It was a lot to take in. "Jesus, it's like joining a damn fraternity, isn't it?"

"Yep, and you're heading into pledge week. I'll show you the secret handshake if you like…" Danny bobbed his fist up-and-down in a pantomime jerk-off.

It was nice to understand how things were.

"So what happens after that?"

"Hard to say. You're off the front burner now that Le Mans is over, so you'll probably sit and stew awhile until they figure out what they want you to do next."

That didn't sound particularly appealing. Or well defined. "But what will I be doing?" I wanted to know.

"You'll be drawing a paycheck," Danny grinned. "Just like the rest of us…"

All of which is how I wound up in Dick Flick's executive-corridor office at 9am sharp on the bleary Tuesday morning after Le Mans. He didn't look happy about being there at all—at least we had that in common—and even less happy about finding me sitting across from him. "I don't know why the hell they dumped you on me," he grumbled as he stroked down imaginary stray hairs in the handsome silvery flashes at his temples.

"I guess because I'm a writer?"

He eyed me like a bad smell. "You're a pain in the ass is what you are. Bob wants you to be some kind of motorsports spy. So why don't you go *be* some kind of motorsports spy and stay the hell out of my hair."

"I lost my job at the magazine," I answered lamely. "I've got no cover anymore..."

"You got fired is what you did. That's how you wound up in my fucking office." He shook his head.

Dick Flick rolled his eyes like he knew all about it. He had this way of looking mildly irritated and yet bored-as-hell when he really wanted you to know how much of his valuable time you were wasting. And then, out of absolutely nowhere: "I don't want you to think you're in for a fucking free ride here, either. They'll be plenty for you to do. More than plenty. You're going to have to learn how to write copy instead of tell stories."

"Isn't it the same thing?"

He glared at me. "When you write for a magazine, you're trying to capture the truth. But when you write ad copy, you're trying to make people think and feel and believe a certain way but have it sound and smell like the truth." He looked me in the eyes. "And I bet you're just barely smart enough to understand the difference."

I didn't say anything.

"When we get this 'Absolute Performance' program rolling, we're going to need someone to go over all the insider drivel in the press releases with a fine-tooth comb. Make sure we've got all the technical shit and buzz-words right for the nutball media outlets. They're picky as hell about that stuff. You'll probably wind up doing some of it yourself if it turns out you know how to use both ends of a pencil." He glared at me some more. "And always remember this: nothing gets released—not *ever!*—until I sign off on it. Do we understand each other?"

I felt my head nod up and down.

"But first you have to learn how we do things around here..."

Trying to adapt to a life split between my new, windowless cubicle in Dick Flick's ad department and my colorless, odorless and tasteless room at the Fairview Inn was a lot like sleep-walking through a dream that didn't go anywhere and didn't mean anything. I did the report Danny told me I'd have to do and then, a week later, I got a dose of second-hand shit from Clifton Toole and Dick Flick and Daryl Starling (by way of Danny Beagle, thank goodness) about the fucked-up traffic in and out of the track at Le Mans and the snotty staff and crappy plumbing at Château Fairway and why the hell did we have a damn *DODGE* motor home, for chrissakes? The basic gist of it was that you couldn't let any rookie employee get away with doing an acceptable job first shot out of the box (why, it was unthinkable!) and, as Danny explained it to me over a couple of cocktails at the Fairview Inn lounge that particular evening, you really wouldn't want that anyway.

"Why is that?" I had to ask.

"Because then expectations get ratcheted way up and then you're even more certain to fuck something up and disappoint people later on." He said it like it was something I should have already understood, and it brought me back to what Ben Abernathy told me that very first night we went out to The Steel Shed together. You know, about how the key to success—or at least survival—in a place like Fairway Tower started and ended with low expectations.

After all, it kept you from disappointing people.

Speaking of Ben Abernathy, he was turning out to be about the best friend I had in Detroit. I mean, Danny was okay—I liked Danny, really I did—but he had a chicken-shit streak a mile wide and his sense of honor and fair play was always going to take a back seat to his minor-league ambitions and survival instincts. I didn't dislike him for that—like I said, I liked him—but that's the way he was and you just have to learn to take people the way they are, because otherwise you'll just get angry with them and make yourself miserable in the bargain. I mean, you're not going to change them, and the sooner you stop thinking that you can, the happier everybody concerned is going to be.

I have to say that my odd plane-ride encounter with H.R. Junior stuck with me like a burr in an old woolen sock, and I was genuinely desperate for somebody to share it with. But of course the only reasonable candidate was Ben Abernathy—I felt I could trust him—and so it all came spewing out over two fat cheeseburgers and a couple cold Stroh's in The Steel Shed on the Friday afternoon after we got back. We were both still pretty shot after the Le Mans trip, and Ben surprised me by showing up in the doorway of my tragically empty little cubicle in Dick Flick's 6th floor ad-copy department at a few minutes after three. You couldn't miss how his eyelids were sagging like the jowls of a prize bloodhound. "Want to cop a sneak?" he rasped.

"I'm supposed to be writing a press release."

"You doing any good?"

I looked at the blank sheet of Fairway Motors letterhead wrapped around the rollers of the big new Remington electric in front of me. "Not so's you'd notice."

"Then screw it."

I looked at him. "Don't you have a pile of urgent stuff on your desk upstairs?"

Ben did his best to roll his eyes, but they wouldn't open far enough. "Nah..." he gave me a little flicker of a grin, *"...there's nothing so urgent today that won't be urgenter tomorrow..."*

"That's Walt Kelly, isn't it?"

"Pogo Possum," Ben nodded approvingly. And then came the wink. "Mabel said she'd cover for me."

"That was nice of her."

"Nah, she just wanted me out of there. She said I was so tired I was screwing things up and I'd just have to un-screw them up on Monday."

Mabel Wozniak was Ben's sweet, harried, long-suffering and somewhat matronly spinster secretary up on the Executive Corridor. She'd been with him a long time—on three different floors of Fairway Tower before they finally made the Executive Corridor together—and she always reminded me of the well-intentioned Classic Literature teacher you might have had back in 7th grade. You know: trying her best to gin up a little enthusiasm for Homer's *Iliad* or one of the Shakespeare histories when none of the kids were paying attention.

"How did she cover for you?"

"If anybody asks—which they won't—she'll tell them I'm down in production or on my way over to the depot to give the transportation guys hell." He tried another wink. "Besides, nobody on The Corridor gives a shit."

"They don't?"

"Nah." He worked up half a shrug. "You couldn't tell it from the piles of shit on my desk, but I only got one job up there."

"Oh? What's that?"

"To make sure it all stops there and that none of the shit disasters on my desk make it any further down the corridor." He nodded towards the elevators. "C'mon, Ernest Hemingway, let's go get a beer."

"But what if Dick Flick comes by?"

"Hell," Ben laughed, "he's been gone since before lunch. Probably shacked up at some motel with his secretary." And with that he turned towards the elevators and started walking, and you can bet I was right behind him.

We got to The Steel Shed well before the shift-ending rush, and so we were pretty much alone in the place except for a couple truck drivers from the transport depot who'd snuck out early. They recognized Ben of course and spent the next few minutes looking the other way or pretending to be fascinated by the yellowed sports-section front pages featuring rare Detroit sports-team triumphs thumb-tacked to the wall. But then Ben sent them over a couple beers to let them know that we were playing hooky, too, and that everything was OK. I went up to the jukebox and played a couple quarter's-worth of Patsy Cline and Porter Wagoner and that ironic, slightly funny and yet pretty much forlorn Billy Walker hit, *Charlie's Shoes*.

When I got back to the bar, I sat down, took a long pull off my Stroh's and let it all come out about my odd and uncomfortably friendly chat with a very drunk Little Harry Dick Fairway on the plane ride back from France.

"Watch out for that," Ben advised as he lit up another Marlboro. "He does that with people from time to time. Lets it all come out. Unburdens his soul. Exercises his demons."

"Don't you mean exorcises?"

"I said what I meant."

"But why me? I'm just a nobody. I mean, he doesn't even know me."

"That's the whole point. He's not about to open himself up to anybody who matters." Ben shot me a headsman's blade of a smile. "Face it, Hank, he picked you *because* you're a nobody. Because you're..." he hunted for the right word, "...you're *expendable.*"

I felt the ends of my mouth bending down.

"But I wouldn't worry," Ben assured me. "He won't remember any of it." He took a bite out of his cheeseburger and chewed as he thought it over. "Or he'll pretend not to, even if he does." Ben looked me in the eye. "The last thing that sonofabitch wants or needs is friends."

I was relieved to hear that. But then, almost without thinking, I felt an involuntary flutter of guilt. "That's kinda sad, though, isn't it? I mean, underneath it all, he's just a lonely, isolated guy with lonely, isolated-guy problems."

"You don't have to go wasting any sympathy on a full-time prick like Little Harry Dick Fairway," Ben pretty much snorted. "There are good people in this world and there are jerks, fuckups, assholes and absolute pricks, and it doesn't take much thought to figure out which category he belongs in."

"I dunno," I told him as I remembered the resigned, even betrayed look in H.R. Junior's half-closed eyes when he talked about his daughter on the plane. "I'd like to think we all have human sides and redeeming qualities."

"I'd like to think my wife looks like Rita Hayworth," Ben grinned around a big bite of cheeseburger, "but that don't make it so."

We had a pretty good laugh off of that.

Chapter 10: Trapped in the Tower

To be honest, my situation at Fairway Motors seemed pretty damn amorphous after Le Mans was over, and I didn't have much of a clue as to what Bob Wright might have planned for me next. You could say I was in pretty much a holding pattern, waiting for my next assignment. Plus I got bored looking through the nonexistent windows of my cubbyhole of an office on the 6th floor and fussing over the crappy little snippets of ad copy and press-release pabulum that one of the third-string dickheads in Dick Flick's ad department kept giving me to write and re-write just so the second-string dickhead above him could blue-pencil the shit out of them and send them back to me for revision two or three times before finally throwing them away. I think they were just trying to get me used to the manic, deadline-driven urgency (which, by the way, came with a lot of attendant monotony, redundancy, ambiguity and anonymity) of life in Fairway Tower. Observing the copy writers in the office cubicles around me, the whole point seemed to be to look terribly busy—totally swamped was even better— even if you were only trying to fill the time before lunch or afternoon coffee break. During which my co-workers mostly talked about their kids and their dogs and their grass seed and their yard fencing and the Supreme Court's shameful and inexplicable school-prayer decision that was going to destroy the fabric and moral fiber (or was it the fiber and moral fabric?) of our nation and all the hot weekend sales coming up on plywood or plush carpeting and how the Tigers were doing—they were in the middle of a rousing 7-game losing streak—and the inevitable *"Hey, did'ja see what happened to Hoss on Bonanza las' night?"* There were even a couple bright-eyed/eager-beaver types who made a big point of bringing their lunch (or afternoon coffee) back to their cubicles so they could push even more exciting new model features, bold new styling concepts, intriguing interior convenience accessories, key sell copy, important bullet points and attendant vowels and consonants around a page during their lunch and break time. Which was brown-nosing of the worst kind as far as I was concerned and made you want to pull cruel, sophomoric pranks on them. Not that I had anything to do with the salt in the coffee-room sugar shaker or the little dead mouse—complete with trap—from one of the factory break rooms that somehow wound up in somebody's paper lunch sack.

Honest.

But the point is I didn't fit in. Not at all. Plus everybody and his brother knew that it was the people further up the advertising department food chain who actually wrote (or at least tweaked) the copy that actually got used in print ads or in radio and TV commercials. Meanwhile, I was stuck down with the rest of the steerage-class plebes in what amounted to Basic Training. Which, like virtually all Basic Training programs everywhere, was essentially there to break your spirit and get you properly in line. Or that was my take on it, anyway.

The only fun part at all was when they let me sit in on a brainstorming session for the Fairway Freeway Frigate "Great Artists Series" Toulouse-Lautrec Special Edition that Amanda Cassandra Fairway had her heart set on. And it was a tough one since Lautrec did mostly faces and figures from the Moulin Rouge and the circus rather than landscapes, still lifes and patterns, and that's hard subject matter to translate into upholstery and trim. We kept winding up with stuff that looked like it belonged on a merry-go-round or a calliope or something. And nobody seized on the genius of my brilliant idea to drop the driver's-side seat cushion five or six inches so even normally-sized drivers could barely peer over the dashboard...

Philistines.

As the days slowly ground by, I found myself lingering over my coffee in the break room and reading the damn Detroit News from cover sheet to cover sheet every day out of sheer, listless boredom. I'd even go hide in the can to do it, even though the only stories that interested me at all were the ones about the growing and worrying number of so-called "U.S. military advisors" in Viet Nam, the problematic SNCC voter-registration drives down south, what was playing at the movies and the sad announcement in the Arts section that revered American novelist William Faulkner had died. Personally, I'd never had much luck slogging through his books—or even some of his paragraphs—although one of my community-college English teachers insisted repeatedly that *The Sound and the Fury* was a genuine masterpiece. And maybe it was. But it was also an awful damn lot of work to read. Or maybe I'm just lazy by nature and more in tune with the straightforward "who-what-where-why-when" approach of plain old news reporting. Which is maybe why I got on so much better with Ernest

Hemingway's novels. God only knows it was easier reading. But if I said anything, my English teacher would bristle up like a threatened porcupine and quote what his man Faulkner had to say about my man Ernest: *"Hemingway has never used a word that would send a reader to the dictionary."* It always galled me that it wasn't until long after I'd left the class (and the school) that I heard about Hemingway's response: *"Poor Faulkner. Does he really think that big emotions come from big words?"*

In line with that, I was sure there were countless long-winded, exquisitely punctuated and excellently embellished eulogies, tributes and memorials to William Faulkner all over the arts pages of every major newspaper and even more of the same in all the literary publications. He obviously spoke to a lot of people. Not people I would necessarily get along with or care to plumb the depths of, but good people nonetheless. Or at least most of them. And I have to admit that it made me sad that he was gone, since in my own small way I knew what it was to stare at a blank sheet of paper wrapped around a typewriter roller and then try to bring the damn thing to life. So I wished his spirit a solemn Godspeed and moved on to the sports section, which was almost all baseball and even less interesting.

No question I was suffering from a severe case of motorsports withdrawal, and I was maybe getting a little panicky that I might have fallen through the cracks at Fairway Tower (and it was big enough that there were plenty of cracks to fall through). I finally got up the nerve to sneak a memo upstairs to Karen Sabelle asking if I could maybe have a few moments of Bob Wright's terrifically valuable time. Much to my surprise, my desk phone rang less than an hour later, and she told me to come up at precisely 1:48pm that afternoon. Not 1:45, mind you, and surely not 1:50. But Bob would be more than happy to see me at 1:48pm.

You can bet your ass I was there on time!

Karen was away from her desk, and I could hear her inside Bob's office. They were going over a four-inch-thick stack of folders—each one with a different problem, question, decision, disaster or opportunity inside—but Bob caught me out of the corner of his eye and immediately waved me in. "Karen said you wanted to see me?"

"Uh, yeah…" I started in. But I could see he was giving me that terribly-busy-and-preoccupied-but-trying-very-hard-to-appear-patient Upper-Executive hairy eyeball. So I just got right down to it: "Well, I was just kind of wondering what's up next for me? I mean, now that Le Mans is over—at least for this year, anyway—and I…"

"That was really a nice job you did, by the way," he said through two-thirds of a hurried smile. "You and, umm…"

"Audrey," I told him. "Audrey Denbeigh."

"Yes, that's it. Really nice job, both of you."

"I'm so glad you were pleased with it. I'm sure Audrey is, too. We…"

"Oh, there were a few things that could have been tweaked or tightened up a bit—there always are—but, overall, well done. Even Karen thought so."

"That's high praise indeed."

He gave me the final one-third of the smile. "Yes, it is," he nodded. "You bet it is." And then the smile vanished just as quickly as it had appeared. "But you have to understand how things work at a company the size of Fairway Motors. Sure, I want to know each and every one of my department heads personally. My special liaisons, too. Like yourself. And I want them to feel free to contact me if they have any kind of problem or concern that can't be addressed through our normal chain of command…"

"I appreciate that," I told him. But I was already getting a sense of where this was going.

"I know you do. I know you do. But the key thing here is proper chain of command. Responsibilities. Delegation of duties. You get that, don't you?"

"Of course I do."

"Sure you do," he nodded like he wasn't really convinced. "I know you do. And that's why we wanted you in the first place. Because you're savvy. Because you're smart. Because you've got the sort of knowledge and contacts we need to accomplish our goals here…" the smile returned, only bigger and broader, like it always got when Bob Wright was trying to sell you something "…and most of all because you're a real *communicator!*"

He made it sound like the best damn thing a human being could ever hope to be. Unless you were maybe Albert Schweitzer or Mother Theresa or that Salk guy who came up with the polio vaccine. So I told him "Thanks." And then I repeated, almost like it was an afterthought: "I was just kind of wondering what you had in mind next for me?"

That's when the other foot dropped. Only so deftly that I hardly felt any pain at all. "Danny'll be taking that up with you when we get our plans settled. We've already had some discussions about it. Trust me, Hank, your situation is evolving."

And that was apparently going to be my answer, because Bob immediately returned his attention to the stack of folders in front of him. I could see from the label that the top one was something about a new casting-and-forging plant Fairway was opening in Cologne, Germany. It was under construction but slightly behind schedule and needed to open early next year.

The message was clear: Bob Wright was an incredibly busy man with an awful lot of things to review, plans to map out and decisions to make, and the door to his office was only open when he invited you in to tell you something, ask you something or pick your brain. And he was damn near surgical when it came to that particular process. Outside of that, you needed to go through normal channels and report to your immediate superior.

Which, in my case, meant Danny Beagle.

And I must admit I understood the sense of it. I mean, Fairway Motors' upcoming cannonball-plunge into the world of motorsports would surely have a massive impact, but it was but one tiny (if highly visible) facet of Fairway's overall corporate universe. I mean, what the hell did I know about the construction details of some new casting and forging operation in Cologne? Without ever having to say it in so many words, Bob Wright had made me feel like an insignificant and perhaps even impertinent little speck of lint on the underside of his socks. And meanwhile, Karen Sabelle was busily going over a column of figures and I might as well have been standing on the dark side of the moon. So I quietly excused myself and headed back down to the 6th floor to write some more dumb ad copy that no one in the greater automotive consumer world would ever see.

It wasn't an hour later that Danny Beagle's head popped into my doorway. "You got a minute?"

"Sure," I told him. "I'm no good at this shit anyway."

"Don't sell yourself short."

"I'm not. When I said 'shit,' I meant it."

That earned me a strained sort-of smile. Then Danny asked if I'd join him for a coffee in one of the little, most-likely-bugged conference cubicles on the 13th floor. The obvious implication was that whatever we were going to talk about wasn't for general consumption, and if anybody was going to listen in, it would be either H.R. Junior himself or one of Scully Mungo's security guys with top-tier clearance.

Once we got to the little conference room, Danny closed the door behind us and sat down across from me. "I hear you dropped in at Bob Wright's office."

"I didn't just 'drop in.' I asked Karen Sabelle for an appointment."

"And she gave you one?"

I nodded, and Danny looked impressed with my answer.

"And what exactly did you learn from that appointment?"

I pretended to think it over. "Not to ask for another one?"

"You're a slow learner, but eventually you get it, don't you?"

"Look, I didn't mean to step out of line, it's just…"

Danny cut me off: "But you *did!*" And then a look of sneaky curiosity blossomed on his face. "So tell me…did he cut you off at the knees?"

"Bob?"

Danny nodded.

"Yeah. More or less. But he did it so quick and clean I hardly felt it."

"That's Bob, all right." He nodded respectfully. "But it was bound to happen sooner or later."

"Oh?"

"Sure. You're a square peg in a round hole."

"Believe me, I know that."

"And like I told you on the bus: you're off the front burner now."

"I just wasn't expecting it, that's all. I mean, he's always seemed so friendly."

"Sure he is. Hell, he's famous for it. But don't go confusing 'friendly' with 'friendship'…They're two different things."

"I can see that now."

"Just remember: Bob's got a lot of plates spinning and a lot of balls in the air. What he does and how he does it is…well, it's pretty damn incredible if you think about it."

"I can see that, too."

"And he's damn good at what he does. Damn good." Danny shook his head. "Sometimes I don't know how the hell he does it."

"It is amazing all right."

"Sure it is. In fact, 'amazing' doesn't begin to cover it…"

I nodded.

"…but you gotta remember: Bob's not like normal people. He's *different*. He's got this, this *thing* inside of him, driving him all the time. He's like a damn shark. He's got to keep moving and seeking and hunting and devouring things or he dies."

I looked over at Danny. "You ever want to be like that?"

Danny thought it over. "I guess I thought I did. Way back when. But you come to see that some people have that vision and that spark and that organization and knack for leadership and that relentless drive to get ahead and, well…" he gave me a shrug, "…I guess the best thing for a guy like me is to find a guy like that and hitch my wagon to his star."

"So you ascend right along with him, right?"

"Or I flame out and fizzle to nothing with him…It can go either way."

"You don't look especially worried about it."

"Why should I be? Bob's on the upswing now. Our run is just starting. And if—or maybe I should make that 'when'—he goes too far or fucks something up or steps on Little Harry Dick Fairway's toes that once too often and gets his butt fired, other companies will come looking for him with checkbooks in hand. That's what happens once you get up there where the air is thin."

"And what happens to you?"

"If I've done my job right and said and done the right sort of things and stayed in the shadows like I'm supposed to, I'll go right along with him. So will Karen Sabelle."

"So he's loyal that way?"

"I'm the one who's loyal. Bob's just practical. He knows what he's got with me, and that's a better option than trying to break in somebody new that he doesn't know anything about."

"That makes sense."

Danny tilted his chair back until it was leaning against the wall. "So anyway, what did he tell you?"

"He said I ought to talk to you."

"He's right. You should."

"So you're more or less my handler?"

"Always have been. Right from Day One."

And that was certainly true. All the way back to our very first meeting in the empty press room at Daytona after that first-ever Daytona Continental World Manufacturers' Championship race back in February.

"So you have any idea what's up next for me?"

"If I were you, I wouldn't be so damn eager. Rest your ass cheeks on your laurels a little while they're still soft and cushy."

"My ass cheeks?"

"No, your laurels."

"That's probably good advice. But I'm antsy as hell. And curious, too. Bob said you'd already talked about what might be up next for me."

"We've talked, and there are a bunch of things Bob wants you to do for us. I know he's planning to send you on a tour of some of our retail dealerships with Manny Streets. You need to know about that stuff."

"I've been in a lot of car dealerships."

"This is different. Dealer relationships are way up there for any car company." He held up an important forefinger. "The first and by far the most important people any car company has to sell to are its own dealers. We've got to get them pumped-up and excited and *believing* in our new car lines every model year—that goes without saying— but we've got to sell them on our message, too. On the *campaign*. And you're likely going to wind up as first assistant spear-carrier for this 'Absolute Performance' thing."

"Me?"

"Who knows it better?"

He had me there. But it really didn't sound very appealing. "So I've got to go meet a bunch of car dealers?" I said like he'd asked me to muck out a latrine. I mean, I'd known a lot of car dealers and car salesmen in my time and, except for the rare ones who were also involved in racing, we didn't have much in common. And I said as much.

"Face it," Danny told me, "this job is not all about doing what you like."

"I'm beginning to understand that."

"Sure, you'll get to do the stuff you enjoy. You'll be a really important part of it now and then. But your job will also be about getting the word out. And, more importantly, getting the right word out to the right people. And at the top of that list will be our dealers. That's where it really has to start."

"But most of them don't give two shits about motorsports."

Danny gave me a toothpaste-ad grin: "My point exactly."

There wasn't much I could say.

"But don't worry. That won't be coming up for a while. Probably during new model-year introductions. We do introduction weekends for the dealer principals."

"But that's not until September, isn't it?"

He looked at me like I was genuinely stupid.

"The production lines are gearing down right now for model turnover. In fact, we're behind schedule already. But that's par for the course. And then we've got the dealer product introductions to set up. Manny and Dick Flick's people work together on those. You'll be in on some of it."

I tried to look excited.

"But we've still got some time in hand, so Bob was thinking about sending you out to Shelby's place in California again to see how things are progressing." Danny leaned in a little closer. "Bob worries sometimes that Shelby's a little bit of a hustler."

"A hustler?"

"You know…a snake-oil salesman."

"Most people really like him."

"Of course they like him. He's a natural-born charmer. And Bob figures he can do a lot of good things for us without much at all in the way of risk exposure. But he wants to keep a little bit of an eye on him, too. And you're the right guy to do it. You're an insider and he knows you from before. You wrote a lot of nice things about him."

"Hey, he was an easy guy to write nice things about. He's a big character with a great smile and a lot of personal magnetism. He can charm the birds out of the trees when he wants to. And he was one hell of a racing driver, too. There weren't many American drivers making their mark over in Europe back then."

"We still want to keep an eye on him. His business and personal life have been all over the map, and somebody told us he had more pairs of expensive Italian shoes than Dick Flick."

"Or Billie Sol Estes."

Danny smiled. "That's a lot of fancy shoes either way, and you can bet somebody's paying for them."

"You can't blame a guy for wanting to look nice."

"Hey, don't get me wrong. We *like* this guy. We're *working* with this guy. We've got *faith* in this guy. We're *spending money* with this guy. But we also want to peek over his shoulder a little bit, too..."

To be perfectly honest, I wasn't particularly thrilled about becoming essentially a company spy out at Shelby's place in Venice. But it did sound better than hanging around writing crappy ad copy on the 6th floor of Fairway Tower. Plus I really liked the prospect of getting back to the familiar sunshine, smog and hot-car culture of Southern California again. And the blessed freedom of being on my own again, of course. The bad part is that it was roughly 2,000 miles in exactly the wrong direction as far as spending more time with Audrey was concerned.

Only then came a very pleasant surprise:

"...And we've got some people working on setting up that business-magazine interview with Mr. Ferrari over in Italy..."

"You *do?*"

Danny looked at me like I didn't know how to salt an egg. "Of course we do. Bob wants to know more about Ferrari's organization. His business. His finances. His key people. His board of directors. That sort of thing."

I wanted to say *"Do you really think I'm the right kind of guy for that assignment?"* but I bit my tongue. I mean, traveling to Maranello to do an interview with Ferrari would very likely mean I'd need an interpreter. And I had just the person in mind. But Fairway's people in Italy probably had their own interpreters on tap, so I figured it might help my case if I could kind of bank-shot the trip through London.

"You know," I started in like I'd had a really, really good idea, "I should probably drop in on Eric Broadley's shop in Bromley to see how he's doing on that new Le Mans car."

"Eric Broadley?"

"That racecar constructor I talked to Bob about over in England. You know, Lola."

Danny gave me a blank look.

"The guy Bob air-freighted a couple of the new V8s to."

I could see a vague flicker of light in Danny's eyes. And then he looked at me kind of sideways. "You just want to see that Audrey Denbeigh again, don't you?"

"That's not it at all!" I huffed like you always do when you're caught red-handed.

But of course that was it, and we both knew it.

"She's an excellent interpreter..." I added defensively.

"Hey, I don't blame you," Danny pretty much snickered, "she's quite the little piece."

I didn't know exactly how to respond to that, but my initial reaction—which I instantly stifled—was to punch Danny Beagle square in the nose. No question my hormones and emotions were running well past the redline where Audrey was concerned. And I can't say I was 100% comfortable with that. I mean, it wasn't all skittles and beer being on my own as a bottom-of-the-food-chain, lone-wolf American race reporter over on the far side of the Atlantic, but at least everything was in its proper place and there was a certain order and security and familiarity to it. Thinking about somebody else all the time—or at least a lot of the time—and wondering where they are and what they're thinking (and particularly what they're thinking about *you*) can get a little confusing. And frustrating. And irritating. And unnerving.

But I kept all that to myself. I mean, it wasn't anybody else's business anyway.

Speaking of Audrey, I was genuinely missing the living shit out of the European racing scene, and all I could get in Detroit was an occasional, 2-line snippet in the back pages of the sports section when something really big happened. Like the surprising—even shocking—news that Californian Dan Gurney had scored his and Porsche's first-ever Grand Prix win at the French Grand Prix at Rouen on July 8th! Wow! I was a huge Dan Gurney fan and had been for years but, even though it was an enormous improvement on their tubby old 4-cylinder cars, Porsche's new flat-8 machine still looked a little crude, bulbous and clumsy compared to the sleek, slender and slippery new crop of British V8s from Lotus, Lola, BRM and Cooper. So I was absolutely dying to know the details, and called Audrey from my desk the second I set the newspaper down. She was over at that fancy house in Mayfair running herd on the children and couldn't really talk, but we did a little quick phone nuzzling and she told me to call her back later after she got home. So I tried calling Hal Crockett, but there was no answer. And I couldn't really bring myself to call that shit-weasel Eric Gibbon who'd been at the grand prix essentially doing my job. So I counted the minutes like a condemned man until 6:30pm London time, sneaked off to one of the empty small conference rooms for privacy and dialed long distance.

Just my luck, Walter answered.

"Is Audrey there?"

"Who wants to know?"

"You know who this is," I said as nicely as I could. "Can I speak to Audrey?"

"And what if I don't want you to?"

"I'd still like to speak to her."

I heard her in the background, and then there was some muffled stuff with his hand over the receiver and then I guess she pretty much took it away from him.

"Hank?"

I could still hear him cursing and grumbling behind her. He could be a nasty bastard when he put his mind to it. And that was most always whenever I called.

"Hank?"

"He really doesn't like me much, does he?"

She covered the phone with her hand again and there was silence for what seemed like a very long time. And when she came back on, it was dead quiet behind her.

"Is he still there?"

"I sent him off to the kitchen."

"You know, he's really going to have to get used to this."

"Let's not go into it now, Hank. There's no point. You're over there and I'm here and we can't really sort this out until you're back in England."

That was true enough.

"I miss you," I told her.

"I miss you, too."

A long silence. And then, all business: "You'd asked about the race."

Audrey had been there doing lap charts for the Bowmaker team and was more than happy to fill me in. "I suppose you'd have to call it a bit of a lucky win," she allowed right off the bat, "but you have to give credit where it's due: Dan and the Porsche were there to take advantage when the opportunity presented itself."

I pressed her for the details.

"Well, the Ferraris didn't show—something about a metalworker's strike in Italy—and everyone was complaining about all the rough patches and bad pavement on the circuit."

"The drivers didn't like it?"

"Oh, the top drivers loved it! Lots of broad, sweeping corners and very scenic. But everyone knew going in that it was going to be hard on the cars." Now I'd never seen a French Grand Prix at Rouen because the race had been held at Reims for the past four years, but all the press-room types spoke reverently about Fangio's masterful, come-from-behind win there for Maserati in 1957 over the combined might of the Ferrari factory team. But of course I was just a cub race reporter out in California back then, and only got to read about it. And there were a lot of politics involved, as both Reims and Rouen dearly wanted to run the French Grand Prix thanks to all the prestige involved (not to mention the crowds and the cash and the full-to-overflowing local hotels, restaurants and guest rooms), so a kind of uneasy agreement was worked out whereby Rouen-Les-Essarts would get the '62 grand prix and then it would revert back to Reims for 1963. After which it would supposedly alternate between the two circuits. But the gentlemen from Reims were still unhappy about having "their" race taken away, and insisted on running a non-championship F1 race at Reims the week before. Harrumph.

Now the track at Rouen was made up of ordinary French roads through beautiful, wooded countryside, and featured a steep, dramatic, high-speed downhill section of fluid, sweeping corners, a tight, dumb hairpin at the bottom and then a climb back up through more fast, daunting sweepers to complete the lap. It was four miles around and terrifically challenging, but there wasn't much in the way of runoff area and the pavement was in pretty rough condition—patched in many places—and would likely play hell with delicate formula-one suspensions and drivelines.

"After qualifying, it was Clark and the Lotus 25 on pole again with Graham Hill in the P57 BRM next to him and McLaren in the works Cooper on the outside. Brabham in his own Lotus 24 and John Surtees in our Lola had the second row, and Gurney's Porsche was in 6th on the inside of the third row."

It was obvious Dan had far from the quickest car. "So how did he pull off the win?"

"I suppose you could say he had help. Starting with the circuit itself."

I waited impatiently for the rest of it.

"John got an absolutely brilliant start in our Lola—he's an amazing driver, really—and Jimmy Clark lit up his tires and got it a bit sideways while Hill surged away in the BRM, and that's how Surtees knifed through to be right in their wheeltracks as they went out of sight. He managed to get past Jimmy somewhere out on the back part, and he was pushing Graham Hill's BRM hard for the lead by the end of the second lap…"

I could almost see it.

"…So far so good, as far as we were concerned! And it stayed that way for a bit with Hill under heavy pressure from our Lola, a few ticks back to Clark followed by McLaren in the Cooper and then a gap to Jack Brabham's privateer Lotus."

"Sounds exciting."

"Oh, it *was…*" she pretty much gushed. Only then you could feel the excitement drain right out of her: "…and then it all started to unravel."

"Oh?"

I could see her nod on the other end. "First it was McLaren with shifter problems. He went for fourth and there was nothing there and so he spun it off the road. Completely out of character for Bruce, but it was hardly his fault and he was fortunate not to collect anything."

"Lucky."

"Lucky indeed at a circuit like Rouen."

"So he was out?"

"No, he managed to get going again and brought it into the pits. The crew worked on it a bit and sent him off again, but he'd fallen well down the order. And while that was happening, Brabham brought his Lotus in with a fractured front suspension."

I muttered something pithy about "customer cars from Lotus."

Audrey sighed into the receiver. "And then, sadly, it was our turn. John brought the Lola in with our own shift-linkage problem. A bolt had worked itself loose. I suppose it was down to the rough surface. In any case, they were able to make a few wrench-passes at it and put it right. But by then he'd dropped all the way from second to eleventh…"

"That's a damn shame."

"Yes, it is." She paused for a moment. "You know, when people look back at the early races of this season, they're never going to realize how bloody well John drove or what a brilliant little car the Lola was." And that was certainly true. Surtees had kept the new Lola up at the sharp end since qualifying for the very first grand prix of the year at Zandvoort. But things kept going wrong and the results just simply hadn't followed. And remember: this was Eric Broadley's first-ever F1 car and only the fourth design in the company's entire résumé. That was pretty damn impressive. Not to mention that Bowmaker was essentially a privateer effort and didn't have quite the resources or connections of the other top teams.

But I wanted to hear the rest about Gurney and the Porsche.

"Well, the race settled down a bit after that. Graham Hill had established a solid margin of something like 15 seconds over Clark, and looked set to more or less cruise the rest of the way home. Only then he got collected while lapping a backmarker in a privateer Cooper. Rotten luck, really. Graham was already past when the Cooper driver shunted him up the backside. Claimed he'd run out of brakes. And maybe he did. But it was rotten just the same."

I rolled my eyes, but she couldn't see it.

"Hill got going again, but by that time Clark had passed into the lead. Only then Clark came in with something gone wrong in his left-front suspension and he was out of it."

"Lotus strikes again."

"…and then it was Hill again with a big lead on Gurney and the rest mostly walking wounded…Surtees had our Lola back up to fourth by that point, if you can believe it."

"So what happened to give Dan the win?"

"With the race all but won, Graham Hill's BRM came by sputtering again. And then it quit altogether half way 'round with something gone wrong in the fuel injection."

"Geez, that's too bad."

"Yes, it was. For Graham. But it moved our Lola up to 3rd place!"

"Hey, for every loser there's a winner."

"Indeed. But the race was far from over. Graham managed to fix the injection linkage enough to limp back to the pits and retire, and by that time Surtees had clawed our Lola all the way to second—albeit a distant second—behind Gurney's Porsche. Only then the gearbox started playing up again and sticking in gear. It was all he could do to limp the rest of the way home with even the backmarkers passing him."

"That must've really hurt."

"It was worse than you can imagine. And then it got even worse than that. John was just struggling along and pulled to the side as soon as he crossed the line because he didn't think the car would make it around another lap. By then the gendarmes had swarmed onto the circuit—ostensibly to hold the crowd back—even though cars were still coming 'round at speed. The blockage gave poor Maurice Trintignant no place to go in Rob Walker's Lotus, and as he swerved to avoid John and the crowd and the gendarmes, he collected Trevor Taylor's works Lotus—at something well over 120—after they'd both passed under the flag."

"Jesus, was anybody hurt?"

"No, but it was just damn lucky they weren't. Stupid, really. And that's after both cars had been in and out of the pits with problems and were just trying to make the end. The cars were both pretty badly mangled, but at least the drivers came out of it all right."

I shook my head at the stupidity of it. And then, slowly, it dawned on me all over again how fantastic it was—regardless of luck or circumstances—that tall, lanky, all-American hometown boy Dan Gurney and the Porsche factory over in Stuttgart had both scored their first-ever Grand Prix victories! That was huge news indeed. Although it was apparently no big surprise to one of the major participants:

"Dan had a bad cold during qualifying," Audrey added because she knew I was a fan, "but I overheard him tell one of the British television interviewers that he thought he and the Porsche might be looking pretty good by the end of the race."

Dan was very savvy about those kinds of things. He was one hell of a driver—right up there with Moss and Clark as far as I was concerned—but he was also a thinker. Plus that was the thing about Porsche. They didn't always have the best car or the prettiest car or the fastest car or the cleverest car or the most elegant car—although they were never very far off—but the damn things were intelligently designed, carefully made, incredibly well screwed-together and would usually keep droning on and pounding out the miles long after all the brilliant stuff from other factories had either come undone or shaken themselves to pieces. The harder the course and the longer the race, the better off you were wheeling a Porsche.

Chapter 11: A Night Visitor

Although I was feeling pretty much marooned in Fairway Tower, I was finding some solace in calling Audrey on the company's international lines—I knew the pass code from when we worked on Le Mans together—and spending a lot of time not really saying much of anything and wishing I were there with her so I could put an arm around her shoulders or muss her hair a little or maybe even massage her shoulders or scratch her back or rub her feet. She liked that, as I'd discovered when we'd spent that night together in that Dodge motor home at Le Mans, and I'd even been thinking about ways I could do it better. Sure, it was exciting when we did the other thing, but it was also nice to know you could make somebody else feel good. Especially somebody you really, really cared about.

Like I said, we spent a lot of time just hanging on the phone together, thinking about stuff like that—or at least I was, anyway—and not saying much of anything.

And then I'd go back to my desk and write some more bullshit ad copy that nobody cared about and wait for my marching orders to come through. About the only other worthwhile thing I had going was spending time at The Steel Shed and the Black Mamba Lounge, listening to a little music and chewing the fat with Ben Abernathy. I'd really come to like and respect that old warhorse, and there was a lot to learn from the way he'd managed to rise through the ranks and moreover survive in Fairway Tower. Sure, he walked on eggs around H.R. Junior like everybody else on the executive corridor. But he also knew that he was near retirement, didn't have any upward ambitions anymore and worked his ass off every day taking care of all the haywire transportation logistics, four-alarm plant problems and myriad manufacturing minutiae that nobody else on the executive corridor wanted to fuck with. And he knew how to keep his nose buried in whatever kind of shit disasters were dumped across his desk or exploding out of his phone lines at any given moment and quietly lurk around in the shadows the rest of the time—particularly at Bob Wright's weekly Management Team meetings—so he didn't have to waste his time and self-respect toadying up to anybody. Not even Little Harry Dick Fairway himself! Not that he ever confronted the pompous little prick over anything. But he'd turned avoiding him into a damn art form. Like when HR Junior would swivel his eyes around and ask some stupid, hair-trigger/cocked-pistol/impossible-to-answer question at one of their Management Team meetings, everybody would avoid his eyes and maybe even cower a little—particularly Daryl Starling—but Ben Abernathy would meet his eyes and make it look like he was ready—like the star student everybody hates in high-school chemistry class—with a long, boring, detailed, accurate, well-thought-out and experience-based answer. And that somehow made Little Harry Dick Fairway's eyes move along to some other, more worried-looking face around that long maple table. He probably thought he was fucking Ben up worse by *not* letting him talk, you know? And that's just the way Ben wanted it.

More than that, Ben had taken a genuine shine to me. Probably because we were both kind of grunt-level car guys at heart, even though we hobnobbed around with a lot of upper-echelon management types. And I knew he really liked my insider racing insights and enjoyed the hell out of our trip to Le Mans. Even if it damn near killed him. Plus we both liked music and people who weren't quite so impressed with themselves as the folks on the executive corridor, so he and I spent a lot of nights going out to The Steel Shed or, more likely, the Black Mamba Lounge to listen to a little music—some of it even live—and shoot the blue-collar, plant-floor shit with all the white or black union workers who gathered there. The week after the French Grand Prix, most of it was grousing about the upcoming layoffs for model-year changeover, the usual pissing and moaning about the Detroit Tigers, nasty gossip about the asshole shift bosses and Scully Mungo's undercover spies, the good and the bad (opinions always varied) about the new records on the jukebox and even occasional mentions by the few souls who read a newspaper in the john every day when they were really supposed to be on the job about the French essentially being thrown out of Algeria on their asses and the giddy, exultant, patriotic, partisan and highly enthusiastic local street celebrations that followed and occasionally included the bloody beatings and outright murder of as many as half-a-hundred left-behind Europeans. On a somewhat happier note was the launching of the new Telstar telecommunications satellite, which was the first-ever private space-launching and made big headlines in all the papers on what was otherwise a pretty slow news day. According to the guy at the end of the bar, American networks would now be able to bounce their television signals off of that Telstar satellite and have them come back down on the other side of the Atlantic—like a bank shot on the pool table in back, the way he explained it—so the folks over there could see live TV from right here in the states. And visa-versa. According to what he read in the paper, the Telstar would make a complete orbit around the earth every two-and-a-half hours—that seemed pretty damn incredible to me—but that you could only bounce TV signals off of it (and across the ocean) during the first 20 minutes of each orbit. That made it sound pretty damn useless as far as most of the folks in The Steel Shed could figure, but it was pretty damn amazing all the same. Meanwhile, on a more frightening and ironic note, both America and Soviet Russia were busy testing powerful and terrifying new hydrogen bombs—including a big one of ours out in the Pacific that lit up the skies over New Zealand and scared the hell out of everybody—while cautious, skeptical, in-no-big-hurry-at-all negotiators from both sides fussed, fought and fumed over the details of a much-publicized test-ban treaty. And that brought a solemn hush down over the bar attendees at The Steel Shed while each one mulled over what it might be like to have New York (or Chicago, or Detroit) suddenly and summarily get vaporized by the blast of an ICBM's warhead. Including sobering inner visions of what it would look like when you, your family and everybody on your block got deep-fried in a flash of molten-hot atomic radiation. Or at least what it would look like until the goop inside your eyeballs boiled up like hot lava and they exploded from the inside out.

It was something to think and worry about, all right…

And then a couple heartbeats would pass and somebody with a grudge or suspicion and maybe a few too many drinks under their belt would speculate out loud about just who might be an undercover shift spy for Scully Mungo. And then somebody else would bring up the line worker who got in trouble for punching out one of the time-study guys from the shift-management team (although rumor had it he'd been getting entirely too chummy with the guy's wife) and then somebody else would start grousing out loud about the crappy relief pitching on the Tiger bench and the conversation would be back to normal again.

I liked going to The Steel Shed with Ben. But I think I liked the Black Mamba Lounge even better. I didn't feel as comfortable there—hey, Ben and I were usually the only white folks in the place—but we were more or less tolerated and it felt a lot more interesting and exotic and exciting than The Steel Shed. And I really loved the blues music. I even ran into Otis Jenkins and Zenobia Smith a few times. Otis was always friendly enough in a wary, guarded sort of way, but Zenobia flat-out didn't like me. She had one of those gnarly, in-your-face black attitudes about white people—and especially white people who came into an all-black place like the Black Mamba Lounge and moreover tried to come off like they were trying to be your friend—and it was every bit as ugly and unreasonable as the prejudice against black people that ran wall-to-wall and floor-to-ceiling through The Steel Shed on the other side of the Fairway plant complex. And all that was getting worse—or at least running a lot closer to the surface—thanks to the newspapers and TV and radio stations devoting so much coverage to Stokely Carmichael and Martin Luther King Junior and all the sit-ins and Freedom Riders down south.

Otis Jenkins didn't care too much about all that. He just wanted to get along, have a little fun, play good football at Michigan State and be able to make a genuine career out of being a pro halfback one day. Even if he had to play for the Lions. But he was on edge around me because he didn't really trust me. Or white people in general, I think. Not to mention that he was worried I'd say something stupid or let something slip about meeting him for the first time in Amanda Cassandra Fairway's signature-edition, Androuet du Cerceau garden maze the night of Amelia Camellia Fairway's seventeenth birthday. But he needn't have worried. I knew how to keep my mouth shut. Even after I'd had a couple. Or even a couple more.

I also ran into Willie Shorter, the sly, cool drug pusher with the cream-colored sport coat and matching Panama hat, and sometimes I'd even make a purchase. Usually it was a couple lids for Amelia Camellia Fairway and her rich-punk friends waiting in the bamboo-cream Pontiac Grand Prix outside. I don't know how the hell she found out where I was staying, but I'll never forget the night there was a soft knock on my door at the Fairview Inn. Ben and I had been out at The Steel Shed that night listening to a little country and western and having a few too many cold bottles of Stroh's, and so I was probably a little groggy. More than probably, in fact. At first, I thought it might be somebody at a door across the hall or something, because the only person who ever knocked on my door was the cleaning lady at something like 10:30 in the morning. And if I was around to hear it, you can bet your ass I'd been out late at The Steel Shed or the Black Mamba Lounge the night before and, unless it was a Saturday or Sunday, I was in big trouble on the 6th floor of The Tower.

Only this particular knock didn't sound like the cleaning lady. It was daintier. And then it rapped again, only more urgently this time. I looked over at the eerie, illuminated green numbers on my alarm clock. Jesus Christ, it was two-fifteen in the fucking morning! On a fucking Wednesday! And then the knuckles rapped again. Really loud this time. So I got up and shuffled over to the door and leaned my forehead against it for support. I didn't turn on the light.

"You sure you got the right room?" I mumbled into the door. "This is Henry Lyons room."

"It's me," a familiar female voice whispered on the other side. I knew that voice. And it sent cold fear sizzling right through me.

"Jesus Christ!" I just about shouted. "That's you, isn't it?"

"Of course it's me," Amelia Camellia Fairway answered back like it should have been obvious. "Now open the door and let me in."

No question this was all sorts of bad. "I d-don't think I should do that," I told her through the door.

"Oh, don't be an asshole," she chided. And there was a little bit of a challenge in it, too. "Now open the door and let me in."

"Listen," I told her through the door, "this could get me into real serious trouble…"

"It'll get you into even more trouble if I start yelling out here."

"Why in hell would you do that?"

"Because you wouldn't let me in."

How could this be happening to me?

"…But of course, I'll tell people I'd already been inside, and that you just threw me out in the hall when you were done with me." She was fucking with me. I knew that. It was nothing but a big game to her. And I could tell she was really enjoying it. No question she had a cruel, sadistic, mean and manipulative streak inside of her…just like her fucking father.

"Do you want to get me fired?"

"If I were you," she went on ominously while letting her voice creep up a few decibels, "I think I'd open this door."

I didn't know what the hell to do. So I put the chain lock on and opened the door a crack. I could see her out there in the shadows of the hallway night lights with her hair all tousled up on top and hanging all stringy over her eyes and with her rumpled denim work shirt opened about five buttons with nothing on underneath.

This was trouble with a capital T.

"Look," I told her as firmly as I could manage, "I'm not going to let you in. You can scream your fucking head off if you want to. And it'll probably get me fired. Or maybe even worse. But I'm not letting you in, Amelia, and that's all there is to it." I stared at her shadowy form out there in the hallway. And I must admit, rumpled and disheveled or not, she was pretty damn special to look at, and I couldn't help feeling a few dark, dangerous urges stirring around in me like dumb, hungry carnivores waking up from a nap. But I stifled them. Amelia Camellia Fairway didn't give a shit about anyone or anything. She was all lizards, snakes and scorpions on the inside, and I knew it.

"How the hell did you find me, anyway?"

She tilted her face up into the half-light so I could see its features and she favored me with a contemptuous little sneer. "It didn't take fucking Sherlock Holmes, that's for sure. Daddy's company always puts their short-term people over here at the Fairview."

I didn't like the way she said "short-term" much at all. But I had more important things to deal with. "Look, why don't you just go home like a good girl?"

"I'm not a good girl," she said like she was proud of it. "And I'm bored shitless. There's nobody around and nothing to do and no place interesting to go. And you should be flattered. I had to steal my mom's car to get over here."

"Oh, great," I moaned into the chain lock.

"And there's something else…"

"Oh?"

"Yeah. I don't have any weed left. So c'mon, why don'cha let me in and we'll smoke some reefer?"

"That would be about the dumbest thing I ever did," I told her as sternly as I could muster. "And why the hell are you interested in me anyway? I mean, I'm way too old for you, and I'm not rich or exciting or good looking…"

"You can say that again," she pretty much sneered.

"Geez, you don't have to agree with me."

"Hey, I saw a shot and I had to take it."

God help me, we both laughed. In spite of everything, I caught myself starting to warm up to her. And that was a perilous feeling indeed.

"Look," I started in again, trying to sound as serious and adult and reasonable as possible, "you've had black star athletes and scraggly-beard folk singers and poets and philosophers and even fix-the-world political organizers. And God only knows who the hell else. What could you possibly see in me?"

"You're different. I mean, I've never had a real writer before. Not really. I'm pretty sure the guy who called himself a poet was just trying to get laid."

"I'm just a motorsports writer," I argued. "It's not like I've written any novels or anything…" I looked down at the hallway carpet and noticed for the first time that she was barefoot. "…And I'm not even that any more. I just work for your father's company these days."

"That's the other thing," she went on as she slowly twirled a few strands of hair around the ends of her fingertips. "I've never balled anybody who worked for my father before," she said like it was something you could get a damn merit badge for. "I'm thinking it could be kind of fun." She looked up at me with all that smooth, teenaged skin and soft, pouty lips and those big, phony-innocent eyes. "You're a fun guy, aren't you?"

You couldn't miss that her pupils were the size of buffalo nickels.

"I'm more like a dead duck here," I told her. "You're every kind of trouble I could possibly imagine."

"But I'm *legal*," she insisted. "I'm seventeen…"

"That's not the point," I insisted. "And I'm pretty sure the law in this state is eighteen."

"No, it isn't," she argued right back. "I looked it up."

"You looked it up?"

"Well, I had my brother look it up."

"Oh, that's just *great*," I pretty much groaned. And then I took in a long, deep breath, straightened my spine up a notch or two and tried my very best to sound like a fully-formed adult. "Look, Amelia, I have to admit that I'm really, really flattered that you think you're attracted to me…"

"I'm not attracted. I just want to smoke some reefer and ball you…That's all."

"Well, that's not going to happen. Not even if you scream and stomp and get the cops up here…" I let out a long, slow exhale. "…And now I'm really, really tired, so I'm going to just close this door and lock it and go back to bed. You can yell or scream or do whatever the hell you want to and it won't make any difference. If you get me in trouble, you get me in trouble and there's not one damn thing I can do about it."

Her seventeen-year-old lips curled down into an injured pout. "That's all right," she said in a voice that fairly dripped with sadness, loneliness and betrayal. "I didn't really come here to get laid anyway."

"You didn't?"

"Nah. I already got laid tonight."

I couldn't believe how matter-of-fact she was about it.

"Then what the hell did you come here for?"

"Just to give you some shit…" she looked up at me with those beautifully wicked, mischievous, unpredictable eyes, "…I told you I was bored."

I tried to give her a scowl, but I'm afraid there was a little bit of a smile hidden somewhere inside of it. "Look, you've had your fun now, so why don't you scoot on home."

"Well, there *was* something else…"

"What?"

"You got any reefer?"

"Jesus!" I rasped at her. *"Keep your fucking voice down!"*

"But do you have any?"

"No!"

"You sure?"

I pretended to think it over. But of course it was all bullshit since I knew for a fact I still had that two-thirds of a joint of Willie Shorter's excellent weed hidden away inside that eviscerated Fairway Motors ballpoint pen clipped in the inside pocket of my Fairway-blue blazer hanging in the closet. Where I figured nobody would ever, *ever* think of looking for it, you know? And particularly the cleaning lady, who I was pretty sure went through my drawers and toiletries and such every day out of simple, professional curiosity.

"Would you look for me?" she went on in a little-girl, singsong voice.

At that point, I felt as much as saw the sweep of headlights across the backside of the draperies. A car was coming into the Fairview Inn parking lot. Probably somebody coming home late from a party or something. But it could also be the police out looking for her. Or some of Scully Mungo's guys who were tailing her. And her mother's fucking car was parked right outside! All sorts of terrifying scenarios involving handcuffs and jail cells started playing out in my head. So I spun around like I was on ice skates, reached into the closet, rummaged around for that ballpoint pen in the inside pocket of my blazer, unscrewed it, weaseled out the remains of the joint and passed it to her under the chain lock with anxious, trembling fingers.

"You wanna smoke it with me?"

There was the muffled sound of a car door closing outside.

"Look," I told her with genuine desperation in my voice, "you gotta get the hell outta here *now!*"

"Sure," she shrugged like she was in no fucking hurry at all. "More for me…"

I heard muffled voices in the stairwell downstairs.

"…Besides, I don't want to get you in trouble, Hank. Not really…"

"Thanks," I snapped impatiently. "That's good to know."

"…only there is one other thing."

"What's that?"

"We need you to score some more pot for us."

She stuck a fistful of rumpled tens and twenties through the crack in the door.

There were footsteps on the stairway now.

"Look," I damn near begged her, "I can't be doing this, okay? I just can't possibly be doing this."

"Sure you can."

"I could get in *so much* trouble…"

"You'll get in trouble for sure if you don't."

"Are you threatening me?"

"I'm just trying to persuade you, that's all. I want us to be friends, see…"

"Jesus, that's not how friends treat each other! Friends look out for each other! They do things for each other!"

"And that's why you're gonna do this for *me!*" she giggled as she dropped the money on the floor. We could both hear the footsteps coming to the top of the stairs. And I watched there, helplessly, as Amelia Camellia Fairway gave me one last, nasty, triumphant teenaged smile and sauntered off towards the opposite end of the hallway.

"Just make sure you don't come back here again!" I hissed at the tails of her un-tucked denim work shirt.

Needless to say, my strange, middle-of-the-night/through the chain-lock encounter with Amelia Camellia Fairway at the Fairview Inn stayed with me like a brain tumor. In fact, I couldn't shake it, and I caught her creeping through the darkest, least civilized recesses of my mind like the spreading black oil slick you inevitably see underneath a blown motor. It's not like I *wanted* to think about her—Jesus, she was poison, pure and simple, and I knew it—but I couldn't seem to stop it. Or the way it got me terrified and yet intrigued in equal measure. She was trouble in spades and I knew it, but there was something exciting and even arousing about the whole thing in a sick, twisted, dark-alley, forbidden-fruit kind of way. And the danger and risk of getting caught made it suicidally enticing. Don't ask me why the average male of the species thinks or feels or reacts that way, but I can assure you, with all applicable lack of good sense or dignity, that they occasionally do. And it's not like it's just us humans, either. I mean, look at the poor praying mantis: the female gives the male a big, enticing wink and maybe shows him a little thorax cleavage, the male gets all properly hot and bothered like nature intended, he proceeds to give the female praying mantis the good, workmanlike servicing she's looking for and then, for dessert, instead of lighting up a couple French cigarettes, she eats his head. Which would strike almost anybody as an odd way of saying "thank you." But the point is that I couldn't get that spoiled, rotten, nasty, not-to-be-trusted, pretty, pouty, smooth-skinned and morally bankrupt little teenaged sorceress out of my head. And naturally that would make me feel instantly guilty and horrible and ashamed because of Audrey—even though I hadn't actually done anything—and I'd be afraid that she could hear it in my voice when I talked to her on our regular long-distance phone calls. I'd usually try to catch her in the morning when she was getting herself and her father ready to go out for the day, and sometimes she'd be in a rush and it would be all strained and hurried and awkward—particularly when her father was in the room glaring at her—but every now and then I'd catch her late in the afternoon London time at that mansion in Mayfair when her little monsters were at least pretending to take their naps, and we'd spend a lot of time talking about missing each other and our night in the motor home at Le Mans and how that compared to my embarrassing little flat over the commercial bakery and how things were going with her father and at the Lola shops and, more than anything, when we might see each other again. And other times, we'd just hang there on the phone and not have to say anything at all. That was almost the best part, just kind of "being there" together.

To be honest, I was running up one hell of a long-distance phone bill for somebody. But I tried to be careful when I called her from The Tower because I was pretty sure Scully Mungo or Clifton Toole's people probably went over the phone records as a matter of course and might wonder why I spent so many hours of the company's time and phone money calling some numbers in England that nobody could really recognize. So now and then I'd sneak up to those little executive conference rooms on the thirteenth floor or across to the employee break room at The Tower end of the final assembly line with a sack of quarters that I kept hidden away in my desk and call from the pay phone there. On my own nickel, you know? Sure, it was kind of noisy, since the Fairway Freeway/Freeway Frigate assembly line was running full-tilt just outside the break-room doorway and so there was clanking and shouting and the hiss of steam and the sputter of air guns and the clatter of the line itself as the cars rolled slowly along towards the roll-off point where they hopefully fired up without a hitch and drove off to one of the random-inspection stations or to one of the holding-pen lots outside. Yeah, it was noisy, but if I went there during normal shift hours, I didn't have to worry at all about being disturbed…

Or that's what I thought, anyway, until one of Scully Mungo's security guys came to see me one day at my desk in the ad department. He was a pale, short, bulky-looking guy with a pudding-fat gut, big shoulders, a twenty-inch neck under a Marine crew cut, a knowing sneer and a highly accusatory look in his eye.

"We had a hell of a time tracking you down, Lyons," he said like I knew exactly what he was talking about. Which of course I didn't. But no question he intimidated the hell out of me and put me instantly on the defensive.

"Tracking me down? Why would you have to track me down?"

Visions of Amelia Camellia Fairway passing me money and making thoroughly indecent suggestions through the chain-locked door of my room at the Fairview Inn flashed though my head like the coming-attraction trailer for a monster movie.

The guy stared at me like we both knew I'd been getting away with something for quite some time. "You're not on the regular company payroll. There's no blue file on you in the security department."

"Blue file?" It didn't occur to me until much later that there might be some sort of bank-shot, reverse-English connection with the mysterious blue folder Little Harry Dick Fairway carried around with him. But for the moment, I was just too damn scared, worried, blind-sided and confused to think much about it. All I knew is that it sounded like I was in some kind of extremely serious trouble. And of course the next thing that flashed through my mind was that he was some kind of federal narcotics detective and that I was about to get busted for supplying illegal drugs to a bunch of underage punks from wealthy, well-connected families. Including, in fact, the daughter of the guy whose family name was on the front of the damn building. And a lot of other buildings in the Detroit area, too. I remembered that pasty-faced punk in the bamboo-cream Pontiac whining about how selling marijuana—he called it "pushing"—was a mandatory, statutory, no-way-out/do not pass "go"/do not collect two-hundred-dollars 30 years-to-life in the state of Michigan. And that got me visualizing myself in solemn prison gray like Jimmy Cagney in *"White Heat"* (or would it be those black-and-white-striped pajama things like in those old Charlie Chaplin/Mack Sennet comedy shorts?) with a hopeless look on my face and a big, mean, scarred and sullen three-time armed-robbery, rape and murder loser named Roosevelt for a cellmate. Who, by the way, thought I looked genuinely adorable in prison fatigues.

There goes that imagination thing again.

And what the hell was I going to tell Audrey? I felt my stomach do a slow Dutch roll. "W-what's this all about?" I more or less stammered.

He looked me right in the eyes. "You're the one who's been sneaking over to make phone calls in the break room, aren't you?"

I felt a confused rush of relief as it dawned on me that he wasn't a federal, state or local narcotics detective. And that made sense because he never said he was or flashed a badge, and that's the first thing they always do in the movies or on TV. But then who the hell was he? The only possible answer was that he was one of Scully Mungo's in-house security people. And that got me wondering how he knew I'd been over in the employee break room during shift making calls on the pay phone?

"Long-distance phone calls," he went on with kind of a smirk. "Long ones. Lots of them, too. To three different phone numbers in and around the city of London, England."

Now how the fuck did he know *that?* I was still plenty worried, but starting to get a little pissed off as well. "Look," I told him. "I haven't been sneaking around any-where…" my mind was racing, but at least it was staying ahead of my mouth, "…I have a good friend over there—a *very* good friend—and we've done a lot of work for the company together. Why, I need to talk to her all the time. On company business. You can ask Danny Beagle."

"But then why do you have to sneak over to the break room to call?"

"Because her father's sick and there's nobody else to look after him and so I like to call her now and then to see how she's doing…" I was really pleased at the way it was all coming together, "…but, since it's not company business, I figured I'd better call from a pay phone. And there's never anybody around that phone during shift, so I figured we'd have some privacy."

"Why d'ya need so much privacy? You talk dirty to her sometimes?" He gave me the hairy eyeball. "Sometimes you're on there for half-an-hour," he said like that was a felony all by itself. "Once you were on for damn near an hour."

How the fuck did he know that?

"Like I said," I went on as evenly as I could, "she's a very good friend. More than a friend, in fact."

"Oh?"

"Yeah," I told him. "We may even get married some day." I had no idea where that came from, but there it was.

"But why over to the break room?" he asked like I was trying to hide something.

"Like I said: because I didn't think it would be right to do it here from my desk on the company's nickel. Those long-distance calls are expensive."

He mulled that over for a moment. And meanwhile, I was trying to figure out where the cameras and listening devices might be hidden in the employee break room. And where else might they be, too?

But he wasn't about to give up. "Aren't you supposed to be working for the company right here at your desk when you're over in the break room on company time playing long-distance kissy-face to London?"

That pissed me off. *"Look,"* I just about snarled at him, *"if you've got something you're not happy about with about my work, why don't you take it up with Danny Beagle? Or Ben Abernathy? Or Karen Sabelle? Or why don't you just take it all the way up to Bob Wright's office at the end of the executive corridor?"*

I'm sure when the guy walked into my cubicle, he thought I was just another 6th floor office drone who was working some slimy little side deal on company time or sneaking company styling, new-product or advertising secrets out to Leyland or BMC or The Rootes Group over in England. Not that any of that bunch posed much of a threat to Fairway Motors anyway. And now that I'd rolled out some heavy-duty, thirteenth-floor executive-corridor names, all of a sudden *he* was the one on the defensive.

"Hey, I'm just doing my job is all," he said defensively. "My department's here to provide security and that's what we do. When something doesn't look right or smell right, I'm supposed to look into it. That's what my department does every day of the week."

"So you spy on the employee break room?"

"We don't spy on anyone!" he insisted. But you couldn't miss that his voice had gone up a half-octave or so. "Nobody in our department spies on anyone. Not ever. And anybody who says different is a liar."

Now it was my turn to glare at him. "There's no other way you could know that much about those phone calls."

He was starting to turn a little red. "We don't spy on anyone," he repeated nervously. "And anybody who says different can't prove a thing."

I looked him up and down. He was your classic tin-badge security cop: pudgy fingers, low forehead, neck like a tree stump, beady, darting eyes…

"What's your name?" I growled at him as menacingly as I could.

"My *what?*"

"Your name!" I demanded. *"What the hell is your fucking name?"*

"T-t-that's none of your damn business!" he more or less stammered as he backed his way out of my cubicle. And maybe it wasn't. But he sure took off like a shot once he got his ass out in the hallway.

Chapter 12: An Ocean Away

I'll never forget opening my July 14th copy of *Competition Press,* which was waiting on the carpet by the doorway of my room at the Fairview when I got home from The Tower the following evening. The little, bold-type "late news" box in the upper right-hand corner trumpeted a few quick, breathless lines about Dan Gurney's and Porsche's breakthrough grand prix win at Rouen—that was old news already as far as I was concerned—and the banner headline and lead story were all about the triumphant Ferrari steamroller act at Le Mans that had taken place damn near a month ago. And of course I was there when it happened, so I didn't really need *Competition Press* to fill me in on all the details. Although I always enjoyed reading Henry Manney's stuff no matter what he was going on about.

And then, down in the lower left-hand corner of page one, there was an item in a small, oddly shaped box with a heavy black outline around it. The headline said simply:

PETER RYAN DIES OF INJURIES

It froze me up solid inside before I even read it. The dateline was Paris, July 2nd—over two weeks ago!—and it seemed impossible that this could have happened to the talented, fast, bright, thoughtful, modest and self-effacing young Canadian driver that I'd been standing around the pits talking and joking with just a few weeks ago at Le Mans. I was stunned! First because it had happened at all, and second because I hadn't heard anything about it! That's how far away it all was now and how far out of the damn loop I'd fallen! Sure, it was a thoughtless and selfish sort of thing to feel, but it was there all the same. And it simmered there for a moment while I recognized and felt ashamed about it. And then my thoughts went back to Peter Ryan.

He had a big, friendly smile and was earnest, honest, cheerful and straightforward in that uncomplicated, almost throwback Canadian way, and I'd really only come to know him when he wound up co-driving with Cal Carrington. But I'd heard about him—everybody had—and most insiders thought that, although he was very, very young, he was a terrific talent and had a genuine shot at becoming one of those "special" drivers. Sure, he had an occasional over-supply of boyish self-confidence, would always listen politely to advice from car-owners and team-managers but wouldn't necessarily heed it and there was always a bit of an edge to it on my end because Cal was my friend, and it's endemic in the world of motorsports that your keenest rival in any racing situation is inevitably your own teammate. He's the first guy you'll be compared to and measured against, and that means he's the first guy you have to beat. Always. But he's also the person you have to work with and make allowances for and compromises with if you want to get any kind of a decent result...especially in a long endurance race. So you smile and shake hands—most usually in front of the crew—and then, over to the side and away from everybody, you promise each other earnestly that you're not going to beat the crap out of the car in an effort to make yourself look faster. And, by extension, make the other guy look slow. And sometimes you actually mean it and sometimes you don't. You have to understand that every young racing driver is eager and ambitious and dangerously competitive, and even the quiet, introspective ones are bubbling over inside with self-belief.

It's hard to keep that kind of chemistry under control.

But Cal and Peter had done a pretty good job of it in spite of Peter being perceived as a hot young prospect on the rise—he had just turned 22 two weeks before Le Mans—while Cal was somewhat unfairly seen as toppling over the apogee of his career following his dismissal from Ferrari at the Targa Florio. So they both had a lot to prove and a lot at stake. But they got along well and they were both able to, if not actually park their egos, at least keep them idling at the curb outside. And the end result was that they actually did take care of the cars and turned disciplined and damn near identical lap times in similar conditions. Although there always seemed to be unfortunate car assignments or mechanical problems or simple bad luck that kept them from scoring the good result they really deserved together.

That's just the way things go sometimes in motor racing. It's not a fair sport.

I had to read the story a couple of times before it all sank in—it was only a hundred or so words all told—and I was amazed at how much there was I didn't know about Peter. Like Cal, Peter came from some old, old family money—his great-great grandfather was some kind of major-league copper and mining tycoon—so he was able to pay in front or slip a little something under-the-table when necessary to secure a good ride. I already knew that part. I'd always thought he was Canadian, but the news story said he was originally from Philadelphia. Or at least that's where he was born. But his father

Joe Ryan (who was described in various places as "an adventurer," "an entrepreneur" or "an eccentric millionaire" depending on who was doing the describing), was also an avid skier who loved the unspoiled Canadian wilderness of the Laurentian Mountains in Quebec. When he and friend, famous broadcaster and fellow ski enthusiast Lowell Thomas skied and trekked their way to the top of Mt. Tremblant back in 1937—all 2871 feet of it!—he thought it was the most spectacular place he'd ever seen. But it was extremely hard to get to, and Joe Ryan decided on the spot that he was going to fix things so a lot more keen skiers could enjoy the area. And he had the resources to do it, too. Or at least he thought he did at the time.

What followed was a real soap opera of negotiations to buy Mt. Tremblant outright from the Province of Quebec so he could develop it as a ski area. But the Province wasn't particularly interested in selling. Following a series of blind alleys, dead ends, tilts with provincial government officials and administrations, possible backroom pay-offs and lots of political intrigue—he enlisted the help of a famously well-connected New York stockbroker to grease the deal along—Joe Ryan prevailed, and the deal was signed by the outgoing Premier of Quebec literally on his way out the door after losing a vote of confidence. He was able to purchase essentially the entire mountain—less the very peak, which remained a provincial park—with the proviso that he spend well over half-a-million 1939 dollars developing the property into a first-class ski area. And get it all finished in an impossibly short two-year timeframe!

But, either due to genius, ambition, dumb innocence or pure, cussed stubbornness, Joe Ryan got it done. Or most of it, anyway. And the result became one of the premier ski-resort areas in all of North America—or the world, for that matter—and his son Peter literally grew up on skis there. And the kid had a natural talent for it, too. Sadly, his father was killed in a mysterious (or possibly even suspicious?) fall from the window of his 22nd-story room at The Warwick Hotel in New York in September of 1950—the more refined newspapers called it "an accident," while the tabloids trumpeted "possible suicide"—when Peter was only ten. But his mother took over running the ski resort on Mount Tremblant and Peter kept right on skiing.

He proved something of a prodigy as a downhill racer, and although he attended quietly top-tier private institutions in the states for his schooling—including the exclusive Hotchkiss prep school in Lakeville, Connecticut—Peter devoted most of his time, energy and passion to skiing. And he was damned good at it. He won a National Ski Association junior downhill event at Mount Rose, Nevada, in 1957, skiing as a Canadian. A furor quickly broke out over whether a Canadian could win a U.S. Championship and as to whether he was really a Canadian or an American. Although the real issue was which country's Olympic team he would ski for at the 1960 Winter Olympics in Squaw Valley, California. Peter quietly professed his preference for his longtime friends on the Canadian team, but he also didn't want to give up his American citizenship. But it all became moot when he suffered a serious skiing accident in 1959—it broke both of his legs—and he switched his attention and interest to sports car racing, which arguably required a lot of the same skills and talents. And he was damn good at that, too.

The old Canadian vs. American thing reared its head again in the motorsports world, but this time the choice was simple. In America, Peter couldn't start racing until he was 21, but he could start at 18 in Canada. Case closed. He initially started out in a well-used but worthy Porsche Spyder and quickly began attracting attention in local Canadian races. In May of 1960, then 19-year-old Peter Ryan finished a close second to Roger Penske's somewhat newer RSK at the O'Keefe Sundown Grand Prix at Harewood Acres in Ontario. Come October, he and Penske teamed up as co-drivers for an endurance race at the same track, and they won again. Somewhat ironically, Peter was invited to drive the clever but brutish Comstock Racing Sadler/Chevrolet in a race at the new Meadowdale racetrack outside of Chicago the following July, and found himself squared off once more against Roger Penske.

Now the Sadler/Chev was a homegrown Canadian special featuring a chuffing great Chevrolet V8 stuffed in the back of a mid-engined, somewhat Lotus 19-like chassis. Only stouter, as you might expect of anything Canadian. It was a good car and well-conceived and executed but, like everybody else at the time, car-builder Bill Sadler couldn't find a suitable transaxle to handle the brute torque of a big American V8. So he built his own. It was a simple, clever and ingenious solution, and basically amounted to making a rugged 2-speed transaxle out of Halibrand quick-change rear end. Sadler figured that the massive torque of the Chevy wouldn't require more than two gears to take on the mostly 2.5-liter DOHC 4-banger racing engines from Europe. And he just about had it right.

Peter and the grumbling, stubby-looking Sadler/Chev two-speed wound up sharing the front row with Roger Penske's bright-red and typically immaculate "Telar Special" Maserati Birdcage, and both cars and drivers proved very evenly matched. A corner-worker friend of mine named Dale Strimple was at that race—stationed on Doane's Corner, which was the second-to-last corner on the track—and he said it was as close and exciting an automobile race as he had ever seen. And Dale had seen a lot, since he'd been pretty much a lifer corner worker with Lake Erie Communications and knew—as they all did—that the long, early-morning till late evening hours of numbing, ho-hum boredom in searing sun, stifling heat, bitter cold, biting wind or pouring rain (or all of those last three mixed together) were now and then rewarded with the best close-up view imaginable of some really great motor races. Not to mention occasional explosive moments of excitement, anxiety, great responsibility and—sometimes—sheer, stark terror. Corner workers (and particularly run-in-packs bunched like the Lake Erie Communications crew) are like a mixture of a strange, white-clad cult, a seasoned combat unit and a wonderful, have-fun/hard-partying social club. They all have terminal cases of the motorsports bug, but generally can't scratch that itch on the driving side (usually due to plain old economics) yet want to be a lot more involved than just standing along the stupid spectator fences. It's hard work and long hours in whatever sort of weather old Mother Nature feels like dishing out, and all they usually get out of it is a couple kegs of beer and some pretty decent food (and even when it's not that decent, there's always plenty of it) come the end of the day. But they get to be on the inside—part of the show!—and get a participant's view of what's going on that not even the winning drivers or car owners get to see. Then throw in the lasting friendships, great corps camaraderie and the feeling that they're doing something vital, necessary, important and worthwhile for the sport they all love. I mean, let's face it, you couldn't run a damn motor race without them. They're the drivers' eyes where they can't see and ears where they can't hear, and every once in a great while they're called to action by dangerous, difficult, demanding, occasionally life-threatening emergency situations where what they do and how quickly and correctly they react is going to make all the difference. And that can make you feel pretty damn special indeed.

In any case, my corner-worker friend Dale had seen it all from Sebring to Laguna Seca, and when he told me that the race at Meadowdale between Roger Penske's Telar Birdcage and Peter Ryan's Sadler-Chev was something special, I knew I wanted to hear the rest: "Why, they were nose-to-tail the whole blessed way!" he told me excitedly. "But you really need to understand a little about the track first. They call the last turn The Monza Wall, because it's a fast, steeply-banked sweeper like that famous Monza banking over in Italy. It's the signature feature of the track and they've got it front-and-center on all the press releases but, to be honest, it reminds you of one end of a stock-car oval. Only rougher. See, when they were paving it, they smoothed the asphalt down by running a roller down and up from the top rail. So there's a seam every three feet or so and it's kind of uneven. It was supposed to come out smooth, but it didn't. And then it got even worse over the winters when everything shifted and settled a little. Some of the drivers say you can't even focus going through there because the car is shaking and pounding and juddering so bad. But it's very fast, and there's a pretty long straight leading up to it and a *really* long straight afterwards, so that's all kind of a power section. Then there's a bunch of downhill-uphill twisty stuff that all the good drivers really like (but where it's pretty damn hard to get around), and then there's a long back straight leading to Doane's Corner, which is where I was stationed. Now Doane's is a sort of flat, three-quarter carousel right-hander with a kind-of dogleg left leading into it, and it's a fairly good spot to try and get by under braking. Only once you're into the corner, it's single file and that's all there is to it."

I was getting a pretty good mental picture of it. "So what happened with Penske and Peter Ryan?"

"Oh, they were side-by-side on the front row and kind of eyeballing each other all the way around on the pace lap. But Ryan really anticipated and got his nose in front when the green waved—I couldn't see it from where I was, but the starter told me he damn near jumped the start—and the Chevy engine in the Sadler had enough grunt to keep him there as they headed into the first corner. And once Ryan got there, he did a hell of a job playing cork-in-the-bottle to Roger's Maserati. You could see the Sadler was stronger on sheer power but that the Maserati was maybe better balanced and braked and handled a little better. But Peter Ryan had that figured out pretty well and did his best to kill the Maserati's momentum coming out of the corners. He'd brake as late as he dared, turn in and then ease back out of it in the middle of the key corners to make Roger back out of it, too—he damn near plowed right into Peter a couple times!—and then he'd set himself up to take the best line and get on the power as early as possible coming onto the long straightaways, where the big Chevy's torque would allow him to pull away enough so Roger couldn't try to dive-bomb him into the next corner. And there the Maserati would be: all over the Sadler again and scratching and pawing for a way by, but with Peter leaving him no real opportunity to get around!"

"Sounds like one hell of a show."

"Oh, it *was!* Lap after lap after lap."

"So what finally happened?"

"Oh, it came right down to the end—the very last lap, I think—and Roger finally gave Peter a little nudge…"

"A *nudge?*"

I could almost see Dale nodding at the other end of the line. "Oh, it wasn't much of a nudge," he allowed, "and it might not have even been intentional."

"Might not?"

The line went quiet for a moment while he thought it over. And then: "I think *'might not have even been intentional'* is probably the fairest way to put it."

Like any motorsports writer, I knew that you sometimes needed to be vague in order to stay accurate. Not to mention keep your friends. "So what happened?"

"Oh, the Maserati gave the Sadler a little love tap in the right-rear about two-thirds of the way around Doane's Corner—like I said, it's just a big, flat carousel—and that was all it took. The Sadler got all loose in back and spun around, and by the time Peter got it gathered back up again, Roger was long gone."

"Was he pissed off afterwards?"

"A little, I guess. But he knew Roger and Roger knew him and, like I said, it was one hell of a great race…"

But although he was young, boyish and enthusiastic on the outside, Peter's ambition went well past stateside club races and all the way up to Formula One. So he bought himself a Lotus 20 formula junior (which most people thought was the best car to have at the time) and furthered his reputation the first weekend in August by winning the Vanderbilt Cup formula junior race at Bridgehampton over an extremely tough field. Including Walt Hansgen in Briggs Cunningham's Cooper. Then he backed that up by winning the so-called "Canadian Grand Prix for Sports Cars" at Mosport in Comstock Racing's Lotus 19. Several established continental stars were on hand that day (including Stirling Moss and Olivier Gendebien in U.D.T.-Laystall Lotus 19s and Pedro and Ricardo Rodriguez in a pair of Carlo Sebastian's quasi-factory Ferraris) and Peter almost apologized for winning afterwards, acknowledging that pole-sitter Stirling Moss most assuredly would have beaten him if Moss hadn't run into gearbox problems. That was pretty damn decent of Peter—not to mention honest and modest—but that's just the kind of driver and young man he was. Then he did the 1961 United States Grand Prix at Watkins Glen in a somewhat outdated "semi-works" Lotus (although the car was entered and run by a privateer team), and Peter finished a creditable 9th overall. After which Lotus signed him to one of Colin Chapman's famous contracts—you can bet some money changed hands…in Chapman's direction!—only when he got to England, Peter discovered he'd been essentially subcontracted to Ian Walker's formula junior team. Which wasn't really such a bad place to start for a young man who didn't know his way around any of the English or European circuits yet. Peter was also somewhat dumbfounded to learn that he had to build up his own racecar from, as he called it, "a bushel basket of parts." But he got on with it—without complaint—and also filled his time doing the early-season long-distance races with Cal. Followed by their problematic run together at Le Mans. But Peter's real goal, like any aspiring young driver, was to race in Formula One. And formula junior in England and Europe had emerged as the natural stepping stone. But it was tough going, competing against a whole crop of eager, steely, even desperate young drivers who were also out to prove themselves and moreover knew the circuits. The competition at the front was at a keen, even dangerous, level. "I'm here to find out how good I am and how much I have to learn," he told one of my scribe friends at his first formula junior race in England. "The times are very, very close and the drivers are really, really good."

He struggled to make it into the bottom of the top 10 that day. But he was confident there was more and better to come. And that, in a nutshell, is how Peter Ryan came to get himself killed in a dumb, who-cares formula junior curtain-raiser for the non-championship F1 race at Reims the week before the French Grand Prix. He'd been dicing hard with a guy named Bill Moss (no relation) driving an advanced, aerodynamically slick Gemini junior, and the two of them somehow touched wheels in the last, fast Crucifix corner leading onto the pit straightaway at Reims. It was apparently a terrible, horrific accident that sent Peter's fragile Lotus somersaulting into the barriers. But while Bill Moss was released from the hospital after being treated for relatively minor bumps and bruises, Peter was in a deep coma with multiple fractures and grave internal injuries. His mother flew immediately to Paris and drove to the hospital at Reims to be with him, only to find that he'd been air-lifted to another, better-equipped hospital in Paris. But there wasn't much of anything they could do for him, and she made it to his bedside essentially in time to see him die the next day.

It was pretty brutal stuff.

I sat on the bed in my room for a long time after that, thinking about the things you always think about—or try not to think about—when those kinds of things happen in racing. Fortunately, the human brain has a way of numbing itself when it wants to or needs to, and so I mostly just sat there like I was trying to remember something that wouldn't quite come back to me. Then I went down to the bar and had a couple drinks, but the place was empty except for a pair of loudmouth-drunk salesmen who were trying hard to get their line of bullshit properly lubricated so they could sell a million-gazillion dash-clock bezels or window-crank gears or brake-lining rivets or whatever to one of the pinched-in little purchasing dickheads on the third floor of The Tower.

"So this guy over at Caterpillar wants me to sell him 20,000 at the 100,000 price. And then he wants me to pick up the fucking freight on it, too!"

"Unbelievable!"

"Yeah, that's what I said!"

"That's why there's an art to selling. Any asshole can give stuff away."

"Amen."

"You ever try to sell them over at Caterpillar?"

"Which plant?"

"Corporate. Over in Peoria. You ever been there?"

"Yeah, I been there."

"What a shit town."

"I'll say."

It went on and on like that.

I really wanted to drink some more, but I just had to get out of there. Then I had a notion about going over to The Steel Shed or the Black Mamba Lounge to listen to some music, but I really didn't want to be around a lot of noise and people. So I went back to my room, took a long, hot shower, turned on some dumb TV show and just as quickly turned it off again and then tried to thumb my way through the rest of *Competition Press* without looking at the first page again. Roger Penske had notched up yet another SCCA National win at Lime Rock Park (two days after his son was born, according to the story) and lapped the entire field in the process. And that of course made me think about Peter Ryan again. Especially since Lime Rock sits literally right down the road from the exclusive Hotchkiss School Peter attended in Lakeville.

I flipped through to page 3 to get away from that and stumbled on a story about an entertaining (if poorly attended) USAC stock-car race on the Mosport road course up in Canada. And that also made me think about Peter, since he'd scored his first big win at that track just last year. I shook my head to try and get rid of it and went back to the story. Ray Nichels Engineering Pontiacs had finished first and second in the hands of Paul Goldsmith and Roger Ward, while tough-as-nails T.J. Huston got himself shoved into a wall (or maybe he was the guy doing the shoving?) and apparently wound up in a fistfight over it back in the paddock. The story didn't exactly say that in so many words, but you could get the gist of it if you read between the lines. I also saw that my favorite stock-car/road-racing hero Freddie Fritter wound up a fairly dismal fifth overall. But he was the highest finishing Fairway Freeway in the field, and it led me to mull over how much work needed to be done and how much ground would have to be made up before Fairway Freeways would be able to run with—let alone beat—the well-established and well-funded Pontiac teams. Sadly, only a handful of people showed up to watch that race at Mosport, but the story said that the regular fans were genuinely amazed by how fast those big American taxicabs went around the racetrack and how good the front-running drivers were.

Back on page 2, right at the top, was a picture of an absolutely gorgeous, Bertone-bodied, Corvette-engined GT coupe from Italy called an Iso Rivolta (a name that made you wonder if anybody at the factory spoke English?) and, across from it and half-a-column down, a photo spread and description of a new, Lotus 23-style racecar from the Huffaker Engineering shop out in California. They called it a "Genie" and it looked pretty slick, but the second paragraph revealed that the pictured prototype had been pretty comprehensively crunched during its debut race outing at Laguna Seca. According to the story, it had been "going like the clappers" before its driver got "forced off course." But that was pretty standard if you were writing about a car, a shop or a driver you knew personally. You had to pump up the car that got wrecked so they could maybe sell a few copies and make sure you let the driver off the hook as well. At least if you wanted to stay friendly with everybody and be welcome back in the shop. I didn't really know the guys at Huffaker Engineering too well because they were from San Francisco and, as virtually any California enthusiast will tell you, that's almost a different state (not to mention a different state of mind) as far as the Los Angeles-based racer types are concerned.

And then I came on Denise McCluggage's slender column right in the middle of the page. It was ostensibly about her drive in an Austin Mini Cooper in the eight-hour Little Le Mans small-sedan Enduro at Lime Rock Park. Only her car blew a crank seal after just 35 minutes, and she was out of it. And then I got to the bottom half of her column:

"Roger Penske had been there for practice, but he received a call from Canada and flew to Montreal to serve as a pallbearer in young Peter Ryan's funeral.

"Every man's death diminishes me, it is written, but I think some more than others. Those of us who follow racing closely have lost many friends to this strange sport. Yet we are affected differently by each. Peter Ryan's death is one that I cannot think about. I cannot believe it. It is difficult to accept that that much spirit, that much big blonde burst of youth can be killed by a race car.

"My way is the coward's way. I avoid the thought. Then months later I will allow it to come into my mind and then I will think: 'but that happened long ago, long ago.'

"But now my sympathies are keen for those who must live with this shattering reality every day. Every hour.

"And yet we race. And yet we live."

I was in a deep, sullen funk for the next several days after reading the news about Peter Ryan. It was one of those things that just gnaws at you and won't leave you alone. It's not like we were great friends or anything, but I'd gotten to know him a little when he was co-driving with Cal, and he was so young and eager and well-mannered and friendly and guileless and full of enthusiasm and energy and life that you couldn't help liking him. And his combination of natural talent and good-natured confidence made him seem, I don't know...invulnerable. But of course that's not the way it works in motor racing. Just as in wartime, people get hurt. People get killed. And then you just have to get on with it. But it's a lot easier when you're there in the thick of it—when there's always another race that needs to be prepared for and gotten to and battled out on the track and then written about afterwards for the folks back home. But of course I didn't have any of that any more, and so the dark, gloomy cloud just kind of hung over me and peed down rain for four straight days.

"You're in a hell of a lousy mood," Ben Abernathy observed over coffee one morning.

"Yes I am," I snarled back like it was none of his damn business.

He eyeballed me while he took a slow sip of coffee and a drag off his latest Marlboro. "You wanna go hear some music Friday night?"

I shook my head like it was a stupid damn question. "I don't want to go anywhere," I told him. "I don't want to do anything."

Ben started to say something more, but stopped himself. He was a good kind of friend that way. A lot of folks would turn it around with one of those dumb, hurt-looking *"Sorry, I was just trying to help"* things, but not Ben Abernathy. He'd let you have the space you needed to be a jerk when that's what you needed to be.

I called Audrey of course, but Walter was there and we just kind of waltzed around the edges of really talking about anything. Yes, she'd heard about what happened to Peter Ryan and, yes, it was a terrible shame. But she kept her distance from it, and I couldn't help thinking about that young racing driver she got involved with back when she wasn't much more than a kid—Neal Clifton, that was his name—who was her first real romance and who crashed and burned to death at Dundrod when she'd snuck off to the races with him back in September of 1955. So I could understand. Besides, she had the British Grand Prix with the Bowmaker Lola bunch coming up that weekend—it was up in the north at Aintree again instead of Silverstone—and Walter was coming along since it was relatively close by. I could tell that she was on edge about that. I could hear it in her voice. But there wasn't much of anything I could say because I was feeling adrift inside and terribly far away.

"It'll work out fine," I told her without much in the way of conviction.

"Of course it will," she agreed with even less.

"I miss you," I told her, but even those words sounded hollow.

I tried calling Cal, too, but couldn't locate him. He'd been staying at the Hotel Real Fini in Modena when he was driving for Ferrari, and he'd been known to drop in on a rather notorious flat outside of London where several young, up-and-coming drivers bunked in between races. But I couldn't find him there, either. And I wasn't really sure what I would have said to him anyway.

Work was terrible, too. I couldn't even write stupid shit copy for a damn press release. It just wouldn't come out. And I was so damn bored and angry and antsy and heartsick and empty inside that I wanted to sneak down to the ugly concrete workers' john in the forge building, with all those monstrous steam hammers pounding molten-orange steel into parts right outside the door and just scream my fucking head off until I ran out of breath.

And then Danny Beagle appeared at my doorway.

"We've got it all set," he told me through a Cheshire Cat smile.

"Got what set?"

"The interview."

"What interview?"

"The interview with Enzo Ferrari. For *Business Week*. It's all set."

It took a few heartbeats for it all to register.

His grin got broader: "And you're going to really owe me on this one."

"Oh? How so?"

"You're going to owe me because I've got it set up where you fly into London next week to check up on that thing over at Lola…"

That was pretty good news.

"…and Karen's agreed that you can use Audrey as your interpreter. She's already cleared the schedule with her…"

That was even better news.

"…We'll be supplying you a courtesy car, and you can drive down from London together…"

That was the best news of all.

His smile faded. "…But separate rooms when you're traveling on company business, understand?"

Hey, I didn't give a shit if Fairway Motors felt like paying for an empty hotel room or two along the way. That was their business and, as far as I was concerned, they were more than welcome to it.

Chapter 13: Back in Old Blighty

I called Audrey right away, of course, and it didn't take long for us to hatch a master plan whereby I'd fly to London on Sunday, July 29th, visit Fairway's English HQ in Dangleton to pick up our car and meet a few people and then drop in on Lola on Monday—Audrey had to be with the Monsters of Mayfair until evening that day—and then we'd leave for Italy at the crack of dawn on Tuesday. We'd stay someplace along the way, arrive in Maranello sometime late Wednesday morning, have our afternoon interview with Mr. Ferrari, stay overnight at the Real Fini (Karen Sabelle had arranged two rooms for us there, but it wasn't terribly difficult because damn near everybody in Italy is away on vacation during the first two weeks of August), and then we'd head off on another long slog north to take us back up through Switzerland and Germany to the Nurburgring for the German Grand Prix that weekend. Audrey had to be there in time for first practice, since she'd be timing and scoring for the Bowmaker team again, while I'd be essentially wandering around feeling excited, thrilled to be there and utterly useless.

The mad scramble to get my good shoes perfectly shined and all my best clothes cleaned and pressed and neatly packed away for the flight to London—including stopping off at a news stand to grab a fistful of stiff-looking business magazines so I could study up on how they wrote and what they focused on and what kind of language they used during my plane trip over—gave me the first genuine sense of purpose I'd had since Le Mans. I can't tell you how good and even therapeutic it felt to be rushed and busy and actually *anticipating* something again! Then I caught another lucky break when the desk clerk at the Fairview flagged me down and handed me my latest, special-delivery copy of *Comp Press* literally as I was heading out the door for my drive to the airport. Obviously those business magazines were going to have to wait until somewhere over the middle of the Atlantic.

Of course, I already knew about Dan Gurney's breakthrough win for Porsche at the French Grand Prix, but I read Henry N. Manney's race report on it anyway. He was always an entertaining read and usually good for a laugh or two as well. Or at the very least a snicker. And then, back on page 6, I was thrilled to learn that Dan had backed up that attrition-aided "survival" win at Rouen with a solid, no-excuses victory in the non-championship F1 race at the sweeping, challenging Solitude road circuit in Germany just one week later. Albeit against somewhat tepid opposition. Oh, Colin Chapman's Lotus team showed up to collect their "star attraction" share of the starting money (they were odds-on favorites for the prize money as well) with the sleek Lotus 25 monocoque for Jim Clark and an older, tube-framed 24 for Trevor Taylor to replace the 25 that got turned into scrap metal in that stupid, dangerous, after-the-blessed-checkered-flag wreck at Rouen. But Cooper, BRM and Bowmaker Lola all headed home after the French Grand Prix and Ferrari remained in Maranello, so the field at Solitude was made up of mostly British and European privateers with second-string "customer" cars and a few older-spec engines. Except for Porsche, that is. Solitude was only a few kilometers from Porsche's home base in Stuttgart, and it was essentially a home-circuit race for them. So they showed up with the full factory F1 effort and were eager to perform well in front of an enormous and highly enthusiastic local crowd still overjoyed by Porsche's first-ever grand prix win at Rouen just one week before.

But of course Lotus was there and, as expected, Jim Clark qualified fastest at the head of a somewhat sketchy, 14-car starting grid. But Gurney's flat-8 Porsche was right there next to him and, in spite of the apparent superiority of the Lotus in both handling and aerodynamics, Dan was determined to give the hometown fans something to cheer about. Clark duly spurted away at the start, but Gurney's Porsche was right there in his wheeltracks. They came around the hairpin side-by-side on the very first lap—the Porsche on the outside, by the way—and, jaw set, Dan forced his way past into the lead. At which point the stands erupted into a thundering avalanche of cheers and applause. But there was still an entire race to run. And the weather was looking iffy as well. But Dan did a magnificent job of playing cork-in-the-bottle to a presumably faster car and simply didn't leave Clark's Lotus even a sliver of an opening to get by.

It was one hell of a drive!

To be fair, the race report did mention that the Climax V8 in Jimmy's car was sounding a little fluffy and sputtery coming off the corners, and that was surely hampering his attempts to re-take the lead. But Dan was also driving with tremendous skill, commitment and confidence.

And then, on lap 20, it started to rain…

But Gurney kept on top of things on the narrow, fast and now dangerously slick racetrack, while Clark somewhat uncharacteristically slithered off and collected a fence. He managed to limp the Lotus back to the pits, but his race was run. Which left Dan to motor serenely on to another excellent win—with the sun now back out and Porsche teammate Jo Bonnier emerging solidly in second place as well—in front of an ecstatic hometown crowd. Dan had proved yet again that he belonged up there with the very best of them. And, like every other American fan or enthusiast on the planet, that made me feel pretty damn special indeed. And it was good to feel close to it again, even if it was only in print. I read every last word in that issue of *Comp Press*. Even the damn classifieds on the back page.

Opposite the French GP story on page one was Henry N. Manney's report on the British Grand Prix at Aintree just one week after Dan Gurney's win at Solitude. Only this time Lotus got it right. Jimmy Clark qualified the sleek 25 on pole, led from the start and essentially ran away and hid from the rest of the field. He made it look easy, too, and along the way tacked a full 10mph onto the existing lap record (which had been set just one season ago by the then all-conquering/now-nowhere Ferrari 156s). My, how things had changed! Speaking of Ferrari, the *Commendatore* was still grousing about the Italian metal-workers' strike that supposedly kept the team from appearing at Rouen (and where they actually might have done pretty well considering the well-proven ruggedness of Ferrari racecars) and he'd threatened to be a no-show again at Aintree. Which was a flat, straightforward and fairly surgical circuit where, to be honest, his existing 156s didn't figure to be particularly competitive. And that's putting it kindly. But there was also starting money to consider, and the Aintree organizers knew they wouldn't have much to hoot about in their pre-race press releases without the magic of the Ferrari name and the presence of reigning world champion Phil Hill. In the end, an almost right-sized bag of gold must have been proffered, and *Il Commendatore* relented and sent a single car up for Phil to drive. To be honest, it was a pretty half-hearted effort and really only there to collect the starting money. You need to under-stand that each team has their own, highly private deal with the organizers regarding what sort of starting money they'll get (assuming the car qualifies and runs a certain, specific percentage of the race), and the amount offered has everything to do with what cars and which drivers the spectators will pay good money to see. So while Ferrari were definitely in the doldrums, they were still the reigning world champs and had won the British Grand Prix (and just about everything else) the year before. Plus you really didn't have much of a grand prix without the red cars from Maranello, and everybody knew it. Surely it would have been fun to eavesdrop on the negotiations (one can imagine the organizers clutching tightly to their purse strings and old Enzo getting very huffy and insulted indeed) and sending just a single car was Ferrari's way of taking the money and extending his middle finger to the race promoters simultaneously. Phil did his best, of course—he always did—but the fast-aging 156 was simply outclassed, and he struggled to a dismal 12th spot on the grid and in the race his car expired at half-distance with a dropped valve. Which gave team manager Dragoni yet another opportunity to complain about Phil's lack of fire and, barely a heartbeat later, berate him for being too damn hard on the equipment. It was a difficult situation for Phil and, as far as I could see, it didn't figure to get any better.

You also felt sympathy for poor Innes Ireland, who had done a hell of a job qualifying the privateer BRP Lotus—still an old-spec, tube-framed "customer" 24—on the outside of the front row. But he lost first and second gears on the blessed reconnaissance lap and was left standing when the green waved and the rest of the field stormed off into the distance. Too bad. And Dan Gurney, who had qualified a decent and perhaps more representative 6th on the grid in the flat-8 Porsche, made another brilliant start and had the silver car up to 3rd in the early going before a slipping clutch dropped him back down the field. Then again, luck and mechanical glitches do tend to even out over time. But the thing that really caught my eye was how John Surtees had qualified the Bowmaker Lola an excellent second to Clark's Lotus, and held that position from the flutter of the green all the way to the checker in spite of losing second gear. No question things were going to be feeling upbeat when I dropped in at the Lola shop in Bromley the following day!

I was also intrigued by a short piece about a meeting the fledgling Grand Prix Drivers' Association (GPDA) held in their fast-recovering chairman Stirling Moss's suite at the Mayfair Hotel in London the week before the British Grand Prix. Of course, what everybody really wanted to know was when (or if) Stirling would be able to return to racing. But there was nothing about it except for a brief mention of how his recovery, progress and rigorous training regimen were continuing to amaze his doctors. Besides that, the story was all about the points under discussion at the meeting. Including the increasing number of serious accidents in formula junior races (really no big surprise, since it was acknowledged as the proving ground for and stepping stone to a professional racing career). The end result was that you had all sorts of eager young talent out to show the world what they could do. And there's just no way at all to pull the fuse out of a situation like that. More reasonable was a desire to establish some sort of standards for driver credentialing at Le Mans, which had become somewhat infamous for inexperienced duffers and hobbyists making life difficult—not to mention dangerous—for the real professional drivers in much faster cars. Although any notion of dictating to the French organizers from the *Automobile Club de l'Ouest* how to run their own damn race would likely fall on deaf ears. And there was also a discussion about the complete removal of batteries from grand prix cars. After Moss's terrible wreck at Goodwood, he said it took the course workers well over half an hour to cut him out of the car, and more than half of that was devoted to removing the battery to reduce the possibility of fire. Still, it didn't sound very practical to me. But it wasn't anything to worry about, since getting any group of racing drivers—and particularly those at the very top of the game—to agree on damn near anything is pretty much impossible. Between their natural competitiveness, their varied languages, national prides, cultural and social backgrounds and the fact that they have to fight it out with each other every damn weekend makes any kind of accord a highly remote possibility.

There was also plenty of coverage from our side of the pond, and it was clear that "friendly" amateur sports car racing was alive and well (but still offering no prize money) all over North America. But there were also some ominous rumblings of professionalism. The Indianapolis-based United States Auto Club (USAC) had taken over the Indy 500 and most of the rest of the professional, prize-money-paying, open-wheel oval-track racing in North America after the AAA pulled out of racing completely in the wake of the horrific Le Mans disaster of 1955. And now they were tentatively putting their toe in the water in both stock-car racing and sports car racing to see if they could draw decent fields and audiences and if there was any real money to be made.

They'd actually combined both ideas at that recent stock car event up at Mosport, but the spectator turnout had been pretty damn abysmal. And they'd run a formula car, open-wheel pro event at the somewhat Frankenstein-monster road circuit at Indianapolis Raceway Park just the previous weekend (although the results and race report wouldn't appear until the next issue of *Comp Press)*. But the old-guard SCCA hierarchy didn't much like their "amateur" drivers competing for prize money (it brought in the wrong sort of people and attitudes, don't you know?), and they'd fire off occasional letters and directives threatening to pull people's licenses if they ran with USAC. But they seemed to be okay with genuine international road-course events (although I have no idea why that should be any different?), and I was excited to see that there was a full, F.I.A.-sanctioned "Double 400" GT points race planned for the Bridgehampton track on Long Island in mid-September. There weren't many points-and-prize-money F.I.A. Manufacturers' Championship races in America—just Daytona and Sebring, really— and it ran through my head that it would be really cool if I could be there to see it happen (and even better if I could be there covering it for a magazine!).

On the amateur side, a pair of Volvo 122S models finished 1-2 after 8 grueling, claustrophobic hours of heavy traffic in the "L'il Le Mans" small-sedan race on the fast and scenic but twisty and tiny little 1.5-mile racetrack at Lime Rock, Connecticut. I always liked Volvos, and no question they were hell for rugged. There was also a short piece about how dentist/Corvette ace Dr. Dick Thompson had a 2-way radio hidden away in the passenger compartment of his car at some backwater SCCA amateur race in Lake Garnett, Kansas. That sounded like a pretty good idea.

Back on the older side of the Atlantic, my friend Tommy Edwards apparently had a pretty good run in somebody's howling, heeled-over Jaguar Mk. II to take 2nd in class and 3rd overall at a minor-league 12-hour sedan race at the Nurburgring. It was hardly the sort of thing to get his name back in the limelight (and he and his co-driver did get beaten into 2nd overall by a Lancia Flaminia) but it was still a good result and I was happy for him. You always want to see the drivers you know and like doing well. It makes you feel warm and proud inside. And it's unsettling when you don't see their names somewhere in the agate type or hear about them through the grapevine. Like my friend Cal Carrington, for example, who seemed to have dropped off the edge of the earth and had me wondering and worrying where he'd gone and what might be happening to him. Racing careers can be incredibly fragile things, and a lot of them run out of opportunities or confidence long before they run out of skill or talent.

By that point I was well into the back pages of *Competition Press,* and I actually think I started reading a little slower and lingering over all the grainy, tabloid-quality pictures to try and make it last a little longer. To the point that I read every single one of the classified ads—every damn word!—like I had all sorts of money to spend and was actually thinking about buying myself a new used racecar or a flashy, exotic street cruiser or something. One guy had a brand-new, never-raced (and now pretty much outclassed and outdated) Lister Corvette for sale for 3500 bucks. That was as much as a new Freeway Frigate (although not quite enough for one of Amanda Cassandra Fairway's "great artists" special editions). I wondered who'd be stupid enough to want such a thing at that price when, just one column over, you could buy yourself a gorgeous, sexy, 4-year-old Ferrari 212 Pininfarina coupe for a hundred bucks less? Although then you'd have to feed it and take care of it, and my guess was that wouldn't come cheap. Hell, my friend Buddy Palumbo was getting ready to move his family and business up to Connecticut thanks to taking care of cars like that. And cars like that white-elephant Lister Corvette, too. It ran through my head that I really hadn't seen Buddy in a long time, and I wondered what he was up to. If I somehow managed to get to that F.I.A. pro race out at Bridgehampton in September, maybe I could drop in on him? Or maybe he could find the time to join me there? And maybe Cal could join us? Maybe he'd even have a decent ride? That would be great! My brain spent a little time daydreaming and visualizing and wallowing around in how much fun that would be. And then I went back to the classifieds. Like always, a few of them were heartbreak soap-opera stories all by themselves:

"1962 Corvette racecar. Very competitive. All options. Fully prodified. Many extras, spares. Zero races on new engine. Must sell. Drafted. $3900."

It almost put a tear in your eye.

But eventually I got to the very last price at the end of the very last classified on the very last page of *Comp Press,* and I had to face the fact that it was time to try muddling through one of the business magazines I'd brought with me. Which, to be honest, was about as appealing as wading through a pool of lukewarm baby barf after all the hot motorsports news and insider stuff in *Competition Press.* Phooey.

I started out with a short, overwrought piece on the after-effects of the terrible "Blue Monday" stock-market crash I hadn't even been aware of back on May 28, and followed that up with a few worrying paragraphs on the precipitous state of America's ever-dwindling gold reserves. But the thing I kept wondering about was who the hell *cared* if there was a little less gold in Fort Knox? I mean, did it make any real difference? What the heck was the stuff good for anyway, except for filling a few bad teeth, making fancy jewelry that rich old ladies wore or putting on the outside of space satellites to protect them from solar heat or radiation or gamma rays or something? I mean, you couldn't eat it or drink it or burn it for fuel or cast a damn engine block or grind a damn camshaft or even make a decent, operational sewing-machine mechanism out of it. Not even the damn needle. And God knows it was cold to the touch and ridiculously heavy and hard as hell to move around. It seemed to me that the only reason gold was valuable in the first place was because a bunch of people way back when decided to shake hands and agree it was valuable—*oooh, shiny!*—and people had been fighting wars over it and hoarding it and scheming to get more of it ever since.

It just seemed dumb to me, you know?

I flipped over to a big, breathless spread about the situation between England and the European Common Market (Would they join? Could they join? Why was the French government of Charles de Gaulle so opposed to it? How did it affect U.S. interests?) with a sidebar about proposed, promised and/or predicted common markets emerging in the Arab middle east and central Africa. To be honest, it sounded like a lot of bullshit double-talk and grand generalities and I couldn't really wrap my brain around it (although I was quite sure it must be important, or why else would people be buying these fucking magazines?). I mean, who really cared? It was frankly amazing to me that all these earth-shaking financial events could be taking place while John Q., Fred Average and the rest of the rank-and-file American public—me included—remained essentially oblivious. Or at least all the people I knew, anyway. Excepting, of course, the financial stiffs on Clifton Toole's staff, who were always carrying around the latest edition of *The Wall Street Journal* like it was parchment from The Dead Sea Scrolls. Even though *The Journal* had neither a sports section nor a proper comics page, which you normally get with any decent, full-service newspaper.

I was yawning by that point.

So I flipped to another story about innovative retailing magnates Eugene Ferkauf and his buddy Joe Zwillenberg, who'd made a great success of their E. J. Korvette's discount chain by opening up stores in new suburban shopping malls instead of traditional, central-urban shopping district locations and, more importantly, taking a sneaky end-run around "suggested retail prices" (not to mention—at least according to the article—the fair price/anti-discounting provisions of the Robinson-Patman Act of 1936) and discounting the shit out of everything. There were a bunch of footnotes citing reference materials and charts and bar graphs to illustrate, but I didn't really understand any of those, either. And that's about when I drifted off to sleep...

I took a taxi to the hotel Karen Sabelle had booked me into near Fairway Motors' British HQ in Dangleton and dropped in the next morning in my Fairway blazer and tie to pick up our courtesy car—it was one of their up-market, "executive class" Chancellors—and meet a few people that Danny wanted me to meet. They passed me off from one to the next like it was some kind of who-can-get-rid-of-him-quickest parlor game, and they were all extremely friendly, attentive and courteous in that wonderful British way that lets you know that they don't trust you one bit and are quite sure that you're a complete waste of their time. Then again, they probably all saw me as the prying eyes and antenna ears of the executive corridor back at Fairway Tower in Detroit, and that could only mean trouble as far as they were concerned.

And who could blame them?

I did like Roy Lunney, who was a Brit by birth, an engineer, toolmaker and designer by temperament, trade and training, an ex-RAF pilot and had done a bit of racing and rallying. He'd also been with AC cars, Aston Martin and Jowett as chief designer before he came to Fairway, so he knew what he was about. He'd actually emigrated to the states several years before and worked out of Fairway Tower most of the time, but he hopped back and forth occasionally on various projects and assignments. I took a liking to him right away. He seemed just slightly less eager than the rest to get rid of me as quickly as possible...

Things made a lot more sense when I dropped in at the Lola shop in Bromley later that day to see how things were progressing with some things I actually knew and cared about. They were fooling with the back of the gearbox and doing a frame-alignment check on the existing Bowmaker Formula One car (Surtees still wasn't happy with it, and particularly compared to Clark's Lotus 25, which he'd had an excellent opportunity to view from behind at Aintree) while work was progressing on a new F1 chassis with some frame and suspension modifications suggested mostly by the driver. Surtees had some very definite ideas about how he wanted things, and when a driver is delivering the goods on track like he was, the team tends to listen. But they'd decided to stick with the existing, 5-speed Colotti gearbox rather than trying Colotti's new 6-speed, as they'd already experienced so many gear- and shifting-related problems during the races that they felt more comfortable with the can of worms they already knew rather than opening up a brand, new can of worms while trying to sort out a new chassis.

Not to take anything away from Valerio Colotti. He was a sharp, resourceful and experienced Italian designer/engineer with an impressive motorsports résumé. He'd worked for both Ferrari and Maserati and was credited with a lot of the chassis work on the classic Maserati 250F grand prix car, which won a pair of races for Juan Manuel Fangio in his 1954 championship year before Fangio's Mercedes ride was ready, took Moss to his first-ever grand prix wins in 1956 and carried Fangio to his final grand prix championship in 1957 with four outright wins. But by then Maserati was struggling financially and the move to rear engines was on. So he set up his own shop and did some excellent work for Rob Walker's team in England. Including designing and building an entire new transaxle for the Lotus F1 cars Stirling Moss drove after Walker's head mechanic and tech wizard, Alf Francis, decided that Lotus's own, sequential-shift "queerbox" was, as Alf himself would have put it: "too clever by half."

And now he was building transaxle gearboxes for a lot of the British Formula One teams. BRM of course built their own—they insisted on building everything in-house whether it was wise to do so or not—and the Cooper team also had their own and the Lotus factory team had an exclusive deal with ZF in Germany, but all the rest of the British teams were using Colottis.

"It's a real problem with these little, high-winding, multi-cylinder grand prix motors," Peter Bryant offered while he ratcheted the small nuts and locking washers onto the Colotti 5-speed's back-cover studs. "The power is way up high and peaky, and they don't have the torque to peel the skin off a bloody custard. So you really need to keep them on the boil to get the most out of them. Ferrari's got a 6-speed and so does Porsche, and it looks like that's where everybody's heading. But it gets problematic when you're trying to keep everything light and compact as possible, so you wind up with a very small box full of skinny little gears and all these dainty little forks and dogs and detents and such to stir them. It's like a bloody watchworks in there, and they don't much care for the constant gear-changing, pounding and vibration of a full-on grand prix distance."

"Henry N. Manney said these new grand prix engines have torque curves as steep as the back of God's neck."

That got a polite little chuff of a laugh out of Peter Bryant.

Over to the side, a couple of the Mk. 5 formula juniors that looked very much like skinny-tired versions of the grand prix car were going through the build process and a few older-model juniors and club-racing sports/racers were in for freshening or to have crash damage repaired. Well over to the side, I could see that Clive Stanley's Imperial Tea Aston Zagato was hidden away under a cotton twill car cover and that the cover itself was covered by a fine film of shop dust. The car was obviously very much as it had finished at Le Mans more than a month earlier, and that made me wonder what was happening with my friend Tommy Edwards. I didn't have to wait long to find out.

"Hello, Sport!" a familiar voice chirped from over my shoulder.

I turned and there he was, suited up in perfectly knotted regimental tie and nice tweed jacket with his salt-and-pepper hair and mustache—more salt by far than pepper these days—neatly trimmed and combed into place. He was looking sharp, keen and fit, and I was glad to see it. Why, his shoes were even shined.

"Good to see you," I told him.

"Good to be seen."

"You've been well?"

"Barely visible," he grinned, "but well."

"That's good."

"It beats the alternative."

He started showing me around like you do whenever you're in a racing shop. There are always a lot of things to see. Like Audrey's father working a lathe in the machine-shop area in the far corner. Making rear hubs, I think. But he pretended not to notice me, and I returned the favor. I'd be picking Audrey up later that afternoon when she got done with her Monsters of Mayfair, and then we had a little shopping to do. We'd be heading off for Italy together early the next morning, and surely Walter knew all about it and couldn't have been well pleased. So we avoided acknowledging each other or even letting our eyes meet. There'd be plenty of time for all of that later. Too much time, most likely. I turned my attention back to Tommy: "You know, I saw your name in the funny papers yesterday."

"You did?"

"Third overall and second in class at the Nurburgring. Or at least that's what it said in *Competition Press*."

Tommy looked embarrassed. "It wasn't much more than a glorified bloody club race that went on too long," he started in apologetically, "dodging in and out of a bunch of Germans in rinky-dink DKW 3-cylinders, NSU Prinzes and BMW 700s. In the middle of the bloody night, mind you! Around the bloody Nurburgring! Can you imagine?"

"Not without difficulty. But then, I've always been short on imagination."

"To be honest, I'm surprised you even heard about it."

"Read about it on the flight over. Although the type was pretty small, now that you mention it. But I borrowed a pair of reading glasses from some old dowager sitting next to me and…"

"I said it was a small event," he pretended to growl, "You don't have to be bloody rude about it."

"Just trying to get it all straight in my head, that's all. Someday I may have to write your autobiography or something."

"My obituary, more likely."

"I'd rather the autobiography. They tend to be longer, and I generally get paid by the word."

"I'll pay you now not to."

It was great to be bantering back and forth with Tommy again. And particularly with him looking as sharp and sounding as upbeat and cheeky as he did now. So I naturally had to put another dig in:

"It said in the results that you got beaten by a Lancia Flaminia."

"Bloody works entry," he laughed. "Really it was. Damn good car, too."

And of course that was true enough. Being a pedantic motoring scribe by trade, I couldn't resist rattling it all off for him: Lancia was one of the oldest and most respected car manufacturers on the planet. Lancia started building cars way back in 1906 and, in spite of the death of founder Vincenzo Lancia in 1937 (the company was passed on to his wife and son), ongoing financial problems and a buyout by the Presenti family in 1956, they'd amassed one hell of a history and a heritage of innovation. They'd introduced what was surely the world's first-ever monocoque, unibody chassis on their Lambda model in 1922, pioneered independent front and rear suspension systems (not to mention V6 engines and rear transaxles) and had hired brilliant designer Vittorio Jano away from Alfa to lead their engineering staff before the war. And Jano was a genius. His postwar "saddle-tank" Lancia D50 grand prix cars were both fast and clever (although not quite up to the well-funded Mercedes juggernaut), but the Presenti buyout, financial troubles, Mercedes' steamroller dominance, the Le Mans disaster and the death of beloved team leader and Italian national hero Alberto Ascari led Lancia to fold up their tent and essentially turn their entire team over to Enzo Ferrari in the middle of the '55 season. Ferrari also got a little backing from Fiat and Vittorio Jano as well. A slightly revamped and re-badged version of the D50 won Juan Manuel Fangio his fourth World Championship the following year after Mercedes pulled out and...

"I know the bloody history!" Tommy snapped, rolling his eyes in mock exasperation.

"But the point I'm trying to make is that I know their cars are really, really good. So it's no real shame to come second to one."

"You don't have to make excuses for me," Tommy laughed. "The Jaguar was the faster car. Full stop. The Jag that won the bloody race proved that..." I watched a little glimmer come up in his eyes. "...And I would be omitting a significant detail if I didn't admit to being the quickest driver on the team and taking the least out of the car as well."

"Bully for you."

I could see a little color creeping up his neck, but it was all in good fun.

"So," I had to ask, "how did you manage to lose?"

"Well, you could start with the fact that the Lancias were a full factory effort. Decent drivers. Well-prepared cars. Good pit stops. To tell the bloody truth, we would have come third behind both of them, but we were fortunate in that one of them ran into mechanical problems."

"I see."

"And then you could add in that my teammate—who was a good enough sort and extremely enthusiastic—had glasses this thick…" he held his thumb and forefinger a quarter-inch apart, "and couldn't see much further than the back end of the Jag's bloody hood ornament…"

"I could see where that would be a problem."

"…but he was also the car's owner, so it would have been rather unseemly to make an issue of it."

"Indeed it would."

"And he did spend some time searching through the hedgerows for missing couples during his night stint."

"Hey, someone's got to do it."

"You'd think the circuit would have people for that."

"Yes, you would."

It was good having Tommy looking and sounding like his old self again.

"But I can't complain. It was a decent ride in a half-decent car, and it even paid a few pounds. And the owner's invited me back to drive it again in the saloon race at the Brands Hatch International on Bank Holiday Monday."

"That sounds promising."

"Not so sure about 'promising,' but it should be a bit of fun. And at least it keeps me out there." He nodded towards the dust cover over Clive Stanley's Aston Zagato. "And I'm trying to talk old Clive into letting me have a go in that one again in the GT race."

"Oh?"

"They won't give us much in the way of starting money what with all the real name drivers already signed up in Ferrari GTOs—Bowmaker's running Surtees in one for the English distributor—but I know Brands, and we might do all right by the end."

"So what are the chances?"

Tommy shrugged. "It would be fairly easy to get things ready, but Clive's got to want to do it. That's the real problem."

"Oh?"

Tommy gave off a little wince of a smile. "He had a bit of a blowup with Ian—it was well overdue, and I suppose it was actually good for my prospects—only now he seems to have taken a fancy to hot-air ballooning…."

I could see where this was going. It happened all the time with wealthy car owners. "Well, good luck with it."

"It would be fun if it happened. So keep your fingers crossed."

I looked him up and down. "I must say, you're looking pretty sharp these days."

"Have to. I'm flogging cars for Mr. Broadley."

"Oh?"

Tommy gave me an apologetic grin. "It's not like I'm very good at it."

"You know the cars and you probably know a lot of the clientele."

"I suppose…" he allowed, "…but selling cars is never simple or straightforward."

"How so?"

"Oh, there's almost always an old car to be gotten rid of—see that lot over there…" he nodded towards the small, tatty collection of older, front-engined Juniors and Lola Mk. I sports-racers huddled in the corner. "…Most blokes want to simply trade them in when they pick up a new one."

"That's pretty standard procedure in the car business, isn't it?"

"But it's different with racing cars. You don't want your operating money or profit tied up in knackered old racing cars that nobody wants."

"I could see where that could be a problem."

"That's why you really want to work through your distributors. You see, most racing-car customers seem to confuse what they have *in* a bloody car with what they think it's worth."

"I think that applies to just about all trade-ins, not just racing cars." I'd heard all about that from Buddy's great friend and mentor Big Ed Baumstein when they had the VW dealership in New Jersey. "I can see where you're better off working through dealers."

"We have them, of course, but they always come with their own set of problems."

"Like what?"

"Money, mostly. Credit. Terms. Getting them to pay in a timely fashion. And negotiating the price they're supposed to be paying in the first place."

"Isn't there a list price and a standard dealer discount?"

"Of course there is. But that's always just the starting point. I'll get some bloke on the line…" he switched to a side-of-his-mouth cockney accent: *"Oi wanner buy five a'them new Mark Five Juniors y'got comin' on-line now."*

"So what's wrong with that? Sounds pretty straightforward to me."

"Of course it does. Only once he gets you down to a fair price for five, he tells you he only wants one or two of the bloody things now and the other three at the beginning of next season. And that's assuming the cars continue to do well and that Lotus doesn't pull some demon new Junior model out of their backside again…"

"Sounds frustrating."

"Oh, it's not so bad," Tommy shrugged. "You just need to stay calm, remain firm and have a thick skin sometimes. Besides, Eric's busy with more important things and really can't be bothered. Plus it's nice that a few people still seem to remember my name…"

"So are you doing any good at it?"

"Not too horrible," Tommy allowed. "I've sold a few of the Juniors—it's a nice, tidy little car—and the way John's been going in the Bowmaker job surely helps."

"He really did well at Aintree, didn't he?"

"And at Rouen until he lost the bloody gears. And don't forget he was on pole at Zandvoort."

"A lot of the scribes thought he was just a bike man and would never amount to much in Formula One."

"Oh, he's the business, all right," Tommy said respectfully. "Maybe the best I've ever come across."

"Really?"

Tommy nodded.

"Better than Clark or Gurney?"

Tommy shrugged.

"Better than Stirling Moss?"

Tommy had to think that one over. "Different from Moss," he finally allowed. "He seems gentle on the outside, but Surtees has an unbelievable will to win. And his technique and racecraft are good as anybody's. Maybe even better."

"You seem to think a lot of him."

"When people ask questions or make comparisons about John—and they always do, especially you scribes—he always gives off a little smile and says, without any bluster or bravado or braggadocio: *Put us in equal cars and I like my chances.*" Tommy shook his head. "Oh, he can be a little difficult about things on the car sometimes but, after he's done letting you know what a heap of rubbish it is, he gets in and drives the bloody wheels off the thing."

No question I'd been impressed, along with everyone else, by Surtees's speed, skill and tenacity ever since he made the switch from two wheels to four. But, looking back over the young season, you wondered if he was happy with the Lola and the Bowmaker team. Everyone knew he'd had a contract offer from Chapman, but he apparently figured he'd be playing second-fiddle to Clark at Lotus, and Lotus number twos had a long history of winding up with second-string cars and fizzled-out careers. So he'd turned Chapman down and taken a chance on the new Lola. But would he stay?

"It's hard to say," Tommy answered diplomatically. "It's a new car and a new team, and we've certainly had our share of problems. Although the car's performance has been more than promising. Especially for a brand-new car."

"No question about it."

"And you can't fault John's effort. He's done the job."

"Yes he has."

"But you wonder if he may get a more attractive offer elsewhere. You know, he's damn near a national hero in Italy."

I nodded. "He took—what was it—seven motorcycle world championships riding for Count Agusta? He can't even buy his own meals down in Italy." I mulled it over in my head. "But who would he drive for?" I mused. "He'd be stark, raving mad to go drive for Ferrari."

"Oh, they're down now," Tommy cautioned, "but you count old man Ferrari out at your own bloody peril."

"But he's lost most of the people on his staff!" I argued. And then I started rattling them off: "Chiti, Bizzarrini, Tavoni…"

"Blokes and geniuses come and go at Ferrari. Always have and always will. But the old man's the one who bloody shakes them up and stirs them around and makes it all happen. He's the best there ever was at it. They'll be back on top again, mark my words…They'll be back."

"That's probably true," I had to agree. "At least if the past is any guide…"

Tommy nodded. "And even if the F1 cars are in a bit of a slump, he's still got things his own bloody way with the sports cars and GTs."

And that was true enough. There was no one to really challenge Ferrari's supremacy in either category. At least not yet. "That reminds me," I quickly added, "how's Eric's new Le Mans car coming along?"

Tommy looked at me sideways. He obviously wanted to know who was asking.

"Look, I'm on your side on this," I assured him. "Sure, I keep my eye on things for the people in The Tower. That's what I'm supposed to do. That's what they pay me for. But I'm the one who mentioned Lola to them in the first place. I'm the one who got Eric those Fairway V8s, remember?"

Tommy frowned as he thought it over. And then the frown melted into a smile. "Look, Sport, I don't want you quoting me on this…"

"I'm not in that end of the business anymore."

"You may not be writing it for publication, but you're still a bloody snoop out sniffing around for the inside story…"

"A leopard can't change his spots."

"So keep this close to your chest, all right?"

"Mum's the word," I promised.

He leaned in close and whispered: "To tell the truth, the Le Mans car is still mostly sketches and drawings right now—a few bits, maybe—but we've been awfully busy. I mean, it's the middle of the bloody season."

"So when do you think?"

Tommy shrugged again. "Hard to say. Resources are tight and we're spread thin as fish paper. But Eric's got it in his head that he wants to roll the new car out at the London racing-car show in January. We'll need to pull some budget out of somewhere and work flat-out over the bloody holidays to make it happen, but that's really nothing new…I've learned not to doubt Eric when he commits himself to getting something done. He's pretty bloody amazing that way."

"Has he figured out yet what he's going to use for a gearbox?"

Tommy looked surprised. "Don't you know about it?"

"About what?"

"Alf Francis's bloke. Valerio Colotti."

"I know about the new six-speed for F1. Peter and I were just talking about it."

"Well, you didn't hear it from me," Tommy half whispered, "but supposedly Colotti's got something brand-new in the works that can handle the weight and torque of a big American V8."

"He *does?*" This was the first I'd heard about it. And of course the next thing I wanted to know was who'd commissioned the project. Independent operators like Valerio Colotti couldn't afford to do anything like that unless somebody else was paying the bills. And I wanted to know just who that somebody might be.

Tommy did his best to answer. "The scuttlebutt I've heard is that it's a big, stout four-speed and that he's doing it for Colin Chapman over at Lotus."

That was big news indeed. But it also didn't ring entirely true. Chapman was busy with a lot of things besides his newly ascendant F1 team and building and selling as many of his Type 22 formula juniors and Type 23 club sports/racers as possible. He had the Elite and Lotus 7 so-called "road cars" in production as both complete cars and tax-avoiding kits, and everyone in the business knew he was planning to launch his intriguing and innovative new backbone-frame Elan sportscar in the fall. So why would he want to expend money and effort on a beefy new transaxle that could handle the power of an American V8 when there was nothing in his current or future plans that might use such a thing?

Tommy gave me a quizzical look. "The rumor I've heard is that they may be building something rather special for Indianapolis…"

"*Indianapolis???*" I just about gasped. "But who the hell's *paying* for it? And what the hell kind of motor are they planning to use?"

Tommy nodded towards the two Fairway V8s that Bob Wright had air-freighted over to the Lola shop. One was up on a stand with its ancillaries and exhaust manifolds stripped off so Eric's guys could take its measurements, while the second was still strapped to its wooden shipping skid underneath a work bench, wrapped in plastic sheeting.

"*FAIRWAY???!!!*"

Tommy nodded. "I'm bloody amazed you don't already know about it."

"So am I," I pretty much mumbled. "So am I."

As soon as I left the Lola shop, I headed straight across the street to a fish-and-chips shop and called Detroit collect on the pay phone. I caught Danny Beagle at his desk, thank goodness, and I think I may have sounded a little agitated.

"*What's all this shit about Fairway Motors going to Indianapolis?*" I damn near screamed into the receiver.

Dead silence for a moment. And then, real innocent: "All what shit?"

"*Look, don't fuck with me, Danny,*" I fumed. "*Everybody over here seems to know about it…*"

Even more innocent: "Know about what?"

"*That Fairway's got an Indy project in the works with Lotus!*"

Dead silence.

"*… And I don't know one fucking thing about it!*"

More silence.

"*Did you HEAR me?*" I pretty much hollered.

"Look, Hank…" Danny started in, trying to both pull rank and sound reasonable at the same time, "…you don't need to know about everything. That's not in your job description."

"*But I thought I was supposed to be your European racing guy!*"

"You are. That's why we hired you."

"*Then why the fuck am I out of the loop on this?*"

"Calm down, OK? You're not out of the loop. You just don't know about it yet, that's all."

"But I should have been IN on it!"

"Maybe," Danny allowed. "But if you really want to get technical about it, Indianapolis is an *American* race."

"Go fuck yourself."

"You don't need to take that kind of attitude with me, Hank. I don't deserve it. Who got you out of the bushes and safely home—and, need I remind you, you were higher than a damn kite that night—from that party at H.R. Junior's house? "

He was right about that. But I was pissed and feeling, I don't know, maybe a little betrayed. "For God's sake, Danny," I hissed at him, "I'm the one who introduced Bob to fucking Colin Chapman in the first place."

"Yes, you did. You introduced them and they shook hands. And you can rest assured that Bob appreciates that. We all do."

"Then how come I'm not in on it?"

"Well, Dan Gurney kind of brought the idea in to us."

"But I should have been in on it."

He had to think his answer through before he gave it to me. "You will be," he promised. "Why, you'll be writing the copy and bringing the whole damn world on board once we get ready to go public. But we're not ready to do that yet, and we don't want a bunch of rumors floating around and people asking questions and peering in over our shoulders."

"You think I'd leak secrets out or tell all sorts of people?" I was feeling more hurt than betrayed now.

"Of course you wouldn't. Didn't Bob tell you right out front about the new Ferret project? He trusts you, Hank. Really he does."

I had to admit that he had shown me the top-secret new Ferret model on my very first visit to his office.

"But this is a little different," Danny went on. "An awful lot of things have to come together to make this work. And this Chapman guy's got a reputation for…well, let's just say he has a reputation…"

"I could have told you that."

"So we thought it might be best to have one of our English guys dealing with him. Keeping an eye on him, you know? Making sure the project is moving along the way it should. The way we want it to. That's not something you could do very well from here in Detroit."

"But I don't *like* being in Detroit. I'd rather be over here doing that job."

"And I'd rather be sitting in Little Harry Dick's office getting a blowjob from Francine Niblitz. Only that's not my job either, is it? Just like the Indianapolis thing isn't yours." And then he went on the offensive. Only gently. Softly. So it really hammered home. "You'd think you'd be happy with what you've got, travelling down to Italy with your girlfriend Audrey Denbeigh in a brand-new, top-of-the-line Fairway Chancellor, staying wherever the hell you want—within reason, of course—all expenses paid…"

I was starting to feel bad about getting angry with Danny. "Look," I mumbled apologetically, "I'm sorry I got hot with you."

"That's OK," he told me. "That's what I'm here for. That's what we're all here for: to serve as a buffer—a kind of information filter and shock absorber—between one level of management and the next one up the line…"

It was a decent and probably even truthful explanation, but it wasn't especially comforting.

"…and you need to understand Bob's position on sensitive projects in general."

"Oh? What is it?"

"It's simple, Hank. And it goes something like this: *If you don't need to know, you don't need to know…*'"

Chapter 14: Mission to Maranello

I suppose if I was any kind of proper writer I could tell you about the arduous but amazing road trip Audrey and I took down to the Ferrari factory and offices in Maranello, then up to the Nurburgring for the German Grand Prix that weekend and back across The Channel for the Brands Hatch International with Clive Stanley's Aston Martin Zagato team the very next day on Bank Holiday Monday (yes, Tommy had talked him into entering, but not until the very last minute) and have you feel and understand what it was like. But I'm not really sure I have the words to capture it—not sure if any writer could—but I'll do my best and you'll just have to kind of fill in the blank spots and gray areas. It's not like it was all romance and violin music—Audrey's just not like that and I suppose neither am I—and when you spend that many hours locked in a moving car together and trying to make meaningful or at least inoffensive small talk or arguing about which route to take or where and when to stop to take a pee or grab a bite to eat or fussing around the edges of where the hell to spend the night…well, learning how to share time and space with another person is complicated. Especially when you really like that other person and really want it to work out, but are also rather used to being on your own and not having to worry about what you say or how you say it or what someone else is thinking or feeling about things or how your peculiarities, peccadilloes and personal eating, sleeping or hygiene habits may look through another person's eyes. Companionship and intimacy aren't that easy to just whip up out of thin air, and I could tell Audrey was suffering through the same sort of feelings, thoughts and misgivings as I was. But we did our best to, as she put it, "put a brave face on and have a go at it," and there were some wonderfully pleasant, relaxed, comfortable stretches in there along with the lurking, edgy strangeness and long, awkward silences.

Fairway had offered us a courtesy car, and Fairway's British division arranged for me to pick up one of their new, top-of-the-line Chancellor models—labeled as a press courtesy car, of course—at their British HQ in Dangleton. It struck me all over again how different it was from the cars Fairway was building back in the States. But the British auto industry (and their entire economy, in fact) had been forced to more or less rebuild itself in the bleak, austere, shy on capital and raw materials aftermath of

World War Two. Plus everything was prodded and guided along by government tariffs and regulations that desperately sought to increase exports and bring in those Yankee greenbacks. Plus there were severe restrictions on using imported materials or components in an effort to bolster home-based industries. So there wasn't much in the way of either budget or resources lying about for grand new technical directions or from-the-ground-up engineering. In short, there was an awful lot of "making do" going on in the postwar British automobile industry. Including utilizing as many available, out-of-the-parts-bin chassis and driveline bits as possible, even if they traced their lineage back to damn near the days of King Arthur. It helped, of course, that the Brits have always had a great sense of tradition, a deep respect for the past and are keenly, stubbornly, even obstinately xenophobic about home-designed, home-built English products. Even when they're pure, unadulterated crap.

Which brings us around to Fairway of England's new Chancellor model, which amounted to kind of a forced, stuffy attempt at tarting up their dull and uninspiring Wren economy sedan with some leather upholstery, a little burl walnut veneer on the dash and door panels and a semi-ancient three-liter motor and sending the whole mess several hundred pounds up-market to do battle with BMC's Austin A99 Westminster and the Vanden Plas Princess 3-Liter Mk. II. It was quite a nice car on the inside—all rolled and piped leather upholstery and handsome walnut veneer—even if it looked a little jukebox-gaudy on the outside with its vestigial tailfins, two-tone paint and fussy grille treatment. They'd stretched the Wren's wheelbase by five inches and the track by two for more leg, butt and shoulder room, raised the roof an inch-and-a-half so it would clear, if not a top hat, perhaps a bowler on a man of average height and replaced the Wren's wheezy, lumpy four with a leaden, long-stroke six out of their commercial truck line. I explained to Audrey that it had been a very successful military truck motor in the Allied advance across Europe during the closing stages of World War Two.

"So it's got quite a pedigree, then."

"If a dray horse can have a pedigree, then this one surely does."

But we didn't say much more than that as we drove south towards the Channel Ferry under a gray, sad-looking early morning sky with a meager spit of rain dripping out of it. And that pretty much matched our moods, since the scene when I picked her up at her father's row house had been far less than pleasant. Not that Walter yelled or cursed or made a scene or anything. Far from it. But he was up and dressed in his shop clothes even though it was still dark outside, and he never said a word. Not one. Just hovered around like a damn stone vulture and stared at us in cold, angry silence.

"There's milk and eggs and some chicken and a couple of wrapped sandwiches in the fridge, and Mrs. Wallen will be coming around in the mornings to see you off and later on to bring your dinners."

Nothing.

"There's a number there for the car when you're ready to go to work in the morning."

You could hear the fizz of the electric filament in the light bulb in the hallway.

"Tommy said he'd see you get home in the afternoons."

More fizz.

She gave him a nasty, exasperated look, but that didn't work, either. So she let out a sigh like a truck exhaust, pecked him on the cheek, reminded him one more time that we'd only be gone a week and followed me out to the car. He was still standing there in the doorway like a damn cement gargoyle as we headed off.

"Pleasant chap," I offered.

"Let's not talk about it."

"Are you all right?"

She gave me a look that discouraged further inquiry. That's one of the things you need to learn about people you hope to spend a lot of time with: when to stop trying to be nice and just shut the fuck up.

The morning brightened up nicely on the ferry ride across the Channel, and things seemed to be thawing out between Audrey and me as we moved further and further away from Walter. We stood up at the bow end for a while with a late-July sun overhead and a warm summer wind in our faces and the water breaking like an endless, frothing auger bit along the hull line below. We chatted a little about not much at all—Clive Stanley's hilariously impeccable wardrobe and the big Ferris wheel that we never got to ride on together at Le Mans and whether we should take the route south through Geneva or the more mountainous one through Lucerne (I wanted to save that one for the trip back north to the Nurburgring) and what sort of food we might want to eat along the way—and I remember I had my arm around her and it felt like it belonged there.

That was really nice.

You could see a lot of the spark had come back up in her eyes and manner by the time we'd disembarked and, not having much of anything else to talk about, I started razzing her a little with a semi-comic (or at least I hoped it was) British magazine-style review on our courtesy car: "The Chancellor is a sterling example of the great tradition of fine British motorcar design that traces its lineage all the way back to the storied days of the Victorian and Edwardian eras. The same, time-honored methods, sturdy, British-made materials and solid, seasoned-ash-and-pig-iron componentry that served us so well at Hastings, Naseby and Waterloo have yielded up a modern road vehicle of great substance, bearing, charm, presence and pedigree, if not actual over-the-road performance."

"You love sniping at us, don't you?"

"Sniping at who?"

"The English."

"Hey, I love sniping at *everybody*. It's what writers do. We're a bunch of cynical, mean-spirited malcontents, really. But at least we're entertaining."

"Oh? And who said you're entertaining?"

"Now you're the one who's sniping."

Silence. And then, out of nowhere: "It really needs a name, doesn't it?"

"What does?"

"Why, our car, of course."

"It's just a car," I told her, "and not a particularly exciting one at that."

"Nonsense," she insisted. "It's going to be our traveling companion. We really need to give it a name."

"We do?"

"Of course we do. After all, it *is* a Chancellor."

I gave her the snake-eye. "Why is it women always want to name inanimate objects?"

Audrey looked at me like it was the silliest question in the world. "Because they *need* names," she said like it should have been obvious. "Not all cars, of course. Just the ones you wind up getting to know. The ones you spend time in that become, I don't know…traveling companions. It's almost like they're members of the family."

"Did your father name his cars?"

"Of course he didn't," she answered flatly. "But my mother always did. We had an Austin named 'Reginald' for a bit after the war—before she got sick—and my father had a very nice old Siddeley Special that she called 'Errol' when he was working at de Havilland. He was very impressed by the aluminum-alloy engine, but he had to patch it up a few times and decided it was rubbish."

"Errol?"

"After Errol Flynn the actor. She quite fancied him…and in a way that I don't think Walter ever appreciated."

"But they're all just bolted-together lumps of metal," I argued just for the pure, contrarian pleasure of it. "Cars aren't alive. They're not conscious of being. They don't have souls or feelings or personalities."

"Of course they do!" Audrey argued right back. "And don't pretend you don't know it. Why, you write about that sort of thing all the time when you do your reviews for the car magazines or write that awful ad copy for the sales brochures. All you talk about is a car's character and personality."

"But that's different," I told her. "I'm talking about a general type or model then, not a single, specific example." I looked over at her. "Men don't give cars pet names like dogs or cats or horses. Only women do things like that…"

I could feel her bristle a little, even though she was still smiling.

"…Oh, sure," I allowed, "You've got your poets and artists and poufters—they give their cars names—but, by and large, it's the female of the species who does things like that." I gave her a prosecutorial stare. "So tell me: why do women do that?"

"Why do men pee on the floor around the toilet?" she answered back immediately while changing the subject completely.

But I was ready for it: "Why do women always change the subject instead of answering a direct question?"

"We do not!" she insisted playfully. And then her eyes lit up. "And aren't *you* the one who started calling that awful Challenger thing at Sebring 'Rasputin?'"

She had me there. And yet it felt kind of good to be had that way.

In the end, we agreed to name our car "Lord Chamberlain"—Audrey's idea, of course—and as we drove deeper into France, she began endowing him with likes, dislikes and personality traits, and even decided to come up with her own, pithy magazine review of Lord Chamberlain. She was pretty damn funny at it, too. My favorite was: *"The new Fairway Chancellor: the car that does absolutely everything, but most of it slowly and none of it especially well."*

"You should write ad copy for Dick Flick."

"He was the sleek-looking one with the love bites on his neck at Le Mans, wasn't he?"

"That's him."

"He dresses very nicely."

"Rumor has it he undresses very nicely, too."

"I'm sure he does. But he's not really my type."

"Most women find him terribly attractive."

"It's the 'terribly' part that puts me off. And the 'most women,' too. I don't particularly enjoy crowds or long lines."

"Me, either."

"You work for him now, don't you?"

"I don't know if I'd put it that way. They've just got me in kind of a holding pattern at a desk in his department."

"You just sit there all day?"

"Oh, they give me things to do—copy to write—but it's all rubbish and I know they're never going to use it. But they can't stand to have anybody working in The Tower who's not swamped and overwhelmed and overloaded and rushing like mad to get things done."

"Doesn't sound particularly efficient."

"Efficiency isn't the point. Activity is. Or that and watching your backside, anyway."

"I'd imagine Mr. Flick is quite adept at watching backsides."

"That he is." And that led to telling Audrey about Dick Flick's slender and beautiful (although now a little gaunt-looking) fashion-model wife and his secretary Wanda Peters who seemed to be a bit more than a secretary to him and all the scurrying copywriters and paste-up people and media-time buyers in Dick Flick's department and especially the ones who brought their lunches and coffee-break snacks back to their desks in order to appear even busier. And then I told her about all the other characters on the 13th floor executive corridor and particularly about the enormous, shrieking heap of disasters, meltdowns and missed connections that were forever piling up on my friend Ben Abernathy's desk, and how his only real job was to stop them dead in their tracks right there and keep them from going any further. And that segued into something about the nights we'd spent listening to music and talking to the white and black plant workers at The Steel Shed and the Black Mamba Lounge and…

"You should really write some of this down, Hank," she told me. "Some of it is really priceless."

"I don't think it would go down especially well with the people who are paying for this trip."

"And provided us with Lord Chamberlain!" she added as she patted the emaciated roll of leather on top of our Chancellor's dash. "But you couldn't write it now anyway. You have to wait and see how it all comes out in the end. But I think it would make a wonderful story."

"It might," I agreed. "But it would sure as hell get me fired."

"Oh, you'll be over by then, too, Hank. Things like this don't last. They're not meant to last. They're not part of the way real life is."

I wanted to argue with her about that, but I knew she was right. Big automobile manufacturers come and go in the world of motor sports. Always have and always will. In fact, there were only two companies I could think of, Ferrari and Porsche, where racing was part of both their essence and their day-to-day existence. Those companies *lived* to race. And, of the two, only Ferrari was building big-bore sports cars aimed at overall World Manufacturers' Championship wins on a regular basis. Although the feisty little Porsches would sneak in now and then and snatch one away from the red cars—like they had at Sebring in 1960 and three different times at the tough, rugged and twisty

Targa Florio in Sicily. But it made you wonder what would happen and how it would all play out if a company with the size, power, resources and mind-numbing corporate bureaucracy of Fairway Motors tried to take on (or maybe even take over?) a tiny, complicated, successful and well-entrenched little divine-right autocracy like Ferrari.

"You know," I told Audrey as we motored on into the afternoon, "it might make a pretty good story at that. After it's all over, I mean…"

Our original plan was to drive straight through to Modena, but it was an awfully long haul and the main autoroutes were clogged with trucks and summer-vacation traffic. We ate mostly gas station snacks on our way through France, but finally stopped for a sit-down dinner at a little roadside tavern south of Dijon. The old French lady behind the counter took us for a married couple and called Audrey "madame" instead of "mademoiselle," and I was pleased that Audrey didn't say anything to correct her. We had a good meal like you almost always do in the south of France, and over coffee we talked about what our plans should be for the night. It was turning out to be an awkward subject for both of us.

"Well, what do you think?" I asked her. "I don't think we can make it all the way to Modena."

"I thought that was a bit ambitious from the beginning."

"It looked plausible on the map."

"You could have asked, and I would have told you."

"Is this an *I-told-you-so?*"

"It sounds rather like one, doesn't it?"

"Yes, it does. But that still begs the question as to where we stop."

"I suppose we could do another hour or two in Lord Chamberlain."

"That should get us about to Geneva."

"I've heard there are some wonderful places to stay there."

"Any one in particular?"

"No, just in general."

"Okay. We'll just drive until we see one we like."

I paid the old lady behind the counter—I remember she smiled at us approvingly as she handed over the change—and we headed back to the car. It was coming on dark by then and a soft rain was starting to fall.

"Do you want me to drive?" Audrey asked.

"I like the driving," I told her. "It relaxes me."

"I think you're just afraid to ride with me. You don't have to be, you know."

"Not at all," I pretended to insist. "I've always been more at ease driving than riding. Ever since I can remember. The time just seems to go faster."

"You don't have to worry, Henry," she said with an edge in her voice. "I'm quite a good driver."

"I'm sure you are," I told her as I slid myself behind the wheel.

"You men are such egomaniacal bastards."

"Just me, or men in general?"

"Men in general. You're actually one of the better ones, I think. But you're still rotten with it. You just can't help lording it over people."

"Hey," I agreed. "Like you said: we can't help it."

"The worst of it is that you don't even try."

Things had been pretty easy and relaxed between us up until that point, but now you could feel a little tension. Getting on each other's nerves, you know. It's bound to happen when you're stuck in close quarters together for hours on end.

"I'll get even with you tomorrow," she warned. "I'm taking first stint, and there's not one bloody thing you can do about it."

I forced out a laugh. "You really want to drive through the mountains?"

"Why not?"

"And then go up against the crazy Italians on their home turf?"

"The Italians don't scare me," she scoffed, and folded her arms across her chest. *"They're* the ones who should be bloody well worried."

"Do you know how to shake your fist out the window and swear?"

"I have quite a colorful repertoire should I require it. Filthy language and rude gestures as well. You'll see."

"I can hardly wait."

The rain started pounding down pretty heavily as we continued south to Bourg-en-Bresse, and I had the wipers flap-flap-flapping back-and-forth across Lord Chamberlain's windshield and the lights coming the opposite way carried eerie, illuminated halos that made you squint and search for the edge of the road in order to stay in your lane. To be honest, I was plenty tired by then and a little worried about the section through the hills into Geneva. But you know how it is when you're traveling: if you're not on a predetermined schedule, you always want to make that few kilometers more. And then a few kilometers more after that. Only the miles were coming longer and slower now, and we were both dead tired and feeling the sweat and tension of long hours on the road in difficult weather. Not to mention thinking and worrying about what was going to happen when we finally stopped for the night. We'd been avoiding any discussions about it, and I think we were both feeling a little nervous and uncertain.

I know I was.

But the rain eased up a bit as we went over the crest and descended down towards Geneva, and by the time we reached the outskirts of the city, it was fine and clear with pinpoint stars scattered across the sky and just a tiny little sliver of a moon. We passed several likely looking places to stay, but I avoided pulling in, kind of waiting for the right moment to present itself. But of course it never came.

"Are we going all the way to Modena tonight?" Audrey asked impatiently. We were both pretty damn irritable by that point, and I almost put us into a ditch as I swerved Lord Chamberlain into the parking lot of the very next place we saw. It was a handsome, chalet-style inn up on a ridge with a view of the lake off in the distance, and it looked just about perfect for a warm, romantic sort of evening. But the parking lot looked ominously full of Mercedes sedans, Citröens, Peugeots, Alfas and Lancias. I slid Lord Chamberlain to a crunching halt on the gravel and switched off the key.

"Well, I guess this is it," I heard myself saying.

Audrey crawled out of the passenger side and stretched herself against the door. You could just make out the tall, purplish-black shadows of the hills behind us, and the lake far below looked like softly hammered pewter. "This is a lovely spot, Hank," she yawned without looking at me.

"It is that," I agreed. I had a sudden urge to wrap her up in my arms and kiss her. But she was on the other side of the car and, even if I'd been there next to her, I wasn't sure I knew how to pull it off. So I just said, "It's one of the prettiest places I've ever seen," and kept looking at the sky.

But of course that inn was full. And so was the next. And the next one after that. After all, it was the last day of July and August is always vacation month all across Italy and most of France, so a lot of people were already on the road. But the man at the third inn told Audrey about a converted farmhouse a few dozen kilometers up the road that catered mostly to motorcyclists and might still have room. As we made our way back to Lord Chamberlain, the cloud cover caught up with us again and it started to rain. By the time we finally found the farmhouse, the moon and stars had disappeared and the rain was really pelting down.

The farmhouse turned out to be a cheap, dingy old place with a camp yard full of motorcycles and tents in back and no view of anything except the highway and some railroad tracks. We had to wake the wizened old guy who ran the inn, and it was obvious that he'd had a few drinks before heading off to bed and was none too happy to see us. And then he explained in an awkward combination of English and French that all they had left was one long, narrow couch in the sitting area by the window in the front room where guests normally gathered over bottles of wine and beer in the evening to swap trip stories. But it was a comfy-looking old couch—or at least it looked like that to us at the time—and the old guy assured us no one would be coming through until breakfast time the next morning. And he had plenty of blankets and pillows and there was a bathroom with a tub in it down at the end of the hall. There were a couple of regular guest rooms on either side of that hall, but the doors were all closed. He called our accommodations "semi-private," and was not above charging us a three-star hotel rate. Audrey bristled at that—she didn't like being taken advantage of—but I just peeled off the bills and laid them on the counter. What else could I do?

"I was hoping we could do a little better than this," I apologized after the old guy stumbled off to get the blankets and pillows. "This is more like the places I usually stay when I'm traveling for the magazine."

"You really know how to show a girl a good time, don't you?"

"I'm really sorry," I told her. And I meant it. "I suppose I should have planned ahead better. But it seemed so, you know, free and romantic to just drive until we felt like stopping."

"Do you have something particular against making proper arrangements?"

I told her I was sorry again.

"Oh, it looks clean enough," Audrey yawned. "Besides, aren't these the sort of adventures that people remember when they get old?"

"Yeah, I guess."

And so that's how Audrey and I spent our first night on the road together: in the "semi-private" front room of that motorcycle guest house near Geneva, pretty much jammed together on that narrow little couch by the window. But we made the best of it. We drew the curtains and took our turns in the bathroom at the end of the hall and turned off the lamp on the table and it was actually pretty quiet and cozy there in the front room. And, after the first few awkward minutes, it felt pretty damn wonderful to have Audrey there next to me. I could feel her skin and her heat and the muscle right underneath and then I was nuzzling into her hair and trying to kiss her a little, but she kept shushing me and telling me to keep quiet and hissing in a hard whisper that we were going to make too much noise and wake everybody up.

But she didn't try to stop me.

So we made love in a strange, kind of sideways position with her whispering in my ear the whole time that we had to keep quiet and me kind of holding my breath as we got towards the end where it was feeling like we were rushing down the same swirling tunnel together and I was biting my lip to keep from panting out loud and I'm pretty sure she was doing the same and then…

Well, you get the idea.

I think I let out one big, pent-up gasp right there at the very end, and she gave me a kind of elbow-in-the-ribs for it. But then she started laughing about it. Only she was trying to stifle it, so it came out all muffled like some furry-cheeked little rodent rustling around in cotton bedding. And then I was laughing and stifling it, too. And then it got very, very peaceful.

"Tomorrow night we're going to have a proper bed in a proper hotel room," I whispered after everything had settled down.

"Sssh!"

"I'm whispering, for God's sake."

"You're too bloody loud!" she whispered back angrily. And then: *"Do you think anybody heard us?"*

"I doubt it. We were pretty damn quiet. Hell, we should get some kind of award for how quiet we were."

"You sounded like a bloody steam boiler exploding there at the end."

"I couldn't help it."

"Sssh!"

And it was right about then, as we were whispering back and forth and she was shushing me repeatedly for making too much noise, that a motorcycle puttered its way into the parking area outside. Judging from the throb of the engine, it was a BMW flat twin. Then it switched off, and we heard voices and laughing. It was hard to make out, but it sounded like German. Or maybe it was Polish. Or Czech. All we knew for sure was that it wasn't English, was generally unintelligible and no question they'd been off drinking and having a lot of fun somewhere. Then a side door banged and the motorcycle couple clomped into the hallway and into one of the guest rooms. They were both wearing bike boots, and they were both pretty beefy. One by one they used the bathroom at the end of the hall, and you could tell by the sounds that they'd probably had themselves a big, greasy dinner with lots of sausage and red cabbage and beer.

Geez, they were loud.

But that was nothing compared to about fifteen minutes later, when they started screwing. They were panting and gasping and grunting like pigs and making the damn bedsprings squeak like mice in a vise and banging the damn headboard against the wall something awful! *"It's like a damn earthquake!"* I whispered to Audrey.

But we were both kind of laughing.

The noise built to a mighty but early conclusion—thank goodness!—and then there were a few more grunts and groans, some muffled gibberish and then, within moments, the snoring that went on all night. Or I assume it went on all night, since it was still going on when Audrey and I finally fell asleep.

Come morning, when the other guests and the campers from outside started coming in for their coffee and breakfast rolls, it was like they'd all heard it, too. Hell, you'd have to be deaf not to. And, judging by the looks and odd glances they flashed, they thought it was *us* making all that noise. Only there was no polite way to tell them: *"No, we were the ones fucking very quietly and demurely here on the couch. It was the German or Czech or whatever couple down the hall going at it like a pair of rampaging rhinoceroses."*

We were out the door and down the road pretty quickly, as I recall.

Audrey made good on her threat to take the wheel that morning, and she was absolutely right about her driving. She was sharp, relaxed and confident, maintained a good pace and watched all the signs, driveways and side roads just as I would have. She was excellent on the run through the mountains and more than up to the swarm of typically mad and aggressive Italian drivers as we descended into Italy. We passed through a short, isolated thunderstorm—one of those light, lush summer rains where you can smell all the crop fields and greenery—and it was actually kind of nice to be in the passenger seat for a change, watching the cars and the clouds and the rain and the scenery rolling by. Especially when the sun broke through and made a vivid double rainbow on the opposite horizon. To be honest, it felt like a pretty damn special time to be alive.

The weather brightened up considerably as we traveled south on the autostrada towards Milan, and Audrey did a fine job in spite of the busy and highly competitive Italian traffic. She gave as good as she got, passing farm trucks and tourist buses and the usual legion of Fiat 500s and 600s, but Lord Chamberlain had to give way to the Alfas and Lancias, the hurtling, light-flashing Mercedes sedans with mostly Swiss or German plates and the occasional Ferraris and Maseratis that flew past in a howling blur on their way to Modena. Not to mention the crazy Italian motorcyclists crouched down tight on their café-racer Ducatis, Parillas and MV Agustas with loud pipes, hard solo seats and clip-on bars, the more sedate tourers in leathers and helmets running close to our pace on their BMWs and Moto Guzzis and all the straining, wound-out Vespa and Lambretta motor scooters in the hands of their thoroughly oblivious and occasionally suicidal *pilotos.*

You had to love Italy. It was so vibrant and alive that it made the rest of Europe look like it was half asleep.

Out of boredom, we started playing stupid word games like you do when you're traveling with kids, and we both really liked 'Who Am I?', where you pretend to become some famous person from history or politics or religion or sports or the entertainment world or even fictional characters from books or movies or mythology or Norse legends or whatever, and then the other person asks yes/no questions until they either get it or give up. I had her going for awhile on Tarzan and Flash Gordon, and she had absolutely no idea who Barney Oldfield was. But she stumped me completely with the last Czar's star-crossed youngest daughter Anastasia (even though I'd seen the movie with Ingrid Bergman and Yul Brynner) and also Josephine Baker and Madame Curie. But Audrey played that game regularly with the kids she tutored, so I decided she was really a bit of a ringer. Plus it wasn't really fair of her to keep springing women on me.

We arrived at Modena in the heat of the early afternoon and checked into the Real Fini for a quick freshen-up before heading over to Maranello for our 4pm interview with Enzo Ferrari. And I've got to say we were both pretty nervous about it. He was famous for being distant, intimidating and imperious, and it didn't help that we were going there under essentially false pretenses. But Audrey put on that same, pretty sun dress she'd worn at Sebring—the one with the bright flower print and the somewhat revealing, square-cut neckline—and I was pretty sure he would like that a lot. I know I did. Meanwhile I shaved and put on my pressed shirt, business jacket and tie and we headed over before three so as to arrive at those famous red brick walls on the Abetone road well before our assigned interview time.

It was a bright, hot and sunny August afternoon and we were both sweating a little and nervous as hell, and the guard at the front gate made it even worse when he looked Lord Chamberlain over—I suppose we really should have washed him after the rain on the trip down—and asked us rather pointedly in Italian to leave him parked on the street outside. In spite of myself, I was beginning to develop a soft spot for that car, and really hoped that his feelings weren't hurt.

We were both feeling pretty well intimidated by the time we walked through the front gate. Being at Ferrari did that to you. There was an almost religious sense of awe about the place that you just couldn't ignore. "It feels like the bloody Vatican," Audrey whispered as we made our way across the courtyard. It was vacation, so there were only a few muffled sounds of compressors pumping and lathes spinning and mechanical clunking and whirring coming from behind the hallowed factory walls where Mr.

Ferrari's boulevard-bound chassis and drivelines came together. They were perceived as the world's ultimate sports and GT cars, and most experts agreed that they were.

We were scheduled to meet first with the assistant to Ferrari's interim personal secretary with whom I'd spoken on the phone, and along the way I explained that race-team manager Romolo Tavoni had served as Ferrari's right-hand man for many years—even though their differences of opinion and fights were downright legendary—but Tavoni had left with Chiti and the rest in the "defection of the brains" the previous November, so things were a bit up in the air on the administrative and management sides at Ferrari. Not that you ever would have known it. All appeared to be under perfect, measured control at the Ferrari factory. Just like always.

The English-speaking assistant looked almost exactly as I'd imagined her: trim, tall and severe and just a little bit haughty. She was dressed in an ivory silk blouse and tailored skirt and wore her hair pulled back from her face and a pair of designer bifocals dangled from a slender silver chain around her neck. She looked like a more stylish, sophisticated and cosmopolitan version of Karen Sabelle. "So nice to finally meet you," she said as she gave us a dismissive once-over. "Please follow me."

She led us into a long brick hallway with tall, cathedral-like windows along one wall and smaller windows looking out into Ferrari's famous customer race shop on the opposite side. "Is that the race shop?" Audrey asked in a hushed whisper.

"No, it's behind the next wall. This shop is where privately owned Ferrari racecars come in for repair, updating and service." And then I explained that Ferrari liked having some of his competition cars and the work his people did on them on display—especially when prospective racing customers came through—but he wasn't about to put his latest Formula One or top-secret sports or GT models out where just anyone could see them. No, the *real* Scuderia Ferrari race shop was hidden away behind a low wall, so no one except the team mechanics, a few drivers and selected insiders ever got to see its contents. But there were lots of impressive cars in the customer shop—mostly older, V12 Testa Rossas and competition-spec Short Wheelbase Berlinettas plus two GTOs being readied for the Tourist Trophy race at Goodwood on August 18th—and I was surprised to see one of Count Volpi's Scuderia Serenissima cars in for service considering the well-publicized rift between old man Ferrari and our young yachting friend Count Giovanni. Rumor had it that the count had already pulled his financial backing from the A.T.S. venture that the Ferrari renegades had set up across town, but grudges and vendettas tend to last a long, long time in Italy.

We turned a corner into a narrower, darker hallway with the same tall exterior windows, only this time they faced another red brick wall so not much light came in. There were a few pictures and plaques and several nicely framed letters that came from people like the mayor of Modena and film director Roberto Rossellini and King Leopold III of Belgium (both well-known Ferrari owners and marque enthusiasts) and maybe even the Pope and Jesus Christ Himself. All we could hear was the staccato click of our heels on the bricks and the sound of our own breathing. At the end of that hall were a line of low leather chairs, and the assistant to Ferrari's interim private secretary halted us there, nodded for us to sit, smiled icily and clicked off down the hall. Audrey and I looked at each other. "It's a wee bit creepy, isn't it?" she whispered.

"Yes, it is," I whispered back.

"If the whole idea is to make you feel intrusive and insignificant, they've made quite a success of it."

"It's what they do."

We sat there for maybe twenty minutes—maybe more—before we heard another slower, heavier set of footsteps coming from around the corner. A short, bulky, middle-aged gentleman with thinning hair, a workman's hands, a bright yellow Ferrari knit shirt and a weary but engaging smile said *"He canna see you now"* in heavily accented English, and nodded for us to follow him. He took us a short ways down another hall and then through a set of French doors into a modest office with somber blue walls, a scant few books, folders and mementoes, a red leather desk set and small, perfect models of favorite Ferrari racecars in small glass display cases arranged around the room. On the wall across from the desk, lit by a single beam of light, was a portrait of Ferrari's dead son Alfredino—known as simply "Dino"—mounted in a heavy black frame. It was of course part of Ferrari's legend how much he doted on the child, and how he'd grieved—and continued to grieve—after his passing. Ferrari had sent him to the finest engineering and business schools in Europe to groom him as his successor. But the boy contracted a tragic, debilitating illness just as he was blossoming into manhood, and died a few years later in 1956 at the age of 24. Ferrari himself refused to talk about the circumstances of his son's death—it was far too painful for him—and most insiders thought he'd had muscular dystrophy complicated by nephritis. But others (like Eric Gibbon) enjoyed insinuating that young Dino's illness was somehow darker and more sinister. And that there was perhaps another, illegitimate Ferrari heir lurking within the factory's walls. But it didn't really matter. Dino was gone and his father's grief and sense of loss were both immense and inconsolable. He famously visited the cemetery to stand by Dino's graveside every single day, and helped spread and reinforce the story about how young Dino worked from his hospital bed to design (or, at the very least, help Vitorrio Jano design) the lightweight, V6 formula-two motor that ultimately evolved into an entire generation of championship-winning grand prix and sports car engines that ultimately bore his name. Dino's tragic and protracted death had a lot to do with the ominous darkness of Ferrari's personality and mystique, and that portrait across from Ferrari's desk—along with the knowledge of what it represented—put you on edge.

But then, it was supposed to…

Across from us sat the man himself: tall, grave, serious and imposing with graying hair and cold, suspicious eyes. He was looking through a leather dossier, frowning ominously, and it was anyone's guess if it was the latest drawings out of the drafting office or sales figures from the North American market or plans for re-tooling some part of the road-car manufacturing process or landscaping plans for one of his villas or smuggled-out transcript notes from the recent F.I.A. meetings on possible rulebook changes for the upcoming season. Or perhaps the menu specials from the Cavallino restaurant across the street where he took his lunch every day. But whatever it was, he was giving it his undivided attention, and didn't even seem to notice as we filed into his office and sat down in the leather chairs across from him. And right there you had a glimpse into the essence of Ferrari's power and presence. Hell, he *had* to notice when we were ushered into his office. And yet he pretended not to notice at all, just kept reading, concentrating and considering like there was no one else in the room. And you *believed* it, too. You sat there, waiting, ill at ease, unable to find a comfortable position and with your face hanging out like an overripe pear with a worm sticking out of it. And then you sat there some more while the worm raised up a bit, felt the chill, curled around and sucked back into its hole.

Ferrari finally looked up from his dossier. He wasn't wearing his trademark dark sunglasses, but you still couldn't read anything in his eyes. Nothing. He looked at us, first at Audrey, then to me, then back to Audrey, where his eyes lingered approvingly…like an aging lion might look at a fine young antelope with a broken leg. It was obvious he was waiting for one of us to say something, and it was *very* uncomfortable. I could actually hear my heart pumping inside my ears. I finally decided I had to say something: "On behalf of the magazine I'd like to thank you. It was very kind of you to grant us this interview."

Audrey translated into Italian. She had a beautiful voice. And Ferrari never took his eyes off of her.

Then it was quiet for what seemed like a very long time. And then he said something quite long in Italian and Audrey translated it back to me: "It is always my pleasure to speak to the press. I often dreamed of being a reporter myself when I was young. I have a great respect for it. So tell me—*prego*—what would you like to know?"

So I did my best to explain that almost all of the magazine and newspaper coverage on Ferrari dealt with either the exciting new road and racing cars or the race team and their successes at the racetrack, but no one had ever written about the *business* of Ferrari. How was it structured, how was it doing and was it as successful as the racing team?

Audrey translated, and the old man turned his eyes to me. They were like armor plate. "This is not something I can discuss in any depth with you," he answered in Italian, "because I have many covenants and restraints." I swear, he never even blinked. "But I can tell you that I do have a board of directors that I rely on—they're mostly Europeans and, of course, their identities must remain confidential for obvious reasons…"

"Oh, of course."

"…But they do understand and agree that the essence of Ferrari—not just the outward image, but the true value and soul of it—comes through our motor sports programs. Without our commitment to those programs, there would not be—there could not be—a Ferrari company or any Ferrari road cars."

"Some journalists have said that the Ferrari road-car program is only there to fund the racing."

Ferrari gave off a third of a shrug. "Does the dog wag its tail or does the tail wag the dog? Who knows? The two ends are inevitably connected."

When it came to being vague, this guy was a genuine master.

"But your sales numbers?" I asked, trying to sound businesslike. "Can you share them with us?"

"I'm afraid those numbers are also confidential. Besides, in business it is never a matter of how many of a thing you sell, but rather at what price."

I wasn't sure where to go from there, but there wasn't much doubt I'd been made to look pretty damn stupid. Only then Audrey said something all on her own in Italian, and Mr. Ferrari considered it carefully before favoring her with a thin smile and answering her back. I asked her what she'd asked him.

"I asked him if he was pleased with his margins and if the business was profitable, and he answered that you always want your margins to be better, but that he would no longer be able to continue in this office if the business weren't profitable."

Now it was my turn: "It's been rumored that you've reached out to other companies like Fiat—and even the Italian government—for help with your racing budgets."

His eyes swiveled over to me. "I've always remembered you as a motor sports journalist," he said evenly, "so you would know this already. Racing has always been expensive. It rides on the crest of technology, and that technology is forever changing and evolving. And one must keep up. We've come to a stage where keeping up—and keeping ahead of the opposition—has become a far more intense challenge. The science and resources required become more challenging every day. So it is hardly unreasonable for a small company like mine to seek assistance from those who also benefit from what we do and share in the glory and publicity of our successes."

"But have they come through for you?"

The corners of his mouth curled down into a frown. "I'm afraid they are by nature short-sighted. As they see it: why would a man pay for something he is already getting for free?"

"So what will you do?"

Ferrari shrugged. "I will continue on as I have always done. That is my plan." And then his lips slowly opened like theater curtains rising at an opera house and he favored Audrey with a smile. It was well known that Ferrari fancied himself as a ladies' man. There were well-circulated rumors of his dalliances, liaisons and affairs, and it was a matter of record that many of his drivers—usually the Italian ones—traveled to the races openly with women other than their wives. It was as much a part of the Ferrari legend as the ripping-silk howl of their engines. But even so, I didn't like the way he was looking at Audrey. Not one bit. But then he rotated his eyes back to me. "You might wish to go back to motor sports writing," he advised me in Italian. "I think it may be a more comfortable field for you. It has more substance and subtext and passion."

And that was undoubtedly true.

Then he gave Audrey another crocodile smile, rose from his chair, picked up his famous dark sunglasses from the edge of his desk, folded them into his breast pocket, walked past us, turned at the door, nodded a curt goodbye and disappeared down the hallway. The interview was obviously over. Why, it hadn't even been fifteen minutes! Audrey and I looked back and forth at each other. And then we just sat there for what seemed like an awfully long time. But then we heard another, even heavier set of footsteps approaching down the hallway. It was the short, bulky guy in the yellow knit shirt again. He had the hands of a shop mechanic.

"Hah!" he said through the same earnest, weary grin. "Ahm a-Guido, anna Ingegnere Ferrari wanna me show you aroun' ever'ting." Then he cocked his head for us to follow him.

And so we did.

It turned out that Guido Antonio Palducci was a very important man at Ferrari (and he was happy to tell us so!) because he—personally—was in charge of the transmission and driveline unit-room work in Ferrari's customer racing shop and as such had to not only take care of maintenance, repairs and rebuilding service for all the very latest Ferrari transmissions, transaxles and rear ends but also had to occasionally attend to the needs, whims and worries of the customers themselves. "At'sa why I gotta speaka English so good," he said proudly. "I live inna Buffalo for t'ree years widda my sister Philomena's family anna I work a-for Carlo Sebastian in Nueva York for a year, too." A mock shiver went through him. "Better back a-here inna Maranello."

Guido took us on a truly impressive tour of the entire Ferrari factory. He started with the customer race shop we had already seen through the windows. *"I'm a-no shoulda take you inside,"* Guido explained in a low, conspiratorial voice. *"But I'm a-like a-you, see, so I'm a-do it anyway."* And with that he opened a metal fire door and marched us grandly down the center aisle at a pace that made sure we wouldn't see much of anything that mattered. We visited his own small, tidy space with its jigs and pullers and bearing presses and hot-oil baths where the transmissions and rear ends came apart and went back together, and he even gave us a peek over the low wall that separated the factory race shop from the customer race shop. But the grand prix cars had already been loaded up and sent off to the Nurburgring and there was no activity at all going on around the sports cars. Then he took us back across to the dark brick corridor of business offices, followed by the bright, florescent-lit drafting offices, across the way to the hot, oppressive foundry building and the whirring machine shop with its smell of curling-hot metal and cutting oil—both about half empty since it was vacation time in Italy—and then on to the assembly floor where the road-car chassis and drivelines came together. Then out an overhead door to the transportation depot where completed chassis were shipped off to specialist *carrozzerria* to have their bodies put on and interiors installed (mostly to Pininfarina by then, but a few to Scaglietti, who also did the majority of the racing cars), the warehouse garage for finished cars ready to be road tested and sent on their way to dealers and the tile-floor customer-delivery area for those who arranged to pick their new Ferraris up at the factory. There was only one car on the floor, a gorgeous, dark metallic blue 400 Superamerica cabriolet waiting to be inspected by its American oilman owner before being shipped off to Texas. Guido couldn't tell me his name, but I was pretty sure it was probably John Mecom Jr. He'd bought a lot of Ferraris in the past few years—racecars, mostly—and he and his father had been regular visitors at the Ferrari factory. There were even some whispers about the Mecoms possibly buying into the business, but nobody put much credence into them.

And then Guido led us around a corner, along another brick wall, across a small strip of grass and through a portal in yet another brick wall to a small, metal fire door. *"It's been a-such a pleasure,"* he told us warmly, and bowed in Audrey's general direction. *"I'm a-enjoy myself a-so much!"* He undid the lock and opened the door for us. I'd gotten completely turned around while we were wandering through the maze of brick walls, long hallways, shops, shipping garages, warehouses and side rooms on our tour, and I was frankly amazed to see that we were right around the corner from the front entrance of the factory again, and I could see where Lord Chamberlain was parked outside the front entrance. *"I'm a-shu you canna finna you' way now,"* Guido nodded pleasantly. And with that, our tour guide and justly proud Ferrari driveline shop manager Guido Antonio Palducci gave us a warm smile, bid us a fond farewell and swung the steel fire door closed in our faces.

We looked back and forth at each other, not quite sure what had happened. And right on cue, we watched Enzo Ferrari and one of his lieutenants or bodyguards (wearing sunglasses and a suit much like his own, of course) emerge from the little *Il Cavallino* restaurant across the street. The lieutenant looked both ways twice while Ferrari worked away at a bit of chicken or veal with a toothpick. Then they crossed the street together—the lieutenant slightly ahead and continually looking both ways—passed through the entranceway and disappeared inside without so much as a glance or a wave. I mean, we were standing *right there,* for Christ's sake! There was no way in hell he could have missed us!

Chapter 15: A Brush with Hollywood

It wasn't even five when we got back to the hotel, and whom should we find in the bar there but our old friend Cal Carrington, looking trim and tanned and well-groomed in his usual, upper-crust prep-school early-evening outfit—pressed white button-collar shirt with the sleeves rolled up precisely two turns, light linen slacks, Bass Weejun penny loafers with matching belt but no socks, etc.—and he seemed glad and even relieved to see us. But it wasn't in his character to get excited or make a fuss…Cal was always far too cool for that.

"Hey, long time no see."

"Since Le Mans, wasn't it?" Audrey smiled as he leaned over and gave her a friendly peck on the cheek. To be honest, I didn't much care for that. But that was Cal, and you can't expect a leopard to change his spots, can you?

I told him he was looking good.

"Hey, it's all part of the deception," he grinned. And then his eyes went back and forth between Audrey and me. Then his eyebrows arched suggestively. "So have you two been an item since then?"

"Hardly!" Audrey laughed.

"And I've been stuck in Detroit until just a couple days ago."

"Detroit?" Cal scoffed. "That's like a damn death sentence."

"It's not so bad," I lied. "After all, we've got the Tigers."

"The *who?*"

"The Detroit Tigers."

"Didn't they used to be a baseball team?"

"That's them. But it's just about all they talk about at this country-western bar I go to."

"You go to a country-western bar?"

"I go with a friend from work. We go to hear the music and talk with the rabble."

"You go to hear country-western music?"

"It's good. Really it is…or some of it is, anyway. It's what the working class listens to."

"That's probably why I don't pay attention to it. I'm allergic to work."

"We go listen to rhythm-and-blues music sometimes, too."

"I don't pay much attention to that, either."

"Well, if you had a choice between that and the Detroit Tigers…"

"You're right. I'd probably take the music."

I looked him up and down again. "And how about you? I thought you'd dropped off the edge of the earth."

"Not quite. Only as far as California."

"What the hell were you doing in California?"

"Oh, there's a car somebody offered me to drive in the fall pro races. I went to take a look at it."

"You went to California in the middle of the European racing season?"

"Hey, when you don't have a ride, you're probably better off being remembered and thought about fondly from afar than moping around a damn paddock with your helmet bag in your hand."

That was true enough.

"So how was the car?"

"Not too awful. It's a Lotus 19 chassis that some genius is dropping a Buick aluminum V8 into."

"That could be good."

Cal gave a noncommittal shrug. "'Could' would be the operative word there."

"Look, I need to freshen up," Audrey broke in. "It's hot as blazes here in the summertime, and I feel like a wet sponge. Besides," she flashed us a wink, "who wants to listen to you two talk shop?"

"Go ahead. We'll have a drink and catch up while you do. And then maybe we can all go to dinner…" I flashed Cal a big, proud smile. *"I've* got an expense account."

Cal looked properly amazed.

"That sounds like fun," Audrey agreed.

"I dunno," Cal allowed. "I was kind of planning on heading out. I've already checked out of my room."

"You won't be hitting the road by the time I get done buying you drinks. Hell, you'll be lucky to make it up to your damn room."

"Speaking of which, we've also got a spare room," Audrey added. And the color started rising in her cheeks as soon as she'd said it. "Or, what I mean to say is that we have a second room that we most likely won't be requiring." She was somewhere between rose and crimson red by the end of her sentence.

Cal's face melted into an oily leer. "Oh, so *that's* the way it is."

I gave him a hard jab in the ribs. "Go to hell, Cal."

So Cal and I ordered ourselves a couple tall gin-and-tonics like we were proper Englishmen on holiday and brought each other up to date while Audrey went back to the room to do whatever it is women do when they go back to hotel rooms.

"So where did you go in California?" I asked, just to get things rolling.

"L.A."

"How was it?"

"Sunny. Hot. Smoggy. Hell, you should know…you grew up there."

"Yeah, but it's a fucking biblical paradise compared to Detroit."

"I'll drink to that."

And then something else occurred to me: Gina LaScala was based in L.A.

"You didn't by any chance drop in on a certain young Hollywood actress while you were out there?"

Cal stared down into his drink with his brow all knitted up, and I knew right away that he had.

"So how did it go?"

"It was okay," he answered without looking up.

"Just *'okay?'*"

"Okay, maybe a little bit better than just okay."

"That's good to hear."

"Yeah, I guess." He swirled the ice around in his glass. "Oh, the first two days were great. Better than great. But then she started shooting some comedy/mystery thing at Warner Brothers, so she was off to the studio before dawn every morning and she had to go over lines with her coach every night so we really didn't get to spend much time together. It was pretty shitty, actually. I finally gave up and went down to my folks' place in Florida for a week or so. Just hung around the pool like an asshole and didn't do much of anything…"

"So the spark's still there between you two?"

He gave an "I don't really give a shit" shrug that neither one of us much believed.

"And when she's done with this one, her agent's got another one lined up for her in London."

"Oh?"

"Yeah. It's some kind of spy movie. Big budget. Lots of special effects. I don't really know much about it."

"That'd be hell for convenient if you're racing over here."

"Yeah…" he agreed, and took a pull off his drink. "…*if.*"

"You got any prospects?"

"That's pretty much why I'm here."

"Oh?"

Turns out he'd come to Italy for a meeting with ex-Ferrari men Carlo Chiti and Romolo Tavoni over at the new ATS shop near Bologna.

"How'd it go?"

"Oh, it was great," he pretty much scoffed. "To hear them tell it, they've already got the fucking world championship by the tail."

"How's the car?"

"What car? It's all dreams and drawings right now. And they're spread way too thin. There's supposed to be a Formula One car and a mid-engined, V8 GT to compete with Ferrari's Berlinettas. Not too ambitious. And I think there may be money troubles, too. Everybody's heard that Count Volpi is already out of it as a backer, and it's hard to see how they're going to make it all come together."

"So it looks pretty bad?"

"Yeah, I guess. But the other side of the coin is that Chiti and Bizzarrini and Tavoni and the rest are nobody's fools. They're damn clever and they built a lot of front-running, championship-winning cars when they were working together at Ferrari."

"But can they do the same without the old man looking over their shoulders, pushing them and prodding them and encouraging them and insulting them and playing them off against one another?"

"That's the $64,000 question, isn't it?"

"Did they offer you the F1 drive?"

"Not in so many words. We talked about it and they said they were keen to do it. But I know they've been talking to Phil, too—it'd be great to be on a team with him again—and there's probably a lot of home-team sentiment to get one of their own Italian guys in there…"

"Anybody in particular?"

"Most likely Baghetti, but I think just about anybody whose name ends in a vowel would do."

I ordered us another round of drinks.

"You got any other prospects in the works?"

"Nah, not really. I went over to see DeTomaso's deal yesterday."

"The new F1 car?"

Cal gave me an eighth-inch nod.

"I saw a cutaway drawing of it in *Comp Press.*"

"How did it look?"

"Ambitious. And maybe a little clunky."

Cal took his hand off his glass and slowly rotated it into a thumbs-down position.

"How about the English teams?"

"I'm heading up there to nose around again after the grand prix this weekend, but you know as well as I do that all the plum seats are filled. I could probably pick up something with one of the privateers, but those guys usually want you to bring money."

"But you could do that, couldn't you?"

Cal flashed me an icy look. And of course he was right. People who actually have wealth—and especially if it's old, multi-generational family money—never want to discuss their financial situations in public. It's just not done. Only then he added: "And even if I could, those are mostly backmarkers and no-hopers—starting-money specials—and where would I go from there?"

"It's like Big Ed Baumstein always said about selling cars: *'you can always go down when you're negotiating, but once you go down, you can never go back up again.'*"

"True enough."

"Speaking of selling cars, guess who I saw in London a few days ago?"

Cal gave me a blank look.

"Tommy Edwards. He's selling racecars for Eric Broadley over at Lola."

"Oh? How's he doing at it?"

"As he put it, *'Well, at least I haven't got the sack yet.'*"

"Is he getting any driving in?"

"A little. Mostly club stuff and some national events in GTs and sedans. He got a pretty good result out of it at the Nurburgring…"

"Good for him."

"You could probably pick up as much of that sort of thing as you want."

"Yeah, maybe. I've got a drive lined up with Count Volpi's team for the Guards Trophy at Brands Hatch next Monday."

"That's damn nice of him. Which car?"

"I wanted the Testa Rossa, of course. But I think they're putting me in that hunchbacked Breadvan thing in the GT class."

"That's a pretty good car. Should be interesting."

"We'll see. But I'm not sure it'll do much for my future."

And that was true enough. Sought-after, top-line drivers had to wheel a lot of different cars—F1, F2, Juniors, sports cars, GTs, sedans, maybe even a crack at Indianapolis—but you really had to have a decent grand prix drive for people to take you seriously as a top-echelon driver. And it was an easy perch to fall from. Especially in the middle of the damn season when all the good factory seats were already under contract.

"And how about you?" Cal asked, as much to end the discussion about his own situation as anything else.

So I told him about my "consulting" deal with Fairway Motors and my stupid holding-pattern cubicle in Dick Flick's advertising department in Fairway Tower and, like him, how much I missed being on the circuit and being a part of it—even when it got ugly and terrible and miserable—and by then it was time for another drink. And it was probably that third drink that prompted me to tell him—in absolute, strictest confidence, of course—all about Fairway Motors upcoming cannonball-dive into the motorsports world and about the top-secret Ferret project and even about Carroll Shelby's Fairway-funded, back-door hybrid deal out in L.A. and how there might be some good opportunities coming up for a quick, good-looking young American driver with proven ability. And particularly if he had a little insider knowledge on the European racing scene in general and Scuderia Ferrari in particular…

"Tell me who to call."

"I will when the right time comes," I promised. "And in the meantime, next time you're out in L.A. sniffing around Gina LaScala, you should plan on dropping by Shelby's place in Venice. It's right near the beach."

He clinked our glasses together. "I'll make a point of it."

Cal knew all the good places in and around Modena and even spoke a little grotesque Italian (or that's what Audrey called it, anyway) thanks to his season on the Ferrari team. So he took us to a nice little restaurant just walking-distance away with a lovely back courtyard covered in vines and ivy and a sky full of stars. We had a really wonderful dinner with good wine and talked mostly about old times rather than the future, which was more comfortable for everybody. To be honest, the future was a topic Audrey and I had been pretty much avoiding ever since I'd picked her up in London. But we'd both been thinking about it. I could tell. And that just made us want to avoid it even more. After all, we were living an ocean apart and, although I was making a little money now, my situation at Fairway felt more like a short- or middle-term assignment rather than a permanent position, and my prospects beyond that wavered somewhere between bleak, vague and non-existent. Unless I decided to become one of the constantly buzzing copy drones in Dick Flick's 6th-floor advertising department. And who the hell wanted to live in Detroit anyway?

On her end, Audrey and her father had their small row house near Bromley and were apparently getting by for money, but surely no more than that. And her future was irrevocably intertwined with his on every possible level: economic, emotional, familial duty and responsibility, guilt…as Audrey herself would put it, she "ticked all the boxes" when it came to being hopelessly and irrevocably trapped. I know we'd both daydreamed about getting together on a more permanent and interdependent basis sometime in the future (I was afraid to put a simpler, more recognizable word on it for fear of scaring the shit out of both of us and maybe ruining what we already had), but the plain fact was that it didn't look possible. Or even practical. But that didn't keep me from thinking about it. And I had the feeling she was doing the same. We were like two young school kids skating around a hole in the ice, pretending it wasn't there.

So, in a way, it was good having Cal with us, because it helped keep everything light and fun. And that's why I didn't mind too much when Audrey asked Cal if he'd like to travel up to the Nurburgring with us. He'd said he had to be at Brands Hatch on Monday for the Guards Trophy race and he'd been planning to drop in on some team in Belgium along the way, but that part sounded pretty half-hearted. Mostly, I don't think he wanted to wind up skulking around the pits and paddock in Germany like a guy without a ride. But you could tell he didn't have much of anything better to do and that a large part of him really wanted to go.

"But what about my rental car?" he protested over dessert and coffee.

"We'll turn it in here and you can ride with us," Audrey assured him. "There'll be a penalty on the rental, of course, but it'll still likely be cheaper than keeping it through the weekend."

"But I haven't got a place to stay up at the 'Ring."

"We've got two rooms booked everywhere we go," I laughed. "Karen Sabelle insisted on it!"

Cal didn't have to think it over very long.

Back at our hotel, we saw Cal to his room—all three of us a little wobbly, I'm afraid—and then Audrey and I headed down the hall to our room, kind of leaning our shoulders into each other like a wandering teepee and not feeling any pain. I let her use the bathroom first and then it was my turn, and the amazing thing was how easy and natural and un-self-conscious it all felt. Although I'm sure the wine helped. But the point is that it seemed so magnificently and spectacularly *ordinary*. And naturally I had to mention it as soon as I switched off the light and got into bed next to her.

"You talk such rubbish sometimes," she scoffed as she nuzzled in next to me. "You know, you don't always have to go examining and explaining things all the time."

"But it's what I *do!*" I explained emphatically to her and the darkened ceiling with its ancient plaster moldings that you couldn't see in the dark and the little sliver of moonlight or street light or whatever coming in at the edge of the curtains. "I can't help it."

"Of course you can't," she agreed through a yawn. "Now why don't you put the great writer to bed and see if there's a great massage artist in your bag of personalities."

"Do you need a back rub?"

"That would be wonderful. My lower back and shoulders are absolutely killing me."

"I'm not sure how good I am at this," I told her. "I haven't had much practice."

"Well then, here's a chance to polish up on your technique."

"How should I start?"

"You didn't have to ask that when we had sex the other night."

"That part seems to come pretty naturally."

"Then just do what comes naturally here. I'm sure you'll figure it out."

So I started massaging her shoulders. And she was right: it did seem to come naturally. And so did her neck and the base of her skull. And her upper arms. And the low-country hollows on either side at the base of her spine. She was almost purring from it, for God's sake, and that can make you feel pretty damn special if you're the one making it happen.

As you can probably imagine, it just went on from there.

Come the morning, we woke up kind of wrapped up with each other and, wine hangovers aside, feeling totally relaxed and ever-so-slightly marvelous. Although it was hell's own job getting out of bed, and we'd probably still be there if it wasn't for our bladders. Not to mention check-out time and the journey ahead.

To be honest, I had mixed feelings about driving up to Germany and sharing our precious time together with Cal. But it turned out to be a good thing. At least if you discounted the fact that Cal was never in a hurry to do anything once he was out of a racing car. So we got started almost an hour late—all three of us feeling a little rocky—because we were late down from our rooms and Cal was even later. And then it got worse because the girl at the car-rental counter couldn't seem to wrap her brain around why Cal wanted to turn his car in here and now in Italy instead of three days later at the Brussels airport like it said on the contract. But Audrey got involved and there was a lot of posturing and gesturing and argumentative back-and-forth in the time-honored Italian style until Cal grew tired of it and just tossed her the keys, told Audrey to tell her it was parked outside and then added, in English, what she could do with those keys if she had a problem with it. And then he just turned us all around and escorted us out the door with the rental-car lady still yelling at our backsides. It was pretty funny, actually.

"Don't you worry about the charges?" Audrey asked him as we headed towards Lord Chambelain.

"My credit card people are used to dealing with shit like this. I mean, that's what they're there for, isn't it?"

Audrey and I looked at each other, both of us wondering what it must be like to live in Cal Carrington's world.

Naturally there was a brief confrontation once we got to the car as to who should drive and who would sit where, and of course Cal wanted to take the wheel because he'd get us there faster and we could neck or whatever in the back seat, and that of course got Audrey's hackles up a little and I argued that he wasn't listed on the paperwork and that I should drive and he countered that he (or his family) could cover it if he accidentally drove us off a cliff and we'd probably be dead anyway so what difference would it make? By that point Audrey was well past exasperated with both of us, and so she simply opened the driver's door, climbed behind the wheel and demanded the keys. And who in their right mind was going to argue with her?

So we headed north with Audrey driving and me next to her with the road map spread out on my lap and Cal kind of lounging across Lord Chamberlain's back seat more or less pouting. But at least he had the sense to stifle the impulse—and you could see he had plenty of them—to critique Audrey's driving. It helped that I was giving him the old snake eye every time he looked like he was about to do it.

There was a ton of vacation traffic on the Autostrada, but it was a fine August day and our hangovers faded to almost nothing by the time we reached Milan. After that, it was kind of fun. We were making reasonable time, and we introduced Cal to the 'Who Am I?' game, and it turned out the sonofabitch knew a hell of a lot about European history—Lord only knows where he picked it up, since you could tell he never paid much attention in school—and he damn near stumped us with medieval twice-king-of-England Ethelred the Unready (although Audrey finally got it), and had us going for quite a while with Wilbur and Orville Wright. But it was fun and helped the time go by. Oh, I didn't much like the way he'd get playful and flirty with Audrey now and then, but he couldn't really help himself. He was just being Cal, and Cal had always been sort of a charming cad by nature. Besides, he mentioned Gina once or twice, and it was pretty obvious that he was still carrying a torch for her (even if he tried to make it sound like it was no big deal to him one way or the other).

We wanted to make it to the tourist hotel we were booked into near the Nurburgring that night, since practice for the race was scheduled to start bright and early Friday morning. And it really shouldn't have been a problem. But then Cal took the wheel when we stopped for gas and a pee break just north of Lake Como, and "suggested" (insisted is more like it) that we should take a slight detour west near Andermatt so we could take the famous and scenic old Furka pass through the mountains.

"We really need to be getting along," Audrey told him with a schoolmistress edge in her voice.

"Hey," Cal argued, "what damn difference does it make if we get in at 11 or at midnight?"

"I have to be at the track early tomorrow."

"You'll be there!" Cal insisted. "And we really need to see this. Phil said it's absolutely spectacular. He said it was the first paved route ever over the Alps, and everybody says that the road and scenery are amazing. Besides, there's not supposed to be much except some tourist-trap town where they sell wood carvings on the other side, so the traffic should be a lot lighter."

I was about to take Audrey's side and argue with him, but by then he'd already signaled and made the left, so there was nothing Audrey and I could do but hang on, enjoy the scenery (it really was spectacular) and try not to lose our breakfasts while Cal put Lord Chamberlain's steering, brakes, shock absorbers and tire sidewalls through an extensive, even painful workout.

"This thing handles like a pregnant water buffalo," he laughed as he cranked on more and more steering lock through one tight, buttonhook mountain bend after another. The climb uphill wasn't too bad, as the steep grade, the car's weight and its dreary engine performance made it sag like a deflating balloon coming out of all the tight corners. But downhill was another matter entirely, as now the car's weight combined with an assist from old man gravity made it an exciting drive, indeed.

"I can smell the brakes," I advised as an acrid smell filtered through the interior.

"Of course you do," Cal grinned as he pumped the pedal to bring it up again. "That just tells you they're working hard."

"You'll lose that smile in a hurry if you boil the fluid."

"You'll lose yours even quicker when we go shooting off a cliff."

"I'll be yelling *I told you so!* all the way down."

"Then maybe I should turn on the radio to drown you out." He reached out for the radio knobs.

"You keep your fucking hands on the wheel!"

It was like baiting a damn crocodile, you know?

I looked into the back and there was a stoic but pale and queasy look on Audrey's face. "Hey, maybe you should ease off a little," I suggested as gently as I could.

"Hey, this is only six-tenths," Cal insisted.

Mind you, our tires were scrabbling at the gravel on the edge of the road coming out of some of those tight, buttonhook U-turns, and there wasn't much except thin air and a long, steep drop on the other side.

"Okay," he corrected himself, "maybe more like seven-tenths."

The thing that struck you, though—I mean besides the feeling that you were about to lose your stomach—was how smooth and unruffled Cal seemed even though he was pushing that clumsy Fairway Chancellor and its howling Dunlop Gold Seals to the very limit of what they could manage. He had a gift for driving, all right. There was a genuine joy in it, too. In fact, it was almost like a privilege watching him. At least if you could keep your food down.

I looked in the back again. Audrey was really very pale.

"You know, it's different when you're the guy behind the wheel," I reminded Cal.

"Don't I know it!" Cal more or less cackled, and threw Lord Chamberlain into yet another massive, tire-squealing drift.

But—fortunately—that was the last of the buttonhooks, and we came out at the bottom in a lovely, green valley with a view almost all the way to the lake. "I could use a bloody rest stop," Audrey advised us weakly from the back seat. She didn't sound particularly happy.

So we stopped at a little eatery and decided to have a late lunch while we were there, and it was hard to miss the elegant, silver-blue Bentley Continental S2 cabriolet with English number plates parked outside. "Wonder who belongs to that one?" I mumbled as we headed inside. It was early afternoon and off the beaten path a bit, so the place was pretty much empty except for two gentlemen—a bulky, Italian-American guy with a mane of longish, gray-tinged hair, big glasses and a streetwise, New York accent and manner sitting across from a more reedy and angular Brit with a slightly receding hairline. They were smoking and arguing with each other over coffee at one of the tables—but they were doing it in an animated, more or less friendly way—and both of them using their hands a lot. You couldn't miss that the Brit had a movie director's viewfinder hanging around his neck. He was smoking an English cigarette and holding it from underneath in the French way, while the Italian-looking guy had this long, dark cigarillo thing that he waved through the air like a baton whenever he was trying to make a point. Judging by the number of butts in their ashtray, they'd been there for quite a while.

Even though the place was empty, the waitress decided to put us at the table next to theirs. Maybe because we all spoke English? Or maybe because she'd just finished cleaning up from lunch and didn't want us to mess up another part of the room? But the point is we wound up next to them, and we couldn't help overhearing that they were arguing about some kind of film shot.

"You can't get all three levels in one bloody shot," the Brit with the director's viewfinder around his neck was arguing. "There's no bloody way, Cubby. The Rolls will be too far away to make out. You'll have to do it with layers and cutting."

The Italian-looking guy waved his cigarillo through the air: "But we don't want to lose all the scale and scenery here. That's the shit we came for!"

"We won't lose the scale and the scenery. We'll establish that part first. Then we'll cut from one level to the next to get it all in: the girl with the rifle and Bond with the Aston Martin and then on to the Rolls down below..."

"Excuse me," I couldn't help interrupting, "did you say Aston Martin?"

They both stared at me like I'd broken through a front door. But then the British one gave me an irritated smile. "Yes, we did," he admitted. "Why should that concern you?"

"It's not like it *concerns* me," I started in apologetically, and in about two minutes flat I'd brought them up-to-date on who we were and how I was a vagabond motorsports journalist and Audrey did timing and scoring for a team that actually ran an Aston Martin Zagato and how Cal was a bona fide racing driver with a rising star of a Hollywood actress starlet for a girlfriend. Maybe.

Their look of irritation faded to mild curiosity. And then the one with the graying mane of hair and the New York accent explained that they were out scouting locations for a movie.

Of course I wanted to know which one. And that's where the Italian guy's story started to get complicated. It seems this one was going to be the third picture in the series, and he'd originally wanted this guy—he gave a faint nod towards the guy across from him—to direct them all. But he'd had other commitments and couldn't do it, and so they'd brought in another guy to do the first two movies. And he did okay. The first one was already in the late stages of editing and on its way "into the can"—it was due for release in October in the UK and next spring in America—and the second one was already shooting in England. But now everyone's schedules had gotten straightened out and so the guy across from him was going to finally come on board to direct the third one. He said it all in such a way that you knew he thought a lot of the guy with the viewfinder around his neck.

"So we snuck away to get away from everybody a little and talk and maybe scout out a few locations," he grinned expansively. "Those are the two best times on a picture: scouting locations before you've made any mistakes or done anything stupid, and after it's in the can and on its way out to the distributors...when you can't do anything to make it worse!"

He said it in a way that made it sound like a lot of fun.

"That's quite a commitment," I observed. "You're already working on the third installment when the first one hasn't even come out yet?"

The big guy just smiled. So did his British pal, only not quite so confidently or convincingly."

"That sounds really interesting," Audrey offered. "Working in films, I mean."

"It's all an illusion..." the big guy explained, waving his cigarillo like a baton, "... just like it is in the movie theaters. It seems much more fascinating when you're sitting

The Los Angeles Times presents the 5th annual

GRAND PRIX

FOR SPORTS CARS

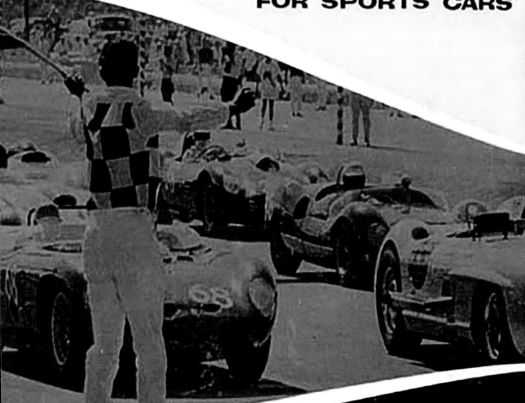

RIVERSIDE
INTERNATIONAL RACEWAY

FRIDAY · SATURDAY · SUNDAY   **OCTOBER 12·13·14, 1962**

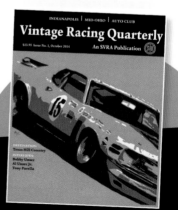

OUR WONDERFUL SPONSORS & SUPPORTERS!

Without you, none of this would be profitable...I mean, "possible."

Get Well Tony Adamowicz!
Alan Brody
Joe Alexander
Rob Alley
Jim & Patti Arnieri
Anatoly Arutunoff
Gord Ballentine
Bill & Sandra Barkley
John Barrett
Mike & Bev Belfer
William Borokhovich
The Bondon Family
Peter Bourassa
Ross Bremer & Karen Perrin
Del Bruce & his scotch
Jim Cantrell
Lee Chapman
Sir Winston Churchill
Randy Cook
David Cooper
Scott & Janet Cracraft
Joe Curto
Charles Darrow
Michael Delaney
Don Denomme
Bill & Shirley Dentinger
Bob DeShane
Bob Dillon
John Dohmen
John Doonan & Family
In Memory of Art Eastman
Bernard Ecclestone
Roy Fine
Lee A. Fischer
Rick & Karen Fiske

Ross Fossbender
Terry Fritz
FOT (Friends of Triumph)
Carl George
Glenda Gephardt
Richard Gustafson
J. C. Hassall
David "no-longer the Boy Wonder" Hinton
Bill Hollingsworth
Jan Hyde
Ed Hyman
Jamie Jackson
Ron Keck
Chris & Judy Kellner
Gordon King
Dan Kirby
Ernie Knight
In Memory of Charlie Kolb
Deb & Mike Korneli
Ken Kotyk
Diane & Ron Kramer
Rex & Bev LaBrie
Phil "Speedy" Lamont
Neil Lefley
Steve & Kevin Levy
Richard Liebhaber
Larry Ligas & Family
Bob Lucurell
Amy Markle
Chris Meyers
MG Vintage Racers
J.R. & Elaine Mitchell
Martin & Graham Nance
Gregory Nel
Robert M. Newman, Jr.

Marc Nichols
Rick Norris
David Oliver
John O'Malley
Rob Orander
Tony Parella
Jeff Palmer
In Memory of Bill Parish
Lou Pascuzzi
Spencer Pumpelly
James Redman
Francis Rivette
Kyle Rohde
James Rzegocki
Kevin Samp
Dennis Sbertoli
Jeremy Seiler
Lynn Serra
Tony, Janet, Lian & Maya Shoviak
Rich Sorensen
Dave Stall
Glenn Stephens
Steve & Sally Styers
Keith Tanner
Ed & Larry at the Two for the Road Garage
Tina Van Curren
Sue & Duck Waddle
Bill Warner
In memory of David Whiteside
Dede Whiteside
Miles "The Mensch" Whitlock
David Yando
Tod & Wendy Willson
David Yando

In memory of Henry Adamson, who truly was "the smartest guy in the room."

GORILLA CARS: As a driver, I'm generally associated with effete little sit-down-to-pee race cars from Europe, but, hey, I'm an American, and I love the big, muscle-bound power, urge and thunder of our homegrown iron as much as anybody. Especially when I get a chance to slide behind the wheel. Like at Road Atlanta a couple years back, when I lucked into a celebrity-guest drive with Lux Performance in the SRT Viper Pro Cup Series. Yep, that's a gorilla car, all right. Speaking of which, check out my "celebrity guest" team-mate: past NFL star and WWF wrestling champion GOLDBERG! He's a real "car guy," by the way...

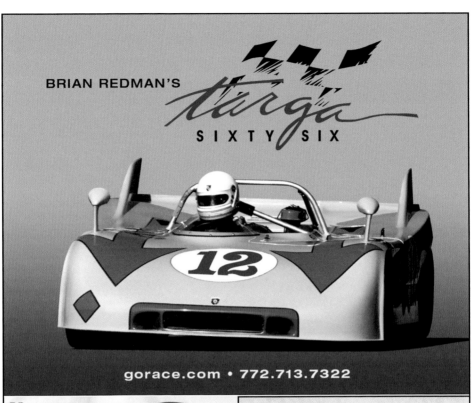

Steve Crowley sez: *"It's Spamtastic!"*

SPAM

Yeah, I've run a few Alfas...

7

I can't really say enough about this place, this concept or these people. It's much more than a car collection and much more than a museum. Miles Collier, Scott George and the entire staff are totally dedicated to improving, perpetuating and disseminating the craft, ideology, skills and science of significant automobile preservation and stewardship. They run a damn good racing team, too, and their intent is always to have their incredible racecars fully prepared and in race-ready condition, but also out on track at important events with genuine, world-class drivers behind the wheel so the enthusiast public can see and hear them doing what they were always meant to do. And, through their association with the unique Revs Program at Stanford University, The Revs Institute is helping pass on our shared interest, knowledge, history and passion to the next generation of automotive enthusiasts and professionals.

They have also kindly allowed me out on track—at speed!—in cars I never dreamed I'd ever get to drive. Thanks to all of you for everything you do!

Burt Levy

9

Where it all started for me: shitbox TR3s, The Midwestern Council, NSSCC and lifelong friends.

From a senior in a Junior to a Pro on the pole, there's a reason they're both on Dunlops.

For racers like us, Dunlop has the most complete line of vintage and historic racing tyres in North America. Authentic, proper and best of all, fun and safer to race on. Every tyre we make is closer to the original size, tread pattern and grip than most of our competitors tyres.

That means right, for _your_ car.

And for Modern Car Racers, Dunlop has a full line of radial racing slicks for formula, GT & sports cars.

110 years of race wins has taught us how to get you to the checker... fast and safely.

VINTAGE TYRES LIMITED

255 Southwest Cove Road, Hubbards, Nova Scotia B0J 1T0
Tel: (902) 228-2335
e-mail: vintyre@gmail.com

Vintage Tyres Limited is the distributor of Dunlop Racing Tires in North America and agent for Dunlop Classic Road Tires, MWS Wire Wheels, Weller and Panasport Racing Wheels.

DUNLOP www.racedunlop.com

In Canada: **BRITAIN WEST MOTORSPORT**
36 Godby Road, Brantford, ON N3T 5L5 • Tel: (519) 756-1610

In the U.S.A.: **SASCOSPORTS INC.**
1010 Ryan's Way, Alton, VA 24520 • Tel: (877) 377-7811 Fax: (434) 822-7300

ROGER KRAUS RACING
2896 Grove Way, Castro Valley, CA 94546 • Tel: (800) 510-7223 Fax: (510) 886-5605

"I was going 200mph!"

Traqmate GPS Verified
2 MPH Steamroller

Finzio's Store

Holiday Gift Catalog

It's July already. Why aren't you shopping yet?

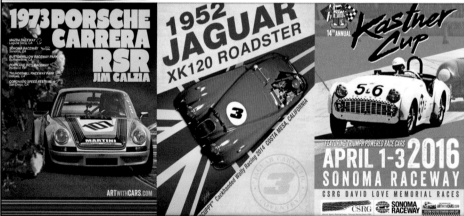
16

Nothing like that could ever happen in *real* racing...

Burt is often engaged to speak at various Club Banquets, Racing Dinners, Car Shows & other assorted enthusiast gatherings that can't afford to hire somebody famous...

Burt mouthing off as the after-dinner speaker at the VSCCA/VRG race at Thompson, CT, 6/20/15.

"THE MOST ENTERTAINING SPEAKER WE'VE EVER HAD!"
Glenda Gephardt, IMMRC

Burt explaining the difference between a Ferrari and a Porsche at the Amelia Island concours.

Burt talking with his hands at the International Motor Racing Research Center in Watkins Glen.

Finzio's Gas Station Prints by Art Eastman
Sweltering Summer Heat or Frigid Winter Cold
$20.00 each or both for $35.00*

Finzio's Gas Station Prints by the late, great Art Eastman

available exclusively from Finzio's Store on the website at
www.lastopenroad.com or call (708) 383-7203

*plus $6.50 per order for shipping & handling

20

21

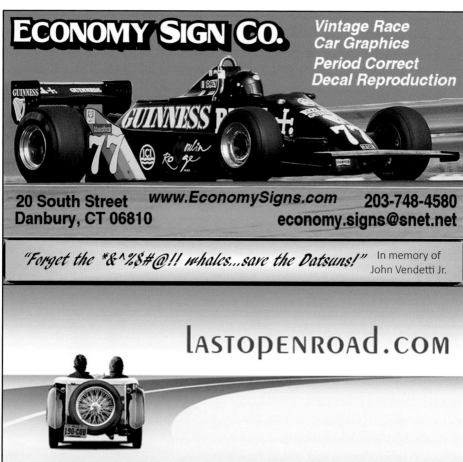

Burt doing his level best
to break some very nice cars!
Huge thanks to *ALL* the Bondons!

BURT...WE'VE SHARED SOME GREAT RIDES!

SPLINTER GROUP RACING TEAM

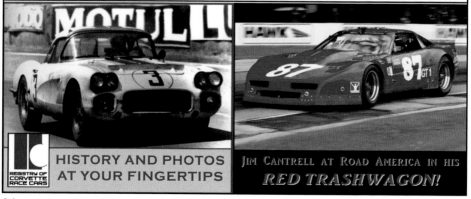

JIM CANTRELL AT ROAD AMERICA IN HIS
RED TRASHWAGON!

Sometimes racing drivers put towels over their heads so as not to be recognized when they're talking to Burt!

ZAPATA RACING
NASHVILLE, TN

1970 Triumph Spitfire Mk. III (V6 Conversion)
Ernie Knight

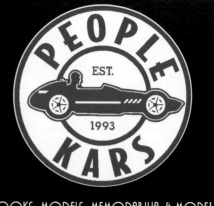

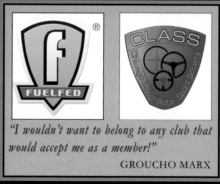

Two days before this book went to press, I was saddened by the news that my good friend, fellow racer and motorsports author Mike Argetsinger had passed away. I'd raced with Mike and against Mike, we shared some cars, became fast friends and once he and wife Lee even bailed me out of jail. Like everyone else in the motorsports community who knew him, I miss him greatly. Godspeed.

Mike wrote some amazingly accurate, detailed, wonderfully researched, utterly human and beautifully written and produced books about Walt Hansgen, Mark Donohue and the days of Formula One Grand Prix racing at Watkins Glen. And he knew those subjects intimately because he grew up with them as the backdrop of his life. They're still available from David Bull Publishing (www.bullpublishing.com) and I recommend them highly.

300,000 MILES. RUNS GREAT.
RACED ONLY ON WEEKENDS.

THIS '94 MIATA HAD 300,000 MILES ON IT BEFORE KENT PRATHER TURNED IT INTO A RACE CAR. FOR 10 YEARS IT SERVED HIM WELL, FINISHING EVERY SINGLE RACE AND WINNING FIVE NATIONAL CHAMPIONSHIPS TO BOOT. BUT THAT CAR IS FAR FROM FINISHED, BECAUSE IT'S STILL OUT RACING TODAY. THIS KIND OF RELIABILITY IS WHY ON ANY GIVEN WEEKEND, MORE MAZDAS ARE RACED THAN ANY OTHER CAR.

zoom-zoom

DRIVING MATTERS™ mazda

with your popcorn and soda watching the finished product than when you're on the inside actually trying to make the damn thing." He looked over at Audrey. "You know what my poppa used to say when we were poor stinking farmers on Long Island?"

Audrey shook her head.

"When the snow melts…" he waved his hand across so you could see a beautiful white carpet of snow, *"…you can see the dog shit!"*

We had a pretty good laugh off of that.

The British movie director extended his hand: "Hi. I'm Guy Hamilton. And this is Cubby Broccoli."

"But you never saw us here!" Cubby Broccoli laughed. "I'm supposed to be at Pinewood Studios in London right now!"

We said our hellos and jawed back and forth a little while the waitress brought our lunches, and the big guy was curious about exactly which Hollywood starlet our friend Cal was pursuing.

"I wouldn't exactly call it 'pursuing,'" Cal said defensively.

"Courting, then?"

"I wouldn't call it that, either."

"It's Gina LaScala," I interjected, "and let's just say they're 'involved.'" You could see her name registered with both of them. "Only it always seems like one wants to be more involved than the other."

"Oh, really?" the director asked. "Which one?"

"It goes back and forth," I pretty much laughed. "That's the sticky part."

You could tell he appreciated the plot possibilities.

The scowl on Cal's face told me he didn't much appreciate any of this, so I quickly changed the subject by asking Guy Hamilton about his film credits. It turned out that he'd worked as an assistant director under Carol Reed on one of my very favorite movies of all time, *The Third Man,* with Orson Welles and Joseph Cotton and a great plot and dark, moody black-and-white cinematography of bombed-out Vienna and this haunting zither music that you couldn't get out of your head. Turned out that Audrey loved it, too (but of course she would!). Based on that, I assured him that we'd surely go see this new movie they were working on whenever it was done.

"I'm hoping they're all going to be huge hits," Cubby grinned. "But you never know in this business. Often as not the cream sinks and the crap rises to the top. It's just the way it is when you're dealing with critics and the public. But if we hit it just right and get a little lucky with the press, and the audiences like it…" he let his voice trail off and the room got very, very quiet.

"You haven't said what they're about," Audrey ventured to break the silence.

Cubby looked at her for a moment—not like he was trying to hide anything but just trying to build up the suspense a little—and then he leaned over closer to our table and let his voice go down to a husky stage whisper: "You know the James Bond books?"

"The spy novels?" Audrey asked.

The big guy nodded solemnly.

And of course we'd all heard of them, even though none of us had actually read one. We were all kind of embarrassed to admit it. "But Georgie Smales reads them constantly," Audrey added emphatically. "Reads them in the transporter when they're traveling and in his room at the races. He can't get enough of them."

"They're popular, all right," Cubby Broccoli allowed. "And we're hoping they'll be-come even more popular." He looked across at Guy Hamilton. "I keep telling Guy and everybody else that we've got a tiger by the tail on this one. All we need is for all the million little pieces to fall neatly into place…"

The waitress brought us our coffee and dessert, and we lingered over them to talk some more about the movies and the movie business: what we liked, what we didn't like, what certain notorious actors and actresses were really like off the screen—all the scandal magazine stuff!—and we could have easily gone on like that all afternoon. It was such good fun. And a little bit sad, too. And that's where I tossed in one of my very favorite two-cents-worth opinions: "You really don't want to know too much about the personal lives or feet-of-clay weaknesses of your heroes and heroines. Not in history, not in politics, not in the arts, not in sports and most definitely not in the movies. It just messes up your ability to appreciate them when they're up on the screen doing what you love them for."

Everybody at both tables seemed to agree.

Only now it was time for Audrey to bring us back to reality. "It's been truly fascinating meeting you both," she said gently but firmly, "but we've really got to be getting on the road. We have an awful lot of distance to cover before we find our way to our beds tonight." And of course she was right.

So we made our goodbyes and shook hands all around. And then one more thing occurred to me: "You know, you said there were going to be three levels in that shot you were talking about, right?"

The question caught them off guard, but then they both nodded.

"And you've got the Rolls-Royce down below and the Aston Martin in the middle…"

They nodded again

"…so what kind of car's going to be on top?"

"We haven't quite figured that out yet," Guy Hamilton shrugged. "We were thinking of perhaps an MG or a Triumph, but they don't really fit properly…"

"…and there's probably not much money in it from those guys!" Cubby interjected with a laugh.

"…You need to understand that the young girl who drives it is young, athletic, determined, committed and independent. She's self-directed and very much on a mission…we're just not sure what sort of car might be right for her yet."

I took out one of my fake business-magazine cards and scrawled Dick Flick's name and direct number on the back. "Give this guy a call. I'll tell him what you're up to when I get back to Detroit. If the timing works out, I think he's going to have exactly what you're looking for. And they'll probably be willing to throw in a very large sack of gold for the privilege."

You could tell Cubby Broccoli liked the sound of that!

Chapter 16: Hurried, Heavenly, Horrid and Heroic

It was a hell of a slog up to the Nurburgring after Cal's impromptu detour through the Furka Pass and our unexpected (albeit highly entertaining) late-lunch visit with Guy Hamilton and Cubby Broccoli, and we didn't reach our hotel near Adenau until well after midnight. I took the first stint with Audrey sitting next to me with the map on her lap, but I could feel Cal's eyes right behind me, watching and critiquing my every move and muttering under his breath now and then whenever I wasn't going fast enough or missed a passing opportunity out of sheer cowardice (or good judgment, take your pick). To be honest, it was more nerve-wracking than riding with him. There was no way around it, he *was* the better driver and he would get us there a lot quicker. So we swapped around on a late-afternoon pee-and-coffee stop (tea for Audrey, of course) around dusk and Cal took over. There wasn't much navigating to do since it was all A3 Autobahn and Cal had been up that way before, so I got in back with Audrey and we did our best to kind of snuggle together and try to get some sleep. But there's just no way you can relax when you've got somebody like Cal behind the wheel trying to make time. He had the gas pedal flat-to-the-floorboards floored the whole way. So we just nuzzled against each other on Lord Chamberlain's thin leather upholstery and listened to the wind noise and the straining, granular hum of that poor old 6-cylinder truck engine up front and felt the occasional, abrupt, sphincter-tightening shift of equilibrium when Cal made an aggressive passing maneuver or had to take evasive action when some poor soul didn't realize he was up against an out-of-work grand prix driver. You could hear him muttering curses under his breath whenever that happened, because it broke his rhythm. It was just enough to keep us on edge, even with our eyes closed, and by the time we got to the hotel, all three of us were feeling sullen, cranky and annoyed. But that's the way it always seems to go on long road trips. Like my real dad used to say way back when on family vacations to California state parks that I could barely remember: *"Hey, Hank, even in heaven they don't sing all the time…"*

It was about all we could do to just check in—with Audrey handling the translating, of course—and lug our bags up to our rooms. It was an old German place that dated back to who-knows-when and was maybe a little faded and musty, but it was scrupulously clean and with nice, soft feather beds and decent plumbing. I half-heartedly tried massaging Audrey's back and shoulders again once we got under the covers, but she just groaned and made it quite obvious that she wanted no part of it. Or me, for that matter. Or anything else but a good night's sleep. And I could understand that, because I was asleep myself almost before I knew it.

We woke up feeling rested and refreshed after a solid night's sleep, and the morning looked fine and bright outside our window. You could see the low, lush mountains all around us and hear birds in the trees and smell the crisp scent of the forest mixed up with the smell of breakfast rolls baking in an oven somewhere. That smell reminded me crappy little flat in London, only the surroundings were much, much nicer. We were both awake but hadn't said anything—just kind of lying there, you know—and the hard part was trying to get ourselves up out of bed. Or it was more like the hard part trying to keep us in bed, if you catch my drift.

"You'll just have to save that bit for later on tonight," Audrey scolded while I tried to hang onto her arm and keep her from getting up. "I've got to be at the track, and I'd just as soon not be used as a convenient repository beforehand."

"It's not like that at all," I lied as she pulled away from me, but of course that was the little head doing the talking. I made one final, half-hearted lunge at her as she rolled off the sheet and stood up, and naturally I missed her completely and banged my forehead smartly against the corner of the nightstand. It was just stupid and clumsy and not really serious, and it made us both laugh like an old Charlie Chaplin movie.

"You see what you get?" she snorted as she walked into the bathroom.

Damn, it was great being with her.

Then she asked if I could perhaps go downstairs and get her a cup of tea. And I told her I would, as soon as the swelling went down.

"Your forehead?"

"No, the other thing."

"Oh."

So a few minutes later, I threw on some pants and went down to get coffee for me and tea for her, and of course the dining room was full of racing people talking over their breakfasts and getting ready to head to the track. I recognized a lot of them— some of the mechanics from the Filipinetti team and a PR guy from Ferodo and a French photographer I knew and two German spark-plug-and-ignition technicians from Bosch wearing company shirts—and I was really starting to get that old buzz in my gut from being at an actual grand prix again. It seemed impossible, but I hadn't been to one all season—not *one!*—and there was always so much going on and so many things to see and talk about and so much wonderful gossip. Like I heard the Ferodo guy and the Bosch guys in deep conversation about the hot new rumor that Honda— yes, *Honda!*—was building a grand prix car for next season! Wow! There had never been a Japanese team in Formula One and they'd have an awful lot to learn, but you had to take a company like Honda seriously. They'd come out of nowhere to take on the established European teams in motorcycle racing, and the previous year they'd taken both the 125cc and 250cc world championships with Tom Phillips and Mike Hailwood. That was pretty damn impressive. According to my scribe friends on the bike side, Honda had top-down commitment to their racing programs, excellent design and engineering talent, a willingness to learn and a unique and genuine humility. That, more than anything, might make them a force to reckon with in Formula One. It was just about killing me that I wasn't covering it for the magazine! And that put me in somewhat the same boat as Cal, who was late coming down again and looked pretty damn grim. Audrey and I did our best to cheer him up, but you pick up on it pretty quickly when even your best efforts are simply bouncing off and rolling away.

The schedule had practices for the support races first—GT cars and sedans and even one for go-karts—and that gave me time to stop in at the press room and try to catch up on things. Fortunately the track press relations guy remembered my face and didn't even ask to see my credential, and it was great to see all my friends and colleagues and compatriots like Hal Crockett and Vinci Pittacora and Denis Jenkinson and Bernard Cahier and Henry N. Manney again. Less so Eric Gibbon, who made a point of pretending to look the other way, then came at me directly when that started to feel uncomfortable and asked me point-blank, in a typically snide and abrasive voice, just whom I might be writing for these days? He made sure he was loud enough for the press relations guy to hear. But I just ignored the sonofabitch and so did the track press guy, and that was more than a little satisfying.

But I was eager to see what was going on outside, so I spent the next hour or so wandering around the paddock. So much had changed since last season! It was my first time seeing the new Lotus 25 in the flesh, and it was so slender and small and sleek and elegant that you couldn't escape thinking it looked brilliant. Although perhaps a little delicate. And no way could a driver much taller or wider than Jimmy Clark—Dan Gurney, for example—even dream of fitting himself inside. The Lola and BRM were about tied for second place in the "looks like the class of the field" sweepstakes (at least to my eyes) while the Coopers were just that little bit stouter and clunkier by comparison. Twice world champ Jack Brabham had brought out his own eponymous grand prix car for its maiden outing, and the Brabham/Ron Tauranac design looked very neat, tidy, straightforward and sharp in its bright turquoise livery with a gold scallop around the nose. But they were still thrashing on it like mad to get it ready, and you could see they were never going to make first practice.

The Porsche 804s looked odd to me in that cold, mechanical German way, what with kind of a stocky build (at least compared to the best of the British cars), exposed horizontal cooling fans over their flat-8 motors and singularly blunt front ends. But you knew they were well-engineered and meticulously screwed together, and that they'd probably be running as strong at the end of a race as they were at the beginning. And that counted for a lot in any sort of race. You couldn't miss the big, empty space in the paddock where the Ferrari transporter should have been, and that seemed curious to me since I knew they'd left Maranello several hours before we did. Hmm.

The German Grand Prix had attracted an unusually large group of independents and privateer entries with older cars—some still running the old, 4-cylinder Climax motors from last year—plus the brand new and quite handsome Gilby BRM, which was more or less what we'd call a "backyard special" back in America and of which not much was expected. But they all flocked to the Nurburgring because the organizers were generous with their starting money—even for the little, no-hoper teams—because you needed a lot of cars to make a decent spectator show at a track the size of the Nurburgring.

You have to understand that the Nurburgring represents a unique proposition in the world of motorsports. For drivers and fans alike. It's all beautiful, deep-green countryside full of lush, dense forests and occasional, rolling meadows like an immense foliage carpet over the hillsides of the Eifel Mountains. Simply beautiful! The Southcurve U-turn around the pits and the start/finish line sit on a high plateau (just over 2000 feet), with the crumbling ruins of a gaunt medieval castle up on a hill just a stone's throw from the circuit. Nurburg Castle gives the place a unique sense of history, majesty and wonder. But the track itself is diabolical: a hedge-lined, 14-mile blacksnake that curls and twists as it plummets steeply downhill a full thousand feet (!!!) to the low point at Breidscheid, then climbs and claws its way back up again through more twists, turns, humps, jumps, odd cambers and unsettling pavement irregularities back to the start/finish line. It's a difficult place to even remember in proper sequence, let alone dream of mastering.

Because of its size, you couldn't really hike around the circuit from one vantage point to another. It was simply too big. So you had to pick the general area where you wanted to watch and be content with that. And that's precisely what Cal and I decided to do— as much to get away from all the people he knew in the paddock as anything else—and so we borrowed a motorbike from someone he knew and headed up to the fairly flat, flowing ess leading to the deceptive left at Hatzenbach to watch first practice. Thanks to the circuit's length, we'd only get to see the cars every 9 minutes or so, which meant there was a lot of waiting and anticipating and you had no idea what was going on the rest of the way around or whether missing cars had gone off into the hedge rows or simply stopped at the pits. To be honest, it made you wonder why so many spectators turned out to watch from the fences. But the Germans love their motor sport, and the crowd around us—many of them camping there for the whole weekend—waved and cheered wildly every time Gurney or Bonnier came by in their Porsches. They both seemed to be going really well, but Porsche had been testing extensively at the Nurburgring, so their drivers had more familiarity with the place and the confidence that generally comes with it. And confidence is everything in a racing car.

We moved on from Hatzenbach to the famous blind crest at Flugplatz ("flying place") for a while, and it was thrilling and even frightening to see cars launch over the top with all four wheels in the air and then come down like shrieking ski-jumpers further down the road. It always gave me chills when a car came off not quite level or square to the road and landed all catty wumpus, but Cal watched it like a damn judge holding up scoring cards at a high-diving contest. He never so much as flinched. But I guess that's the difference between doing things and writing about them.

We rode the motorbike back to the paddock after practice, and by then the Ferrari transporter had finally arrived and unloaded. And there was quite a surprise in store! Ferrari rolled out a brand-new, lower-slung "English-style" 156 with a lighter, skinnier frame, revised suspension, a far more reclined driving position and an "English" nose without the split front nostrils that had been the trademark of Ferrari grand prix cars since the new formula was introduced. Then again, the "shark nose" was always identified with engineering director Carlo Chiti and racing manager Romolo Tavoni, who were among the renegade defectors (or fired employees, depending on who was telling the story) who left Ferrari the previous November. So no question a change was coming. Phil Hill was supposed to drive the new car, but they'd stopped for a quick shakedown test at the Modena Autodromo on their way (that explained why they'd arrived so late), and Phil found the handling unsorted and seating position impossible because he kept slipping down into the cockpit. So he elected to drive his Aintree car with the latest, 120-degree V6 (and which, unlike the others, had its transmission mounted ahead of the rear axle and the clutch hung out behind) and the new one was given to Bandini, who didn't like it much either. There was a freshened-up 120-degree V6 for Baghetti and one of last year's cars with the older-spec, 65-degree V6 for young Ricardo Rodriguez, who surely must have felt slighted and was out to show everyone—and particularly the old man back in Maranello and team manager Dragoni—what he thought of it!

You could always count on plenty of drama, emotion and politics at Ferrari, even when the cars weren't genuine front-runners.

Things started to come into clearer focus during the afternoon session. Phil Hill had wowed everyone the previous year by being the first man ever to lap the Ring in under 9 minutes (8:55.2) but this went by the boards pretty quickly, and you couldn't miss all the cars coming in and out of the pits to have shocks stiffened or softened, springs re-set or ride heights adjusted to keep them from crashing down *hard!* into the pavement after some of the more hair-raising jumps. I was glad to see Gurney, Graham Hill, Clark and Surtees going well and topping the time sheets in that order, but there was a very scary (and arguably avoidable) moment towards the end of the session that caused quite an up-roar. De Beaufort's older, privateer Porsche (one of the stubby, fat-looking ones with a 4-cylinder engine) had been fitted with a movie camera to take some on-car footage for

German television, and the damn mount broke and the thing fell off in the middle of the fast, steeply downhill Fuchsrohre section. You couldn't see it from the other side of the rise and moments later Graham Hill arrived, doing something like 140, only to find this large, heavy object sitting in the middle of the road! There was no way in hell he could avoid it. The impact ripped off the BRM's oil radiator and feed lines—liberally oiling the track—and the car pinwheeled instantly and spun into the hedges, ripping off the right-rear wheel and suspension in the process. Hill was incredibly lucky, and wound up with nothing worse than bumps and bruises and a torn-up racecar. But he was badly shaken. Fortunately for the team, he'd been in the training car and not his actual racecar.

And the mayhem wasn't over.

Bruce McLaren in the works Cooper was next on the scene, but he saw the dust and bits of shrubbery flying as he came over the crest and slowed right down. He would have stopped to check on the driver, as the corner stations are generally quite a distance apart at the Nurburgring, but Graham waved that he was all right and so McLaren continued on. Not so lucky was his teammate Tony Maggs in the second works Cooper, who came over the top after the dust and debris had settled and had no visual clue that anything was amiss. He hit the BRM's oil at full speed and spun hard into the bushes and fencing. But he, too, escaped with nothing worse than bumps and bruises and a pair of large, vibrating eyeballs. His car, however, kept the team mechanics busy all night and into the following day rebuilding it for the race.

As you can imagine, there was a huge brouhaha afterwards with lots of angry voices, shaken fists and finger-pointing, and the wisdom of mounting television cameras during regular race-weekend practice and qualifying sessions was surely a major topic at the Grand Prix Drivers Association meeting in the paddock the following afternoon. Not that you could get that bunch to ever agree on a unified course of action…

We went back to our hotel after practice and enjoyed a nice dinner with Cal and some friends, and then they went into the bar and Audrey and I went outside for a walk. It felt like a front might be coming through as there was a chill in the air even though it was August, but Audrey had a light sweater and I had my arm around her and you could hear the chatter and jabber of race fans and racers and hangers-on coming out of lighted windows and doorways all through town. We walked for quite a long time that night, not saying much of anything except dumb small talk, and then we went back to the room and curled up in that soft featherbed with each other and, well, this is one of those blank spots you'll just have to fill in for yourself.

But it was pretty damn good.

"That was really kind of special," I whispered to her afterwards.

"Just kind of?"

"Well, more than kind of."

"You really don't know when to bloody well keep quiet, do you?"

I shrugged against the pillow. And then I leaned over and kissed her forehead and said, *"I love you,"* for maybe the first time ever. And I was glad that it didn't come out mushy or gushy or flowery or stupid or ridiculous, but just like a plain, clean fact.

And then I waited.

But Audrey didn't say anything.

I finally got sick of waiting. *"Hey, aren't you supposed to say it back to me?"*

"Oh? Is that how it works?"

She was screwing with me. I could feel her eyes dancing, even in the dark.

"I'm pretty sure that's the way it's supposed to work," I deadpanned back at her.

"And how would you know?"

"I wouldn't. At least not personally. But I've read a few books and I watch a lot of movies."

"So it's really all fiction and hearsay, isn't it?" And then she goosed me under the covers. Right out of nowhere. And then we kissed and kissed some more and did it all over again. Even better. And the best part about it was that I seemed able to make her feel good, too. Better than good, even. Not that it's any of your damn business.

I laid awake for awhile after Audrey drifted off to sleep, just lying there in the darkness with my arm around her shoulders feeling a million miles away from everything. Just floating, you know? And then I started listening in on some English race fans drinking beer in a circle of coolers and upturned buckets and folding chairs next to their camping trailer in the parking lot outside. They were talking mostly about the BRM chassis and engine versus the Lotus chassis with its Coventry-Climax V8, and Hill (their dapper and mustachioed Graham, not our American Phil, of course) versus

Jimmy Clark as drivers. The general consensus was that Graham was the surer, steadier, more workmanlike hand, while Clark was the more fluid and naturally gifted, and I was pleased to hear a passing mention of Surtees and the Bowmaker Lola as a legitimate contender in that company. Conspicuously missing was any talk of Gurney and the Porsche 804 (except for one wag's opinion that they'd only lucked into the win at Rouen because all the best—read "British"—cars had broken or been slowed by problems) and nothing at all about Ferrari except that the bloody red cars were finally getting what was bloody well coming to them. And bloody well right!

There was also a lot of chatter and supposition about their hero Stirling Moss, who had emerged from the hospital the third week in June—albeit on crutches and apparently against the advice of some of his doctors—and had recently taken off for a holiday in Nassau, where he had always enjoyed the climate and the relaxed, island ambience. He'd won quite a few races there as well during the Nassau Speed Weeks.

"'el be back in a car before too long," one of them enthused. *"an' then the rest of the lads better bloody well watch out!"*

"'oi heard he took all of 'is nurses out t'dinner and bought 'em all gifts."

"The paipers said he was up t'go swimmin' in Nassau, too."

There was a tremendous amount of interest swirling around the subject of Stirling's recovery and possible return to racing. It was all over the English press and had become something of a national obsession. Surely his incredible recuperative powers had amazed the doctors and hospital staff. But I'd talked to people on the inside in the press room that day, and so I knew that the plucky, full-of-promise interview that had appeared in the *Daily Express* was pretty much fabricated from whole cloth, and that the actual encounter had left the reporter convinced that Stirling would never fully regain his abilities and should never race again. Only you couldn't tell people that. And, most especially, you couldn't tell Stirling that. Not that he would have accepted it. But he'd had a terribly serious, probably life-altering head injury, and he was having an understandably difficult time coming to terms with what it had done to him. Probably the worst of it was his lack of memory of the incident itself. Stirling had always been the most precise, scientific, exacting and disciplined of drivers, and yet he could neither seem to remember nor find out by way of investigation whether he had made a mistake or if perhaps his Lotus and Graham Hill's BRM had accidently touched wheels as he made his ballsy try around the outside. Or if the car had jumped out of gear again or if a driveshaft had snapped or if something in the suspension had possibly broken. It was maddening not to know, and he was utterly determined to find out what happened. And yet it all remained blank and empty. My English friends in the press room said it was affecting him terribly, even though he did his best to smile and wave and remain genial and upbeat with all the myriad photographers, reporters, fans and well-wishers. They said his vision still wasn't right, his depth perception was iffy and his hand-eye coordination was nothing like it used to be. So even if his bones and joints were healing beyond all expectations and he was looking more and more fit and ready every day in the tabloid photographs, there were other things that weren't coming together so well and that might not ever heal. Only you didn't dare write about it or talk about it in public. Especially in England. It just wasn't done.

I drifted off to sleep listening to the lot outside, and it occurred to me that Hope was indeed an amazing thing. It gave you strength and courage and optimism and confidence even when you weren't really entitled to them. But what did it matter if it all turned to ashes in the end? You still got the magic out of it. You still got the illumination.

The sky looked grim and threatening the next morning as we headed off to the track, and the weather went back-and-forth from light drizzle to fleeting moments of sunshine and back to sprinkles of rain all day. Which was nothing unusual at the Nurburgring. But it meant the times would be off and so Friday afternoon's times would set the grid for Sunday's race. So there wasn't much in the way of meaningful track activity except for testing wet setups and experimenting with tire pressures and trying out the cars that had to be repaired after Friday incidents. But the sun broke through beautifully for the only real highlight of the day: a demonstration run by one of the monstrous 1939 Mercedes-Benz W154 grand prix cars with original team driver Hermann Lang at the controls. Sure, it was hard to get around the politics of the damn thing. The cars were built with Herr Hitler's urging, support and financial encouragement in order to demonstrate to the rest of Europe—already teetering precipitously on the brink of war—the crushing superiority of Germany's technical and organizational capabilities. Which they did.

Along with their counterparts/rivals from Auto Union in Zwickau, the two German teams swept all before them in what some might think of as the very first blitzkrieg. So it was hard to separate those cars from the Nazi regime that backed them, spurred them on and used them as propaganda. Only then you had the incredible engineering and mechanical genius of the machines themselves, and it was impossible not to be awed and excited by their presence, sound and spectacle. In fact, the hellacious, deep-throated howl of that two-stage supercharged, 3-liter, DOHC V-12 made hands and cheers rise all around the racecourse. It also made the delicate, wasp-swarm buzz of the current crop of grand prix cars seem downright puny by comparison.

It started to rain in earnest during the middle of the night, and race-day Sunday turned into about as cold, wet and miserable a day as I have ever spent at a racetrack. There was hard rain pounding down and a heavy, wet mist hanging over the loop around the start/finish line as the scheduled 2pm starting time approached, and you can bet none of the drivers were looking forward to going out in that mess. Cal was standing next to me under the pit awning and you could see how his jaw was tense and tight just thinking about it. Oh, he would have been out there in a heartbeat if someone had offered him a car, but he also knew how tough it was going to be and couldn't help but have a little sympathy for the guys who would have to go out there and face it. The Ring was a difficult racetrack under any circumstances and iffy weather that could change in a moment—or from one part of the track to another—was often part of the deal. But this was exceptionally bad. Visibility was damn near nil on the high, start/finish line plateau, and the hammering rain had washed some of the earthen banks clear across the road, leaving dangerous, slippery smears of mud here and there around the circuit.

And the rain just kept coming down in bone-chilling torrents.

The amazing thing was that the German fans, many of them camping for the weekend, were still lining the circuit all the way around in their rain suits and umbrellas and makeshift awnings and blankets covered with ponchos—the press relations guy said 350,000 of them!—waiting patiently in the downpour to see their heroes race.

The organizers wisely decided to postpone the start until the drivers could maybe see the track, and so there was nothing to do but wait in the cold and damp and listen to the crackly German music being feebly pumped out over the PA system. You could barely hear it over the pounding of the rain. I decided to borrow an umbrella and take my chances going over to the press room in hopes of getting some hot coffee and maybe a paper cup of tea to bring back for Audrey. As you can imagine, the room was packed with scribes and photogs and hangers-on with dubious press passes trying to get out of the weather, and once again the track press guy just nodded me in without asking to see my credential. I had an idea he maybe did it just to screw with Eric Gibbon. But he was one of your typical, stone-faced Germans who didn't show much of what they were thinking even when they smiled. But I swear I thought I saw him wink.

I found my Italian scribe friend Vinci Pittacora sitting by the window looking sad and miserable, but of course that was because it was a cold, ugly day and Ferrari's prospects were looking about the same. Ricardo Rodriguez had shown just about everyone what he thought about being assigned to last year's car and pulled out another brave and impressive performance to qualify quickest of the team's four entries, but even so the first red car was mired down in tenth place with Phil Hill just a few ticks behind him in 12th on the inside of the fourth row and Baghetti just to Phil's left in 13th. Poor Bandini in the supposedly new-and-improved, "English-style" Ferrari was a thoroughly miserable 18th and not enjoying the car at all.

"Don't worry," I told him. "They'll be back. Maybe not this year. Maybe not even next. But you know old man Ferrari. He never stays down for long."

Vinci gave me an exaggerated, even operatic shrug. "I believe a-that, too, my friend, but it's a-difficult to watch them struggle a-so this year."

"Yeah, but remember what they did *last* season…"

That earned me a big, melancholy smile. And then a sigh. "It's the money I'm a-worry about. It a-cost so very much nowadays…"

And that was true enough. Not to mention offering a perfect opportunity to grill Vinci a little about Ferrari's finances and such for my friends back in Fairway Tower. So I gave him the same phony line about working on a freelance story for some American business magazine about "Ferrari the Company" and, given that the rain was pouring down and there was nothing but wet and cold and feeble, crappy oom-pah-pah music going on outside, Vinci filled me in a little. Of course he wanted to be sure and play his cards close to the vest because he only got his favored, insider position at Ferrari by being a total company man, an unabashed cheerleader and a willing shill and mouthpiece for *Il Commendatore* whenever he needed one in the motoring press. But my Italian friend also liked to talk and show off what he knew—what journo doesn't?—and so I picked up a lot of useful tidbits about Ferrari's actual production numbers, his dealings with the various *carrozzeria* who put the sexy bodywork on his cars, his semi-invisible board of directors (including the secretive French foundry owner who occasionally got "special" cars that couldn't be found in the company catalog) and his bank relationships and lawyers that I never came close to getting down in Maranello. I couldn't really write it down while we were talking—that would have shut Vinci up in a heartbeat—but as soon as I got back outside, I huddled next to the building with Audrey's tea jammed under my elbow and scribbled as much of it as I could remember on the back of a soggy grid sheet. A lot of it was good stuff, and would maybe make me look like a little less of an idiot when I reported back to Bob Wright and Danny Beagle at The Tower come Tuesday morning.

The mist started to lift a bit and the rain had eased off to a slow, steady patter as 3pm approached, and the organizers decided it was as good a time as any to get the show on the road. But the conditions were still pretty miserable, so they also decided—wisely—to let the drivers take one reconnaissance lap before the start so they could see and evaluate the track conditions for themselves. It was strange and even a little eerie to hear the whole pack trundle away from the grid and echo through the surrounding hills and forests at grumbling, impatient engine speeds, and one could only imagine what the drivers were seeing (or couldn't see) through the rain, mist and spray.

But they were grand prix drivers and knew their jobs and racing in the slop was part of it, so they duly lined up in their assigned grid positions, switched their motors off and waited on the extraordinarily large and silent 4-3-4-3-4-3-4-1 grid. With poor Lotus #2 Trevor Taylor all by himself on that last row. The organizers thought he hadn't completed enough official laps to qualify, but Colin Chapman argued vehemently that he had, and in the end the officials relented and allowed him to start. Not that it did him much good.

And there they sat in eerie silence, glistening with beaded-up rainwater and with the sky still dark and spitting down rain while the crews topped up their fuel tanks and perhaps tried final, take-a-chance/last-minute adjustments to tire pressures or swaybars or brake balance or whatever. And meanwhile the drivers wiped their goggles inside and out, and those that carried spares made sure they were clean as well and hanging at the ready around their necks. You could hear the rain pattering lightly on the metal pit awning above us and the squish of the mechanics' shoes as they bustled around the cars that one last time, taking their makeshift rain covers off the carburetor and fuel-injection intake trumpets before clearing the grid...

Then the order came to fire them up, and suddenly the soft, steady patter of the rain exploded into the whirr, sputter, pop, wail and crackle of 26 tiny, tightly wound little racing engines with cylinders the size of polite teacups. Out of the corner of my eye, I could see Jimmy Clark was still wiping furiously away at the fog of mist in his goggles. He was sitting third on the four-wide Gurney/Porsche, G. Hill/BRM, Clark/Lotus, Surtees/Lola front row. The starter looked them over as the drivers stared him down, blipped their throttles and tried to get the revs and the clutch and the angle of the front wheels just right, and then it seemed like everything stayed suspended in mid-air for a moment—engines and heartbeats racing crazily—before the flag swirled down.

And then all hell broke loose.

Poor Clark had been so busy wiping his goggles that he'd quite forgotten to switch on his fuel pump, and just as the flag waved—wouldn't you know it—the float bowls on his carburetors ran dry and his engine stuttered, stumbled and stalled. Dead. Which naturally sent those behind him scrambling every which way to try and get around. The fact that no one collected the Lotus (or anyone else) was a tribute to both the awareness and skill of the drivers and pure, dumb luck! Clark realized his error immediately and had his pumps switched on and the starter grinding before half the field had passed, but he still couldn't avoid dropping from the front row to the very back pack as the field streamed away. He had to be furious with himself for that mistake, and no question he'd be determined to make up for it.

Meanwhile Gurney got the revs and clutch just right and surged away from pole in the Porsche, hugging the right-hand side of the road on the concrete surface of pit lane where the traction seemed better and holding a slight advantage over Hill in the BRM and Surtees in the Lola as they slithered away towards the first corner complex. Phil Hill made an absolute brilliant start from 12th spot, way back in the 4th row, and came hurtling up the pit-lane concrete to be an amazing fifth by the braking zone for the very first corner! Wow! We watched the rest of the field stream out of sight and there was nothing to do but wait and listen as the cars and drivers fought their way around the Nurburgring's 14 daunting miles of twists, turns, wet pavement, standing water and mud smears across the road.

I didn't envy them.

It took almost eleven minutes for the cars to make it back around—that tells you all you need to know about the conditions—but they all made it except for poor Trevor Taylor in his second-string Lotus 24. It was bad enough that he was stuck with "the old nail" and had to start at the back because he was unable to complete a single lap on Friday due to car problems. And now there was apparently water somewhere in either the fuel feed or the electrics and his engine was halting and sputtering and refusing to run clean. Damn. Only then, in a stroke of good fortune and bad all rolled up into one, the Coventry Climax V8 suddenly cleaned itself out, came on cam with a bang and pitched him straight into the barriers.

There was nothing he could do.

And now all he could do was sit by the car, wait the long hours in the cold and rain for the damn race to be over and try to figure out just what the hell he was going to tell Colin Chapman…

Damn again.

Up at the front, Gurney was under heavy pressure from Graham Hill in the BRM and a surging Phil Hill, who knew the 'Ring as well as anybody and had somewhat miraculously carried his aging Ferrari up to third, just ahead of Surtees! Cal and I both cheered and whooped as he went by. Even though we were pretty certain it wouldn't last. And you couldn't miss that Jimmy Clark had passed no less than 17 cars on that opening lap! Sure, he was in arguably the best car and he was cleaving his way through essentially back-markers, but it was still a hell of an accomplishment.

Then another long, nervous wait—still over 10 minutes—and although it was still raining there at the start/finish plateau, there were reports that the rain had slacked off or even stopped completely at other places around the circuit. Which meant the track surface was changing not just from lap to lap, but from corner to corner! Usually, when you have conditions like that, the race tends to string out into a long, boring procession. But not today at the Nurburgring! In spite of the rain and mist and cold and mud, it turned out to be a cracking good race.

Graham Hill finally managed to get up alongside Gurney and slip past into the lead, but Dan wasn't about to let him get away, and the three of them—Hill, Gurney and Surtees—stayed in incredibly close, competitive company all afternoon. It was heartstopping stuff. Meanwhile, Phil Hill's excellent run was interrupted by an emergency pit stop for a clean visor—his old one was smeared with mud and oil and badly fogged on the inside—after which he continued, only now well behind. Damn.

And then Dan Gurney had a hell of a moment when the battery box in his car broke loose and started banging and bouncing around in the cockpit. It couldn't have been lost on Dan that there were fuel tanks and fumes all around him and that if one of the battery's terminals grounded against something metal, it could set off a very nasty spark. But Dan wasn't about to give up or call at the pits for repairs, and he did his best to hold the battery box wedged against the frame with his lower leg and just kept driving. He slipped wide at one point while trying to hold it there and Surtees and the Lola were past in a flash. But Dan hung on onto him and the race went on.

Meanwhile, Graham Hill was having footwell problems of his own. His fire extinguisher had broken loose from its bracket and was rolling around on the floor underneath his legs. There was no way he could reach down and stop it or try to grab it and throw it over the side, and the worst part is that it would roll forward into the back of his heels under braking. God only knows what would happen if it got fouled up in the pedal assembly, and he worried that it might interfere with his footwork and cause an accident. Or at the very least let his pursuers sneak by. There was nothing he could do but make the best of it and carry on. Then again, that's what Graham was always best at.

While all this had been going on, Clark had been absolutely charging through the field, taking incredible liberties with the car and cornering in wild, heart-stopping slides, and by the middle of the race was putting pressure on McLaren's Cooper in 4th. That was pretty damn amazing. I also noticed that some of the older, 4-cylinder cars seemed to be going surprisingly well, and Cal agreed that their friendlier torque curves and more gradual power delivery could be smoother and easier to deal with in the wet. And especially on a tortuous track like The 'Ring.

By the end of lap 8, Clark had gotten around McLaren and was closing on the three leaders at something like 5 seconds a lap. But he was still a long way back. And a lap after that, a disgusted, drained and dispirited Phil Hill brought his Ferrari slowly into the pits to retire. Something had gone wrong in the rear suspension—he said it felt like the shock absorbers had broken—and so the car was bouncing and skipping and jittering all over the road, and that's just not what you want on a wet, narrow, twisting, bumpy racetrack with hedge rows down either side. Naturally, Dragoni was mightily displeased with Phil's decision to retire the car. He was pretty damn vocal about it, too. But that went without saying.

Meanwhile Audrey and the rest of the Bowmaker crew were damn near vibrating with excitement since Surtees had closed right up on Graham Hill's exhausts and was looking and hunting and feinting for a way by. He even got his front wheels up inside Graham's rears a couple times—including a strong bid going into the Southcurve, right behind us—but Hill held him off. Barely. We found out afterwards that John had made many other attempts, but Hill always seemed to cover them—just—and stay in front. Of course part of that was just the nature of racing on a wet but somewhat drying track: the favored line is what all the drivers want to use, and so it gets a little drier and grippier than the off-line pavement around it. So trying to go around another car that's using the favored, dry line is a little like stepping out onto an oil slick.

As Jimmy Clark discovered when he got off-line a little and damn near stuffed the Lotus into the barriers. He'd been spectacular in his brilliant but occasionally frightening pursuit of the leaders, but now only a few laps were left and he was still more than 15 seconds behind (not to mention that there were no backup Lotus 25s available should he accidentally wad this one up). So he wisely elected to back off, pocket the points for an incredibly well-deserved 4th place and race for the lead again some other day.

And so the laps wound down on one of the most dramatic, competitive, exciting and downright heroic Formula One races I'd ever seen. The order at the front held until the checker, but it was pins-and-needles all the way, and all I can say is that at the end of two hours and 38 minutes of racing on the world's most challenging racetrack and under the most difficult conditions imaginable, the gap covering Graham Hill in first, John Surtees in second and Dan Gurney came down to 4.4 seconds at the flag.

Wow!

Chapter 17: A Damp Day at Brands

Naturally everybody was limp from excitement after that incredible race at the Nurburgring (not to mention shivering cold and soaking wet) but we had to scramble for the exits as soon as we got Audrey's timing gear packed up because we had to get her to Brands Hatch by early the following morning. Cal had arranged himself a ride with several other drivers on their way to Brands in a team principle's brand-new, twin-engined Beechcraft Baron, and so Audrey and I were back on our own again. And, to be honest, feeling pretty tired, wet and worn out after our long weekend. Not to mention a little silent, strained and edgy in the wake of what had gone on between us over the previous several days. I wanted to find some way to break the ice again, of course, but all my attempts at small talk fell flat as we ground our way towards the car ferry to Dover. I finally just gave up and we drove on in silence with Audrey just staring out the windshield with unfocused eyes, not saying anything. And then, out of absolutely nowhere: "Did you ever even once consider the possibility of getting me pregnant?"

The question stunned me. But she didn't sound angry. More like sad. And disappointed.

"Of course I did," I answered immediately. And that was essentially true. But it was also true that I promptly set it aside and forgot about it every time the proposition sneaked into my mind.

"So you just left it to me," she went on in the same disappointed, even disgusted tone.

"I just thought…" I started in. Only then I couldn't think of a single worthwhile thing to say. It had started to spit a little rain again and so I switched on the wipers. But there wasn't enough water and they squeaked loudly as they scraped across the windshield.

"You needn't worry," she went on matter-of-factly as she watched the wipers squeak one way and then the other. "I'm off-time on my cycle." She looked over at me. "I checked it very carefully before we left. I'm always quite regular that way." Then she looked back out through the windshield. But not really at anything. You could tell this was terribly hard for her. Almost like she was going to cry. And then she continued in a dry, cracking voice: "…But we'll have to make some other sort of arrangements going forward…" The words choked off in her throat and she put her forehead down into her hands. I knew I had to say something. Only what?

"Are you sorry you...I mean we..."

"No," she sobbed softly into her fingers. "It's not that at all..." And then she looked up at me with a thin, pasted-on smile and a renegade tear leaking down her cheek. "...It was lovely, Hank," she said like she was in agony. "...Really it was."

I understood what she was feeling because I was feeling a big, hollow dose of it myself. The problem for both of us was the same:

Where the hell do we go from here?

And the answer was already carved in stone. I was taking her to Brands Hatch for yet another day of racing and attending to time sheets, and then it'd be back to the empty bedroom in the row house she shared with Walter and looking after the monsters of Mayfair three to five days a week and making travel arrangements as necessary for the racing teams and, well, more of the same. And meanwhile I had a plane ticket in my pocket for my flight back to Detroit Monday evening and a meeting with Danny Beagle and Bob Wright scheduled for 10ayem the following morning and then...

Well, I really didn't know what would come after that, except that I'd be living out of a damn suitcase at the Fairview Inn for God knows how long and we'd be an ocean apart again with no real plan or idea about when we might see each other. And I knew for certain that she was thinking the same exact thing.

I reached over for her hand. "This is really the shits, isn't it?"

She gave me a hopeful but pitiful smile. "Yes it is," she nodded, "it most certainly is."

"Maybe I should just quit the thing at Fairway and move back to London."

"Oh, that would be just lovely," she sneered. "You could go back to your awful flat over the bakery, and we could spend our bloody nights there. Then you could drive me home before dawn every morning so I could get my father on his way."

"It wouldn't have to be like that..."

"Of course it would!" She glared at me. "...And what would you *do?*"

She had me there. All I really knew was motorsports writing, and there weren't really any job prospects for me in England. Not to mention that it didn't pay enough for two people to even starve on. "They might hire me on at the bakery?" I told her, only half-joking.

"Oh, I'm sure you'd be a bloody whiz at that. And think of how rewarding it would be for advancing your career."

"You mean the money or the job satisfaction?"

"Oh, take your bloody choice!" She was fighting to keep from crying again. Audrey wasn't really the type to lose her composure or carry on, and it made her angry with herself when she did. And at me, by extension, since I was the cause of it.

"Maybe I could do something else?" I offered hopefully.

"Oh?" she snapped. "Like what? A clerk in a bloody shop? A waiter? Tending bar in some neighborhood pub?"

"But I want to be with you, Audrey. All the time, I mean…"

Oh, what the hell:

"…we might even get married."

"Oh, that would be just bloody wonderful!" she spat out. "You with some rubbish job and me taking care of those children and my father. Why, you could move right in with us. Think of how lovely that would be! He could be reading his newspaper in bed with his tea every evening and we could be in the next room, going at it like rabbits. And then we could all have breakfast together in the morning…" that made her laugh even while she was trying to keep from crying. I had to laugh, too. And then it got quiet again, with just the sound of the windshield wipers flapping across the glass. The rain was coming down a little harder now, so they were making a kind of squeegee noise instead of squeaking.

"It's really a fucked-up situation, isn't it?"

"I wish you wouldn't use that word."

"It's not a word. It's an expression."

"Then I wish you wouldn't use that expression."

You could feel that we were coming to the end of it, when all the heat, anger and frustration have steamed away and you're nothing but hollow, spent and empty inside. And no closer to any kind of solution or conclusion or resolution than when you started.

I needed to say something. Do something.

"Maybe I could get the company to transfer me to England?"

"You've just barely started there," she reminded me quietly. "You're just a tiny little cog in an enormous, uncaring machine." She looked over at me again. "No, you need to do what they want you to do, Hank. That's got to be your future right now, and both of us bloody well know it."

"But there's the new Le Mans car coming together in Broadley's shop, and they've got the Indianapolis program started up with Colin Chapman. They'll *need* someone to keep traveling back and forth over here to keep an eye on things."

She didn't look convinced.

Neither was I, come to think of it. I was just trying to sound hopeful.

Audrey let out a long, slow sigh. "We need to face it, Hank. We're going to have to just go along with the bloody status quo for a while and see where it leaves us."

"That stinks."

"Yes, it does."

"Besides…" she looked down into her hands, "I've also got my bloody father to think about."

"But he's a selfish, vindictive, mean-spirited sonofabitch," I answered back without thinking. The words made her stiffen and her eyes went hard and cold. But then, very slowly, they softened again. "He's my responsibility," she said in a low, resolute whisper. "I need to look after him. I promised my mother before she died. And his health is… well, you know…"

I could feel a wave of anger and frustration building up inside. "He uses that for all he can get, Audrey. You know it and so do I. He's fucking *using* you."

"*Oh?*" she glared at me. "And you're not?"

"It's not the same!"

"*Isn't it?*"

And then, very slowly again, I watched her anger melt away. "Look, Hank," she finally continued, "we'll have to take things the way they are, not the way we want them to be. So you'll get on a plane and fly back to Detroit and I'll go back to doing whatever the bloody hell it is that I do and we'll see each other when and where we can and make the bloody best of it."

And of course she was right.

And it stunk.

Lord Chamberlain made good time from the ferry landing to Brands Hatch (as he should have, since it was the middle of the damn night) but we couldn't find a place to grab a few hours sleep close by and really didn't want to continue on to Audrey's father's place and open that can of worms. So we pulled into the parking lot of a darkened pub nearby, drove around behind the building, shut Lord Chamberlin down and kind of leaned in against each other and nodded into a sort of exhausted, nervous half-sleep until the sky started grudgingly turning light and it was time to head for the racetrack. We both felt pretty much like shit, and the plane ticket in my jacket pocket might as well have been a thin slab of ice.

It rained on and off all that day at Brands, and by prior arrangement Tommy Edwards brought Walter along since the race was so close to home. Audrey ran over and gave him a frozen sort of hug when she saw him—she was looking over his shoulder at me the whole time—and the bastard wouldn't even acknowledge that I was there. He'd just stare off the other way whenever I was in the vicinity. And that was okay with me, since I didn't really have the energy or inclination on tap to try to be nice to him. Plus it was eating away at me like a slow acid bath that I'd have to be on my way to the airport long before the day's racing was over. Oh, it looked like a rotten enough day, and it was clear already that whatever Audrey and I had going would have to, as she put it, *"be put on the shelf until we can be together alone again."* What she really meant was away from him, and we both knew it. But there really wasn't much of anything I could say with him lurking around in my peripheral vision like a damn vulture on a rock. Even so, I hated the idea of leaving. Hating the notion of letting the door swing closed on the closest and best and most comfortable I'd ever felt with anybody. And moreover knowing—or at least thinking I knew—that she was feeling the same way, too.

I'd called to see if there was maybe a later flight out of Heathrow, but there was nothing available, and I knew the traffic out of the racetrack would be sheer murder at the end of the day. Not to mention that the damn airport was all the way on the other side of London. Plus I had to make arrangements to have Lord Chamberlin either returned or picked up, and the three-day weekend holiday road traffic would surely be a mess everywhere. But even so I didn't want to leave. I was like a kid wandering around the scene of a fireworks display the next morning, when all that's left are a few burned-out cardboard shells and some soggy flakes of confetti scattered in the mud.

With gray skies overhead and rain threatening and Audrey busy with her charts and watches and Walter sitting right next to her on the timing bench and no real desire or energy on tap to go out on a corner to watch practice and qualifying, I sat down on a folding chair with a copy of the race program and read it through from cover to cover like it was a damn magazine.

The Guards Trophy meeting at Brands Hatch was billed as an "International" event, but it didn't count towards the World Manufacturers Championship (or any other kind of championship, to be honest), and I always considered it more of a glorified national event. But the schedule and entry list convinced me that the promoters had worked hard at providing an entertaining day at the racetrack. Things would kick off right after lunch with the 25-lap Peco Trophy race for GT cars at 12:30, and the entry featured no less than *six* of Ferrari's amazing and impressive new GTOs. Including the Bow-maker team/Maranello Concessionaires entry with our stalwart John Surtees at the wheel, another Maranello Concessionaires GTO looked after by Tommy Sopwith's Ecurie Endeavour bunch with favorite English hotshoe Mike Parkes handling the driving, Count Volpi's lone GTO (remember, old man Enzo wouldn't sell him another one after their falling out) for regular Scuderia Serenissima driver Colin Davis and a sea-sick-green U.D.T.-Laystall GTO for Innes Ireland. Plus Graham Hill in John Coombs's very quick and well-prepared lightweight E-Type to keep them all honest. And then you had Aston regular Mike Salmon and my friend Tommy Edwards in their privateer Aston Zagatos, which were truly lovely cars and just about competitive with Ferrari's old Short Wheelbase Berlinettas, but not really on the same level as Enzo's new GTOs. South African Bob Olthoff was also entered in the top class in a stiff-upper-lip Austin-Healey 3000, but it seemed sort of like (as Tommy put it) "a working-class bloke in coveralls happening through a track-and-field meet." The Healey would probably have looked more at home in the smaller-displacement classes—among the Morgans and TVRs and Sunbeam Alpines and what-have-you—but its boat-anchor of a 2912cc truck engine put it up against the Ferraris and Astons and such. Oh, Healey 3000s could occasionally do well against that bunch in long, tough endurance races like Sebring where ruggedness was often more important than sheer, blinding speed, but it was surely in over its head in a flat-out sprint. There was also a somewhat unusual, Roy Winklemann-entered Chevrolet Corvette in the top class driven by a generally unknown

American from Colorado named Danny Collins. I was curious about that one so I asked around, and it turned out that Danny was a nice enough fellow who'd done well in some club racing back in the states and was well thought of in Colorado, but he clearly had a lot to learn at this level. Plus the car was a bit of a brick. Maybe even more than a bit, if you want the truth of it. Far more intriguing was entrant Roy Winklemann's story, which was both vague and deliciously mysterious. Winklemann was an ex-pat Brit who grew up in Utah, studied criminology in college in California, got into the Air Force as some kind of special investigator and was now based in England again, doing a little racing and entering of cars here and there, transporting a bit of gold bullion in armored cars, running a security service that specialized in surveillance issues and finding and neutralizing electronic bugs and maybe, just maybe, working for the C.I.A. Hmm. A lot of creepy cold-war spying, espionage, manipulating and maneuvering was going on all over Europe and England—particularly in the wake of the Russians building the Berlin Wall—and motor racing was a great way to meet, rub shoulders and exchange information with some of the mighty, powerful folks who might (or might not? or might be enticed to?) be or become involved. It reminded me of what Cubby Broccoli told us at our lunch at the bottom of the Furka Pass just a few days before: *"This shit may have the whole damn human race chewing on their fingernails thinking they're teetering on the brink of extinction, but it's been a fucking gold mine for Ian Fleming, and I'm hoping it'll be even bigger for us!"*

One man's meat, you know…

Following the Peco Trophy, they had the Molyslip saloon car race scheduled, which would surely come down to a slew of bulky, heavy, high-center-of-gravity Jaguar Mk. IIs careening around in massive, tail-out slides while heeled over so far that sparks damn near flew off the rocker panels! Plus there were Minis in the small-displacement class—including the number 126 driven by a very pretty, fast and popular female driver named Christabel Carlisle, who was a great crowd favorite—and they were always fun to watch. Especially in the rain, where the faster Minis would inevitably be nipping at the heels of some of the front-running Jaguars.

The third race on the schedule was the 50-lap Guards Trophy feature, which had attracted an impressive, genuinely international entry of big, crowd-pleasing sports-racing cars thanks to a selective but liberal distribution of starting money (not to mention the one-day, Bank Holiday Monday format that made it the only fixture on the European calendar). The lion's share of that starting money surely went to Enzo Ferrari, who duly sent up one of his 246 Dino sports/prototypes (along with a handful of factory race mechanics) and had it assigned to sometime Scuderia Ferrari sports car ace and acknowledged Brands Hatch expert Mike Parkes.

Now Mike was an interesting story. He was a second-generation automotive engineer (his father John worked for and eventually became chairman at Alvis), and he'd worked at Rootes Group for years. He was team leader (along with his friend, co-worker and fellow motorsports enthusiast Tim Fry) on the company's "Apex" project for a new economy sedan to rival BMC's Mini. It was still very hush-hush, but the rumor mill said it was going to be quite radical, what with the engine in the back, fully independent suspension at both ends and a motor supposedly derived from the all-alloy, overhead-camshaft Coventry-Climax "FW" series of racing engines. Pretty exciting stuff. But it was all mostly winks and whispers in August of 1962.

Mike had also enjoyed quite a career as a racing driver. He claimed it was nothing more than a hobby, but he was damned good at it, and you always got the sense that he yearned for more. He'd started off in his MG TDs and a vintage, chain-drive Frazer-Nash, and was invited to drive some other people's cars because of his approach and ability. Including two character-building seasons in a rather radical but ultimately unsuccessful mid-engined Formula Two special. But his talent ultimately caught the attention of some major car owners because of his extraordinary mechanical sympathy and fast, committed driving style. Not to mention his car set-up capabilities and reserved, polite and gentlemanly demeanor out of the car. He became a regular driver for Tommy Sopwith's Ecurie Endeavour team, and racked up quite a few wins for them in Jaguar sedans and E-types. That caught the attention of the English Ferrari importer, Maranello Concessionaires, who helped put him in a Short-Wheelbase Berlinetta for Ecurie Endeavour (he'd won with it at Brands the year before) and recommended him to the factory team in Maranello. Although he always claimed racing was "just an avocation," Mike had a passion for it and even carried aspirations towards Formula One. But his height worked against him, as his 6-foot-4 frame made fitting into one of Ferrari's 156 grand prix cars damn near impossible. And particularly since Ferrari was always playing musical chairs with his Formula One cars and drivers. But Mike did get some good sports car drives for Ferrari, including second overall in a Testa Rossa at Le Mans in '61 with Wild Willy Mairesse as his co-driver. But he'd infamously put his 4-liter Ferrari coupe on a sand bank during the very first lap at Le Mans back in June (although he steadfastly maintained that an Aston driver had put him off), and that was surely something he wanted people to forget.

Speaking of red cars, Count Volpi sent up his Sebring-winner Testa Rossa for Jo Bonnier to drive in the Guards Trophy race along with his odd-but-intriguing "Bread-van" Ferrari hotrod (which had to run as a sports/prototype even though it was really more of a GT) for my friend Cal Carrington. Innes Ireland was back in U.D.T.-Laystall's wire-wheeled Lotus 19, Jim Clark was at the helm of a semi-factory Lotus 23 entered by Essex Racing (several "customer" 23s were also on hand), Roger Penske was trying a bit of British racing in the same bright-red, 2.7-liter "Telar Special"-liveried Cooper Monaco he'd run in the Daytona Continental in February, and Lucien Bianchi was entered in the Maserati France Tipo 151 that we'd seen at Le Mans. What a monster! The rest of the field was mostly amateur/borderline-professional British drivers in a hodge-podge of semi-outdated Lister-Jaguars, Aston Martins, D-Types and what-have-you (plus assorted Lotus, Elva, Cooper, Lola and Merlyn sports/racers running in the smaller-displacement classes), but they still filled up the track nicely and made it look like the guys at the front were actually beating somebody.

One of the things I kept thinking about was that the grand prix drivers racing at Brands Hatch that Monday had been slogging around in the cold and the rain at the Nurburgring in Germany not 24 hours before! And now they were going to run in two (or maybe even three!) sprint races in England the very next day! Wow.

I had lunch in the paddock with the Bowmaker bunch and Clive Stanley's team, and the sky was looking dark and threatening off to the west of us. Things would surely get worse before the afternoon was over. Audrey had her father in a folding chair at a little, fold-up camp table, and she was kind of hovering around him—no question he was making her feel as guilty as he could about going away with me—and Tommy Edwards was over to the side, looking a lot more tense and serious than usual. It's not that he minded racing in the rain—heck, British drivers grow up on it—but you could tell he was feeling a lot of pressure. An older, more experienced driver can be a great asset in a long endurance grind where steadiness and judgment are generally more important than flat-out speed—particularly in the wet—but in a balls-to-the-wall sprint race, you've just got to be fast. Period. And Tommy had come out of morning qualifying pretty far down the order. On a track he knew well. Sure, Clive Stanley's Aston had been hurried together in a rush to make the race, but that was something no one knew or cared about on the far side of the fences...

And maybe it was just him?

By contrast, our friend Cal came wandering by wearing a big, confident smile. He was in a situation of very low expectations with the Breadvan—especially since he had to run it against the all-out sports/prototypes—and yet morning practice and qualifying had convinced him it was really a damn good car. He'd driven Short Wheelbase Berlinettas before, and this was really a lower, lighter, more powerful and more agile version of the same exact thing. Oh, it was cramped inside thanks to Bizzarrini moving the engine down and back as far as it would go in the chassis, but that also meant it was pleasantly warm inside and that the windshield might not fog up so much compared to the other cars. And the engine power and the balance felt really, really good to him. Not quite as good as a Testa Rossa, perhaps, but awfully damn good. In fact, his qualifying time would have put him on pole in the Peco Trophy GT race. And that was a heck of a boost considering the six GTOs entered and the formidable cast of characters wielding them. There's almost nothing better from a driver's perspective than being assigned to an underdog that's actually a lot better than everyone thinks it is. "Oh, it's not as good as having the fastest car in the field," Cal grinned, "but at least you've got the opportunity to shock the hell out of people."

It was clear he was planning to have some fun with it!

Then the time came and they called the GT cars to grid, and although it was still more or less dry, you could feel the rain threatening and no question it would likely arrive before the race was over. Tommy Edwards had told me that Mike Parkes was always brilliant at Brands, and had an uncanny knack and feel for the place. He was slotted third on the four-wide front row with Surtees in the Bowmaker GTO on pole,

Salvadori in John Coombs's GTO next to him and Graham Hill in Coombs's lightweight Jag E-Type on the outside. Surtees had the inside line heading into the first corner and took advantage of it, but Mike made a great start along with Graham Hill's torquey XKE next to him, and it was those two side-by-side—the Jag maybe half-a-nose ahead but on the outside—as they charged down towards turn one. At which point Hill tried to make a bid but Mike Parkes was having none of it and the two cars bumped as Parkes forced his way through. Hill went wide and dropped to sixth, but Mike was off in hot pursuit of Surtees and wasted little time in getting by. And then he simply ran away and hid, increasing his lead with every lap. Even when it started to rain. The wet track caused problems for many of the drivers—Colin Davis stuffed the nose of Count Volpi's GTO into the barriers after a spin, and even John Surtees spun in the rain—but Mike Parkes just cruised serenely on. It was a very impressive performance. And I was pleased to see Tommy Edwards turning in a workmanlike job in Clive Stanley's Aston Zagato. He came patiently through the field and cracked well into the top ten—which is where I thought the car should have been—and didn't put a wheel wrong all race. It was the kind of performance you don't really notice unless you're looking for it, but I was thrilled for him. He looked pretty damn pleased about it himself afterwards. Not that he was the type to do much more than smile and shrug and thank Clive and the two mechanics.

Next up was the Molyslip race for sedans, held on a soaking-wet track in (as the Brits always call it) "pissing rain." It was probably going to be a Jaguar benefit with the Minis thrown in for entertainment, but the car that interested me was the 360hp, Corvette-engined Chevy II that a guy named Chuck Kelsey had brought over to harass the Jaguars. He'd run it a couple of times before and I heard he even eked out a close win over a couple of Mk. IIs in a minor-league amateur race at Brands. But this was the big time against top-class cars and star-level drivers (not to mention the weather), and he was well off the pace and clearly struggling in a car that mostly spun its rear tires and threatened to come around or understeered like a tugboat. He finally retired the damn thing at about three-quarters' distance, but at least he didn't wind up in the scenery like some folks!

Graham Hill's Jag Mk. II grabbed the lead at the start, but he had Mike Parkes's similar car breathing down his neck, and it wasn't long before Parkes was through and away. Poor Christabel Carlisle's Mini got squeezed off by a spinning Mercedes 220 coming down Paddock Hill and dropped all the way to the back. After which she put up a stunning drive all the way up to 8th place overall and 3rd in class (just behind the two works Minis!) come the checker. Meanwhile, up at the front of the queue, Mike Parkes was simply driving away from the other Jag sedans like he had special tires or something. It was uncanny to watch him come around the corners in massive, frightening, even desperate-looking slides. But he kept on doing it, lap after lap and inch-perfect every time, and you got the feeling that he was really quite comfortable.

He was really having himself one hell of a day!

And he wasn't done yet. I knew I had to be heading off for the airport, but I hung around anyway to watch the start and the first few laps of the Guards Trophy feature. And it looked like more of the same as Mike took Mr. Ferrari's 246 Dino to an incredible four-second lead by the end of the first lap, and he continued to stretch it out like that with every circuit. Pretty damn impressive. Ireland was running second in the U.D.T. Lotus 19 with Clark a somewhat surprising third in the 1498cc Essex Racing Lotus 23, then Penske in his red Telar Cooper followed by Bonnier in Count Volpi's Testa Rossa, and then our boy Cal doing an amazingly good job on the wet track with Count Volpi's GT-hotrod Ferrari Breadvan. I wanted to stay and watch the rest, of course—you always do—not to mention possibly getting in a little private time in with Audrey before I left. But she was under a makeshift awning with her head buried in her watches and timing sheets and her father sitting like a stone-faced gargoyle just a foot away, and all I could do was sneak up behind, tap her gently on the shoulder and whisper haltingly into the ear opposite her father: *"…gotta go now…plane to catch…it was…I mean, you know how it was…everything…you know…"* I was wracking my brain for something meaningful and memorable to say, but the best I could come up with was: *"…I'll call you…"*

As I turned to leave, Walter's hand shot out like a striking viper and grabbed me by the arm. His fingers were bony and vise-like just above my wrist. I looked up, and he was staring right at me with rainwater dripping down from his hairline—he wouldn't wear a damn hat—and his eyes full of…well, it was hard to say what they were full of.

It wasn't quite anger and it wasn't quite hate and it wasn't exactly disdain and it surely wasn't fear. But it wasn't anything nice, either.

"*I want to thank you for looking after my Audrey,*" he hissed between his teeth. There was no recognizable friendliness, warmth or kindness in his voice. Only then the corners of his mouth curled slowly up into a strange, cold, executioner-style smile. "*Have a thought for what it's like on my bloody side of the fence sometime,*" he said simply. And then he let go of my arm and rotated his attention back to the racetrack like I wasn't even there.

I didn't really know what to make of it.

But maybe that was the whole idea.

Traffic was even worse than I expected heading to the airport and of course when I stopped to call Fairway's British headquarters about what to do with the damn car, nobody was there because of the holiday. I really should have planned ahead better than that—Audrey surely would have—but it was like I was avoiding anything that had to do with heading back to Detroit and my road trip with Audrey coming to an end. I decided the best course of action was to just drive Lord Chamberlain to Heathrow, find some gas-station garage or attended car park where I could leave him and call Danny Beagle long distance in Detroit to tell him what I'd done. That sounded like a reasonable plan. Only then the traffic ground to a solid halt because some stupid caravan trailer had sheared its axle or hub or whatever and lost a wheel (they do that, you know), so now I was running so late I might miss my plane. And I think maybe half of me wanted it that way. But then what was I going to do? Besides, they'd be waiting for me in the tower on Tuesday morning, and I knew I sure as hell better be there.

With my sense of panic rising, I finally pulled out of line and tried to go around on the grassy verge that sloped steeply downhill into a ditch—people were honking and shaking their fists and muttering angrily as I crawled past—and I damn near had the car get away from me and slither down the wet grass into a mud puddle the size of Lake Elsinore. And then the grass verge pretty much disappeared, and I had to put on my most desperate, pleading, basset-hound eyes, stick my arm out the window and beg, beseech, inch, creep and insinuate my way back into the regular traffic lanes.

People hate you when you do shit like that.

But eventually I got around the mess, rushed like crazy to get the rest of the way to Heathrow and wound up doing a Cal Carrington and just leaving poor old Lord Chamberlain at the curb with the keys over the driver's-side sun visor as I grabbed my bags and bolted for the lobby. And of course there was a line at least a dozen people deep at the ticket counter, and each one seemed to be taking their own, sweet time getting checked in. Only when I finally got to the front, it turned out that my flight had been delayed by more than an hour! So I checked my bag and then wandered back towards the front windows—looking as innocent as an altar boy, of course—and peered through the glass. By that time Lord Chamberlain was gone.

Then again, he *was* parked in a loading zone….

So I went over to a pay phone and called Danny's office in Detroit long distance, but thankfully he was out to lunch and so I got away with just leaving a message with his secretary. Something to the effect that the car had been rudely towed away while I was bringing my bags inside and dropping them off at the ticket counter. There was simply nothing I could do about it. Sure, it sounded like pure bullshit—even to my own ears—but it was like all those lame stories you tell your mom or your teachers or whomever when you're growing up. The idea is not to actually have them believe it, but rather to discourage further inquiry. Oh, they'll give you the old *"harrumph"* or the snake eye or the eye roll (or maybe all three, and sometimes with the old arms-folded-tightly-across-their-chests thrown in for good measure) but, if you're lucky, that's usually the end of it.

After I hung up on Danny's secretary, it slowly started dawning on me that I had time to kill. A whole lot of time if you counted the damn plane ride back to Detroit. So I went into the closest airport bar and had the first of what would ultimately be far too many drinks and started thinking about Audrey and what her father had said to me right there at the end—what the hell did he mean by that, anyway?—and that I probably could have stayed and watched the end of the damn race. And didn't Mike Parkes have himself one hell of a fine day in the rain and slop at Brands Hatch? And filtering through all of that were tiny, will-o'-the-wisp, now-you-see-it/now-you-don't recollections from Audrey and my road trip down to Maranello and up to the Nurburgring and back. It seemed so far away now, even though the end was barely a day ago. Sometimes I couldn't make myself believe it had actually happened.

Somewhere around halfway through my second (or was it third?) Black Label and water, it occurred to me that I had a meeting with Danny and Bob Wright coming up in The Tower the next morning, and that it wouldn't really do to show up hung over. Or, worse yet, still three sheets to the wind. But there were a lot of hours in between, and I told myself that the liquor would just help me sleep on the plane. So I ordered another Black Label with a splash and tried to remember our trip a little more.

Eventually it was time to go and I grabbed my bag off the stool next to me and headed for the gate. Along the way, I picked up a late-edition copy of the *Daily Express* to read on the plane. And what a shock when I opened it up as the DC-8 taxied towards its runway: right there on the front page—complete with photo—was the startling news that Marilyn Monroe had apparently committed suicide! It was hard to wrap your brain around. And of course it was the kind of story every yellow-journalism news writer and scandal-sheet scribe can't wait to run through their typewriters. It had everything: sex, death, drugs, fame, nudity, sorrow, celebrity, scandal, innuendo…it was a damn gold mine! Why, it was like a hanging and a horrible train wreck all rolled into one. Sure, you wanted to look the other way, but you just couldn't help yourself. And so I read every blessed word. Just like everybody else. And while I was doing it, I was remembering—also just like everybody else—how sexy she was and how she looked as *Playboy's* first-ever Playmate, and how she talked and moved and acted in movies like *The Seven Year Itch* and *Some Like It Hot* (what was it Jack Lemmon said about the way she walked: *"like Jello on springs"?)* or when she cooed *"Happy Birthday, Mr. President"* to President Kennedy in a way that made the hairs inside your ears curl.

And now she was nothing but a shapely, 36-year-old corpse with a stomach full of sleeping pills. The story said they found her naked in bed with a phone in her hand—like she'd maybe changed her mind and was trying to call for help?—and you couldn't help but feel sad and titillated and then maybe a little ashamed for being so damn interested and then you went back and read it again to make sure you didn't miss anything. In fact, you maybe grabbed another paper the first chance you got to see if there were any new details you might have missed.

To be honest, it made everything else in the newspaper bland, dull, pale and unimportant by comparison. Even the frightening news about the Russians "testing" the second-biggest nuclear bomb in history—40 megatons worth!—by exploding it high up in the atmosphere over some arctic island. That was very scary stuff indeed. In fact, it might conceivably lead to the annihilation of the whole damn human race! But who cared?

I tried meandering my way through the rest of the paper and had a few more drinks that I really didn't need and tried to drop off to sleep. But I couldn't. I just kind of hung there with an airline pillow under ear and my forehead leaning against the window glass, listening to the drone of the engines, trying like hell to remember and even re-live what had happened and wondering and worrying about what was coming up next. I guess I finally dozed off somewhere over western New York State, and so I'd only been asleep for a half-hour or so when the wheels banged down at Detroit Metro. Which is probably worse than no sleep at all. And I was still feeling half-drunk/half-hungover when I showed up for my meeting at Fairway Tower later that morning. I was looking pretty disheveled, too.

"Jesus, you look like hell," Danny Beagle said disgustedly as soon as I walked into his office.

"I feel like hell. Came here straight from the fucking airport. My plane got delayed last night."

"Looks like you had a rough trip," he observed as he herded me towards a conference room.

"I couldn't sleep."

He looked me up and down. "Things didn't go well?"

"Oh, they went fine for most of it. Better than fine, even. But it was solid rain for the last three days, and then it kind of went to shit right there at the end."

"Well, you'd better pull yourself together. Bob is gonna be here in a few minutes, and he might have some other people with him?"

"Like who?"

Danny gave me a nasty sort of smile: "Who would you least like to see?"

I didn't have a chance to answer (or to tell him it should have been *"Whom* would you least like to see?"*) when Bob Wright, Karen Sabelle, Dick Flick, Randall Perrune, Clifton Toole and none other than Little Harry Dick himself came parading into the conference room. *"Jesus H. Christ!"* I muttered under my breath.

Danny Beagle leaned over and whispered: *"No, I don't think he's coming...."*

Well, it probably should have gone a lot worse than it did. I did my best to straighten myself up, and Danny was nice enough to give me a little send-off introduction that included how I'd been up for about 30 hours and that my plane had been delayed and blah-blah-blah, and meanwhile they were all looking me over like you might look at a derelict wino passed out across a city sidewalk. But I had my notes from my conversation with Vinci Pittacora, and I started out by saying how coy, guarded and cagey old Enzo Ferrari was and how hard it was to get any kind of a straight answer out of him. But then I went right into the stuff about his board members and his bankers and his lawyers and my best insider guess as to his actual production numbers for the previous year. Which, as far as I could tell, amounted to something like 385 "road" cars in steel-bodied Short Wheelbase Berlinetta coupes, sexy 250GT California Spyder ragtops (mostly for the American market), slightly more elegant 250GT Cabriolet convertibles, 250GTE 2+2 coupes with a so-called "rear seat" for small, spoiled children or legless dwarfs (all of the above with Ferrari's justly famous and mellifluous 3.0-liter V12 under the sheet metal and mostly Pininfarina—although occasionally Scaglietti—bodywork) plus a few 400 Superamerica coupes and cabriolets with Enzo's big, 4.0-liter V12 under the hood for very special Ferrari customers who just *had* to have the meanest dog on the block. And on top of that, you had the racing cars—and it was pretty damn impressive when you looked back at the year old man Ferrari had for himself in 1961—including the five shark-nosed 156 F1 cars that totally dominated the grand prix scene that year, the 246 Dino mid-engined prototypes and older-style, front-engined 3.0 liter Testa Rossas that did the same in the World Manufacturers' Championship, 19 special, hotted-up, drilled-out, plastic-windowed and alloy-bodied Short Wheelbase Berlinettas that utterly flattened the opposition in the big-bore GT classes worldwide and, as if that wasn't enough, the GTO prototype that Stirling Moss drove a few times and ran away and hid from all those lightweight Short Wheelbase Berlinettas. Plus a leftover, 1960-issue front-engined F1 car that got sold and shipped off to a customer in New Zealand with a 3.0-liter Testa Rossa V12 stuffed under the hood scoop. And what an exciting ride that must have been! I went into a lot of detail on all the racecar stuff and the *carozzeria* body-builder stuff on the road cars—hey, I was finally into something I understood and knew about—and that seemed to satisfy everybody that I'd actually accomplished something useful while I was over in Italy.

Then Randall Perrune asked me some questions I couldn't answer about what kind of corporate structure Ferrari had and what sort of succession plan he had in place, and then Clifton Toole wanted to know about the profit margins on the road cars and what sort of dealer discount program Ferrari had worked out with his dealers and distributors, and I really didn't know any of that stuff, either. And because I was exhausted and still a little drunk and generally feeling like my world was coming to an end no matter what the hell I said, I just told him I had no idea, but that I'd sure as heck try to do a little more investigating to see if I could maybe find out. And that seemed to be the end of it. Besides, it was getting on towards lunchtime, and you could tell by the expressions on most of them—Randall Perrune and Dick Flick and Clifton Toole, in particular—that they thought our meeting was a complete waste of time and that the fortunes and future of some tiny, medieval-fiefdom of a sports car manufacturer in Maranello, Italy, had nothing whatsoever to do with making a gargantuan, global-sized profit off a gargantuan, global-sized automotive colossus like Fairway Motors.

So everything was kind of hanging there in an uncomfortable, unfinished silence. I could see Bob Wright was about to say something—he was a master at wrapping things up when there was nothing but loose ends lying around—but Little Harry Dick Fairway decided it was time to assert himself and beat him to it. Hell, he hadn't lambasted, berated or threatened to fire anybody since he came into the room! He swiveled his head around like a tank turret, and I just about froze when his eyes landed and locked directly on me. You could tell he was about to unload. You could damn near hear it churning and gurgling and fulminating inside of him. But he must have been having an off day, because all he came up with was, "You look like shit, Lyons."

"I know I do," I answered meekly. "Danny already told me."

"Do you even know a damn dry cleaner?"

"I came straight from the airport, sir."

"You don't ever hear Bob or me making lame excuses like that, do you?"

"No, I don't," I barely whispered.

"…Or Dick Flick, either. Hell, he always looks like a fucking magazine ad…" his eyes swiveled over to Dick Flick, "…at least so long as he keeps his fucking pants on, anyway…" I thought I was in the clear now, but then H.R. Junior's eyes snapped back to me. "I don't want to ever see you showing up at a fucking meeting looking like that again..." he turned the glare up a few thousand watts, "...do I make myself clear?"

"Yes, sir!" He looked like he was waiting for more. "Of course you do." That still wasn't enough. "Like I said, Danny already told me..."

And now it was too much. HR Junior rolled his eyes like he was in agony. Then he shook his head. "Well, I hate to agree with that stupid sonofabitch..." his eyes moved over to Danny Beagle. You could almost feel Danny's legs start to quiver and flinch down below the table where nobody could see. "..but for a change he got something right." Then Little Harry Dick stood up, gave an abrupt little snort with a lot of snot in it and stalked out of the room. Everybody else followed except Danny.

"You really got lucky there," he whispered after everybody had left.

"Don't I know it..." I agreed, and laid my head down on top of my arms. I needed some sleep. "You got any idea what's up next for me?" I yawned into my knuckles.

"I think Karen's got you scheduled for some new-model-year dealer introductions with Manny Streets."

But by then I was snoring.

Chapter 18: Dealing with the Dealers

Manny Streets was the only V.P. on the executive corridor who was hardly ever there. But that's because he was always out in the field handling problems, kissing up to pissed-off dealers, settling territorial disputes between zone reps and pushing those reps to get their dealers to take more cars whenever the holding lots around the assembly plants were overflowing with inventory and the old supply line was threatening to back up like a bad case of constipation. And it was a tough sell when the dealers' own lots and showrooms were filled with unsold cars from back fence to sidewalk. But Manny was always there to remind those dealers—right from the top floor of Fairway Tower—that friendly company financing was likely available and how their willingness to help out would be remembered when supply got tight sometime in the future. And it would. Particularly on those hot new models and color combinations that everybody and his brother wanted to buy. So Manny spent most of his time on the road, sweet-talking dealership principals, browbeating zone managers, un-ruffling ruffled feathers, pouring oil (or occasional gift bottles of 12-year-old scotch) on troubled waters and making countless promises, compromises and excuses on behalf of the company that nobody much believed would happen exactly as he'd laid them out. But you need to remember he was dealing with automobile dealers, so honesty was more of a fungible commodity than a character trait.

Another facet of Manny's job involved coming up with special deals, incentives, spiffs, promotions and trip-to-Hawaii sales contests to help move slow-selling models and trim packages that nobody really wanted to buy. Like Amanda Cassandra Fairway's beloved "Great Artists" series of Freeway Frigates, which most dealership salesmen agreed were just about sale-proof and which had hit a new low with the introduction of the Jackson Pollack, Joan Miró, Wassily Kandinsky and particularly the dizzying, vertigo-inspiring M.C. Escher special editions.

I got to know Manny Streets pretty well over the next several weeks and, like all great salespeople, he was instantly likable and even more instantly believable. Even when he was spinning gold thread out of pure bullshit. Manny was a short, natty little guy with a sort of pitiful attempt at a trendy, Elvis-style haircut (that you could incidentally see through in the right light and from the proper angle in back) and thick glasses in heavy black frames like Walter Cronkite reading the TV news. Manny had a sort of perpetual, world-weary smile, a serious oversupply of nervous energy and eyes as soulful and reassuring as your family Labrador retriever. He worked very hard at being agreeable and understanding even when he was telling you that you weren't going to get what you wanted—no fucking way!—and he could dial up a "what-can-you-do" shrug that would de-fuse almost any volatile situation. And his low, soothing, "just-be-tween-you-and-me" manner could put even the most infuriated car dealers at ease. And that was a genuine talent.

Manny was a sharp dresser in a way that most any car-dealership salesman could appreciate. Which is to say *not* in the sort of finely styled Italian or bespoke Savile Row suits favored by Dick Flick and occasionally copied (albeit with far less savoir faire and on a far dumpier frame) by Little Harry Dick Fairway himself. No, Manny preferred slightly loud but well-tailored suits, blazers and sport coats featuring lots of shoulder padding in assorted pinstripe, houndstooth check and windowpane plaid fabrics (always with complementary silk ties, of course), wore a fat, star-sapphire pinky ring on his right hand to balance the heavy psychological weight of the gold wedding band on his left and expensive oxblood, brown or black wing-tip oxfords that were always shined to a glow-from-within gleam.

I got to observe Manny working with the dealer principals and working over the zone reps at the new-model-year introductions he took me to during those last few weeks of August and through the beginning of September, and it was a fascinating study. Manny was a fidgety, nervous type of guy and animated by nature, but he could come across as calm, smooth and soothing when the situation required and he talked with his hands all the time like a Jewish stand-up comic. In fact, Ben Abernathy said you'd strike him damn near mute if you ever tied his arms behind his back. There were even rumors around the Tower that he might actually *be* Jewish, but Manny insisted he only had "maybe a few little drops of it, and just on the left side" like he was talking about mumps or something. Then again, there hadn't really been any Jews up on the executive corridor of Fairway Tower before—H.R. Senior was a real stickler about that, and H.R. Junior was only too happy to carry on the family tradition—and Manny sure as hell didn't want to be labeled as the first. I mean, who needed the aggravation? Besides, he'd married himself a nice Italian Catholic girl, and all three of their kids got baptized until they damn near drowned from it and attended school at Our Lady of Unrelenting Penance (or Saint Braggadocio's two suburbs further northeast after Manny got his promotion and his new office on the executive corridor and moved his family to a nicer neighborhood). To be honest, he wondered why everybody couldn't shut up with the damn questions and whispers about his heritage and just forget about it? He just wanted to do his job.

And he was damn good at it, too. He could be tough in a nice way, nice in a tough way, stern or calming as required and never, ever lost his temper. Or at least not so you could see it. He was well paid for what he did, but it was a tough and largely thankless task, and there was always more of it waiting in the stack of urgent, angry and/or desperate (or all three) phone messages piled up on his desk whenever he did make it back to Fairway Tower. As I got to know him better, I realized he had maybe the second-toughest day-to-day job on the executive corridor (right behind my friend Ben Abernathy, of course) but Manny knew how to handle it. After all, he'd grown up in the car-retailing business and he knew it backwards and forwards and from every high perch and sneaky low angle imaginable. He'd seen and heard it all. Which is precisely what made him the perfect choice to handle Fairway Motors's occasionally delicate, sometimes strained front-line, in-the-trenches field relationships with its extensive— and, need I remind you, privately-owned—dealership network.

And here I should probably explain that most dealership principals are successful, hard-driving, self-centered, flamboyant big-shot/larger-than-life personalities who want and expect special treatment. Most of them are demanding, entrepreneurial, self-made maverick types (or, like Little Harry Dick Fairway, the spoiled-sperm scions of demanding, entrepreneurial, self-made maverick types) and, taken as a whole, they tend to be outwardly gregarious, inwardly wary, almost invariably sly, shrewd, self-absorbed, skeptical, highly aggressive, even more highly competitive, cautious by nature but shoot-from-the-hip reckless when pressed (or when the mood strikes, take your pick), occasionally outrageous, cynical of head yet cautiously optimistic of heart and subject to passing moods of dark, brooding paranoia. Plus the vast majority carry around egos the size of ocean-going luxury liners.

But if anybody knew how to deal with them, Manny Streets did.

Like I said, he'd grown up in the business.

Manny's dad had a used car lot on Woodward Avenue back when Manny was a just a kid during the mid- and late-1920s, and the old man specialized in purveying slightly past-their-prime Lincolns, Packards, Auburns, Franklins, Stutzes, Pierce-Arrows and Cadillacs to upwardly-mobile folks who dreamed of someday buying themselves a brand-new luxury car (but probably never would) as well as street-wise, not-to-be-taken types who simply didn't trust new-car dealerships. Often with good reason. Over time, Manny's dad developed an extensive clientele of meat, fish, fruit, poultry and vegetable wholesalers, up-and-coming criminal and divorce lawyers, likewise tax accountants, dignified church elders and not-so-dignified public servants, cops on the take, building inspectors ditto and a large following of traveling salesmen, new restaurant owners and showy storefront businessmen who wanted to appear like they were doing better than they really were. Along with some well-connected local gentlemen of Sicilian extraction who wore wide-brimmed fedoras and long overcoats even in the summertime and were always on the lookout for something new and different to drive. Or, in other words, something that nobody from the police department or any of the other local Sicilian families might recognize as their own personal car. On occasion they could also be looking to trade in a clean, low-mileage luxury sedan that had maybe a few unsightly stains on the trunk floor or a shattered rear or side window or had been observed somewhere near a shooting or a restaurant fire-bombing or had perhaps come down with a row of unsightly bullet holes across the spare tire cover. And they liked dealing with Manny's dad because he had no qualms about handling large wads of well-used tens and twenties—he'd never even raise an eyebrow—or putting titles in the names of assorted wives, cousins or business associates who might not be present at the time of the transaction.

Manny's dad worked hard and did pretty well for himself throughout the latter part of the 1920s, but times got a lot tougher after the crash of '29. Oh, he was always a resourceful type—*hey, when you get lemons, you make lemonade!*—and Manny's dad bought a lot of prime, first-class merchandise off the estates, ex-wives and suicide widows of guys who'd lost their shirts and everything else in the stock market crash. And by the time that well started to run dry, he'd already established himself as a well-known gypper, which is a particular type of used-car trader who cultivates symbiotic relationships with all the new-car retailers in town and buys their trade-ins in wholesale, odd-lot, sometimes "pay-you-by-the-end-of-next-week" bunches. It takes a lot of time, sweet-talk and coming through with what you promised to build up that kind of trust with car dealers, but Manny's dad managed it pretty well.

As you can imagine, some of the fine used cars Manny's dad bought off the dealerships needed a little work (or even a lot of work) to show well and be truly roadworthy, but his dad had a pretty good Czechoslovakian mechanic named Mirko Zajicek who worked out of a nondescript, back-alley garage that none of Manny's dad's customers ever saw just six blocks from his lot. He also had an Italian bodyman a couple streets over who could do wonders with a little lead, a little putty, a little paint, some chicken wire and a few pounds of shredded newspapers.

Manny washed cars for his old man after school when he was little and, once his feet could reach the pedals, moved them around on the lot for him (it was important to make it look like your inventory was turning) and back-and-forth to Mirko's back-alley garage and the Italian's body shop. His dad had a big sign with shaded outdoor lights over it (he got them at salvage from a miniature golf course over on Telegraph that went bust in the wake of a divorce settlement) so people could see it and read it even at night:

HONEST HERB STREETS SELECTED AND INSPECTED USED CARS
"LET STREETS PUT _YOU_ ON THE ROAD!"
—IF THE HORN HONKS, WE'LL TAKE IT IN TRADE—

Manny's dad was a real natural in the used-car business. Like Manny, he was friendly, likeable and easy to get along with. Plus he understood the art of deal-making and had a whippet-fast head for numbers. Almost more importantly, he was able to maintain a free-floating (if occasionally dubious) line of credit with just about everybody in town. He had a sixth sense about who had to be paid when and a line of bullshit that always seemed able to cover over the gaps. It helped that he had the cool, rattle-free nerves of a riverboat gambler and knew how to duck out the back door and hide in the alley in order to make himself "temporarily unavailable" when that was the necessary course of action. "Never let 'em see you sweat," he always told Manny, "And that goes double for bankers, landlords, process servers and anybody who thinks they've got you by the balls."

By the time Manny was in his teens, his dad would have him watch the lot and schmooze the tire-kickers while he made his rounds of the franchise dealerships in town. Once there, he'd walk up and down the rows of back-lot rats and recent trade-ins to see what might appeal to his occasionally threadbare but always upwardly aspiring clientele. And there had to be a dog in the mix. That was the real key if you were seeking a truly sharp deal on some cars you really wanted. So you'd throw in some crappy, worthless, clapped-out piece-of-shit that the dealer hadn't really wanted to take in trade in the first place and had no idea what to do with. Manny called those "Zajicek Specials," because he'd always pawn them off on Mirko in exchange for some engine work or brake work or putting a half-pound of sawdust into a noisy transmission or rear end. And Mirko would inevitably wind up selling them to some poor, hardscrabble, *barely-speeka-the-English* immigrant family that badly needed a motor car and didn't own a handgun.

But the point is that taking the dog off the dealership's hands (and moreover making it look like you were giving good money for it) was often a way to get a real bargain on some more appealing units. And it was a good deal for the dealerships, too, since they could liquidate a whole handful of cars—including the dog—in one fell swoop and get them the hell off the books. I mean, you didn't want a lot of your operating capital (or, worse yet, your credit line from the bank) tied up in merchandise that would just sit there because it wasn't right for your lot. Plus there was always a lot of haggling, dickering, posturing, head-shaking, shoulder-shrugging and horse-trading involved in a multi-car gypper deal, and if there's one thing car dealers love to do, it's make those complex, confusing, intricate and nuanced kinds of deals with a lot of moving parts and one big number at the end of it.

Manny's dad was pretty damn good at it.

But it didn't stop there. Because now he had to turn that merchandise around in a timely fashion so that everybody who needed to be paid got paid before they sent somebody around to break his arm or rearrange his face. But Manny's dad usually had a quick home in mind for at least one of the cars even as he was making the original deal. Like he'd maybe take in a real cream-puff of a low-mileage, not-even-year-old Lincoln Model K in a four-car buy from some Packard dealer, and no question it was maybe a little too new and too nice (not to mention too expensive) for his own lot. So he'd hustle it over to the Lincoln dealership on the other side of town that very afternoon and use it as the bargaining chip in a fast-turnaround, two not-quite-so-nice older cars for one damn-near-perfect Lincoln Model K swap that would also likely net him a fistful of twenties in operating capital. And then he'd drive one of those not-quite-so-nice older cars—say a hard-starting and slightly shopworn but still sharp-looking two-tone Kissel White Eagle Speedster with a balky engine, a fender dent, a bent front bumper, a lot of miles on the odometer, a rumble seat that wouldn't open and an iffy set of tires—over to Mirko's garage to have the motor looked at. Oh, it was pumping a little oil, but the real problem was the loose contact plate inside the distributor and a couple duff plug wires, which Mirko had fixed that very afternoon. He even cleaned the gunk and oil residue off the sparkplugs and re-set the timing and damn if it didn't run fine. Or pretty fine, anyway. Then Manny hustled it over to the Italian body man to get the bent bumper and the dinged front fender straightened out and the rumble seat jimmied open (turns out the Italian guy had to cut a hole in the floorboards and come up through the bottom to get at the latch, but he was smart enough to cut the hole underneath the seat cushion and flop it out of the way so nobody would ever be the wiser unless they had the damn thing up on a lift!). And then Manny's dad would send Manny over to rummage through the stack of used tires he kept in the lean-to shed behind Mirko's garage to see if he could maybe find a matching, presentable pair for the Kissel. He really only needed two because the back tires on the Kissel were borderline decent, and he could put those two on one side of the car and the two matching ones from his tire stacks on the other—hey, *nobody* can see both sides of a car at once!—and stick the best of the two bald, patched fronts in back as the spare. Hell, it was inside a metal spare-tire cover and nobody could see it anyway. Then his old man would have Manny wash and wax and polish that Kissel until it sparkled like Shirley Temple's smile. And who really cared that it was a seven-year-old car with a *lot* of miles on it (why, you could easily get rid of ten or twenty thousand—or as many as you liked, really—if you chucked up the speedometer cable in an electric drill and just let the damn thing spin until you got it where you wanted) or that it pumped a little oil or that the Kissel Motor Car Company itself had gone tits-up bankrupt back in 1931. Hey, it still looked sharp as all getout…

Only then you had to get the word out. You had to put it where people could see it. And not just in the stupid newspaper classifieds with all the rest of the new-car deal-erships and used-car lots. No, you had to be creative. So by the end of the week, Manny's dad would have that shiny, sharp-looking Kissel parked in front of a Rotary Club function in Southfield or St. Clair Shores or Sterling Heights or a Moose Lodge meeting in Farmington or Ferndale on Friday night and then have Manny shuttle it over by a park where a little-league game was playing on Saturday afternoon. And come Sunday, it would be in the no-parking zone right in front of a church or two or three just as services were getting out and maybe in front of the clubhouse at a second- or third-rate golf course on Sunday afternoon. And always with his dealer tag on the back and "JUST IN" scrawled across the passenger side of the front window in white-soap lettering and a fistful of business cards stuck behind the windshield wiper. As if he'd just grabbed it out of stock to drive it there for services or a round of golf or whatever, you know? Although Manny's dad never actually attended those church services or played in any golf games, since he'd have Manny pick him up and take him back to the lot for another one—a high-mile Caddy Limo or a slightly faded Packard Phaeton or whatever—and they'd do it all over again. Manny and his dad worked their asses off on the weekends—particularly on Sunday—but the phone would usually be ringing come Monday morning.

Manny liked working at his dad's used-car lot. But it scared him a little bit, too. He liked the hustle and the action of it, and also the slow times on weekday mornings and early afternoons when he and his dad could have a cup of coffee and read the sports section or listen to a Tigers game on the radio while worrying about where the heck their next nickel was coming from. That was the thing about the retail automobile busi-ness: it was an up-and-down, feast-or-famine kind of proposition and, as Manny him-self told me (at least once we'd gotten to know each other a little on a few airplane rides), he discovered that he really didn't have the temperament for it. "I worried too much…" he admitted as our Lockheed Electra turboprop leveled off for the short, easy hop to Chicago. "…And I was maybe a little too honest…" he gave off a helpless little shrug, "…not a *lot* too honest, you understand…" he held up his thumb and forefinger less than a quarter-of-an-inch apart, "…Just a little…"

So the uncertainty bothered him. Especially after he got married and had his first kid. And then there were the inevitable scary, uncomfortable moments. Like when stern-faced people in ill-fitting suits came by looking for money when sales were slow. Or when angry customers showed up after their "new" used car had broken down and left them stranded when a connecting rod blew through the side of the engine block or a damn wheel fell off. Some of those people could get very irate indeed. And then Manny's dad had to try to calm them down by showing tremendous interest, respect, sympathy and concern over the terrible, terrible thing that had happened to (and I quote): *"the car you now own…"*

Then the war came, and Manny went down and enlisted the very day his draft notice showed up in the mailbox. He thought that might get him better duty, and the fact that he could hardly see without his glasses, couldn't do a single chin-up, knew a little something about automobiles and business and had a good head for figures led the Army to make him a stateside supply-line clerk (and eventual liaison) dealing with tank, ambulance, and transport-truck manufacturing contracts, quotas and allotments. Which is how he first came in contact with Little Harry Dick Fairway, who was just a spoiled young punk at the time and passed Manny's desk without so much as a nod on his way to taking Manny's superior officers out for dinner, drinks and "entertainment" on occasional Friday evenings. Sometimes they wouldn't turn up again until Tuesday morning. None of them. But Manny was never a part of those evenings, since he was just a damn clerk and essentially part of the furniture as far as Little Harry Dick Fairway (and Manny's superiors, for that matter) were concerned.

Manny spent most of his time in the service doing tedious, pencil-pushing, paper-shuffling bureaucratic bullshit. He hated the dreary military order and hierarchy of things, but he enjoyed the structure and security of it and the fact that his paychecks came regularly. And that was more than he could say for his dad's struggling used-car business on Woodward Avenue. Sure, the war had been hell for everybody, but especially for new-car dealerships because they couldn't get cars to sell since all the damn manufacturers were working overtime grinding out tanks and fighter planes and command jeeps and military haulers for the war effort. Not to mention the wartime gasoline rationing and the wartime tire shortage and the fact that a large portion of every dealership's prime prospective customers were overseas getting shot at by the Germans and the Japanese. And, very occasionally, the Italians.

But times were even tougher for an independent operator like Manny's dad. All the new-car dealerships were hanging onto their used car inventory with a death grip—often it was the only merchandise they had to sell—and the last thing they really needed or wanted was low-overhead competition. In spite of everything he could do or try, including selling used pianos and church organs as a sideline, Manny's dad's used-car lot finally folded just a week after the Normandy landing. It was a bitter, bitter pill for Manny's dad to swallow, and his level of alcohol consumption increased even as the quality and selling price of the alcohol he consumed went in the opposite direction. Manny was eventually able to help his dad find a little semi-government work arranging the collection and sale of used American farm tractors to the Russians, but of course the ruble was shaky, and it was hard to do international commerce involving live chickens, mother-of-pearl-inlaid mandolins and 50-gallon barrels of borscht.

When the war finally ended and automobile production slowly, haltingly resumed, Manny's dad found work as the used-car manager for a big Hudson dealership in Royal Oak, and it wasn't long before they made him general manager, since he knew the business inside and out, could still run numbers in his head like a bookie and knew how to deal with people whether they liked him, hated him, thought he was trying to cheat them, thought they were pulling a fast one on him or wanted to stab him in the back with a pair of rusty garden shears. Manny's dad had several really good years there where he made good money. But almost everybody in the business was making good money back then. Demand was huge and cars were in short supply so it was a true sellers' market right after the war, and the only window stickers in sight were the ones the dealers themselves printed up, typed in their own offices and pasted on the glass. So you could charge pretty much whatever the market would bear. And it would bear one hell of a lot in the late 1940s and early 1950s.

Then the guy who owned the Hudson dealership got sick (Or maybe it was just sick and tired of running it? Or maybe it was that third wife and second divorce settlement? Or maybe he had an inkling of what was coming?), and he made Manny's dad what looked like a hell of a good deal to buy the dealership outright in the fall of 1952. It was expensive, and Manny's dad had to leverage his ass all the way up to the top of the crack to get it done, but he was thrilled to be captain of his own ship again and, considering how things were going, looked forward to a bright and profitable future. Hudson had a pretty decent customer following at the time and a solid reputation going all the way back to 1909, and that was the kind of thing Americans could put their faith in. Plus the company's low-slung, low-center-of-gravity "step-down" Hudson Hornets were very possibly the best-handling cars on the market, and their optional dual-carburetor, "Twin H-Power" intake manifolds made them arguably the highest-performance cars in America. No question they were absolutely cleaning up in stock-car racing (although a lot of that came down to a clever Daytona garage-operator named Smoky Yunick, who built some awfully fast Hudson stock cars and could pick through a blessed rule book like a spring robin looking for worms). The end result was that Hudson's racing Hornets were making Detroit's "Big Three" look pretty damn lame by comparison.

Only then the bottom more or less dropped out.

First off, manufacturing supply caught up with demand, so the postwar seller's market faded as more and more cars became available and, as any first-year economics undergrad would be only too happy to explain, a cut-throat buyer's market quickly replaced it. Plus Hudson was struggling because they didn't have the capital to develop stunning new models or exciting new engineering innovations like GM's OHV V8s or Chrysler's FirePower and FireDome engines with their fancy hemispherical combustion chambers. No, all Hudson could do was facelift their existing cars with new grilles and trim, and that reduced their appeal somewhat and put a damper on showroom traffic. But not nearly so much as the brutal, death-struggle price war the Big Three waged against each other in the face of too damn many cars sitting on dealership lots and even more backed up in the supply line all the way to the factory gates. There was simply no way Hudson—or its dealers—could compete with that. And it got even worse with the largely government-induced mini-recession of 1953, which cut back even further on consumer demand. In fact, the main thing keeping Hudson going were its government military contracts feeding the ongoing (but essentially and—at least from Hudson's point-of-view—thankfully stalemated) Korean War. And then the worst finally happened in July of 1953, when the Korean Armistice Agreement was signed bringing an end to overt hostilities. And that left Hudson pretty much teetering on the brink. In a last-gasp effort in May of 1954, a desperate Hudson grudgingly merged with Nash-Kelvinator to form American Motors. And there was actually some promise to the idea, as George Romney wound up at the helm of the company and steered it in the direction of smaller, cheaper, more sensible/more economical cars aimed directly at the great, soft underbelly of America's middle class. But of course the problem for dealerships and dealership salesmen was that you couldn't make nearly as much money selling smaller, cheaper automobiles.

Not that it mattered much to Manny's dad, since by that point his dealership had long since gone under.

But you've got to take your lumps and keep bouncing back if you plan to survive in the retail automobile business (either that or turn into a degenerate drunk, which is always the popular alternative) and Manny's dad spent a lot of time reminiscing and ruminating and recriminating with old Jim Beam and his less-expensive cousins over the weeks and months that followed. But then his wife got sick, and he straightened himself up enough to get hired on as the second-in-command general manager of a well-established Packard dealership. Which quickly became a Studebaker/Packard dealership as those two companies merged in another American auto-industry marriage of two separately struggling, desperate situations joining together to form a single, larger, even more desperate-and-struggling situation. *"Hell, I'd rather be selling Packards and Studebakers than fucking Ramblers for Romney,"* Manny's dad would grumble angrily into his tumbler of old Julius Kessler's "smooth as silk" blended whiskey. He was drinking again and thinking and remembering maybe a little too much about those grand old days when his used-car-lot business was booming on Woodward Avenue and the good times right after the war with the Hudson dealership when the money was just rolling in and seemed like it would never stop. Plus it was occurring to him with increasing regularity that he was getting a little old, worn-down and tired for the game. And by now his wife was really sick and in the hospital as often as not and then she finally passed away. And three days after the funeral, Manny's dad went home from work early and drank himself into a coma.

He never woke up.

So Manny had seen it all. And then some. He'd grown up in the retail American automobile business and understood all of its highs, lows, vagaries, defeats and uncertainties, and although he hated his job in the military, he could appreciate the advantages of stable employment and a regular paycheck. Especially now that he was married himself and had a couple kids. So becoming a zone rep for a big, solid company like Fairway Motors was a perfect fit for him. And it didn't take long for him to advance up the ladder as the marketing landscape changed and it got tougher and tougher for dealers to enjoy the kind of freewheeling business practices and occasional outright piracy they'd grown accustomed to in the wake of World War II. If it wasn't dubious model mixes and nagging quality-control issues from the factories, it was dwindling profit margins from the sales wars. And it surely didn't help when a do-gooder Oklahoma Senator named Almer Stillwell "Mike" Monroney came up with a bill requiring actual *factory* window stickers on all new cars that showed the exact, same-in-every-dealership retail price of every blessed model, trim package and optional extra on their showroom floors.

It took all the fun out of it, you know?

But if there's one thing that's true about car-dealership principals, it's that they're survivors. They're resilient. They can adapt. They can change locations or even the lines they carry. They can go bust with Studebaker/Packard and be up-and-running with an AMC deal or a Chrysler/Plymouth deal or a Volkswagen import deal or even a Citröen/Renault deal (God help them) before the next model year comes around. I don't really understand just how they do it, but meeting a bunch of them face-to-face surely gave me some insight. And it all starts with big balls, big dreams, big egos and a serious oversupply of ambition. Sure, capital helps and credit is absolutely necessary, but you're not going anywhere in the retail automobile business unless you live for and truly love that razor-edged, high-wire balancing act between risk and reward.

To be honest, I didn't really fit in at the new-model-year introductions I attended with Manny Streets. I missed being around the people I knew and understood at the racetrack, and I missed Audrey even more. But I sure got to see some sides of the automobile business and meet some incredible, indelible characters that I never would have run into in the grandstands, paddocks and press rooms at the races. It was an education and another world all wrapped into one, and I had to keep reminding myself that the sport I loved was just one tiny, shiny little facet of the huge, world-wide automobile industry, and that motorsports wouldn't even exist except to pimp, pump-up and promote the big corporate factories and their brand-name dealerships up and down Main Street, U.S.A.

Now the new-model-year introductions in each zone were generally held at some big, fancy place with good food, an attentive staff and a large lawn or pavilion or something where the new cars could be displayed. Private golf clubs were good because you wanted to maintain a curtain of secrecy around the new models (although a whispered leak and a grainy snapshot or two were always good—Dick Flick was a master at planting them—to get a little murmur of anticipation started), although most of Fairway's "all-new"1963 offerings amounted to little more than face-lifted styling and new hubcaps, chrome trim and grille bangles pretty much across the line. The new Ferret was more than a year away and still very hush-hush (we were allowed to hint that "something really big" and even "an entirely new kind of personal car" was coming, but that was about it), and the one really new thing in the model lineup wasn't even on display. And that of course was the new, sloped-back roofline on the full-size Fairway Freeway "Sport Coupe" models that had been developed in a damn wind tunnel under the watchful eye of Harlon Lee and his guys and figured—along with the monster new 427 V8—to make Fairway's stock cars damn near unbeatable on the NASCAR superspeedways. But all that stuff was still under wraps until the lid was ready to blow off Bob Wright's "Absolute Performance" program in the spring of 1963, and the last thing Bob or Harlon Lee or anybody else on the inside wanted was to give the other factory race teams an early peek at the new roofline and possibly even copy it. Or protest it. So the new "Sport Coupe" roof was scheduled (for the first time ever, in fact) as a "mid-year model addition," which meant pictures, specifications and brochures would break cover sometime after the first of the year. Or, in other words, right about the time the transporters with Fairway racecars inside would be loading up in Georgia and Tennessee and North Carolina and heading towards Daytona for the first race of the season…

Not that many of the dealer principals gave a shit about any of that. Most of them had no interest in motorsports whatsoever, thought racing was a huge waste of time and money and that they'd probably rather have another full-page ad in *Good House-keeping* or another 30-second sponsor spot on *Gunsmoke* instead. Power and performance tended to bring a lot of wild-eyed, itchy-palmed, indifferently groomed, motorsports-crazy tire-kickers into their dealerships, who would proceed to waste their salesmen's time asking about ring-and-pinion ratios and limited-slip differentials and special "Heavy Duty" option packages that no one ever heard of. Then they'd scare the living shit out of those same salesmen on test drives (at least if you were stupid enough to give them the opportunity) and never buy a damn thing. And that's because most of them were LOFs (dealer slang for "Lack of Funds") and drove up in rumbling, six-year-old Chevies with primer spots on the sides and glass-pack mufflers that made the damn showroom windows rattle.

I asked one of the dealers—you know, one car guy to another—what his favorite car was? And he just looked at me for the longest time like he didn't understand what I meant. "My favorite car?" he repeated. And then he smiled. "Why, that would be the one going out my overhead door, over the curb and into the street with all the paperwork signed and the money already on its way to the bank…"

But I did find one or two genuine enthusiasts among the dealer principals. Like Richard Fisher, who was an Englishman by birth (and you know how nuts about motor racing the Brits are), and had a pretty successful Fairway dealership in Evanston, Illinois. Most of his customers were ordinary, somewhat conservative suburban-family types from Chicago's well-to-do North Shore—he sold a lot of Freeway Frigate Broughams to the husbands, Esquire Estate station wagons for the wives and base-model Freeway Flyers for when the kids turned 16 or headed off to college—but he flat couldn't wait for the new Fairway performance models and the exciting new racing and advertising programs he'd heard whispers about. "How the hell did you hear about that?" I had to ask.

"Oh, nothing over here," he said with a nudge. "But I've still got a few connections back in England, and I heard from a cousin who has a friend who delivers gas bottles for a living—the type used for welding and brazing, you know?—that you've got a bloody Indianapolis car in the works over at Colin Chapman's Lotus shop in Cheshunt…"

And that's why you can't keep any damn thing a secret in motor racing. Or at least not for very long. Hell, there was a piece about the Fairway/Lotus Indianapolis rumor on the front page of *Competition Press* not two weeks later. It seems Mickey Thompson had somewhat bitterly leaked the story during an interview when somebody asked him if Dan Gurney would be driving for him again at Indy. He replied rather pointedly that Dan had a fancy new contract with Fairway Motors for Indianapolis, and that he'd put the Fairway brass and Colin Chapman together—right under Mickey's nose in the damn pit lane at Indianapolis!—when they were gathered around his own rear-engined, stock-block Harvey Aluminum special the year before. And then he added that there was no way a little, homespun, made-in-America hot-rodder effort like his could compete with Fairway Motors money and resources and that, to the best of his knowledge, they were already hard at work on their own stock-block, rear-engined Indycar (an awful lot like his, in fact!) over in England! And you really couldn't blame Mickey for being a little bitter. But he'd always been in bed with GM, and that's what you tend to get when you start playing with the big dogs. What was killing me was that I wasn't over there being a part of it and helping make it happen (on behalf of the parent company, of course!) instead of doing fucking new-model-year introductions with Manny Streets.

Damn.

But even if I was suffering from a serious case of motorsports withdrawal and missing the shit out of Audrey, I learned an awful lot about the retail automobile business and the regularly unusual personalities, predilections and proclivities of car-dealership principals. Not to mention hearing a lot of great car-retailing stories and picking up on some of the insider, car-dealership jargon that goes with it. Like I learned that "a lay-down" (also known as "a bunny") was someone who walked in the front door and took whatever the hell the dealership offered without any haggling or hesitation. Even better were the "get-me-dones," who couldn't care less how much they paid so long as the dealership could get them financed. The only thing those types ever wanted to know was, *"What are the monthly payments going to be?"* Or, in certain neighborhoods: *"Whut be muh'note?"* A dealership could actually make more money off a get-me-done deal than a lay-down, but it was sleazier work and probably earned you a middling stretch in purgatory if the Catholic Church has things right.

The whole thing made me feel pretty damn uncomfortable. Like I was at a party where I didn't know anybody and didn't really belong. Mostly the dealer principals couldn't have cared less about the new-for-'63 Fairway model line. Oh, they'd walk up and maybe even walk around them a couple times, but none of them looked like they cared much one way or the other. No, what they really wanted to do was have a few drinks and eat prime steaks and smoke expensive cigars and play friendly with each other like they were long-lost pals—even though they were bitter rivals every other day of the year—while engaging in endless, high-dollar rounds of *"can you top this?"* on everything from new showroom floors and ceiling fixtures to new service areas to new additions on their personal houses to new condos in Florida or summer cottages on a lake somewhere or even exotic safari vacations to someplace in Africa where the lions roar and the elephants stomp and the bugs are the size of hummingbirds. Plus there was an endless supply of dealership humor and horror stories, and some of them were truly worth hearing. And repeating.

Like the one this dealer principal with a fat Cuban cigar in his fist and a big, blond wife by his side with hair a foot high, lots of sparkling jewelry and a cleavage like the Grand Canyon told about the well-groomed, well-spoken prospective customer who came back to his friend's Mercedes-Benz dealership in downtown Chicago twice during the Christmas holidays to look at this used Rolls-Royce Silver Wraith that they'd taken in trade. "It was all creamy white with creamy white leather…a real nice-looking piece with that fancy, stand-up Rolls grille and lines like a damn chorus girl. Only it had a few little service problems going on underneath, including a patched and wired-together exhaust system that was about one rough railroad crossing away from falling clear off the bottom of the car. That's really why the guy traded it in." He leaned in over the table. "You don't even want to guess at the price of a new Rolls-Royce exhaust system…"

In any case, the well-groomed, well-spoken prospective customer showed up in a Cadillac limo on his first visit (it turned out to be a hire car), but it was right around rush hour on the Friday night of New Year's Eve weekend, and so the salesman couldn't do much more than ride him around the block in bumper-to-bumper traffic. So the prospective customer says he'll be back at 10am the next morning. Which of course just happens to be a Saturday and, co-incidentally, New Year's Eve day. And damn if the guy doesn't show up. Only on foot this time. But still in his very expensive suit, tie and topcoat. So they go out for another test drive—a long one—and damn if the guy doesn't pull a gun and explain that he's going to put the salesman in the trunk so he can drop him off in some cold, lonely stretch of forest preserve where the salesman won't know where the hell he is or how to find a phone to call the police so the well-groomed, well-spoken car thief can make off with the Rolls. Only the salesman knows that the Rolls has a bad exhaust system (although it hardly seems a propitious time to mention it to the gentleman with the gun) and that if he gets in the trunk, it will very likely be the last thing he ever does. Plus the guy with the gun may also be planning to shoot him once they get to some quiet, secluded place where he's supposedly going in the trunk. So they pull up to a stop sign in the middle of nowhere and there are thankfully a few other cars around, and the salesman realizes that he'd better do something (and *fast!*) and so he hollers out in a panic: *"Look, if you're gonna shoot me, you're gonna do it in front of all these people!"* and he bolts out of the Rolls like it has a damn ejector seat.

The story had everyone around the table leaning forward in their seats.

And then the guy just left us dangling while he took a long, satisfying draw on his cigar and waited for somebody (it was me, actually) to ask breathlessly, *"So what the hell happened???"*

"Oh, the guy takes off, of course. And the salesman gets picked up by one of the other cars and he's on a pay phone in less than ten minutes making a police report."

"So do they get the guy?"

"Nah. He vanishes."

"Vanishes?" one of the other dealership principals asks. *"In a fucking white-on-white Rolls-Royce Wraith?"*

The dealer telling the story nods. And then adds a little explanation: "Y'gotta understand that it's New Year's Eve day, see. So there's just a skeleton crew of cops working—the rest come on duty later when most of the fun and mayhem starts—and we all figure that the guy's a pro and that the car's probably headed overseas somewhere or maybe down to South America."

"So is that what happened?"

A big, wide smile blossoms around the guy's cigar. "You'd think so. Only it didn't exactly work out that way. Turns out the guy's a fucking amateur who stole the car for his own personal use. Not as a daily driver, you understand, but as sort of a special car for weekend dates and stuff."

"But how the hell did he get away with it?"

"Oh, I suppose he told people he had some rich uncle drop dead and leave it to him. Who the hell knows…"

"So what finally happened?"

"Oh, it gets real cute from there. It seems he gets in a little trouble at work—by this point his regular car is coming down with something, and so he's been driving the damn Rolls there a couple times a week—and he winds up getting his ass fired. And by now, the car's getting pretty rough from lack of mechanical attention and it's making all kinds of noise on account of the exhaust system's about falling off, and so now he's got a Rolls-Royce Silver Wraith on his hands that sounds like some high-school punk's '55 Chevy! And he can't really bring it in anywhere to have it fixed on account of he doesn't have any money. Not to mention that the cops are probably still on the lookout for it. So he winds up at some backwoods car dealership in Indiana trying to trade it in on a Jaguar-sedan demonstrator. Like he could afford to keep one of those damn things running, you know? Only the GM at the dealership is also a part-time sheriff's deputy and he remembers about the stolen Rolls-Royce out of Chicago. So they nab the guy, and the poor insurance company eventually gets the car back. Only it's in crap shape now, so they're truly up shit's creek and really would have been better off if the damn thing never showed up again at all."

"That's a hell of a story."

"There's one more little piece to it."

"Oh?"

The guy telling the story nods. And then he waits for a heartbeat or two. Just to build up the suspense. And then: "Guess what the guy who stole the car did for a living?"

"You mean the job he lost?"

And then the guesses start coming in from around the table. But they're all off base. Finally the guy with the blond wife with the big boobs and the big, black cigar waves them all off, takes one final drag off his smoke and gives us the punch line: "He was a corrections officer at an Indiana prison…"

Everybody around the table kind of gasps. Although there are several skeptical—even incredulous—looks on the faces of some of the other dealer principals. They don't like being one-upped. And especially by another local car dealer.

"It's the emis!" the guy telling the story swears. "I even know the damn salesman. His name is Levy. Used to work for us before he switched over to the Mercedes dealership."

And that was pretty much the end of it.

But the silence didn't last long because, like nature, car-dealership principals abhor a vacuum. So one of them started telling me the story most of them already knew about the wizened but feisty little Fairway dealer principal sitting two tables over. His name was Joe Rubin, and he had a block-long dealership in the Edgewater neighborhood on the far north side and a wife who liked to travel overseas and buy all sorts of stone statues and ceramic figurines and such for her garden, wraparound front porch and entrance foyer at home. She bought them in France and Greece and Spain and England and Italy, and Joe always complained that it cost him a fucking fortune to ship the damn things home to Chicago.

I was sure she'd get along famously with Amanda Cassandra Fairway.

But the point is she'd bought these two large, stone lions off of some destitute Italian aristocrat's estate that they were tearing down to build an amusement park. Only when they finally got home, it was apparent the instant the sweating delivery men finished unloading the damn things that they were waaaaay too big for the foyer. Or the garden. Or the wraparound front porch. Or anyplace else, for that matter. But the dealer had paid good money for them (and even more to ship them home) and he was damned if he was going to let them go to waste. Besides, he had an idea. And, in fairly short order, he had them trucked over to his dealership and hoisted by rented crane onto the far opposite corners of the dealership's roof. And then he proceeded to infuriate all the other dealers in the zone by putting big, full-page ads in all the Sunday auto-section supplements in all the Chicago Sunday newspapers featuring the following headline in huge, blast-you-in-the-eyeballs 72-point boldface:

WORLD'S LARGEST FAIRWAY DEALER!

And then, below that, in much smaller type (and also in French) the following line:

avec deux lions sur le toit

Which is of course French for *"with two lions on the roof."* Oh, other dealers threatened to sue him for false advertising and called the Better Business Bureau and the Chamber of Commerce and raised bloody hell with the Fairway zone rep about it, but wizened, feisty little Joe Rubin from the North Side just smiled, shrugged, rolled his palms helplessly toward the heavens and told them all to go fuck themselves.

You had to love a guy like that.

Then Manny told a story he knew they'd all appreciate about a somewhat famous (or at least notorious) car deal his own dad was working on back at the Hudson dealership. It was one of those grind-it-out situations where the salesman was going back-and-forth with the customer and they'd gotten Manny's dad involved because, besides being the used-car manager, he was also the "T.O." man. Now that's dealership slang for the Take-Over man, which is the guy who gets brought in when the deal is hanging in the balance and the prospective customer is threatening to walk. Usually it's some big, bulky, angry-looking guy with his lower jaw jutted out like a fucking bulldog and a mousy wife in tow, and he's read everything he can about the car he's thinking about buying in the newspapers and magazines and thinks he knows it all. And on top of that, he's showing off for his wife because he's probably got some crappy, low-paying job (otherwise why would he be trying to buy a damn near sale-proof Hudson Jet "economy compact?") where he has to take crap off everybody all day long and can't talk back to any of them. Plus the mechanic he uses at the gas station down the street has probably just told him what it's going to cost to put a new clutch and a rebuilt transmission in his rat of a '46 Nash 2-door parked outside.

Now you need to understand that in every car deal, three figures are usually in play. The first is the new car's asking price (which, thanks to Senator Monroney, is now on the blessed window sticker for everybody to see). The second is the actual dealer cost on that car, which the customer isn't supposed to know but often thinks they do. And even when they're on the low side by half-a-thousand bucks or more, there's no way you can talk them out of it. And then you have the renegade loose cannon in the deal: the value of the trade-in. And it's always the used-car manager at any dealership who has to figure that out. Or, in the jargon of the industry, "put a line on the trade."

There's a bit of Kabuki theater that goes along with this, because the really sly, shrewd, thinks-he's-sneaky customer will always start off by saying he's going to give his old car to his cousin or his brother-in-law or sell it to the Puerto Rican guy who cuts his lawn (who, by the way, says he really, really wants it), and so this will be a straight cash deal on the new car. Assuming the guy can get his ass financed, of course…but that comes later. Much later. In the meantime, he's looking for your very best, cash-on-the-barrelhead/don't-you-fuck-with-me/drive-it-home-today price. And he mentions that maybe fifteen or twenty times while you're going over the cars the dealership has in inventory and the options and color combinations he and his wife want. Then, when you finally get him "on a unit" (you need to do that before you can start in on any kind of deal), you take him and his wife for a test drive. And she *loves* it (but of course she does after riding around in that piece-of-shit Nash), and then you walk them through the service area and lie about how good your mechanics are and how long they've been with the company and then you buy them each a coffee and get them over to your sales desk and right away, before he's even finished sitting down in the damn chair, the guy wants to know "how much?" And so you fake fiddling around with some numbers on a deal worksheet and then you go see the general manager and stay in his office for maybe twenty minutes talking about sports or the good-looking girl in the business office that got herself knocked up by one of the guys in the parts department and then he writes a number in red pencil on the worksheet that's maybe eighty bucks off the full list price on the window sticker and you hold your head next to the heater duct for a few minutes so it looks like you've been working hard when you come back out again. And then you push the deal worksheet over in front of the guy and show him the number the sales manager wrote in red pencil and the guy blows his fucking stack. Which is exactly what he's supposed to do. And after he's done calling you names and the manager names and questioning both of your ancestry, you quietly turn the tables on the asshole by saying, with tremendous, even obsequious respect: *"Well, you're obviously an intelligent, well-informed consumer who has certainly done his homework on the situation…*[insert long pause here]*…tell me, fine sir: what do YOU think a fair price would be so that the two of you can take that brand-new Hudson Jet that your wife loves so much home with you today?"*

Now you know before he opens his mouth that the guy is going to come up with some impossible, unworkable number that the dealership can no way even consider. But that's not the point. The real point is getting him to make the *mental commitment* to buy the car. After that it's just a matter of negotiating the final price. And the dealership has a real advantage there, since the drool and his wife probably buy a car once every eight years or so (assuming, once again, that he can get his ass financed) while the dealership does it over and over again every fucking day of the year. And so you go back-and-forth and back-and-forth and grind and grind and grind, and if it's a really tough one, you bring in the T.O. man to explain through a sincere but condescending smile—*what are you, a fucking idiot?*—that the dealership can't stay in business selling its cars at a loss and fine customers like yourselves really need us to be here to take care of you in the service department after the sale and *"we really need to get a bit more realistic here"* and blah, blah, blah. And then, after the guy has threatened to leave maybe fifteen or twenty times while you and the T.O. man grind and grind and grind him up to something like a hundred-and-fifty bucks below dead-nuts dealer cost, he decides that maybe his cousin or brother-in-law might not really need that old Nash or that the Puerto Rican guy who cuts his neighbor's lawn might not really have enough cash on hand to buy it, so what would you give him on a trade-in? He figures he's really being sneaky here, while the salesman and the T.O. man and the sales manager have never seen anything as sly and shrewd and clever as this since, oh, say, 10:30 that very morning.

So the salesman asks for the keys and hands them over to the used-car manager (who is also the T.O. man and the general manager in this case, and all three of them are Manny's dad), who takes them outside to that piece-of-shit Nash with the slipping clutch and the shot-to-hell 2nd-gear and drives it around the block. And he makes sure to take a good, long time doing it, so the guy and his wife can sit and sweat and stew for awhile. Now the used-car manager (who is also incidentally the general manager and the T.O.

man) knows he's already upside-down on the deal, so the only way he can get back on the plus side is to grossly under-value the trade. And that can be a tough thing to do when the damn car is borderline worthless to begin with. But it could easily wind up as the dog in a gypper deal come Tuesday morning (hell, it was made for the part), and if he can just get the nose of the deal to poke above water, they can maybe pick up some profit on the back end with the financing. I mean, you can look at this guy and his trade-in and the clothes his fucking wife is wearing and *know* he's not paying cash.

So then comes the second moment of truth: when you tell the guy what his trade-in is worth. And of course he blows his stack again and cusses out the salesman and the T.O. man and the used-car manager and all the way down the line to the route guy who puts pop bottles in the vending machine over by the service counter. Which means everybody involved (except the pop-route guy, of course) has to start grinding and grinding and grinding all over again. And the used-car manager (Manny's dad, remember) makes sure to mention how bad the Nash's clutch is slipping and how the transmission grinds going into second gear and he really isn't so sure he didn't over-value it and that they'd have to wholesale it because they wouldn't be caught dead trying to pawn off a piece-of-shit car like that off on one of the dealership's own fine customers.

If it's a really tough deal, the time always seems to come when the sonofabitch prospective customer finally stands up, leans menacingly over the desk, tells the salesman to go fuck himself and stalks right out of the building. But it's just more Kabuki theater, because he can't drive off. Or at least not as long as the used-car manager is still holding the keys to his prospective trade. So he sticks his head back in the door and screams for his fucking keys. And that's when Manny's dad walks slowly across the showroom floor, steps outside, holds the Nash keys right up in front of the guy's eyes and then, in one swift, smooth, totally unexpected motion, hurls them up onto the dealership's roof!

"So what the hell happened?" everybody at our table asked in unison.

"The guy wound up buying the fucking Hudson, of course," Manny explained proudly. "After all, that's what the sonofabitch came in for…"

Chapter 19: Suitcase Racers

When I wasn't flying off to new-car introductions with Manny Streets, I was mostly either hanging around the coffee machine on the 6th floor of Fairway Tower or hiding out in the men's bathroom just down the hall reading a newspaper (or, every other week, my latest, air-mail copy of *Competition Press)*. To be honest, there wasn't much of interest to me in the regular news. The Reverend Martin Luther King Jr. got himself arrested again at some anti-segregation prayer-vigil demonstration in Albany, Georgia, after which he was thrown into jail for two weeks, brought to trial, found guilty and then pretty much let go. You got the feeling that the folks down south were beginning to realize that the more they tried to hang onto their old ways and fight against what they saw as outside interference, the more damn attention they got from the newspapers and the TV commentators and the hated federal government up in Washington, DC. And that just brought in more damn marchers, sign-holders, slogan-shouters, bus-riders, lunch-counter sitters, gospel singers, left-wing agitators, bored opportunists, socially committed clergymen, idealistic Yankee college kids who needed a shave or a bath (or both), nosy newsmen and all-purpose busybody do-gooders from Up North with nothing much better to do.

When you get right down to it, most people don't really care much for change.

On the international front, the Cold War was still giving folks nervous chills, sleepless nights and regular cases of goosebumps on both sides of the Berlin Wall, and some poor East German guy got himself shot to death by the border guards when he tried to climb over that wall and escape to the west. There were pictures, too. And it didn't help that everybody on both sides knew there were pointy nuclear warheads sitting on top of fire-spitting long-range ballistic missiles scattered here and there around the globe. It gave you the cold sweats every now and then, even if you were doing your level best to ignore it.

oh and e e cummings

the famous harvard educated poet

who didn't care much for punctuation

or capitalization

died of a stroke

on labor day

As you can undoubtedly tell, I had a lot of time to kill. And when I wasn't busy trying to avoid Dick Flick and his people in Fairway Tower, I spent most of the rest of it holed up in my room at the Fairview watching crap television or trying to get a call through to Audrey. It was always great talking to her—even if it was hard to come up with enough new things to say once I got her on the line—and it helped a lot when she had fresh, insider racing news to pass along. Jesus, I missed being on the road on my own and covering the damn races. So I really enjoyed her timely, day-after report on the big Tourist Trophy GT race at Goodwood, the entry list of which included no less than six of Enzo's magnificent new GTOs. Mike Parkes was in the same one he'd driven so successfully at Brands Hatch a couple weeks before, Innes Ireland had the pale green U.D.T.-Laystall car, Graham Hill was in John Coombs's example, effective privateer David Piper had his own GTO, John Surtees was in the Bowmaker/Maranello Concessionaires entry that Audrey was timing and a somewhat mysterious "number 7" Rob Walker GTO was listed on the entry for none other than Stirling Moss (although neither car nor driver ultimately showed up). Up against the GTOs were Jim Clark, Graham Warner, Mike Salmon and my friend Tommy Edwards in Aston-Martin Zagatos, Salvadori, Lumsden and Protheroe in Jaguar E-Types (Salvadori's car had been rebuilt from a wreck by the factory, and Audrey said it had some interesting new mechanical and aerodynamic tweaks and didn't weigh nearly as much as the other two) and the semi-hopeless Winklemann Corvette for American Danny Collins filled out the big-bore field. Plus a lot of Lotus Elites (ten, to be exact), Morgans, Sunbeams, Sprites, TVRs and a lone privateer Porsche Carrera Abarth in the tiddler class below.

Ireland had a slight crash in practice when the steering wheel apparently broke in his hands (and what a surprise that must have been!), but his crew got it repaired, and he more than made up for it by scampering across the track to be first away from the Le Mans-style start. But he was hardly alone, as Surtees and Graham Hill in two of the other quick GTOs were right with him, along with Clark doing his best in the heavy and recalcitrant Aston. Audrey's father was out watching on one of the corners, and Walter said Clark's Aston was wallowing through in massive, tail-out slides and looking terrifically clumsy compared to the Ferraris.

Meanwhile, up front, Surtees was really on his game, and he dispatched Ireland after a few laps and began pulling away from the field. Which was pretty damn impressive considering all the front-runners were top-tier grand prix pilots in supposedly identical GTOs, and I could readily imagine the excitement in the Bowmaker pits. And Surtees just kept padding his lead, held it easily through the fuel-and-tire stops and seemed set to cruise to a well-deserved win. Only then he came up on Clark in the ill-handling Aston Zagato, and Jimmy uncharacteristically spun right in front of him (or maybe he saw John coming and tried to politely move aside, which all too often results in the exact opposite of the intended outcome). Regardless of how it started, Clark's car pirouetted around backwards and poor Surtees had no place to go and plowed right into him! So instead of drinking victory champagne, the Bowmaker team wound up with a badly crunched Ferrari and looking forward to a lot of straightening and panel beating back at the shop.

Damn.

Meanwhile, Ireland's crew made an excellent call on the pit stop, short-filling their GTO with (hopefully) just enough fuel to make the finish, and that provided enough of a gap to give Ireland a narrow, 3.4-second win over Graham Hill's GTO at the checker.

"Sounds like a pretty good race."

"Oh, I suppose it was. But it was bloody miserable for our people. They were gutted when John crashed out."

"Yeah, that pretty much stinks."

"And you could tell the spectators were really missing the big sports prototypes. Limiting the field to GT cars just isn't as exciting."

"A lot of people feel that way. And not just in England."

"It seems rather stupid, doesn't it?"

"Yes, it does. I've written about it. Or at least I did back when I was writing for the magazine…"

I hear my voice trail off and then the line went quiet.

Too quiet.

I'd inadvertently led us into one of those awkward, dead-calm spells that just seem to hang there. And then hang there some more.

"I miss you," I finally mumbled to fill the silence.

"I miss you, too."

Another pause.

"It doesn't sound like much, does it?"

"No, it really doesn't."

More silence.

"I'm trying to see if I can get myself over to England again. Soon, I mean."

"That would be nice."

Quiet.

"How have the monsters of Mayfair been?"

"Generally tolerable. But no better than that."

"And the Lola shop?"

"Busy."

"And how about Walter?"

Audrey didn't say anything at first. And then she told me she was worried that he might have had another small stroke because he seemed sullen and angry and irascible all the time. I wanted to ask her how the hell she could tell the difference, but it was a mean crack and so I kept it to myself. It was killing me how far away and distant she sounded, and it was getting to where I couldn't really remember our trip to Italy together. I mean, I could remember what had happened—every blessed detail of it, in fact—but I couldn't really wrap my brain and my insides around what it *felt* like. It was almost like I'd heard about it somewhere or that it had happened to somebody else.

In the end, we wound up swapping a couple more hollow-sounding *"I miss yous"* and hung up. And then I just stared at the receiver in my hand for the longest time. It was strange, but talking to Audrey always left me feeling even more empty and alone, and so afterwards I'd generally go downstairs to the lounge and have a few too many drinks. Or sneak over to that school playground down the street and smoke a little pot underneath that kids' slide if I had any. Or maybe I'd do both. But none of it was doing much except making me feel even more bewildered, anxious and isolated. To make matters worse, Ben Abernathy's oldest daughter was getting married—good for him!—and so he was busy with all sorts of family wedding shit (he told me that if you're really, really bad in this life, you come back as a father of the bride) and couldn't go out to The Steel Shed or the Black Mamba Lounge with me on Friday nights to listen to some music. And it just wasn't the same going on my own. I went one night to hear Junior Wells and Little Walter and try to pick up a little something to smoke from Willie Shorter, and the crowd and the music made me feel all strange and jittery and paranoid and like everybody was staring at me. So I left. And then I couldn't sleep when I got back to my room—just tossing and turning there in the dark with nothing but the luminous green numerals on my alarm clock for company—and an hour or so after I finally dozed off, there was this faint little knock at my door. It was soft and hesitant at first, but it quickly got louder and more impatient.

"Who is it?" I asked as I stumbled towards the noise.

"It's Jeffrey, man." The voice was high and reedy, but trying very hard to sound cool. I kind of half-recognized it, but couldn't really place it. And then I opened the door a crack, and who the hell is standing out in the hallway but that insolent little twerp friend of Amelia Camellia Fairway's. You know: the one with the tousled blonde hair and the shirt tail perpetually hanging out who drove the Bamboo Cream Pontiac Grand Prix with the glass-pack mufflers and the 8-lug aluminum wheels that his folks surely paid for…

"What the hell are you doing here?" I growled.

He gave me a little punk shrug and said, right out loud and standing in the fucking Fairview Inn hallway with room doors up-and-down either side, "I just wanted to pick up some weed, that's all…"

I shut the door in his face.

Only then he started knocking again. *"C'mon, man…"* he kind of whinnied through the door, *"…Amelia says you can always get some…"*

Jesus, he was going to get me fucking arrested. And sent to jail. And fired on top of it.

"Go away!" I hissed at the door.

"Aw, c'mon, man…" he whimpered back. Only a little louder this time. *"Amelia says you do it for her all the time…"*

I opened the door, grabbed the scrawny little sonofabitch by the shirt collar and yanked him right up in front of my face. His eyes went a little wide when I did it.

"Look," I snarled at him, *"I don't have anything. I can't get anything. I don't want anything. And the last thing I need is for some high-school punk like you coming around here where I live asking about it. Do you know how much fucking trouble you can get me into?"*

"Geez, man, don't get all twisted up about it. I was only looking for a lousy lid, Hank…"

"Don't call me 'Hank'!" I damn near screamed. And then I realized where I was and started to worry and look around. But the hallway was still empty. And then, almost without thinking, I knew what I had to do. I tightened my grip on his collar, frog-marched him down the hall, down the stairs, into the vestibule and out the side door. In my fucking underwear. I could see the Bamboo Cream Pontiac sitting in the lot across from us. The other young high-school punk with the bad skin and the oily dark hair was sitting in the passenger's seat. With the fucking interior light on! *"Now you listen to me!"* I rasped at the kid named Jeffrey, *"You ever come around here again and I'm going to call your fucking folks. Do you hear me?"*

"Hey, don't get all mad at me, Hank," he said like I was picking on him. "I was only doin' it 'cause Amelia said you'd have some for us. She said she got some from you here lots of times…"

"Well…" I was stumbling for something to say, *"…she wasn't telling the truth!"*

"But she said…"

"I don't give a fuck WHAT she said!" I tightened my grip even more. You could see his face was getting pretty red. *"Look, you little dipshit, I don't know you and you sure as hell don't know me. And that's the way it's going to stay!"* I eased up my grip on his collar. And then, right out of nowhere, I heard myself ask: "Where is she, anyway?"

Jeffery looked down towards the asphalt. "Aw, she met some college guy from Wayne State. We don't really see her much anymore."

I started to say something, but instantly thought better of it. The less I knew or saw or cared or thought about Amelia Camellia Fairway, the better off I was going to be. And that was for sure. I turned my attention back to Jeffrey, tightened my grip again and played tough: *"Now you and your pimply-faced buddy get the fuck out of here. And don't come back…not EVER! I've got nothing for you, I don't want to see you and I swear to God-fucking-Almighty that I'll call your folks and tell them what the hell you're up to if you ever pull this shit again!"*

I let go of his collar and pushed him away. You could see him trying to get his snotty little teen-age swagger back as he headed towards the Pontiac. *"You'll get in trouble, too…"* he whined back over his shoulder. He sounded like some kindergarten kid whose mommy wouldn't buy him a chocolate bar in the supermarket check-out lane.

The sickening part was that he was right.

Boy, was he ever right…

I finally got a reprieve from the new-car introductions when Bob Wright (via Danny Beagle, of course) sent me out to L.A. again to see how things were progressing at Shelby's shop on Princeton Drive. Carroll knew I wasn't much more than a company spy but, unlike in England, that got me the royal treatment rather than the stink eye from just about everybody on the staff. Ol' Shel always understood which side of his bread the butter went on (and, more importantly, who was supplying that butter). And that always included so-called "members of the motoring press," who had fallen all over themselves heaping praise on his new Cobra (and why not, since it reared up on its haunches and slammed you back in the seat upholstery like no other sports car they'd ever experienced), and none of them had caught on that they were all testing the same blessed car with different paint colors sprayed over it. Or that Shelby's guys were regularly replacing the clutch and rebuilding the driveline and rear end between magazine test dates. Then again, magazine road testers are genuinely famous for ham-fisted brutality (even if they all seem to think they're the second coming of Juan Manuel Fangio), and so abuse was to be expected. In fact, Carroll *wanted* them to wail the living shit out of his car. *"I want them to come back with their eyes wide, their palms sweaty and a fresh, new peak in the seat-cushion!"* he drawled, and you had to love the twinkle that danced in his eyes when he said it. After a lifetime of grand plans and business schemes that always seemed to fold up, fizzle out or come to nothing, he knew he had a tiger by the tail….

There was another big motorsports deal going on in Southern California while I was out there, and it all pivoted around an L.A. press conference by the fast-recuperating Stirling Moss, who had flown up from his place in the Bahamas to film a segment for some TV news-and-entertainment show. And also to meet with a couple high-flyer Hollywood types who had shown interest in perhaps buying the rights to his life story for the movies. It all came in the wake of Stirling's extensive, incisive and somewhat controversial magazine feature (penned by well-respected auto writer/author Ken Purdy) that appeared in the September issue of *Playboy* magazine. Equally controversial was the news that Stirling was going to meet with *Playboy* editor/publisher Hugh Hefner and maybe even share a meal with him while he was in Los Angeles. To be fair, there was a lot of excellent editorial content in that September issue of *Playboy* (and, as everybody knows, most *Playboy* purchasers buy it for the articles…). Including a revealing interview with reclusive jazz great Miles Davis, an article titled "Wall Street in Crisis" by none other than J. Paul Getty himself, an excerpt from James Jones's blockbuster new war novel *The Thin Red Line,* a satirical look at the advertising world on Madison Avenue and a fall football forecast for the shoulder pad-and-pigskin set. Along with a few random photo spreads of comely, artfully-posed young ladies with large breasts, supple thighs, perfect skin, great hair and makeup and little if anything in the way of clothing. As you can imagine, the *Playboy* story raised a few eyebrows (not to mention hackles) among the motorsports community. Particularly my good friend Denise Mc-Cluggage, who had a somewhat different take on fine motorsports reporting wrapped around bosomy centerfolds than the rest of the motorsport press corps.

Imagine that?

Now I was supposed to go to Riverside that day to watch the fledgling Cobra racecar get wrung out (or, as Warren Olsen put it: "see what's going to break next"), but Shelby's guys were waiting for some new rear-end parts so the test was postponed. And that allowed me to cadge a fly-on-the-wall invite to the Moss press conference thanks to some old L.A. scribe connections. To tell the truth, I was both impressed and disheartened by what I saw and heard. Moss was looking quite fit and tanned—even a little sunburned on top—from recuperating at his home in the Bahamas. He sounded good, too. But you could see he still favored his left leg—he had trouble getting in and out of a Lotus Formula Junior they'd brought around for the occasion—and he still had limited (although much improved) use of his left hand. He assured everyone that he was all right and doing just fine, but admitted that he'd set repeated timetables for his return to racing and yet had to keep pushing them back because he still wasn't ready. And the physical things you could see were only part of it. "Concentration is my problem now," he admitted candidly. "I can do things all right, but not automatically. I have to think about reaching out for a door handle. And at times I have split vision, although the doctors assure me time will cure that…"

It was chilling stuff. Especially in the straightforward, matter-of-fact way Stirling delivered it. You knew that he was (or at least had been) the best damn racing driver on the planet. And you also knew how much it meant to him. Racing was his life, plain and simple. And here he was, at age 33, recovering from a horrific, life-changing accident that damn near killed him and facing the very real possibility that his racing career might be over. But he didn't whine or agonize or carry on about it. That wouldn't be like him. And I was absolutely fascinated—especially considering the accident and its aftermath—by his thoughts and opinions on driver safety, which remained very old-school and British. "No, I won't wear an 'American' [full coverage] helmet in the future…" he told all the reporters gathered around with their pens poised over their note pads. "…And, no, I still don't approve of rollover bars and seat belts in my racing cars…These things should not be mandatory." He paused for an instant, then added: "If I want to die, I should have the choice of poison, shouldn't I?"

It's hard to argue with an attitude and thought process like that, even if you believe deep down inside that it's misguided.

I wished him the best after it was over—I was pleased that he remembered me—and wondered what it must be like putting on a brave face while walking along the edge of what was very likely a bottomless abyss. Then again, racing drivers tend to be stoic by nature and terribly, even brutally realistic about everything save their own chances for survival and the depth of their own talent.

It's just the way they're built.

I went out testing at Riverside with Shelby's guys two days later, but there were overheating problems that took some time to properly diagnose. At first they thought it might be a head gasket. Only the engine was still running fine and it wasn't losing power. But it was sure as hell losing coolant. In the end, it turned out to be nothing more than a stupid seam crack in the radiator's header tank. But you couldn't really fix it properly in the car and we didn't have a spare one in the truck (although there were plenty back at the shop, of course). So they tried adding some Bars-Leak, and that helped for awhile. But the seam finally split wide open from the shaking and vibration, so the team didn't get many laps in. After that, there was nothing left to do but pack everything up and head back to Shelby's place in Venice with everybody feeling pretty much disgusted. But that's the way things go sometimes in testing. You come out to try one thing (or several "one things"), but you wind up battling something stupid and unexpected that has nothing whatsoever to do with anything and you don't get much accomplished.

It's a pretty shitty feeling.

Back in Shelby's shop on Princeton Drive, the so-called Cobra "production line" was more sputtering, clanking and grinding to a halt rather than humming along mellifluously and spitting out motor cars one right after the other. But that was okay, since the development of the new Cobra was still very much a work in progress, and they really needed a little more time to get everything properly sorted out. Or at least pretty much sorted out, anyway. Besides, most of them were racers at heart, and they had this racecar to get ready for Riverside…

Everybody knew from Day One that the Cobra would be raced, and everybody also knew (and especially the shop veterans who'd been through the mill with the Scarab projects) that you couldn't just drop a big, powerful American V8 into a chassis that was never meant to handle it, slap a number on the side and go racing. No way. Particularly when you're also trying to get the street car business rolling and the dealer orders filled and keeping all the motoring scribes happy, wide-eyed and panting. Not to mention keeping all the purse-string people back in Fairway Tower pleased with your progress and publicity. In racing, the day of reckoning always arrives before you're really ready for it. In the Cobra's case, the plan was to enter the new red #98 in the three-hour "production car" enduro at Riverside that served as the "Saturday Feature" curtain-raiser for the big *Los Angeles Times Sports Car Grand Prix* on Sunday, October 14th. And everybody knew that Chevrolet was going to be there with a couple of their brand-new, fuel-injected, independent-rear-suspension Sting Rays entered (albeit from independent local back-door Chevy "performance" shops run by guys like Mickey Thompson and Bill Thomas, since GM still wasn't involved in racing…*hah!).*

So the stage was pretty much set for a showdown.

You can bet your ass I planned to be there.

I was even doing a little lobbying to see if I could maybe get Cal Carrington the Cobra drive at Riverside. I mean, he was a fast, popular, personable and good-looking young

American driver with an established following and an impressive international résumé. Plus I knew he'd jump at the chance. But I also knew that plenty of other California hotshoes were knocking on the door, calling on the phone and making themselves not-so-subtly available. But Shelby kept the decision-making process to himself and refused to let anybody know who his pick might be. And I don't think he was trying to be clever or coy or sneaky…he just hadn't made up his mind yet. Shelby had been on both sides of that particular deal, and he knew that picking race drivers was a sensitive, difficult and politically charged undertaking. Sure, it was tough to be a driver looking for rides. But it was maybe even tougher trying to pick the right hotshoe to sit in your racecar.

You were going to disappoint some people.

You were going to piss them off.

Including people whose opinions you valued and whose company you enjoyed.

People who used to like you…

There were two big races over the weekend of September 15-16, and I witnessed both of them from the fucking window seat of a Douglas DC8 somewhere over Nevada, Colorado, Kansas, Iowa, Missouri, Illinois and Lake Michigan on my way back to Detroit with the latest copy of *Competition Press* spread out across my tray table. The Italian Grand Prix turned out to be another high-speed slipstreaming battle at Monza where any group of cars running in even a semi-cooperative pack were inevitably faster than any single car running on its own. Which made it virtually impossible for anyone to make a break from one of those packs and sneak away. As Dan Gurney put it: "You could do a corner really well and gain some distance, but then you'd glance in your mirrors and see them reeling you in again as soon as you got back on those long Monza straightaways." It had always been like that at Monza, but it became even worse after the anemic 1500cc F1 engine formula was adapted for 1961. Oh, the cars were getting faster in an absolute sense thanks to lighter weight, improved handling, reduced frontal area and better aerodynamics, but that just exacerbated the importance of running in packs and slipstreaming. The Monza organizers had also decided they could increase the spectacle of the whole thing by making the race a full 500 kilometers—which is *long* for an F1 race—and so a lot of teams were adding additional fuel tanks or even contemplating pit stops for fuel and, if necessary, fresh tires.

As you can imagine, Ferrari was out in force for their home grand prix, and for a change everybody on the team had a blessed car to drive. But there was nothing really new among the red cars (the lightweight, "English-style" car that had run but ultimately crashed out at the Nurburgring was still the latest and freshest thing on hand), and not even the combined bravery and talent of Giancarlo Baghetti, Willy Mairesse, Lorenzo Bandini, Ricardo Rodriguez and Phil Hill could get any of them much above the very bottom of the top ten. Which had to be pretty embarrassing back in Maranello. But they were still looking better than the fresh-out-of-the-shop new DeTomaso, which only made a few fitful laps in practice and was never a threat to so much as qualify. Audrey said she'd heard that DeTomaso only brought it out to show the world—and his investors— that there really *was* a running DeTomaso F1 car. Even if it didn't run very fast.

Or for very long, come to that.

Practice showed that the fuel-injected BRM V8s of Graham Hill and Richie Ginther were really strong on power, while the Lotus effort was pretty much a shambles at Monza. Clark had two gearboxes break, the team flew another one down from England, the crew stayed up all night putting it in and then a tappet in the valve train broke in the very next session. Teammate Trevor Taylor was likewise having teething troubles with his new, just-finished Lotus 25 monocoque. In the end, they swapped numbers around and Clark took Taylor's car out for a few laps at the very end of qualifying… and put it on pole! But not by much, as he was just a scant few hundredths clear of Graham's BRM (while BRM teammate Ginther was right behind Clark in 3rd). Porsche was trying a bunch of new tricks on Gurney's car what with a freewheeling cooling fan that declutched at high speed to provide a little more power down the long Monza straights and some aerodynamic tweaks like full-coverage wheel discs and fairings over the suspension links to hopefully reduce drag. But they were still off the pace of the Lotuses and the BRMs (although ahead of the Ferraris, to the undoubted disappoint-ment and even anguish of the huge and highly partisan Italian crowd).

The race itself quickly broke into slipstreaming packs, with the British V8 bunch up front (the BRM, Lotus, Lola and Cooper works cars along with the independent U.D.T.-Laystall Lotuses of Innes Ireland and Masten Gregory) and the silver Porsches hanging on grimly, followed by a growing gap down to the red cars and privateers. Then the transmission in Clark's Lotus played up again and he had to make a pit stop, Ireland ditto with a carburetion issue, and that left the BRM of Graham Hill out front while teammate Ginther held second just ahead of John Surtees in the Bowmaker Lola. And maybe holding him up just a bit to allow his team leader to get away? Gurney was mixing it up with whomever he could behind that bunch—sometimes passing and re-passing several times a lap—but he could never get away and was dead meat on his own as even the scrambling pack of Ferraris could reel him in then. Except for poor Phil Hill, whose engine was sounding sour as curdled milk and who kept slipping further and further backwards. He probably had to resist the temptation to just put the damn clutch in and blow it up, but he knew someone on the fences would hear it and know what it was…

Then the engine note on Surtees's Lola went flat and he had to park it a lap later—really too bad since he was sitting second in the points going into the Italian race—and twenty-some laps later, the transmission in Gurney's Porsche gave up and he also had to retire after a typically gallant (if thankless) effort. And that was pretty much it. Graham Hill went on to win and further pad his championship points lead with teammate Ginther something like a half-minute behind in second place. Then came McLaren another half-minute back in third and just barely holding off the inspired, never-say-die Willy Mairesse in the best of the Ferraris, who had driven like a madman, used the slipstream skillfully and reeled the Cooper in during the late stages of the race to finish just a few feet short in a near photo-finish. To the massive delight of the Italian crowd. And meanwhile, poor Phil Hill soldiered around to finish a dismal eleventh, five laps behind.

Hell, he'd won both the race and the blessed world championship for Ferrari at Monza the year before.

Back over on our side of the ocean, they held the first-ever World Manufacturers' Championship points race outside of Florida at the Bridgehampton "Double 400" on Long Island. It drew fairly decent (if sparse) fields for both the smallbore (category II) GT race on Saturday and the "big gun" run on Sunday, and the organizers had wisely decided to follow the lead of Sebring and Le Mans and include a special, "experimental" class for sports/prototypes up to four liters. You can bet your next paycheck that Carlo Sebastian had something to do with it, since he showed up with the same, one-of-a-kind, 4.0-liter Ferrari Testa Rossa that had won at Le Mans earlier in the year (only now with a US-style rollover bar and without the tall, ugly, wraparound windscreen and the "wing-style" fairing behind the cockpit that it wore in France). Older brother Pedro Rodriguez was handling the wheel-work, and they were far and away the class of the field. Although quick SCCA "gentleman driver" Alan Connell was there to give chase with his 2.5-liter Cooper Monaco and Briggs Cunningham had brought both of his monstrous Maserati 151 Le Mans coupes to see what they could do.

The Saturday smallbore race was won in a walkover by Bob Holbert in a borrowed Porsche Carrera Abarth (it was the only one on hand, and the owner was only too happy to step aside and let proven Porsche ace Holbert drive it), while well-to-do local boy/sometime artist/topnotch racer Bob Grossman took the 1000cc class and 3rd overall in a Fiat Abarth 1000. But not without one heck of a battle. Briggs Cunningham was there with three other Abarth 1000s for Walt Hansgen, Roger Penske and my friend Cal Carrington, and they were ready to make a race out of it. Penske's car dropped out almost immediately with clutch trouble, but Cal, Bob Grossman and Walt Hansgen had themselves one incredible and stupendous motor race! There were only a few lines about it in the *Comp Press* story (I mean, it was only the "tiddler" feature on Saturday) but Cal told me all about it when I ran into him on the Thursday test day before the big Times Grand Prix weekend at Riverside. "Oh, the three of us were going around like we were connected with elastic bands!" he explained through a wide, happy smile. "We were passing and re-passing for the sheer damn fun of it, and nobody was able to sneak away." He shook his head. "Oh, that was one hell of a lot of fun! The cars were so damn equal, and that track…" he shook his head again, "…you ever been to Bridgehampton?"

"Not really."

He looked at me somewhat incredulously.

"I was based out in California, remember," I did my best to explain, "and they never really had a major race there before this. It was all small-time amateur stuff. And damn if the magazine was going to pop for plane fare—or even gas money—to go see some grassroots regional race out east. They'd get some local guy to do for thirty-five bucks and no expenses. With maybe five bucks more for a picture if he knew how to focus a damn camera…."

"Well, you've missed a really good one. That turn one-two-three combination will shrink your balls up to the size of raisins!" He shook his head one more time, but still grinning. "Downhill. Blind. Fast…it's really something special. And the track's right by

Long Island Sound, so there's all these sand dunes all around. And if the wind gets to blowing or if somebody drops a wheel or two off, the sand gets all over the asphalt and it gets *really* slippery. Like at Zandvoort in Holland."

"So it was a good race?"

"Oh, it was a *hell* of a good race. Nose-to-tail and doorhandle-to-doorhandle. Even if you managed to sneak your way to the front and even if you did that last corner dead, solid perfect, there's this long, kinda uphill straight that follows and the other two guys would just draft right back up to you and steam right past—or try to steam right past—heading into one. And it's pretty damn hairy through there, believe me."

"Sounds like fun."

"Oh, it was! The Cunningham cars had a little more power—Alf Momo saw to that—but Bob's car was handling better. Plus Bob and Walt both know that place really, really well. To be honest, I was mostly following in their wheeltracks and hanging on for dear life the first few laps trying to figure it all out…" he gave me a little hint of a wink, "…but I got it eventually."

"So how'd it turn out?"

"Tires."

"Tires?"

Cal nodded. "We were running Michelin X's on the Cunningham cars, but Bob had a set of Goodyear race tires on his, and the surface is pretty damn abrasive at Bridgehampton—you spend a lot of your time sliding around in these glorious, 4-wheel drifts—and as we got towards the end, Walt and I are starting to slide all over the place and we're losing the back end on all the right-handers. And when you get a little, low-powered car like that sideways, it just scrubs off all the speed and you can no way get it back." He lifted his shoulders up in a helpless shrug. "I actually stopped at the pits to see if I maybe had a tire going down or an oil leak getting goo under the left-rear or something—I mean, the last thing I wanted to do was put one of Briggs's Abarths on its head again like I did at Sebring—but it was just the left-rear tire worn down to the fucking belts. You could see the damn cords! But it was right close to the end when I stopped, and Alf Momo told me to just go back out and putter around to the checker."

"What happened to Walt?"

"Oh, he slowly but surely lost touch with Bob and dropped back. It was one of those 'the harder I try, the slower I go' deals. And by then I'd made my stop and so Alf hung out a 'LR TIRE!!!' pit board to warn him. So Walt backed right out of it and settled for second-in-class."

"That's too bad."

"Yeah, I suppose. But you gotta give Bob Grossman and his guys credit for making the right call on the tires. And he drove one hell of a race, too. Can't take it away from him."

"And that's about it?"

"Oh, this guy named Mark Donohue looked really good again in this odd little TVR Grantura thing—he was driving the fucking wheels off of it—only then it broke and he was gone."

"Anything else interesting happen?"

"Not on Saturday. But Sunday was pretty interesting."

"Oh?"

And that's when Cal told me about his race in the Cunningham Maserati coupe. The same one, in fact, that he'd be driving here at Riverside. Briggs had two of the damn things and didn't really know what to do with them. They were built primarily for Le Mans, where that big, 4.0-liter Maserati V8 and the strange but supposedly aerodynamic coupe bodywork would make them really fast in a straight line. And no question they were among the fastest cars in France back in June, getting up to something like a hair over 180 on that long, long straightaway towards Mulsanne. But they'd all run into problems—mostly with the goofy, articulated rear suspension—and now they were in kind of a strange place competitively speaking. The cash-strapped factory had only built three of them, all to order (two for Briggs and one for the French Maserati distributor) so they could no way qualify as production GT cars. Although a lot of people—Cal included—thought they could blow the doors off of Enzo's GTOs if they could only run in the same class. But they couldn't. And the new crop of mid-engined sports prototypes like the Lotus 19, Cooper Monaco and Ferrari's 246 Dinos were just a lot lighter and handier. Particularly over shorter distances and even more particularly if you didn't have a convenient 8-kilometer straightaway on hand where you could let the damn thing loose to do what it did best. So the 151 was kind of iffy as a competitive proposition. But it was still damn fast—one of the fastest racecars around, in fact—and besides, Briggs owned two of them that weren't even half-a-season old and, assuming that the rear suspension problems had been sorted out, they were going to be pretty reliable. So he'd brought both cars to Bridgehampton, one for Cal and one for Augie Pabst, who had pretty much recovered from his harrowing wreck at Daytona back in February. Lead team driver Walt Hansgen was busy handling the Cunningham XKE in the GT class, going for the F.I.A. Manufacturers' Championship points on behalf of the Jaguar factory.

And that left Cal in one of the Maseratis. "Oh, most everybody seems to think they're monsters to drive," Cal confided, "but that's mostly on account of how they look. I mean, they *are* pretty nasty on the eyes."

"Vinci Pittacora says they look like the hunchback of Notre Dame."

"Yeah, kinda. They drive that way, too. The back end steers one way when you get on the gas and the other way when you lift off. You just have to get used to it. But they actually go around corners pretty well. Or at least fast sweepers like they have at Bridgehampton. You can get them into these fantastic drifts—totally predictable, you know?—and it feels absolutely marvelous. And that big V8 has got a *lot* of grunt in a straight line…"

"So they're actually *nice* to drive?"

"I didn't quite say that," Cal laughed. "They're hotter'n hell inside and the ass end steers and the noise is like a damn artillery barrage. And you can't see the corner apexes real well over the front fenders and even less out the back. And they do get to feeling clumsy around the little roundhouse carousel over on the backside of the circuit at Bridgehampton."

"Clumsy?"

"Oh, the car kinda wants to roll over onto the left-front tire and just plow through there. And the harder you push it, the worse it wants to plow. And if you try to compensate by chucking the back end out to get it turned, you just get all sideways and burn up the back tires."

"That doesn't sound like much fun."

"Ah, it's OK. You just gotta be patient through there and let the car do the best it can. Hell, it's great around the rest of the circuit. It's got torque like you can't believe, and it *really* hooks up through those two fast sweepers after the bridge. I was enjoying the heck out of it."

"So how'd you do?"

Cal's smile faded. "Oh, you know how it is: *It's not really what you're driving, it's who they put you in against...*"

I told Cal I understood.

"...Rodriguez and the big Ferrari were just too damn strong. I think we had almost as much horsepower and maybe even a little more on the torque end, but the Ferrari was a smidge lighter and sat a little lower to the ground and it poked a smaller hole in the air and, well, try as I might, I couldn't get quite down to his times. Neither could Augie in the other car. But we were reasonably close."

"Was anybody else in the hunt?"

"Oh, there was this Alan Connell guy up from Texas in a brand-new Cooper Monaco—the new-style kind with the pointy fins in back—and he drove it really well. It was magic through all the swoopy stuff. I think that's the car I really would've rather been driving, even though it had less power. And there was some guy named Colombosian on the entry list with a Lotus 19 with a Buick aluminum V8 stuffed in back. Now *that* would've been the car to have! Only it never showed up." He leaned in close and whispered: "I know for a fact that Cunningham's got something like that in the works out in Reventlow's shop in California—only in a Cooper chassis—but Walt will probably get the drive. I mean, he's their guy, isn't he?"

I had to agree that he was. And that he'd earned it, too, what with all sorts of victories and championships in Cunningham cars. But the talk about the Lotus 19/Buick and the Cooper Monaco/Buick got me thinking again about Eric Broadley's mid-engined Le Mans project back in the Lola shop in Bromley. "You know what're they planning to use for a transaxle on the Cooper?"

"Who the hell knows? I just drive the damn things."

Which naturally led to asking him how his race in that monster Maserati worked out at Bridgehampton?

"Oh, it was one of those stupid Le Mans start deals. And I'd have to say I did pretty good considering I had to open the damn door and climb in while most of the guys could just vault over the side. So there were a bunch of Porsches and shit in front of me by the time we funneled down through 1, 2 and 3 on the opening lap. But I stayed patient and waited till the pit straight, and then I just opened up that big old Maserati V8 and blew right past 'em." He gave me a big grin. "That's a pretty good feeling, you know?"

"I can imagine."

"By the time everything sorted itself out, I was running third with Augie right behind me in the other Maser and I could see Rodriguez in the Ferrari and Connell in the Cooper up ahead. But they had some distance already, so I was really only watching. And they were getting away from us. Not by a lot, you understand, but just that odd couple of tenths here and there every lap. And there wasn't a damn thing we could do about it."

"Sounds frustrating."

"Hey," Cal shrugged, "you do what you can do. You try to do more than that and they wind up calling a wrecker and plucking you out of the damn scenery."

It was interesting to see how Cal had matured. I could still remember the spoiled, cocky, *"I can do everything with anything"* kid who came out to California direct from the paddock at Road America to drive Ernesto Julio's Ferraris. That was only seven years before, but it felt like half a lifetime. Maybe even more than half…

I told him to go on with the story.

"It was probably a pretty good show to watch, actually. You could see that the Ferrari had more steam and would pull out a pretty good lead on the power sections, but Connell's Cooper was harassing the shit out of it through the corners."

"So what happened?"

"Nothing. You're just not going to rattle one of the Rodriguez brothers. Not either one of them. Pedro just drove like the Cooper wasn't even there, putting in one good, solid lap after another, and pretty soon he started to ease away. Not by a lot, you understand, but it only takes a little to break the other guy's spirit if you're doing it every lap. And then the ring and pinion went south on the Cooper and Connell was out of it. Brand new car, too."

"So what happened then?"

"Well, at that point I'm up to second place—mind you, it's still early on—and I've got Augie in my mirrors in the other 151. But he's not breaking either of our balls trying to get around—I mean, we're supposed to be teammates, right?—and so we're just kind of circulating around in formation and marking time. We both know there's no way either one of us are gonna catch Rodriguez in the Ferrari. And then all of a sudden, I see a cloud of smoke in my mirrors and Augie goes missing."

"Oh?"

Cal nodded.

"What was it?"

"They didn't tear it down at the racetrack, but Alf Momo said it looked like a broken piston. Probably trashed a lot of other stuff inside the motor, too."

"Geez. That's too bad."

"I'll say. And those Maserati V8s are *not* cheap on the rebuilds. Or that's what Briggs said, anyway."

"And what happened with you?"

"Aw, hell, I was just cruising around on my way to an easy second place. Money in the bank, you know?" He shook his head. "And then it all went to shit."

"Oh?"

Cal nodded. "Stripped ring and pinion. Just like Connell's Cooper."

"It broke just like that?"

"Nah, it was one of those Slow Death deals."

"Like a Chinese water torture?"

"Yeah, that's it." I watched his eyes go far-away unfocused as he remembered it: "I heard it first. Like this deep, soft, off-key humming noise that sort of fades in and out. And at first you're not sure if you're really hearing it or if it's just your ears playing tricks on you because you're all alone on the track with nobody to race. Only then it gets a little louder and you notice that you're hearing it mostly when you've got the car loaded up in right-hand corners. Which is like about two-thirds of the damn circuit at Bridgehampton. And then it gets even louder and more off-key and strident and now it's turning into this nasty, painful sort of metal-on-metal warble. And now there's a vibration you can actually feel coming through the seat of your pants and the steering wheel. You can smell it, too: that stinky, burnt-metal foundry smell like somebody's roasting crank fragments marinated in gear lube on a hot plate."

"Sounds unpleasant."

"Oh, you know you're fucked—I mean, the race is supposed to be 400 kilometers and it's still less than half over—but you do your best to try and baby it around and keep going. And by now there's even some smoke and fumes filtering into the cockpit and it smells to high heaven. You can even start to feel the heat of it on your backside—you're damn near sitting on the rear axle in one of those things—and you know the gas tank is back there, too, so now you start thinking how inconvenient it would be if the damn thing burst into flames. I mean, it would take a little time and distance to get the thing whoa'd down from 150 or so. Not to mention finding a friendly place to park it and bail out. And then of course it would probably just burn to the ground right there by the side of the road. And you wouldn't want that, either." He let off a slow, sad sigh. "So you decide to back out of it and head for the pits, and by now it's chattering and gnashing and grinding back there like a bucket of bolts being fed through a sausage grinder..." Cal's voice trailed off. And then he added, somewhat sheepishly, "I probably should've brought the damn thing in the lap before, but I was still kidding myself that I could make it to the end."

"That's really too bad."

He rolled his palms up. "Hey, what can you do?" And then he looked thoughtful for a moment. "You know, there was actually a lot of that going on at Bridgehampton."

"A lot of what?"

"Rear-end problems. Cars chewing up their differential gears." He looked over at me again. "Alf Momo said it's because you spend so damn much time loaded up and sliding through those long sweepers and fighting your way around the carousel. It puts a lot of load on the ring-and-pinion gears and the support bearings."

"Makes sense."

"Hey, what do I know? I'm no mechanic. Back when I used to drive the cars Buddy used to put together, he told me I was the poorest excuse for a mechanic he'd ever seen in his life. Said he didn't want me around the car with anything sharper or heavier than a shop rag."

We had a good laugh off of that.

"Did you see Buddy while you were out east?"

"Oh, I stopped by his shop between Bridgehampton and the race at Watkins Glen the next weekend."

"Oh? How's he doing?"

"Looks like he's doing really well for himself. He's got a new shop all picked out up in Connecticut. He says it doesn't look like much on the outside, but it's big inside and the roof and the heat are good and there's a graded lot outside and some sheds and out-buildings for storing stuff. And Julie found an old Victorian house she really likes that he says needs a million things and that they can't really afford. But she likes it and she says the schools are good and you and I both know how that deal's gonna turn out."

"That we do."

"So he's got the house and his shop in Jersey on the market and money down already on the two places up in Connecticut. But he's got money. He came away smelling like a rose from that VW dealership thing with Big Ed."

"Good for him. He worked hard for it."

"That he did."

"Is he looking forward to the move?"

"Not to hear him tell it. He says he'd rather put a bullet in his head."

"Is he still doing a lot of racecar stuff?"

"Oh, he's got this fat Costin Lister that some masochist's dropping a Chevy in and that same Lotus 17 the owner doesn't know what to do with—only that one's outside under a tarp and some plastic sheeting now—and he's still got Carson's Healey 3000 and his own Giulietta packed away in the corner under car covers. Plus this really nice E-Type club-racer that he looks after for that Buster Jones guy—you remember him?—but he hardly ever takes it out and runs it anymore."

"It's like Buddy always said: if you still have the car, you can still tell everybody in the joint you're a racing driver…"

"I guess."

"So what else is in the shop?"

"Oh, he looks after some exotic street stuff—a couple Ferraris and Maseratis from Bergen County and quite a few Jaguars."

"He was always good with Jaguars."

"Hell, he grew up with them," Cal shrugged. "And most of the owners have had it up to here with the dealership service departments."

"Amen to that."

"But he's doing more and more of those long-term restoration projects. Old stuff, you know? Classics. Says he really enjoys it when he can take his time and get things right."

"Yeah, the racecar stuff always seems pretty frantic," I had to agree. "Sure, it's fun. Best fun there is. But you're always in a hurry and there's always too much to do and not enough time and some kind of deadline looming. When that green flag waves, you sure as hell better be there and be ready…" I ran it around in my mind. It was familiar territory. "…And then there's all the travel and the crap rooms and the long tows to get there and get home again. Living out of a damn suitcase can get pretty old."

Cal knew exactly what I was talking about.

"…Oh, I guess it's fine if you're a young guy on your own. But it gets different when you've got kids and a family to take care of…" I gave Cal a little shrug. "…some guys just get burned out along the way…"

I could see that the subject didn't sit too well with Cal. He'd been on the road so damn long he didn't really have a home base anymore. Oh, he'd always been a lone-wolf type and his family had several really nice houses—a mansion that was damn near a castle in New Jersey and a summer home out in the Hamptons and a winter place down in Palm Beach—where he could go and stay for as long as he liked whenever the hell he felt like it. But that's not really the same thing, is it? I decided it might be best if I bailed out of the subject and asked him to tell me more about Buddy's shop. And he was more than ready to do it:

"Oh, he's got this enormous 1916 Packard Twin-Six touring car in a million pieces. Says it's a near-twin to the Russian imperial state limousine. The czar and czarina and their kids used to ride around in it before the Bolsheviks took over and filled them full of lead."

"Cheery thought."

"Well, there always has to be a story, doesn't there?"

"Sure there does. A little romance. A little mystery. A little magic. Just ask Dick Flick about it."

"Who?"

"Never mind," I waved him off. "Tell me more about the cars."

"Oh, he's got all kinds of neat stuff. He's doing a Bugatti for one guy and a Bentley Speed Six for another, and there's an old Alfa 8C he just got in that's plain gorgeous."

"Sounds like he's keeping busy."

"The best part is that these guys can afford the work and they don't rush him too much. Or at least not once he's talked to them about 'Time and Materials' and doing things the right way. He said that was the hard part at first."

"Oh?"

Cal nodded. "He said he damn near went broke on his first few restoration jobs. He figured he had to finish the damn things before he could ask for any money."

"I bet he learned that lesson pretty quick."

"Hey, he's not the sharpest businessman in the world—hell, he'd be the first one to tell you that—but Julie took one look at where they were and told him point-blank that he had to bill his restoration work out every month if he wanted to keep doing it. Time and Materials. Every fucking month." Cal gave me an insider smile. "And you don't go arguing with a ball-buster like Julie Finzio if you know what the hell's good for you."

"Amen to that!" I agreed. And that's when I realized I hadn't seen Buddy—or Julie or their kids—since Cal and I drove up there from Florida on a crazy whim between Daytona and Sebring what seemed like a hundred years ago.

"You should really drop in on him some day," Cal advised.

"I'd like to."

"It looks like he's doing really well."

"Good. He deserves it."

"And he looks reasonably happy, too. Home life seems to agree with him. He's even put on a little weight."

"He's married to an Italian," I laughed out loud. "What do you expect?"

Chapter 20: In the Paddock at Riverside

It was great being back in Southern California again, and even better being back at Riverside for its biggest event of the year. SoCal had always been sports-car country—hey, it was just made for loud, fast, exotic, sharp-looking cars and top-down motoring—but the L.A. area never had a real world-class racing circuit until Riverside opened in 1957. It was out in the middle of what was almost a damn desert and the heat, wind, grit and dust were almost always a problem. But noise wasn't, since it was right next door to March Air Force Base, where all sorts of jet fighters, SAC bombers, tankers, military cargo planes and an entire squadron of piston-engined Fairchild C-119 Flying Boxcars were forever taking off and landing. And that was a good thing. Plus Riverside was big (3.3 miles per lap on the full "long course" lap) and it was fast and challenging and there were grand, sweeping esses and camber and elevation changes that made the cars go all light and queasy just where you didn't want them to. Not to mention a back straightaway that went on for just over a full mile (!!!) with what amounted to a claustrophobic little oval-style U-turn with a very solid wall around the outside when you got to the far end! Although for this race they were using the somewhat slower, 2.54-mile "club" circuit that added a big, connector "S" bend, cut out the Turn 8 "boot" and shortened the back straight to six-tenths of a mile. Which would hopefully keep the faster cars from flirting with 190 or so before they had to lean on the binders. Even so, a lot of people thought Riverside was dangerous because it was so fast and unforgiving in spots—people had died there—but all the sportycar types around Los Angeles were absolutely thrilled with it and had turned out in impressive numbers to watch the LA Times Grand Prix (sic) for Sports Cars since the very first time it was run back in 1958. And why not, since it was the biggest damn professional road race of the year in Southern California.

It was wonderful wandering through the Riverside paddock again and seeing so many of my old L.A. racing friends. I hadn't seen some of them for years. Plus there was a sizable international contingent on hand thanks to an impressive wad of prize money and the fact that all the drivers were already over on this side of the Atlantic for the United States Grand Prix at Watkins Glen the previous weekend. Not to mention the money race at Kent, Washington, the week before that and the Mosport pro race the week before Kent.

I really wanted to be at all of them, of course—particularly the USGP—even though I knew in advance that Audrey wouldn't be there because she didn't want to leave Walter alone for five or six days. He groused about that, of course. Told her the team needed her and that she should get the bloody hell out. But he'd apparently lifted something way too heavy at the Lola shop and screwed up his lower back so badly that he could barely get out of his bed or his telly chair and crawl to the damn bathroom on his hands and knees. And of course he was furious about that and re-sented being incapacitated and not being able to go to work and resented Audrey even more for trying to help. You could lay it off by saying he was just an angry, bitter, ungrateful, mean-spirited old sonofabitch and let it go at that, but I kept think-ing about that strange, almost frozen moment in the pits at Brands Hatch, when we were standing there in the drooling rain and I was just getting ready to leave for the airport. I didn't want to go, of course, since I knew I'd be flying back to that sterile, empty room at the Fairview and all the stupid company bullshit in Fairway Tower and Audrey would be staying there in London and who the hell knew when I'd get a chance to see her and be with her again? So I'd kind of hung around longer than I should have. And it was just about the time I realized that I'd better get my ass on the road or I'd miss my plane when Walter's hand shot out of nowhere like a snake strike and grabbed hold of my forearm. I can still remember the grip of those strong, bony fingers. And then he looked me right in the eyes, thanked me without warmth or emotion for looking after Audrey, curled the corners of his mouth up into a cold, executioner's smile and added, in this strange, icy monotone: *"Have a thought for what it's like on my bloody side of the fence sometime…"*

It made me feel sad for him even while I was busy being angry as hell at him for keeping us apart and moreover fucking up her life with his incessant needs and de-mands. It's kind of confusing when you feel sorry for someone even while you're wish-ing that they could be conveniently found dead under a bus or drowned in a bathtub or stretched out cold and motionless on the floor from a cooperative heart attack. I didn't wish him any pain or suffering, mind you. Just death. Or disappearance. That would work, too. And then of course I felt guilty as hell for even thinking such a thing.

And then I thought it all over again…

I hadn't seen Audrey since the race at Brands Hatch—it was two months now—and I was missing her terribly and even losing touch with what it was like to be around her. And that's a desolate feeling indeed. But even though she wasn't going to be there, I was still mad as hell that I'd missed the only genuine grand prix in North America at Watkins Glen. Oh, there was another one coming in Mexico next season (and a non-championship round there in a couple weeks to allow the circuit and the teams to get to know each other and "prove out" the track and the organization to the grand-prix movers and shakers) and I knew the Canadians wanted one, too. But for 1962, the USGP at Watkins Glen was the only genuine F1 grand prix on the North American continent. And there was a great (if long-shot) world-championship battle going on between Jim Clark's Lotus and points-leader Graham Hill's BRM to add spice and story line to the weekend. Plus The Glen wasn't all that many hours from my adopted-but-unloved home base in Detroit. But we had this big wind-up meeting/de-briefing/brain-storming session on the Thursday and Friday where everybody who was in any way involved in those dealership-principal new-car-line introductions had to get together to present their reports, hash out how things went, explain what they thought they'd accomplished and think ahead to how they might do it all better next year. It was pure bullshit, of course—even Dick Flick thought so—but Danny Beagle told me I sure as hell better be there because Bob Wright would be heading up the program, and he believed very strongly that communal corporate dissection, discussion and development would help build what he called "team and task unity" in The Tower and improve, at least over time, (and I quote here verbatim from his opening remarks:) *the dealership-principal relationship, experience and education that ultimately translates into the front-line, out-on-Main-Street face and identity of Fairway Motors to the car-buying public."* And that sounded like bullshit to me, too. Only it had a near-evangelical believability when Bob Wright was the guy up on the podium giving it to you in person. Plus Little Harry Dick Fairway himself came sauntering in just about the time Bob Wright was wrapping up his *"This is important to all of us! Go-get-'em!"* speech. So you didn't dare crack wise. Or even snicker.

H.R. Junior walked in like he owned the place, of course (which, when you get right down to it, he more or less did), and in his wake was his favorite and generally terrified new house pet: computer modeling/consumer data specialist Hubert C. Bean. *"We're gonna get this shit all down into our computers now,"* H.R. Junior bellowed with the usual edge of warning in his voice, *"so I want all of you to give everything you got and everything you come up with to Hubert here. He knows what to do with it."*

To be honest, if anybody since the dawn of creation looked less like they knew what to do with anything, I don't know who it might be. But Hubert just radiated his best deer-in-the-headlights smile—it was more like a grimace, actually—and timidly made his way to a seat in the far back corner of the room as soon as Little Harry Dick made his exit.

Like I said, it was all bullshit.

So that was Thursday and Friday shot to hell (while practice for the damn grand prix was going on not all that many hours away at Watkins Glen), and Ben Abernathy's daughter was getting married on the Sunday and he'd damn near begged me to attend. He told me he saw way too much of his own family and his wife's family already (not to mention all the Tower people he was pretty much doomed to invite), and he didn't much care for the guy his daughter was marrying and even less for his family. "I need somebody to sneak out back with, Hank," he pleaded. And of course I knew what he was talking about. We'd never actually smoked any pot together (or even talked about it...I mean, you really don't know who you can trust with that kind of information), but the subject came up somewhat casually when we were discussing Little Harry Dick's wayward, spoiled-rotten, insolent and potentially dangerous teenage daughter. That's when Ben kind of let on that he'd tried it out on the darkened edge of the Black Mamba Lounge's parking lot a time or two and I kind of let on that I had, too, and from that moment on, we had an unspoken understanding that we could sneak off and do it together the next time we had an appropriate opportunity. And that opportunity was apparently going to come up at his daughter's wedding. Which, I must admit, was tremendously—even hilariously!—amusing after we'd snuck out back of the rental hall together and passed a joint of Willie Shorter's weed back and forth in the shadow of the alley dumpsters. Ben would start to sputter trying to hold it down and one time he went on this coughing jag that actually scared me.

"Jesus, Ben, do you really think you oughta be doing this?"

"Look," he gasped when he could finally get a word out, "I'm less than two years from retirement."

"So?"

"So you see all those people inside?"

I nodded.

"That's my future, Hank…" he rasped as he sucked in another hit, "…Hanging around with those assholes…"

We smoked it down to a stub so small you couldn't hold it between your thumb and forefinger, and then we looked up at the moon and stars for a while—or maybe it was the fucking streetlamp, it didn't make any difference—and then the two of us went back inside and pretty much laid waste to the appetizer and dessert tables. Not to mention the bar.

And so that's how I spent the Sunday of the United States Grand Prix at Watkins Glen, pushing frosted slices of strawberry-goo-filled wedding cake, repeated scoops of creamy vanilla ice cream and entirely too many chocolate-covered glazed pecan squares into my face like I was some sort of one-man sweet-table demolition squad. I couldn't stop myself, you know? And that's why I didn't really get a full update on the F1 race until I ran into Geoff Britten and Peter Bryant wandering through the paddock at Riverside a week later. "So how did it go?" I asked them both.

Peter pretended to spit at the ground. "It was shit for us…that's for damn sure."

"Oh?"

Peter nodded emphatically, and Geoff Britten added a terse little half-nod of agreement.

"So what happened?"

"John crashed the Lola in Friday afternoon practice. Not his fault at all. Bloody steering arm fractured up by the ball joint. Happened out of nowhere and sent him hurtling off into the woods. Big bloody wreck."

"Jesus…was he OK?"

"Shaken up a bit, but OK."

"Bloody lucky, though. Some poor bloke got himself killed not far from that spot in an amateur race just two weeks before. Went off and collected a tree in an old Lotus Mk. IX that some bloody genius had stuffed an ally Buick V8 into."

"Those things were a bundle of sticks to start with," Geoff grumbled disapprovingly. "They were designed to take Ford Tens and hotted-up TC motors. Or perhaps a Coventry-Climax FW if you had the budget for it. But they were marginal even then. No one in their right mind would attempt putting an American V8 in one…"

"That may be," Peter interrupted, "but once you're headed into the bloody scenery, what sort of box you're in doesn't make as much difference as what you're about to hit and how bloody hard you're going to hit it. Shitbox or Formula One car, it's all down to speed and angle of impact at that point."

Geoff opened his mouth to argue, but thought better of it.

"I'll tell you this, mate," Peter Bryant continued, "I believe our Mr. Surtees is getting damn bloody tired of having the rug ripped out from under him like that."

I knew what Peter was talking about. The worst thing for any racing driver is an unexpected mechanical failure. And particularly if it has anything to do with brakes or steering. There you are, streaking along at damn near the limit, with all of your attention and concentration focused into this all-consuming funnel of speed when—completely out of nowhere!—there's a *bang!* or a *snap!* (or sometimes there's no warning sound at all!), and you're suddenly and irrevocably out of control and headed wherever your fucking vector, velocity and momentum feel like taking you. It's a pretty damn sobering sensation, and sometimes you get away with it and sometimes there's a truly hard *thump!* or *whump!* or *crunch!* at the end. Followed by an ambulance ride. Or, worse yet, nothing at all.

"John was all right," Geoff quickly explained, "but you can be sure it didn't do much for his confidence in the car."

"I'll bloody say," Peter snorted. "Mind you, the Lola's a good car, don't get me wrong. In fact, for a first-time effort, it's bloody damn brilliant! But I'm sure this 'test pilot' business is getting pretty old from John's point of view. And I can't say as I bloody well blame him."

I could understand that, too.

And that made it even more impressive when John took over team-mate Salvadori's older car for the race on Sunday. It takes huge balls and/or a very short memory to do things like that.

Peter looked over at Geoff as if for approval before continuing in a low, confidential whisper: "None of us really knows what's going to happen for next year. There's rumors Bowmaker may have had about enough of F1 and the old checkbook may be closing."

"That's never good."

"No, it isn't. But it does bloody happen. In fact, it's one of the few things in motor sport you can count on. Money comes, money goes…"

Geoff Britten added another imperceptible nod.

"Plus I think old Enzo may be whispering in Surtees's ear."

"Oh?"

Peter nodded.

"Wouldn't he be crazy to take it? I mean, they've been way off the pace this year, and the Lola's been pretty damn quick."

"Indeed it has, indeed it has. But the bloody wheels keep snapping off. And whatever you can say about the red cars, they're built bloody stout. Always have been."

"And Ferrari aren't fools," Geoff noted. "They've seen what our English cars are all about and they'll have their own take on it soon enough. They won't be down forever in Formula One. They'll bounce back. You can count on it."

Peter gave me the insider eyeball. "And John likes it in Italy. He's a bloody national hero down there from the bike days with MV."

And that was surely true.

I got the rest of the story on The Glen weekend as we sat down over a typically greasy racetrack-concession-stand breakfast. You know: slimy eggs, slippery sausages, a sodden lump of hash browns and soggy slice of toast with way too much butter. They put it on with a damn paintbrush! And you know what? It tasted *wonderful*.

Turns out Phil Hill was out of a ride again at Watkins Glen since Ferrari didn't even bother to send cars over (Enzo claimed it was because of the strikes in Italy, but nobody much believed it). And rumors were circulating that Phil was either already sacked or about to be sacked by Dragoni. Perhaps the Old Man had heard whispers about Phil's conversations with Chiti and the rest of the Ferrari renegades over at ATS? If so, that couldn't have gone down very well in Maranello. In any case, Phil was seen wandering around the pits looking a bit lost, and Dan Gurney managed to talk Porsche into letting him have some laps in Bonnier's car on Saturday since Jo was suffering from lower back problems (although he was back in the Porsche for the race).

Speaking of Gurney, both he and Richie Ginther (and Masten Gregory in the pale green U.D.T.-Laystall Lotus 24 with BRM power) were showing that little extra shot of speed, guts and grace that race drivers always seem to whip together for their home-country grand prix. Richie's BRM actually out-qualified team-and-championship leader Graham Hill (albeit by only a tenth of a second) to sit on the outside front row of the staggered, two-by-two starting grid, and Gurney once again had the air-cooled Porsche flat 8 punching well above its weight just behind the BRM boys in 4th, while Gregory was by far quickest of the non-works entries in 7th. That had to make you feel good if you were an American. And particularly if you could wave it around under Eric Gibbon's nose like a bad-smelling piece of cheese. Although solidly on pole (and the only driver to dip into the 1:15s with a 1:15.8) was Jimmy Clark and the Lotus 25. Mind you, G. Hill in the BRM had a fairly comfortable points lead going in, but it was obvious Jimmy and the Lotus intended to make a fight of it.

And that's precisely how the race played out. Much to the delight of the large turnout of fans, who braved overcast skies and typically chilly October weather to see a tremendous battle between the two championship contenders. Jimmy got away quickest at the start, but Graham Hill fought back and even managed to snatch the lead away for several laps after Jimmy got balked working his way through some backmarkers. But the Lotus's superiority—at least on this day and at this particular racetrack—was not to be denied, as Jimmy reeled the BRM in (setting a new lap record in the process), re-took the lead on lap 19 and eased away to an impressively solid victory. Which must have brought a smile to Colin Chapman's face, since the USGP paid by far the largest purse on the entire grand prix calendar. Plus it set up a cliff-hanger, winner-take-all scenario for the final GP of the season in South Africa on December 29th. If Clark won again, he would be world champion. If he didn't, Graham Hill would take the crown.

You couldn't write it up any better as fiction.

"How'd Gurney make out?" I wanted to know.

"He drove like a bloody tiger, as always—I put him on the short list with the very best of them—and he charged his way up to third early on and held it through most of the race. To my way of thinking, he was running ahead of several cars—cars with very good drivers, mind you—that really should have been quicker. But he's one of the special ones, Gurney is…"

"So how did it all turn out?"

"Seemed to me that the Porsche faded a bit as the race wore on, and McLaren in the Cooper and then Brabham in his own car got by. But Dan did finish 5th, and the way I saw it, he carried that bloody car on his back most of the way."

"He always gives a great effort."

"That he does. And what a touch! He never looks frantic or messy…just bloody *fast!*"

"Anything else special?"

"Oh, your Kansas City boy Masten Gregory took a nice 6th in U.D.T.'s Lotus/BRM hybrid, and a few of your home American drivers made the race and didn't embarrass themselves. That Roger Penske fellow qualified 12th and finished 9th in a rented-and-repainted BRP Lotus, and those Chaparral boys—Jim Hall and Hap Sharp—showed up with an out-of-date Lotus and an out-of-date Cooper, and they did tolerably well. Hall's car broke something in the motor and didn't make the start, but Sharp put in a very workmanlike performance for a big man in a small car with just an old 4-cylinder Climax for power. The car was a bloody antique, to be honest. But he did the full distance and brought it home 11th at the flag."

That was good to hear.

And then I wanted to know about something else. "So," I asked as I chewed on my over-buttered piece of toast, "how's Audrey doing?"

"Oh, she's all right. You know how it is."

"No, I don't know how it is," I corrected him. "That's why I asked."

"Well, you know Walter's been a bit laid up."

"She said it's his back."

"Dumb bastard tried to lift a Climax V8 onto the workbench all by himself. Stupid bloody thing to do. Oh, it's alloy and it didn't have the heads on it, but the bloody crank, rods and pistons were all inside."

"What the hell was he thinking?"

"Who knows? But he knew right away he'd bunged himself up. Tried to hide it, of course, but he couldn't."

"So what happens now?"

"Oh, there's docs and therapy—there'll be more therapy once he can get around a bit more—but it's tough on the old bird."

"I bet it's tougher on Audrey."

"Oh, you can bloody bank on it. He's no daisy even when he's at his best."

I felt this grim, sinking sensation inside. I knew that I should really *be* there for her. Even if there wasn't much of anything I could do. And then I started picking through my head again for plausible excuses that might take me back to London. But the only things I could think of were the Lola Le Mans coupe that was hopefully coming together with a Fairway V8 in back in Eric Broadley's shop and the now-everybody-knows "secret" Indianapolis racer—also with Fairway power—under construction over at Lotus. But Danny Beagle had been less than lukewarm regarding my need or value on either of those projects. The next "real" thing on the agenda was the Olympia Racing Car Show at the end of January, and that was more than three fucking months away.

Damn.

But race weekends have a way of sweeping you up in their slipstream and leaving the cares and concerns of your everyday life, if not behind, at least in the shadows until Monday rolls around and you realize once again that you're miserable. Not to mention exhausted, sunburned (or chilled, sniffling and coughing…or all of those things put together) and generally beat to shit. And it starts with all the people you run into that you haven't seen in quite awhile and all the stories you need to catch up on. Like what happened just two weeks before the US Grand Prix, when the Canadian organizers at Mosport and the SCCA folks at Watkins Glen managed to put two of their biggest sports car events of the year on the same damn weekend! Although they're in different countries, those two tracks are just 275 driving miles apart (or 135 miles as the crow or Cessna flies it) and feed off the selfsame pool of spectators and volunteer workers. It was no good and everybody knew it. But, like sanctioning bodies everywhere, the two groups just set their jaws and dug their heels in and absolutely *insisted* that "the other bunch" were the ones who'd gotten it all wrong…

Some things never change.

To be fair, the Glen race was an SCCA amateur deal while the Canadian race paid actual prize money, but it put everybody involved on either side of the St. Lawrence

Seaway in a quandary as to which race to attend or support. And that made it a particularly difficult choice for the volunteer workers who were needed to staff both events. Like my corner-worker friend Dale Strimple from Lake Erie Communications, whom I instantly recognized from the back in the Riverside paddock: white worker coveralls with "Lake Erie Communications" embroidered across the back, wide-brimmed Australian sun-or-rain hat (he's no fool), longish grey hair and beard and comfortable boots performing a happy but beleaguered sort of shuffle as he directed racecars to the false grid for Thursday morning practice.

"Hey, Dale!" I shouted at his back. *"What the hell are you doing out here in California?"*

He recognized my voice and turned around. And then answered, kind of sheepishly, "Well…y'see…I'm not really here…."

"You're not?"

Dale shook his head. "Nah," he admitted, "I'm home sick in bed. Been that way since Wednesday morning. Or that's when I called it in, anyway…" he tossed in a guilty smile, "…don't expect I'll be feelin' well enough to go back t'work until Tuesday. And I guarantee I'll be lookin' right poorly when I do show up…"

"You're playing hooky, aren't you?"

"I don't know as I'd call it *that,*" he started in, "but I was off for the F1 race at Watkins Glen and for Mosport two weeks before that—my boss is usually pretty good on that stuff so long as I get all my work done—but there's just no way I could miss this one."

And I could understand why. The *Times Grand Prix* at Riverside was going to have the best entry of top-level cars and drivers *ever* in these United States—the latest Lotus and Cooper sports models, Ferrari Testa Rossas, Maserati Birdcages and 151 Le Mans coupes, V8-powered American specials and hybrids, cream-of-the-crop European drivers, home-grown road-racing and Indianapolis stars…you name it—and it would be tough for a guy like Dale not to want to be there and be a part of it. He leaned in a little closer and whispered the details:

"There's four of us who came out. This guy named Ken Kotyk—he's a Lake Erie guy, too—he's got one of those Volkswagen bus things. A camper, you know? So on the way back from Mosport we got to talking about how cool it would be if we could all just sneak out to Riverside for this one. I mean, we weren't really serious about it or anything. It was just talk. But by the time we got back to Ohio, we'd just about convinced ourselves that we could do it. I mean, we'd have to leave Tuesday pretty much right after work, drive straight through, get here in time for the worker briefing Thursday morning for the test day, do the weekend, leave right after the race, drive straight through again and be maybe just a little bit late for work on Tuesday morning."

I shook my head. "You guys are *nuts!*"

He gave me a toothy grin. "Hey, it beats nine-to-five'n it!"

And that was true enough.

Then I had a question: "What made you guys pick Mosport over The Glen?"

"Hard to say. But we knew we was gonna be at The Glen for the F1 race two weeks later, so it just seemed like the right thing to do. Plus we all love it up in Canada. The people are friendly as anything and they always treat us great. Bob DeShane is president of the club up there, and he always makes sure we're well taken care of. Besides, we'd heard that Stirling Moss was gonna be there."

"Stirling Moss?"

"Yep," he nodded. "Some Canadian guy who made a fortune in wieners and sausages paid for him to be there."

"Wieners and sausages?"

"Sure," he went on like it made perfect sense. "He makes and sells these 'Shopsy's Wieners' all over Canada. And that's a lot of damn wieners. Anyhow, he's a big race fan and so he paid to have Moss come up to be the honorary starter."

I thought about the Moss press interview I'd attended just a few weeks before, and I couldn't help thinking what it had to be like for him, showing up at one of his favorite North American racetracks as an honorary, pomp-and-circumstance-style figurehead instead of a driver. He'd won both heats in dominating style at the Players 200 at Mosport the previous June, and finished third after radiator and gearbox problems (although he sat on pole and set a new lap record) in the fall race there. It had to be tough.

"So how'd the weekend go?"

"Oh, it was a pretty good race," Dale allowed. "In spite of the rain and wet and the cold."

"It rained?"

"Just on race-day morning," he gave me a helpless little shrug. "It was pretty miserable there for awhile. But then it cleared some before the start and actually dried out during the first part of the race. It was still pretty cold, though." He didn't look particularly upset about it. Then again, corner workers are used to crappy weather. They deal with it all the time—searing heat, bitter cold, blazing sun, whipping wind or rain pouring down in torrents—they've seen it all and they know how to prepare for it. It's just part of the adventure.

As I've said before, Mosport is one of those fast, flowing and yet terrifically intimidating racetracks, and that makes it the kind of place where a truly gifted, calm-in-his-heart driver—like Moss, for example—can really make a difference. And so it was no surprise to learn that Dan Gurney had once again put the Arciero Brothers Lotus 19 on pole and set a new qualifying record in the process. But it took a lot of doing since another team had hired away the Arciero Brothers' longtime mechanic and crew chief Jerry Eisert, and so the learning curve for their new guy, Bob Harris, was just about vertical. It's tough stepping into some other guy's shoes (not to mention his shop and whatever projects he's got taken apart or is in the process of putting back together) and so the car arrived late, and Dan and Bob spent all of Friday's practice time in a local gas station going through it since the engine and driveline had just been re-installed. And come Saturday, the engine had a recurring flat spot at the top end. They'd put fresh plugs in (warm-up plugs, in fact, because the weather was so blessed cold) and get three good laps out of it, but then the miss came back, and the damn thing wouldn't pull over 6000rpm. They went through everything they could think of—carburetion, electrics, you name it—looking for the cause, but the problem reappeared on the pace lap and Dan never got higher than 3rd place. He ultimately made a pit stop to change the plugs again, and one of them was sooty black and obviously not firing properly. But by then Dan was back out and, sure enough, two laps later the problem reappeared. It wasn't until the second pit stop that they finally located the cause...a bad plug lead that was leaking the sparks out all over the engine! By that point, Dan and the Lotus were hopelessly behind, but he sure showed what he and the car could do, catching and passing the leaders—twice!—and knocking off Moss's existing race-lap record in the process as he clawed his way back up through the field until...until the damn gearbox broke around five laps from the checker and put him out for good! Typical Gurney luck!

But the race was pretty interesting anyway, as "Kansas City Flash" Masten Gregory had one of his hit-or-miss brilliant race days in the U.D.T.-Laystall Lotus 19. Oh, he may have looked more like a biology grad assistant than a racing driver, but no question Masten had balls the size of grapefruits—even Cal said so—and he was always at his best on scary, daunting racetracks (like Spa, for example) that put other drivers on edge. Plus some days—and especially on difficult tracks—Masten somehow found that little extra dose of grace or touch or spunk or tiger or whatever the hell it was, and he'd put in a truly flawless performance. But it was far from easy at Mosport, since he'd had car troubles in qualifying and didn't get a single qualifying lap in the books. So he had to start from the very last row. But sometimes that just gets a driver revved up, and fortunately his crew guys had found the problem and sorted it out so his car was good for the race.

Only like I said, he had to start at the back.

But Masten had come up with a clever and cunning little strategy to deal with the situation. As the field came around to take the green on a damp-but-drying track, Masten cut hard to the right at the very last instant and dove into pit lane. And then he just plain *nailed* it. The pea-soup green Lotus came blasting through pit lane like a damn rocket sled—almost collecting some poor movie cameraman who was looking the other way through his Bolex to film the start—and swooped out pit exit to rejoin the pack about twenty places further up the field! Not to mention damn near taking out a popular young local driver named Jack Boxstrom in an ever-so-slightly antique Lotus Mk. IX when he swerved into the pits. Poor Jack was just tooling along, minding his own business at the back end of the starting field when Masten's Lotus suddenly chopped across his bows and barreled into pit lane. It caught the local driver completely by surprise, and it was only his quick reactions and acute sense of thrift (Canadian drivers are world-renowned for avoiding situations that they may ultimately have to fix with their own money) that prevented a serious incident.

Speaking of Canadians, everyone was astonished to see that the leader at the end of lap one was none other than an ex-pat Brit/now Canadian driver named John Cannon in the absolutely brutal-looking (and also homegrown Canadian) Dailu-Chev. John had quietly made a reputation for himself racing his own Elva Courier and then a well-used D-Type Jaguar, and he proved his speed was no fluke when he was brought in to drive Montrealer Dave Greenblatt's ferocious new racing special. It had been built over the winter months by Greenblatt and his mechanic, Luigi Cassiani, and it was along the lines of Jim Hall's Chaparral what with a big Chevy motor in front and independent suspension all around. But it was black instead of white, hugged tighter to the ground and looked far wickeder than Hall's Chaparral. Greenblatt had driven it himself in a few local amateur races while they worked out the bugs, and then they brought Canon in to run the money races.

Now big, bellowing, 368-cubic-inch front-engined V8 racing specials are not what you would expect at the head of the queue on a difficult and demanding—not to mention damp!—racetrack like Mosport. Especially against genuine, international-grade competition in the very latest, lightest and lithest Lotus and Cooper chassis. But there John Cannon and the Dailu were, and (according to Dale, anyway) the Canadian crowd was going absolutely and understandably apeshit along the fences. I mean, he was keeping some really *good* people (Penske's Telar Cooper, Gurney, Gregory's leap-frogging Lotus, etc.) bottled up behind…

But of course it couldn't last. Gregory was on a mission and soon swept past to take the lead (although the Canadian officials were already deep in conversation about his impromptu and dangerous shortcut though pit lane). And meanwhile Gurney's engine had gone off-song and then poor John Cannon—who was putting in the drive of his life—had to make successive pit stops for an engine pulley that had come apart and then a distributor rotor. That dropped him well back, but it was still one hell of a drive. Then Penske's Cooper blew up with lots of smoke (but not much noise) and Gurney made his pit stop to change plugs and Jim Hall's Chaparral holed a piston and Innes Ireland had the nose blow off the other U.D.T.-Laystall Lotus 19 (no, really), all of which left Gregory damn near a lap ahead by the time they reached half-distance. But there was still the little problem with the race officials regarding his blast through pit lane on the start. Masten's U.D.T. crew chief had pleaded and wheedled and argued and begged the officials not to give him an immediate black flag and stick him back behind all that traffic again, and the powers-that-be finally relented and agreed to let him stay out, but stipulated that a one-minute penalty would be added in at the end of the race. Which sounded pretty damn fair from my point of view. I think Canadian officials tend to be a bit more flexible and practical in that regard than some other folks I could mention on both sides of the Atlantic. Then again, most of the officials up in Canada are racers themselves, and that makes a big difference.

In the end it was all pretty academic, since Masten went on to win by over a lap from Pedro Rodriguez in Carlo Sebastian's 4-liter Testa Rossa and "Canada's Fastest Bus Driver" Francis Bradley in a locally entered Lotus 19. And wily old Jack Brabham took next spot and the Under-2-Liter prize money in a Lotus 23. But the Canadians had something to cheer about since their own Luwig Heimrath came home fifth overall (and second in the under-2-liter class) in a two-year-old, 1600cc Porsche RS60, which was one place better than the latest, factory-entered 2000cc/8-cylinder Porsche with team ace Joakim Bonnier at the wheel.

"Sounds like a pretty good weekend."

"Yah, it was," Dale grinned. "But they're almost all good weekends." He gave off another helpless shrug. "The hard parts are always the work weeks in between."

I could relate to that.

I could also relate to the exhausted, almost shell-shocked look in his eyes, so I had to ask the obvious next question: "So how was your drive out?"

"Oh, you know how it goes. We had four of us so we could share in on the drivin', an' there's plenty of room in one a'those VW microbuses so long as you're not too particular about being comfortable or getting anywhere fast…"

"How long did it take you?"

"Well, we picked up three hours on account of the time zones and all—we'll lose it again goin' back—but I figure we were right around 38-and-a-half-hours all told. Maybe 39. Give or take…"

"That's pretty good time for a fully-loaded VW bus," I told him. In my mind's eye, I could see them droning across the vast, empty expanses of, oh, say, Utah or Nevada with the throttle mashed to the floorboards and the VW doing a giddy 65 or maybe even 70 if there wasn't any headwind. Or (God help them!) straining through the Colorado Rockies with that noisy little 1200cc four-banger fighting for every uphill mile, its puny, single-throat Solex damn near strangling on the thin, 11,000-foot mountain air.

"So how was it going through the mountains?"

"Oh, we damn near had to get out behind and push a time or two going up through the Rockies. And we lost two fanbelts along the way. The first one was Ken's fault 'cause he never checked it before we left and the second was Mark's 'cause he didn't set the tension right with the shim washers when he put the new one on—he said he knew what he was doin', but he didn't—an' then we stopped for a nighttime pee break someplace out in the middle of the damn desert and I wandered off the road aways into the desert scrub and all of a sudden I hear all these rattlesnakes rattlin' all around me…"

"Jesus."

"Yep, that's what I said, too. And all I had on were m'damn sneakers! But I just kinda backed up towards the road—same way I'd come, one careful little step after th' other—and they all quieted down again."

"Sounds like one hell of a road trip."

"Prob'ly sounds like more fun than it really was," he grinned. "I mean, it's a long, *long* way. And the way back'll seem even longer. But it'll make for one hell of a beer-keg story. Assuming we make it home in one piece, of course."

"Oh, you'll make it," I assured him. "Maybe not in time to save any of your fucking jobs, but you'll make it."

We had a pretty good laugh off of that.

It was always great to see my corner-worker friends again. They have a lot different perspective on things than the wags and so-called "experts" up in the press room. Or the folks looking down from the top floor of Fairway Tower. No, if you really want to know what's going on in the world of racing, you've got to be right there on top of it. Even better, be a part of it. You and your best buddies. And that's why corner-worker types travel all over hell and gone on the cheap and sleep out in tents or campers and do it all for nothing but a few blessed meals and a keg of beer or two.

"You guys are nuts," I told him.

"Yep, I s'pose we are" Dale agreed, "but there's nothin' I ever found I like better…"

I was glad to hear from one of my California scribe friends that Dan Gurney (and his new crew chief) finally had everything go right for them at the USAC pro sports car race up at Kent, Washington, two weeks before. The field wasn't as strong as at Mosport (Gregory and Innes Ireland were there in the U.D.T.-Laystall Lotus 19s, but the rest of the international contingent were no-shows) but for a change the Arciero Brothers' Lotus 19 ran flawlessly, and Dan flat blitzed the field in both heats to take a well-deserved—and long overdue—victory. It was pretty amazing when you thought about the insane amount of traveling—let alone racing—a top driver like Dan had to do. He'd done the Italian GP at Monza for the Porsche F1 team on September 16th, was racing the Arciero Lotus 19 at Mosport just east of Toronto the following weekend, turned up with the same car on the far west end of the North American continent for the Kent, Washington, race just one week later, then scrambled back east to be in the Porsche again for the USGP at Watkins Glen in upstate New York the weekend after that and now, just four days later, he was entered in the Lotus and practice was starting for the Times Grand Prix sports car race in Riverside, California. Whew! But that was nothing compared to his schedule back in May and early June, when he had his rookie test, qualifying and his first-ever Indianapolis 500 (in the ever-so-slightly squirrelly Mickey Thompson car) all tangled up with the Targa Florio in Sicily on May 6th, the Dutch Grand Prix in Holland two weeks later, the Nurburgring 1000Ks in Germany the week after that, the 500 in Indiana just three days after the Nurburgring, practice sessions for the Grand Prix of Monaco starting just two days after Indy, back in the Lotus 19 again for the Players 200 at Mosport the following weekend, the Belgian GP at Spa the week after that and then, just seven days later, the 24 Hours of Le Mans…

It made your head spin.

Now all the top drivers had to do stuff like that—it was part of the job but not very many of them hop-scotched back and forth across the Atlantic (and across the continents on both sides of it) like Dan. And yet he seemed to thrive on it. He never seemed to lose his enthusiasm for the next race or the grand Gurney smile that was always waiting to flash through between the serious, contemplative, disappointed, thoughtful and exasperated expressions that were all part of the game. I do know that my friend Cal Carrington envied the hell out of Dan's bewildering and surely exhausting race schedule. Cal had fallen into a kind of ace-driver limbo where he could still get rides, but not the sort he really needed to revive his career. Although he was looking pretty relaxed and happy for a guy stuck in a less-than-competitive racecar when I ran into him later in the Cunningham bivouac.

I figured right away that he must have spent some time in the Hollywood area with Angelina Scalabrini (or was she truly just Gina LaScala these days?) between races. "Yeah, I saw her," he said through an easy, self-satisfied smile. "She's between pictures right now, and we got to spend a couple days together." We leaned back against the hulking Maserati coupe he was slated to drive at Riverside. "She just finished a ten-city promotional tour for some dumb costume epic about the French revolution, and her agent's getting things lined up for some south seas adventure thing where she has to learn how to use SCUBA gear and swim with sharks."

"Swim with sharks?"

"It's not as bad as it sounds. They've got a stunt double for all the dicey stuff and she'll be doing most of her scuba diving in a pool or a hotel lagoon. They've got an underwater fence and support boats and stuff, and they'll do the close-up shark scenes with mirrors or a panel of bulletproof glass or something in between."

"You're taking all the magic out of it."

"Hey," he grinned, "it's what I do."

I must admit, I hadn't seen Cal looking this upbeat for quite some time. "So it was good seeing her?"

"Yeah," he said almost apologetically, "She's got a pretty nice place for herself now in Toluca Lake. Not one of those big, garish places like in Beverly Hills, you know. But nice. And I gotta own up to it…it was *really* good to see her again."

"You should maybe think about making it permanent."

"You sound like my fucking sister. That's what she keeps saying."

"Maybe she has a point?"

"Nah. She just wants to be related to a movie star, that's all. So she can brag to all of her stuck-up asshole friends about it. That's all she cares about. She doesn't give two shits about me. Never did." He looked over at me. "And you know what? I don't give two shits about her, either. So it's even-steven all the way around."

"You've always been the sentimental type."

Cal shrugged and looked off into the quiet, dusty air. "It wouldn't work out anyway. Gina's got her life and I've got mine and there's no way either one of us would want to give that shit up." He kicked at an imaginary stone. "It just wouldn't work out, that's all. We've talked about it and we both know we'd drive each other nuts…." his eyes swiveled over to me, "…and how about you? What's going on with that Audrey Denbeigh deal over in England?"

It was my turn to look off into the distance as I tried to think my way to an answer. There was always a lot of dust swirling around in the air over Riverside. But what do you expect for a fucking desert? "It's hard to pin down," I finally told him. "We're in kind of suspended animation right now."

"You mean you're stuck over here and she's stuck over there?"

"That's about the size of it. Only it's more complicated than that. In fact, it's a *lot* more complicated than that."

"I dunno," he allowed like he didn't really give a shit one way or the other, "it sounds pretty simple to me. You want to be over there with her, you find some way to make it happen. That's all there is to it."

"You've got a real fucking gift for oversimplifying things when you're talking about other people's lives."

"I've never been much for complexity. Complexity breeds contempt."

"It's *familiarity* that breeds contempt," I corrected him.

"Sure it does…" he agreed, "…but that comes *later*…."

Talking about Audrey was making me uncomfortable. It was all so unresolved. And looking like it was destined to stay that way. So I steered the conversation back to racing. Cal and all the Cunningham guys had gone to the SCCA race at Watkins Glen the same weekend as Mosport, and Walt Hansgen had pretty much steamrollered everybody (although it was a fairly weak field) with Alf Momo's Cooper Monaco/Buick hybrid. "He had Reventlow's guys out in California build one of those aluminum-block Buick V8s for Briggs's Cooper Monaco, and it's a pretty damn marvelous combination. Walt lapped the whole damn field with it. Augie was in the other Monaco with the Maserati four-banger in back and he would've finished second, but the oil pressure went south on the last lap and so he had to push it across the line to take third."

"How about you?"

"I was supposed to be in the 151 again," he patted the Maserati's tall, ugly windshield, "but we had a fuel pump crap out on the pace lap."

"Gee, that's too bad."

"No, it isn't," Cal laughed. And then he leaned in close like he didn't want the car to hear: "It just saved us both a lot of embarrassment. The Glen wasn't really the right track for this old girl anyway. At least not running in the same class as Walt in the Cooper/Buick. Hell, we would've got our asses lapped like everybody else."

I ran my eyes over the brutish-looking Maserati. "Jesus, Cal, this is one ugly racecar."

"Hey, you watch what you say about my baby!" He patted the 151 on its bulbous hood scoop.

"I don't know, Cal," I offered uncertainly. "This doesn't exactly look like a great ride for a 200-mile sprint race at a track like Riverside. Most of the press-room types think these are pretty awful cars."

"This is a *great* car!" he corrected me through a perfectly straight face. "Why, you could walk away from people like they were tied to a post with this car…" I saw the sly old Cal Carrington smile bubbling up to the surface, "…four or five years ago."

That made us both laugh. But only on the outside. You could feel all the bleak, Hopeless Situation stuff swirling around underneath the surface. Cal walked us around behind the trailer to where the Cunningham team had set up a canopy for shade with some lawn chairs, a half-dozen or so water and soft drink coolers and an industrial-sized fan plugged into a generator and blowing in from one side. It threw up a hell of a lot of dust, so Alf Momo had insisted that they put it around on the back side of the trailer. But it was hot at Riverside, so it drew a lot of customers anyway. Cal stood directly in front of the fan and let it blow through his T-shirt. "So," I had to ask, "Why'd you take the drive?"

"If you must know, nobody else asked."

"Nobody else asked?"

Cal shook his head. And then the smile came back. "Oh, there's some mad-doctor type from West Hollywood who was trying to shoehorn a NASCAR Pontiac into a Lotus 23 and wanted me to drive it. But I went by his shop, and it was a mess. He didn't tell me on the phone that he was starting out with a wreck. Or that he didn't have any money." Cal snorted out a weak, helpless laugh. "He was a little nuts, too. He had that look in his eyes, you know?"

"Like the guys in the circus sideshows who bite the heads off live chickens?"

"That's the one!"

"You don't need to be taking rides like that at this stage of your career."

"You don't need to be taking rides like that at *any* stage of your career," he laughed. "Although I guess we all did on the way up."

"I've heard the stories from Buddy."

"I bet you have."

Cal pulled a couple cold sodas out of the cooler and handed one over. "Anyhow, I was pretty much out of a drive at that point. And then I got a call from Briggs about running one of his Maseratis." He took a long, gulping slug of soda. "I really didn't have a lot of options at that point." He looked me in the eye. "What I'd really like is a crack at that Cooper/Buick thing, but you can't expect Briggs to stick me in it ahead of Walt just because I got fired off the Ferrari factory team in Europe."

"I guess not."

"Hell, I'm lucky just to be here."

I clinked our soda bottles together. "You're lucky to be anywhere, right?"

"That's right!" he agreed. "Hell, I'm lucky to be anywhere." He took another long pull on his soda and leaned back against the trailer. "Anyhow, it's not so bad. Briggs runs a good team. And Alf Momo is one of the best in the business. The cars are well-prepared and nothing falls off or comes off in your hand and there's none of the fucking pressure and intrigue and in-fighting like at Ferrari." I watched the grin spread back across his face. "Besides, nobody expects me to do shit with this car. So if I just keep my nose clean, stay out of trouble, keep it on the black part and make it all the way to the end, I'll finish in the top eight or ten and surprise a few people." He drained the last of his pop and let out a long, exaggerated belch. "You gotta keep your name out there, you know? Keep people talking…"

"So how's that working out for you?"

"Hey, it got me a drive in a Sunbeam Alpine!"

"A what?"

"A Sunbeam Alpine. In Saturday's enduro. I'm going to be in one of Ken Miles's cars."

"Oh?"

Cal nodded. "It's not much, I know, but my teammates are Jack Brabham and Bruce McLaren."

"You're kidding."

"Like hell I am. The local Rootes guys wanted to put some famous-name drivers in a few of their cars."

"So how did you make the cut?"

"Very funny. But I used to win a lot of races out here for Ernesto Julio."

"I know you did. And you're probably the only driver here who got himself fired off the Ferrari factory Formula One team."

"How about Dan Gurney?"

"He didn't get fired. He quit."

"So you say," he sneered back at me. And then he gave off a helpless little shrug. "Anyhow, it should be fun if the car holds together. I mean, they're entering six Sunbeams out of two shops, and you know what that means."

"I do?"

"Sure you do: It means they've been thrashing like hell to get them finished—all except Ken Miles's own car and the one for Jerry Titus…they've been campaigning those pretty actively all season—and that no two of them will be alike."

"They won't?"

"They never are," he said like it meant something. But then the smile came back. "But what the hell, eh? I mean, if it's good enough for Brabham and McLaren, I'm thinking it's more than likely good enough for me. Besides, the money's pretty good."

"It is?"

"It is for racing a fucking Sunbeam Alpine!"

Cal took a last swallow of pop and headed us around to the other side of the trailer where the Tipo 151 was parked. I ran my eyes down its hunchbacked silhouette. "So tell me, what's it like inside a Maserati 151 at Riverside?"

"It's not too bad," he allowed. "At least if you don't mind watching the handier cars walk away from you through the corners and the more powerful ones blowing you off on the straights. Or taking a sauna bath inside a kettledrum, come to that."

"How about the handling?"

"Oh, it's not as bad as its reputation…" Cal grinned broadly, "…but then again, what could be?"

"How d'ya think it'll run here?"

"Hot."

"Hot?"

"Not the engine. The driver." He shook his head. "It's gonna be brutal hot in there." He thought it over for a moment or two and a wistful look came into his eyes. "I sure wish we were running the old layout with the mile-long back straight."

"That would be good for this car, wouldn't it?"

"Sure it would. But, hey, you gotta play 'em the way they're dealt, right?"

"That's what I hear."

"We brought Briggs's Tipo 64 Birdcage, too, but it's not really running right. Plus it's just a 3-liter, and we figure the 151 with the 4-liter'll probably be faster here." He leaned in closer and added: "Alf put an even bigger engine into the one Augie blew up at Bridgehampton."

"Oh?"

Cal nodded. "They came up with a 5.6-liter Maserati engine someplace and dropped that monster into the other 151."

"Jesus."

"They got Chuck Daigh to drive it, too, and he's supposed to be something of a local expert here at Riverside."

"He won the first Times Grand Prix here in a Scarab. In fact, he won a *lot* of races in those Scarabs. He was Reventlow's number-one guy."

"What the hell," Cal shrugged. "There's nothing as great for your career as driving what appears to be the same damn car your teammate has, only he's got a hundred more horsepower."

"Is it that much?"

"Nobody knows for sure...the Italians always lie about horsepower anyway."

"Indeed they do."

"I'm thinking they only did it because they got a deal someplace on the five-point-six. It was going to cost them a bundle to rebuild the 4-liter..." A wistful look came into his eyes. "What I'd really like is a shot in the Cooper/Buick," he said again, "but Walt's got that deal locked up solid. And I guess he pretty much deserves it. He's been their guy for a long time, and he's brought home a lot of hardware for them. And Briggs is real big on loyalty. You gotta respect that."

"Especially in this business."

Cal's head bobbed up and down in agreement.

"If you could have anything you wanted to drive here, what would you pick to race?"

"Oh, it'd be nice to have a drive in a decent Lotus 19. That's probably the car to have right now."

"Any prospects?"

Cal shook his head. "Nah. There's six of the damn things here, but the seats are all filled and nobody's looking for any chauffeurs…" he swiveled his eyes over to mine. "T.J. Huston's in one of them."

"T.J. Huston?"

"You know, the Indianapolis driver."

"Of course I know him. I owe him ten bucks."

"You do?"

"It's a long story."

"Everything with you is a long story."

"Hey, that's happens when they pay you by the word…"

We shared a pretty good laugh off of that.

There were a lot of interesting cars to see in the Riverside paddock, and I was really taken by Lance Reventlow's new mid-engined, Mk. IV Scarab. It was basically a wide-body, 2-seater edition of their ill-fated, mid-engined F1 car that never got to run in a single grand prix. They finished it too late to make the tail-end of the 2.5-liter Formula One in 1960 (a lot of people thought the new, 1.5-liter F1 was a dumb idea and that the "big cars" would continue to race and draw fans in something called "Formula Continental," but it pretty much fizzled out. In any case, the new Scarab sports car was gorgeous to look at, beautifully constructed and had a hotted-up Buick aluminum V8 in back. The body sculpturing, paint and detailing on that car were Southern California speed-shop exquisite. I thought it was the prettiest damn car in the paddock. Bar none. Plus Reventlow's crew had found an unexpected source of income building modified

Buick aluminum V8s—complete with big, twin-choke Weber DCOEs on elegant, cross-ram custom intake manifolds—for other teams to stuff into assorted Cooper and Lotus chassis. Like the Cooper-Buick hybrid that Cunningham's team had put together for Walt Hansgen. It was really starting to look like the coming thing: big, cheap, powerful, well-developed pushrod American V8s shoehorned into English-style, mid-engined racing chassis. At least if somebody could come up with a transaxle stout enough to handle the torque, anyway. And you wouldn't necessarily have to limit it to GM's Buick-Olds-Pontiac aluminum V8s, either. Sure, it was nice to have that light-weight aluminum engine block in back, but those motors were only three-and-a-half liters, and you could get a *lot* more power out of bigger V8s like the hot-rodder-favorite Chevy 327 and Fairway's new and reasonably lightweight, thinwall-cast iron V8. Hell, you could get American racing V8s all the way up to 7 liters if you could just find a way to handle the power and carry the weight. And that of course got me thinking about the Le Mans GT project that had to be coming together that very moment in Eric Broadley's Lola shop over in Bromley.

And that got me thinking about Audrey again.

Only there wasn't much of anything I could do about it.

But then my attention landed on a car that stopped me dead in my tracks. It was just being rolled out of its trailer—incredibly low, incredibly slippery, immaculately presented and bright lipstick red—and, at least to my way of thinking (not to mention a lot of other people's), totally illegal! Sure enough, Roger Penske had shown up with a radical, barely-finished-in-time-to-make-the-race device he called the "Zerex-Duralite Special." But it was really nothing more than a year-old Cooper Formula One car clothed in central-seat, full-coverage "sports car" bodywork and stuffed full of the consensus-pick strongest damn 2.7-liter Climax FPF racing engine on the planet. It was the spare from Indianapolis, and Roger had used that engine to very good effect several times in his "Telar Special" Cooper Monaco. Everybody knew how quick it was. But he'd sold the Monaco off to a well-fixed, up-and-coming young American driver named Timmy Mayer (or more correctly to his father), although the Mayer car strangely enough ran into serious engine problems with the replacement unit at Riverside.

Imagine that!

But Roger didn't need the Monaco anymore, because he was ready to unleash his new track toy. And it had eyes rolling and tongues clucking all around the Riverside paddock. Plus it was a really interesting story, so I was disappointed as hell not to be writing it up for the magazine. Unlike most good racecar stories, this one actually *started* with a wreck (whereas the vast majority generally tend to *end* with a wreck). It seems Walt Hansgen had somewhat uncharacteristically crashed Briggs Cunningham's T-53 Cooper F1 car during the 1961 USGP at Watkins Glen. Although, to be fair, he did it when another driver spun right in front of him, and so it really wasn't his fault. In any case, the car had some suspension and a lot of bodywork damage, and cagey young Roger made a deal to buy the remains—as is, but less engine—at what one can only assume was a bargain-basement price. And then, in complete and utter secrecy, he and mechanic/friend LeeRoy Ganc began converting it into the "Zerex-Duralite Special." Which basically amounted to straightening out the chassis, dropping in the bigger/ex-Indianapolis-spare 2.7-liter Climax FPF engine that Roger owned and fitting a svelte, low, hip-hugging/wind-cheating central-seater body over it (which was hammered out in a local Pennsylvania body shop by a talented panel-beater named Harry Ditmarsh) with an extra "passenger seat" hidden away underneath the left-side alloy "door." Which was more like a tonneau cover than a door, if you want the truth of it.

Now the Riverside race (and the entire, three-race "West Coast Pro Series," for that matter) were being sanctioned and run by USAC since the SCCA still didn't want anything to do with "professional" sports car races that paid actual prize money. And the F.I.A. "Appendix C" rulebook and the parroting USAC "sports car" regulations were pretty damn clear: a sports/racing car had to have, and I quote: "two seats of equal dimensions located on either side of the longitudinal axis of the car." Which Roger's new car surely did not. But Roger knew that USAC was already offering waivers for door and windshield variations from the F.I.A. rules so that Lotus 19s, Cooper Monacos and American specials like the Scarabs and the Chaparrals could run the series. And there was precedent, since Cooper's own Type 39 "Manx-tail" had used central seating with a vestigial, "side passenger seat" configuration all the way back to 1955, and those cars had competed regularly on both sides of the Atlantic and even ran at Le Mans. So Roger sent a query off to USAC to see if his car would be legal, and they responded with a half-committal "why not?"

So now there it was in the Riverside paddock. And it really looked superb. And then Roger went out and set fast time with it in the first official practice session on Friday, and that immediately amped up all the grousing and whining and cries of "foul." Only by then it was too late, since the USAC rules also stated that vehicle protests had to be lodged within an hour of the close of tech inspection. And the other thing was that, like virtually all really great racing cars, the awesome speed of Penske's new special wasn't down to just one concept or a single, radical idea (although it did sit very low to the ground and, thanks in part to the central seating, poked a *very* small hole in the air), but rather to an enormous collection of small details thought carefully through and done exactly right. Plus the threat of Dan Gurney's Arciero Brothers Lotus 19 hadn't been there for Thursday practice or Friday qualifying (they were busy going through it at the Arciero shop after Dan's two hard weekends on it at Mosport and Kent, Washington), and everybody in the press room figured that would surely be the car to beat at Riverside.

If it lasted the distance, that is.

As for my roundy-round hero T.J. Huston, he was proving—just like Freddie Fritter did at Daytona what seemed like half-a-lifetime ago—that a great racing driver is a great racing driver, and even if he came up through dirt-track ovals and the Indianapolis 500, it wouldn't take him long to get a handle on "this here road-racin' stuff." In fact, he was up in the top half-dozen on the time sheets after the first practice session, and that was pretty damn good for a guy driving a new type of car on a new type of race-track. Although, to be fair, he'd landed a ride in a very well-prepared Lotus 19. It was being looked after by Jerry Eisert, the hired-away crew chief that used to take care of the Arciero Brothers Lotus 19 that Dan Gurney had gone so damn fast and done so damn well in, and no question Jerry was a true ace—maybe even a magician—when it came to race-preparing Lotus 19s.

In any case, I figured I ought to wander over to T.J.'s paddock spot and re-introduce myself. But not before stopping at one of the concession stands (which were already pretty busy, even though it was only Friday morning), buying myself a coffee and a sweet roll with a rumpled twenty and asking for the crispest, straightest tenspot in the register as part of my change. The lady looked at me kind of funny, but then produced a truly mint-condition sawbuck. Which I handed over to T.J. in lieu of a handshake the moment I saw him. He stopped chewing his trademark, three-stick wad of gum for a moment and looked at it. Then his eyes swiveled slowly back to me.

"You hit a hot streak at the tables or sum'thin?" he deadpanned. And then he started in on his gum again.

"Nah, I got a different job now."

"Honest work?"

"Not really."

"That figures."

With guys like T.J.—and, in fact, most racing people—heckling and insults are simply signs of respect. Or at the very least acceptance. "So how d'ya like the Lotus?" I asked.

He gave me a wink you almost couldn't see. "Y'know, y'can take a reporter off'n a dang magazine, but'cha can't take the nosey nature outta his heart."

"I can't help it, T.J. Questions just pop into my head when I'm around a racetrack."

"I'm a li'l surprised they manage t'stay in there…" he deadpanned some more. "…I mean, without rollin' out yer ears when y'tip yer head over t'one side."

I couldn't really think of a comeback for that one. And so I pretended that he'd hurt my feelings. Or maybe it wasn't entirely pretending. In any case, he apparently felt bad about it, clapped his arm around my shoulder and led me over by his racecar. He nodded down at the Lotus and continued:

"Now this here thing is pretty darn clever—I'll admit that—but it was built by guys who don't know how'ta weld fer sour apples. I seen wads a'chewin' gum with a better bead on 'em. And everything's built way too light. Ain't nothin' around you but a bunch a'damn conduit pipe. Hell, I wouldn't run lamp wires through that shit."

"The 19s are fast," I reminded him.

"Yeah, they're fast, but that don't do you no good if the damn thing falls apart on you. You put a dang Offy in one a'these here an' the frame'd shake itself t'pieces in ten laps," he glanced over to check my reaction. And I guess I must've been smiling, because he went right on: "An' don't they have nobody sells car wax or metal polish over there in England? Hell, I got half a mind t'send 'em a few tins. Free, I mean. Postage paid an' everything."

He was obviously going to keep it up until I sent him off in some other direction. "So how about the power?"

He gave me a sorrowful head shake. "T'tell th'honest truth, I came in after the first few laps wonderin' if we maybe had a plug lead off…"

He was messing with me, and I knew it.

"But how do you like driving it?"

T.J. gave off a noncommittal shrug. "Oh, it hannels purty good. I'll say that for it. An' I can find most a'the gears most a'the time with th'shifter. At least if I bother t'*look* for 'em…"

"How about the steering?"

"I'm pretty sure it works on th' front wheels…just like my Indianapolis cars."

He was screwing with me again.

"Would you rather be driving something else?"

"I didn't exactly say that, now did I? A racecar's a racecar far as I'm concerned. I drive whatever they pay me t'drive."

"But is there anything here you like better?" In the back of my mind, I was thinking how much Cal would like to be out of the Cunningham Maserati 151 and sliding his butt down into T.J.'s apparently well-prepared Lotus 19.

"It don't matter all that much t'me," he lied. "I've learned it's a real waste of time t'go around coveting some other driver's racecar. All that ever does is make things worse." He tapped his forehead. "Up here, I mean…"

"But if you could have any car in the paddock?"

He knitted up his brow for a second thinking about it and followed up with a miniscule shrug. "Aw, I dunno. I know everybody's real keen on these mid-engined Lotuses and Coopers an' stuff, but I'm kinda partial to that Troutman-Barnes car."

"The Chaparral?"

T.J. nodded. "Aw, it's prob'ly got th'dang engine in the wrong end, but it's the right kinda engine for these here straightaways. And it's built simple and clean and solid. Like an Indianapolis car, y'know?" He looked me in the eye. "Dick Troutman an' Tom Barnes built it. You know who they are?"

"Of course I do," I said like it was a damn stupid question. That got me just the tiniest little hint of a smile. I think.

"Well, Rodger Ward's got hisself a ride in one—Troutman an' Barnes entered it—an' he says he really likes it. Sure, it won't go around corners quite as good as one a'these here things," he nodded down towards the Lotus, "but it'll get through traffic a lot better thanks t'that big ole Chevy motor…" T.J. looked up at me again, "…But like I said: it don't do any good coveting other people's racecars. Y'just go out there an' do yer best an' if somebody else shows up with a better mousetrap, well, about alls you can do is try to get yourself inta that seat—or one jest like it—fr'the next race."

That made perfect sense to me.

"And how about the track?" I asked him. "How do you like Riverside?"

He made like he was thinking it over very carefully. "How much did you say the purse was for this here race?"

"If you believe this morning's paper, it's over 30,000 dollars."

That big old gum-smacking smile flashed across his face again. "Then I like it just fine…" he nodded. "…I like it just fine indeed."

Chapter 21: The Snake Strikes

Motor racing is loaded with irony. In fact, it's downright lousy with it. And some of those ironies are funny and some are grim and some are so damn dark and strange that they make you question the reasonableness of your own thinking. Like what happened to 1962 Indianapolis 500 winner Rodger Ward in the straightforward, nicely designed, well-crafted and solidly built Troutman-Barnes Chaparral that T.J. Huston liked so much. It was during practice on Friday, when Rodger was just getting down to some serious lap times. That's when, right out of nowhere, a front brake disc pretty much exploded. And sent a hefty chunk of itself right through the steering linkage. Which in turn sent Rodger's solidly built Chaparral hurtling through a double wall of hay bales, launching off an eight-foot embankment and crash-landing *hard* on its wheels in a thankfully vacant spectator area. It was a brutal hit, and Rodger suffered a serious lower back injury—somebody said it was a compressed disc or something—that would keep him out of the cockpit for months to come.

It was bad, but it so easily could have been much, much worse.

And that's the way it goes sometimes. You take what you think is the strongest, safest, best-built car in the whole damn paddock and even then some sneering little gremlin can rip the rug out from under your feet and send you off to the hospital. In the case of the Chaparral, it was probably a defective part or a hairline crack or lousy metallurgy or manufacturing or who the hell knew? It was a brand-new car, and for sure everything had been inspected and magnafluxed or zyglo'd or whatever before assembly. But sometimes iffy stuff still manages to squeak by, and that brake rotor got to its critical-mass point with use and abuse and molten-hot temperatures and simply shattered into pieces. At which point the brake pedal went straight to the firewall, the steering wheel was no longer connected to anything and Rodger couldn't do much more than mumble the first three words of a prayer and brace for impact.

Now all race drivers wind up taking that sort of ride sooner or later. And the amazing thing is how they all seem able to shrug or swagger or shake it off and get back in a damn car again. It's part of what makes them special.

Or maybe a little nuts?

The other thing we learned during Friday qualifying was that the "other" Roger—Penske, I mean—was fast as stink in his new, central-seater (some said "cheater," although nobody bothered to protest) Zerex-Duralite special. He took pole with the fastest time of all on Friday—an impressive 1:35 flat—followed a half-second back by Bruce McLaren in the latest, factory-entered Cooper Monaco (which, like Penske's car, was sporting one of the rare, 2.7-liter Climax engines). Those two were followed by a trio of American V8 hybrids: Cal's teammate Walt Hansgen in the Cunningham Cooper/Buick at 1:35.7, Jim Hall's powerful but front-engined Chaparral at 1:36.1 and Pac Northwest star Jerry Grant in a Pacific Raceways-sponsored Lotus 19 with yet another Buick aluminum V8 shoehorned in back. Then we got to the more normal, as-God-and-the-factory-in-England-intended Lotus 19s and Cooper Monacos fitted with the standard, British-built, double-overhead-camshaft, 2495cc Climax FPF racing engines. Masten Gregory was quickest of those in the U.D.T.-Laystall car (run in cooperation with rich cattle-and-oil Texan Tom O'Connor's new Rosebud Racing Team for this "west coast pro series"), but next up was none other than my ten-dollars-richer pal T.J. Huston, who was indeed "getting the hang of this here road racin' stuff" with the Jerry Eisert-prepped Lotus 19. And good for him. Eighth and ninth were another pair of late-style Cooper Monacos with American amateur-cum-pro Alan Connell doing an excellent job in his own car at 1:37.1 and F1 world championship points-leader Graham Hill (!!!) two-tenths further back in Nevada SCCA driver Bill Sturgis's privateer entry. Graham can't have been very pleased with that. Filling out the top 10 was Jo Bonnier in the factory-entered Porsche Flat 8 that was also the first of the U2L contenders. There were a couple strong entries going for the Under-2-Liter prize money, including Innes Ireland in 13th grid slot in a U.D.T./Rosebud Racing Lotus 19 with a 2.0-liter Climax FPF, a whole passel of Porsche RSKs and RS 61s (most of which figured to still be around at the end of 200 miles) led by Bob Holbert in 16th, wily old Jack Brabham at exactly the same lap time (1:40 dead) in 17th in his own Lotus 23, Pac Northwest pro-am ace Pat Pigott just a few spots back in a similar car and on and on. It was a truly spectacular entry at Riverside—the best sports car field anyone had ever seen, in fact—but there were also the usual ageing has-beens like Ted Petersen and Lew Florence in Costin-bodied Listers (Jaguar- and Corvette-powered respectively) and Bill Wuesthoff in the once-dominant/now long-in-the-tooth Scarab-Chev that had won the very first Times GP at Riverside with Chuck Daigh way back in 1958. It was now part of brewery heir Harry Heuer's Meister-Brauser team out of Chicago, but Harry himself was driving the team's Chaparral (he was gridded 14th), which was really kind of an improved, second-generation Scarab anyway. And hawk-nosed, ex-pat Brit/L.A. racing, repair-shop and special-building legend Ken Miles had a drive in Harry A. Finer's ex-Bill Krause (and pretty much raced-to-exhaustion) Maserati Birdcage. That car had a *lot* of miles and hours on it, but Ken flat loved to race and he couldn't pass up a chance to be in the biggest show ever in Southern Cal. Whispers were circulating that his North Hollywood sports car shop was struggling a bit financially, but that's what tends to happen when racers try to run retail car shops. Like I said, Ken loved to race—lived for it, in fact—and he had kind of a factory deal with the local Rootes Motors distributor to run a couple Sunbeam Alpines in area club races, and it was more or less a full-time job trying to beat the Porsche 1600 Normals with an Alpine. Not to mention the time and effort involved in getting two more Alpines race-prepped and ready for this weekend's big enduro. So, as you can imagine, his bread-and-butter everyday business was suffering. And that's hardly a rare or unusual story when it comes to racers running car-repair shops.

The huge field was filled out with the usual backmarkers, spear-carriers and semi-scary homebuilts (like Bill Boldt's frightening old Kurtis Kraft with a 421 cubic-inch Pontiac engine under its hood, André Gessner's Chrysler-powered, Allard-based contraption that he called the Twareg Mk. II and Paul Cunningham in his gnarly and spindly-looking "Terrible Tempest" special, which was essentially a much-modified MG TC with a 3.5-liter Pontiac Tempest version of GM's new aluminum V8 jammed between the frame rails). Sure, they were all no-hopers, but they wanted to make the show. Just to be there. Even at the tail end of the grid.

And then you had the inevitable hard-luck stories. Led by the Rodger Ward wreck mentioned earlier and a Thursday practice crash (fortunately without injury) that broke a rear hub carrier on Lance Reventlow's gorgeous new mid-engined Scarab and essentially parked it for the rest of the weekend. But all of that paled compared to the mad scramble back at Bob Challman's Lotus dealership trying to get the engine and gearbox in Dan Gurney's Lotus 19 rebuilt and race-ready following its win at Kent two weeks before and its long trek out to Mosport the week before that. The Arciero car didn't show up until qualifying was already over on Friday, but the stewards kindly allowed Dan a few "hardship laps" late in the day to make sure everything was screwed back together properly. Dan would have to run the 10-lap "consolation" race on Sunday morning (which he won with ease) in order to make the field, and then start the 200-mile feature way back in 28th grid slot. In, mind you, what most insiders reckoned to be the fastest damn car-and-driver combination in the paddock.

It was a shame, really.

As for Cal and the 4.0-liter Maserati coupe, he managed a workmanlike 1:39.9 (which put him a highly respectable 15th on the grid, just behind Harry Heuer in the Meister-Brauser Chaparral and just ahead of Bob Holbert in the fastest RS-61 Porsche), but even so he was a full second off the other Cunningham Maserati with, as he put it, "the 100-inch bigger motor hidden under its hood."

"It's not hidden," I needled him. "They've got a clear plastic cover over the carbu-retors. You can see the whole damn thing."

"Screw you."

"And besides," I needled some more, "it's only 97 cubic inches bigger, not 100."

"Okay," he scowled, "but how much bigger is that percentage-wise?"

"How the hell would I know?"

"C'mon. You're the damn writer. You're supposed to be the smart guy. Figure it out."

So I did. Later on. When I came across a pencil and the back of an old Thursday time sheet in the press room. And it worked out that the V8 in the other 151 was a whopping *40%* bigger than the one in Cal's car. And yet the cars weighed about the same. So Cal's job in the smaller-engined Maserati was looking pretty damn solid indeed. The bad part was that I was about the only person on the premises who knew about it.

Everybody else figured he was just being out-driven.

But of course I wasn't really there to watch the epic, 200-mile Times Grand Prix for Sports Cars on Sunday. No, I was destined to be on my way to the fucking airport long before it was over. Oh, I'd get to see the start and maybe the first hour or so. But I had to be in Bob Wright's office at 8:30 the following morning with my report on the Shelby Cobra's racing debut in Saturday's 3-hour "amateur" enduro for production cars and smaller-displacement sports/racers. And the flight Karen Sabelle had me booked on was wheels-up at 4:20pm Sunday afternoon, and it would likely take me two full hours—maybe more—to get from Riverside to LAX in typical weekend traffic. And that's if I left well before the inevitable bumper-to-bumper, mass-exit traffic jam following the checkered flag.

Now the 3-hour Saturday enduro had attracted quite an impressive entry. Not to mention a lot of fans. The grandstands, car parks and spectator viewing areas were all pretty much jammed, the lines were long and slow at both the johns and the concession stands and I couldn't believe this was only Saturday! But there was a lot to see, what with a small-bore sprint race for club racers, a formula junior open-wheeler race and fully 45 cars lined up along Riverside's front straightaway for the Le Mans-style start of the enduro. Ken Miles had no less than five Sunbeam Alpines to look after: one for himself, one for friend and up-and-coming journalist/racer Jerry Titus (who would of course write about it for *Sports Car Graphic* and give the folks over at the Rootes distributorship a little return on their investment) plus a pair of cars for—wait for it—twice world champ Jack Brabham and current Cooper number one Bruce McLaren and one for my friend Cal Carrington! Now I guess you'd have to call those last three "ringers" in an amateur, just-for-giggles-and-trophies club-racing enduro (and Cal had already told me they were getting cash money to do it) but it sure added a lot of interest to the proceedings. As did the new MGB entered by Hollywood Sports Cars, which was making its stateside competition debut with local hotshoe Ronnie Bucknum behind the wheel (although the car didn't really seem sorted out yet). Plus there were a couple good FP Porsche 1600s for the Alpines to chase after and a super-quick Porsche Carrera Speedster with the 4-cam Fuhrman engine in it up against Corvette chassis guru Dick Guldstrand in an older, solid-rear-axle Corvette in the B-Production class. Not to mention the always-fast Lew Spencer in his crowd-favorite, Kingfisher Blue-with-white-numerals #45 Morgan SS (that's the really lightweight one with the alloy body panels) that he called "Baby Doll."

But the cars everybody had their eyes on were running in the so-called "experimental" class: four brand-new/hardly-even-in-showrooms-yet Corvette Stingray coupes, all with the Z-06 "Special Duty" factory racing option plus a bit of additional tweaking and massaging by local, back-door Chevy-affiliated race-prep artists like Mickey Thompson and Bill Thomas and Max Balchowsky. Plus all four were assigned to proven Corvette hotshoes including Dave MacDonald, Bob Bondurant, Jerry Grant and Doug Hooper. And, up against them, our lone, red #98 Shelby Cobra with Billy Krause at the wheel.

In fact, you could feel the excitement sizzling like sausages in a frypan as they rolled the cars into position for the Le Mans start, and the paddock was buzzing with chatter and opinions about the long-awaited showdown between Shelby's new Cobra and Chevrolet's new, independent-rear-suspension Corvette Sting Ray. And the bulk of the conjecture was focused on the #98 Bill Krause Cobra and the #00 Dave MacDonald Sting Ray out of Max Balchowsky's shop right up at the front of the line. I couldn't wait to see how it all played out.

It seemed to take forever to get all the cars lined up in their proper places—under a broiling hot sun, of course—and meanwhile the concession stands were doing a land-office business in cold beer and soda pop and the lines for the porta-johns stretched all the way back to the grandstands. But the time finally came, the anticipatory silence descended like a thick woolen blanket, everybody held their breath, the flag dropped to the soft patter of feet as the drivers scampered across to their cars and then everything exploded like a damn fragmentation bomb as the field bellowed, howled, screamed, swarmed, screeched and thundered away in a cloud of dust and noise and stink. Followed by the inevitable stragglers like Cal Carrington's Alpine, which took several long, agonizing seconds to start because the engine was apparently flooded. Then came the inevitable long, itchy silence as everybody on pit row waited to see who would come barreling out of Turn 9 at the head of the queue. And we were hardly disappointed, as for several thrilling laps we were treated to the show everybody had come to see: Dave MacDonald in the quickest of the Z06 Sting Rays and Billy Krause in the #98 Cobra scrapping like gladiators at the front of the field. And pretty much leaving everybody else behind in the process. You had to be really impressed—hell, make that *incredibly* impressed!—with the way Dave MacDonald hauled, hurled and manhandled that bulky #00 Sting Ray coupe around the racetrack. Not only was he sideways most of the time, but he was *graceful* sideways. *Smooth* sideways. *Fluid* sideways. Not many people could do that in a bull-elephant brute like a Sting Ray. But Dave MacDonald could. He was frankly amazing. And yet you got the feeling that Billy Krause was just biding his time and enjoying the show. He knew the Cobra had the Sting Ray covered—and then some—and it was just a matter of waiting for the right moment, finding his way by and pulling away.

And that's exactly the way it played out. Krause finally managed to get by under braking and make it stick on lap 9, and once he was clear of MacDonald, the Cobra just motored slowly but inexorably off into the distance. There was nothing the Corvette driver could do about it! To tell the truth, I was getting pretty excited about the race report I'd have for Bob Wright and Danny Beagle on Monday morning. But only fairy tales have happy endings, and I can't say I was overly surprised—disappointed, yes, but not surprised—when the Cobra's left-rear stub axle sheared and the wheel fell off just five laps later.

Damn.

Oh, well…

MacDonald's Corvette also lost its left-rear wheel some nine laps nine after that (opinion in pit lane held that Riverside's roundabout, near-carousel Turn 9 put one hell of a strain on that side of the car) and that left the lead to…I had to do a little head-scratching here…could it be Ed McKay in an old Lotus Eleven with an Alfa-Romeo engine? It was kind of hard to be sure, because we were an hour into the race and there had been a lot of passing and lapping and attrition and pit stops for problems. But I had taken notice of a new guy who looked pretty impressive coming through Turn 9 in somebody-or-other's Alfa Spider. It was only a 1300, but he had it heeled over in these beautiful-yet-economical 4-wheel drifts and had it running well above the middle of the field with it while it lasted. I looked in the program and the driver was named George Follmer, and I figured he might actually go someplace in racing if he ever got a break or two. Not that things like that happen very often. I'd also been keeping track of the Sunbeam Alpines, and that was kind of fun to watch. Lean-looking Ken Miles made by far the best run-and-jump-in start and got away first of the Sunbeams (but all mixed up with two of the quick Porsche Speedsters) followed a bit further back by Brabham and McLaren, then another dozen cars or so to Jerry Titus (who'd taken three tries to get his blessed lap belts fastened) and Cal way down at the tail of the field with the engine running all spluttery from the flooding (although it cleared up by the end of the first lap and ran fine after that).

It became obvious pretty quickly that the Ken Miles car and the one with his friend Jerry Titus in it were the quickest Alpines in the race. You could hear it in the damn engine note when they came by. Particularly Titus's car, which was apparently sporting more compression, a wilder cam, a higher redline and a taller rear-end gear than any of the other Sunbeams. He caught and passed both Brabham and McLaren without much difficulty and then proceeded to reel in Ken Miles (who was leading in class by that point). You need to understand here that the Sunbeam factory had sent some sort of "race-prep expert" over from England to help set up the "celebrity guest driver" cars for Brabham and McLaren (and the one Cal was driving, which it turns out was originally earmarked for Steve McQueen, only he couldn't make it because he was off shooting *The Great Escape* with James Garner). In any case, it was clear that Ken Miles wanted to show the Rootes people in England (in a way that they could readily understand, don't you know?) that his California crew could do a more effective job of race-preparing Sunbeam Alpines than the stiff they'd sent over from the factory. I mean, there was no way a transplanted, hawk-nosed ex-pat Brit North Hollywood car-shop owner and a small-time, nobody-ever-heard-of-him club racer/journalist from California could be *out-driving* genuine, top-of-their-game grand-prix stars like Jack Brabham and Bruce McLaren, was there?

An interesting side note was that Ken and Jerry were using experimental, in-helmet radios supplied by Bell. They couldn't talk to their people in the pits, but they could hear them, and it helped a great deal when it came to knowing where they were relative to the competition, knowing their target pace and the time remaining and particularly letting them know when a wrecker had been dispatched to retrieve a wounded car. I could see right away that this was destined to catch on virtually everywhere in the motorsports world.

It was that good.

As for Cal, he got a handle on the Alpine pretty quickly and was doing a hell of a job climbing up through the field after his dismal start in the third "British-prepared" Alpine. In fact, he was slowly but surely reeling in Brabham and McLaren in their similar cars. Although, to be fair, Brabham was babying his car a bit because of this odd, squealing noise coming from the engine compartment. Turns out the bolt on the generator bracket had worked itself loose so the fan belt was slipping like crazy and making a heck of a racket. Eventually it threw the belt and cooked the engine. But not before Cal had caught him and passed him! And can you believe it: McLaren's car suffered the same exact problem—thrown fan belt—and would ultimately retire with a blown head gasket. Cal backed right out of it after he saw the other two Alpines in the pits with their hoods up and steam issuing forth. He figured it would be worth a small piece of honor to be the only one of the three to make the finish. Which he did. And finished one place (although more than a full lap) behind Ken Miles in his more tweaked-and-sorted Alpine.

As for Jerry Titus in the "California hotrod" Sunbeam, he'd pulled away from Miles, caught and passed the class-leading Porsche 1600 Normal of Dave Jordan and at one point was running a giddy third overall with a 25-second class lead! The guy could drive, no question about it. Although the car definitely had more power and was pulling more revs than any of the other Sunbeams. Only then those taller rear-end gears started making noise. And once that happens, you know it's not going to do anything but get worse. Sure enough, the ring-and-pinion stripped just a few laps later. Afterwards, back in the shop, Ken said it looked like the teeth had pretty much melted right off the pinion. But the bottom line was that Jerry's fine drive went for nothing. Even so, the "preparation specialist" gent from Rootes had to be impressed with the "California" Sunbeam Alpines. Not to mention a wee bit embarrassed.

But back to the race. At around the halfway point (with a lot of cars already having visited the pits with assorted mechanical agonies, the trackside dotted here and there with abandoned cars and a lot of those still running falling into the "walking wounded" category), the Lotus Eleven/Alfa hybrid that race control seemed to think was leading started having engine difficulties. They turned out to be terminal, and that left first place to…aah, I'll have it for you in a moment…California Corvette veteran Doug Hooper in the Mickey Thompson Z06 Sting Ray. He'd driven a smart, conservative, carefully judged race (especially for a brand-new brute of car that had never run anywhere before), and Doug and Mickey were duly rewarded with a fine first overall and first in the "experimental" class at the checker. Well done. Second, a lap back and taking the BP class win was the Kirby/Johnson Porsche Carrera, and a serene and trouble-free third overall (along with the CP class honors) went to the lovely and amazing Kingfisher Blue Morgan of Lew Spencer. Everybody loved "Baby Doll," and it was hardly a surprise to see her do so well and run so reliably.

But of course the big news was the new Corvette Sting Ray's solid overall win in its first-ever race appearance. No question the top brass and the "non-existent" racing department at Chevrolet were highly pleased with the outcome. And don't think for a moment that they weren't paying attention.

But the handwriting was on the wall as far as Shelby's new Cobra was concerned, and everybody knew it.

I suppose the smart thing would have been to head straight for the airport on Sunday morning rather than watch the first hour or so of Sunday's *Times GP* feature and then have to tear myself away and battle through L.A. traffic to make my flight. That's an awful thing to have to do, and especially if the race has some excitement and drama to it. And this one surely did. I'd parked my Fairway Flyer courtesy car right near the Highway 60 exit so I could make a fast getaway, and that put me out with the rest of the rank-and-file race fans at the at the bottom of the 4th-gear esses and the hard, slightly uphill braking zone into the decreasing-radius buttonhook of Turn 6. It was a pretty decent place to watch. And I wasn't the only one who thought so. The grandstands were absolutely packed with spectators, the concession stands had run out of everything but mustard and pickle relish and the, umm, "sanitary facilities" were totally inadequate and anything but sanitary. You were better off to go hide behind a car someplace. But Southern Californians are nuts about sports car racing, so I guess that was to be expected. And they were about to be treated to a really good show. At least from what I got to see of it, anyway.

The crowd cheered and clapped and stomped so much they made the damn grandstands shake as the cars jostled and snorted their way around on an excruciatingly slow pace lap, and no question a lot of the fans around me were rooting for their hometown boy Dan Gurney (even if he did originally come from Long Island) who was mired way at the back of the field in the #96 Arciero Brothers Lotus 19 after missing qualifying. But everybody knew he'd be coming through the field like a bullet once the race got underway. And I of course took note of Cal in the Maserati coupe, and noticed he was swiveling his head around this way and that in the cockpit. I couldn't figure out what he was doing, but he told me all about it later that night on the phone:

"So I'm sitting there on the grid, getting myself fastened in and waiting until the last second to have the guys close the doors because it's already hot as hell in there and I haven't even fired up the damn engine yet. Not that there's really a breeze worth talking about anywhere at Riverside."

"Only when it's there to blow the dust and sand around."

"That's right," he laughed. I could almost see him giving me one of those big, helpless grins. "So they give us the five-minute board, and I figure I'll wait until three—I mean, the guys have already warmed up the engine and switched over to the race plugs—and then we get down to the three and I nod for them to close the doors and I give my belt a little make-sure tug, check over the dash one more time and hit the button. It fires right up and the noise is like thunder in a fucking kettledrum. It makes the car shudder and shake like crazy—I'm almost kinda used to it now—and I check over the gauges and everything looks OK and so I give the gas pedal a little goose like you do and the whole car gives a little yank-twist to the right in response—all pretty standard stuff—and so I blip it again…and that's when the damn rear-view mirror falls off in my lap!"

It took a moment to register. "You're *kidding!*"

"Like hell I am."

"So what did you do?"

"What could I do? I'm in the middle of a wicked-fast 33-car grid and they're showing the 1-minute board now and all I've got time to do is throw the damn mirror out the window so it's not flying around loose in the cockpit!"

"Jesus."

"That's what I said."

"So what did you do?"

"What could I do? We're heading out onto the fucking track now! And I'm blind as a bat from the rear. Those damn things don't have any side or fender mirrors—too much fucking wind resistance, right?—and so I'm trying to look over my shoulders on the pace lap to see if I can see anything. But I can't. And I know for sure that there's faster cars out there and more powerful cars out there and better handling cars out there and better braking cars out there and…" his voice kind of trailed off to nothing.

"But you stayed out."

"What the hell else was I gonna do? I mean, I don't use the mirrors all that much anyway. Sure, it's nice to know who's about to run into you or over you or try a crazy, kamikaze dive-bomb move down the inside, but you can usually rely on the corner workers to show you the blue flags and, well, I wasn't about to pull in and start whimpering to the crew about a damn mirror. Not on the first fucking lap of the race…"

And right there is the thing about motor racing: the more inside of it you get and the more aware you become of all the little dramas and glitches and nuances and subtleties and problems and back stories going on, the more fascinating and compelling it becomes. But if you're on the outside (as exemplified by the wife of the guy sitting next to me in the grandstand, who'd obviously been dragged out to Riverside against her will), it's a different thing entirely. She was a big, loud, heavyset blonde in a white sun visor and about a half-pound of sun-block, and she asked him repeatedly (and with increasing dismay and disgust every time): *You tell me, Erwin: How much noise, heat, dust, grease and beer does a person need in one lifetime?*

I eventually pretended to get up to go to the john (or, more precisely, get into that long, long line to get to the john) and relocated myself along the fences. It was crowded and I wound up looking through a bunch of heads and couldn't really see as much, but it was still a much nicer place to watch the race.

Which went pretty much like this:

At the start, Walt Hansgen in the Cunningham Cooper/Buick muscled his way past McLaren in the factory Cooper Monaco so it was Penske in his bright red "cheater"

Zerex-Duralite Special and Walt in the Cooper-Buick followed by an almost endless, bellowing, feinting and jostling stream of cars snaking down the esses and bluffing their way into the braking zone for Turn 6. I'd never seen a field of sports-racing cars like that before in my life.

Nobody had.

It was fucking spectacular.

Things stayed tight at first like they always do, but you could see that Penske was inching away from the Hansgen car a little more each lap, followed by Hall in the white Chaparral. Masten Gregory in the U.D.T. Lotus and my neophyte road-racing pal T.J. Huston in his 19 had made big improvements on their starting positions at the expense of McLaren and some others, but you got the sense that McLaren was in it for the long haul and looking for a nice, safe, fairly empty piece of track where he could run his own pace and wait to see how things unfolded. I mean, 200 miles is a long, long way, and a lot of the cars running ahead of him were surely not going to be around at the end. So he settled into a gap between Hansgen's Cooper-Buick (which was already suffering from a long brake pedal) and T.J. Huston in the privateer 19. He was only 25 years old, but Bruce already had a ton of experience to go along with his natural speed, and I figured him to be one of the most thoughtful and intelligent drivers out there.

In the meantime, Gurney was making an amazing and yet methodical charge up from the back of the field. He didn't make scary moves or take crazy chances, but he was just so damn much *faster* than the others that he could pretty much pick his spots. It was almost like the track he was on was smoother, faster and wider than the one everybody else was driving. By the 14th lap he'd worked his way up to second place ahead of Gregory (while Hansgen had pulled into the pits with brake problems that ultimately proved terminal) and then, little by little, he closed on the leader. And there was nothing Roger Penske and his "cheater" car could do about it. And meanwhile, Jo Bonnier's factory Porsche had dropped out with engine woes and so it was Innes Ireland in the 2.0-liter U.D.T./Rosebud Lotus 19 leading the U2L class with the Pac Northwest's Pat Pigott doing a wonderful job to run second-in-class just a few spots further back in his privateer Lotus 23. Good for him.

As for the Cunningham Maseratis, they were involved in one of the most entertaining scraps of the day. Cal had caught up to Chuck Daigh in the larger-engined car, and the two of them were doing what he later called "clumsy ballet" with those monsters. "Yeah, he had a little more poke," Cal told me over the phone that night, "but it's not like the long course at Riverside where you can really use the power so much. I found that if I could stay in his slipstream heading down into nine, he couldn't really gain that much. But if I was ahead, he could suck right up next to me by the time we got to the braking zone so we'd be side-by-side and that would slow both of us down. So I guess we both kinda figured it would be best to keep running around in tandem and see where that took us."

All I knew is that it looked absolutely marvelous from the sidelines, as those two ungainly-looking Maserati coupes came down the esses in a nose-to-tail, pas-de-deux series of tail-out broadslides! It was fabulous stuff! Plus they were sneaking up the overall order here and there as more and more of the front-runners ran into trouble.

By this point I was glancing at my watch every five or six seconds to see how close I could shave it before sprinting to my car and heading off for LAX. Even though Gurney had caught right up to Penske by then, and you could see he was scratching for a way by. *DAMN!* I kept looking at my watch and then out over the mountains in the general direction of the airport and muttering *"one more lap"* to myself over and over again while my feet did a little panic dance under my knees. With the two leaders still nose-to-tail, I finally caved in and went sprinting full speed for my car. And naturally some inconsiderate asshole had parked so close behind me that I had to wrestle it out an eighth-of-an-inch at a time and then I had to drive like a crazy man to try and make the airport in time. I really thought I was going to miss my plane when I got stuck in a typical Los Angeles traffic jam with the airport almost in sight. I was sweating and swearing and damn near pounding my fist through the fucking dashboard. So I tried listening to the radio to take some of the edge off. Only it seemed like the new, chart-topping hit *"Sherry"* by the 4 Seasons was playing on every fucking station. Or at least when they weren't playing the last, out-going/chart-topping dance-craze hit *"The Loco-Motion"* by somebody called "Little Eva." You would have thought they were the only two records in the entire fucking universe. And all the while and on top of everything else, I was dying to know what the hell was going on back at Riverside…

Turns out Dan finally swept past Roger Penske with a ballsy *outside* move into Turn 9 to take the lead on lap 38 (of 77) and immediately started pulling away. He and the Arciero Lotus had everybody covered, no question about it. And Dan was pretty much cruising at that point (or cruising for him, anyway, which sits on a somewhat higher plane than it does for most drivers) when the old Gurney Luck struck once more. Throttle linkage this time. The cable must've been chafing against something and it finally snapped in two in the middle of Turn 9. The sudden power drop sent the rear of the red Lotus squirting out sideways and it bounced off the outside retaining wall. Which didn't do a tremendous amount of damage, but it did break the latch on the thoroughly useless left-hand-side "passenger" door. Fortunately the pit entrance was right there, and Dan dove for it and trundled to his pit box on the idle jets so the crew could take a look underneath and maybe try to work out a fix. He finally got going again with a pair of mini vise-grips holding the two frayed ends of the throttle cable together! Worse yet, Dan had to hold the far-side door closed with his left hand to keep it from flopping open (which would surely earn him a black flag) while trying his damndest to steer and shift with his right! He did his very best, of course (although now four laps down), but the linkage started coming apart again and he finally had to pull in and park it.

Damn.

To be honest, I was glad I wasn't there to see it and wouldn't have to write about it for a magazine. I mean, it was tough watching an incredibly talented (and moreover genuinely nice) guy like Dan Gurney going through shit like that again. It just didn't seem fair.

So I flew home to my non-home in Detroit while Roger Penske went on to score an impressive debut win in his new, central-seater/really-a-converted-F1-car Zerex-Duralite Special. It won him more than $12,000. And a brand-new Pontiac. And you'd have to say he really deserved it on both the driving and car-building ends. It was a hell of a performance. But there were a lot of impressive performances at Riverside. Starting with Dan Gurney's incredible but ultimately futile run through the pack, Jim Hall's solid second place in the maybe not-so-antiquated front-engined Chaparral and Masten Gregory's typically gritty and determined drive to third place in the U.D.T./Rosebud Lotus 19, which was just four seconds behind the Chaparral at the checker. As for T.J.

Huston, he actually managed to get around Bruce McLaren in the factory Cooper for fourth, only then the gearbox packed up on him just a few laps from the finish. Hey, he'd said he was having trouble finding gears with it. And even if he ultimately wound up a DNF, all the sportycar types came away mighty impressed.

The guy could *drive*.

So T.J.'s retirement left fourth to McLaren, and Innes Ireland put in an excellent run to take the Under-2-liter class honors and 5th overall in the U.D.T./Rosebud Lotus 19 with the 2-liter engine. And I was glad to hear that Ken Miles somehow kept Harry Finer's raced-to-death, ex-Bill Krause Maserati Birdcage in one piece through a combination of skill and mechanical sympathy to come home sixth overall (I was sure he could use the prize money) and just a few car-lengths ahead of Cal in the 4-liter Maserati coupe. I got all the insider details when Cal called me—collect, of course—at something like 3:30 in the morning Detroit time.

"Do you have any idea what the hell time it is?" I groused at him. But I was glad he'd called.

"I'm guessing it's pretty late where you are. I know it's late here."

"Has anybody ever told you that you're an inconsiderate S.O.B.?"

"I believe I've heard that a time or two."

"Well, now that you've gotten me up," I growled into the receiver, "you might as well tell me the rest of it. How'd the car run?"

"The damn thing ran like a freight train all afternoon!" Cal hooted on the other end. "Handled sorta like one, too."

He'd had a good, solid run, and it was obvious he'd been doing a little celebrating.

"So you wound up seventh overall? In that sled?" I needled him.

"You be careful what you say about Lucrezia."

"Lucrezia?"

"Yeah. That's what one of the guys called her after the race. Lucrezia. It kinda fit."

"You're not going sentimental on me, are you?"

"It wouldn't be my style, would it?"

"No, it wouldn't."

I could hear there was someone else in the room.

"Nobody gives a shit about who finished seventh," I needled him some more.

"Ahh, go fuck yourself."

"Is that the best you've got? 'Go fuck yourself?'"

"Yeah, that's the best I got. It's late." He took another swig of something. "But I'm not a big, important professional wordsmith like some people…" A taunting edge crept into his voice: "But then, you aren't anymore either, are you?"

"Go fuck yourself."

"Is that the best you've got?" he parroted back at me. "'Go fuck yourself?'"

"Okay. *Touché.*"

We both laughed. And somewhere behind him, I could hear the echo of a high, silly giggle.

"Well, now that you've gotten me up, you might as well tell me what the hell happened. And I mean besides who the fuck finished seventh. Nobody cares about that."

"Sure they do."

"No they don't. And don't try to kid yourself that they do. Not even your mother cares."

"She never cared."

"How tragic that must have been for you."

"I don't know why I even bothered to call you."

"Who else would take the fucking call?"

"Buddy would."

"Yeah? Then why the hell didn't you call *him?*"

There was a long pause at the other end. "I already did," Cal kind of mumbled.

"You did?"

"Uh-huh."

"At this hour?"

Silence.

"So how's he doing?"

"I have no idea…" this time the pause was even longer "…Julie answered."

"Oh? How's she doing? And the kids?"

"Couldn't tell you. When I heard it was her, I hung up."

"That was a stinking thing to do."

"Well, she sounded pretty pissed off."

And of course that was something I could understand. I loved Buddy like a brother—better than a brother, in fact!—but you have to take people you care about with the wives and families that come with them. Like Walter with Audrey, for example. And in Julie's particular case, that meant staying the hell out of the way when she got angry. And she could get angry as the business end of a blowtorch and at the proverbial drop of a hat. Over all sorts of stupid things. And waking her and her kids up at 3:30 in the morning on a school night would surely be one of them. "Do you think she knew it was you?"

"I didn't say anything, but I have a feeling she knew. She's got kind of a sixth sense for who's at the other end."

"Most wives do. Besides, who the hell else would call at this hour?"

I had him there.

"So," I started in again, "how the hell did Ken Miles get around you in that beat-to-death Maserati Birdcage?"

"Hey, that's a good car," Cal protested.

"It *was* a good car…" I pretended to agree, "…back during the Eisenhower administration."

"Go fuck yourself."

"So how'd it happen?"

"Aw, I'd backed off towards the end 'cause I was running shy of brakes a little. And I couldn't see out the back, remember. Ken kinda crept up on me, and I guess the crew thought he was a lap down or something and didn't let me know he was coming. And then, all of a sudden—*whoa!*—there he was up the inside of me. I never had a chance to fight back."

"How about Chuck in the other 151."

"You mean the one with the cheater engine?"

"I mean the one with the bigger engine."

"Same difference."

"So how'd you get away from him? You guys looked damn near equal while I was watching."

"We were. But I caught a lucky break in traffic. We came up to lap two cars that were in the process of trying to get around another car that was even further back, and Chuck just picked the wrong guy to tuck in behind. It happens. So he got boxed in, and I found an opening around the outside that was kinda half in the dirt and—what the hell—I made a fucking break for it!" I could just about see the sheepish look on his face. "I didn't really do it on purpose or anything, but there it was right in front of me and by God I took it."

"So you finished ahead of him?"

"Yeah, I did. I didn't have a mirror so I couldn't see behind me and I didn't know where he was, but I drove my fucking ass off after that until Alf Momo hung out an 'E-Z' sign."

"So you left the other Maserati behind?"

"Well, it'd be nice to say I did, but it wasn't entirely fair there towards the end."

"Oh?"

Cal nodded into the phone. "I got by him fair and square—or thanks to that break in traffic, anyway—and then I did put in some really solid laps. Just stitched 'em together, one after the other."

"And he couldn't reel you back in?"

"I was worried that he could. But it was hot and the other Maser started having fuel starvation problems. Vapor lock, you know?"

"Probably from the bigger motor. More heat."

"Could be. But whatever it was, his motor went all fluffy there towards the end, and there wasn't much he or any other driver could've done about it."

"That's nice of you to acknowledge."

"Hey, I'm only saying it 'cause I know you're not writing it up for a damn magazine. I wouldn't say it if I thought it would wind up in print someplace. Besides, there was a long yellow there at the end and everybody had to pretty much hold station. That's why I never got Miles back."

I heard some rustling and giggling in the background. "Lissen, Hank, I really gotta go now. Something's come up."

"I just bet it has!" I laughed. "But you said there was a long yellow. What happened?"

Cal's voice turned sober instantly, and I heard him say: *"Hey, cut it out!"* to whomever was in the room with him. Then came a silence so long and deep I could count the heartbeats on the inside of my eardrum. And then his voice came, very softly: "I thought you already knew."

"Knew what?"

Another long silence. And then, in a voice that sounded very far away: "Did you know Pat Pigott?"

"Sure. The Lotus racer from Washington. He was running second in Under 2-Liter and into the top ten when I left."

"That's the one."

I remembered seeing him in some of the west coast races before I left for Europe, and knew he'd won the Saturday Formula Junior curtain-raiser—against some really good drivers—at the pro-race weekend at Laguna Seca in 1960. "Geez," I asked, "did he get hurt?"

There was a long, hard silence at the other end.

"He got worse than hurt."

That all-too-familiar *"oh, no!"* feeling raced through me and left a cold, hollow vacuum in its wake. And then came the inevitable: "So how'd it happen?" I don't know why, but you always seem to want to know how it happened. Like it somehow makes a difference.

Cal's voice went so low I could hardly hear it. "He'd been running really well all day long. Timing and scoring had him running a solid second to Ireland in the 2-Liter class. But then his exhaust came loose, and it was dragging on the pavement so he had no choice but to stop in the pits and have it wired up, and that cost him an awful lot of time. You know how it is when you've got a volunteer crew in too much of a hurry trying to handle hot exhaust pipes. And that really had to be disheartening for him. You put in a great run and you're all set for a really decent finish and then everything falls to shit right at the end. But eventually his guys got the exhaust pipe wired up and sent him back out to finish the race, and I'm sure all he really wanted at that point was just to make it to the end. There were only about fifteen minutes to go…" his voice trailed off again.

"But he didn't make it?"

Cal let out a long, sad sigh. "Nobody seems to know if he got gassed by the fumes from the broken exhaust…" I remembered how that happened to Jimmy Clark in the factory 23 at the Nurburgring earlier in the year, "…or if it damaged something underneath when the exhaust was banging around, but with maybe ten minutes left, the Lotus suddenly shot off the end of Turn 9 and buried itself in the guardrail…"

I could almost hear the crunch and see the wheels and chunks of fiberglass flying.

"Did something break?"

"Who knows? Most people thought something must have, because he went off at a place and at an angle that you wouldn't expect. But you couldn't tell from looking at it. The car was so damn low the nose went right under the guardrail. It was a hell of a mess…" Cal paused for a moment, and then continued. "…It took the safety crews almost half an hour to cut him out of the wreckage…"

I felt my stomach turn.

"It gets worse," Cal went on miserably. "The race was over by the time they finally got him out, and the ambulance got stuck in traffic trying to get him out of the damn racetrack. It should have only taken minutes to get him to the hospital they use over at March Air Force Base, but because of the traffic it took them damn near an hour." Cal let out a long, labored sigh. "…Anyhow, that's where they pronounced him dead."

"God, that's awful," I said numbly. "You all must have felt terrible."

"We had no idea!" Cal insisted. "Oh, we knew there'd been a wreck and that there were tow trucks and safety vehicles around it, but they just hung out the yellow and the race was over a couple laps later and we all pulled into the paddock thinking everything was okay. There was a victory circle thing for Roger and I got some nice congratulations from the Cunningham crew and none of us had any idea how bad it was. I mean, there was nothing over the PA speakers or anything."

"There never is."

And so that's how the 1962 *Los Angeles Times Grand Prix for Sports Cars* came to an end. To be perfectly honest, I didn't feel bad about missing out on it. I'd already experienced that cold, sick feeling inside more than enough times coming home from racetracks. Even if it wasn't anybody you knew particularly well—or knew at all, come to that—it was still usually someone you'd seen around and maybe even heard laughing or cussing somebody out as recently as that very morning. And now they were gone—vanished!—and that was the hard part to deal with as you tiptoed past the empty trailer that everybody in the paddock was trying to avoid…

Chapter 22: Bright Lights and Shadows

As you can imagine, I was groggy as hell when I finally made my report to Danny Beagle and Bob Wright in Fairway Tower the following morning. But they seemed pleased with what I had to tell them about the speed Shelby's new Cobra had shown at Riverside. For fourteen laps, anyway. "So you think it's faster than Chevy's new Corvette?" Bob asked point-blank when I was done.

"I don't *think* it is," I told him, "I *know* it is."

Bob and Danny exchanged glances.

"In fact," I added guardedly, "given a little proper effort and massaging, I think it might even be faster than one of Ferrari's new GTOs."

"Faster than a Ferrari?" Danny asked with a little edge of incredulity to his voice.

"Oh, not right now," I quickly back-tracked. "And certainly not over any meaningful distance. But I really think the potential is there. I mean, in the end, it all comes down to power-to-weight ratios and development, doesn't it? And reliability. And tires. And aerodynamics, too…especially at Le Mans."

Bob Wright rubbed his chin and thought it over. And then he asked the absolutely perfect next question: "So what do you think they need?"

I knew the answer right away, but I pretended to give it serious thought. "They need time more than anything. Time to get the damn thing sorted out and developed and find all the weaknesses. Right now, that car is as rough and raw as it can be."

"So how much time do you think they'll need?"

This time I really did have to think it over. "That depends on a lot of things," I finally answered. "They need enough people—and I mean the *right* people, not just warm bodies or engineers in lab coats—and enough budget so they're not scrambling to stay afloat building the street cars."

Bob looked over at Danny and then back at me. "I think we could work something out along those lines if what you say is true."

"Oh, it's true all right," I assured them both.

"And what about Shelby as an administrator?"

I stifled a laugh. "Well," I allowed carefully, "he's a hell of a hustler and an idea man. But you may want to give him a little backup on the administration and management end." Now I liked Carroll Shelby—really liked him—and no question he was a top-echelon race driver when he did that for a living, and he was an absolutely incorrigible entrepreneur by nature. Not to mention a near-irresistible charmer when he had to be and one hell of a snake oil salesman. But behind his back, some of his own employees called him "Billie Sol" in reference to the self-made Texas billionaire who also talked in a Lone-Star drawl, liked fancy suits and fine Italian shoes and was all over the newspapers because he was just going to trial in Washington on fraud, bribery and conspiracy charges that went all the way up through the Agriculture Department.

"So he's not entirely trustworthy?" Danny asked.

"That's not what I said. You let him do what he's good at and he'll make you more damn press and publicity than you've ever seen before. And it'll hit right smack dead-center on your new 'Absolute Performance' program. The timing is perfect."

Bob Wright rubbed his chin some more as he mulled it over. I had the feeling he was going to come through and back Carroll Shelby with whatever he might need. And that was surely going to shake up a lot of people—like Zora Arkus-Duntov's entire, "non-existent" Corvette racing department over at Chevrolet—and make a lot of other people (like the California racecar-builders, mechanics and fabricators who hadn't had a steady, dependable paycheck since the Reventlow Formula One effort fizzled out) very, very happy. And I was glad (or at least hopeful) for every one of them.

Bob had another meeting scheduled—something about that new engine plant in Germany, I think—and so Karen Sabelle led us out of his office and Danny took me to one of the little, most-likely-bugged conference rooms with the golden-bronze-tinted plate-glass windows that overlooked the vast, soot-colored expanse of Fairway Motors' Detroit plant. I think it was the same, cold little room he took me to that very first time I came to Fairway Tower back in February...could it be just 10 months ago?

We sat down across from each other again and Danny set a manila folder with my name on it in front of him then gave me one of those annoying, toying-with-you Cheshire-cat smiles. "I've got a little surprise for you," he finally said through his grin.

"And I've got one for you, too."

"Oh, really?"

I nodded.

"Go ahead," he insisted. "You go first."

And that's when I let him in on the little bombshell I'd heard from one of the other motorsports scribes at Riverside. It wasn't really public knowledge yet—it would be confirmed in the next issue of *Competition Press* at the end of the month—and I'd even called that asshole Eric Gibbon (of all people) in London to make sure that it was true. And it was. I figured it might just be the hook I needed to get myself back to London so I could see and be with Audrey again. But I had to handle it carefully. I had to make Danny and Bob Wright and Karen Sabelle believe that sending me back to England was important. That it was in the company's best interests. Better yet, to make Bob think it was *his* idea. So I had to set it up properly. I looked over at Danny like I was trying to organize my thoughts. "Do you know what happened in Paris last Wednesday?" I finally asked him.

Danny shook his head.

"The Sporting Commission of the F.I.A. had a meeting there. You know who they are, right?"

"Of course I know who they are," he answered like it was an insulting question. "They're the guys in Paris who pull all the strings. We were with you at Le Mans, remember?" He wanted me to get to the point.

"Well," I told him, "the Sporting Commission of the F.I.A. made a pretty big announcement on Wednesday."

"Oh?"

I nodded emphatically. "As of last Wednesday, they've lifted the displacement limit on sports/racing cars and prototypes for 1963 and beyond…" I gave that a moment to sink in.

"So what does that mean to Fairway Motors?" Danny wanted to know.

Now it was time to spring it: "You know that Lola GT racer that Eric Broadley's been working on?"

"Of course. We sent him a couple motors. Air freight. Cost us a pretty large stack of nickels."

"Dick Flick spends more than that on a pair of shoes."

Danny bristled a little at that. But I saw the tiny flicker of a smile at the corners of his mouth. "So where is all of this going?"

"Well, I always thought that Lola GT was a really good idea. A *really* good idea. But I wondered if it had any kind of future since there's no way Eric Broadley could ever build and sell enough of them to get it homologated as a legitimate GT car."

"So?"

"So now there's no displacement limit on sports/racers and prototypes. You can stuff whatever size motor you want wherever you want to stick it, and there's no minimum build quantity for homologation."

"So what does that mean to us?"

"It means that Eric's car can run for the top prize at Le Mans. And I mean right away. Next June. With a hot-rodded Fairway V8 in back!"

Danny pretended to think it over. And then he sprang *his* little surprise. "That's actually fairly interesting," he allowed like it he wasn't particularly interested at all, "and maybe you should drop in for a look-see while you're over there this week."

"I beg your pardon?"

The Cheshire-cat smile came back in a flash. "I told you I had a surprise for you."

I didn't know what to say.

"You're flying out to London tomorrow morning."

"I *am?*"

Danny nodded.

I was afraid to say anything at that point. I mean, I didn't want to jinx it. But curiosity was eating away at me. "So what's the occasion?" I finally had to ask.

"Well, as far as the rest of the world knows, you're going over as an ad flake for Dick Flick. You're going to drop in on the London Motor Show that starts Wednesday at Earls Court. And we want you to hang around right through the weekend. I don't think Karen's got you booked for a flight back until the following Wednesday…."

I flat couldn't believe it! In fact, half of me wanted to bolt right out of that conference room and find a phone someplace so I could call Audrey. But the other half wanted to know what was up. "I'm not quite sure I get this," I told him.

"There's nothing to get."

"But what, exactly, do you expect me to do at the Earls Court show?"

"We want you to be our eyes and ears, of course. Check out all the new models. The advertising pitches. The marketing. Ours and the competition's. And then report back to us…you know the drill."

Something didn't sound right. "And *that's* why you're sending me to London?"

"Of course not," Danny said like we both knew better. And then he smiled that Cheshire-cat smile again while I waited for the other shoe to drop. "The thing is," he started in, "we want to make use of a few of your motorsports connections while you're over there."

"My motorsports connections?"

"That's right," Danny nodded. "Sure, we want you to stop in at Lotus and see how the Indianapolis car is progressing…"

My best guess was that it wasn't progressing much at all. I knew Colin Chapman would be launching his new Elan sports car at the Earls Court show, and so he was surely up to his ass with that and building and selling all the type 23 sports/racers and type 22 formula juniors that people all over the world were lined up to buy. Not to mention looking ahead to his Formula One team's last, title-deciding grand prix of the season in South Africa on December 29. So I was pretty sure the Indianapolis car was a long way from reaching critical mass in Colin Chapman's universe. But I also knew he'd get it done. Probably at the last fucking moment (what else?), but he *would* get it done. And it would surely be spectacular. So I kept my mouth shut.

"…and you're right," Danny continued, "you should also drop in on Broadley's shop and take a look at that new Lola…"

"But that's not the real reason you want me over there, is it?"

Danny gave me his very best rendition of an inscrutable smile. He was going to let me hang there for a bit. Just so he could savor it, you know?

"Let's put it this way," he finally said. "I know you've got important personal reasons for wanting to be back to England."

"That's hardly a secret."

"Of course it isn't. And I don't blame you. She's worth it."

"Thanks," I told him as the heat came up in my cheeks. "I think so, too. And I'll be sure and tell her you said that."

"Good," Danny nodded. "And that's precisely why we think you're the perfect guy for this assignment. You want like hell to be over there, and that's why you're going to be smart and astute and clever and discreet about this."

"Smart and astute and clever and discreet about *what?*"

He leaned back in his chair. "It's two things, really. First off, we hear that Ferrari has been trying to get money out of Fiat—and the Italian government—for quite some time now."

"That's pretty much common knowledge, isn't it?"

"Well, we want a reading on it. How much is he looking for? And how close is he to putting a deal together?"

"To hear him tell it, he's not getting anything from anybody."

"Yes…" Danny nodded. "…to hear him tell it. But Bob Wright wants to know what stage the negotiations are at. Or if there really are any negotiations. And he wants to know what the figure is, too."

"I can probably find that out for you." I was thinking of my racing-scribe friend Vinci Pittacora, of course.

"And then we want you to do one more thing."

"Oh?"

"Bob wants you to leak something."

"*Leak* something?"

Danny nodded. "I don't know exactly how you're going to do it, but we want to get word back to Ferrari—actually more like a rumor back to Ferrari—that a large American automobile company may just be interested in a joint venture. And I mean with all the money he'd ever need attached."

That made me think back to my first-ever visit to the executive corridor of Fairway Tower. And particularly to that short, uncomfortable introductory meeting in Little Harry Dick Fairway's corner office where he asked in his arrogant, ignorant, dismissive and classless way why the hell Fairway Motors didn't just *buy* Ferrari. Outright. Lock, stock and barrel. I remember it sounded thoroughly absurd at the time.

It didn't sound nearly so absurd now.

I found out later on that H.R. Junior was on board with the idea again because he'd really wanted to buy Rolls-Royce. You have to follow me here. Out at the Grosse Pointe country club where he played golf three or four mornings a week when the weather was nice, he'd run into some obnoxious ant-trap-and-roach-spray magnate who'd just bought himself a brand-new Rolls-Royce Silver Cloud II drophead in kind of a rich Madeira-wine color with Wilton-wool carpets and creamy off-white (I think they called it "magnolia") hand-stitched Connolly-hide leather upholstery. And of course the ass-hole was going on and on about what a magnificent and exquisite car it was and how it made men take notice and women swoon and that at a hundred miles an hour—top up *or* down!—the only sound you could hear was the ticking of the damn dash clock.

"So you're saying the dash clock's real loud?" Little Harry Dick needled back at him. "Maybe you oughta take it in for service…."

But the worst of it was the deferential, kowtowing, sycophantic way all the valet car-parkers treated the guy. And his fucking car. And that was enough to put the creaky, wobbly, out-of-balance and likewise out-of-round wheels spinning in H.R. Junior's head. And that's how he happened to waltz into a Rolls-Royce showroom in Palm Beach on a whim a couple weeks later while his wife was out shopping for oversized, carved-stone garden gnomes with her latest new favorite landscaping genius, Pierre Patou *("You say eet like when you spit"),* who actually came from Poughkeepsie rather than Paris and whose real name was Morty Finkelstein. And I got that directly from Harold Richard Fairway the Third in the maple-paneled library of the Fairway mansion on McEligott Lane at Amanda Cassandra Fairway's annual holiday party at the end of December.

But I'm getting ahead of my story.

The point is that H.R. Junior wandered into this fancy Florida Rolls-Royce dealership because he had nothing better to do and started looking at cars and asking all sorts of dumb questions. Now the sales guy in the Rolls dealership—one of those tall, elegant Brits with impeccable grooming and just the tiniest hint of refined condescension in his voice—finally blew him off after twenty minutes or so as a fucking time-waster. Which you get a lot of at a Rolls-Royce dealership. And no question H.R. Junior was, since he had no in-tention whatsoever of buying a Rolls-Royce on that or any other day. But he'd taken up the salesman's time sitting in the driver's seat and the passenger seat and the back seat and looking under the hood and into the cavernous trunk of virtually every Rolls Royce Silver

Cloud on the showroom floor. While smoking a cigar, of course. And then, since his wife was apparently still occupied with Pierre Patou and his carved-stone garden gnomes, Little Harry Dick Fairway asked to see all the special-order color chips, smooth Connolly leather samples and deep-pile Wilton-wool carpet swatches on the premises.

Did I mention he was wearing bright yellow Bermuda shorts with over-the-calf brown socks and a Popeye t-shirt?

And that's about when the salesman excused himself "to return an important overseas phone inquiry on a special-order car" and disappeared into hiding in the back of the dealership parts department.

As you can imagine, H.R. Junior didn't much like getting blown off as a time-waster. Or being treated like a spoiled, boorish, obtuse, ignorant and uncultured American asshole. A well-heeled British Rolls-Royce salesman can do that with little more than a glance and a sniff, don't you know. And that's why Little Harry Dick decided that he wanted to buy the Rolls-Royce, Limited, motor-car company in Crewe, England. So he could personally go over there and fire the living shit out of everybody.

So H.R. Junior called Bob Wright into his office the very first thing (which would have been around 10:30am) on the very first morning he was back in The Tower, and asked him right out of left-field why the hell Fairway Motors couldn't buy Rolls-Royce? After all, it wouldn't do for him to show up at his country club in anything but a Fairway product, and it would surely settle things with that asshole at the country club and all those peon, country-club valet car parkers if he showed up in a fucking Rolls. Only with a nice, tasteful Fairway badge stuck at the top of that tall, stately grille. Right under the Spirit of Ecstasy's tits, in fact.

Now Bob Wright didn't think that was a particularly wonderful idea (or that the gentlemen at Rolls-Royce in Crewe would take very kindly to it), but he felt compelled to have a little basic scouting done just so he would have something to report in case H.R. Junior ever asked him about it again. And naturally he handed the job off to Danny Beagle and, just as naturally, Danny Beagle decided to hand it off to me.

"I don't really know any of the people at Rolls-Royce," I more or less protested.

"That's what makes you the perfect man for the job," he explained like it should have been obvious.

"I don't get it."

"Look, Bob doesn't want to embarrass our company by making overtures formally through our English division."

"Why not? Isn't that the way it's usually done?"

"Of course it is. But it looks bad if they blow us off. And they probably will."

"So why even bother?"

"Because he needs to be able to tell H.R. Junior that we've looked into it. So humor me on this. Get the word over to Rolls-Royce that we're sniffing around and that we just might be interested in making an offer."

"To buy them out?"

Danny nodded. "Don't mention any numbers, of course. If that comes up, just tell them the offer would be 'sufficient'..." a little smile crept its way across Bob's face, "...isn't that what they say about their horsepower?"

I nodded.

"And let them know we'd keep everything just as it is, only they'd be operating as a separate and mostly fully independent division of Fairway Motors."

"Mostly fully independent?"

"Mostly fully independent," he repeated like there could actually be such a thing.

"It sounds a little far-fetched to me," I had to tell him.

"Oh, it's absolutely ridiculous," he agreed. "But we have to do ridiculous things now and then to keep the peace around here." He looked me in the eye. "In upper management, you need to save your leverage and built-up political capital for the fights you really want to win...."

And that was pretty much the end of it.

Only Rolls-Royce wasn't really for sale at the time, and it was Bob Wright who once again managed to divert and re-direct Little Harry Dick's remarkably short attention span so he was back to wanting to buy Ferrari again. Bob Wright had a real knack for handling H.R. Junior. But it was chancy work—like handling rattlesnakes or taming lions and tigers in the same fucking cage—and there was always the possibility (some even might say the inevitability) that he would turn on you. Which is why everybody else on the executive corridor did their level best to stay the hell out of his way.

So that's how I wound up back in England again just three days after the *Times GP* at Riverside, and I can't tell you how great it was to see Audrey again. And the reason I can't tell you how great it was is because it really wasn't great at all. In fact, it was kind of uncomfortable at first. And strange. And edgy. You build up all this anticipation for somebody you really, really care about and whom you haven't been able to see for quite some time and, well, it gets you a little over-wound. And that makes everything feel all awkward and stilted and odd when you finally wind up face-to-face with them again. And it surely didn't help that I came calling for her at her father's place straight from the airport (I'd caught the red-eye over from the states and so it was just coming up on lunchtime) and he was sitting right there behind her, only about half-upright in his telly chair with a couple pillows stuffed in behind his back and looking even gaunter and more dissatisfied with life than I remembered. His back wasn't improving, and you could see by how faded his complexion had gotten and how sunken his cheeks looked that he wasn't doing well at all with being essentially immobilized.

So I kind of shuffled around from one foot to the other there in the doorway and when I tried to kiss Audrey—not a big, deep kiss, just a friendly little "hello" peck—I got it all wrong and caught her when she was turning her head so it landed more or less on the side of her nose. Which made us both feel pretty stupid. But she did seem awfully glad to see me, and she'd arranged for the nurse who lived a few doors down to drop in from time to time to look after Walter while we were out. But I could see she wasn't really comfortable with the idea. So everything felt kind of strange and out of-kilter as I walked her out to the new Fairway Frobisher II courtesy car I had parked by the curb. The Frobisher was Fairway's brand-new replacement for the stodgy-but-popular Curmudgeon series of two-rungs-up-from-the-bottom family sedans, and it had been strategically and patriotically named after famous British sea captain and ex-plorer Martin Frobisher, who made three successive and surely harrowing voyages to the New World in the late 1570s in search of the elusive (and ultimately non-existent) Northwest Passage. He never found it, of course, but did manage to bring back 1500 tons of what he assumed was high-grade gold ore but which turned out, after much smelting, melting and refining, to be pretty much worthless as anything but ballast. Captain Frobisher ultimately did a bit better for himself in the piracy business, taking and looting many fine French ships with the wink-and-nod approval of Her Majesty Queen Elizabeth (as you can see, the cross-the-channel animosity between the French and the English has a rich and lengthy history) and made his mark as one of the brave and justly famous English privateers who amazed the entire world when they defeated the mighty Spanish Armada in 1588. That was stirring stuff to any patriotic Englishman (and you won't find many who aren't!) and so in spite of its odd, stubby tailfins, awkward two-tone paintwork and grille treatment like a mouth full of dental braces, it was a decent enough thing to drive and sure to find acceptance in the home marketplace. I know all the British Fairway brass in Dangleton were absolutely counting on it. But I had other, more important things on my mind as I opened the Frobisher's off-side passenger door for Audrey. It made a nice, clean, new-car squeak when I did it.

We drove off from the curb in a strange, heavy silence that was almost like a smell. I tried breaking it about a mile or two down the road by telling her how great she looked and how great it was to see her again, and she said pretty much the same about me. And then it got real quiet again.

Jesus.

"You've been taking care of him pretty much full time, then?" I finally asked.

"Oh, I'm still working for the family in Mayfair most days and I do still drop in at the Lola shop once or twice a week. But Clive Stanley's pretty much given it all up as a bad try—I think he's involved with some bloody thing to do with horses and stables and such now—and it looks like the Bowmaker team is winding down a bit as well."

"Oh?"

"They want to keep on running, of course, and they will be taking the cars down to East London for the last grand prix at the end of December. But I'm pretty sure the sponsorship money from Bowmaker is going away and everybody seems to think Surtees is leaving as well to go drive for Ferrari."

"You can't really blame him, can you?"

"Of course you can't. And it's just as well on my end. Walter needs a bit more attention now what with the therapy and all and everything seems to be working out so I can give it to him."

"It's not much of a life for you, though, is it?"

She looked over at me, and I thought I saw her chin tremble just a bit. "Let's not talk about that now, Hank. It'll just spoil things." She gave me a sad sort of smile. "It's just the way things have worked out, that's all."

I started to say something, but I stopped myself. There'd be plenty of time for that later. So I tried cheering her up by telling her Karen Sabelle had arranged a nice suite for us at the historic old George Hotel just a block away from the Earls Court exhibition center. It had three stars in most of the tourist guides, and a few of them even gave it four. But Audrey didn't seem particularly excited about the prospect. And then she felt badly about not acting excited and that just made things worse.

"I just don't like leaving my father, that's all," she said by way of explanation.

"Look," I said as gently as I could, "we're going to have to get around to talking about it sooner or later."

"Then let's make it later, all right?" And with that she leaned her head over and rested it against my shoulder. Although that felt a little odd and stilted, too.

So we checked into the hotel and my internal clock was all run down and Audrey looked worn out, too, so we went to bed at something like 2:30 in the afternoon and made love that didn't really feel like there was much love in it and then we just laid there, looking up at the ceiling and listening to the afternoon traffic outside. "So is this the way it's going to be?" she finally asked. "Bloody company hotel rooms in the middle of the afternoon?"

"Jesus, I hope not."

"You're not angry with me, are you?"

"Of course not, Audrey. It just all seems so unreal seeing you again and being with you again and…"

She put her finger over my lips. "Ssshhh," she said gently. "Let's stop trying so bloody hard. It'll come back around."

"What'll come back around?"

"You know. How we feel about each other. I promise we've not lost it."

And, just that quickly, we had it back again. Only now with the disconcerting knowledge that it could come and go whenever it wanted. And that was a little unsettling.

"You know," I whispered into her hair, "I think we need to set things up so we're together more often."

"How much more often did you have in mind?" She was teasing me a little, but there was something dead serious underneath.

I took a quick breath, thought for half-a-heartbeat and let it come out: "All the time, actually."

She looked across the pillow at me. "So what exactly are you saying?"

I felt a little rattle of fear go through me…like a pair of tiny, ragged claws scuttling across the ocean floor. "I, umm…" I swallowed a couple of times while I tried to form the words and work my courage up, "…I mean, I guess what I'm trying to say is that I want to be around you all the time…"

A pleased, surprised and yet suspicious look came into her eyes. "You mean you want to *marry* me?"

"I…I guess that's what I mean."

"You know," she said with needling disapproval, "most blokes put it in the form of a question. I believe that's the way it's bloody properly done."

"I'm sorry," I apologized. "It's just…"

"And isn't there usually some sort of ring involved?"

"Jesus, Audrey, I just…"

"Oh, don't worry a thing about it. I'm far past expecting a Yank scribbler like yourself to have proper manners or breeding or to understand proper social protocols."

Now she was just fucking with me.

"Look, Audrey," I started in. But she stopped me. And she sounded serious this time when she spoke:

"It sounds awfully nice, Hank. Really and truly it does. But I wonder how possible or practical it is? I mean, it's always great to see you and we do get on well together, but you're still based out of bloody Detroit and I've got Walter to look after and…"

And, just like that, we were back to Square One again.

Only this time we talked it out. And it wasn't easy. We hashed and thrashed through all the stupid roadblocks and impossibilities and inconveniences, and I told her about the things that were going on at Fairway Tower and that I just might be able to get my ass transferred back to London sometime next year. Now I had no real reason to believe that I could actually make that happen, but I also had this inner feeling (or maybe it was just hope?) that I could. And if determination counted for anything, I would.

We also talked about Walter's situation, of course, and that got a little tacky and testy here and there, but I could tell that she agreed with me in principle: looking after her father was a pretty dead-end sort of life for her. Sure, she'd been riddled with guilt just trying to pass even a small part of that responsibility along to other people, but the bare fact was that he might live a long, long time—possibly as an invalid—and while that responsibility surely had to be *part* of her life, it would take away every other possibility if she made it the only thing that mattered. And I promised I'd help. I meant it, too. Although, as Audrey pointed out, promises made in bed tend to be balloons filled with resolve and good intentions, and you never know how they'll fare or how long they'll last out in the wind and weather.

It was tough going talking our way through all that stuff. And we didn't fully resolve a single thing. But we did decide we were going out shopping for an engagement ring while I was in town, and furthermore that she was going to wear it every day and show it to her father and that I was going to work like a damn commando team on a mission trying to get the powers-that-be in Fairway Tower to transfer me back to London.

And then we made love again. I mean *really* made love. Like in the movies.

The next morning we had a lovely room-service breakfast at the hotel—Audrey called to check in with the nurse down the street while we were waiting for the eggs and breakfast cakes to arrive—and then we got ourselves cleaned up and headed over to Earls Court. It was walking distance, really. We held hands while we walked, too. "You're lucky I was able to arrange a day off," she said dreamily.

"And lucky you…you get to spend it with me!"

"Yes," she gushed, "going to a bloody car show! Lucky me, indeed."

"It's a press day," I told her. "You'll like it. Really you will."

She didn't look entirely convinced.

"Look," I finally told her, "let's just try to have a good time today. Forget about things. Maybe we can even go out to dinner or a club afterwards. Just the two of us."

"I do need to be back by ten-thirty. Walter's nurse has a shift at the hospital."

"That's a lifetime from now."

She tilted her head back and regarded me through a pair of detached, faintly disapproving eyes. "Do you know why I love you, Henry?" she asked out of nowhere.

That caught me off-guard. "N-no, not really," I stammered as the heat rose up my cheeks.

"Well, that's the odd thing, isn't it? Neither do I."

She was fucking with me again.

It felt exciting and yet wonderfully familiar to be back on the hall floor of the Earls Court Motor Show during the press preview day. And it was fun showing it all off to Audrey. We were surrounded by carpeted displays featuring all the latest, shiniest new British auto-industry offerings, and many of them were being shown off by leggy, bosomy models with big hairdos and way too much eye makeup wearing everything from scoop-necked formal gowns to incredibly short, trendy miniskirts. It was hard not to stare at some of them. And even harder not to be caught staring. Meanwhile, nervous-looking company representatives flitted around in the background like suit-and-tie hummingbirds, ready to answer any questions from the press before the models had a chance to fluff them and hoping desperately for some positive ink in the newspapers and magazines. But of course most of the reporters weren't looking for much more than some free food and drink, a company-logo fountain pen, tire gauge or tie clip, a few brochures, a perfunctory, down-the-nose once-over of the cars and an eyeful of cleavage. They'd already seen it all before, don't you know. And did you see the knockers on that one over there?

Most of the insider, behind-the-hand chatter on the show floor circled around England's proposed entry into the European Common Market the following year and how it would affect the British auto industry. Most of the company executives on hand professed (at least publicly) that it would be a real boost for the home-market manufacturers. But I had my doubts, since open trade tends to be a two-way street that seems to go uphill in one direction and decidedly downhill in the other. And when you looked at the products of the British industry compared to the best of what the Germans and the Italians and the French and even the Swedes were doing, it made you wonder how well they'd stand up to the comparison. Then again, de Gaulle was making ugly noises about not wanting England in the Common Market at all thanks to their subsidized farming and cheaper food prices, so it was hardly a sure thing.

But of course the real stars of any motor show are the cars, and Fairway Motors' English division fell all over itself promoting their new Frobisher II and their much-ballyhooed Fairway Firefly economy sedan. It was Fairway of England's latest offering and aimed directly at the biggest segment in the market, but Audrey and I both thought it looked a bit dull and ordinary in spite of dramatic lighting and modish models with huge hair and breasts showing it off on an elevated, rotating turntable. Not to mention constant polishing and flicking off of imaginary lint particles on its dazzling, pale-blue finish. They'd really worked hard on that show model in the paint shops. You could tell. Even if it did look like the paint layers might actually be thicker than the fender metal underneath.

It was common knowledge throughout the company that there'd been quite a corporate row over the naming of the new model, and that none other than Dick Flick ultimately had come over as Bob Wright's personal representative to help settle things and sign off on it. Dick liked traveling to England because he'd been introduced to a very striking (and strikingly accommodating!) young woman who worked in a somewhat undefined capacity for the company that supplied most of Fairway English Division's felt gaskets and rubber seals. Suffice to say that the high-thread-count Egyptian cotton sheets got quite a workout in the fancy hotel room at The Savoy that Karen Sabelle booked for Dick whenever he traveled to the U.K. Along with the bedclothes that inevitably wound up scattered all over the floor in the cozy little flat near Dangleton that the felt gasket and rubber seal company listed on its books as a "field office."

Even so, Dick Flick didn't much enjoy meeting with the English Fairway executives, who dickered and dithered on forever about every little thing and clearly resented, as any Englishman would, paying fealty to some slick-looking upstart from the colonies who wore shiny, razor-creased Italian suits (rather than traditional Saville Row) whenever he was in town—just to piss them off—and had, if push came to shove, their corporate nuts in his back pocket. But that didn't keep some of them from being sniffy, stodgy or outright, down-their-noses disdainful. Especially after lunch. And the naming of this key new British model had several of them arched up and ready for a fight. A few of them (along with Daryl Starling back on the 13th floor of Fairway Tower) were high on calling their new economy sedan "the Fairway Fawn," while others on the executive staff thought it was far too weak and effeminate. "It's warm and endearing," one of the Fawn supporters argued as manfully as he could.

"It's fey, limp-wristed and prissy," a mustachioed opponent angrily shot back. He'd been a tail gunner on a Lancaster bomber crew during the war years and had the eyes and scars to prove it. And he'd moreover had a few stiff whiskeys at lunch. But then, so had several of the others. Plus he was married to the sister of the English C.E.O.'s wife, and that (along with the whisky) gave him a certain sense of invulnerability. "Why don't we call it the bloody Wasp?" he almost snarled. "That's a good, solid name with a real sting in its tail."

"We can't," Dick Flick explained firmly.

"Why the bloody hell not?"

Dick shot him a withering stare. "Because it doesn't start with 'F.' All Fairway model names have to start with an 'F.' That's corporate policy."

"But it's bloody stupid," the tail gunner mumbled feebly. "And what about the bloody 'Chancellor?'"

"That one was grandfathered in. Going forward, corporate wants all the new model names to start with 'F'."

"But it's bloody stupid," the tail gunner repeated.

To be honest, Dick was in silent personal agreement with that sentiment. But he knew better than to let on. The very first major decision Little Harry Dick Fairway ever made when he took over the helm of the company after his father's death was to decree that all Fairway model names would henceforth and forever begin with the letter 'F' because, and I quote, "it sounded better." Not that Little Harry Dick Fairway could so much as spell "alliteration," much less define it. But he proclaimed it with his lower jaw jutted out like a bulldog with a severe under-bite and then glared his way around the big mahogany conference table in his recently inherited office suite on the 13th floor of Fairway Tower. Just to see if anyone dared to make so much as a tiny peep about it.

Nobody did.

And so that's the way things were.

Period.

When Bob Wright ascended to his position of President and Chief Executive Officer at Fairway, he chose—wisely—to avoid the issue rather than contest it. Hell, there were plenty of good F-words in the dictionary. Besides, it made more sense to save his confrontations with Little Harry Dick Fairway for things that really mattered. But the policy inevitably created problems, confusion and endless arguments during the new model naming process, and the F-section of the dictionaries in Fairway corporate offices around the world had been thumbed scruffy and tattered as a result.

"Why don't we just call it the 'Fuck-all' and be done with it?" the tail gunner groused.

"You're not being constructive here."

"Or how about 'Furball,' 'Fecker' or 'Fartleberry?'" an unidentified voice tittered from the far end of the table.

"That's enough of that!" the English Fairway CEO growled as he kicked his brother-in-law the tail gunner under the table. "Let's be serious here."

Many names came up for consideration. Including Fox *("I think someone else already has that")*, Fawn *("too bloody fruity")*, Fennec *("What the hell is a Fennec?")*, Fer-de-Lance *("too bloody French")* and Friendly but, in the end—and with the firm guidance and full agreement of Dick Flick from the corporate offices in Detroit—the model name "Firefly" was ultimately settled and signed off on by all concerned. And now here it was in the metal on a dramatically lit, elevated rotating platform at the Earls Court Motor Show, resplendent in many gleaming, glistening layers of robin's-egg blue and displayed between two huge, piled-up blonde hairdos and two even more impressive cleavages to show it off!

Even so, it looked a bit underwhelming.

"It's about as inspiring as oatmeal," I observed.

"We call it porridge," Audrey corrected me.

"Then it's about as inspiring as porridge."

And so it was. Although Colin Chapman had lent his name and a few engine-and-chassis tweaks (and a special paint job) to a hotted-up, Lotus-badged "performance" version that was also on display at Earls Court. And that looked pretty interesting.

Across the aisle, BMC was playing up its new MG- and Morris-badged 1100 sedans, which were essentially slightly stretched, more powerful versions of the popular Austin Mini and featured a new, interconnected, fluid-filled Hydrolastic suspension system that promised an amazingly smooth ride for a short-wheelbase car with small wheels along with plenty of service headaches for BMC dealers on both sides of the Atlantic in the coming months and years. BMC was also showing off tarted-up, Riley Elf- and

Wolseley Hornet-badged editions of their popular Mini along with a bulldog-aggressive, rallye-spec Cooper Mini with a more powerful engine, fatter wheels and tires and a whole bank of fog and driving lights plastered across the front. I was kicking myself for not being on staff at a magazine, because I really wanted to drive one. Drive it *hard!* And then simply hand back the keys and smile (as smoke and stench rose gently from the hood, brakes and exhaust), say "thank you very much, then" and walk away.

Boy, I missed road-testing all the neat new cars!

You got to pound the living shit out of them…

You'd have to say that the Mini was one of those cars that flat captured people's hearts and imaginations. Even though designer Alec Issigonis was simply trying to create a cheap, simple, workmanlike, no-frills, small-on-the-outside/roomy-on-the-inside economy car along the lines of what Ferdinand Porsche did for Herr Hitler's Reich when he designed the Volkswagen Beetle some 21 years before. But the runty little Mini, perched up on its tiny, 10-inch road wheels, turned out to be even more loveable and adorable than it was practical or economical. Plus it didn't hurt that it was a four-alarm ball to drive. "You may not be going very fast," I wrote after my first-ever Mini press drive in April of 1959, "but there's an awful lot going on and it's incredibly entertaining!" And the snotty, cheeky little Mini seemed to fit right in with the new, hip, "mod" British lifestyle that had just started taking over the trendier sections of London.

Against all odds and logic, the Mini was also beginning to make a name for itself in racing and rallying (something designer Issigonis surely never envisioned nor desired!) in spite of its tiny engine, tiny brakes, tiny tires, cheap componentry, a stupidly high center of gravity, the aerodynamics of a garden shed and wrong-wheel drive. But give an Englishman a lump of metal and he's bound to try and make it go faster, and soon well-sorted, well-driven Minis were giving fits to bigger, supposedly faster and far more expensive cars with far more illustrious nameplates and bloodlines. And that made people love them even more.

Behind the various Mini variants was a powder-blue MGB roadster, one of the boxy Mark II Healey Sprites (which, although more practical, had none of the charm or character of the original, frog-eyed version), plus an evolved, Mk. III edition of the gutty, torquey and broad-shouldered Austin Healey 3000. Now with a proper central shifter and a genuine, walnut-veneer dashboard that it probably didn't need. I liked Big Healeys a lot, but also knew that they were heavy, noisy, antiquated old lumps, rode like ox-carts (although they'd raised them up enough that you didn't rip the whole damn exhaust system off every time you went over a railroad crossing!) and were hot as hell inside in the summertime. Especially the U.S.- and Euro-spec left-hand-drive editions, where the exhausts ran under the drivers'-side floor rather than the passengers' side like the proper R.H.D. English cars. I once overheard a British Healey enthusiast who'd just returned from the states and had driven an L.H.D. example on a hot summer day over there musing: *"I don't know why in blazes anyone in America would buy one of the bloody things…"*

Jaguar's E-Type was well past brand-new by October of 1962, but a brilliant white example still looked absolutely stunning on the Jaguar stand. Although I always thought peering out of the cockpit over that long, long hood was like navigating from the back end of a war canoe. And trying to park one in tight city quarters was a good way to find out how much those oh-so-stylish (but somewhat useless) front and rear bumperettes cost to replace. But it was still a gorgeous thing, offered a tremendous amount of style and performance for the money and looked sexy as all getout. Although, as one Jaguar exec quietly whispered to me behind his hand, those exact virtues had unfortunately attracted far too many of the wrong type of buyers. Buyers who had no appreciation of the marque's history or heritage or the sporting spirit and mechanical sympathy required to be a proper Jaguar owner. Particularly over in the States, where (at least in his opinion) an inordinately large number of E-type buyers didn't know enough to come in out of the rain.

Rolls-Royce/Bentley had the next stand over (surrounded by brass standards and burgundy velvet ropes, of course) and I can't say I was particularly wild about the new quad-headlight treatment on their Silver Cloud III and Bentley S3 models. In fact, they both looked like shit. Although Audrey and I thought Bentley's 2-door Continental convertible was rather nice. At the far opposite end of the ragtop spectrum, Standard-Triumph was showing off their sporty little entry-level Spitfire roadster to compete with the Austin-Healey Sprite and its sister-under-the-nose-badge MG Midget sibling. Standard-Triumph was understandably proud of the new Spitfire's fully independent, swing-axle rear suspension layout that promised a more supple, sophisticated ride (even if it tended to jack the back end up under spirited cornering until the outside rear wheel folded under like the landing gear on a carrier-based fighter plane). In any case, the new Spitfire looked bright, spirited, game, gutsy and terrifically cheap and tinny all at the same time…in the very best Standard-Triumph tradition!

Audrey had never been to a press preview day before, and so she wasn't used to the lack of crowds or the toadying personal attention from all the hurriedly coached models and nervous manufacturer PR-types looking to get good reviews. And I could feel her sense of excitement when she saw TV crews setting up here and there with their lights, cameras, sound men and haven't-I-seen-that-face-on-the-telly-before screen commentators filming their show-preview reports. I tried to act nonchalant about it all, of course, and I think she was genuinely impressed by how many of the manufacturers' people seemed to know me and wanted to talk to me and get my opinions. Then again, they were car-industry types, not racers, and so not many of them knew I wasn't writing for *Car and Track* any more. And I wasn't about to tell them.

But of course I was really there at Earls Court to find Colin Chapman and get an update on Bob Wright's top-secret Indianapolis project, and sure enough we found him bustling around the Lotus stand, which was towards the back of the hall just ahead of the other, even smaller-volume British boutique manufacturers like Jensen, Elva, Fairthorpe, Turner and TVR. As Buddy Palumbo always said, anyone with a pile of scrap metal and a welder can go into the car-manufacturing business in England. All you have to do is hang out a shingle. Although there was no doubt by then that Lotus had truly emerged from the "kit car" category and that Chapman's new Lotus Elan was one of the genuine stars of the show. It was a terrifically clever and ambitious little sportscar that featured a lightweight, attractive fiberglass body shell dropped over an ingenious, pressed-steel "backbone" frame that forked out at both ends to hold the driveline and suspension. Plus it was powered by Lotus' own, in-house, 1499cc twincam engine—basically a detuned version of the same exact motor that had proved so devastatingly effective in Chapman's Type 23 sports/racer—and everyone loved the way the fold-away headlights allowed for a smooth, sleek front end and then seemed to wink at passers-by when they popped up into operational position. And it surely didn't hurt that Lotus was riding a virtual tidal wave of positive publicity thanks to the way Jimmy Clark and the monocoque Type 25 grand prix car had been showing its pea-shooter exhausts to the entire Formula One field all season long.

Naturally the British magazines were falling all over themselves heaping praise on the new Elan. They went on and on about its radical yet deceptively simple chassis design, its elegant engineering, its willing, race-bred engine, its incredible over-the-road nimbleness and its sublimely supple suspension. Although they did tend to leave out how the rubber doughnut couplings in the rear halfshafts tended to wind up and then snap back like fucking mousetrap springs if you were anything less than delicate on takeoff. Best guess was that they'd need plenty of regular servicing and replacement, too.

To be honest, the Elan represented an enormous gamble for a small but emerging young sports car company like Lotus, and the verdict was still very much out as to whether Chapman could build and sell enough of them to make it a viable business venture. Road-going Lotuses had always lived in an unusual and in some ways unenviable market niche. They weren't cost-no-object supercars like Ferraris or Maseratis or Aston Martins, didn't have big power or spectacular straight-line speed like the not-that-much-more-expensive Jaguar XKEs or Corvette Sting Rays and came with an unfortunate (but unfortunately well-deserved) reputation for indifferent build quality, poor reliability and being screwed together out of various and sundry "parts-bin bits" from mass-market sedans.

But that's not what Lotuses were all about. They were built for a very special, cerebral, discerning, cultish and moreover forgiving sort of customer who valued their lightness, handling, race-bred heritage and cutting-edge engineering over all else. Including resale value, component reliability and assembly quality! Plus the company had dropped a bundle on Chapman's previous road-going sports car venture, the lovely but problematic and expensive little Lotus Elite. They'd sold right around 1000 of the little jewels, but lost money on every one thanks to the high cost of manufacturing the fiberglass monocoque chassis-cum-body. So the Elan was a make-or-break proposition for Lotus, with the company's very survival hanging in the balance. Sure, Chapman had his racing successes and plenty of headlines going for him, but printer's ink and notoriety never amount to much when it comes to signing checks to suppliers or paying workers' wages. So the risk was great, the stakes were incredibly high and money was terribly tight, and Colin had a deserved reputation for being a tough thinker, a shrewd negotiator and a clever—some might even say shifty or slippery—sort of character. But he'd persevered and kept everything together, and you had to respect the hell out of that. To my mind, the only other person who'd managed that sort of thing (albeit in a completely different way) was Enzo Ferrari. They were both genuine geniuses and, like all geniuses, it set them apart from ordinary people. But that also tended to isolate them with their dreams, desires and demons. So if Colin appeared at times to be impatient, abrupt, sharp-tongued, short-tempered, irritated, angry, brusque, aloof or preoccupied, it was easy to understand why.

When we arrived at the stand, Colin was rotating quickly between hurried, whispered conversations with Lotus employees and bright, glad-hand greetings for all the press-corps interviewers and TV types. I saw him notice me out of the corner of his eye while he was talking into a BBC microphone, and the fleeting look of exasperation that flashed through his eyes was unmistakable. But it was gone before the camera could notice, and he didn't skip a beat throughout the interview. Then he had another quick word with one of his assistants, checked a schedule on someone's clipboard and made sure there was a charger running under the new Elan so the lights would be burning when they flipped up into position. He also checked on the tiny electric fish-tank pump they had whirring away underneath the car to maintain the vacuum in the actuating cylinders so the headlights would indeed pop up in perfect unison whenever they were supposed to. Those things attended to, Colin headed straight over, greeted me with a perfunctory handshake and a flinty smile and assured me that the Lotus/Fairway Indianapolis project was coming along nicely and would be ready when it needed to be. And then he casually mentioned that he needed more money, of course.

After the show, Audrey and I went out to dinner in the up-and-coming, fashion-forward Carnaby Street district, and after that we took a long walk and peered into the shop windows at all the outrageous new styles that were becoming all the rage. I have to admit I kind of liked the way bell-bottom pants looked on the mannequins, but they didn't seem particularly practical to me. Especially for driving something with three small pedals placed very close together. And some of the new miniskirts took "mini" to the most extreme interpretation of its meaning. "You'd look great in that," I told Audrey as we stared in slack-jawed awe at a glistening little band of miniskirt made out of perhaps 30 square inches of lipstick-red vinyl.

"I'd look like a tart. And a bloody fat tart at that."

"You're not fat."

"Put me in that and I'd look fat." She wrinkled her nose. "Do you know why they call it 'Mod?'"

I shook my head.

"Because only skinny little models can wear the bloody things! The rest of us look like stuffed bloody sausages."

"All the trendy people are wearing them."

"And they all look like stuffed bloody sausages," she laughed. "And they must feel one hell of a bloody draft in the wintertime...."

We found a place called The Marquee Club at the end of the street, and we could hear the sounds of a band setting up inside—the quick riff of an electric guitar, a sputter of drum beats, a few heavy throbs out of an electric bass—and we decided to stop in for a drink and give them a listen. It turned out to be a new, on-their-way-up band called The Rolling Stones, and the people sitting around us said they were awfully good. So we stuck around to hear them play a few sets. They were a rough, scruffy, raw-looking bunch—upper-middle-class white English kids trying to look a lot older, tougher and more street-wise than they were—but the music they played was the same, gut-level blues I'd been listening to and enjoying so much at The Black Mamba Lounge in Detroit! Sure, it sounded odd coming out of a bunch of skinny, pasty-faced young white guys with London accents. But the sound was all lean meat once they got rolling. And I couldn't believe the way the lead singer could go from hard, angry pounding to mournful, soulful pleading to damn-near terrifying Satanic as he snaked and pranced and postured his way around the stage. I had a feeling that the world would be seeing and hearing a lot more from this bunch...

Chapter 23: A Diamond, Fear and Death

It turned out to be easier than I imagined to leak Bob Wright's purposely hazy message about "some large American automobile company" having an interest in possibly acquiring (or entering into some sort of joint venture with) a smaller—you could even say tiny—Italian manufacturer that produced exotic, expensive automobiles, had an impressive sporting pedigree, a fine competition history and ongoing money troubles. But the important thing was that it had to be no more than a vague rumor. Especially when it came to which "large American automobile company" might be involved and which small Italian specialty-car builder might be of interest. Ferrari? Maserati? OSCA? DeTomaso? Who knew? The key thing, according to Bob Wright, was "getting the chum in the water." And I got the whole thing accomplished in a single afternoon.

It started out when I ran into my sad-eyed Italian scribbler buddy Vinci Pittacora at the Earls Court Motor Show. He'd missed the press day because…well, I'm not really privy to the details of why he missed the press day, but he told me it was *"bellissima"* and that he definitely left her smiling. Plus he had the 1000km GT points race to cover on the half-oval/half-road-circuit track at Montlhéry just south of Paris on the October 20-21 weekend. So Vinci didn't get to England until the following Tuesday and, to tell the truth, I'd been up and down the aisles and in and out of the press room at Earls Court for several days trolling for him. The good part was that I lucked into having it seem like a thoroughly casual, unplanned encounter. And Vinci was really glad to see me. He said he missed me out on the circuit and I told him I missed the hell out of hanging around with him and being there in the press rooms and paddocks and pit lanes. We wound up going out to lunch together at a little Italian sit-down place he knew not far from the exhibition hall where it was quiet and the food was good and you didn't have to stand in line and pay stupid, exhibition-hall prices just to eat crap sandwiches out of paper wrappers while standing against a damn wall.

We talked about the Formula One season and all the Jim Clark-vs.-Graham Hill/Lotus-vs.-B.R.M. drama building up to that final grand prix of the year in South Africa on December 29th, and also about the non-championship F1 round coming up just over a week away in Mexico. Vinci wasn't going to that one because, once again, Ferrari wasn't sending any cars. And you couldn't really disagree with that decision, since it was a non-championship race that didn't really count for anything and the organizers probably weren't offering enough starting money to make the trip worthwhile. Not to mention that the Ferraris were sadly out-of-date and off-the-pace at that point and so why make even a token, show-the-flag appearance in North America (which, by the way, had already become Ferrari's largest market) when it was just going to make you look bad?

Then I filled Vinci in on the Riverside race and the excellent field it attracted. He was sorry he missed it, as he'd heard a lot about the beautiful, suntanned girls out in California—was it true they were all blondes?—and then it was his turn to fill me in on the Paris 1000 GT race. There was a pretty decent entry since it counted towards the GT-only World Manufacturers' Championship, and he was sorry to tell me that French DB driver Paul Armagac was killed during practice. We both knew him, as he'd been pursuing the Index of Performance and Index of Thermal Efficiency awards at Le Mans for years in streamlined little French cars that I'd always somewhat derisively referred to as "tiddlers" in my race reports. And now I felt guilty, because he was a good guy and he and his teammates were just as dedicated, hard-working and serious about the Index wins they were pursuing as the overall leaders were about theirs. Plus it proved once again that you could kill yourself just as dead in a DB (or a Sprite) as you could in a Ferrari. The Ferrari would just get you there quicker.

As for the race, it was of course another Ferrari benefit. The Rodriguez brothers were teamed up in Carlo Sebastian's "American" GTO (which was brand-new and fresh from the factory with all the latest tweaks and mods) and they pretty much ran away from everybody from the drop of the green. And some pretty formidable teams were lined up behind them. But both Rodriguez brothers had established themselves as top-shelf, world-class racers by then—even though Pedro was only 22 and his brother Ricardo was just 20—and they used the new GTO's slight power advantage to good effect, separating themselves from a strong field of pursuers and, at least according to Vinci, never putting a foot wrong. John Surtees and Mike Parkes teamed up to take a distant second place, a full lap back, in British Ferrari distributor Ronnie Hoare's much-raced GTO, and I was very pleased to hear that my young yachting friend Count Giovanni's striking and unusual "Breadvan" orphan had been allowed in as a GT car and took an impressive third place (Ludovico Scarfiotti/Colin Davis) ahead of three more "factory-style" GTOs. Jim Clark had mixed it up with some of the non-Rodriguez

GTOs early on in John Ogier's Aston Zagato, but according to Vinci that was down more to Clark's brilliance than the car's capabilities. He finally spun it, got going again, handed over to co-driver Sir John Whitmore and then the engine broke. Oh, well. The best they could have hoped for was a "class" among the non-Ferraris, and not surprisingly that fell to the U2L-winning Porsche Carrera Abarth of Herbert Linge and Gerhard Koch. Vinci allowed that overall it was a pretty good weekend—Paris was never hard to take under any circumstances—and he was of course proud of how the Ferraris had taken the first seven places. Then again, who could stand up to them?

We talked about the rest of my journo friends in the press corps (even that asshole Eric Gibbon who'd taken my job at the magazine) and about the prospects for next year. Vinci was very high on Ferrari's choice as new technical director: a 27-year-old Modenese native and creative-yet-conservative engineer named Mauro Forghieri. There was also a particularly sharp and precocious young assistant engineer working under him, Paolo Dallara, and Vinci was absolutely convinced those two were the right guys to lead Ferrari's Formula One team out of the wilderness. And then of course I asked him about the rumor that John Surtees was going to drive for Ferrari. Vinci balked at first, but the look in his eyes confirmed what I was pretty sure I already knew…it was a done deal.

By that point we'd had a few glasses of red and the conversation was flowing freely, and I decided it was probably the right time to do what I'd been sent over there to do. And I knew how to do it, too. I simply asked it in the form of a question: "So tell me, have you heard anything about a big Detroit manufacturer trying to buy into Ferrari or Maserati?"

Now I knew the last thing *any* journalist wants to admit is that they're out-of-the-loop on anything as important and earth-shaking and with as many ramifications as that. So Vinci didn't even flicker an eyelash when I mentioned it. Just gave off a disinterested, noncommittal sort of shrug and asked, in a thoroughly offhand way, "So what have a-*you* heard?"

"Not much, really. It's just something I thought I overheard at a cocktail party in Detroit. I was on my way to the john, actually. Don't know which American manufacturer they were talking about or whether it was Ferrari or Maserati or whoever…."

"You should have a-stayed to hear a little more."

"I really had to go. Too much wine and coffee. You know how that is."

"Sure I do," he nodded. But you could see his brain going a million miles an hour already behind his eyes.

Mission accomplished.

Audrey and I did go ring shopping on the Friday before I left, and we were able to find a nice—she called it "suitable"—one that fit right out of the jeweler's case. There was a much finer, more expensive one that I know she really liked, but it would have to be re-sized and it was quite a bit more money. So she called it "gaudy" for my benefit and said: "Let's do take this one. It's so pretty and we can have it right away."

So we did. And then we went straight over to the Lola shop in Bromley to show it off. Everyone was very complimentary about it (although Peter Bryant asked if Walter had seen it yet?) and I was pleased to see that the Lola GT project was coming along fairly nicely. It had to be third-tier work after the customer race cars and the work for the formula-one team, but the monocoque was mostly finished and I was told the suspension bits and the sub-contracted fiberglass body panels were also in process. Eric Broadley assured me that the car would indeed make its debut at the Olympia Racing Car Show in January. Even if they had to roll it in while they were still bolting bits onto it! Of course the big bugaboo was an appropriate transaxle, but it seems Colin Chapman had ordered up a new, heavier-duty unit from Colotti for his Fairway-powered Indianapolis car, and Lola was on the list for one as well. So all the necessary pieces were either promised or in the pipeline. The only problem left was getting them in time and putting them all together for the show.

And then I got a little unexpected bonus when John Surtees walked in to have a look at some modifications on the F1 car and talk about travel plans for the South African Grand Prix in East London, the non-championship Rand Grand Prix at Kyalami two weeks before and the non-championship "New Zealand Grand Prix" at Pukekohe on January 5th. And also, I found out later, to privately confirm to Eric Broadley and Reg Parnell—face-to-face—that he would indeed be leaving to drive for Ferrari the following season. But also assure them that they would have his very best efforts, as always, in his final events for the team in South Africa and down under. He wanted to do that in person rather than by letter or phone call or, worse yet, having them read about it somewhere after Ferrari made his official announcement in early December.

Surtees was a real gentleman that way, and you had to respect him for it.

His appearance at the shop gave me an unexpected opportunity to double-down on my Fairway Tower "plant the rumor" mission, and so over a cup of tea at the little shop across the street, I asked him the same leading question I'd posed to Vinci Pittacora the day before. He of course told me he hadn't heard a thing about it. But he did say he'd ask around for me.

I chalked that up as another solid score for the Fairway Tower team.

It was tough saying good-bye to Audrey at the airport on Wednesday morning, but at least we were both feeling a little more settled and committed about things. Jesus, I loved being around her, and I almost couldn't believe she seemed to feel the same about me. Although of course she wasn't the type to get all gushy or maudlin or misty about it. That was more or less my job. And I'm happy to say that Walter was less miserable than expected when we showed him the ring and gave him the news. All he wanted to know was if we'd set a date yet—of course we hadn't, since I really didn't know when I'd be back in England again—although he did give off a gaunt, grudging nod of approval when we told him we were planning to do whatever it was we were about to do in England, and that there were absolutely zero plans for Audrey to re-locate with me back to Detroit. God forbid.

All of which made me feel pretty damn upbeat as I boarded the 707 bound for Detroit late that morning. As far as I could see, I'd accomplished my mission for the company, got the girl, faced the dragon and was headed home with all sorts of promising news for the gents in Fairway Tower. It was like a fucking Hollywood movie script, you know? Although my steady supply of in-flight scotch-and-waters surely helped elevate my general sense of euphoria. They also helped me plan and scheme ahead for another trip back to London (at the company's expense, of course) for the Lola GT's launch at the Olympia Racing Car Show in early January.

So everything was right with the world.

Until I landed in Detroit, anyway.

I'll never forget arriving at Detroit Metro that Wednesday afternoon. It was October 24th, and I noticed as soon as I came down the jetway that everybody in the terminal looked a little pale. A little frightened. A little shell-shocked. Or maybe all three of those at once. You could see it in their eyes. Perfect strangers were whispering back and forth to each other at the gates and in the corridors while others gathered anxiously around TV sets in the airport bars or listened intently to transistor radios pressed up against their ears, trying to hear through the static. I knew something was up, but didn't really understand what it was until I saw the headline on the last copy of *The Detroit Free Press* left on the news stand:

NUCLEAR SHOWDOWN ON THE HIGH SEAS!
U.S. Warships and Russian Missile Ships on Collision Course!

That sobered me up in a hurry!

Of course I was aware that tensions had been running high over "the Cuban situation" ever since fatigues-wearing, cigar-chomping Ruthless Communist Dictator Fidel Castro swept into power on what most Americans viewed as a misguided groundswell of Marxist-Leninist mob rule. And meanwhile, the highly cooperative, US-friendly and fun-to-be-around (at least if you had money and the right connections) government of Ruthless Capitalist Dictator Fulgencio Batista beat it out the back door with pockets crammed full of whatever would fit. Now our government in Washington wasn't real thrilled about having a Russian-backed communist dictatorship and a firebrand populist rabble-rouser like Fidel Castro just 90 miles off the American coastline. And unhappier still were the displaced, disenfranchised Cubans who'd been doing pretty damn well for themselves during the Batista regime, thank you very much, and were now living in unhappy exile in Florida, Texas and Louisiana. Also pissed off were a fat handful of powerful, well-connected "American gaming entrepreneurs" (most from large eastern cities and with last names ending in vowels, if you catch my drift) who were equally upset about all the lucrative, high-class Havana gambling joints and attendant "hospitality businesses" they'd lost to the Castro revolution. The situation had simmered and festered for several years, and there were even rumors of abortive attempts to get rid of Fidel Castro in the time-honored Sicilian way (which, by the sheerest of coincidences, was also the time-honored communist way) by sending him poisoned and/or exploding cigars. But none of them worked out. So a bunch of Cuban ex-pats got together with some shady gangster types and black-hole American C.I.A. operatives to stage an invasion and put things back the way they used to be. But the key to the whole plan—at least in military terms—was the American air support that was supposedly going to show up but never actually did on invasion day at the Bay of Pigs. Now some said it was all a big misunderstanding, while others claimed that President Kennedy froze up like a popsicle when the time came to give the launch order for the planes. But it also seems there may have been a security leak or two, since the Cubans appeared to be ready and waiting for the assault forces with open arms and plenty of ammunition. The end result was a certifiable disaster on both the military and political fronts and an enormous black eye for American prestige. But you'd have to say it was worse yet for the poor soldiers who got stranded on the beach with no air support.

In any case, you couldn't really blame Cuba or its allies for being a little nervous about what Washington might try next. And that's why old Nikita Khrushchev decided to send his pal Castro a nice new set of Russian-built mid-range nuclear missiles that he could lob over at the United States anytime they were getting a bit too frisky regarding Cuban sovereignty. And that didn't sit well at all with the folks in Washington. Once our spy planes confirmed that missile bases were being built and that several shiploads of large, suspicious-looking, tarp-covered metal cylinders with little fins on one end and pointy, cone-shaped warhead tops on the other were on their way across the Atlantic, President Kennedy ordered a lockdown naval blockade—the official term was "quarantine," since a blockade was considered an act of war—to keep them from getting through. Things ratcheted up in a hurry from there, what with threats and counter-threats and demands and counter-demands flying back-and-forth between Moscow and Washington and screaming headlines and half-hourly news bulletins about the rapidly escalating danger of all-out nuclear war!

No matter how you tried to slice it, the ships carrying those Russian missiles and US Navy warships carrying plenty of firepower were steaming inexorably towards each other in the middle of the Atlantic. And it all came to a head the day I landed at Detroit Metro. That's the day the whole damn planet held its breath as the two biggest, most powerful, most heavily armed countries in the whole damn history of the world seemed loaded, cocked and hair-trigger ready to blow each other (and everything else in creation) into atoms. And all any ordinary citizen on either side could do was worry and ponder and pray and pick at their meals and count their rosary beads one after the other while waiting to see if Kennedy and Khrushchev were going to brinksmanship themselves all the way into World War Three. And, thanks to haunting nuclear-apocalypse movies like *On the Beach* (which did feature a pretty cool sports car race), the general feeling was that if they did, it wouldn't be like any war anybody had ever fought before. It would be over (if not exactly settled) in a hurry, and it would transform most of the major metropolitan areas on both sides into bombed-out, radioactive wastelands…

So we read the papers and crowded around TV sets and listened to our car radios and tried to wrap our heads and hearts around the notion that America and Russia were squaring off like a couple of belligerent drunks at closing time. And all any average-Joe citizen on either side could do was just wait and worry and wonder if this was really going to be The End. Fortunately, cooler heads ultimately prevailed and a complicated, behind-closed-doors compromise was worked out whereby the Russian missile ships veered off course and pretty much headed home with their tails between their legs, and our side grudgingly agreed (under-the-table, of course) to pull our own, somewhat out-of-date ICBMs out of Italy and Turkey, which were likewise uncomfortably close to the Russian heartland. And particularly to Moscow, where all the communist-party bigwigs lived with their families and their mistresses and their favorite theaters and libraries and restaurants and museums and night clubs and bath houses and drinking establishments.

So the crisis passed over like the shadow of Terrible Death itself, then slowly ebbed away. But no one who was anywhere in America (or Cuba, or Russia, or damn near anywhere else on the planet that day!) will ever forget it. We'd all found ourselves suddenly, inexplicably and terrifyingly standing on the edge and staring into an abyss. And there wasn't a lot of comfort in knowing that the fear was communal, regardless of which side you were on.

It was just over a week later—at something like 2 am Detroit time on Friday morning, November 2nd—that I got a thoroughly unexpected call from my ace race-photographer pal Hal Crockett. He was calling from some hotel bar in Mexico City with loud music playing in the background, and I could tell that he'd been drinking. A lot more than usual, in fact. "This is a hell of a time to call," I groaned into the receiver. "It's fucking two am here, Hal."

"It couldn't be helped," he slurred in my ear.

"It couldn't be helped?"

"I couldn't sleep."

"You're not getting like Cal on me, are you?"

"It's the damn phone system here," he snarled. "I couldn't get through for a fucking hour."

"So you were planning to call me at one am instead of two?"

"I needed to talk to somebody," he answered morosely. "I figured you'd do."

"Thanks a lot."

"Don't be a prick, okay? It's been a tough day at the office." The surly, half-angry/half-miserable tone of his voice told me something bad had happened. I'd heard that sort of voice before—too many times, in fact—and it never failed to send a cold little shiver through my gut.

"So tell me about it. What happened?"

No response.

"Come on, Hal," I prodded. "You called me at two the fuck in the morning on a work day. So what is it?"

"Rodriguez," he mumbled into the receiver.

That startled me. Why, they'd just teamed up to win that GT points race at Monthléry together not two weeks before. And then came the unavoidable question: "Which one?"

"The younger one. Ricardo."

I waited for the details, but nothing came.

"He's dead?"

I could feel Hal nod at the other end of the line.

And then silence.

A lot of silence.

"So how'd it happen?"

"How does it usually happen at a fucking racetrack?" He growled into the phone. "He tried to go too fast or something broke or who-the-fuck knows? But the bottom line is that he crashed and he's dead."

To be honest, I wasn't entirely surprised. Shocked, horrified and saddened, yes. But not completely surprised. My brain flashed back to the chat I'd had with Count Giovanni on his yacht at Daytona. The one about how Papa Rodriguez was perhaps pushing his boys along too ambitiously. And stoking the natural rivalry between them to make them go even faster. They were proud, privileged, competitive and determined young men and both genuine talents—no question about that part—but they were also terribly young and had come up incredibly fast thanks to all the money, connections and opportunities their father eagerly supplied. To my mind (and Hal's, and Vinci Pittacora's, and even that asshole Eric Gibbon's), Pedro was arguably the more polished, more thoughtful and more mechanically sympathetic of the two. But Ricardo was perceived to have that little something extra. That special, uncanny gift or grace for it. Along with the frightening kind of bravery that only comes from not thinking about— or perhaps not really comprehending—the potential consequences. Like his brother, Ricardo started racing bicycles and then motorcycles when he was no more than a boy, and he'd won several championships in Mexico.

His father couldn't wait to get him started in cars.

I remembered seeing him for the first time at Riverside in September of 1957. That's the weekend he showed up out of nowhere in a Porsche 550 Spyder with "MEXICO" spelled out over the rear wheel openings. Rumors quickly spread that he was only fifteen—not even old enough to hold a driver's license in California!—but that didn't keep him from blowing off all the best under-1500cc sports/racers and drivers on the West Coast and taking a solid win.

It was a pretty damn phenomenal performance.

His older brother Pedro was really good, too, although generally saddled with the family's more powerful but less nimble Ferrari Testa Rossa. The two of them had already driven in—and won—many national races in Mexico, and extended their reputations with impressive showings all over the United States and down at the Nassau Speed Weeks. That led to co-drives in *concessionaire* Ferraris for Carlo Sebastian (with quiet money backing from their father, of course) in international-level endurance races. Ricardo's youth, speed and bravery caught the eye of Enzo Ferrari, and he arranged a one-off "tryout" drive for Ricardo in the Italian Grand Prix at Monza in September of 1961. Most people remember that race only for the horrific accident where the presumptive World Champion and a handful of innocent spectators were killed. But Ricardo put in a pretty damn amazing performance in the shadow of that tragedy. He qualified an impressive 2nd on the grid in an older car (and this in his first-ever Grand Prix!), and battled back-and-forth for the lead with his more-experienced Ferrari teammates Phil Hill and Richie Ginther until forced to retire with fuel-feed problems. At age 19, he was the youngest driver to ever start a world-championship grand prix, and his performance at Monza was enough to earn him a full, factory-team ride with Ferrari for 1962. But following the defection (or was it firing?) of Chiti, Bizzarrini and the rest, Ferrari's warmed-over '61 car wasn't fast enough to match the new chassis and engines from England. Or the air-cooled flat-8 from Porsche in Dan Gurney's hands. Plus Ricardo had to struggle against his own teammates in the usual Ferrari fashion, and was regularly beaten on accumulated skills and racecraft by Phil Hill and thanks to bursts of inspired madness by wild Willy Mairesse. But you had to remember that Ricardo was only 20 and on his first full season in Europe, while his teammates had raced there for several years and knew the dangers, nuances and subtleties of both the tracks and the lifestyle that went with them. Ricardo did manage a 4th behind Hill's Ferrari at Spa and a 6th in Germany (where he out-qualified all of his teammates on the supremely difficult Nurburgring circuit), and scored his first World Manufacturers' Championship victory for Ferrari at the Targa Florio in a 246 Dino shared with Mairesse and Gendebien. Pedro had a solid solo win (admittedly over weaker opposition) when he drove the one-off, Le Mans-winning 4.0-liter Testa Rossa to a dominating victory at the first-ever "Bridgehampton Double 400" World Manufacturers' Championship race on Long Island. And then, just two weeks before the fateful day in Mexico, Ricardo and Pedro teamed up to beat a strong field of GT cars with a flag-to-flag win in the 1000 km of Paris driving Carlo Sebastian's fresh-from-the-factory GTO.

As you can imagine, the Rodriguez brothers' burgeoning success had made them national and international heroes—Ricardo's face was featured on the cover of the March, 1962 issue of *Sports Illustrated*—and that in turn was fueling an enormous resurgence of racing fever in Mexico. This was the country, after all, that had essentially shut down its new (and only!) major highway in order to stage a flat-out, 5-day, 2200-mile-long and singularly difficult, dangerous and dramatic *I a Carrera Panamericana* road race from Tuxtla Gutierrez in the south all the way up to Ciudad Juarez near the Texas border. I was there with Buddy and Big Ed Baumstein back in 1952 and witnessed an incredible, back-and-forth, once-in-a-lifetime battle between the Ferrari and Mercedes factory teams. I also saw firsthand the passion the Mexican people had for motor racing. But there were too many fatalities, and the wild, one-of-a-kind *La Carrera* was shut down after the 1954 running—and probably rightly so—and no question Mexican aficionados had been waiting impatiently for something like the Rodriguez brothers to come along and rekindle the magic.

And that's how plans came about to host a real, F.I.A.-sanctioned *Gran Primio de Mexico* so the new national heartthrobs could perform in front of their home crowd. The Magdalena Mixhuca circuit had opened on the outskirts of Mexico City in 1959 and seemed a perfect location (especially since it was a home track for the Rodriguez brothers), but there wasn't enough time or international clout on tap to get a full World Championship event sanctioned for the '62 season. Plus the F.I.A. in Paris—perhaps recalling the wild and wooly *La Carrera* and its notorious lack of crowd control—was wary of the Mexican organizers' ability to pull it off. So it was agreed that a non-championship, non-points "Mexican Grand Prix" would be held the first weekend of November, with a full World Championship round promised for the '63 season if all went well. Mexican enthusiasts were thrilled, and no question an enormous crowd would turn out to see the show and cheer their heroes on.

The major problem was that the acknowledged star of the event, Mexico's own, meteoric young Ricardo Rodriguez, didn't have a ride! Many of the Grand Prix teams readily agreed to attend the Mexican race because the starting money was attractive, their cars were already in the States for the U.S. Grand Prix at Watkins Glen a month earlier and many of the top drivers had stayed on to do the three-race "West Coast Pro Series" at Kent, Riverside and Laguna Seca in between.

But Ferrari had elected not to send his Formula One team to North America just so they could be humiliated by the new-generation British machines. The decision was understandable, but it left poor Ricardo without a drive. A deal was ultimately made to put him in one of Rob Walker's older-style, tube-frame Lotus 24s, and although it was hardly the best car in the field (what with Team Lotus regulars Jimmy Clark and Trevor Taylor there in the monocoque-chassis Type 25s), it was far from the worst and a top finish was surely in the cards on his home track. Ricardo also helped arrange a drive for his older brother Pedro in Wolfgang Seidel's BRM-powered Lotus 24, and rumors were swirling that they were going to be side-by-side again as factory-driver teammates at Scuderia Ferrari for the upcoming season.

But all was not perfect in Mexico. The high altitude made carburetion problems damn near epidemic. Plus Ricardo was used to driving Ferraris, and there were significant differences between a Lotus Formula One car and a Ferrari. "Ferraris are pretty damn tough," was the way Cal summed it up the night we consumed way too much wine and grappa after he got fired off the Ferrari factory team at the Targa. "You can treat them rough now and then and get away with it." But a Lotus was something else again. Sure, everyone agreed that the limits were much higher in a Lotus—especially through fast, high-speed sweepers—but the edge was far keener and not nearly so easy to sense. A driver might occasionally be able to *force* a Ferrari to do something, but you could never get away with that sort of thing in a Lotus. You had to kind of creep up on them. Finesse them. Almost *seduce* them into yielding their ultimate performance.

And you surely didn't want to step over the edge in a Lotus….

The other problem for Ricardo was John Surtees. John's Bowmaker Lola had escorted him into a huge wreck during practice for the U.S. Grand Prix at Watkins Glen a few weeks before—fortunately without injury—and when it became clear that the frame was badly bent and that the wreck was caused by a fractured steering arm, Surtees elected to use the team's backup Lotus 24 for the non-championship race in Mexico. Or, in other words, the same exact chassis-and-engine combination that young Ricardo was driving.

I had a feeling I knew what was coming.

"It was *Thursday!*" Hal moaned into the phone line. *"First fucking day of practice! Nothing counts for anything on a Thursday!"*

I waited for him to go on. But it took a bit of time for him to gather himself together. And when he started in again, his voice was low and sullen and gravelly: "They've got this last corner there called the Peraltada, see. And it's a real monster. Like a fucking oval corner, really. Super fast, 180-degrees, slightly banked, bump in the middle, daunting as hell…It had all the drivers on edge." Hal paused to take a drink of something "…So we're pretty much done with Thursday practice, and Surtees has gone a little bit quicker than Ricardo in the same kind of car."

"Surtees is damn good."

"You bet your ass he's good! He didn't get to be a five-time world motorcycle champion without a really serious set of balls on him."

"He's smart, too."

"Smart enough to keep on this side of the grass," Hal agreed. "…And walking around on it, too! That's not easy on bikes."

There was no argument to that. People got hurt all the time racing motorcycles. It was part of the deal.

"So what happened?" I prodded.

Hal blew a long, slow sigh. "Well, Ricardo had some carburetion problems—just about everybody did—and the mechanics had been working on it all afternoon. He was already changed into street clothes and getting ready to leave for the reception, but then the mechanics asked him to take it out again to see if they'd gotten the carburetion fixed. So he put his racing overalls back on and headed out. It was around 5 o'clock and he was the only car on the track…" Hal's voice trailed off.

"Go on," I finally urged.

"I was out trying to get some of that good, late light on the cars," he continued almost dreamily. "You can get some really lucky shots sometimes when it's late in the year and late in the afternoon and the sun's all low and golden and the light's…" his voice trailed off. And then I heard him take another slug of whatever he was drinking. "You could hear the sound of the engine as he went around on that first warm-up lap. It sounded a lot sharper and smoother than it had all day. You could hear the difference. And that might have given him ideas, you know?"

"Ideas?"

"Sure. About putting in a quick one and showing his father and his brother and the mechanics and John Surtees and all of Mexico and fucking Enzo Ferrari back in Maranello and everybody else in fucking creation what he could do. You could tell he was on a flier. Just from the noise."

"Go on."

"From what I could see and hear, it seemed like he tried taking the Peraltada *flat!* Without lifting!" Hal paused for a moment while the vision replayed itself in his head. "He damn near made it, too…"

"But he didn't?"

"No, he didn't. Not quite. Not all the way. He hit that bump in the middle and either the car snapped away from him or something broke in the suspension—I couldn't really tell you which—and he just arrowed right up into the guardrail. It was a hell of an impact. A *huge* crash. It would have made you fucking sick if you saw it." There was another long pause. "You know," he barely mumbled, "I called to talk to someone about this, but now I really don't feel like it anymore."

I told him I understood. And I did. But I was still morbidly curious about how it all played out. "Can you tell me anything else?" I finally asked.

"Oh, it was messy stuff. Ugly. Terrible. He got thrown out of the car and the windscreen damn near cut him in half...."

I felt my stomach twist into a knot.

"...the corner workers ran over as quickly as they could and his brother Pedro came over from the pits on a motorbike and by then there were gawkers and photographers swarming all around like fucking ants on a piece of candy. I don't know where they all came from. Pedro tried to push them away, of course, but there were too damn many of them."

"That's awful."

"To be honest, I'm pretty sure he was dead right there. But later on, some press-room asshole started spreading a rumor around that he died on the way to the hospital. And what he supposedly said right there at the end."

"Oh?"

Hal choked back a sob. "They said he was begging the ambulance crew: *'Please, don't let me die'.*"

I shook my head.

Hal's voice turned angry: "Why would you ever say anything like that? Even if you knew it was true, why the fuck would you go around telling people? It just doesn't do anybody any good."

"People like to hear that kind of stuff," I reminded him.

"But *why?*"

"Hell, I write shit like that sometimes, and I'm damned if I know. It's just the way people are."

"Well, the way people are fucking stinks!" he yelled so loud it echoed. And then the line went quiet again, with just some soft, low static crackling through it.

"You okay?" I finally asked.

"No, I'm not," he said matter-of-factly. "I'm drunk and I'm sad and I'm angry as hell...I think I oughta try and get some sleep."

"That's probably a good idea. You'll feel better in the morning."

"No, I won't."

"Okay, so you won't. But you ought to try and get some sleep anyway."

"Maybe I'll have another drink."

"Maybe you should."

"It's a damn shame about Ricardo."

"Yeah," I agreed. "Rest in Peace."

"Yeah," he sighed. "Rest in Peace."

"You okay?"

"Yeah. I'm okay."

"I'm going to hang up now."

"Go ahead."

"You sure?"

"Yeah. Sure. I'll see you at the fucking races."

Click.

And now I was the one who couldn't sleep.

Chapter 24: Freakish Holiday Festivities

Amanda Cassandra Fairway threw another of her famous holiday-season blowout party extravaganzas the Friday night between December 25th and New Years' Eve, and naturally I was invited along with all the other folks who regularly passed through the brass-and-nickel, art-deco elevator doors on the 13th floor of Fairway Tower. I would have much rather been somewhere around the East London circuit on the South African coastline that particular December 28th, waiting with supreme anticipation for the last Grand Prix of the season that would take place the very next day.

The fierce championship battle between Jimmy Clark in the Lotus 25 and Graham Hill's BRM P57 was still very much up for grabs, and there was no question it would be settled at East London. While Jimmy and the Lotus had generally been quicker (although the BRM was very close and had arguably better power and particularly more torque), the Lotus had let Jimmy down many times when it didn't win while Hill's BRM had been stunningly reliable, with just a single DNF in France. So although Graham and Jimmy were tied even-up at three wins apiece, Clark had just his unfortunate 4th place at the Nurburgring (when he stalled on the grid after forgetting to switch his fuel pumps on) to back them up, while Hill had two solid 2nd-place finishes—behind Clark, of course—at Spa and Watkins Glen. Since a driver could only count his five best finishes towards his championship total, it meant Clark needed to win outright in South Africa to take the title. Nothing else would do. But he'd been on a hell of a roll with pole position, fastest race lap and a decisive win over Hill's BRM at the U.S. Grand Prix at Watkins Glen in October. Followed by an even more impressive victory in the non-championship Mexican round where poor Ricardo Rodriguez had been killed.

BRM didn't attend the Mexican race, preferring instead to concentrate on the championship rounds, and so Clark was on pole by almost a full second. He squirted off to an immediate lead, but was forced to pull in and retire with mechanical problems. In a highly unusual move, Chapman brought teammate Trevor Taylor in so that Clark could take over his car. In spite of a near minute-long pit stop to make the driver change, Clark proceeded to storm back through the field, re-take the lead by two-thirds distance and score yet another crushing victory. And the winning continued at the two non-championship South African rounds that preceded the points-paying race at East London. Clark and Taylor qualified and finished 1-2 in their Lotus 25s in the so-called

"Rand Grand Prix" at Kyalami and reversed that order at the so-called "Natal Grand Prix" at Westmead after Clark suffered fuel vaporization in the preliminary and had to fight his way up from the back of the grid to take second.

So it was shaping up to be one hell of a showdown for the championship! And here I was, riding along the fucking shoreline of fucking Lake St. Clair with Danny fucking Beagle, on my fucking way to Amanda Cassandra Fairway's fucking Christmas-cum-New Year's holiday party in a fucking ostentatious, oversized fucking mansion with an exact fucking 8/10ths-scale reproduction of the famous fucking garden maze at fucking Charleval out back and way too many fucking over-decorated, over-redecorated and over-re-redecorated rooms inside. Hell, the damn race would be starting around the crack of dawn Detroit time, and I didn't even know who was qualified where on the fucking grid! It was eating me up! And instead of a race program or a timing sheet, sitting next to me on the front seat was one of the embossed, linen-finish and somewhat message-confused invitations that the Fairways had sent out to all the upper-management types from the 12th and 13th floors of Fairway Tower. Who in turn invited favorites from among their staff plus a smattering of carefully selected individuals from the lower floors who had caught their eye because they appeared to be either (a) eager, ambitious, respectful and intelligent young men on the way up or (b) eager, ambitious, well-endowed young ladies with a suspected likelihood of going in entirely the opposite direction. The invitation was honestly a little hard to fathom, what with a solemn, peaceful, pious and serene Three Wise Men staring up adoringly at a gold-stamped Star of Bethlehem on the outside and a big cartoon Santa Claus wearing a New Year's party hat and blowing on a roll-out noisemaker on the inside. The supposed reasoning behind the whole thing was that Amanda Cassandra Fairway's party would be a great opportunity for many of Fairway Motors' key people to enjoy each other's company in a festive holiday setting, get to know one another a little better and socialize with the same damn people they saw and worked with every fucking day of the year... including immediate superiors, their immediate superiors, project managers, department heads, their bosses, their bosses' bosses and on and on up Fairway Motors' convoluted chain of command all the way to the double-hung mahogany doors at the far end of the executive corridor that separated Little Harry Dick Fairway's private office suite from the rest of the known universe.

All of which meant that everybody invited had sure as hell better be there at the end of McElligot Lane as requested come Friday night, December 28th, had better be appropriately dressed and groomed and had better bring some sort of gaily wrapped holiday gift in the general shape of a fruit basket, a really nice box of candies or pastries or an expensive bottle of hooch. And they had moreover better watch their step and be on their very best behavior if they knew what the hell was good for them. And also hope like hell that their wives, husbands, boyfriends, girlfriends or whomever the hell else they brought along did the same and didn't get too loud, drunk, flirty, overly friendly, underly dressed, off-color or obnoxious. Or God forbid proposition anybody (or get propositioned by anybody) higher up on the old corporate ladder.

But of course the *real* reason for Amanda Cassandra's party was to allow her to unveil, just in time for the holidays, the stunning new "Middle Eastern motif" makeover theme for her beloved main entrance hall that she, favorite-designer-of-the-moment Sean Shawn and several dozen tradesmen working double-overtime shifts for the past three weeks had rushed to hurried completion only a few hours before. To be honest, I would have much rather been either down in South Africa for the race or back in London with Audrey than arcing through the stone-gate portals of McEligott Lane with Danny Beagle in one of the generally sale-proof Fairway Freeway Frigate Fragonard Special Editions that had been doled out as company cars to get them the fuck off the inventory books.

I remember we were listening to The Tornados' neat instrumental hit *"Telstar"* on the Freeway Frigate's radio, and I was bracing myself for what I was quite sure would be another long, loud, dull, edgy, awkward and uncomfortable evening of Fairway-mansion hospitality. Considering how things had turned out the last time I was there, I'd quietly vowed to avoid anything much stiffer than a few ginger ales and maybe a glass or two of champagne. As Buddy Palumbo's great friend and mentor Big Ed Baumstein always put it: *"It's no damn fun getting drunk around people you wouldn't want to be drunk with."*

And of course he was right.

Losing your inhibitions, equilibrium and/or the ability to form complete sentences around people you don't really know, care about or feel comfortable with (or, worse yet, work with every day) is usually a pretty bad idea.

At the very least, no good can come of it.

And speaking of things no good could come of, I was pretty damn sure I wanted to avoid spoiled daughter/troublemaker/harpy-in-training Amelia Camellia Fairway, who looked very likely to get me into some very serious trouble—or worse—and yet still sent a strange, peculiar fizz through my gut every time I thought about her. Or maybe it was lower than my gut. And I had to admit that I thought about her more often than I cared to think about. It's not like I was terribly attracted to her (in fact, she made me terrifically uncomfortable), but no question there was something about her insolent, predatory, angry-at-the-world/who-gives-a-shit forbidden-fruit sexuality that made her hard to ignore. Plus there's always been something train-wreck fascinating about the wanton, amoral boredom of the rich, young and privileged. It's like way too much sugar frosting with a little dash of alcohol, pot and snake venom mixed in.

As you can imagine, the Fairway mansion was damn near ablaze with holiday lights, and you damn near needed sunglasses to keep your irises from snapping down to *f*22 pinpoints. And right in the middle of everything was this dazzling, eight-story-high, trucked-directly-in-from-Canada-on-a-flatbed-semi-trailer-at-enormous-and-exhorbi-tant-expense Fraser Fir Christmas tree decorated with more fucking colored lights and blinking, glittering, flashing holiday doohickies than Times Square. It looked like a flash-frozen fireworks display erupting out of the center of Amanda Cassandra Fairway's driveway. It was a massive, stupefying, totally overpowering thing, and as you got closer you could see that tiny, near-silent electric fans were hidden away inside to make the tinsel shimmer. Not to mention all the beautiful, hand-blown mercury-glass ornaments in the shape of favorite fruits and vegetables and the insect pests that plague them. "That was Sean's idea," Amanda Cassandra Fairway tittered excitedly from the top of the entrance stairs. "He wanted to make one of his statements." She took another healthy swig of high-octane eggnog out of an engraved-for-the-occasion crystal mug. "He's *so* evolved…"

Our hostess was resplendent in a draped, platinum lamé cocktail gown, an aggressively cheery holiday smile, a holly-and-berry-motif necklace-and-earrings set made out of sparkling rubies and emeralds (real ones!) and a darling little red-velvet Santa Claus cap with genuine arctic fox trim. Spread out around her at the foot of the stairs and scattered out across the lawn were illuminated ice sculptures of the holy family and the three wise men gathered around a crèche scene, Santa and Mrs. Claus, Santa's sleigh and reindeer (with a blinking red light in Rudolph's nose, of course), a bunch of Santa's elves carrying presents, a line of toy soldiers, dancing sugar-plum fairies, Frosty the Snowman, Susie Snowflake, the Cinnamon Bear and assorted kid-favorite Disney characters like Mickey Mouse, Minnie Mouse, Goofy, Pluto, Donald and Daisy Duck plus the little black lawn jockey who was more or less a permanent fixture on the Fairway mansion's entrance drive (although he'd been decked out in a felt Santa hat for the occasion). But it seemed a bit odd to me that Mickey Mouse, Minnie Mouse, Frosty, Goofy and the Cinnamon Bear all appeared to be part of the crèche scene.

But the *piéce de resistance* was the gaily painted, three-foot-high Little Drummer Boy standing right next to Amanda Fairway in the entranceway. "He came all the way from Germany," she cooed to Dick Flick and his wife, who were just ahead of us on the stairs. Amanda Fairway reached down for what was surely the fiftieth or sixtieth time that evening and pressed a small, red button on the back of the Little Drummer Boy's neck. Followed by the gnash of hidden gears as a tightly wound mainspring ratcheted her Little Drummer Boy into action. His eyes rolled maniacally and his arms jerked spastically up and down as he pounded out what sounded like the first sixteen bars of a Third Reich marching song on his little tin drum. He reminded me of something out of a creepy *Inner Sanctum* episode. "Sean found him in some horrid little junk shop in Munich, and we just *had* to have him," Amanda Fairway gushed. "He was in absolutely *terrible* condition. All rusty and one of his dear little eyes wouldn't work. And his gears or whatever were all frozen up inside." She let out an elaborate sigh. "And he was in this absolutely *horrid* old gray uniform!"

"You've done wonders with him," Dick Flick's wife assured her.

"Oh, it wasn't *me!*" she insisted, damn near bursting with modesty. "It was Sean. *He's* the one who saw the potential. Saw what he could be…" her face brightened like a stage light had hit it "…and just look at him *now!*" She pressed the button again and her Little Drummer Boy rapped off a few more spine-rattling bars of Heil Hitler marching music, his eyes rattling left-to-right like windshield wipers as he scanned the crowd on Amanda Cassandra Fairway's front steps for any undetected Gypsies, Jews, communists or homosexuals. But his mainspring tension was starting to run a little low by then, and I watched with a combination of horror and fascination as he ground awkwardly to a halt. Right at the end he sounded like a bunch of tired old bottle caps bouncing off an ashcan lid. She switched him off and summoned one of the car parkers to wind him up again. I noticed right away that it was my Black Mamba Lounge friend Otis Jenkins, but all we could do was make a little silent eye contact before he bent down to re-wind the key in the Little Drummer Boy's back. You could see it took quite a bit of effort, even for a future star halfback for the Michigan State Spartans.

Amanda Fairway took another slug of her eggnog, leaned in a little closer to Dick Flick and his wife and stage-whispered: "Of course, Richard could have bought himself another Chris Craft for what the damn thing cost to restore."

"He's just darling," Dick's wife assured her.

"Isn't he?" Amanda agreed, and nodded them inside. That left Danny and me next in line, and to be honest, I don't think Amanda Fairway recognized me.

"What a marvelous job you've done with the decorations!" I told her as I handed over a professionally wrapped bottle of Napoleon brandy. I mean with coiled gold ribbons around the neck and everything. And then I tried to sneak inside. Only Amanda Fairway reached her hand out and stopped me. Or maybe she just needed something to lean on? She'd obviously been sampling quite a bit of the eggnog to make sure that each new batch was properly mixed. Amanda Fairway gave me a grand, who-the-fuck-are-you smile, leaned in close and whispered, *"It's not an easy thing to do."*

"I'm sure it isn't," I whispered back like I had some idea what she was talking about.

She nodded knowingly, leaned her forehead in against mine and confided, *"Getting the theme and the food and the decorations just right is SUCH a challenge."*

"Oh, I'm sure it is," I confided right back.

"It's a pain in the ass, if you want the truth of it!" she confided some more. And then she leaned her head back and laughed like it was all so terribly amusing. Poignant, too.

"I'm sure it is!" I laughed and poignant-ed right back at her.

She grabbed my collar and pulled me in close again: *"And Richard isn't much help at all, if you know what I mean."*

"I'm sure he isn't," I whispered back.

She rolled her eyes in a grand, exaggerated swoon. "But of course I understand how things are," she continued with a self-sacrificial lilt. "I know he's *terribly* busy with the cars and the company and all…."

"There's a lot on his shoulders, all right."

At which point Amanda Fairway drew back a half-foot and regarded me like she was seeing me for the very first time. A puzzled, inebriated look descended over her face like a window shade. "Do I *know* you?"

"W-we've met a few times," I more or less stammered. "I was here for your daughter Amelia's 17th birthday party last spring."

Her face brightened like a stage light had found it again. "You're Bill Phlegm from accounting, aren't you?"

"Uh…actually, no. I'm not."

Her smile melted into a frown. "You're *not?*"

I shook my head.

"Then who *are* you?"

"Hank. Hank Lyons. I kind of work for Bob Wright."

"Oh, of *course!*" she gushed. By then, a few more people were coming up behind us, and she'd obviously realized that I was nobody of consequence. So she smiled at Danny and nodded us inside, took another slug of eggnog and got ready to run through her Little Drummer Boy routine again for the people behind us.

The Middle Eastern-motif makeover of Amanda Cassandra Fairway's Grand Entrance Hall was truly something to see. Gone were the Baroque/Rococo styling cues, grand flourishes, swirling gold-leaf filigrees and the exact scale replica of the Trevi Fountain, all of it replaced by a sort of muddled Moorish/Moroccan/Byzantine theme complete with graceful masonry arches, slender, stalk-like columns, ornate geometric moldings and inlaid tile mosaics. And right in the middle of everything—where the African Veldt watering hole had once been and the scale replica of the Trevi Fountain after that—stood a larger-than-life-size and somewhat out-of-place Bethlehem crèche scene carved out of pure Italian marble. It must have taken a damn forklift to move the pieces into position. Joseph, the blessed mother and assorted heavenly angels, cherubim and seraphim hanging above them on near-invisible wires were all in purest white (the infant baby Jesus was so white he seemed to almost glow from within) while the surrounding shepherds and sheep were more ivory-colored and the three wise men and their camels were a decidedly more yellowish. Well, they were supposed to be from the Orient, weren't they?

I got myself a drink—a ginger ale to start with—and wandered over to where Ben Abernathy and his wife were standing next to the Steinway grand with a fat stack of holiday sheet music piled on top of it. No question Christmas caroling was on the agenda once Amanda Fairway finished with her reception duties and all of the guests were properly lubricated. Ben and I exchanged hellos and shot the shit for awhile, but you couldn't miss that Ben's wife was acting a bit cool towards me. Apparently she'd figured out just who the hell had been accompanying Ben over to The Steel Shed for a few beers and a little shit-kicker music after work. Or over to the Black Mamba Lounge for some live blues now and then on Friday nights. She didn't look particularly happy about it.

As for Ben, I could tell by the way he kept looking around and sighing and checking his watch every five minutes that he was just waiting for a socially acceptable amount of time to pass so he and his wife could say their good-byes and get the hell out of there. But it's hard to judge that sort of thing, and a good rule of thumb is that you don't want to be the first, second or third couple out the door (medical, child, pet and babysitter emergencies excepted, of course), and you should always try to insinuate yourself into a larger group of exiting guests so as not to call attention to yourself. So Ben and his wife were obviously going to be stuck there at least until the caroling started. And I didn't want to be anywhere around that grand piano when it happened. I don't much like to sing unless I'm terribly, sloppily, tell-everybody-around-you-how-much-you-love-them drunk, and I've been advised by good friends whom I trust and who have moreover see me in that condition that I have no ear for music along with one of the five or six worst singing voices in recorded human history.

Ben gave me the old eye-roll as soon as his wife was looking the other way, and I knew right away what he had in mind. But I shook my head. I had a feeling that getting stoned on some of Willie Shorter's excellent weed and coming back into a room like this could be scary indeed. Besides, after last time, I'd promised myself to stay 100% straight and at least 70% sober this particular evening.

Or 60%, anyway.

So I gave Ben an apologetic little head shake and went wandering around the room, mostly flitting from appetizer table to appetizer table and doing my best to stay away from the six or eight bars they had set up at strategic intervals. Not to mention the big, frothy fountain of high-test eggnog right in the middle of everything and the endlessly circulating waiters carrying trays of long-stemmed, freezer-frosted champagne glasses. It's not like I was planning to be a teetotaler all evening, but I did have fixed dead-center in my mind that I didn't want to get stinking, fall-down drunk again. And that's a terribly easy thing to do if you're feeling out-of-place and uncomfortable and there's a lot of free hooch being passed around. Especially when you're not blessed with an excess of natural capacity. I mean, it's not like I was Little Harry Dick or Amanda Cassandra Fairway, who had virtually everybody on the premises by the short hairs and really didn't give a good God damn about what people thought.

I walked up the three marble steps to the gold-and-silver-garland-decorated French doors leading out onto the terrace and ran my eyes around the room, searching for someone—hell, anyone!—that I really felt like talking to. But Amanda Fairway's Grand Ballroom was packed full of noise and chatter and dumb, forced laughter, and a few tentative tinkles on the piano keys left no doubt that Christmas carols (plus at least six or seven achingly maudlin renditions of *Auld Lang Syne*) were about to begin.

God, I felt lonely.

So I grabbed myself a mug of eggnog—just one, you understand—and headed off down the hallway looking for a place where I could nurse my lonely eggnog and feel morose and sorry for myself in peace and quiet and not have to deal with anybody. We've all felt like that at parties now and then, haven't we? And particularly around the holidays, when everybody's trying so fucking hard to be cheerful. I decided to head down to the library to see if I could maybe find something to read. Or just something to thumb through and look at the pictures. Books are good for that. They give you a place to hide along with a perfectly reasonable excuse for not wanting to talk to anybody, either.

But I wasn't the only person with that idea, and whom should I find in the library again but resident mansion teenage prodigy H.R. Fairway the Third. He was coiled up in that big leather chair by the desk and concentrating mightily as he worked his way through the pages of the second volume of a near-priceless, calf-leather-bound edition of Edward Gibbon's monumental *The History of the Decline and Fall of the Roman Empire*. "That's pretty heavy reading, isn't it?" I asked him softly.

H.R. the Third's eyes rose up over the binding and he smiled at me. "It's a little windy," he allowed. "But there's some good stuff in here, too."

"Got another book report to do?"

"Nah," he yawned, and laid the heavy book across his chest. "I've got this history teacher who thinks Gibbon ought to have a statue erected in his honor. Says he pretty much *invented* the causal interpretation of history."

"Oh?" I asked, trying to pretend like I knew what the hell he was talking about. "Didn't he?"

H.R. the Third stifled another yawn. "It's hard to say, but I figured I ought totry and find out for myself."

"And did you?"

A weary frown creased his face. "I'm halfway through this one and I've got two volumes still to go and, to be honest, it's pretty slow going." He tapped the binding with his forefinger. "You ever read this?"

I started to hem and haw, but I had no place to go and I knew it. "I always *meant* to read it…"

"You and everybody else!" he laughed. "Nobody but an old academic mossback like my honors history teacher can get through the darn thing."

"So is it worth it?"

"Well, the guy's obviously quite a thinker," H.R. the Third acknowledged. "But he goes on and on and on about things. And it's just full of personal opinions and unsubstantiated conclusions masquerading as unarguable facts…" he stifled another yawn "…Or that's how I see it, anyway."

"Oh?"

H.R. the Third nodded. "It seems to me that you can look at human history from two different and distinctly opposite angles."

"Do tell?"

"One is to assume that things happen randomly and chaotically—often without reason—and the crazy mess you end up with when all is said and done is human history."

I regarded him as seriously as I'd ever regarded a high-school student in my life. "So what's the other way?"

"Oh, that's Gibbon's way. You look back at history and it all seems to have structure and make sense. Like there's a direct, cause-and-effect relationship between everything that has happened and everything that will happen. If you believe that, then we can empirically *explain* and *understand* why things change and evolve and develop like they do."

"And can we?"

H.R. the Third answered with a small, ambivalent shrug.

"But what do *you* think?" I prodded.

"I dunno. I guess it's a little bit of both."

I let out a low whistle. "Boy, are *you* ever ready for college."

"You really think so?"

"Trust me," I laughed. "You're *past* ready."

A smile curled up the corners of his mouth. He leaned back into the leather upholstery, stretched like a cat and closed his eyes. "I can hardly wait," he said so softly you could barely hear it.

"Can't wait to go away to school?"

"Can't wait not to have to live here anymore!" Only then he realized what he'd said, and his eyes opened warily. "But I'd just as soon keep that quiet if it's all the same to you. I don't need things to get any more, um, you know...*difficult* for me here."

"Hey, I don't give a shit one way or the other. It's no skin off my nose."

I watched his shoulders relax. "Thanks," he said simply And then: "I really don't need any more grief with my parents."

"They give you a hard time?"

"Nah, not really. My sister's the one who's always getting into trouble." He flashed me an exasperated grimace. "She goes out and *looks* for things that'll piss them off. It's like some sort of stupid crusade for her."

"But you don't feel that way?"

"Nah, it's not worth it. Old people can't help being how they are. It's not like you're going to change them."

"You're wise beyond your years."

"Nah, not really. But what's the point of swimming upstream? You just get into big fights that go 'round and 'round and 'round and never get anywhere."

"And it doesn't bother you?"

"*Sure* it bothers me. My parents bother the shit out of me. I hate it that they're so damn rich and stupid and arrogant and ignorant and irritating and irrelevant…" his voice trailed off and his eyes slowly closed. "I know it's a terrible thing to say, but I really can't stand them. Either one of them. I'm just not like them at all."

I almost said something, but thought better of it. Even bright, smart, level-headed kids like H.R. the Third can repeat things they've heard in the heat of fighting with their parents. I figured I was better off to just sit there and nod.

Down the hall, the first few rounds of Christmas carols were cranking up around the gleaming black Steinway in the ballroom. *Deck the Halls*, in fact. But it sounded a little weak to me. Like it needed a little more eggnog, you know? For singers and listeners alike.

I got up and closed the door. It was a big, heavy door and it muffled the caroling pretty well. Then I looked down into my glass. It was empty. I had an urge to go back to the ballroom and get another, but I really didn't want to.

"You want something more to drink?" H.R. the Third asked like he was reading my mind. "There's a full bar behind that fake set of Encyclopedia Britannicas over there. You just need to pull on the copy of *Roget's Thesaurus* on the shelf above it. But you'd better lock the door first. I'm not supposed to know it's there."

So I did. And, sure enough, the entire A-to-Z shelf of Britannicas turned out to be a fold-out, polished-maple shelf with a full wet bar and a small ice freezer—like a wall safe, you know?—behind it. I poured myself a generous glass of Napoleon brandy. "You want anything?"

"I'm not really a drinker yet."

It was easy to forget how old H.R. the Third was.

Or how young, to be more accurate.

I let my eyes swivel slowly around the room, taking inventory or all the fabulous books that would probably never be opened again once H.R. the Third went off to college. "It's kind of a shame, isn't it?" I said to nobody in particular.

"What is?"

"These books. They seem so—I don't know—*lonely*. I mean, it's like they're nothing more than decorating here."

"That's all they are. But time will pass and my folks will get old and die and somebody will buy this house and they'll probably wind up being given away to some charitable foundation for a big tax writeoff. They may even wind up in a small college somewhere."

"That would be nice."

"It could happen that way."

"You've got a very positive view of the future."

"Not really. I think everything's going straight to hell and we're all going to die and that'll be the end of it. But I like to keep a good thought now and then."

"You think there's going to be a nuclear war?"

"I don't think we'll be that lucky."

"Oh?"

H.R. the Third shook his head. "Nah. That's just a romantic notion. See, everybody dreams about this huge, cataclysmic disaster that will end everything like the big flares, bombs and rockets finale of a fireworks display. Something that will end all of our little miseries at once and tie everything up neatly with a fancy radioactive ribbon."

"And you don't?"

"Nah. It's too neat. Too easy." He looked up at me. "You know that poem?"

"What poem?"

"You know: *this is the way the world ends…not with a bang, but a whimper.*"

"That's T.S. Eliot, isn't it? *The Love Song of J. Alfred Prufrock,* I think."

He looked at me sheepishly. "You've got the right guy," he said almost like he was apologizing for correcting me, "but that line is from *The Hollow Men.*" He must have seen the dispirited look on my face and so he added, even more apologetically: "It's an easy mistakc to make. They're all good poems and they all sound pretty much the same…"

I wanted to tell him what an amazing sort of kid he was. But before I could, there was a harsh, impatient knock on the door. Followed by Amelia Camellia Fairway's insolent, strident and thoroughly unmistakable voice: *"Who the fuck is in there, huh? And why's the fucking door locked?"*

"It's just me," H.R. the Third answered meekly.

"Are you playing with yourself again in there?"

"No…" H.R. the Third blushed. "No, I'm not. And I'm not alone, either. So I wish you'd watch your mouth a little."

"Who's in there with you? You don't have a girl in there, do you?"

H.R. the Third slowly uncoiled from his chair and went over to the door to let his sister in. Amelia Camellia padded into the room barefoot with just a plaid flannel bathrobe around her. Her hair was all scraggly, and she looked like she'd just woken up, and I could see that she wasn't wearing anything under the bathrobe. But it wasn't like she was trying to be sexy or provocative. She just plain didn't give a shit.

"You'd better not let mom and dad see you like that," H.R. the Third warned. "They've got one of their parties going on."

"I know," she yawned. "I heard the fucking caroling. That's what woke me up. What the hell time is it anyway?"

I checked my watch. "It's a little past nine."

Amelia Camellia's eyes slid over to me. "What the fuck are you doing here? And what're you guys doing in here anyway?" You could sense the frost between her and her brother. But I guess that's pretty normal among siblings. And particularly if the bloodline may not be exactly the same.

"We were talking about Gibbon's *The History of the Decline and Fall of the Roman Empire*, if you must know," H.R. the Third said like it was way over her head.

"Sure you were," she taunted right back at him.

"No, really," I assured her. "That's what we were doing."

She eyeballed me suspiciously. "Sounds awfully boring," she yawned some more.

"You think *everything's* boring," H.R. the Third sneered.

"I can't help it," she grumbled. "Everything *is* boring." She walked over to the bar and poured herself half a tumbler of vodka.

"Maybe if you weren't sleeping all day and getting high with those stupid friends of yours all the time…."

"They're not my friends," she said as she downed three fingers of vodka in one gulp. "They're just people I know. And then she looked over at me like we had some sort of sly, special secret going on between us. I couldn't help noticing that her robe was hanging about halfway open and that the skin underneath looked smooth and creamy and dangerous. "I like getting high," she said like she was proud of it. And then she looked me in the eyes again. "In fact, I'd like to get high right now."

I could feel H.R. the Third's eyes going back and forth between us—I'm sure he saw me looking down her bathrobe—and immediately the heat started rushing into my cheeks.

"Look, I don't really care what you do one way or the other," he growled disgustedly. "I don't give a crap how you mess up your life."

"Why should you?" she demanded. *"It's none of your fucking business!"*

"I don't!"

"And that's just fine with me!"

"Good. That's just fine with me, too!"

"And you can go straight the fuck to hell while you're at it!" She wrinkled her nose at him like a pissed-off housecat.

H.R. the Third answered with a disapproving sneer.

"H-hey, look," I ventured, "I should really be getting back to your folks' party. I mean, it might not look right me being in here with you two."

"Nobody'll give a fuck," Amelia Camellia assured me while still glaring at her brother. "Nobody'll even notice. Besides, it's boring out there with all the apes and idiots. You *really* want to sing fucking Christmas carols?" She turned to me with an artless but unmistakably flirty smile. It made me *very* uncomfortable. Especially in front of her brother. But she acted like he wasn't even there. "I got some pretty good stuff hidden away in my mother's sewing room upstairs," she went on in a teasing, singsong voice.

I could feel her brother's eyes on me like a set of driving lights.

I have to admit there was a tiny, ugly little urge inside to go with her, but the rest of me was all sirens, air horns and crash-dive alarms. No question it was time to excuse myself and head back to the party.

"Thanks for the offer," I said as diplomatically as I could, "but I don't think that would be a very good career move for me." I looked over at her brother with a helpless shrug. "Good to see you again," I told him as I headed for the door. "Let me know how *The History of the Decline and Fall of the Roman Empire* turns out."

"I'm pretty sure the barbarians win," he called after me as I headed back to the party.

Chapter 25: Winners, Losers, Wax and Polish

As I headed back to my room at the Fairview at a little past midnight, I knew the entire grand prix traveling circus—patrons, *pilotos,* participants, parts-chasers, press pimps, posers, pretenders, and hangers-on—was just starting to wake up in East London, South Africa. The better-fixed ones in swanky hotels overlooking the gently rolling surf of the Indian Ocean, the shooters, scribblers and mechanics that hadn't been up all night wrenching in dank little rooms that smelled of grease and pee. But they'd all shower and dress and grab some breakfast-on-the-run, then head off to the racetrack for the season-finale/title-deciding South African Grand Prix.

Jesus, I wanted to be there!

But the best I could do was give my crotchety, cantankerous photographer friend Hal Crockett a call to see what the hell was happening. And if he didn't want me bothering him at 6:15am on race-day morning, he shouldn't have given me the number at his fucking hotel.

"Whozzis?" he grunted into the receiver. I believe I woke him up.

"It's me."

"I know who it is. Who the fuck else would call me at the crack of dawn?" He sounded a little hung-over. Maybe even more than a little.

"Good party last night?"

He thought that over for a moment or two. Maybe longer. Like he was actually trying to decide. And then, quite groggily, "I guess it must have been."

"You're not sure?"

"Too early to be sure. Check with me later on. You get sure too early in the morning and you just wind up taking it back later."

"You still sound a little drunk."

"Can't be drunk…I know that because I've got a terrible hangover. You can't still be drunk and have a terrible hangover at the same time. It's one of the standard rules."

Hal was making perfect sense and no sense at all, and so I knew he was starting to come around.

"I was at a party last night myself…" I bragged. And then paused for proper dramatic effect, "…in a real, live *mansion.*"

He didn't seem impressed: "I bet mine was better."

"Probably. But what makes you so sure?"

"The people. I was getting drunk with Peter Bryant and Georgie Smales and a couple of the local South African guys who're filling out the field. You were probably with a bunch of assholes."

"How do you know?"

"The fact that you're calling me at—what is it, just past midnight there?—to find out what's happening here instead of still out carousing or sleeping it off like somebody who actually had a good time."

He had me there.

So I asked him what was happening at the racetrack.

He told me Clark's Lotus was on pole again with Graham Hill's BRM right beside him—barely three/tenths of a second off—and that those two were a full second-and-a-half faster than anyone else. So the stage was set for a real, classic, *mano-a-mano* championship showdown between the two cars and drivers that had dominated the entire season. Hell, you couldn't write it up any better as fiction! Although Hal allowed that the field was a little sparse since Ferrari again didn't send any cars to be humiliated and neither did Porsche. There were rumors from several quarters that Porsche was getting ready to fold up its tent and give up grand prix racing as a bad try.

"That's kind of a shame."

"Yeah, it is," Hal agreed. "But to spend that much money, effort and manpower and get so little to show for it, well…" he let his voice trail off.

"Especially when you've got one of the best damn drivers on earth right now on your payroll."

"Amen to that. Gurney's one of the special ones all right."

"Makes you proud to be an American."

"That it does."

"So where do you think he'll go?"

I could feel Hal shrug at the other end of the line. "Nobody knows. At least not yet, anyway. But he'll find a slot. He's too good not to."

"It'd be great to see him in a Lotus."

"I don't think he'd fit in one. Chapman always hires those little jockey-sized guys like Clark and Taylor and Stacey and Arundell. They're the only ones who can fit in the damn cars…"

That was true enough.

"…And besides, Chapman's already on a roll with what he's got. They had a pair of non-championship rounds at Kyalami and Westmead over the past two weekends, and the Lotus 25s finished 1-2 in both of them. Clark won easily at Kyalami with Taylor right in his wheeltracks. And it was nice to see Surtees take third in the Lola."

"I heard. It's a damn shame to see what's happening to that team. The Lola's a *really* good car."

"It doesn't finish very many races."

"It's their first fucking season!" I protested. "And, when you get right down to it, it's not a real factory effort. Not like Lotus or Porsche or BRM or Ferrari. And it's Broadley's first-ever try at an F1 car! And…"

"Are you on his payroll?" Hal chuckled. "You sound like a fucking press agent."

That brought me up short. "I just think a lot of what he's done, that's all."

"So do I. So does everybody. But in the end, it's all about results, isn't it?"

It was hard to argue with that. Genius and effort aren't worth very much by themselves. You need to have the other part, too.

"So what happened in the other race?"

"Another Lotus 1-2, only Taylor got the win at Westmead because Clark had fuel vaporization problems in his qualifying heat and had to start from the back in the feature. But he came right through the field to take second behind Taylor at the flag. And everybody was happy to see Taylor get the win. It's tough being the teammate of a guy like Jimmy Clark. He's just *so* good. And you know he gets the best of the equipment."

"He's not a very big man, but he casts one hell of a long shadow."

"That he does. And the Lotus 25 is the car-of-the-moment now, isn't it?"

"You can't argue with that."

"Plus Chapman's gotta be pretty damn happy about how that junior thing worked out at Monza in December."

"What junior thing?"

"You haven't heard?"

I shook my head, even though I knew he couldn't see it.

"Well, you know how Colin runs a genuine, factory-effort Formula Junior team, right?"

"Sure I do. And I also know that his cars have been mopping the floor with the opposition just about everywhere they race."

"And they should. I mean, first off, the 22 is probably the best car in the class, and Chapman's fielding a real, professional-level effort with the best motors and topnotch, hired-gun drivers—Peter Arundell's been just about unstoppable in the Lotus juniors this year—along with plenty of testing and tuning and development. And they're running against mostly amateurs and privateer teams."

"Yeah, I know. But it's helped him sell an awful lot of cars. Guys line up all over the world to buy the latest Lotus juniors as soon as they come out."

"That they do. And he keeps coming up with new ones, too."

And that was true enough. Colin Chapman had made quite a successful business venture for himself out of formula junior. And he did it by coming up with successively newer and sleeker and faster cars. First you bought a Lotus 18, because that was the car to have. And then he came out with the 20, and that made your 18 into an instantaneous lump-of-shit that nobody wanted. Or that no *serious* driver wanted, anyway. And then the even slicker and slimmer 22 came along, and all of a sudden your 20 was last year's news. And rumors were already circulating about a new, monocoque-chassis junior that would likewise obsolete the 22. Some North American club drivers (who loved the class, by the way) had even started calling formula junior the "car of the month club."

And that was mostly down to Lotus.

"Hey," I observed, "people always line up money-in-hand to buy the car that's winning all the races."

"Well, it's turned into damn near an annuity for Colin Chapman."

We shared a good laugh off of that.

"So tell me," I prodded, "what happened at Monza?"

"It was pretty funny, actually. And it all starts with some hack reporter who writes for that German magazine, *Auto, Motor und Sport...*"

My ears perked up. I knew Eric Gibbon wrote for that magazine now and then—in German, no less—using an assumed name that he claimed came off the headstone of some World War One German infantry captain who'd led an ill-advised charge across the Western Front's no-man's land and into a nest of .303 Vickers water-cooled machine guns. Like all of Eric's stories, you had no idea how much of it was true, but there was certainly a lot of drama and gore and romance to it. The amazing thing was how he could not only write well in both languages (and French, too, when he needed it), but also switch off his virulent, native-British jingoism and temporarily swap it— for a paycheck, of course—for a more agreeably Teutonic point of view.

I wanted the rest of the story.

"…Well, it seems this German reporter heard a lot of grumbling from some of the other teams about how blinding fast the factory-entered Lotus juniors were. And I don't mean just around corners, if you follow my drift."

"Of course I follow."

"So he asks one of the Lotus drivers about their engines, and the guy tells him they have 'special' engines. Now what the guy actually means is that they have forged, billet-steel crankshafts that allow them to rev higher and make more power without blowing up. But the German reporter thinks he means they're running oversized, 'cheater' motors—1450cc instead of the class-limit 1100cc—in the factory cars. And he says so in print in the fucking magazine."

I let out a low whistle. "You can get yourself into a lot of trouble and make a lot of enemies doing shit like that. Believe me, I know."

"I know you do."

"So how'd it play out?"

"Oh, Chapman gets wind of it—I mean, now it's in the magazine and *everybody's* talking about it—and so he issues a formal, public challenge to the magazine. He bets them a thousand pounds sterling that he can take his cars to any circuit they ran on during the season—the German magazine's pick, you understand—and go as fast or faster than they did during the actual race weekend. And then pass a full technical inspection. Including a complete engine teardown."

"Sounds like fun."

"Oh, it *was!* Chapman's challenge was front-page news in some of the British motorsports rags."

"So what happened?"

"I guess the German magazine balked at first, but then they realized they either had to put up or shut up—I mean, Chapman could have sued them for libel or defamation or misrepresentation or whatever—and so the bet was on."

I could hardly wait to hear the rest of it.

"First off they went round-and-round on picking a track—hey, it's coming on the end of November by then, so everything in England and northern Europe is pretty iffy on the weather. And both sides want it to be on neutral ground. And the Germans want to be careful, because they know how Chapman is about money. So in the end they settle on Monza, which is perfect because it's a horsepower track anyway, and also the place where Arundell absolutely demolished the rest of the field and set a new lap record at the big Italian Lottery race back in June."

"And so they actually did it?"

"You bet your ass they did. And I got to go shoot it, too."

"So how'd it turn out?"

"Hey, it's always great going to Italy in December. Especially if you're getting paid. You can't beat it."

"And what happened?"

"To tell the truth, it was actually pretty boring. The magazine had stipulated and Chapman had agreed to using Arundell's winning average over the same 30-lap distance as the June race as the target speed to settle the wager. Just to keep Chapman from building up some one-lap, hot-rodded 'qualifying special' to win the thousand pounds."

"Not that Colin Chapman would ever do such a thing."

"Oh, of course not. Perish the thought."

"So did they do it?"

"Did they *ever!* Peter took that Lotus junior out and droned around and around all by his lonesome while the stopwatches clicked off his times, and he easily beat the bogey speed—hell, he broke his own lap record eight times in the process!—and all the while Chapman and his guys are nodding and grinning and the guys from the German magazine are standing around eating their livers."

"Serves 'em right."

"Yeah, it did. And in the end Chapman got the speed he needed—and then some—and then they weighed the car and checked all its measurements and tore that motor all the way down to the bare cylinder block. And you know what?"

"Let me guess…it was all perfectly legal."

"Of course it was."

"So what did the magazine do?"

"What could they do? They paid him the money and issued a public apology. In print, I mean…It was pretty fucking wonderful."

"Sounds like it," I laughed. And Hal laughed right along with me.

You get moments like that in motor racing. It's a lot of what makes it so special.

And then of course I wanted to know what was going on in East London.

"Well, as you know, there's a lot at stake. And no question Lotus and BRM are pulling out all the stops on Clark's car and Hill's car. Lotus tried Lucas fuel injection on their latest chassis, but it kept going all fluffy on the front straight once it got hot—at one point they had *three* Bendix pumps on it to try to keep the fuel from percolating—and BRM showed up with a new 'lightweight' car for Hill. It was supposed to be 40 pounds lighter than the old one, but then they actually weighed the damn thing, and it came out to something like five or six pounds less. Maybe seven."

"How about the rest?"

"What rest? Nobody else is even close. And there's a real end-of-term feel to a lot of the teams. Bowmaker in particular. Everybody knows Surtees is going to Ferrari and that the Bowmaker money's probably coming to an end."

"That's too bad."

I could almost see Hal shrug at the other end of the line. What could you do? "Hey, teams come, teams go. Drivers come, drivers go. That's just the way it is in motor racing. You can't afford to get too sentimental about it."

"Yeah," I had to agree, "I know."

Hal promised to phone me right after the checker to fill me in on the actual race, and sure enough he did. I'd treated myself to a big, bacon-egg-and-pancakes room-service breakfast so I'd be sure to be there to take his call, and I couldn't wait to hear the outcome and details. But it turned out the title-deciding race in East London was basically anticlimactic. And also a bit of a microcosm of the entire '62 season: Clark's Lotus 25 bolted from the grid like a rifle shot while Hill's BRM slithered away with its wheels spinning and smoke pouring off its tires, and Clark had a full second lead by the end of the first lap. After that, the Lotus just kept pulling further and further away—he was gaining almost a full second on every single lap—and there was nothing Graham Hill or his BRM could do about it.

At least there was a good scrap going on for third, what with South African native Tony Maggs in the second team Cooper doing predictably well on a familiar track and in front of his home crowd. He held third for quite a while just in front of team-leader Bruce McLaren in the other Cooper and John Surtees giving his usual 100%-plus in his last grand prix for the Bowmaker Lola team. He eventually managed to pass McLaren and then Maggs to take third, but then McLaren passed Maggs and, on lap 19, managed to get around Surtees so the Lola became the meat in a Cooper sandwich. But John was already experiencing engine problems, and pulled in eight laps later to retire yet again, this time with some ugly clattering noises coming from the Climax V8's valvetrain.

I was thinking there ought to be some sort of 1962 hard-luck sweepstakes between John Surtees and Dan Gurney. They'd both driven so incredibly well and yet neither one had much to show for it.

In any case, by that point the race had turned into something of a procession, with Clark unassailably out front, Hill holding a solid, solitary second place (which would leave him shy of the necessary points he needed to secure the world championship) and the two Coopers circulating in relaxed, orderly tandem well behind Hill's BRM. There wasn't much going on, and it surely looked like Clark's and Lotus's world championship to lose...

And that's precisely what happened!

With just 20 laps to go and the championship in sight, the Lotus came by the pits trailing a huge cloud of oil smoke. The engine still sounded fine, and Clark made two more laps before the smoke slowly subsided (the oiling system was finally running dry) and the pressure gauge in the cockpit started fluctuating and dropping to zero through some of the corners. Clark had no choice but to pull it in and retire. I mean, there was no point blowing it up and being stranded out on the circuit with a rod through the block. A post-mortem in the garages revealed that a small, two-inch through-bolt to the jackshaft mounting pedestal had fallen out of the engine—it may have been assembled without its lock-washer and vibrated loose—and that left a hole that allowed a mist of oil to spray out on the exhaust headers. It wasn't a huge leak, but it was enough.

And that was pretty much the end of it.

Clark's retirement allowed Graham Hill to power through to a hugely popular victory and world championship title, and Jim Clark was among the first to come over and congratulate him. It was also a wonderful achievement (not to mention a tremendous relief!) for BRM, who had suffered for so many years with sometimes radical and too-often unreliable designs, and yet appeared in 1962 with a fast, beautiful, elegant, solid and terrifically reliable machine. Its fuel-injected V8 revved higher and arguably had a fatter power band than the Climax V8s in most of the other British contenders, and while the BRM P57 didn't have quite the outright pace of the Lotus 25, it just ran and ran and ran. So while Clark usually won or finished in the pits, Hill's BRM was there to take useful second-place points when the Lotus was first under the checker at Spa and Watkins Glen. And that made the difference. Not to mention that Graham Hill started out as a mechanic, so even if he didn't have quite the natural talent or genius or whatever of a Jimmy Clark (or a Dan Gurney, or a John Surtees), he had more mechanical feel and sympathy than any one of them. And that was surely one of the factors that made his cars so consistent and reliable. It won him the world championship, the way I saw it.

And everyone was happy for him.

And for the team.

Especially in England.

It was during the very first week of 1963 that Bob Wright told Dick Flick and Danny Beagle he'd decided that the perfect spot for me—at least for now—was as Fairway Motors' on-site press-relations guy at the racetracks. Especially now that his new "Absolute Performance" program was about to break cover in earnest. I mean, I knew a lot of the press types already and also the drivers and the teams and the lay of the land and supposedly where most of the bodies were buried, and he figured by then that I was enough of a company man (in other words, I relied on my paychecks) to put the right sort of spin and polish on things to make the company look good. And I guess I was.

So that's what brought me out to California again for NASCAR's first-ever stock-car race at Riverside on the third weekend in January. They'd put together a special, slightly-less-twisty (read: easier on brakes and more time for them to cool down that long, original backstraight) 2.6-mile course for the stockers, and the turnout of star drivers and teams (not to mention fans) was truly incredible. All the big stock-car names were there, including Freddie Fritter in one of the new, "1963½ " Fairway Freeway slope-back coupes out of Harlon Lee's stable, NASCAR standout "Fireball" Roberts in a Banjo Mathews-prepared Pontiac, Richard Petty and Jim Paschal in Plymouths, Paul Goldsmith and '62 NASCAR champ Joe Weatherly in another pair of Pontiacs, west-coast Corvette ace Dave MacDonald in a Chevy, and on and on it went through 44 entries. What a field!

But the guy I had my eye on from the moment I first looked at the entry list was local-and-personal hero Dan Gurney in another one of Harlon Lee's "fastback" Fairway coupes. Dan knew Riverside maybe better than anybody, and that guy could *drive*. But so could all the rest of them. Like my old, gum-smacking "why not let's bet on it?" Indy 500 pal T.J. Huston, who was wheeling another brand-new, Ray Nichels Engineering-prepared Pontiac. Seeing as how there was a whopping $66,245 purse—the largest ever for any kind of road-racing event in North America—T.J. allowed as how he was more than eager to try out "a l'il of this stock-car road-racin' bid'ness." I figured he'd be quick, and he was. So was Parnelli Jones, who led early on until he ran into gearbox problems (as did many of the stock cars on the road course at Riverside) and Fireball Roberts' Pontiac was running towards the front until he lost everything but 4th gear some 50 laps from the end and limped home to take fourth. But the guy who had everybody covered when it counted was Dan Gurney, who mixed just enough speed with just enough me-chanical sympathy to out-run and out-last the rest of the field. It was kind of anti-cli-mactic there at the end, as there was a crash—one of seven or eight during the afternoon, with thankfully none resulting in injuries—and the officials handled it oval-track style with a full-course yellow and a pace car. So the last few laps were spent trundling around behind the pace car, and that took a lot of the sizzle and oomph and glory out of the finish. But it was still a big win for Dan and for Fairway's new, now-brazenly-out-in-the-open racing program, and I was also really pleased to see that T.J. Huston's Pontiac had come home second, also ahead of all the "usual suspect" NASCAR regulars. Although I didn't say much about T.J. or his Pontiac in the decidedly Fairway-oriented press release I had to hammer out afterwards. Which, as we say in the business, "pretty much wrote itself."

Sadly I wasn't able to hang around in California and be there at Riverside two weeks later when new team drivers/Shelby employees Dave MacDonald and Ken Miles took their Cobras to a dominant, one-two finish ahead of a *very* good field of Corvettes (including Bob Bondurant, Paul Reinhart, Dick Guildstrand and original Cobra chauffeur Billy Krause, who'd taken the bait and switched over to driving a new Sting Ray for Mickey Thompson). There was a lot to be said for hiring away the best driver off your top competitor's team (as Shelby did with established Corvette ace MacDonald and Mickey Thompson did for the Chevy folks with Billy Krause) since they could tell you where the other car was worse or better and help you get a handle on things. Plus you were taking away the opposition's best weapon, and that never hurts.

But I couldn't be at Riverside because I had to fly back to England again at the tail-end of January so I could be there for the new, Fairway V8-powered Lola GT's public unveiling at the London Racing Car Show at the Olympia Exposition Center. I was also going over to "just casually drop in on" (Danny Beagle's words) Colin Chapman's race shop to see how the new, radical, mid-engined/stock-block Fairway V8-powered Indianapolis cars were progressing. Little Harry Dick Fairway was always a great believer in the power of The Unannounced Visit—he loved the way it made people squirm and scatter and scurry about—and Bob Wright was rightly convinced that Colin Chapman was spread so thin at that point as to be damn near transparent! And he naturally wanted to make sure that his project was getting the proper attention. He didn't completely trust the update reports from his English colleagues in Dangleton because, well, *they* were British and *Chapman* was British and…do I really have to spell it out for you?

Personally, the whole idea made me a little uncomfortable. I mean, I'd always looked up to Colin Chapman as a brilliant engineer and entrepreneur and creative genius and hero (in spite of all the things I knew and all the stories I'd heard), and the idea of showing up unannounced and poking around like some sort of corporate-flunky spy didn't sit particularly well. Plus I knew whatever I had to say or whatever questions I posed would be greeted with a slightly irritated, *do-you-really-have-to-bother-me-with-this?* smile, a few upbeat words and a small serving of the well-known Chapman charm. After which I'd be shown a few longer suspension arms for the oval-track chassis offset and the bare aluminum monocoque taking some sort of basic, pre-natal shape on a work table in the build shop. After which I'd be ushered politely out the door. And good riddance.

I did find out a little more about Chapman's plans for the Indianapolis cars, and I must say his core strategy had never even occurred to me. I'd always figured the idea was to bring over a pair of modern, up-to-the-minute, F1-style chassis powered by a couple of warmed-over Fairway V8s—much along the line of oversized, slightly off-set-to-the-left grand prix cars—and win the race based on lighter weight, superior handling and better aerodynamics. But the strategic brains in Fairway Tower were insistent that the cars should run on gasoline (like their road cars) rather than the occasionally nitro-spiked methanol blends powering all of the traditional Offy roadsters. So, from the very start, Chapman's cars would be at a significant horsepower disadvantage compared to the old-style, even antiquated (but *very* well-developed) Offenhauser-powered cars.

It was typical of Chapman to look for a way to turn that sort of problem into an advantage. And his answer, of course, was fuel mileage. The gasoline-powered engines in his cars would go a lot further on a load of fuel than the alcohol-burning Offies. And his lightweight chassis would be far easier on tires. So even now, in the middle of fucking winter and with the race still four months away, Chapman was planning for his cars to be almost as fast as the old roadsters on sheer speed, much handier through the turns and through traffic thanks to their lighter weight, better weight distribution, superior aerodynamics and state-of-the-art chassis, and—here's the key—to do the entire, 500-mile race distance on a single fucking pit stop!

Clever doesn't begin to describe Colin Chapman.

Neither does shrewd.

Or sly.

Or devious.

Of course I was also thrilled to be back in England so I could see Audrey again, but this particular trip turned into a bumpy ride. It started out with my company courtesy car, which this time was one of the company's slightly face-lifted, bottom-of-the-corporate-model-line Fairway Farthing economy sedans. I think the boys in Dangleton assigned it to me as a not-so-subtle way of saying *"Bugger off, Yank, we really don't need you peering over our bloody shoulders here."* But what they actually said at the time was, "We know your motoring-journalist credentials and we'd really like some feedback and driving impressions on this one."

"Oh?"

A nod. And then: "We think too many of our Farthing buyers are opting for Austin Minis instead."

"I see. Do you think you can get me a Mini to drive for comparison?" Hey, sometimes you have to be quick on your feet.

"We should be able to arrange that."

"Make it a Cooper if you can."

"I'll see what we can do...."

But for now, I was stuck with the Farthing, and if wheezy engine sounds, tinny sheet metal, tippy handling and poor assembly quality were the hallmarks of great small automobiles, this one would have leaped to the top of the list. But that's not what I was thinking about as I pulled up in front of the brick row house where Walter and Audrey lived. It was early evening—already pitch-dark since it was the end of January—and the shade wasn't drawn. So I could see them through the window even as I pulled up to the curb. And I could tell in a heartbeat that they were having one hell of a row. Or, more accurately, Audrey was telling him off. Loudly. Angrily. With her face all red and furious and contorted. I'd never really seen her like that. And he was just sitting there in his telly chair with his eyes hard and narrowed and his lower jaw jutted out like the front-end of a damn tugboat. I killed the lights, switched off and just sat there for a minute or two, watching.

I was pretty damn sure that they were arguing about me.

I'd gotten Audrey and me a room again—a suite, actually—at the George Hotel near the exposition center. Like the one we'd enjoyed so much the last time I was in town. And it was obvious that Walter wasn't real pleased with that. Or with the prospect of being looked after for a few days by the neighbor lady who was also a nurse. They'd apparently developed a bit of a mutual dislike.

Not that such a thing was hard to understand.

But the thing I couldn't get over was the sheer fury and fire and frustration raging in Audrey's eyes and face. And through her tightly clenched teeth and fists. I'd seen small, fleeting glimpses of her temper before, but she'd always had the manners and breeding and self-control to stifle them and come across as merely bitchy. This was something else. Something new to me. And I waited there in the car for quite some time before I finally got the nerve to step out and walk up to the door. It was obvious when she answered it that she'd been crying a bit as well as yelling.

"Are you all right?"

"I'm fine," she pretty much snapped at me.

"You sure?"

"Let's just get the bloody hell out of here, all right?"

"You sure you don't want me to come in?"

Her eyes flared at me like prison searchlights. "I told you I was bloody well fine. Do you need some sort of detailed-and-indexed explanation?"

"No. Of course not. I just thought…"

"Then don't think, all right? It'll be better off for both of us." She threw her coat over her shoulders, grabbed the small suitcase she had packed and waiting by the door and hurried towards the car.

"I'm sorry about the car," I half-laughed/half-apologized, trying to lighten things up a little. But it's like she wasn't even listening. So I tried again. "Do you want to go out to a restaurant or something?"

"I'm not hungry."

"Do you want to go out for a drink?"

"I want to go out for several drinks. But that's why I bloody well shouldn't."

"So do you just want to go back to the hotel?"

"Why not? That's what we always do, isn't it?" She was mad as hell. You could feel it. I looked over at her. "Jesus, are you OK?"

She gave me those piercing, searchlight eyes again. "It should be bloody well obvious that I'm *not* OK. And it's also none of your bloody business."

"Look, Audrey, there's no way I can help unless I know what's wrong."

"You can't help even if you know. Men are always stupid that way."

Well, of course the fight with Walter was about me and our future together (whatever the hell it was) and what was going to happen to him whenever that finally transpired. And by the time we reached our room at the George, the other, underlying problem had started to dawn on me. You know, the one men are so stupid about?

Sure enough, it was Audrey's time of the month, and it was a really bad one. So she was crampy and cranky and angry and uncomfortable like I'd never seen her before. I ran down and got us a couple stiff double-scotches from the bar downstairs as soon as we'd checked in, and after that she simmered down to mostly sniffles and snorts and occasional, nasty whining about her current discomfort and her asshole father and how much the sonofabitch *needed* her and *relied* on her—he really knew how to stick the old guilt knife in and turn it, you know?—and how was she ever going to take care of that responsibility and get married, too, and…

She eventually whimpered herself off to sleep after another round of double scotches. And I just laid there next to her on the bed with my arm around her in the dark and thought about how complicated things seem to become the further you get into them.

Audrey was feeling a little better the next morning—she looked pale now instead of red-faced and angry—and she kept apologizing for the way she'd acted the night before. I told her not to worry about it, that everything was fine. But I don't think I was particularly convincing. "Hey," I finally said, "in sickness and in health, right?"

"It's not always that bad," she did her best to explain. And then she kind of blushed. But just a little, since most of the color had pretty much drained out of her.

"Don't worry," I told her. "I mean, it's only a couple days a month, right?"

I saw those searchlight eyes start to flare again, but she quickly snuffed them out. "It can't be very much fun for you," she said apologetically.

"Hey, don't worry about it," I repeated grandly. "I mean, we're in this for the long haul, aren't we?"

"I'm hoping that we are."

I wanted to say "So am I," but I figured *'There's no hoping about it: we're going to get married and be together and stay together...that's all there is to it!'* might be a nicer, kinder, more appropriate sort of sentiment. Even though it was hard to say and sounded just a little bit like bullshit. Even to my own ears.

"You're so bloody full of it!" she laughed. And there was a real smile with it, too. One that brought back the old Audrey I knew and loved and had such a hard time connecting with the night before.

"You want some breakfast?"

"I could eat something."

"You want it here in the room?"

"I think I'd rather get cleaned up, fix my face, go downstairs and eat in the hotel restaurant like proper human beings."

So that's what we did.

After which we drove over to a garage about eight miles away and swapped my awkward and thoroughly uninspiring Fairway Farthing for the nice, British Racing Green Mini Cooper with white racing stripes and rallye lights on the front that the PR people in Dangleton had kindly arranged. And was it ever a fun thing to drive! I mean, you could rev it to the redline and stir that school-bus shifter and hurl it into corners on those ridiculous little 10-inch wheels and there was just so much *going on* inside a Mini Cooper. "It may not be fast in an absolute sense," I observed, "but it's sure as hell entertaining!"

I let Audrey drive it, too (of course) and it was great to see her smile as she rowed it through the gears and cut impulsively and decisively in front of double-decker buses and dawdling London taxis. Later on we went over to the London Racing Car Show at Olympia and made the rounds of all the stands. Graham Hill's championship-winning BRM was on display on an elevated, rotating stand—boy, was it ever a handsome thing!—and there were some new formula juniors from Lotus, Gemini and others to look at and wonder over. Plus hop-up, dual-carb/camshaft/header kits for Minis (it had already occurred to me what our frisky little Mini Cooper could do with a little more power!), a sturdy and stately old 4.5-liter blower Bentley from 1928 that once lapped Brooklands at over two-miles-a-minute and a sharp new fiberglass coupe called a "Falcon 515" that looked great from fifty feet away, not quite so great as you got closer and was probably destined for the ever-growing trash-heap of tiny British sports car builders with small budgets and enormous dreams.

But no question the absolute star of the show was Eric Broadley's new, Fairway-powered "Lola GT." It was presented very much as a possible road car with a nice paint finish and no numbers on the sides, but everyone could see the potential. It was state-of-the-art conceptually with its mid-engined layout and monocoque-style chassis, well-designed and well-built, and it relied on a big, cheap, readily available American V8 for power. And now, with the new "no displacement limit for sports/prototypes" rules at Le Mans and elsewhere, it seemed to have one hell of a promising future.

But only time would tell.

Chapter 26: Drama at Daytona

It was the middle of February in Detroit and, just like in most of Manny Streets' dreary, sometimes snowbound Midwestern dealer showrooms, not much was going on. It was inevitably a crappy month for the salesmen, because the new models weren't really new anymore and there was hardly any foot traffic through the front door (except for a few mooches and tire-kickers with nothing much better to do and a few sugar daddies and husbands trying to patch things up around Valentine's Day). Not to mention that it was a short month anyway. Manny always said that if you really wanted to get a good deal on a new car, you hit the showroom just about the time they were getting ready to switch the lights off on the last working day of February. Better yet if it was below zero outside and with a gale-force blizzard blowing to cover up your trade. And then you did your damndest to steal the fucking car. You started out at what you knew (or at least thought you knew) was below dealer cost, and then you just ground and ground and ground and kept switching what you wanted and how you wanted to pay for it and putting the trade into the deal and taking it back out again and keeping the poor salesman and his sales manager there—just the three of you, everybody else had long since gone home—while the wind and the snow picked up outside and both of them are sneaking sideways glances when they think you don't see it at the monthly sales chart tacked up on the wall and thinking how, even at a stupid, below-rock-bottom deal figure, they'd really like to have another unit up there when the boss walks in the next morning to stare at it with hard, squinty eyes, take it down and put the March board up…

I called Audrey in London on Valentine's Day and spent almost twenty bucks of long-distance time not saying particularly much. But it was nice to just kind of "be there" with her—even over the phone—and I'd come around to thinking that the rough patch we went through the last time I was in London was probably a good thing. I told myself that it deepened and enriched our relationship. And I told her the same thing through the phone line. She had a simple, one-word answer for me:

"Bollocks."

But I must admit I remained a little intimidated—you could even say scared—by that red, contorted, teary, angry, wrong-time-of-the-month face I'd seen through the front window when she was telling off her father. It was disconcerting knowing that a face and a mood and raw, angry emotions like that were in her repertoire.

But why wouldn't they be? God knows they were in everybody else's.

Speaking of God, we all know He moves in mysterious ways, and that was the first thing that ran through my mind when I heard about the small, surprise message that came to Fairway Tower—by way of Fairway's German affiliate in Cologne—that an unspecified boutique builder of fine, expensive and greatly respected Italian sports and GT cars might be for sale. Or, at the very least, was sniffing around for an unspecified large, well-established and well-fixed international automaker to partner with or joint-venture. It seems the note had come to Fairway's German affiliate through some trade-department underling in the diplomatic corps, and it had come to his desk—via a long and circuitous route—by way of the Italian consulate in Cologne, who'd gotten it from the Italian embassy in Bonn, who'd gotten it…well, there was no telling how it came to them or how or why or where they decided to pass it along. It didn't take me long to sense the hand and mind of Enzo Ferrari behind the whole thing. He was a master at mystery, intrigue and manipulation, and knew better than anyone how to slip his bait quietly into the water and then wait—patiently, silently and confidently—for his quarry to come to him.

At first, there was speculation on the far end of the executive corridor that the message might be a fake. A ruse. Somebody pulling somebody else's leg. But Little Harry Dick rang up that French Embassy connection of his and had him do a little sniffing around (and he'd better, if he wanted a fat campaign contribution come election time), and, sure enough, the message turned out to be legit. And the boutique Italian specialist builder involved was (to no real surprise on my end), Ferrari!

It all sounded so perfect—and so perfectly timed, what with Fairway's "Absolute Performance" program about to break cover at Daytona in just a few weeks' time— that it made the hairs on the back of my neck curl up. Only with suspicion more than excitement. Sure, Ferrari was getting up there in years. He was just celebrating his 65th birthday about the time that mysterious "sexy and exotic Italian car company seeks manly, powerful and well-funded partner for possible relationship" note popped up in Cologne, and not only had he lost five of his key lieutenants (including the core of his engineering staff) in what Vinci Pittacora labeled "the defection of the brains" in October of '61, he had no real succession plan in place. The portrait of his dead son Dino still brooded morbidly from the wall across from his desk—Vinci told me Enzo visited the cemetery where his son was buried every day before going to work—and there was probably no single human being on earth with the brass and the balls and the knowledge and the need and the intelligence and the experience and the cunning and the raw, predatory hunger and entrepreneurial genius to take over the reins and continue what Enzo had started and built in any case. And yet he could be a veiled, devious, manipulative, hidden-agenda sort of player, and there was always the possibility that he just wanted to use Fairway Motors as a diversionary tactic in some larger, more complex, more nuanced and surely more agreeable strategy.

But I kept my mouth shut. As far as I could see, the whole thing was about getting to travel over to Europe and down to Italy with Audrey just as often and for as long as I could possibly arrange. On the company's behalf, of course (not to mention their expense account) to keep an eye on things in Maranello. I was even thinking they might want to re-locate me there. I mean, who else did they have who understood the history and the people and the pecking order on the racing side? Hell, I was almost having wet dreams about the prospect.

So I kept quiet and just nodded and went along and told Bob Wright and Danny Beagle and even that asshole H.R. Junior what a swell idea and what a wonderful opportunity this was and that we should pursue investigating a possible deal to buy (or at least buy into) Ferrari immediately. And with every source, resource and contact at our disposal before somebody else—maybe even from the other side of town—stepped in and snatched it away.

I made it sound that desperate.

And then I called Audrey. Only from the pay phone at The Steel Shed on the outside of the factory gates. I didn't want to risk using the free-to-anywhere-on-earth desk phones (where one of Scully Mungo's guys might just be listening in?) in the little conference rooms with the big, copper-gold tinted windows on the 13th floor. So I snuck out through the final-assembly line area and hustled over to The Steel Shed at just after 3pm—it was damn near empty at that hour—and got five bucks worth of change from the bartender. He had to open up the damn jukebox to get it for me. And while he was in there, he tripped off a half-dozen freebies just to listen to while he rinsed out beer glasses in the sink and waited for the whistle to blow and the day-shift regulars to start shuffling in. I remember Patsy Cline's "Sweet Dreams" was playing as I dialed the operator to make the long-distance connection. It was a little after 9:00pm over in London, so I figured she'd be home and that it would be OK. Hell, I would have called if it were three in the fucking morning!

I expected Audrey to be excited by the news. And she was. But then she started thinking about it and mulling it over and asking questions like "would you be moving to Italy?" or making comments like "I can't really be re-locating my father to another country, Hank. He's old and he's got his home here and his doctors and his therapy and his work when he can do it and a routine he's bloody used to…"

I obviously hadn't thought this all the way through.

Although what she was saying was making me agitated. And so the next part came out a little testy. Maybe even more than a little. "Look," I told her, "is this whole thing going to wind up being about you and me or you and him?"

She got testy right back at me. "It's going to be about you and me *and* him, Henry. It has to be. There's no other bloody way."

My mouth started moving like it wanted to say something, only my brain couldn't find any words. But then she started in again. Only softer now. Gentler. "Look, Hank, I'd be thrilled if you were re-located to Italy. It's a lot closer than Detroit, and we'd surely be able to see each other more…"

"Look," I interrupted her, "this just came up today, Audrey. This very afternoon, in fact. I don't know any of the details yet because there aren't any. I just wanted to let you know, that's all. I wanted you to start thinking about it."

"But thinking about *what?*"

"Well, that would be the part I don't know yet, wouldn't it?"

"You confuse me sometimes, Hank. It can be a little unsettling."

"Hey," I told her, "sometimes I confuse myself."

And then we both laughed, and for just that brief, fleeting instant, it was almost like she was right there with me.

Almost.

I found myself down at Daytona again two days later for the newly expanded version of the Daytona Speed Weeks, which kicked off with its "sportycar" weekend on February 16-17, followed by a week of bench-racing, wrenching, eating and drinking (hey, let's be honest here) and culminating in the centerpiece Daytona 500 stock car race the following Sunday. I was actually kind of looking forward to that, since I'd never really been on hand for a NASCAR race on a high-banked oval. The conventional wisdom over in Europe was that American stock-car racing was mostly for mouth-breathing, southern-fried backwoods Neanderthals who never made it through grade school. And I'm talking on both sides of the fences here. To be honest, I had a little dose of that condescending, uptown, college-educated (well, junior college, anyway) attitude myself. Or at least I did before I met and got to know guys like Freddie Fritter and Harlon Lee. Once you got around their aw-shucks, deferential, down-home drawl and started figuring out what they really knew and what they were really talking about, it became apparent that these were clever, skillful, knowledgeable, talented and resourceful fellows indeed when it came to motor racing. And I mean any old kind of motor racing, once you gave them a little time to wrap their brains and backsides around it.

Case in point is the frightening hybrid Harlon Lee's shop whipped up for the new, 250-mile American Challenge Cup race that kicked off the week-long festivities on Saturday. Now this was a pretty special sort of "GT race" because it was held exclusively on the high-banked oval. The previous year they'd run the first lap of the 3-hour Daytona Continental on the tri-oval (and it'd cost me ten bucks to T.J. Huston's monster-engined Pontiac Tempest!) but then it dove down into the normal, oval-and-infield Daytona road course. At which point the 7-liter Tempests were shit out of luck. But the Speedway management thought the public (not to mention the American manufacturers!) might enjoy a "Grand Touring" race held on the same tri-oval the stock-car guys used for the Daytona 500. So there were no twisty infield bits to test grace, finesse or handling balance and no hard braking zones where clumsy, heavy, big-inch/big-horsepower American cars would have to bleed off all that speed. Not to mention that the tri-oval was familiar territory to all the stock-car guys (and their mechanics) but a strange new world for the sportycar types. Plus it was *horsepower über alles* when it came to going fast around there, and the speedway had decided that a nice, round, NASCAR-style 428 cubic-inch engine limit would be just the thing for the American Challenge race.

I figured one of the cars to reckon with would be Pontiac stock-car regular Paul Goldsmith in the number 50 Pontiac Tempest, which was an evolved-and-developed version of the 421-cubic-inch Ray Nichels Engineering powerhouse that T.J. Huston had driven and actually led with (for the first lap, anyway) the year before. And I frankly couldn't believe some of the stuff I learned about it in the garages. The bodywork forward of the firewall was aluminum (somebody said it weighed in at 3200 pounds with fully 52% of its weight on the rear wheels…in spite of that enormous, cast-iron V8 in the front). And, speaking of that motor, it had the full NASCAR treatment what with heavy-duty innards, a hot cam and twin four-barrel carburetors, and the scuttlebutt was it produced 420 real horsepower (along with, as Harlon Lee put it, "enough torque to rotate God's earth"). And yet it used the Tempest's controversial and somewhat unloved "rope drive" flexible driveshaft and—I couldn't believe this part—a heavy-duty version of the Tempest's independent rear suspension along with an *automatic* 4-speed transaxle made out of no less than two Pontiac TempesTorque 2-speed automatics running essentially in tandem! And you can bet that little beauty wasn't whipped up in some bozo's back-alley speed shop!

But Pontiac wasn't the only GM division with its eyes on motorsports, and it seems a couple of Chevy's new, 427-cubic-inch "porcupine" NASCAR Mystery Motors somehow found their way down to Smokey Yunick's infamous "Best Damn Garage in Town" skunk works just down the road in Daytona. Where they were quietly dropped into the engine bays of two of Mickey Thompson's Z06 "special-duty option" Corvette Sting Rays just for the American Challenge race! Plus they'd drafted in two experienced Chevy NASCAR drivers, Junior Johnson and Rex White, to handle the brutes around the tri-oval. But, compared to the Pontiac deal, the big-block Sting Rays were very much a last-minute thing and the cars hadn't even turned a wheel before they got to the Speedway.

Up against that bunch were a few 3.0-liter Ferrari GTOs (one with my stock-car friend and hero Freddie Fritter behind the wheel) along with some more standard-issue, 327 cubic-inch fuel-injected Z06 Sting Rays from Mickey Thompson and Ronnie

Kaplan's Nickey Chevrolet shop out of Chicago. My "you-owe-me-ten-bucks" pal T.J. Huston was in that last one. Oh, and there were also four Porsche 356s entered—including one for Porsche motorsports boss Huschke von Hanstein—and looking to drone around the Daytona oval for an hour and forty-five minutes with their throttle pedals mashed to the floorboards and collect the Under 2-Liter prize money. Which was pretty much a sure thing since they were the only U2L cars entered.

But the car everybody was muttering, mumbling and grumbling about from the moment it rolled out of its trailer was the Briggs Cunningham entry. Although the trailer it rolled out of carried a North Carolina rather than a New York or Connecticut license plate and was moreover registered to a certain racecar shop belonging to an aw-shucks and amiable but terrifically talented and astute car-builder named Harlon Lee!

Let me fill you in on the details:

By the finish of the Riverside Times Grand Prix four months before, it had occurred to Briggs Cunningham that the two Maserati 151 coupes he owned were rapidly turning into white elephants. Oh, they would have been devastatingly quick as GT cars and very likely could have blown off Ferrari's all-conquering GTOs. But the Maserati factory only built three of them and so there was no way they could be homologated as production GTs. And there was likewise no way they could be competitive as prototypes anymore, what with the lid off on engine displacement in the prototype class at Le Mans and elsewhere and the move to mid-engines already underway. They'd tried putting the biggest possible version of Maserati's V8—all 5.7 liters of it—into one of the cars, but it wasn't that much faster than the 4.0-liter. So Briggs sold the 4-liter to a San Francisco sports car dealer named Bev Spencer at the Laguna Seca race after Riverside (he planned to campaign it in club races) and the other one…well, it had a somewhat different destiny in store…

Now of course Alf Momo and Harlon Lee knew each other from the racetrack and respected each other greatly, and somehow they got to talking about pulling that enormous and expensive 5.7 Maserati V8 out of Cunningham's "other" 151 and, in Harlon Lee's words, "put a *real* motor in it." The catalyst was of course the upcoming, 7-liter-limit American Challenge race at Daytona, and a little work with a tape measure indicated that one of Fairway's new, 427-cubic-inch NASCAR motors would, with a little plumbing and exhaust-header fiddling, slip right in. As Harlon put it, "Heck, what with them big overhead-cam boxes an' all, that l'il Maserati motor's bigger'n one a'my 427s! Or at least wider, anyways…" And no question Fairway's 7-liter stock-car motor, although far less sophisticated, would crank out more horsepower and a *lot* more torque than any 5.7-liter alternative. The two of them likewise got to thinking that a 7.0-liter, Fairway-engined Maserati Tipo 151 might be just the ticket for Daytona's run-what'cha-brung American Challenge race on the tri-oval. Why, it might even be good for an outright, closed-course World Speed Record attempt! And Harlon Lee moreover happened to have six or seven of those motors just sitting in a corner of his shop with plastic wrap taped over their carburetor intakes, silently waiting for their chance to be used in anger..

It was too damn delicious to pass up, you know?

So Briggs gave the green light and the Maserati went down to North Carolina for its engine transplant and Harlon rang up Freddie Fritter and asked if he'd like to drive it at Daytona when they were done with it? But Freddie had to beg off, because he'd already agreed to drive one of Carlo Sebastian's new Ferrari GTOs at Daytona (and he was really looking forward to it) and, even if he'd wanted the Maserati ride, he wasn't the kind of guy to fink out on a deal. Even if it was just a: "Sure. OK. Glad to. Thanks for thinking of me," over the phone with nothing down in writing.

But Freddie was intrigued with the idea and suggested his and Harlon's old buddy Marvin Panch for the drive. And it was a perfect fit because Marvin knew the Daytona tri-oval like it was his own driveway, didn't have a ride for the American Challenge and was moreover under contract as a Fairway driver anyway and would be running one of Harlon's 1963½ Fairway Freeway "fastbacks" in the Daytona 500 a week later. So the deal was done. And from the moment they unloaded that ungainly-looking-but-most-likely-aerodynamic, monster-engined Maserati coupe from its trailer, all the other American Challenge teams were looking at it sideways out of the corners of their eyes and muttering about it under their breath.

It sure looked like the car to beat.

Until it took to the track Friday morning, anyway. That's when Marvin Panch got in it for the first time and took a couple laps to see how it felt. And it didn't feel all that great. So he dropped back into the pits and talked back-and-forth with Harlon Lee and

Alf Momo and then they rolled it back into the garages and played with the toe-in front and rear and added in a little caster stagger in the steering (that was Harlon Lee's idea) and sent him back out. And now it felt pretty decent, and so Marvin gave them the thumbs-up that they should alert the timing and scoring folks because he was going to take a flyer at a new lap record.

He made it about two-thirds of the way around. That's when, bellowing down the back straight at something around 200+ miles-per-hour, his Maserati pretty much took off. It was air packing up under the front of the car that probably did it, but whatever it was, the nose came up off the ground and then the bottom-side of the car caught all that onrushing air and it just blew up and over like a leaf in the damn wind! Only it was still going *really* fast. It came down on its roof and went sliding off onto the grass, and Marvin said afterwards that he was standing on the brake pedal so blessed hard he was surprised it didn't snap right off. It didn't occur to him until later, in his hospital bed, that the brake pedal doesn't do much good when the car is upside down and all four wheels are pointed towards the sky!

As luck and fate would have it, the Maserati didn't hit anything, and finally slid itself to a halt at the base of the banking between turns three and four. Still upside down. And it was while Marvin was thanking his lucky stars and mumbling heartfelt promises about how he'd go to church every Sunday with his wife and family when he wasn't off racing and remember to be a little kinder and more considerate to his fellow man when he realized he couldn't get out. See, the Maserati 151 had gull-wing doors that hinged up into the roof to make it easier for the drivers to get in and out during pit stops at races like Le Mans and such. Only they flat wouldn't open when the car was upside down. Period. And that's about when the fire started.

To be brutally honest, that would have been the firey, horrific and no-doubt painful end of Marvin Panch right there if it hadn't been for the pickup truck of racing types just coming in through the Turn Four tunnel barely sixty yards away. In it were Firestone tire engineer Steve Petrasek and mechanic Jerry Raborn, and they were quickly joined by drivers Bill Wimble, Ernie Gahan and Dewayne "Tiny" Lund, who'd been watching along the fences nearby. Now Tiny was a veteran driver out of Harlan, Iowa, who'd come south to go stock-car racing 18 years before, didn't have much in the way of a résumé—not to mention any sort of ride at Daytona—but he'd driven down hoping to catch on with somebody's pit crew and be at least part of the action at this biggest-of-all stock car races. He'd gotten the nickname "Tiny" because he was a pretty damn massive edition of a human being at 6-foot-5 and something around 270 pounds, and he and his wife—they got married at a race track—ran a fishing camp in Cross, North Carolina, when he wasn't off racing someplace.

In any case, the guys in the pickup and Tony and the other drivers along the fence realized immediately that it was a desperate situation, and they pulled the truck right up against the fence so the five of them could jump up on the hood and vault over the top to get to the racetrack side. Then they ran over to the inverted Maserati—which was already burning a little, but would surely ignite into a conflagration when the fire reached the fuel tank!—and they tried lifting it up so that Panch could crawl out. Marvin had already levered himself around to try and kick the door open, and he had the lower half of his legs out when—with a mighty, terrifying *"WHOOPMPH!"*—the gas tank went up. The force of it blew them all back and they dropped the car. But they could see Marvin still trying to get out. In fact, he actually heard Steve Petrasek yell, right through the whoosh and crackle of the fire: *"He's still kicking!"* And that's when Steve and Tiny Lund waded into that inferno, lifted up that flaming Maserati with their bare hands and dragged him out. It was one hell of a heroic thing to do and, like all great acts of heroism, it was something neither one of them had time to think about or consider beforehand.

They just *did* it.

Hey, that's what heroism is all about.

Well, the Maserati wreck put Marvin Panch in the hospital with serious burns. But at least he was alive. And ready to tell anybody who would listen that it was true: when you think you're about to die, all the bad things you've ever done go through your mind like a breakneck-speed newsreel. And yet you seem to have time to regret every single one of them. Not to mention worrying and agonizing about how selfish you've been with your life and what's going to happen to the wife you love who's stood behind you all these years and the kids you've had together and…

And that's about when Tiny Lund and Steve Patrasek pulled him out of the fire.

So, from his hospital bed, Marvin Panch gave thanks. And also asked Harlon Lee if maybe he might give the #21 Fairway Freeway he was supposed to drive in the 500 to Tiny Lund. And Harlon said "yes." I mean, it almost seemed like it was destined to be.

Come Saturday, we had the first-ever, oval-only American Challenge 250 at Daytona. And we also had rain. Not a whole lot of rain, but enough to make the prospect of running around the high banks and down that long Daytona back straight at speeds approaching 200mph scary indeed. Junior Johnson opted out of driving his silver Mickey Thompson big-block Sting Ray on the grounds that he didn't have any experience racing in the rain. So the car was handed over to Thompson's new road-racing hotshoe, Billy Krause, who probably figured, "Why the hell not?" After all, there were only 14 cars in the race (most of the serious players were saving their cars for the much bigger-money Daytona Continental 3-Hour the following day) and Mickey Thompson's 427 Corvettes were arguably the fastest cars in the field—on a dry track, that is—so a good finish was a distinct possibility. Besides, the big engine wasn't homologated, so the big-inch Corvettes couldn't really run anywhere else.

The crowd turnout was abysmal because of the weather and the small field, and they ran the first ten laps under caution with a pace car to give the drivers a chance to acclimate themselves to the mist and the damp pavement. And then they turned them loose. I was up in the press box, mostly to stay out of the rain, and so I had to endure one of the know-nothing local stick-and-ball guys getting all patriotic and excited over the 7-liter Corvettes and Pontiac Tempest pulling slowly but inexorably away from Enzo's mega-dollar GTOs. I started to explain that a 7.0-liter racecar was just naturally going to motor away from a 3.0-liter racecar on a big, banked oval where horsepower meant everything. "It's like putting the best middleweight on earth up against an average-Joe pro heavyweight. Unless he manages to tire the other guy out, the middleweight will lose because he simply can't *hurt* the heavyweight.

But I wasn't getting through to the stick-and-ball guy. Or, more accurately, he didn't much care. So I went back to watching the race. And it was a pretty dull affair if you want the truth of it. Paul Goldsmith established himself in front and began pulling away while the Thompson Corvettes ran into the usual new-car troubles. Their front ends were too heavy, and so they handled a little odd (or that's what Billy Krause said after he went spinning down the backstretch in the rain…fortunately without hitting anything) and, worse yet, they were getting water into their interiors through Mickey Thompson's lightweight, more aerodynamic plexiglass side windows, and that water was landing on the floor and making the pedals all slippery. And then, thanks to the engine heat off those big 427 motors, turning to steam inside the car…

Both 427 Corvettes came in with their drivers unable to see and the final solution was to rip out those "lightweight, more aerodynamic" plexiglass side windows and give the drivers a rag to wipe off the inside of their windshields. At 160-plus. In the rain.

In the end, Billy Krause did manage to bring the silver #4 car home third, which was quite an accomplishment given the circumstances. But he was six laps behind Paul Goldsmith in the winning Pontiac Tempest and four laps behind second-place T.J. Huston in the regular, 327-cubic-inch Sting Ray out of Ron Kaplan's Nickey Chevrolet shop in Chicago. And you have to give T.J. tremendous credit for what he was able to do with that car under such difficult conditions. He allowed afterwards that his dirt background helped a lot when the "rain came a l'il harder and it got kinda slippery."

The good news for the stick-and-ball guy in the press box was that all three of those cars finished ahead of the two Ferrari GTOs entered. Fair and square. So there. Nyaahhh. And there was no arguing with the guy, you know? Or, at the very least, it wasn't worth it. But I was happy to see that Freddie Fritter was the first of the Ferraris home in fourth place, and that he finished a full lap ahead of the other GTO. Like T.J. Huston, the guy could really *drive*.

Things were reversed in the Daytona Continental the following day. The weather was clear but chilly, there was a fairly decent crowd and an excellent field of cars—42 of them, in fact—and we were treated to some fine racing. At least right there at the beginning, anyway. Squaring off for the overall win were five Ferrari GTOs in the 3.0-liter class, a pair of Momo-prepared Cunningham E-Types in the 4.0-liter class, a team of four Shelby Cobras in the 5.0-liter class and no less than sixteen Corvettes (!!!) in the over-5.0-liter class. It looked pretty damn good on paper. And I was thrilled to see that my friend Cal Carrington had landed a drive in one of the Shelby Cobras! And even more thrilled to hear that he'd been picked as the "rabbit," which meant he had a special, higher-revving engine with a wilder cam and a lightened flywheel and that he was supposed to run as fast as he could right from the drop of the green and try to break up the opposition. And also find out what would break first, since the Cobras weren't really tested or sorted yet as endurance cars.

"You happy about that?" I asked him in the paddock that morning.

"Hell, I'm happy to have the chance. You may not have noticed it, but my so-called career has been stuck in neutral lately. I could wind up doing amateur club races like Tommy Edwards is doing over in England if I don't get some kind of break somewhere."

"And this might be it?"

"I'm hoping so. I know Shelby's got plans."

"So does Fairway," I told him like I knew something he didn't know. "It'd be a good thing to get in on the ground floor."

"Yeah it would. And look who I've got for a teammate...Dan Gurney! It's really something that they wanted *me* to be the rabbit instead of *him.*"

I had it on pretty good authority that they'd originally wanted Dan to be the rabbit, but then they found a compression leak and had to do a last-minute engine change, so he might not even make the start on time. But I didn't say anything. I mean, what purpose would it serve?

The other big surprise was that Pedro Rodriguez was driving that same new Carlo Sebastian GTO that he and his younger brother had raced together and won with in the Paris 1000kms just four months before. Only now Ricardo was dead and I knew for a fact that Pedro had wrestled with thoughts of retirement after that terrible day in Mexico. But then he did a BMC promotion he'd agreed to with several other name drivers in a squadron of viciously flogged Austin Mini Coopers, and even though it was basically a goof and not really serious, he discovered all over again that he still loved it and enjoyed it and, to get to the real core center of it, would never find anything even remotely close to replacing it. So he was back. And the Daytona Continental was his first real race following his brother's death. And in the very car they'd shared and won with together just a few months before.

As I've said so many times, you couldn't write this stuff as fiction.

Come the start Cal did as he was instructed and blew past Rodriguez and the rest to lead the first 11 laps. And he looked good out there, even though you could see that the Cobra was a little raw and rough in the handling department and ran into something of an aerodynamic brick wall once it got up to 150 or so. Even though it had a smaller engine, Rodriguez's GTO surely had more top end. And it was more graceful and balanced through the infield, too. But the Cobra sure could come squirting out of the corners, and Cal was using that—plus a *lot* of opposite lock—to keep the Mexican driver behind.

Pedro finally got past on lap 11, but Cal wouldn't give up and they swapped places back-and-forth for five more laps until Cal felt a vibration coming through the shifter and floor and the seat of his pants. He wasn't really sure what it was, and it was while he was trying to figure it out that there was a mighty *"BANG!"* as the flywheel pretty much exploded. Chunks of it shattered right through the bell housing and transmission tunnel and Cal was damn lucky it didn't take his leg off. As it was, he got a bad gouge and cracked a bone in his leg. But it so easily could have been much worse.

Meanwhile Pedro motored off on a truly accomplished, masterful drive and had more than a minute in hand by the end of the three hours (ahead of Roger Penske in John Mecom's GTO), and those two were the only cars on the lead lap. Poor Walt Hansgen had a solid third place locked up in the quicker of the Cunningham E-Types, but ran out of gas with the checker almost in sight. And then he got disqualified for receiving a push from his teammate in the other Jag to try and make it to the flag. Which left 3rd overall and first in the over-5.0-liter class to Dr. Dick Thompson after a fine drive in Grady Davis' new and well-prepared Z06 Sting Ray coupe. And Dave MacDonald, who'd been dicing with Penske for second early on, came though to score a solid fourth-overall finish (along with first in the 5.0-liter class) in spite of a long pit stop to replace a water hose.

So, like every good race, there was a lot to take in and all kinds of interesting stories to tell. I was just sad that I wouldn't be the guy telling them.

A week later I was up in the press box again to watch my first-ever Daytona 500 stock-car race, and again it'd been a damp morning with light rain on and off, and even though the weather had cleared a little, they again had to start the race under yellow-flag conditions and behind a pace car to try and dry the track off enough for racing. But after ten laps like that they pulled the pace car in and turned them loose. And I must admit, it put a lump in my throat and a quiver in my gut when that huge, thundering herd of 7-liter stock cars—50 of them!—came charging towards the green flag. Why, it made the whole damn press room shudder! And you could hear the fans—70 thousand of them!—cheering and hooting and screaming right through the thunder!

It was something, all right.

At first, it was Junior Johnson leading in a white '63 Chevrolet with one of Chevy's potent new "Mystery Motor" V8s under the hood. And right in his wheeltracks was Paul Goldsmith in a Ray Nichels '63 Pontiac. They looked like they were running away from everybody. But I knew from some of the looks and nods I'd seen in Harlon Lee's garage area that the Fairway guys were planning to keep it cool, not show their hands, stay on the lead lap and wait until past half distance to really start racing. Harlon figured the race would come back to them. And it did. Junior Johnson's Chevy had distributor trouble, and then Paul Goldsmith's Pontiac had the lead. But then he had to stop for oil, and soon thereafter retired with a broken piston ring. That left the lead to T.J. Huston in yet another Ray Nichels Pontiac, but only until he got swallowed up by G.C. Spencer in another of those monster-motor Chevrolets. But then he had to stop for fuel and, for the very first time, the lead went to one of Harlon Lee's Fairway entries. The one with my down-home hillbilly racer/friend Freddie Fritter behind the wheel. But there were still a lot of good, fast cars running and, hell, the race was just a lap past quarter-distance. Anything could happen.

And so the afternoon ground on and on with racing-for-the-lead and pit stops and hard luck and ailments and retirements. Freddie Fritter was running solidly in front (albeit ahead of a tightly bunched pack of about six cars) when he came in for his second routine pit stop. And that left the lead to Bobby Johns' Pontiac. But he tried to milk it that little bit too far and ran out of gas on his run into the pits two laps later. The crew filled him up, but then it wouldn't start because the carburetor and fuel line had run dry. So they opened up the hood and frantically took off the air cleaner and tried pouring gas down the carb throats while Bobby ground and ground on the starter. Only then the whole engine compartment burst into flames and his crew chief was burned and, well, even though they got him running again, his Pontiac was out of it as far as a lead-lap finish was concerned.

And meanwhile the racing went on.

With a little over 100 miles still to go, it had turned into pretty much a Fairway benefit, with Freddie Fritter in the lead and Ned Jarrett in another Fairway Freeway right behind him. And, lurking back in third place, almost a half-lap back...Tiny Lund! I'd seen him in a low, off-in-the-back-of-the-garage conversation with Harlon Lee before the start, and I'd assumed Harlon was just trying to calm him down since this was, by far, the biggest damn race he'd ever been in. But it turns out they were also talking strategy. "I want you to mind your fuel mileage," Harlon was telling him. "I want'cha t'tuck up tight in them other cars' draft and give that engine a nice, long breathe when y'do it. An' iff'n we figger th' gas wrong an' it starts coughin' out there, I want'cha t'cut the dang motor and come coasting inta th' pits so's y'don't run 'er dry. But then y'gotta switch it back on agin' an' let out th' clutch t'start 'er up once't y'all's safe in pit lane. You unnerstan'?"

Tiny nodded.

And then he went out and did exactly as he was told. And those of us up in the press box started to get an inkling of what might possibly happen when Freddie Fritter came in for his last fuel stop with 44 laps yet to go—that's 110 miles—and Ned Jarrett followed a lap later with 107.5 miles still to run. But old draft-it-and-coast-it Tiny didn't have to pit (he coasted in, of course) until there were just 40 laps left to run. And everybody knew that NASCAR stock cars had 22-gallon fuel tanks....

So now all the drama circulated around if any of them could make it to the end. Tiny was in front thanks to a slightly quicker pit stop from Harlon Lee's guys, but he didn't want to be in front. Hell, he wanted to be behind somebody so he could draft them and save fuel. So he slowed up a little so Freddie Fritter and Ned Jarrett would catch him. But they knew what was happening, and they wanted Tiny out there in front of them so he'd use more fuel. In fact, all three of them slowed down so much that some of the lapped cars came up and passed them. And each time one of them did, Tiny did his best to hang onto the back of them and save a little more fuel.

In the end, Freddie Fritter had to pit with just a handful of laps left for a splash of fuel and Ned Jarrett had to stop two laps later for the same thing. But Tiny kept drafting and coasting and going easy on the throttle whenever he could, and his car finally sputtered and coughed and ran itself out of gas not two hundred yards after he passed under the checker. No shit. And if you think it's easy getting damn near five miles-per-gallon out of a 427 cubic-inch race motor pushing a nearly two-ton stock car around the 2.5-mile high banks of the Daytona International Speedway at something like a 160mph average, you know even less than that stupid stick-and-ball guy who was asleep in the chair next to me in the press room and probably dreaming about baseball double-plays and succulent young football cheerleaders with enormous bosoms.

So Tiny got the race win—his biggest by light-years—in the car that was really supposed to be driven by the guy whose life he'd saved by wading into a boiling wall of flames and pulling him out of that wrecked Maserati with his own two hands. In victory lane, Chris Economaki pushed a microphone in front of his face and asked him: *"That's a pretty big win for you, Tiny. Twenty-five thousand dollars! What are you going to do with all that money?"*

Tiny shrugged kind of sheepishly and answered: *"Pay our bills, I guess."*

He hadn't stopped grinning since the checker came down.

Like I said, you couldn't write this stuff as fiction.

Chapter 27: Diplomacy, Drugs, and no Denouement

I was on another 707 to England a week and a half after Daytona, and I was sorry to read in the paper that country-music star Patsy Cline had been killed in a small plane crash just outside of Nashville the day before. She was on her way back from a Sunday night concert at the Soldiers and Sailors Memorial Hall in Kansas City, Kansas. It was a benefit concert for the family of a local country & western disc jockey named "Cactus" Jack Call, who'd died in a car crash a month before. According to the newspaper, she'd had the flu, but did three full performances anyway—one at 2pm, one at 5:15pm and another one at 8pm—and she closed that last show in a white chiffon dress singing a new song that she'd recorded barely a month before, *I'll Sail My Ship Alone*.

She was planning to leave for Nashville the following day in a Piper Comanche piloted by her manager, Randy Hughes, and with fellow country singers/benefit performers Hackshaw Hawkins and Cowboy Copas coming along for the ride. But the local airport was fogged in on the Monday, so they weren't able to take off until Tuesday. They stopped for fuel in Missouri and again at the municipal airport in Dyersburg, Tennessee, less than two hours from Nashville. The airport manager suggested they stay the night because of high winds and rough weather ahead, but, at least according to the newspaper, Randy Hughes said, "I've already come this far. We'll be there before you know it." The plane went down in heavy weather just twenty minutes later, 90 miles outside of Nashville. Everybody on board was killed.

It was a damn shame.

Ben Abernathy and I really liked her music. Everybody who liked country music did. *I Fall to Pieces, Walkin' After Midnight, Sweet Dreams,* and of course *Crazy*…they were all great. And now she was gone.

Damn.

But I couldn't really dwell on it once my plane landed at Heathrow. I had a lot to do. Things had been progressing at a truly breakneck pace ever since Bob Wright and Little Harry Dick Fairway verified the news that Ferrari was, at least potentially, up for sale. Partially, I should mention, thanks to some behind-the-scenes snooping on the part of that son-of-the-American-ambassador-in-Paris/hoping-to-become-a-second-term-congressman (in spite of some rather unpleasant tabloid publicity involving two Washington-area strippers and a trained seal) old fraternity buddy of H.R. Junior's. And although I wasn't terrifically sure about Old Man Ferrari's true intentions, I was more than happy to go hop-scotching back-and-forth to Italy (with Audrey in tow as my official Fairway Motors interpreter, of course) along with a couple side trips to Colin Chapman's Lotus Components Limited shop at Hethel to see how the new Fairway Indianapolis car was coming along. And I must say, as the month of May drew closer, Chapman's vision was quickly turning into reality. There would ultimately be two cars for the actual race—a Lotus green one with yellow stripes for Jim Clark and a white one with blue for Dan Gurney, who'd really sparked the whole project with Colin and Bob Wright in the first place—but Chapman insisted on building a test mule first to make sure everything worked and went together properly. So Audrey and I had to fly back up to London after our preliminary meeting in Maranello so we could be on hand for the shakedown test of the new Lotus 29 "test mule" at Snetterton on Tuesday, March 7th.

Now Snetterton was one of several ex-World War II airfields that found new life as ad-hoc racing circuits after hostilities ended, and so it was mostly wide, flat-out straights, 90-degree or hairpin corners where the runways came together and not much at all in the way of shade, scenery or ambience. It was a cool, bleak, overcast day and the car really looked pretty cobbly and unfinished, what with no engine cover over its Weber-carbureted Fairway V8, wires and cables and fuel lines running all over the place and crude, unpainted "organ-pipe" exhausts sticking up into the airstream on both sides. But it sounded lean, deep and nasty when they fired it up and, well, it was fast as stink! It easily broke the outright lap record—right out of the box!—and then they crated it up and put it on a plane to America so the Fairway people could have a look at it and do some testing of their own.

I also heard from two of the Lotus mechanics about the hush-hush private test at Goodwood just the Wednesday before. That's when Stirling Moss came out—wearing a full beard now—to drive the pale green BRP Lotus 19 he had driven and won with before. Of course the British motoring press had been following his recovery process and fanning the flames of his "imminent return to racing" for months, but his manager and the team made sure the test took place in absolute secrecy. It would be his first time in a racing car since his horrendous Easter Monday accident at Goodwood, just a year and a week before. And although he was getting around quite well now and had recovered much of his mental acuity, he was a different, damaged, more difficult, more studied, more stilted, more self-conscious sort of man than the best-in-the-world star driver who'd gone off the same track and crashed terribly a year-and-a-week before. It was overcast on the test day and spitting rain now and then, and the circuit was decidedly damp. But Stirling had always excelled in the wet. And he wasn't really there to wring out some new tweaks on a car or try for a new lap record (as he'd done so many times before), but rather to find out if he was right enough and fit enough to go racing again.

He wasn't.

Although his laps were decent enough for the car and the conditions, his old, non-pareil skill and balance and flow and brilliance were gone. He was just another plodder. Even spun once at the chicane. Moss was changed, and he knew it. Damaged. Mortal. Like everybody else. Oh, he went pretty well—most drivers would have been thrilled with his times—but he wasn't anywhere near his own, lofty personal standards. It was like Tommy Edwards always used to say about getting older as a racing driver: *"These days, I've got to think about doing things I used to do without thinking."* Moss' accident—and particularly the brain injury—had accelerated all of that. And he knew it.

He announced his retirement the very next day.

It must have torn him apart inside.

But it was better than going out and being ordinary.

Come Thursday Audrey and I were on another plane hustling our butts back down to Italy for our Friday lunch with Mr. Ferrari. And that was just one of several trips we wound up taking there during the next few weeks. It was a hectic, exhausting, and complicated time for us, but also thrilling and wonderful, since Audrey and I got to spend so much time together—away from Walter—and yet we were never gone for more than a few days at a crack, so her worry and guilt levels never got up to the red-line. More importantly, after all the screwy unease and awkwardness the last time we'd been together, all of a sudden everything was working and feeling right again. It's like we relaxed with each other because we were so damn busy and preoccupied with trying to keep track of all the fucking details and inferences and nuances on the Ferrari negotiations so we could accurately report them back to The Tower. Along with the latest news on the Lotus Indycar project. And the progress on Eric Broadley's new Lola GT. And...

But the real point was that Audrey and I were feeling and working like a genuine team again. Better yet, we were truly enjoying—even with all the damn questions and uncertainties and endless, maddening details—how great it was to work and hang around with somebody you not only loved (hell, "love" can be a pretty vague word a lot of the time), but trusted and respected as well. We were spending a ton of time together and it felt right and safe and comfortable and complete in spite of all the challenges and hassles and the breakneck schedule, and you couldn't miss the sense that both of us wanted it to go on and on and on. I'd never really felt that way before—not ever!—and I don't think she had, either. I knew I could count on her, and I had the feeling (in spite of my own nagging doubts and worries) that she felt the same way about me.

It was exhausting, but it was wonderful.

And so was the sex...not that it's any of your damn business.

But there was so much to do. In Maranello, Ferrari took us to lunch at the little Il Cavallino restaurant across the street from the factory, and he really turned on the charm for Audrey. They talked and laughed back-and-forth in Italian and he told her stories about all the kings and dukes and princes and notorious international scoundrels and important heads-of-state and glittering movie celebrities—like Roberto Rossellini and Ingrid Bergman—who came to Maranello to buy cars from him. And also about the great opera singers he'd heard and known and wonderful local wines and appetizers and pasta dishes to try and...and all I could do was sit there like a lump of suet and smile from time to time like I actually understood a fucking word of it.

To be honest, I was a little jealous.

And I guess it showed, because Audrey needled me relentlessly about it during our ride back to the hotel. "I was just trying to put him at ease," she said with a maddeningly triumphant sparkle in her eyes.

"Did you have to do such a good job of it?"

"You're jealous, aren't you?" she teased.

"Of course I'm not."

"You're jealous *and* a bloody liar," she teased some more.

"Ahh, go fuck yourself."

"That's not very nice." And then she scooted over right next to me and whispered in my ear, *"…besides, I'd rather fuck you…."*

I just about drove off the damn road!

I reached out to put my arm around her, but by then she'd scooted back over to the opposite side of the seat looking awfully damn pleased with herself.

"You look awfully damn pleased with yourself," I groused.

"And why shouldn't I be?"

"And I'm not jealous," I groused some more. "Really, I'm not."

"I won't give it another thought," she laughed. "And don't you worry about it either, Henry…You look bloody marvelous in green."

The gist of things down in Maranello—I mean once you brushed all the charm and posturing and bullshit and double-talk aside—was that Old Man Ferrari had about had it up to here with the road-issue sports/GT manufacturing side of his business. He said it was doing well—at least according to him—and making money (and of course he was proud as hell of it!), but the magic had pretty much gone out of it. He was tired of the relentless, day-to-day operating hassles and keeping his concessionaires in England and France and Switzerland and America and wherever the hell else people wanted to buy Ferraris happy. Not to mention the "special" customers who required special attention (and lots of it) and husbanding the company's resources and looking after its relationships with its coachbuilders and component suppliers and arguing with the fucking unions all the time and worrying about the mass FIAT strike the previous June and the recurring transportation strikes and metal-workers strikes that had become epidemic in Italy and made it damn near impossible to run any sort of industrial man-ufacturing plant there. And then there was cash flow to worry about and plant im-provements and new capital expenditures for the latest and best machinery to consider and…well, who the hell needed it?

What Ferrari was really looking for was some sort of corporate sugar daddy with deep pockets and the right sort of respect, personnel and expertise to take that burden off his shoulders so he could spend his golden years indulging—you could even say wallowing in—his lifelong passion for motorsports. He flat *loved* sending his cars out to go racing. And he loved winning even more. He was addicted to being the best in the world, and he had a desperate, irrational, all-consuming need to keep kicking the living shit out of *everybody!*

And could you blame him?

I mean, he'd done it before. And before that. And before that, too.

It's what the Old Man wanted. Needed. Lived for.

And Fairway Motors sure looked like his answer.

But of course none of it was going to be simple or straightforward.

To begin with, Enzo didn't particularly like dealing with me. Oh, he liked Audrey well enough. Better than well enough, in fact. Why, you could see the old crocodile eyeballing her even from behind those armor-plate sunglasses of his. And particularly when she wore that yellow floral-print sundress with the square-cut neckline. Oh, I think he found me pleasant, deferential, knowledgeable, respectful and intelligent enough. But he didn't like dealing with, as he put it, *"un messaggero."* He figured he ought to be dealing with somebody a little higher up the old corporate ladder, you know? And I can't say as I blamed him. In fact, he was pretty damn adamant that he wanted to deal with *"Signore Fairway"* face-to-face. And of course there was no way that could ever happen. Little Harry Dick Fairway was not about to go traipsing over to fucking Italy just to meet some two-bit, half-pint sports car manufacturer who didn't even sell as many cars in a year as some of Manny Streets' retail dealers. And I'm not even talking the top grossers. No, if that Italian nobody wanted an audience with Little Harry Dick Fairway, he could just get his ass over to Detroit and wait in one of the Barcelona chairs outside the double-hung mahogany doors of his office suite on the thirteenth floor of Fairway Tower until Little Harry Dick Fairway was good and ready to see him.

So there!

But that was actually a good thing, since nobody (and especially me, Danny Beagle, Bob Wright, and all the other regular denizens of the executive corridor) wanted such a thing to happen. First off, Little Harry Dick Fairway was a dumb, artless, rude, lewd, crude, loud, spoiled, unpredictable, ill-mannered, loutish, temperamental, boorish and more-than-occasionally infantile asshole. And I'm sure I've left a few things out. Secondly, he didn't like meetings—or even casual conversations—with people he thought seemed smarter or sharper or cleverer or better educated or more worldly or more experienced or more astute or more gracious or more accomplished than him. And that covered roughly 80% of the world's population as best as I could figure.

Or maybe make that 85%.

On the other hand, I could well understand Enzo Ferrari's desire—no, it was really more like a demand—to be dealing with somebody from the very top of the Fairway chain of command. So I discussed it with Danny Beagle and he discussed it with Bob Wright and, in the end, they did what Fairway Motors always did in such situations: they sent a fucking army. Once we got the preliminary talks out of the way, what amounted to a small invasion took place, including a full squadron of Clifton Toole's skinny-tie-and-crew-cut accounting people, a backup battery of Randall Perrune's legal types plus Ben Abernathy to run his eyes over the manufacturing and supply end and even Hubert C. Bean and a couple of his pasty-faced ciphers from the computer-modeling department because…well, who the hell really knew? The point was to overwhelm Ferrari psychologically as well as physically, do the first real down-to-the-last-fucking-nut-and-bolt inventory and financial review the company had ever endured and soften the old bird up for the final negotiations and the ultimate and inevitable *coup-de-gras* takeover.

Personally, I thought they were underestimating the hell out of *Commendatore* Ferrari. And you do that at your own peril. But I kept my mouth shut and went about my business because it meant more time with Audrey. And maybe even a future over there?

Besides, who would have listened to me anyway?

As far as the people on the executive corridor had it figured, this whole thing was going to be little more than a minor skirmish. A walkover. A blowout. A piece of cake…

Friday the Thirteenth fell on a Saturday in April of 1963, and that meant another extravagant, she-could-have-cared-less-about-it birthday party for renegade daughter Amelia Camellia Fairway at the opulent and ostentatious Fairway mansion at the end of McElligot Lane. I didn't really want to go, if you want the truth of it, but I was in town (in fact, I'd gotten off a plane from Heathrow that very morning) and Danny Beagle made it clear that Mrs. Fairway wanted and expected me to be there.

"Why the hell does she want *me* there?" I grumbled as we wheeled northeast along the shoreline of Lake St. Clair.

"She thinks you like her."

"I don't."

"But she thinks you do. You said some nice things about her décor."

"I was just trying to be polite."

"See what it gets you?"

"Hey, no good deed goes unpunished."

He looked over at me. "Did you just make that up?"

"Nah," I admitted. "I heard it somewhere."

"Well, it's funny."

"Then why aren't you laughing?"

"I guess I heard it before, too." He picked up a small, gaily-wrapped gift package off the front seat and put it in my lap. "Here," he said. "Here's your gift for the little snot."

"What is it?"

"A charm, I think. Real silver. For a charm bracelet, you know?"

"Is it in the shape of a hypodermic needle?"

"Nah, I think it's an animal. Maybe a dog or a cat or something."

"It should be a wild boar. Or maybe one of those praying mantis things...they're the ones who bite the heads off their mates after they screw, aren't they?"

"I wouldn't know."

"You planning on staying long?" I asked as we pulled into the driveway.

"Long enough so it doesn't look rude when I leave."

"Well, I'm pretty bushed. I may fake a headache or something and cab it back to the Fairview."

"Suits me."

"I mean, check for me before you go, OK? But if I'm not there, just go on without me."

"Suits me even better."

One of the car parkers came over and opened the doors for us. I noticed it was an older colored guy, not Otis Jenkins. I almost asked him where Otis was and if he was working that night, but that's just not the sort of thing you do at the far end of McElligot Lane. Especially when your hostess is beaming down at you like a grinning, welcoming, ever-so-tipsy spotlight from the top of her new entrance stairs. She'd done yet another complete makeover of her grand entrance hall, and this time the theme was ancient Mesopotamia. Including lots of authentic, Tigris-Euphrates-inspired Sumerian architectural details copied directly, she assured me, from the famous Great Ziggurat of Ur near Nasiriyah. And, no, I'd never heard of Nasiriyah before, either. The rotunda inside the entranceway was now a confusing, even dizzying mélange of statues and murals and friezes that all looked a little Egyptian to me. Except that you could see both eyes. But what the hell do I know? She took me by the arm (she had a drink in her other hand, of course) and marched us over to a small, illuminated shadow-box where the rough clay figurine of a tall, athletic-looking woman with big breasts, big teeth, strong legs, cascading rolled hair and a sword held high stared wildly back at us.

"Do you know who that is?" Amanda Fairway asked.

"No clue. But I'm not much on ancient Babylon."

"It's not Babylon, it's *Sumeria!*" she insisted. "And this is their goddess *Inanna!*"

"*Yo'mama?*" I parroted, trying to keep a straight face.

"No, no, no!" she corrected. "It's *In-nan-na!*"

"Oh, really?" I did my best to make it sound truly, truly fascinating.

"Yes, sir!" Amanda nodded, and took another swallow of her drink. Then she leaned in a little closer and whispered, "She was top dog as far as female goddesses went in ancient Sumeria. I know. I read up on it."

"Oh?"

She nodded emphatically. And then added, just a little embarrassed: "I really had my son Harold look it up for me—you know Harold, don't you?—but I truly did read all the passages he marked for me. It was several pages in two different books."

"Very impressive."

"Why, thank you!" she beamed, and added an unsteady little three-inch curtsey. I swear, it looked like she was even blushing a little. Or maybe it was just the alcohol.

"So tell me," I continued, "what was she goddess of?"

Amanda Fairway gave me a big, proud smile. "Inanna was the Sumerian goddess of love, war and fertility."

"Wow. That's quite a résumé."

"Sure it is. But she could handle it. She knew what the hell she was doing." At that point Amanda's attention flickered back to her front doorway, where some new guests were just coming up the steps. Which, by the way, were exact copies of the famous run of steps outside the Ziggurat of Agar Quf near Baghdad (although she assured me it was originally called "Dur Kurigalzu" when the Kassite king of Babylon had it built back in the fourteenth century, B.C.).

So Amanda Fairway went to greet her next set of guests, and I wandered into her grand ballroom, grabbed myself a tall scotch-and-water from one of the bars and swept my eyes around looking for somebody—hell, anybody—I really felt like talking to. My old blues-and-country-western-loving buddy Ben Abernathy was there with his wife over by the appetizer table, but you could see he was having another one of his friendly-but-intense political disagreements with Hugo Becker, and I really didn't feel up to getting involved. I mean, once you get much past college, you've already picked out, staked out and fortified your personal political perspective, and no amount of jawing or arguing or reasoning or persuading or even outraged, righteous indignation will change it.

It's like religion that way.

Exactly like religion, in fact.

I decided to grab a drink for my other hand and wander off down the hall. I kind of hoped to find Harold Richard Fairway the Third in the library again, but I guess he was off attending some civic-minded do-gooder meeting or maybe taking in a French movie with subtitles or at some chess club thing or history club thing or physics club thing or dropping in on an existential philosophy forum full of tweed jackets and facial hair at one of the local colleges. I really like H.R. the Third, and I was disappointed not to run into him again. Hell, he was the only one in the family I genuinely liked or admired or felt the least bit comfortable around. But he wasn't there, so I wandered into the library by my lonesome and started looking around. It was really a beautiful, solemn, stately and reverential sort of room, and you just didn't know where to start with all those amazing books. From Galileo to Gutenberg to Ulysses S. Grant to Mohandas Gandhi to J. Paul Getty to Graham Greene to Erle Stanley Gardner, it was all there, all around you. It made me feel humble and unworthy and insignificant, you know?

And it was while I was wandering around in there that I noticed Little Harry Dick Fairway's familiar, mysterious blue folder peeking out from underneath the desk blotter. I mean, I kind of knew what it was, but at the same time, I couldn't imagine for the life of me what might be inside. And without even thinking twice about it, I walked over to that desk and started pulling that scary-but-oh-so-intriguing blue folder out from underneath the blotter. I was frankly dying to know what was inside.

Of course that's when I heard a loud, piggish snort from the hallway and the door banged open so hard and fast that it whapped against the bookshelves! And naturally who is standing there in the doorway but Little Harry Dick Fairway himself? But he looked pretty red-faced and bleary, and I don't think he even noticed as I shoved that blue folder frantically back under his desk blotter and stammered: "H-Hello"

"Oh. It's you," he grunted like I was something he'd discovered on the bottom of his shoe.

"I was just admiring your books," I told him. "You've got a really magnificent collection here."

"Of course I do," he grunted some more. "I pay two guys from the college t'find 'em and pick 'em out fer me."

"Do you ever find enough time to read them?"

"Of course I do!" he snarled at me. *"I've read 'em all!"* You could see he was unsteady and wavering just a bit.

"Why, that's amazing," I told him. "It must have taken a tremendous amount of time."

He eyeballed me suspiciously. "Are you getting smart with me?"

"No, of course not," I apologized. "In fact, I was just leaving."

"Good." And then he added, like he was talking to himself: "Can't stand all these fucking people all over the place. My wife'll have the bastards *singing* pretty soon. It's enough to make you wanna puke."

"Well, I definitely wouldn't want to miss that," I assured him, and headed for the door.

"Close it on your way out," he commanded over his shoulder. And so I did. And left the sonofabitch alone with his blue jerk-off folder and his fucking hand for company.

Which is, I'm quite sure, precisely what he had in mind.

I heard him click the lock as I wandered off down the hall.

I didn't much want to go back to all the noise and pleasantries and political conversation in the grand ballroom, so I went around the other way, through the kitchen with the conservatory-sized, all-glass breakfast nook—all sorts of caterers, cooks, waiters and bartenders were milling around in there, but they pretty much ignored me as they went about their business—and I grabbed myself a half-full bottle of Marsala cooking wine off the counter when nobody was looking and headed through the French doors to the patio and gardens outside. It was pretty chilly out there—in the lower 40s, I think—and I pulled my blazer tighter around my shoulders and took a hefty slug of the Marsala to try and stay warm. But at least it was quiet and peaceful out there. An enormous moon was peeking through feather-edged clouds—there had been a full moon just four days before—and you could see its mirror image shining up out of Amanda Fairway's reflecting pool. I was just trying to figure out what I wanted to do and how I was going to escape back to the Fairview without being seen when I heard voices coming from the shrubbery around the corner of the house. I recognized one of them immediately as birthday girl Amelia Camellia Fairway. The second was that skinny blonde punk with the creamy-yellow Pontiac Grand Prix who'd tried to buy dope from me at my hotel. And there was a third voice, too. A little older and deeper. I couldn't place it. But whomever it was, they were coming my way.

"There's plenty enough here," the older voice said.

"It sure doesn't look like much."

"Just wait. You'll see."

"I heard some people get all paranoid and jump off of buildings."

"I could see where that might happen," the older voice agreed solemnly. "I mean, if you're not in the right place. In your head, I mean. If you're not...*centered.*"

"Why don't we do it right now?" Amelia Fairway pretty much demanded. She was impatient about it. You could tell.

And that's about when she looked up and saw me standing there on the edge of the patio with the half-bottle of cooking wine in my hand.

"What the fuck are *you* doing here?" she wanted to know.

"I'm here for your birthday party," I explained. "You do know they're having another birthday party for you inside?"

"Fuck 'em."

"They've got presents."

"Fuck those, too."

You had to love her attitude. It was like the pure, distilled essence of insolence. It made me feel snotty and mocking and sarcastic, too. Like it was catching, you know?

"Why, *I* even brought you a present," I told her.

"Fuck you, too."

I was really starting to feel the buzz off the scotches and the wine. So I went on. "I mean, it's not like I bought it or shopped for it or picked it out for you or anything. Karen Sabelle probably did all that. And Danny Beagle just gave it to me in the car so I wouldn't have to walk in empty-handed. That's the fucking truth."

She looked at me for a moment like she was puzzled. And then her face blossomed out into a wide, wicked smile. "You oughta come with us," she grinned at me.

"Where are you going?"

"To the boat house. Down by the lake. It's warm in there. And there's a guest bedroom upstairs. More like a suite, actually," she turned up the wattage on her smile. "... we're gonna do some stuff in there."

"Some pot?"

"Sure. We can smoke some pot. I've got plenty." She clicked her head to one side. "C'mon. It'll be fun."

I looked at the skinny kid with the blonde hair—to be honest, I didn't care if he lived or died—and then at the older dude. He was probably near thirty and a little pudgy in the middle with longish brown hair and a blue bandana tied around his forehead. He was wearing the full uniform: a well-worn Salvation Army Thrift Store leather vest over a Sears Roebuck denim work shirt over a faded pair of blue jeans over a battered pair of rough-out Dingo boots. And a string of beads, of course. Indian, I think. The American kind, not the Taj Mahal kind. I also noticed he had a small, fringed leather pouch hanging from his belt and some record albums under his arm.

"You really ought to come with us, man," he advised. "It'll be worth it."

"And if you don't come," Amelia Fairway added, "I'll tell my parents you tried to corner me and rape me."

"WHAT??!!"

"Hey," she laughed. "I'm just fucking with ya, Hank…" it sent a shiver up my back when she called me Hank "…I wouldn't do anything like that to you…" she let it linger for a second, then added: "…*probably.*"

So I went. I mean, there were four of us.

What could possibly happen?

I can't really remember everything that went on in the Fairway family boathouse on Lake St. Clair that night—or not in its proper order or the way it really was, anyway—but I do remember we got there and there was some beer in the refrigerator and a bottle of Bacardi rum and another of brandy under the sink and I poured the last of my Marsala into a clean glass so I wouldn't look like some street bum swilling out of a bottle. Then the guy with the bandana put on one of his records—it was Bob Dylan's new one, *The Freewheelin' Bob Dylan*—and he told us that it wasn't even out yet, but that he had connections in the record business in New York and out in LA and…

He was already starting to get on my nerves.

Not that I really gave a shit one way or the other.

"You ever hear of the Beatles?" I asked, just to take him down a peg.

"The who?"

"No, The Beatles. They're really huge over in England right now."

"How do you know?" he scoffed at me.

"I just got back from London this morning. They're on every fucking station right now. And they're *good,* too."

He curled his nose. "They'll never make it over here."

It wasn't worth arguing with him. Hell, it wasn't even worth talking to him. Only then he opened up that little leather pouch on his waist and took out a small plastic bag with what looked like a half-dozen sugar cubes in it. "I thought we were gonna smoke some reefer or something? What the hell is that?"

He gave me a Cheshire-cat smile. "You ever hear of Dr. Timothy Leary from Harvard?"

I shook my head.

"How about the International Foundation for Internal Freedom?"

"What the hell is that?"

"You'll find out."

He took four sugar cubes out and handed them around. Amelia popped hers into her mouth immediately. The blonde punk looked at his uneasily for a while and then over at Amelia. "Go ahead!" she told him. And so he did, too.

The know-it-all guy with the leather vest held his up in front of his eyes and inspected it—savored it—like it was something far more than a damn sugar cube. And then, very slowly, solemnly and deliberately, he put it on the end of his tongue, drew it back into his mouth and brought his lips back together like a stage curtain coming down.

Then all three of them looked at me.

I remember Bob Dylan's *Blowin' in the Wind* was playing in the background.

"What is it?" I repeated.

"It's LSD, man..." the older guy explained, and raised his eyebrows up towards his headband. "...You know, *Psychedelics!*"

I had the feeling right away that it was something I was better off not doing. "I dunno," I told him. "I just came to drink a little wine and smoke some pot."

"You really ought to," Amelia offered. "It'll make you feel amazing."

"Lemme think about it," I told her, kind of playing for time. "I gotta go pee anyway. Is there a bathroom in here?"

"Right up the stairs."

So I went up and took a pee and decided that, very definitely, I did *not* want to eat one of those sugar cubes. I didn't like the whole idea. Or the setting. Or the people I was with. And I remembered reading somewhere that you stayed high for a long time with LSD. A really long time. And also that it could be pretty damn intense. Even terrifying. So I went back downstairs with every intention of leaving, heading back to the house, finding Danny Beagle or calling a cab and getting my ass back to the Fairview. Only they had a joint going by the time I got downstairs again and so I hung around to help smoke it—I mean, it was pretty good stuff—and finish the last of my wine and listen to Bob Dylan singing *"A Hard Rain's A-Gonna Fall"* and *"Don't Think Twice, It's All Right."*

The odd thing was that I didn't see any real change in any of them. Nothing. Not Amelia or the blonde punk or the asshole with the headband. They just looked a little wasted, that's all. "So when does it start happening?" I asked.

"You'll see," Amelia smiled. It was one of those cobra-snake smiles.

"Whaddaya mean, *'I'll see?'"*

"Just what I said."

"But I didn't take any."

She turned up the cobra smile a little more. "You're wrong about that."

"Whaddaya mean, *'I'm wrong?'"*

"I put one in your wine. You already drank it."

I looked down at the glass in my hand. Sure enough, it was empty. You could even see a soggy little fragment of dissolved sugar residue down at the bottom.

I was angry as hell. And a little scared, too. But also pretty drunk from the wine and high from the grass, and that tends to make you kind of sedentary. So I just sort of growled at her.

"You'll be amazing," she repeated. "Really you will."

And so all I could do was sit there on the floor with my back against a footstool or an ottoman or something and wait for something to happen. I remember the asshole with the bandana—well, maybe he wasn't *really* an asshole—got up to put his Bob Dylan record on again (Jesus, didn't he have anything else to play?), and I noticed that it seemed to be getting brighter in the room. Even though they'd turned off the ceiling fixture and the one in the kitchenette and had just one little desk lamp burning over by the window. The one with the green glass shade the color of a scarab beetle's wing and the light coming out of it all fringed around the edges with little slivers and shivers of neon. It was like everything in the room—hell, everything in the whole fucking universe!—was moving and shifting and swirling and changing and mutating and evolving even while it was sitting absolutely, peacefully still. And I could see the reflection of the moonlight outside that streaming, half-liquid window like some all-powerful (but nonetheless gentle and benign) Force of Nature was swirling enormous, illuminated-from-within globules of mercury around the surface of Lake St. Clair. But of course that couldn't be, because the mercury would be heavier than the water, and it would sink right to the bottom.

It'd poison all the fish, too.

The all-powerful but nonetheless gentle and benign Force of Nature wouldn't like that one bit!

The strange guy with the headband lit a candle in the middle of the table and rolled up another joint. Only he didn't look so strange any more. Just odd. And sad. And lost. I felt sorry for him. Hell, his whole fucking façade was melting off of him like a box of watercolors left out in the rain. He looked nervous, too.

The blonde kid was lying rigid on the floor with his eyes shut so tight and his muscles so desperately clenched that he was damn near vibrating. I felt sorry for him, too. Although I still didn't like him. He was on top of one of those goofy animal-hide carpets made out of some poor, scooped-out zebra or antelope or something. I was pretty sure the Force of Nature wouldn't be real happy about that, either. But—hey—it happened a long time ago, and none of us had anything to do with it. Honest we didn't.

Amelia Fairway had her chin on the edge of the low table where the candle was burning. Her eyes were wide open, and her pupils were big as manhole covers as she stared into the flame. She looked like she was hypnotized. I didn't think she looked particularly pretty. I thought she looked young and sad and terribly out-of-place.

The older guy with the drooling-off façade lit his joint off the candle flame, took a deep drag, held it, and offered it to me. I shook my head. Didn't want it. What was he trying to do, kill me? He passed it over to Amelia and she took a hit and then it went to the kid on the floor, who was still damn near vibrating. She had to hold it to his mouth in order for him to inhale. It made him cough. A lot.

I had to get out of there.

I mean right away.

These people were making me a little panicky.

Especially the guy with his façade melting off.

Besides, I had to get back to my conversation—well, it wasn't really a conversation, it was more like a mutual, communal state of understanding—with that all-powerful but nonetheless gentle and benign Force of Nature who could swirl thousands of gallons of luminous liquid mercury around on the top of Lake St. Clair.

And I had to get out of my clothes, too.

Jesus, they felt like fucking ropes around me.

And I mean those fat, rough, heavy, ugly ropes they use to hold monster steamships and barges and oil tankers to their docksides. The ropes cartoon rats use to tiptoe on board in the middle of the night. Jesus! And who the hell was Jesus, anyway? And how was he related to that Force of Nature thing that was urging me—hell, *insisting!*—that I get the hell out of my clothes before they strangled me.

Suffocated me.

Crushed me.

I would have done it right there, but I still had some small, stretched-out strand of societal decorum left. So I mumbled "I gotta pee again" and headed up the stairs. Where I took off my clothes—all of them—right there in the bathroom and then spent the longest time just staring at myself in the mirror, trying to figure out who the hell I was. It was a friendly enough face. Even if it refused to stay still and kept moving and changing like seaweed in a tide current. Oh, it was a little jaded maybe. A little cynical. But basically it was a nice face. A likeable face. An honest enough face. A generally benign face.

I was using that word a lot.

Maybe even too much.

But can you ever have too much benign?

I didn't think so.

I knew I couldn't stay in the bathroom all night. I mean, to begin with, the light pouring out of the florescent fixture over the mirror felt like it'd blown right down from the arctic. It was that cold. Like the moon when it has a halo of ice crystals around it, you know? And I knew I couldn't go downstairs, either. I didn't have any clothes on. And besides, I'd had about enough of Bob Dylan's moaning and carping and complaining. Sure, the world was fucked up. Everybody knew it. Everybody agreed. And it's great that he felt the need to say something about it in his music. Good for him. But enough is enough, already!

I didn't want to be down there with the other three human creatures, either.

I felt like being alone.

So I opened one of the hallway doors and found a darkened bedroom with gauzy linen curtains with moonlight like a mist you could taste behind them and a dark taffeta bedspread that may have been dark green or dark blue or even purple—you couldn't tell, because it kept changing colors—and that's where I climbed into bed and looked up at a ceiling that looked alive like a movie screen and out the window at the moon that almost talked to me and all of its poisonous, reflective mercury floating around on the top of the water and…

And I can't tell you where all I went and what all I learned or forgot or even how long I was there. But I do know that someone else came into the room sometime in the dark middle of the night and lay down beside me.

It was Amelia.

And she was naked, too.

And she smelled like flowers in a locker room.

And she spoke:

"Are you all right?" she asked.

"Are you?"

"I'm alone."

"We're all alone," I explained for her. "But that's OK, because we're part of the whole thing, too."

She seemed to understand what I was talking about.

I'm not going to lie or prevaricate or make excuses for what happened next. It all started with feeling sorry for her, I think. She just seemed so lost and sad and dissatisfied and unfulfilled and disappointed in herself. Or that's what I thought at the time, anyway. And I felt so sorry for her. Sorry for the whole damn world. It was overwhelming…

like standing under a crashing, cascading waterfall of all the needless suffering and pain and misery and cruelty and loneliness in the universe that I couldn't do anything about. Why was I the lucky one? It didn't seem fair. So I bowed my head inside my head and felt thankful. And by then she was nuzzling into me and the moonlight was waking up on the windowsill like muffled drum beats—and so was I—and then, pretty soon and without even seeming to do anything, I was on top of her and inside of her we were going at it like we were just one of those hot, squishy places where two parts of the living universe pass through each other like a solar eclipse and melt, albeit briefly, into each other. I was working so hard and I could see inside my head and body like I was in an enormous, endless tunnel of humming, throbbing, purring, straining, singing, screaming living cells—muscle cells, brain cells, organ cells, *everything!*—and it was like I was trying to get somewhere...trying so desperately hard to get to wherever it was... and yet at the same time watching it draw further and further away from me...

I'm pretty sure I just stopped and rolled over on my back—exhausted—before I even finished.

"Are you OK?" she asked from what sounded like a million miles away.

"No," I told her. "No, I'm not."

Well, you don't have to tell me what a stupid, idiotic, shameful, immoral and inexcusable thing that was to do, because I already know. And it got even worse a few days later. That's when the itching started. I wasn't sure what it was at first, but then I went to the public library and did a little reading and then casually asked Willie Shorter about it over at the Black Mamba Lounge when I dropped by to listen to some music and buy some more pot.

"Sounds t'me like y'got y'self a dose a'th' crabs," he chuckled.

"Is it serious?"

"It's serious as far as them crabs is concerned."

"Why's that?"

He looked at me like it was a dumb question. "Why, you their housing, son."

"Jesus! What do I do? Do I need to see a doctor?" I was getting worried that there was maybe a health law or something and that I'd have to divulge who I'd been with and who else I might have had sex with?

Well, it was too damn frightening to contemplate.

"I'd go talk to a pharmacist at th' drug store," Willie advised. "He'll know whut y'need t'do."

So that's what I did. Only at a drug store on the other side of town. And I mean *way* on the other side of town. Like south of Wyandotte and across the bridge from Trenton on Grosse Isle. And I waited until nobody else was in the store before I explained my problem in a whisper from the shadow-side of the cash register. The pharmacist regarded me with a disapproving (but also grudgingly admiring) sort of frown. And then he reached down and produced a bottle of A-200 Lotion from behind the counter. "This should take care of it," he said.

"I'll take two. Just in case."

So he rang me up and I had him put both bottles in a brown paper bag and I headed for the door. I couldn't wait to get the hell out of there.

"Good luck," he called after me.

Like I was going fishing or something, you know?

So I went back to my room and read the label—even the fine print—and it assured me that A-200 Lotion was indeed a tested, trusted and time-honored treatment for head lice, body lice and (ahem) pubic lice. I followed the directions and shampooed the heck out of myself "down there" and then did it again just to make sure. And once more after that. So you can imagine how distraught I became a few weeks later when I was down at Indianapolis for the first week of 500 practice and the itching started up again.

Shit.

The pharmacist in Indianapolis explained that it was possible some of the crab lice (or, more likely, given the time lag involved, some crab-lice eggs) had found their way into a pair or two of my undergarments, and that's how they managed to re-infest me all over again! And I was due to fly back to Italy in a few days and meet Audrey again! I toyed with the notion of telling her the whole, sordid story, but I knew I couldn't do it.

I mean, it was just so damn *wrong*.

So I shampooed and shampooed and threw out all my underwear and bought new (and even washed them before I wore them!) and by the way the Lotuses were looking pretty damn good at the Speedway. Not that I was really paying attention. But they were fast right out of the box and handled really well, and both Clark and Gurney seemed pleased with them. Although I've got to say that Clark looked a little spooked by the speedway. I mean, he'd done Eau Rouge and Burnenville and the Masta Kink at Spa—mastered them, in fact—and those were probably the most difficult, intimidating and dangerous corners on earth. But none of them had concrete walls around the outside—so damn close you could almost reach out and touch them!—and that made the Indianapolis Motor Speedway a little different. More than a little, in fact. It was a scary sort of place for someone who'd never done ovals before.

But Jimmy sucked it in when he needed to (after a bit of a talking to from Colin Chapman—in front of the entire fucking team—the night before time trials), and, in spite of the horsepower disadvantage and most of the Offies running large doses of nitro in their fuel mix for qualifying, put his Lotus into the middle of the second row! Which was one hell of a fine performance. Dan Gurney's situation was more problematic, as he scraped the right-front corner off against the wall during practice, and they wound up cobbling his car back together with parts off the old, original mule. So, even after they finished, it wasn't quite right. But he was still doing better than any of Mickey Thompson's drivers in their new, roller-skate-like Harvey Aluminum-sponsored machines with their tiny, 13-inch wheels. World Champ Graham Hill had one hell of a scary spin—right down the middle of the front straightaway, in fact—and eventually told Mickey, "Thank you very much, but no thank you," and headed off to the Grand Prix of Monaco. Which he won. Billy Krause was likewise having trouble getting comfortable with the track and the new Thompson cars. But part of that could be from the spin he had early on, which left him travelling backwards at well over 100 with concrete walls on either side. After which he got walloped—*hard!*—by an oncoming car.

That sort of thing would set anyone back.

And particularly anyone who'd never been to the Speedway before....

Fortunately the crab lice responded the way I wanted them to and decided to go away again, and everything seemed fine as could be when I met up with Audrey at the Milan airport so we could drive down to Maranello together and continue our negotiations with *Commendatore* Ferrari. It was getting really close now—at least according to the legal types and bean counters that Fairway had sent over—and Bob Wright had even flown over to look after the final arrangements and represent Fairway Motors at the signing of the papers. Ferrari was still a little upset (I think insulted might be a better word) that the man with his family name on the company logo hadn't bothered to make the trip. But he understood by then that Bob was the real power behind the throne (for as long as he managed to stay there, anyway) and also knew from his inside-the-industry sources that Little Harry Dick Fairway was two-thirds of an idiot-asshole anyway. Maybe even more than two-thirds.

Commendatore Ferrari seemed in an expansive and gregarious mood. And not without reason, as John Surtees had joined his team and right away produced a dominating win at the 12 Hours of Sebring (co-driving with team-manager Dragoni favorite Ludovico Scarfiotti) in the Scuderia's new, mid-engined 250P prototype. With the sister 250P of Mairesse/Vaccarella a lap back in second. And Pedro Rodriguez and Graham Hill taking third, another lap back, at the wheel of Carlo Sebastian's 4.0-liter front-engined Testa Rossa from the previous year. Followed by no less than *four* GTOs, led home by the blue-and-white John Mecom entry of Roger Penske and Augie Pabst. Ferrari had totally steamrollered the opposition, such as it was, in the GT classes.

There'd been a bit of a freak letdown at the Targa Florio on May 6th, where Jo Bonnier/Carlo Abate eked out a win for Porsche thanks to a solid drive, dramatically changing weather conditions and some confused decision-making by Dragoni in the Ferrari pits regarding who should drive which car and when. Even so, they almost snatched it away, as an inspired Willy Mairesse was closing in on the leading Porsche when—on the very last lap!—another rain squall hit, and he bounced it off a wall and had to limp to the finish.

Oh, well.

But the team rebounded at the Nurburgring just days before our formal signing ceremony (or what we surely thought would be our formal signing ceremony, anyway), as Surtees and Mairesse teamed up to head yet another devastating Ferrari 1-2-3 at the Nurburgring 1000 Ks. And Surtees had qualified an encouraging third and finished a solid fourth at the Monaco Grand Prix in Mauro Forghieri's new T56 grand prix Ferrari! So things were looking rosy indeed for Scuderia Ferrari!

To celebrate all of this, Enzo took Bob Wright out to dinner. Just the two of them. At Ferrari's very favorite restaurant up in the hills overlooking town. And, for transportation, the Old Man selected one of his gorgeous—and *fast!*—250GT "Lusso" models. A special one. With a full-house, 390hp, 4.0-liter Ferrari V12 under its hood! Vinci Pittacora told me later that Enzo had it specially installed for the occasion. And you need to remember here that Ferrari started out as a test driver and racing driver for C.M.N. and then Alfa Romeo long before he ever dreamed of building his own cars. And also that he liked good wine. I didn't actually see any of it, of course, because I was holed up in the Hotel Real Fini with Audrey at the time. But, judging from the harrowing description Bob gave at breakfast the next morning and the color—or rather the *lack* of color—in his face, it was apparent that the good *commendatore* had done his level best to scare the living shit out of him.

But Bob didn't get to where he was without unparalleled focus and commitment, uncommon determination, will and dedication and, when he really needed them, enormous balls, and so he hung onto the seat and the window crank for dear life, didn't utter so much as a word and silently-but-fervently prayed that Enzo Ferrari was as great a driver as he apparently thought he was.

The final signing meeting didn't last very long. It was held in a little conference room just down the hall from Ferrari's office, and Bob Wright, Randall Perrune and two of his assistants, Danny Beagle, Audrey and I were there on behalf of Fairway Motors and across from us were Ferrari, his first lieutenant Franco Gozzi and their company lawyer. Clifton Toole's bean-counters had done an incredibly thorough job and had ultimately come to the conclusion that Ferrari, the company, was both solvent and marginally profitable (not to mention reasonably priced as acquisitions go), and Bob Wright believed to the very core of his being that the value of the Ferrari name, history and prestige—not to mention the racing team and the talent and expertise that came with it—were almost beyond calculation.

He was ready to make a deal.

The papers were drawn up.

They just needed two signatures and it was done.

The general gist of the deal was that the company would be split into two separate (but related) entities. One would be called Fairway-Ferrari, and that would be the road-car company. It would essentially keep running with its existing staff and workers (but under Fairway's stewardship, oversight and control) and continue building, distributing and developing all of Ferrari's road-model cars. The other entity would be Ferrari-Fairway, which would be the racing arm. And that's the one Enzo Ferrari would continue to run and control...under Fairway's guidance, of course.

Everything seemed to be moving along smoothly as the lawyers pored over the paperwork and made notes here and there in the margins. Only then Enzo Ferrari had a question. "Tell me," he asked, using Audrey as his interpreter, "who decides where I race my cars?"

"Why *you* do, of course!" Bob Wright told Audrey to tell him. And then added: "With our approval, naturally."

Audrey translated that, too.

"With your approval?" Ferrari parroted back in Italian. You could see his eyebrows arching up. *"...Cosa significa?"*

Audrey looked at Bob. "He wants to know what you mean."

"I mean 'with our approval,'" Bob repeated.

She translated that to Commendatore Ferrari. He thought it over for a moment and rubbed his chin. *"Tell me, then..."* he started in again in Italian, *"...what happens if I want to race my cars at Indianapolis?"*

He obviously knew about the Lotus-Fairway Indycar—hell, everybody did by that point—and I knew he considered Indianapolis unfinished business. He'd sent a car over there in 1952 for then-world-champ Alberto Ascari to drive, but the best it could do was 19th on the grid and it was one of the first cars out with a broken wire wheel.

All the Indianapolis regulars had long since moved away from wires and on to stronger, lighter, and less maintenance-intensive cast magnesium wheels.

That's not the way Enzo Ferrari wanted to be remembered at Indianapolis.

"What happens if I want to race my cars at Indianapolis?" Audrey translated.

"Well, that depends," Bob Wright answered.

"Depends on *what?"* Ferrari shot back in English. It stunned everybody in the room. Only by then he was back to not speaking or understanding any English again.

"Well, lots of things…" Bob prevaricated. "…Like if we have some other sort of corporate program going on at the time."

Enzo looked over at Audrey and smiled. But he was smiling at her, not at the situation. *"And what if I still want to go?"* he said to her in Italian. She translated it into English for Bob.

Bob Wright squared his shoulders and looked Enzo Ferrari right in the eyes. "Then you do not go," he told the *Commendatore* flatly. And even before Audrey finished translating, it was clear he understood. He cocked his head, slumped ever so slightly back into his chair and smiled. *"Bene,"* he finally muttered, and looked pleased with himself. And then he stood up, turned to his lawyer and his first lieutenant and asked them where they'd like to go to lunch?

"Il Cavallino?" his lieutenant shrugged.

"Il Cavallino," Ferrari nodded. And then he turned to the rest of us, still seated at the table, and said *"It's been nice knowing you,"* in Italian. And then the three of them filed out of the room.

The silence they left behind was like concrete setting up.

Well, it was a tough phone call to Detroit for Bob Wright—Little Harry Dick Fairway was definitely *not* amused by the turn of events in Maranello—and by the time we were on the plane to go home, Bob was talking about Fairway Motors building their own damn car and beating that conniving, manipulative, double-dealing Italian sonofabitch at his own game. And in truth he was just parroting back what Little Dick Fairway had already yelled in his ear over the long-distance phone line. Only Bob used nicer language. And I was seeing a whole new bonanza of fabulous opportunities opening up for me. And Audrey, too. I mean, all the best talent and knowledge and expertise and experience they'd need was in England. And most of it was around London. Plus they already had a bit of a jump-start with Eric Broadley's Lola GT, which certainly looked like it had potential and was surely headed in the right direction. Why, all the best designers and chassis men and race mechanics and team managers in the whole fucking world were around London. And they'd *need* somebody over there to look after things and help arrange things and pick the right talent to hire (or put under consulting contracts) and faithfully report back to the Tower with updates or to get additional instructions.

It was damn near perfect.

By the time the wheels touched down at Detroit Metro, we were already laying out our plans. And I couldn't wait to tell Audrey. So I called her. Even though it was the middle of the fucking night over in London. The phone rang and rang. And then—finally—Walter answered. *"Do you know what bloody time it is?"* he screamed at me.

"I'm sorry," I told him. "But is Audrey there? I need to speak to her."

"She's here, but she doesn't want to talk to you."

"I beg your pardon?"

"You heard me! She bloody well doesn't want to talk to you!"

I didn't understand.

And then he hung up.

Click!

I started to dial again, but thought better of it. Maybe she was fast asleep and he was just taking the opportunity to fuck with me. That would be like him.

So I waited until the next morning—3:30 the next morning Detroit time, to be precise—and tried her again at the Lola shop.

They told me she wasn't in and that they didn't expect her.

So I rummaged around through the loose papers and scribbled notes in my desk drawer and in the pockets of my briefcase until I found the number of that fancy house in Mayfair on the back of an envelope. I dialed it. And it was Audrey's voice that answered, "Hello?"

"It's me."

"You bastard," she snarled.

And then she hung up.

What the fuck?

So I dialed the number again. Only this time I started with: *"Please don't hang up on me!"*

"Why shouldn't I?" she demanded. Boy, was she ever angry.

"Why should you?" I asked while I tried to make sense of it.

"Why should I?" she fired back. *"Because you gave me bloody crab lice, you rotten, stinking bastard!!!"*

I turned icy-white inside.

And then I started backing up like you do when you're impossibly, unforgivably wrong and caught dead-to-rights with no place to go and nothing to say to defend yourself. I was drowning! Flailing around blindly for something—*anything!*—that might save me. And that's when—for the life of me, I don't know where the hell it came from—I uttered the six terrible words I never, *ever* should have said:

"Are you sure it was me?"